By Lee Child

Stories

The Midnight Line

LEE CHILD

Delacorte Press | New York

The Midnight Line

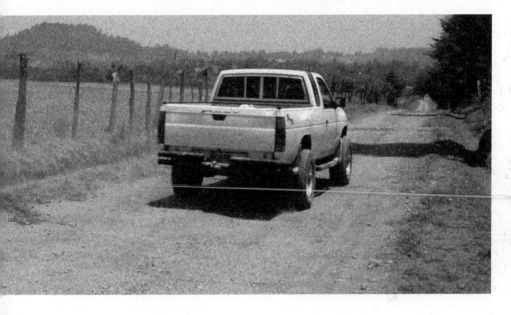

A JACK REACHER NOVEL

Copyright © 2017 by Lee Child

All rights reserved.

Published in the United States by Delacorte Press, an imprint of Random House, a division of Penguin Random House LLC, New York.

DELACORTE PRESS and the HOUSE colophon are registered trademarks of Penguin Random House LLC.

Title page art from an original photograph by FreeImages.com/Ariel de Silva Parreira

LIBRARY OF CONGRESS CATALOGING-IN-PUBLICATION DATA
Names: Child, Lee, author.
Title: The midnight line : a Jack Reacher novel / Lee Child.
Description: First Edition. | New York : Delacorte Press, [2017] | Series: Jack Reacher ; 22
Identifiers: LCCN 2017031499 | ISBN 9780399593482 (hardback) | ISBN 9780399593499 (ebook)
Subjects: LCSH: Reacher, Jack (Fictitious character)—Fiction. | Murder—Investigation—Fiction. | BISAC: FICTION / Suspense. | FICTION / Action & Adventure. | FICTION / Mystery & Detective / General. | GSAFD: Suspense fiction. | Mystery fiction.
Classification: LCC PS3553.H4838 M53 2017 | DDC 813/.54—dc23
LC record available at https://lccn.loc.gov/2017031499

Printed in the United States of America on acid-free paper

randomhousebooks.com

9 8 7 6 5 4 3 2 1

First Edition

Book design by Virginia Norey

So far in our history,
nearly two million Purple Hearts have been awarded.
This book is respectfully dedicated
to each and every recipient.

Chapter 1

Jack Reacher and Michelle Chang spent three days in Milwaukee. On the fourth morning she was gone. Reacher came back to the room with coffee and found a note on his pillow. He had seen such notes before. They all said the same thing. Either directly or indirectly. Chang's note was indirect. And more elegant than most. Not in terms of presentation. It was a ballpoint scrawl on motel notepaper gone wavy with damp. But elegant in terms of expression. She had used a simile, to explain and flatter and apologize all at once. She had written, "You're like New York City. I love to visit, but I could never live there."

He did what he always did. He let her go. He understood. No apology required. He couldn't live anywhere. His whole life was a visit. Who could put up with that? He drank his coffee, and then hers, and took his toothbrush from the bathroom glass, and walked away, through a knot of streets, left and right, toward the bus depot. She would be in a taxi, he guessed. To the airport. She had a gold card and a cell phone.

At the depot he did what he always did. He bought a ticket for the first bus out, no matter where it was going. Which turned out to be an end-of-the-line place way north and west, on the shore of Lake Superior. Fundamentally the wrong direction. Colder, not warmer. But rules were rules, so he climbed aboard. He sat and watched out the window. Wisconsin flashed by, its hayfields baled and stubbly, its pastures worn, its trees dark and heavy. It was the end of summer.

It was the end of several things. She had asked the usual questions. Which were really statements in disguise. She could understand a year. Absolutely. A kid who grew up on bases overseas, and was then deployed to bases overseas, with nothing in between except four years at West Point, which wasn't exactly known as a leisure-heavy institution, then obviously such a guy was going to take a year to travel and see the sights before he settled down. Maybe two years. But not more. And not permanently. Face it. The pathology meter was twitching.

All said with concern, and no judgment. No big deal. Just a two-minute conversation. But the message was clear. As clear as such messages could be. Something about denial. He asked, denial of what? He didn't secretly think his life was a problem.

That proves it, she said.

So he got on the bus to the end-of-the-line place, and he would have ridden it all the way, because rules were rules, except he took a stroll at the second comfort stop, and he saw a ring in a pawn shop window.

The second comfort stop came late in the day, and it was on the sad side of a small town. Possibly a seat of county government. Or some minor part of it. Maybe the county police department was headquartered there. There was a jail in town. That was clear. Reacher could see bail bond offices, and a pawn shop. Full service, right there, side by side on a run-down street beyond the restroom block.

He was stiff from sitting. He scanned the street beyond the restroom block. He started walking toward it. No real reason. Just strolling. Just loosening up. As he got closer he counted the guitars in the pawn shop window. Seven. Sad stories, all of them. Like the songs on country radio. Dreams, unfulfilled. Lower down in the window were glass shelves loaded with smaller stuff. All kinds of jewelry. Including rings. Including class rings. All kinds of high schools. Except one of them wasn't. One of them was West Point 2005.

It was a handsome ring. It was a conventional shape, and a conventional style, with intricate gold filigree, and a black stone, maybe semi-precious, maybe glass, surrounded by an oval hoop that had *West Point* around the top, and *2005* around the bottom. Old-style letters. A classic approach. Either respect for bygone days, or a lack of imagination. West Pointers designed their own rings. Whatever they wanted. An old tradition. Or an old entitlement, perhaps, because West Point class rings had been the first class rings of all.

It was a very small ring.

Reacher wouldn't have gotten it on any of his fingers. Not even his left-hand pinkie, not even past the nail. Certainly not past the first knuckle. It was tiny. It was a woman's ring. Possibly a replica for a girlfriend or a fiancée. That happened. Like a tribute or a souvenir.

But possibly not.

Reacher opened the pawn shop door. He stepped inside. A guy at the register looked up. He was a big bear of a man, scruffy and unkempt. Maybe in his middle thirties, dark, with plenty of fat over a big frame anyway. With some kind of cunning in his eyes. Certainly enough to perfect his response to his sudden six-five two-fifty visitor. Driven purely by instinct. The guy wasn't afraid. He had a loaded gun under the counter. Unless he was an idiot. Which he didn't look. All the same, the guy didn't want to risk sounding aggressive. But he didn't want to sound obsequious, either. A matter of pride.

So he said, "How's it going?"

Not well, Reacher thought. *To be honest.* Chang would be back in Seattle by then. Back in her life.

But he said, "Can't complain."

"Can I help you?"

"Show me your class rings."

The guy threaded the tray backward off the shelf. He put it on the counter. The West Point ring had rolled over, like a tiny golf ball. Reacher picked it up. It was engraved inside. Which meant it wasn't a replica. Not for a fiancée or a girlfriend. Replicas were never engraved. An old tradition. No one knew why.

Not a tribute, not a souvenir. It was the real deal. A cadet's own ring, earned over four hard years. Worn with pride. Obviously. If you weren't proud of the place, you didn't buy a ring. It wasn't compulsory.

The engraving said *S.R.S. 2005*.

The bus blew its horn three times. It was ready to go, but it was a passenger short. Reacher put the ring down and said, "Thank you," and walked out of the store. He hustled back past the restroom block and leaned in the door of the bus and said to the driver, "I'm staying here."

"No refunds."

"Not looking for one."

"You got a bag in the hold?"

"No bag."

"Have a nice day."

The guy pulled a lever and the door sucked shut in Reacher's face. The engine roared and the bus moved off without him. He turned away from the diesel smoke and walked back toward the pawn shop.

Chapter 2

The guy in the pawn shop was a little disgruntled to have to get the ring tray out again so soon after he had put it away. But he did, and he placed it in the same spot on the counter. The West Point ring had rolled over again. Reacher picked it up.

He said, "Do you remember the woman who pawned this?"

"How would I?" the guy said. "I got a million things in here."

"You got records?"

"You a cop?"

"No," Reacher said.

"Everything in here is legal."

"I don't care. All I want is the name of the woman who brought you this ring."

"Why?"

"We went to the same school."

"Where is that? Upstate?"

"East of here," Reacher said.

"You can't be a classmate. Not from 2005. No offense."

"None taken. I was from an earlier generation. But the place doesn't change much. Which means I know how hard she worked for this ring. So now I'm wondering what kind of unlucky circumstance made her give it up."

The guy said, "What kind of a school was it?"

"They teach you practical things."

"Like a trade school?"

"More or less."

"Maybe she died in an accident."

"Maybe she did," Reacher said. Or not in an accident, he thought. There had been Iraq, and there had been Afghanistan: 2005 had been a tough year to graduate. He said, "But I would like to know for sure."

"Why?" the guy said again.

"I can't tell you exactly."

"Is it an honor thing?"

"I guess it could be."

"Trade schools have that?"

"Some of them."

"There was no woman. I bought that ring. With a lot of other stuff."

"When?"

"About a month ago."

"From who?"

"I'm not going to tell you my business. Why should I? It's all legal. It's all perfectly legitimate. The state says so. I have a license and I pass all kinds of inspections."

"Then why be shy about it?"

"It's private information."

Reacher said, "Suppose I buy the ring?"

"It's fifty bucks."

"Thirty."

"Forty."

"Deal," Reacher said. "So now I'm entitled to know its provenance."

"This ain't Sotheby's auction house."

"Even so."

The guy paused a beat.

Then he said, "It was from a guy who helps out with a charity. People donate things and take the deduction. Mostly old cars and boats. But other things, too. The guy gives them an inflated receipt for their tax returns, and then he sells the things he gets wherever he can, for whatever he can, and then he cuts a check to the charity. I buy the small stuff from him. I get what I get, and I hope to turn a profit."

"So you think someone donated this ring to a charity and took a deduction on their income taxes?"

"Makes sense, if the original person died. From 2005. Part of the estate."

"I don't think so," Reacher said. "I think a relative would have kept it."

"Depends if the relative was eating well."

"You got tough times here?"

"I'm OK. But I own the pawn shop."

"Yet people still donate to good causes."

"In exchange for phony receipts. In the end the government eats the tax relief. Welfare by another name."

Reacher said, "Who is the charity guy?"

"I won't tell you that."

"Why not?"

"It's none of your business. I mean, who the hell are you?"

"Just a guy already having a pretty bad day. Not your fault, of course, but if asked to offer advice I would have to say it might prove a dumb idea to make my day worse. You might be the straw that breaks the camel's back."

"You threatening me now?"

"More like the weather report. A public service. Like a tornado warning. Prepare to take cover."

"Get out of my store."

"Fortunately I no longer have a headache. I got hit in the head, but that's all better now. A doctor said so. A friend made me go. Two times. She was worried about me."

The pawn shop guy paused another beat.

Then he said, "Exactly what kind of a school was that ring from?"

Reacher said, "It was a military academy."

"Those are for, excuse me, problem kids. Or disturbed. No offense."

"Don't blame the kids," Reacher said. "Look at the families. Tell the truth, at our school there were a lot of parents who had killed people."

"Really?"

"More than the average."

"So you stick together forever?"

"We don't leave anyone behind."

"The guy won't talk to a stranger."

"Does he have a license and does he pass inspections by the state?"

"What I'm doing here is legal. My lawyer says so. As long as I honestly believe it. And I do. It's from a charity. I've seen the paperwork. All kinds of people do it. They even have commercials on TV. Cars, mostly. Sometimes boats."

"But this particular guy won't talk to me?"

"I would be surprised."

"Does he have no manners?"

"I wouldn't ask him over to a picnic."

"What's his name?"

"Jimmy Rat."

"For real?"

"That's what he goes by."

"Where would I find Mr. Rat?"

"Look for a minimum six Harley-Davidsons. Jimmy will be in whatever bar they're outside of."

Chapter 3

The town was relatively small. Beyond the sad side was a side maybe five years from going sad. Maybe more. Maybe ten. There was hope. There were some boarded-up enterprises, but not many. Most stores were still doing business, at a leisurely rural pace. Big pick-up trucks rolled through, slowly. There was a billiard hall. Not many street lights. It was getting dark. Something about the architecture made it clear it was dairy country. The shape of the stores looked like old-fashioned milking barns. The same DNA was in there somewhere.

There was a bar in a standalone wooden building, with a patch of weedy gravel for parking, and on the gravel were seven Harley-Davidsons, all in a neat line. Possibly not actual Hells Angels as such. Possibly one of many other parallel denominations. Bikers were as split as Baptists. All the same, but different. Apparently these particular guys liked black leather tassels and chromium plating. They liked to lie back and ride with their legs spread wide and their feet sticking out in front of them. Possibly a cooling effect. Perhaps necessary. Generally they wore heavy leather vests. And pants, and boots. All black. Hot, in late summer.

The bikes were all painted dark shiny colors, four with orange flames, three with rune-like symbols outlined in silver. The bar was dull with age, and some shingles had slipped. There was an air conditioner in one of the windows, straining to keep up, dripping water in a puddle below. A cop car rolled past, slowly, its tires hissing on the blacktop. County Police. Probably spent the first half of its watch ginning up municipal revenue with a radar gun out on the highway, now prowling the back streets of the towns in its jurisdiction. Showing the flag. Paying attention to the trouble spots. The cop inside turned his head and gazed at Reacher. The guy was nothing like the pawnbroker. He was all squared away. His face was lean, and his eyes were wise. He was sitting behind the wheel with a ramrod posture, and his haircut was fresh. A whitewall buzz cut. Maybe just a day old. Not more than two.

Reacher stood still and watched him roll away. He heard a motorcycle exhaust in the distance, coming closer, getting louder, heavy as a hammer. An eighth Harley came around the corner, as slow as gravity would allow, a big heavy machine, blatting and popping, the rider lying back with his feet on pegs way out in front. He leaned into a turn and slowed on the gravel. He was wearing a black leather vest over a black T-shirt. He parked last in line. His bike idled like a blacksmith hitting an anvil. Then he shut it down and hauled it up on its stand. Silence came back.

Reacher said, "I'm looking for Jimmy Rat."

The guy glanced at one of the other bikes. Couldn't help himself. But he said, "Don't know him," and walked away, stiff and bowlegged, to the door of the bar. He was pear shaped, and maybe forty years old. Maybe five-ten, and bulky. He had a sallow tan, like his skin was rubbed with motor oil. He pulled the door and stepped inside.

Reacher stayed where he was. The bike the new guy had glanced at was one of the three with silver runes. It was as huge as all the others, but the footrests and the handlebars were set a little closer to the seat than most. About two inches closer than the new guy's, for example.

Which made Jimmy Rat about five-eight, possibly. Maybe skinny, to go with his name. Maybe armed, with a knife or a gun. Maybe vicious.

Reacher walked to the door of the bar. He pulled it open and stepped inside. The air was dark and hot and smelled of spilled beer. The room was rectangular, with a full-length copper bar on the left, and tables on the right. There was an arch in the rear wall, with a narrow corridor beyond. Restrooms and a pay phone and a fire door. Four windows. A total of six potential exits. The first thing an ex-MP counted.

The eight bikers were packed in around two four-tops shoved together by a window. They had beers on the go, in heavy glasses wet with humidity. The new guy was shoehorned in, pear shaped on a chair, with the fullest glass. Six of the others were in a similar category, in terms of size and shape and general visual appeal. One was worse. About five-eight, stringy, with a narrow face and restless eyes.

Reacher stopped at the bar and asked for coffee.

"Don't have any," the barman said. "Sorry."

"Is that Jimmy Rat over there? The small guy?"

"You got a beef with him, you take it outside, OK?"

The barman moved away. Reacher waited. One of the bikers drained his glass and stood up and headed for the restroom corridor. Reacher crossed the room and sat down in his vacant chair. The wood felt hot. The eighth guy made the connection. He stared at Reacher, and then he glanced at Jimmy Rat.

Who said, "This is a private party, bud. You ain't invited."

Reacher said, "I need some information."

"About what?"

"Charitable donations."

Jimmy Rat looked blank. Then he remembered. He glanced at the door, somewhere beyond which lay the pawn shop, where he had made assurances. He said, "Get lost, bud."

Reacher put his left fist on the table. The size of a supermarket chicken. Long thick fingers with knuckles like walnuts. Old nicks and scars healed white against his summer tan. He said, "I don't care what scam you're running. Or who you're stealing from. Or who you're fencing for. I got no interest in any of that. All I want to know is where you got this ring."

He opened his fist. The ring lay in his palm. *West Point 2005*. The gold filigree, the black stone. The tiny size. Jimmy Rat said nothing, but something in his eyes made Reacher believe he recognized the item.

Reacher said, "Another name for West Point is the United States Military Academy. There's a clue right there, in the first two words. This is a federal case."

"You a cop?"

"No, but I got a quarter for the phone."

The missing guy got back from the restroom. He stood behind Reacher's chair, arms spread wide in exaggerated perplexity. As if to say, what the hell is going on here? Who is this guy? Reacher kept one eye on Jimmy Rat, and one on the window alongside him, where he could see a faint ghostly reflection of what was happening behind his shoulder.

Jimmy Rat said, "That's someone's chair."

"Yeah, mine," Reacher said.

"You've got five seconds."

"I've got as long as it takes for you to answer my question."

"You feeling lucky tonight?"

"I won't need to be."

Reacher put his right hand on the table. It was a little larger than his left. Normal for right-handed people. It had a few more nicks and scars, including a white V-shaped blemish that looked like a snake-bite, but had been made by a nail.

Jimmy Rat shrugged, like the whole conversation was really no big deal.

He said, "I'm part of a supply chain. I get stuff from other people who get it from other people. That ring was donated or sold or pawned and not redeemed. I don't know anything more than that."

"What other people did you get it from?"

Jimmy Rat said nothing. Reacher watched the window with his left eye. With his right he saw Jimmy Rat nod. The reflection in the glass showed the guy behind winding up a big roundhouse right. Clearly the plan was to smack Reacher on the ear. Maybe topple him off the chair. At least soften him up a little.

Didn't work.

Reacher chose the path of least resistance. He ducked his head, and let the punch scythe through the empty air above it. Then he bounced back up, and launched from his feet, and twisted, and used his falling-backward momentum to jerk his elbow into the guy's kidney, which was rotating around into position just in time. It was a good solid hit. The guy went down hard. Reacher fell back in his chair and sat there like absolutely nothing had happened.

Jimmy Rat stared.

The barman called, "Take it outside, pal. Like I told you."

He sounded like he meant it.

Jimmy Rat said, "Now you've got trouble."

He sounded like he meant it, too.

Right then Chang would be shopping for dinner. Maybe a small grocery close to her home. Wholesome ingredients. But simple. She was probably tired.

A bad day.

Reacher said, "I've got six fat guys and a runt. That's a walk in the park."

He stood up. He turned and stepped on the guy on the floor and walked over him. Onward to the door. Out to the gravel, and the line of shiny bikes. He turned and saw the others come out after him. The not-very-magnificent seven. Generally stiff and bow-legged, and variously contorted due to beer guts and bad posture. But still, a lot of weight. In the aggregate. Plus fourteen fists, and fourteen boots.

Possibly steel capped.

Maybe a very bad day.

But who cared, really?

The seven guys fanned out in a semicircle, three on Jimmy Rat's left, and three on his right. Reacher kept moving, rotating them the way he wanted, his back to the street. He didn't want to get trapped against someone's rear fence. He didn't want to get jammed in a corner. He didn't plan on running, but an option was always a fine thing to have.

The seven guys tightened their semicircle, but not enough. They stayed about ten feet away, with better than a yard between each one of them. Which made the first two plays obvious. They would come shuffling in, slowly, maybe grunting and glaring, whereupon Reacher would move fast and punch his way through the line, after which everyone would turn around, Reacher now facing a new inverted semicircle, now only six in number. Then rinse and repeat, which would reduce them to five. They wouldn't fall for it a third time, so at that point they would swarm, all except Jimmy Rat, who Reacher figured wouldn't fight at all. Too smart. Which in the end would make it a close-quarters four-on-one brawl.

A bad day.

For someone.

"Last chance," Reacher said. "Tell the little guy to answer my question, and you can all go back to your suds."

No one spoke. They tightened some more and hunched down into crouches and started shuffling forward, hands apart and ready. Reacher picked out his first target and waited. He wanted him five feet away. One pace, not two. Better to save the extra energy for later.

Then he heard tires on the road again, behind him, and in front of him the seven guys straightened up and looked around, with exaggerated wide-eyed innocence all over their faces. Reacher turned and saw the cop car again. The same guy. County Police. The car coasted to a stop and the guy took a good long look. He buzzed his passenger window down, and leaned across inside, and caught Reacher's eye, and said, "Sir, please approach the vehicle."

Which Reacher did, but not on the passenger side. He didn't want to turn his back. Instead he tracked around the trunk to the driver's window. Which buzzed down, while the passenger side buzzed back up. The cop had his gun in his hand. Relaxed, held low in his lap.

The cop said, "Want to tell me what's going on here?"

Reacher said, "Were you army or Marine Corps?"

"Why would I be either?"

"Most of you are, in a place like this. Especially the ones who hike all the way to the nearest PX to get their hair cut."

"I was army."

"Me, too. There's nothing going on here."

"I need to hear the whole story. Lots of guys were in the army. I don't know you."

"Jack Reacher, 110th MP. Terminal at major. Pleased to meet you."

The cop said, "I heard of the 110th MP."

"In a good way, I hope."

"Your HQ was in the Pentagon, right?"

"No, our HQ was in Rock Creek, Virginia. Some ways north and west of the Pentagon. I had the best office there for a couple of years. Was that your security question?"

"You passed the test. Rock Creek it was. Now tell me what's going on. You looked like you were fixing to fight these guys."

"So far we're just talking," Reacher said. "I asked them something. They told me they would prefer to answer me outside in the open air. I don't know why. Maybe they were worried about eavesdroppers."

"What did you ask them?"

"Where they got this ring."

Reacher rested his wrist on the door and opened his hand.

"West Point," the cop said.

"Sold to the pawn shop by these guys. I want to know who they got it from."

"Why?"

"I don't know exactly. I guess I want to know the story."

"These guys won't tell you."

"You know them?"

"Nothing we can prove."

"But?"

"They bring stuff in from South Dakota through Minnesota. Two states away. But never enough to get the Feds interested in an interstate kind of thing. And never enough to put a South Dakota police detective on an airplane. So it's pretty much risk-free for them."

"Where in South Dakota?"

"We don't know."

Reacher said nothing.

The cop said, "You should get in the car. There are seven of them."

"I'll be OK," Reacher said.

"I'll arrest you, if you like. To make it look good. But you need to be gone. Because I need to be gone. I can't stay here my whole watch."

"Don't worry about me."

"Maybe I should arrest you anyway."

"For what? Something that hasn't happened yet?"

"For your own safety."

"I could take offense," Reacher said. "You don't seem very worried about their safety. You talk like it's a foregone conclusion."

"Get in the car. Call it a tactical retreat. You can find out about the ring some other way."

"What other way?"

"Then forget all about it. A buck gets ten there's no story at all. Probably the guy came back all sad and bitter and sold the damn ring as fast as he could. To pay the rent on his trailer."

"Is that how it is around here?"

"Often enough."

"You're doing OK."

"It's a spectrum."

"It wasn't a guy. The ring is too small. It was a woman."

"Women live in trailers, too."

Reacher nodded. He said, "I agree, a buck gets ten it's nothing. But I want to know for sure. Just in case."

Silence for a moment. Just the engine's whispered idle, and a breeze in the telephone wires.

"Last chance," the cop said. "Play it smart. Get in the car."

"I'll be OK," Reacher said again. He stepped back and straightened up. The cop shook his head in exasperation, and waited a beat, and then gave up and drove away, slowly, tires hissing on the blacktop, exhaust fumes trailing. Reacher watched him all the way to the corner, and then he stepped back up on the sidewalk, where the black-clad semicircle re-formed around him.

Chapter 4

The seven bikers resumed their previous positions, and they hunched down into their combat stances again, feet apart, hands held wide and ready. But they didn't move. They didn't want to. Not right away. From their point of view a new factor had been introduced. Their opponent was completely batshit crazy. He had proved it. He had been offered a graceful exit by the county cops, and he had turned it down. He had stayed to fight it out.

Why?

They didn't know.

Reacher waited. At that point he figured Chang would be hauling her packages home. Dumping them on the kitchen counter. Assembling her ingredients. Taking a knife from a drawer. Maybe heating the stove. Dinner for one. A quiet evening. A relief, perhaps.

Still the bikers didn't move.

Reacher said, "You guys having second thoughts now?"

No response.

Reacher said, "Answer my question and I'll let you walk away."

No movement.

Reacher waited.

Then eventually he said, "A person less patient than me might think it's time to shit or get off the pot."

Still no response.

Reacher smiled.

He said, "Then I guess I was just born lucky. This is like winning the slots in Vegas. Ding, ding, ding. I got seven big girls all in a line."

Which got a reaction, like he wanted it to. Like he needed it to. Motion was his friend. He wanted moving mass and momentum. He wanted them raging and blundering. Which he got. They glanced among themselves, outraged, but not wanting to be the first to move, or the last, and then on some kind of unspoken signal they all jerked forward, suddenly mad as hell, all pumped up and vulnerable. Reacher put his original plan in action. It was still good. Still the obvious play. He waited until they were five feet away, and then he launched hard and smashed through the line with a horizontal elbow in his first target's face, and then he turned immediately and launched again, no delay at all, stamping his foot to kill the old momentum and get some new, scything his elbow at the guy to the right of the sudden new gap, who turned straight into it, facing front with all kinds of urgency, meeting the blow like a head-on wreck on the highway.

Two down.

Reacher turned again and stood still. The five survivors formed up in a new semicircle. Reacher took a long step back. Simply to gauge their intentions. Which were exactly as predicted. Jimmy Rat faded backward, and the other four came on forward.

Reacher had graduated most of the specialist combat schools the army had to offer, most of them on posts inside the old Confederacy, all of them staffed by grizzled old veterans who had done things no normal person could imagine. Such schools concluded with secret notes in secret files and a lot of bruises and maybe even broken bones. The rule of thumb in such establishments, when faced with four opponents, was to make it three opponents pretty damn quickly. And then to make it two opponents just as fast, which was the win right there, the whole ball game, because obviously any graduate of any such school could not possibly have the slightest problem going one-on-two, because if he did, it would mean the instructors had done a poor job of instructing, which was of course logically impossible in the army.

Reacher called it getting his retaliation in first. The four guys were all hunched again, arms wide, bow-legged and feet apart. Maybe they thought such poses looked threatening. To Reacher they looked like a target-rich environment. He darted in and picked off the end guy on the left with a kick in the balls, and then danced away at right-angles, in line with them, where the back three couldn't get to him without detouring around the end guy, who by that point was doubled over, retching and puking and gasping.

Reacher stepped back again. The back three came after him, making the detour, the first guy going right, the second left, the third right again. All of which gave Reacher time to slip around behind the line of bikes, to the other side. Which gave the three guys a decision to make. Obviously two would follow one way and one the other, but which one and which way? Obviously the lone guy carried the greatest risk. He was the weak point and would get hit first, and maybe hardest. Who wanted that duty?

Reacher saw Jimmy Rat watching from the sidewalk.

The three guys split up two and one, the two coming around to Reacher's right, the lone guy from the left. Reacher moved to meet him, fast, his mind on the invisible geometry unspooling behind him, figuring he would get just shy of three seconds of pure one-on-one, before the other two arrived behind him.

Three seconds was plenty. The lone guy thought he was ready, but he wasn't. He was thinking all wrong. His subconscious mind was telling him his best play was to hang back a little. Human nature. Millions of years of evolution. Then the front part of his brain was telling him no, if a confrontation was inevitable, then logically his interests would be best served by staging it as close to reinforcements as he could get. Therefore he should move toward the other two. Not away from them.

The stop-start impulses in the guy's head produced a sudden forward lurch, which brought him too close too soon. His mental bandwidth was all taken up with locomotion issues. Time and space. He wasn't thinking about how to defend himself. Until too late. And even then he showed no imagination. He had seen elbows and feet, and he improvised a kind of all-purpose defensive posture against either, but Reacher ignored both and took the last unexpected stride at full speed, and seamlessly head-butted the guy full on the bridge of the nose. Moving mass and momentum. You bet your ass. Game over, right there. A second and a half.

Reacher turned fast and found the last two guys already around behind the line of motorcycles, twelve feet away, coming on at a medium speed, somewhere between eager and obligated. Reacher stepped backward over his head-butted victim and looped back around to the street side of the bikes. He watched the last two follow. Watched them realize. They were on an oval racetrack. They could go around and around all night long.

They split up, one and one. They glanced and paused and coordinated. They waited, one behind the last bike on the left, one behind the last bike on the right. The survivors. The pick of the litter. The smartest, certainly. Always better to go fifth and sixth than first or second.

Then on a silent count of three they stepped forward. Not the worst Reacher had ever seen. Their speed was right, and their angles were right. The textbooks would say it was very likely Reacher would get hit. From one direction or another. It was almost unavoidable. They would arrive together. He would be the turkey in the sandwich.

Probably Chang was sitting down and eating by that point. Whatever she had made. At her kitchen table. With a glass of wine. A small celebration, maybe. Home safe.

Getting hit was a rare event for Reacher. And he intended to keep it rare. Not just vanity. Getting hit was inefficient. It degraded future performance.

He stepped forward, just as the two guys were rounding the ends of the line of bikes. Now the angle was flatter. More of a straight line than a triangle. He took a breath. The two guys got closer. One from his left, and one from his right. They were mincing along, pace for pace, always glancing ahead at the relative distances. Aiming to arrive together.

Human nature. Millions of years of evolution.

Reacher darted left, and two things happened. The left-hand guy reared up backward, because he was surprised, and the right-hand guy sped up forward, to close the gap, because he was in full-on hunting mode, and his prey was getting away.

So Reacher spun back instantly, and the right-hand guy ran full speed straight into his scything elbow, whereupon Reacher turned once more, and found he had half a second to spare, because the left-hand guy was taking some major amount of time to get his rearing-up-backward momentum converted into forward motion again. Which gave Reacher space to pick his spot. He kicked the guy in the knee, which dropped him face down on the gravel, *bang,* and then Reacher kicked him in the head, but left-footed, which was his weaker side. Normal for right-handed people. And appropriate. No need to go too far. Being dumb wasn't a capital crime. Wasn't a crime at all, in fact. Merely a handicap.

He breathed out.

Undefeated.

From the sidewalk Jimmy Rat said, "Feel better now?"

Reacher said, "A little."

"You could work for me, if you want."

"I don't want."

"Is it woman trouble?"

Reacher didn't answer. Instead he squeezed between adjacent handlebars, and he swung his leg over, and he sat down on Jimmy Rat's bike. He pushed back in the saddle and got comfortable and put his foot up on a peg.

"Hey," Jimmy Rat said. "You can't do that. You can't sit on another rider's motorcycle. It's disrespectful. It's a thing, man."

"How big of a thing?"

"It's rule one."

"So what are you going to do about it?"

Jimmy Rat said nothing.

Reacher said, "Answer my question and I'm out of here."

"What question?"

"I want a place and a name in South Dakota, where you got that ring."

No answer.

Reacher said, "I'm happy to sit here all night. Right now there are no witnesses. But sooner or later someone will come along. They'll see me sitting on your bike. With you doing nothing about it. Like a pussy, not a rat. You'll be finished."

Jimmy Rat glanced all around.

He said, "This is not a guy you want to meet."

"Neither were you," Reacher said. "But here I am anyway."

There was the sound of traffic, one block over. Maybe a pick-up truck, rolling slow. Jimmy Rat watched the corner. Would it turn in? It didn't. It hissed away into the distance, and silence came back.

Reacher waited.

There was the sound of another car, a block the other way.

Jimmy Rat said, "He operates out of a laundromat in Rapid City. His name is Arthur Scorpio."

The car on the parallel block was slowing. Preparing to turn toward them. It was thirty seconds from the corner. Reacher got off the bike, and squeezed back between the handlebars again, to the sidewalk. Jimmy Rat went the other way, around the bikes, into the shadows behind the building. Maybe in through the rear door.

The car showed up at the corner, right on time. It was the county cop. Back again.

Chapter 5

The cop paused a beat, with his foot on the brake, and then he hauled on the wheel and stopped on the same curb he had used before. He buzzed his window down and surveyed the scene. Six men, all horizontal, some of them moving. Plus Reacher on the sidewalk, standing straight.

The cop said, "Sir, please approach the vehicle."

Reacher stepped over.

The cop said, "Congratulations."

"On what?"

"What you did here."

"No, this was all self-inflicted. I was just a spectator. They had some kind of a big falling out. I think someone sat on the wrong motorcycle."

"That's your story?"

"You don't believe it?"

"Just theoretically, would I be expected to?"

"The pawnbroker's lawyer says it would be better for us all if you did."

"I want you out of the county."

"Works for me. I'm planning on the first bus."

"Not fast enough."

"Want me to steal a motorbike?"

"I'll drive you."

"You want me gone that bad?"

"It would save a lot of paperwork. For both of us."

"Where would you drive me?"

"I'm guessing they answered your question. So now you're headed west. The county line out there is a straight shot to the I-90 on-ramp. Plenty of friendly folks. You'll get a ride."

So Reacher climbed in, and forty uneventful minutes later he climbed out again, in the middle of nowhere, on a dark two-lane road, next to a sign that said he was leaving one county and entering the next. He waved goodbye to the cop, and walked forward, a hundred yards, two hundred, and then he stopped and looked back. The cop flashed his lights and backed up and turned and drove away. Reacher watched his tail lights disappear, and then he moved on, to a spot where the shoulder widened a little. He waited there. Ahead of him was about sixty miles of two-lane, and then I-90. Which led west through Minnesota, into South Dakota, through Sioux Falls, and all the way to Rapid City.

And onward. All the way to Seattle, if he wanted.

At that moment, more than fifteen hundred miles away, Michelle Chang was eating a delivery pizza at her kitchen table. With a glass of water, not wine. Not a celebration. Just calories. She had been busy all afternoon, catching up on a week's worth of missed chores. She was tired, and partly happy to be on her own, and partly not. She figured Reacher would have gone to Chicago next. Plenty of options from there. She missed him. But it wouldn't have worked. She knew that. She knew it as clearly as she had ever known anything.

* * *

Also at that moment, nearly seven hundred miles away, a phone was ringing on a desk in the Rapid City Police Department's Crimes Against Property unit. It was answered by a detective named Gloria Nakamura. She was small and dark and three years in. No longer a rookie, but not yet a veteran. She was an hour away from the end of her watch. She said, "Property, Nakamura."

It was a tech from Computer Crimes, doing her a favor. He said, "My guy at the phone company called me. Someone named Jimmy on a Wisconsin number just left a voicemail for Arthur Scorpio. On his personal cell. Some kind of warning."

Nakamura said, "What kind?"

"I'll email it to you."

"Owe you," Nakamura said, and hung up. Her email dinged. She clicked on the message, and clicked on a file, and dabbed her volume button. She heard what sounded like a barroom, and then a nervous voice speaking fast. It said, "Arthur, this is Jimmy. I just had a guy inquiring about an item I got from you. He seems set on working his way along the chain of supply. I didn't tell him anything, but he already found me somehow, so what I'm thinking is maybe he'll somehow find you, too. If he does, take him seriously. That's my advice. This guy is like Bigfoot come out of the forest. Heads up, OK?"

Then there was a plastic rattle as a big old receiver was fumbled back in its cradle. Maybe a pay phone on a wall. In a bar in Wisconsin. The Arthur Scorpio file was already three inches thick. Nothing ever stuck. But Rapid City's CID never quit. Every scrap of intelligence was logged. Sooner or later something would click. Nakamura wrote it up. After the narrative summary she added her notes. *No smoking gun, but persuasive about the existence of a supply chain.* Then she opened a search engine and typed *Bigfoot.* She got the gist. A mythic ape-man, hairy, seven feet tall, from the Northwest woods. She reopened her document and added: *Maybe Bigfoot will shake something loose!* She emailed a copy to her lieutenant.

Afterward she felt bad about the exclamation point. It looked girlish. But it had to. Really she meant for her boss to read her note and order an immediate resumption of surveillance. Just in case Scorpio's incoming visitor proved significant. A no-brainer, surely. Obviously Jimmy from Wisconsin was lying when he said he didn't tell the guy anything. That claim wasn't logical. A guy scary enough to warrant a heads-up voicemail was scary enough to elicit the answer to just about any question he wanted to ask. So obviously the guy was already on his way. Time was therefore of the essence. But her boss claimed all executive authority as his own. Nudging was counterproductive. Hence the giggly deflection, to take the sting away. To make the guy think it was his own idea all along.

Then the night shift came in, and Nakamura went home. She decided she would swing by Scorpio's laundromat in the morning. On her way back to work. Thirty minutes or an hour. Just to take a look. It was possible Bigfoot might have arrived by then.

Reacher had no reason to doubt the county cop when he said western Wisconsin was populated by friendly folks. The problem was quantity, not quality. It was a lonely rural road, in the middle of nowhere, and by that point it was late in the evening. There was no traffic. Or almost none, to be exact. A Dodge pick-up truck had blasted by in a howl of warm wind, and five minutes after that a Ford F-150 had slowed down to take a look, before speeding up again and driving on without stopping. Now the eastern horizon was stubbornly dark and silent. But Reacher remained optimistic. It only took one. And there was plenty of time. There was no big strategic hurry. The ring had been in the pawn shop for a month. There was no red-hot trail to follow.

A buck gets ten there's no story at all.

Reacher waited, and eventually he saw distant headlights in the east, just dim twinkles like faraway stars. For a whole minute they seemed to get no closer, because of the head-on perspective, but then the picture sharpened. A pick-up truck, he thought, or an SUV. Because of the height and the spacing of the lights. He stood a yard inside the traffic lane and stuck out his thumb. He turned half sideways, like a Hollywood pose, so his profile was presented at an angle, so visually his bulk was minimized. Nothing he could do about his height. But the less threatening the better. He was an experienced hitchhiker. He knew he was subject to snap decisions.

It was a pick-up truck. A big one. A crew cab. Japanese. Lots of chrome and lots of shiny paint. It slowed down. Came close. The driver's face was lit up red, from the instrument panel. *Not going to happen,* Reacher thought. The driver was a woman. She'd have to be nuts.

The truck stopped.

It was a Honda. Dark red metallic. The window buzzed down. There was a dog on the back seat. Like a German shepherd, but bigger. About the size of a pony. Maybe a freak mutation. It had teeth the size of rifle ammunition. The woman leaned across the console. She had dark hair up in a knot. She was wearing a dark red shirt. She was about forty-five years old.

She said, "Where are you headed?"

Reacher said, "I need to get on I-90."

"Hop right in. That's near where I'm going."

"You sure?"

"About where I'm going?"

"About me hopping in. From the safety point of view. You don't know me. As a matter of fact I'm not a threat, but I would say that anyway, right?"

"I have a savage dog in here."

"I might be armed. The obvious play would be shoot the dog first. Or cut its throat. And then start on you. That's what I would be worried about. Professionally speaking, I mean."

"You a cop?"

"I was in the military police."

"You armed?"

"No."

"Then hop in."

* * *

She was a farmer, she said, with a lot of dairy cattle on a lot of acres. Doing well, Reacher figured, judging by her car. It felt about as wide as a Humvee inside. It was upholstered in quilted leather. It was as silent as a limousine. They talked. He asked if she had always been a farmer, and she said yes, four generations. She asked him what he did for a living, and he said he was between jobs. The giant dog followed the conversation from the back seat, turning its wicked head one way, and then the other.

An hour later she stopped and let him out at the I-90 cloverleaf. He thanked her and waved her away. She was a nice person. One of the random encounters that made his life what it was.

Then he walked to the westbound ramp and started over, standing at an angle, one foot on the rumble strip, the other in the traffic lane, with his thumb out wide.

Nearly seven hundred miles away, in his office behind his laundromat in Rapid City, Arthur Scorpio was clearing the last of the day's texts and emails and voicemails off his phone. He got to Jimmy Rat's message, and heard *I didn't tell him anything, but he already found me somehow, so what I'm thinking is maybe he'll somehow find you, too.* Which, translated into plain English, meant *I snitched on you and a guy is definitely on his way.* So, in the long term, no more business for Jimmy Rat, and in the short term, defensive measures might have to be considered.

Scorpio called his secretary at home. She was on her way to bed. He asked her, "Who or what is Bigfoot?"

She said, "He's a giant ape-man who lives in the woods. On the slopes in the Northwest. About seven feet tall and covered in hair. Eats bears and cattle. One rancher lost a thousand head, over the years."

"Where was this?"

"Nowhere," the secretary said. "It's imaginary. Like a fairy tale."

Scorpio said, "Huh."

Then he disconnected, and made two more calls, both to reliable guys he knew, and then he locked up his laundromat and drove himself home.

Chapter 6

Close to midnight Reacher got a ride in a shiny stainless steel truck carrying five thousand gallons of organic milk in a tank shaped like a boat-tail bullet. It was headed to Sioux Falls, which was the western limit of that particular dairy's distribution area. But which was still more than 350 miles short of Rapid City. Don't worry, the driver said. Onward rides would be easy to get. There was a truck stop with all kinds of traffic, night and day. A real big place, like the crossroads of the world.

Reacher kept the guy talking all the way through Minnesota, which he figured was his job, like human amphetamine. Anything to keep the guy awake. Anything to avoid the old joke: *I want to die peacefully in my sleep like Grandpa. Not screaming in terror like his passengers.* The resulting conversation spiraled off in all kinds of different directions. Institutional injustices in the milk business were exposed. Grievances were aired. Then the guy wanted to hear war stories, so Reacher made some up. The big truck stop came along soon enough. The guy had not been exaggerating. There was an acres-wide fuel stop, and a spreading two-story motel a hundred yards long, and a warehouse-sized family restaurant, blazing with neon outside and fluorescence inside. There were back-to-back eighteen-wheelers wheezing in and out, and all kinds of cars and trucks and panel vans.

Reacher climbed out of the milk tanker and headed straight for the motel office, where he took a room, even though it was already close to dawn. No point arriving in Rapid City all tired and exhausted. No point arriving exactly when expected, either. Obviously Jimmy Rat would have called Arthur Scorpio. Some kind of a get-in-first cover-your-ass play, as in *It wasn't me, honest, but I think someone dimed you out.* Which wouldn't necessarily be believed in every particular, but which would certainly be acted upon, as a distant early warning. *There's something out there.* The oldest fear in human history. Scorpio would post sentries right away. And so in turn Reacher would make them stare at a whole lot of nothing for the first day. To dull them down, to sap their enthusiasm, to make them yawn and blink. Always better to engage at a time of your own choosing. So he ate breakfast in the bustling restaurant, and then he headed back to his room, and took a shower, and went to bed just as the sun rose, with the tiny West Point ring on the night table beside him.

At that point, more than 350 miles away to the west, in Rapid City, Detective Gloria Nakamura was already up and about. She had woken before dawn, and showered and dressed and eaten breakfast. Now she was heading out, a whole hour early. To work, but not yet.

She commuted in her own car, which was a mid-size Chevy sedan. It was pale blue, and as anonymous as a rental. She drove through downtown, and turned off the main drag toward Arthur Scorpio's territory. He owned a whole city block. His laundromat was in the center building. Like a flagship operation. The block fronted on a cracked concrete cross street with a narrow sidewalk featuring a dead tree in a bone-dry pit. Running down the back of the block was a service alley, for deliveries and trash collection.

She tried the alley first. It was patched and narrow. Overhead a skein of power lines and phone wires looped left and right from tilted poles. There was a guy outside the laundromat's back door. He was leaning on the wall, with his arms folded. He was in a short black coat against the dawn chill. A black sweater under it. Black pants, black shoes. He was more than six feet tall, and heavy. About twice Nakamura's size. He was wide awake and watchful.

She wanted to take a cell phone picture. For the endless file. But she couldn't be obvious about it. She had heard nothing from her boss. Surveillance had not been officially reauthorized. So she swiped through to camera, and put the phone to her ear, next to her window, as if she was taking a call, and she drove slowly by, eyes front, furtively dabbing with her thumb, *click click click,* until the sentry was well behind her. Then she turned left out of the alley, and left again, and drove past the front of the building.

There was another guy at the front door. Same deal. Leaning on the wall, watchful, arms crossed. Dressed in black. Like a nightclub bouncer. No velvet rope. Nakamura put her phone to her ear. *Click click click.* She turned right at the end of the block and parked on the street where the guy couldn't see her.

She checked her pictures. Both sets were tilted and blurry and neither had the subject anywhere near the center of the frame. But the building was recognizable. The overall context was clear. The narrative told a story. Scorpio had gotten word from Wisconsin, and had immediately hired security. Local muscle. Two guys. One in front, one in back.

Because Scorpio was at least somewhat worried about Bigfoot.

Who was where?

Incoming, Nakamura thought. Had to be. *He seems set on working his way along the chain of supply.* She got out of her car. She walked back the same way she had come, and turned in on Scorpio's street. She stayed on the opposite sidewalk. The guy at the laundromat's door saw her. She felt his eyes on her. He didn't move. Just watched. She kept walking. There was a breakfast place almost opposite the laundromat. Not Scorpio's. His neighbor's. It had an undersized front window, but if you took the first table and craned up in your chair you got a pretty good view. Nakamura had spent hours in there.

She pushed in the door.

Her table was taken. By a guy with the ruins of a bacon and egg breakfast pushed away from him, and a half-full cup of coffee cradled in its place. He was a neat, compact man, in a collar and tie, and a dark conventional suit made of sensible hardwearing fibers. His hair was neatly brushed. He was somewhere over fifty, but how much over was hard to say. His hair was still brown. He had a lean and ageless face. He could have been sixty. He could have been seventy.

He was watching the laundromat through the window.

Had to be. Nakamura knew the signs. He wasn't craning up in his chair, because although not tall he was taller than she was. But even so, his back was unnaturally straight. Had to be, to get his eye line up over the sill. And his gaze was unwavering. He never looked down. He found his cup by feel, and raised it blind, and watched over the rim while sipping.

Was this Bigfoot?

Take him seriously, the voice from Wisconsin had said. And certainly the guy at the table looked like he should be taken seriously. Deep down there was something hard and competent about him. Not immediately obvious. His expression was amiable. But he had limited patience. He wasn't to be messed with. That was clear. Theoretically it was possible to imagine him as a quiet and deadly foe of some sort. It was possible to imagine him as the kind of man who might merit a whispered heads-up voicemail. With an urgent warning and a pithy description. But the description would not have been *like Bigfoot come out of the forest.* Not for this man. It would have been a reference to a spy movie perhaps, about a faceless KGB killer blending in with the crowd. It would have been about how neat he was. How physically unobtrusive. He was almost dapper. He was the opposite of Bigfoot.

So who was he?

One sure way to find out.

She sat down across from him, and took her badge from her purse. It was in a department-issued vinyl wallet, opposite a photo ID behind a plastic window. *Nakamura, Gloria, Detective,* and her signature and her picture.

The guy took a pair of tortoiseshell reading glasses from an inside pocket and put them on. He glanced at the ID, and glanced away. He took a small notebook from another inside pocket. He opened it with his thumb. He glanced at it, changed pages, and glanced away.

He said, "You're with Property Crimes."

"You got us all listed in there?"

"Yes," he said.

"Why?"

"I like to know who does what in a place."

"What are you doing here?"

"My job."

"What's your name?"

"Bramall," the guy said. "First name Terrence, but you can call me Terry."

"And what's your job, Mr. Bramall?"

"I'm a private investigator."

"From where?"

"Chicago."

"What brings you to Rapid City?"

"A private investigation."

"Of Arthur Scorpio?"

"I'm afraid I'm bound by a certain degree of confidentiality. Unless and until I believe a crime has been or is about to be committed. Which I don't at this moment."

Nakamura said, "I need to know whether you're for him or against him."

"Like that, is it?"

"He won't be voted citizen of the year."

"He's not my client, if that's what you mean."

"Who is?"

"Can't say."

Nakamura asked, "Do you have a partner?"

"Romantically?" Bramall said. "Or professionally?"

"Professionally."

"No."

"Are you part of an agency?"

"Why do you ask?"

"We heard someone was on his way here. Not you. Someone else. He was in Wisconsin yesterday. I wondered if he was an associate."

"Not mine," Bramall said. "I'm a one-man band."

Nakamura took a business card from her purse. She put it on the table, near Bramall's coffee cup. She said, "Call me if you need me. Or if you decide to take the confidentiality stick out of your ass. Or if you need advice. Scorpio is a dangerous man. Never forget that."

"Thank you," Bramall said, his eyes on the window.

Nakamura walked back to her car, with the guy at the laundromat door watching her all the way. She drove to work, and got there early. She woke her computer and opened a search engine. She typed *Bramall, Terrence, private investigator, Chicago*. She got a bunch of hits. The guy was sixty-seven years old. He was retired FBI. A long and distinguished career. Many successful cases. Senior rank. Multiple medals and awards. Now he was in business on his own account. He was high end. He didn't advertise. He was hard to get. He was expensive. He was a true specialist. He offered only one service. All he did was find missing persons.

Chapter 7

Reacher woke himself up when he figured the lunch rush would be over. He felt OK, after his exertions the previous evening. No real aches or pains. He checked the mirror. He had a light bruise on his forehead, from head-butting the fourth guy. And his right forearm was tender. It had dispatched three of them all by itself. Fully fifty percent. Along the bone there was nothing to bruise, but the skin looked about twice as thick as normal. And red, with tiny puncture wounds here and there. Even through his shirtsleeve. Which happened. Teeth, usually, or chips of bone from broken noses, or eye sockets. Collateral damage. But really nothing to worry about. He was in good shape. Same old same old, on another lonely day.

He showered and dressed and walked over to the emptying restaurant and ate off the all-day breakfast menu. He asked for quarters in his change and stopped at a pay phone near the door. He dialed an ancient number from memory.

It rang twice and was answered.

"West Point," a woman's voice said. "Superintendent's office. How may I help you?"

"Good afternoon, ma'am," Reacher said. "I'm a graduate of the academy, and I have an inquiry I'm sure will end up in your office anyway, so I figured I might as well start there."

"May I have your name, sir?"

Reacher gave it, and his date of birth, and his service number, and his graduation year. He heard the woman write it all down.

She said, "What is the nature of your inquiry?"

"I need to identify a female cadet from the class of 2005. Her initials were S.R.S. and she was small. That's all I've got so far."

He heard her write it down.

She said, "Are you a journalist?"

"No, ma'am."

"Do you work in law enforcement?"

"Not currently."

"Then why do you need to make this identification?"

"I have lost property to return."

"You can send it here. We can forward it."

"I know you can," Reacher said. "And I know why you're suggesting we do it that way. You have all kinds of security issues to worry about now. Privacy rights, too. Not like it was when I was there. I understand that completely. You really shouldn't tell me anything. Which is fine. I don't want to put you on the spot, believe me."

"Then we seem to understand each other."

"Just do me one favor. Look her up, and then look me up. Consider all the possible circumstances. Either you'll be kind of happy you didn't give me a name, or you'll be kind of sorry. I'll call you back sometime and you can tell me which it was. Purely out of interest."

"Why would I be sorry I followed procedure?"

"Because in the end you'll realize that right now was the first faint whisper you ever heard that a West Pointer with the initials S.R.S. was in some kind of trouble somewhere. Maybe alone and in need of help. Afterward you'll wish you'd taken it seriously from the beginning. You'll be sorry you didn't tell me sooner."

"Who are you exactly?"

"Look me up," Reacher said.

The voice said, "Call me back."

Reacher walked the length of the motel to an area near the fuel pumps, where a kind of unofficial hitchhiking market was being run, by a homeless-looking guy wearing a coat tied up with rope. He would collect the desired destination from each new arriving hitchhiker, and then he would walk around shouting it out to the drivers in line for the pumps, and sooner or later one or another would wave and agree to some particular destination, and the lucky hitchhiker would tip the shouting guy a dollar and climb up in the cab.

Good business. Reacher was happy to pay a buck. Not that he would need help or luck. Every single driver was going to Rapid City. It was 350 miles away, but it was the first stop. There wasn't much before it. After it there were choices. Wyoming, Montana, Idaho. But everyone had to pass through Rapid City first.

He got a ride inside about a minute and a half, in a huge red truck pulling a white boxed-in trailer. The cab had a quadruple sleeper pod behind the seats, bigger than some accommodations Reacher had been raised in. For cross-country house moving jobs, the driver said. The whole crew could sleep in the vehicle. Saved on motels.

The guy was old, like a lot of drivers. Maybe it was a fading profession. Maybe it had gotten too hard. Reacher thought the last of the frontier would die with it. Those guys were the final generation. The end of the DNA. Now people wanted to be home every night.

The guy said it would be five hours and five minutes to Rapid City. He said it with the kind of confidence that comes from having done it a thousand times before. They rolled out, sitting way up high, with a clear view to the horizon, and they ground up through the gears, and up, and up, until they were bowling along at more than seventy on the flat, and faster still on the down grades. The mile markers flashed past. Five hours and five minutes seemed dead-on plausible.

As always the driver wanted to know where his temporary passenger was traveling to, and why. As if in payment. A long story, for a long distance. For some reason Reacher told him the truth. The pawn shop, the ring, his compulsion to find out what connected the two. Which he said he couldn't entirely explain.

The driver chewed on it all for ten whole miles.

Then he said, "My wife would say you feel guilty about something."

Reacher didn't answer.

"She reads books," the driver said. "She thinks about things."

"I don't even know who this woman is. I don't know her name. I never met her. How could I feel guilty about her? All I know is she sold her ring."

"Doesn't have to be about her. There's a word. Transference, I think. Or projection, although that might be something different. My wife would say you feel guilty about a separate issue."

"Would it have to be related?"

"Broadly, I suppose. Not necessarily that you made some other woman sell her jewelry, too. Doesn't have to be obvious. My wife would say it might be some other failure or injustice."

Reacher said nothing.

"My wife would ask if you had a wife or girlfriend to talk things over with."

Chang would be halfway through her first full day back to work. Maybe she had new cases. Maybe she was already back at the airport.

"Tell your wife to keep on reading," Reacher said. "She sounds like a very smart woman."

As so often, getting from the highway to the city was the hardest part of the trip. The red truck was too big for downtown. Reacher got out at the cloverleaf, at ten to eight in the evening, after five hours and five minutes exactly. He stretched and breathed and set out looking for a local ride. There was plenty of traffic. Plenty of pick-up trucks, and SUVs, and regular cars. But there was the wrong frame of mind. They were all coming off the highway. They were all on their last lap. All almost home. Almost there. Almost to the bar. Almost to the girlfriend's house. Almost to wherever. They all sped past. No one was in the mood to offer a ride. Not then. Did not compute. Rides were offered at the start of a journey. Not at the end.

Best hope in such a situation would always be a guy who had shaken his head three hundred miles ago, and then regretted it all the way since. Mostly a self-image thing. Such a guy was cooler than that. Such a guy would stop in his last few miles, maybe secretly hoping his limited offer would get a rueful refusal, thereby salving his conscience at zero personal cost, but also weirdly happy to actually go ahead and pick a guy up and drive him five or ten miles. In Reacher's experience, given the traffic density, such a guy would come along about every twenty or twenty-five minutes. Visibility was key. The earlier they saw you, the better your chances. More time for the cool-guy thing to kick back in. Enough space to glide to a casual stop, and lean across with a smile.

In the end it took forty minutes. At eight-thirty exactly a Dodge crew cab pulled over. The driver put on a generous but apologetic expression and said he was going only as far as downtown. Reacher said that was great. He said he needed the part with the cheap motels. The guy said he would be passing by that general area, about two streets over, and would be happy to point the way.

The cheap part of downtown was dark. Daylight was long gone. There were lights on some street corners, and some of them worked, but not enough. Reacher got out of the Dodge and walked a long block west, mostly by feel, with visibility about a yard, and then another block just the same, and then he turned left and as promised he found two side-by-side motels, on a strip that also featured a diner and a gas station and a tire shop, which likely meant it was a popular route in and out of town. The right-hand motel had a tall lit-up sign, with come-on offers stacked up vertically, like logs in a pile: *Free Breakfast, Free Cable, Free Wi-Fi, Free Upgrades.*

The left-hand motel had: *Free Everything.*

Which Reacher doubted. Not the actual accommodation itself, surely. But nothing ventured, nothing gained. There was an old lady at the desk. She was slender and refined. She had blue hair, spun as fine as cotton candy. She was maybe eighty. Maybe she was the original owner, from way back long ago. Reacher asked his question, and she smiled and said no, he had to pay for his room, but everything else was included. She said it with a half-amused look in her eye, up and then down, and he sensed she meant *Free Everything* partly as a response to her neighbor's boasting, whether good humored or teasing or edgy all in the eye of the beholder, but also partly she meant it as a despairing lament that these days, whatever you did, there was always someone in the world prepared to do it cheaper. Where could she go after free?

Reacher paid for a room.

He asked her, "Where could I wash my clothes around here?"

"What clothes?" she said. "You don't have a bag."

"Theoretically. Suppose I got a bag."

"You would go to a laundromat."

"How many do you have?"

"How many do you need?"

"Some might be better than others."

"Are you worried about bedbugs? You shouldn't be. That's what laundromats are for. Turn the dryer on high, and you kill them stone dead. That's what I do here. With the sheets."

"Good to know," Reacher said. "How many laundromats are there in Rapid City? I'm curious, is all. I like to know things."

She thought about it and almost answered, but then she stopped herself, too naturally meticulous to rely on memory alone. She wanted corroboration. She took a thin Yellow Pages from a drawer. She checked under L, and again under C, for coin-operated.

"Three," she said.

"Do you know the owners?"

Again she thought about it, at first looking skeptical, as if the question was odd and such acquaintances unlikely, but then her face changed, as if she was recalling old trade associations, and local business campaigns, and rubber chicken, and cocktail parties.

She said, "Actually I do know two of the three."

"What are their names?"

"Does it matter?"

"I'm looking for a man named Arthur Scorpio."

"He's the third of the three," she said. "I don't know him at all."

"But you know the name."

"This is a small town. We gossip."

"And?"

"He's not well spoken of."

"In what way?"

"Just gossip. I shouldn't repeat it. But a friend with a great-nephew in the police department says they have a file on Mr. Scorpio three inches thick."

"He buys and sells stolen property," Reacher said. "That's the story I got."

"Are you a policeman?"

"No. Just a regular guy."

"What do you want from Arthur Scorpio?"

"I want to ask him a question."

"You should proceed with great caution. Mr. Scorpio has a reputation for hostility."

"I'll ask politely," Reacher said.

There was a Rapid City street plan in the front of the Yellow Pages. The old lady tore it out, very carefully, and she marked where the motel was, and where Scorpio's laundromat was. She folded the page in quarters and gave it to Reacher. For the morning, no doubt she assumed, but he went straight there. Nearly ten o'clock in the evening. He walked long pitch-dark blocks, checking the old lady's map wherever he found a bulb that worked, and then up ahead he saw the glow of neon. A late-night convenience store, on a corner. According to the old lady's map, Scorpio's laundromat was across the street and half-way down the block.

Reacher found it right where it should be. Just beyond a dead tree. It was in the middle of the block, in the center unit of a larger structure that ran from corner to corner. It was currently closed for business. The lights were off. The door was locked, and it had a padlocked chain wrapped through the handles. The door was glass, with a wider window next to it. Inside was gloom, with a row of stacked machines on one wall, ghostly white and bulky, and a row of plastic lawn chairs on the other, below dispensers for change and soap and fabric conditioner and dryer sheets. Everything seemed to cost a dollar.

Across the street was the lit-up convenience store way on the left, and then a shoe outlet, and then a couple of empty units dead ahead, and then a little right of center was a breakfast place. A real greasy spoon. Its front window was small, but its line of sight would be good. Its food, too, probably. And its coffee. Reacher made a mental note.

Then he walked around the block, and located the laundromat's rear door, in an alley. It was a blank fireproof slab, made of metal. A standard industrial product. Nothing special. A zoning requirement, maybe, or insurance. It was locked.

He walked back. He paced out the depth of the building, from the alley to the street. Too much. It was about twice the depth he could see through the laundromat's window. Which meant there was another room in back, about equal in size. A storeroom, maybe, or offices. Where business was done, that gave rise to gossip.

He stood in the dark a minute more, and then headed back the way he had come. On the opposite corner he stopped in at the convenience store. He figured a cup of coffee would be a good idea. Maybe a sandwich. He was hungry. There was another guy in there on the same mission. He was standing at the deli counter sipping from a go-cup. He was a small man, neat and compact, in a dark suit and a necktie. Apparently he had ordered an elaborate construction involving a fried egg and a large quantity of grated cheese. Clearly not worried about cholesterol. The counterman finished his work and wrapped the sloppy result first in paper, and then in aluminum foil. He handed it over and the guy in the suit turned and stepped around Reacher and headed for the door.

Reacher ordered his go-to, which was roast beef and Swiss cheese, with mayo and mustard, on white bread. Plus coffee. The counterman turned away and spun up the slicing machine. Reacher asked him, "What do you know about the laundromat down the block?"

The guy turned back. The blade hissed and sung behind him. He looked puzzled at first, and then a little hostile, as if he suspected someone was making fun of him. Then he looked preoccupied, as if he was struggling with a difficult arithmetic calculation, and coming out with an answer he liked but didn't trust.

He said, "That's what the other guy just asked."

Reacher said, "The guy with the fried egg sandwich?"

"But what does that kind of guy need with a laundromat? The suits go to the dry cleaner, and the shirts get starched for a buck and a half. Am I right?"

"I'll be back in a second," Reacher said.

He stepped to the door, and out to the sidewalk.

No sign of the guy in the suit and the tie.

No echo of lonely nighttime footsteps.

Reacher came back in and stepped back to the counter, and the guy making his sandwich said, "He would need to wash his underwear, maybe. And socks. But all the hotels have laundry bags in the closet. A guy like that wouldn't sit and watch the soap suds go around and around."

"You think he's staying in a hotel?"

"He's not local. Did you get a look at him? He's some kind of a professional person. I would say a lawyer, in town to try a big case, but he didn't look rich enough. So now I'm thinking IRS or something. A government worker. And then you asked the same question. About the laundromat. I don't think you're IRS, but you could be a cop. So now I'm thinking Arthur Scorpio has got trouble coming."

"How do you feel about that?"

"Depends."

"On what?"

"Whether it works. Mr. Scorpio has been in trouble before. Nothing ever sticks."

Chapter 8

The next morning Reacher left his not-free room just as the sun was coming up. He retraced his steps from the night before, until the last couple of blocks, which he looped around at a distance, until he was beyond them. Then he doubled back, toward Scorpio's alley from the far side, and he peeked in.

There was a sentry posted at the laundromat's rear door. Leaning on the wall, arms folded, short black coat, black sweater, black pants and shoes. Maybe forty years old, maybe six-two, maybe two-ten.

Reacher backed away, and looped around again at the same distance he had used before, two blocks over, two blocks down, so he could approach the breakfast place unseen, from the rear. He figured it would have an alley of its own behind it. Like Scorpio's place. A necessary amenity. Greasy spoons generated a lot of trash. Eggshells, coffee grounds, packaging, leftovers. Drums of used grease. And where there was an alley would be a kitchen door. It would be open. Almost certainly a legal requirement. *This door must remain unlocked during business hours.* To act as a fire escape for the cook. Another necessary amenity. Greasy spoon kitchens burned like napalm.

Reacher found the alley. Found the door. He went in through the kitchen. Into the dining room. He focused on the window, and stepped left for a better view.

There was a second sentry at the laundromat's front door. Same kind of guy. Same kind of pose. Leaning on the wall, impassive, dressed in black.

Arthur Scorpio was taking precautions.

There's something out there.

Reacher looked away, and looked around the room. And saw the guy he had seen the night before. In the convenience store. In the dark suit and the necktie. He was at the table under the window, looking out.

Detective Gloria Nakamura repeated her routine from the previous day. Up before dawn, showered, dressed, breakfasted, and out the door a whole hour early. To work, but not yet. She parked where she had before, and turned in on Scorpio's street, and felt the guy at the laundromat door watching her all the way. She walked to the breakfast place and went in.

Her table was taken. Again. By the same guy as the day before. *Bramall, Terrence, private investigator, Chicago.* The same dark suit, a fresh shirt, a different tie.

And standing in the middle of the room was Bigfoot.

No doubt about it. The guy was huge. Not quite seven feet, but close. Almost to the ceiling. And he was wide. From shoulder to shoulder he looked like four basketballs in a rack in her high school gym. He had fists like Thanksgiving turkeys. He was wearing canvas work pants and a huge black T-shirt. His forearms were battered and sculpted. His hair was a mess. Like he had toweled it dry but not combed it. Like he didn't even own a comb. He hadn't shaved in days. His face was all bone and stubble. His eyes were pale blue, like her car, and he was looking straight at her.

* * *

Reacher saw a petite Asian woman, wearing a black skirt suit like
a uniform. Five feet nothing, maybe ninety-five pounds soaking wet.
Maybe thirty years old. Long black hair, big dark eyes, cute as a button. But no smile. A severe expression instead, as if she was in charge
of something important. As if looking severe was the only way to stay
in charge of it. Which was possibly true, when you were starting out
from five feet nothing and ninety-five pounds. But whatever, she certainly wasn't shy. She was looking straight back at him, openly, examining him, top to bottom and side to side. With some kind of dawning
recognition in her eyes. Which he didn't understand. Not at first. He
was pretty sure he had never seen her before. He felt he would remember. Then he figured Jimmy Rat would have included a description. In the cover-your-ass phone call he must have made. *A big guy
in a black T-shirt is coming.* Maybe the Asian woman worked for
Arthur Scorpio. Maybe she had been briefed about the emergency.

Or maybe she was just an office worker, grumpy about her early
start.

He looked away.

The guy in the necktie was still staring out the window. His expression was patient and contained. And equable. He looked like the type
of guy who would give a polite answer to a reasonable question. But
maybe only as a professional veneer. As if he held a place in a hierarchy where old-fashioned courtesy oiled the wheels. He reminded
Reacher of army colonels he had known. Squared away, buttoned up,
a little gray and dusty, but driven by some kind of quiet internal vigor
and confidence.

Reacher took a table against the wall, at a distance, where he could
see out the window over the other guy's head. Nothing was happening
out there. The sentry was still leaning on the laundromat wall. Not
moving. The lights were on inside. There were no customers yet.

A waitress came by and Reacher ordered his go-to breakfast, which
was coffee plus a short stack of pancakes with eggs, bacon, and maple

syrup. The coffee arrived first. Black, fresh, hot, and strong. Pretty good.

The Asian woman sat down at his table.

She took a small vinyl wallet from her purse. She opened it up and held it out for inspection. On the left was a gold-colored shield. On the right was a photo ID behind a plastic window. It said *Nakamura, Gloria, Detective, Rapid City Police Department*. It had a picture of her face. Dark eyes, a severe expression.

She said, "Were you in Wisconsin yesterday?"

Which told Reacher that Jimmy Rat had indeed made a phone call. And that the Rapid City PD was tapping Scorpio's line. Which meant there was an active and ongoing investigation. Probably the typed transcript of Jimmy Rat's call was already the new top sheet in the three-inch file.

But out loud he said, "Are you entitled to ask that question, even as a cop? I have the right to privacy, and the right to go where I want. It's a First Amendment thing. And a Fourth."

"Are you declining to answer my question?"

"No choice, I'm afraid. I was in the army. I swore an oath to uphold the Constitution. Can't stop now."

"What's your name?"

"Reacher. First name Jack. No middle initial."

"What did you do in the army, Mr. Reacher?"

"I was a military cop. A detective, just like you."

"And now you're a private investigator?"

She glanced at the guy in the necktie as she said it.

Reacher asked her, "Is that guy a private investigator?"

She said, "I decline to answer your question."

He smiled.

He said, "I'm not a private investigator. Just a private citizen. What did you hear from Wisconsin?"

"I'm not sure I should tell you."

"Cop to cop. Because that's what we are."

"Are we?"

"If you want to be."

She put her ID wallet back in her purse and took out her phone. She swiped through to a section with audio recordings. She chose one and touched an on-screen symbol. Reacher heard a plastic and distorted version of barroom noise, and then Jimmy Rat's voice. He recognized it right away. It sounded fast and nervous. It said, "Arthur, this is Jimmy. I just had a guy inquiring about an item I got from you. He seems set on working his way along the chain of supply. I didn't tell him anything, but he already found me somehow, so what I'm thinking is maybe he'll somehow find you, too."

Nakamura touched the pause symbol.

Reacher said, "Why would that be me?"

She pressed play again.

Jimmy Rat said, "If he does, take him seriously. That's my advice. This guy is like Bigfoot come out of the forest. Heads up, OK?"

Nakamura pressed stop.

"Bigfoot?" Reacher said. "That's not very nice."

She said, "What item?"

"Does it matter? All I want to do is ask Scorpio a question. Then I'll be gone."

"Suppose he doesn't answer?"

"Jimmy in Wisconsin did."

"Scorpio has protection."

"So did Jimmy in Wisconsin."

"What item?" Nakamura said again.

Reacher dug in his pocket and came out with the ring. *West Point 2005.* The gold filigree, the black stone, the tiny size. He put it on the table. Nakamura picked it up. She tried it on. Third finger, right hand. It fit easily. Even loosely. But then, she was five feet nothing and weighed ninety-five pounds. Her fingers were about as thin as pencils.

She took the ring off again. She weighed it in her palm. She looked at the inside, at the engraving. She asked, "Who is S.R.S.?"

"I don't know," Reacher said.

"So what's the story?"

"I found it in a pawn shop in a small town in Wisconsin. It's not the kind of thing you would give up easily. This woman suffered four hard years to get it. Every day they tried to break her and make her quit. That's how West Point works. And 9/11 had just happened. Those were serious years. And what came afterward was worse. Iraq, and Afghanistan. She might have sold her car, or the watch she got from her aunt for Christmas, but she wouldn't have sold her ring."

"Does this guy Jimmy own the pawn shop?"

Reacher shook his head. "He's a local biker. Goes by the name Jimmy Rat. He wholesaled the ring along with a bunch of other trinkets. He told me he got it from Arthur Scorpio, here in Rapid City. So now I want to know who Arthur Scorpio got it from. That's the only question I want to ask him."

"He won't tell you."

"That's what the guy in the pawn shop said about Jimmy Rat."

Nakamura didn't reply. Nothing was happening out the window. The waitress came back with Reacher's meal. Pancakes, eggs, bacon, maple syrup. It looked good. He asked for more coffee. Nakamura ordered hot tea and a bran muffin.

Reacher put the ring back in his pocket.

The guy in the necktie got up and left.

Still nothing happening out the window.

Reacher asked, "What kind of private investigator is he?"

Nakamura said, "I didn't say he was."

"I told you stuff. Now you can tell me stuff."

The waitress brought Nakamura's muffin. It was about as big as her head. She broke off a pea-sized crumb and ate it.

She said, "He's from Chicago. His name is Terry Bramall. He's retired FBI. He finds missing persons."

"Who is he looking for here?"

"I don't know."

"Is Scorpio a kidnapper, too?"

"We don't think so."

"Yet Mr. Bramall from Chicago is watching his place. Not just this morning. He was in the neighborhood last night. I saw him in the convenience store."

"You got in last night?"

Reacher nodded. "Pretty late."

"You came straight here from Wisconsin. This is important to you."

"I could have gotten here sooner. I took a nap in Sioux Falls."

"Exactly how did you get Arthur Scorpio's name from Jimmy Rat?"

"I asked him nicely."

She didn't reply. He carried on eating his breakfast. She sipped her tea. There was a long silence.

Then she said, "Arthur Scorpio is not well liked within the police department."

"Understood," Reacher said.

"Nevertheless I am officially required to warn you against committing any kind of crime inside our jurisdiction."

"Don't worry," Reacher said. "All I'm going to do is ask him a question. No law against that."

"What if he doesn't answer?"

"I suppose that's always a theoretical possibility," Reacher said.

She took a business card from her purse. She put it on the table, near his coffee cup. She said, "Those are my numbers. Office and cell. Call me if you need to talk. Scorpio is a dangerous man. Never forget that."

She put five bucks on the table. For her tea and her muffin. Then she got up and left. Out the door, along the sidewalk, and out of sight.

Still nothing happening out the window.

She had left her muffin. Whole and untouched, apart from the pea-sized crumb she had eaten. So Reacher ate the rest of it, with another mug of coffee. Then he called for his check, and asked for quarters in his change. He stopped in the restroom corridor, where there was a pay phone on the wall. Just like there was in the bar in Wisconsin. Which was where Jimmy Rat had made his call to Arthur Scorpio. The background noise proved it. Reacher had seen the guy loop around the line of bikes, to the rear of the building, where he must have gone in the back door, where he must have seen the phone on the wall, where he must have decided upon an immediate warning. Right there and then. While Reacher was still outside, still talking to the county cop.

Some kind of urgency.

Reacher leaned on the wall, where he could still watch the front window, and he dialed the same ancient number from memory.

The same woman answered.

"West Point," she said. "Superintendent's office. How may I help you?"

"This is Reacher," he said.

"Wait one, major."

She knew his rank. She had read his file. There was a click, and a long silence, and then another click, and a man's voice said, "This is the supe."

The superintendent. The big boss. What any other college would call the president.

Reacher said, "Good morning, general," politely but vaguely, because he didn't know the guy's name. He didn't keep up with alumni affairs. But the supe was always a general. Usually smart and accomplished, sometimes progressive, never a pushover.

The guy said, "Your inquiry yesterday was most irregular."

"Yes, sir," Reacher said, purely out of habit. In such situations there were only three permissible responses at West Point: Yes sir, no sir, no excuse sir.

The guy said, "I would like an explanation."

So Reacher told the same story he had just gotten through telling Nakamura, about the pawn shop, and the ring, and his nagging sense of disquiet.

The supe said, "So this is about a ring."

"It seemed significant."

"Yesterday you implied the former cadet was in danger."

"She might be."

"But you don't know for sure."

"She pawned the ring, or sold it, or had it stolen. Any of which would suggest some kind of misfortune. I think we should find out."

"We?"

"She's one of ours, general."

The guy said, "I read your file. You did well. Not well enough to get a statue on campus, which you wouldn't get anyway, mostly because of the corners you cut."

"No excuse, sir," Reacher said, purely out of habit.

"I have one obvious question. What are you doing now?"

"Nothing."

"What does that mean?"

"It's a long story, general. We shouldn't take the time."

"Major, I'm sure you understand that supplying personal details about current or former military personnel is strictly prohibited about nineteen different ways. The only possible chance it could happen would be a top-secret off-the-record whisper from one West Pointer to another. Purely as a courtesy. Exactly the kind of oak-paneled bullshit we're always being accused of. Therefore naturally you and I face a question of mutual trust. Possibly less important to you than to me. You could put my mind at rest by letting me take your measure."

Reacher was quiet a beat.

"I get uneasy," he said. "I can't stay in one place. I'm sure if you gave the VA enough time, they could come up with a name for it. Maybe I could get a check from the government."

"It's a medical condition?"

"Some would say."

"Does it bother you?"

"Turns out I don't want to stay in one place anyway."

"How frequently do you move around?"

"Constantly."

"Do you think that's a fitting way for a West Pointer to live?"

"I think it's perfectly fitting."

"In what sense?"

"We fought for freedom. This is what freedom looks like."

The guy said, "There are a hundred reasons for selling a ring. Or pawning it. Or losing it, or getting it stolen somehow. Not all the reasons are bad. This could be completely innocent."

"Could be? That's a little lukewarm, general. Sounds like you don't know for sure. Even after reading her file. Which therefore can't have reassured you completely. So now you're hinting about a whisper. Because now you're worried. I think deep down you want to tell me her name. So let me guess. She took off the green suit and now she's under the radar."

"Three years ago."

"After what?"

"Five hard tours in Iraq and Afghanistan."

"Doing what?"

"Unpleasant things, I imagine."

"Is she small?"

"Like a bird."

"That's her," Reacher said. "Now it's decision time, general. What are you going to do?"

The supe didn't answer.

Out the window Reacher saw a black sedan slow up. It stopped on the curb across the street. Outside the laundromat. The driver's door opened. A guy climbed out. He was tall and bony. Maybe fifty years old. He had gray hair cut short. He was wearing a black suit with a white shirt buttoned to the neck, but without a tie. He stood on the sidewalk for a second, and looked a question at the sentry at the door. Who shook his head, as if to say, *No trouble, boss.*

Arthur Scorpio.

Who nodded back at the sentry, and then stepped past him, in through the door.

The sentry stepped across the sidewalk in the other direction and got in Scorpio's car. He drove it away. To park it, presumably. On a side street, or in the alley. Maybe a five-minute absence. The first of two such absences, presumably. He would go retrieve the car at close of business. Two five-minute windows every day.

Good to know.

In Reacher's ear the West Point supe said, "She might not want to be found. Did you consider that? No one comes back whole. Not from five tours."

"I'm not trying to sell her a timeshare in Mexico. If she looks OK from a distance I'll walk away and leave her alone."

"How will you even find her? She's under the radar. Will her name even help?"

"It won't hurt," Reacher said. "Especially not at the end. I'll follow the ring until I find someone who heard of her."

The supe said, "Her name is Serena Rose Sanderson."

Chapter 9

Out the window the front sentry walked back into view, after parking Scorpio's car. He resumed his position, leaning on the wall to the left of the laundromat door, arms folded, impassive.

He had been gone just over five minutes.

Still no customers inside.

Into the phone Reacher said, "Where is Serena Rose Sanderson from?"

"As a cadet her home state was listed as Wyoming," the supe said. "That's all we've got. You think she went back there?"

"Depends," Reacher said. "For some people, home is the first place they go. For others, it's the last. What was she like?"

"She was before my time," the supe said. "But her file is very solid. She was pretty close to outstanding, without ever quite getting there. Never in the top five, always in the top ten. That kind of person. She branched infantry, which was considered a smart choice for a woman, back in '05. She knew she wouldn't see combat, but she guessed the chaos would push her pretty damn near to it. Which I'm sure is what happened. Close support units were always busy. A lot of driving for resupply, which meant a lot of roadside IEDs. Plus vehicle recovery, which would have exposed her out in the open. Off post she would have been armed at all times. I'm sure she was in firefights. Those units took plenty of casualties, same as anyone else. She has a Bronze Star and a Purple Heart. So she was wounded herself at some point."

"Rank?"

"Terminal at major," the guy said. "Like you. On her last tour she was doing a pretty big job. She led her soldiers well. On paper she's a credit to the school."

"OK," Reacher said. "Thank you, general."

"So proceed, but with caution."

"Don't worry."

"I do."

"Why?"

"I read your file," the guy said again. "If you tilt it right and hold it in a sunbeam you can see the invisible writing. You were effective, but reckless."

"Was I?"

"You know you were. You got away with things time after time."

"Did I?"

"One damn thing after another. But you always came up smelling of roses."

"Then draw the appropriate conclusion, general. I wasn't reckless. I was relying on methods I knew had worked before, and would likely work again. I felt I was the opposite of reckless. There's a clue in the word. Reck comes from reckon, and I felt I did more reckoning than most folks. Not less."

"Call me back," the guy said. "Let me know about Sanderson."

For the second day running Gloria Nakamura was early to work. She parked her car and walked up the stairs. The mother hen at the gate to the detectives' pen told her the lieutenant wanted to see her. First thing. Urgent but not critical. The mother hen said his voice on the phone had sounded OK. Not particularly angry.

Nakamura dropped her bag at her desk and headed off down the corridor. The lieutenant's office was a corner suite at the far end of the floor. He was a cancer survivor, worn down to nothing but lacy bone and sinew, but lit up through his papery skin by some kind of crazed internal energy. He had gotten some bonus years, and he was going to slap the shit out of them. He was going to get big things done. Privately Nakamura felt his brush with death had produced an epiphany. He was afraid of being forgotten.

He was at his desk, reading email.

He said, "You sent me a thing about Arthur Scorpio."

She said, "The voicemail from Wisconsin. Yes, boss. There have been developments."

"Has Bigfoot arrived?"

"Yes, boss, I believe he has. But first there was a private eye from Chicago."

"What did he want?"

"He wouldn't say. But I checked him out. He's a missing persons specialist. Very expensive."

"Who's missing?"

"About a million people nationwide."

"Any reason to believe one of them is washing his shorts in Scorpio's place?"

"There's nothing on the wires."

"Tell me about Bigfoot."

"He's a military veteran named Reacher. He found a West Point class ring in a pawn shop and he's tracing its provenance."

"Like a hobby?"

"No, like a matter of military honor. Like a moral obligation. Verging on the sentimental, in my opinion."

"How is Scorpio involved?"

"The likelihood is the ring was stolen property fenced by Scorpio to a Wisconsin biker named Jimmy Rat, who then sold it onward to the pawn shop, where Bigfoot found it. Bigfoot says the pawn shop owner told him Jimmy Rat's name, who told him Arthur Scorpio's name. Now he wants Scorpio to name the next name. Whoever he got the ring from. And so on, all the way down the line. Bigfoot wants to return the ring to its rightful owner. That's my assessment."

"Scorpio won't tell him shit."

"I think he might. I'm not sure Bigfoot was telling the whole truth about what happened in Wisconsin. I don't think a biker with a lucrative trade in stolen property would tell anyone anything. Least of all the name of a supplier. Not voluntarily. You should listen to the audio. Jimmy Rat sounds scared."

"Of Bigfoot?"

"I saw him, boss. You could put him in a zoo."

"You think Scorpio will be scared, too?"

"Either way I think a serious crime is about to be committed. Either Bigfoot will squeeze too hard, or Scorpio will push back too hard."

Then she waited.

The lieutenant said, "I think we should get the surveillance going again."

She said, "Yes, boss," and breathed out.

"Just you. Eyes on at all times. Nothing subtle. Get right up in his grill."

"I might need back up. I might need to intervene."

"No," the guy said. "Don't intervene. Let nature take its course. It's a win-win. If Scorpio hurts the guy, that's great, because then we've got something on him at last. We've got you as an actual eyewitness to a felony assault. On the other hand, if the guy hurts Scorpio, that's good news anyway. The worse the better. Plus you could always arrest the guy afterward. If you wanted to. For a felony assault of his own. If you need to boost your quarterly numbers, I mean."

Reacher left the breakfast place through the kitchen door and slipped away through the alley. He didn't want the front sentry to see him. Not yet. The Bigfoot description would leave the guy in no doubt.

Word would pass instantly to Scorpio inside. Better not to get them too excited too soon.

So he skirted around at a safe radius, and then headed downtown, and started looking for better hotels than his own. The kind of place a retired-FBI gumshoe might choose. No fleapits, but nothing fancy, either. Probably a mid-market national chain. The guy probably had a loyalty card.

Reacher found four possibilities. At the first he went in and asked the clerk for a guest named Terrence Bramall, small guy, neat, in a suit and tie. If he was in a car, it might have Illinois plates. The woman pattered at her keyboard and stared at her screen, and then she said she was sorry, but currently the hotel had no guests with that name.

At the second possibility Reacher was told Terrence Bramall had checked out just thirty minutes before.

Or maybe even less, the clerk said. Maybe only twenty. She called up the closed account, to calibrate her memory. It was twenty-seven minutes ago. The guy had stopped at the desk, in his suit and tie, with a leather traveling bag in one hand, and a leather briefcase in the other. He paid his bill, and headed out to his car, which was in the covered lot. It was a black SUV, with Illinois plates. Bramall loaded his bags, and then got in and drove off, toward the Interstate, but whether he then turned east or west was anyone's guess.

"Do you have his cell phone number?" Reacher asked.

The woman glanced at her screen. Left-hand column, Reacher thought, maybe two-thirds of the way up.

The woman said, "I really can't give it out."

Reacher pointed at the base of the wall behind her.

"Is that a cockroach?" he said.

Not a word hotel keepers liked to hear.

She turned to look. He leaned over the desk and bent his neck. Left-hand column, two-thirds of the way up. Ten digits. Not a prodigious feat of memory.

He straightened up.

She turned back.

"I didn't see anything," she said.

"False alarm," Reacher said. "Sorry. Maybe just a shadow."

Reacher found a pay phone in the lobby of an all-day Chinese restaurant. It was a chromium instrument mounted on a wall of red velvet. Not as glamorous as it looked from a distance. The chrome was pitted and the velvet was threadbare and tacky with grease.

Reacher dialed Bramall's cell number. It rang and rang. It wasn't picked up. No big surprise. The guy was probably on the Interstate. Probably a safety first type of person. Probably had to be, to survive a lifetime in the FBI.

No answer.

A recorded voice came on, inviting Reacher to leave a message.

He said, "Mr. Bramall, my name is Reacher. We waited in line together last night for sandwiches and we were briefly in the breakfast place at the same time this morning. I infer you were watching Arthur Scorpio's place in connection with a missing persons inquiry. I was watching it in connection with trying to trace the source of a piece of stolen property. I think we should put our heads together, to figure out exactly what we both know. Just in case there's more here than meets the eye. Could be useful for one of us, if not both. You can't call me back because I don't have a phone, so I'll try you again at a later time. Thank you. Goodbye."

He hung up.

He stepped out from the velvet lobby to the concrete sidewalk.

Arthur Scorpio's black sedan stopped at the curb.

Right next to him, level with his hip.

The window buzzed down.

The front-door sentry said, "Get in the car."

Chapter 10

The guy had a gun. A revolver. It looked like a worn-out Chief's Special. A .38 five-shooter by Smith & Wesson. Short barrel. It looked small in the guy's hand. His right hand. He was half-twisted behind the wheel, aiming half-sideways through the open passenger window, with a bent arm and a cramped right shoulder.

"In the car," he said again.

Reacher stood still. He had choices. Life was full of them. Easiest thing would be just walk away. Straight ahead along the sidewalk, in the same direction the car had been driving. A right-handed shooter in a left-hand-drive car would have a practical problem with that kind of geometry. His windshield was in the way. Couldn't shoot through it. The bullet would deflect and miss. And afterward there would be a hole in the windshield. Not a smart thing to have. Rapid City was no doubt a tough old town, but it wasn't South-Central LA. Morning gunfire would get called in. Especially downtown, near the hotels and the restaurants. Police cruisers would show up fast. Questions about a bullet hole in a windshield would be hard to answer.

So the guy would have to move. He would have to shift the transmission, and take his foot off the brake, and shrug off his seatbelt, and flip up the armrests, and shuffle his ass across the front bench, and hang his right arm out the passenger window. All of which would take a small but finite amount of time. During which Reacher would be walking farther and farther away. And all the guy had was a worn-out .38 with a two-and-a-half-inch barrel. Not an accurate weapon. More or less a guaranteed miss, with the speed Reacher could walk.

So the better bet would be hang out the driver's window. Much quicker. It was right there. But how? The guy would have to kneel up sideways on the driver's seat, and stick his whole upper body out, and wriggle his right arm free, like putting on a tight sweater, bringing him all the way out of the car up to his waist, and then he would have to twist, and aim, and fire. Except at that point he would also be over-balancing and about to fall out the window. An inaccurate weapon, and a preoccupied shooter clinging to the door mirror. Not a whole lot to worry about.

Which meant the guy's best bet would be step out and brace behind the open door. Like a cop. Except as soon as Reacher heard the creak of the hinge he would duck out of sight into the nearest store or alley. Same thing if he heard the car move off the curb and roll toward him. Stalemate. The whole get-in-the-car thing looked pretty good in the movies, but on the street it was basically optional. Plenty of choices. Keep calm and walk away. Live to fight another day.

But Reacher stayed where he was.

He said, "You want me to get in the car?"

The guy said, "Right now."

"Then put the gun away."

"Or?"

"Or I won't get in the car."

"I could shoot you first and get you in bleeding."

"No," Reacher said. "You really couldn't."

All he had to do was take one fast pace left. Then the guy would be shooting through glass again, or the B-pillar, or the C-pillar, plus anyway his shoulder was tight against the upholstery and wouldn't rotate. Plus again, the cops would come. Lights and sirens. Questions. The guy was stuck.

He was an amateur.

Which was encouraging.

"Put the gun away," Reacher said again.

"How do I know you'll get in?"

"I'm happy to visit with Mr. Scorpio. He has information for me. I was planning to call on him later today, but since you're here, I guess this is as good a time as any."

"How do you know I'm working for Scorpio?"

"Magic," Reacher said.

The guy held still for a second, and then he put the gun back in his coat pocket. Reacher opened the passenger door. The sedan was an ancient Lincoln Town Car. The old square style. The kind that got crashed and burned on the TV shows, because they were cheaper than dirt. The upholstery was red velvet, no better or worse than the restaurant lobby's walls. A little crushed and greasy. Reacher crammed himself in the seat. He put his elbow on the armrest. His left hand hung loose, the size of a dinner plate. The guy stared at it for a second. Long thick fingers, with knuckles like walnuts. Old nicks and scars healed white. The guy looked away. No longer top dog. Uncharted territory, for a man who made his living leaning on walls and scaring people.

"Drive," Reacher said. "I haven't got all day."

They took off, left and right through the downtown blocks, back to the low-rent district. They parked outside the laundromat. The guy took out his gun again. Saving face, in front of Scorpio. Reacher let him. Why not? It cost him nothing. He waited until the guy came around and opened his door, and then he got out, and the guy nodded toward the laundromat entrance. Reacher went in first, to the smell of drains and cold soap, and the back-door sentry leaning on a washing machine, and Arthur Scorpio himself sitting in a plastic lawn chair, as if he was a customer hypnotized by the churning drums.

Up close he had pitted skin on his face, unnaturally white, as if it had been treated with chemicals. The pallor made his eyes look dark. He was tall and thin. Maybe six feet two. Maybe a hundred sixty pounds. But only if he had a dollar's worth of pennies in his pocket. All skin and bone, and awkward as a stepladder.

The back-door sentry pushed himself off the washing machine and came over to stand close. The guy who had driven the car stepped up from behind.

Scorpio said, "What do you want?"

"You fenced a ring to Jimmy Rat," Reacher said. "I want to know who fenced it to you."

"You got the wrong person altogether. I run a laundromat. I don't know any Jimmy Rat."

"Is the laundromat doing well?"

"I'm comfortable."

"And modest. You're doing better than comfortable. Your cash flow is so big you had to hire two guys to watch over it. Except I don't see how. You got no customers."

"You accusing me of something?"

Out the window a pale blue car stopped on the opposite curb. A domestic product. A Chevrolet, possibly. Nothing fancy. A plain specification. In it was a small Asian woman. Black hair, dark eyes. A severe expression. Nakamura. She just sat there, engine off, head turned, watching. A level gaze, over the hood of Scorpio's parked Lincoln. Her eyes were locked on Reacher's, through two layers of glass and thirty feet of air.

Reacher turned back to Scorpio and said, "Jimmy Rat left you a voicemail, which is why you hired these guys. He told you I was coming. And here I am. It's up to you how long I stay."

Scorpio said, "Firstly I don't know what you're talking about, and secondly do you know who that is, in the blue car across the street?"

"She's a cop. Detective Nakamura."

"Who harasses me on a regular basis. As you can see. For completely invented reasons. But this time she can make herself useful for once. You're trespassing, and she can come remove you herself. My tax dollars at work."

"You pay taxes?"

"You accusing me of something?"

"I'm not trespassing. You invited me here. Kind of insisted."

"My point is you can stick your little threats where the sun don't shine. Up to me how long you stay? What are you going to do, with a cop watching?"

"I know her name because we talked. She told me you're not well liked within the police department."

"Mutual."

"It's a code. In plain English it means I could rip your arm off and beat you to death with it, and they wouldn't stop me. They'd sell tickets instead."

"What code? You a cop, too? From somewhere?"

"You expecting one? Not me. I'm just a guy with a question. Tell me the answer, and I'm gone."

Scorpio said, "You never asked how I found you."

Reacher said, "Didn't need to. I already figured it out. From where your boy showed up. Restaurant staff. You slip them a few bucks. They all talk to each other. They all have cell phones. They text. A nice little network. Underpaid and underappreciated. You put the word out. Based on Jimmy Rat's voicemail. Watch out for Bigfoot to come out of the forest. That's what Jimmy said, right?"

"I don't know any Jimmy. Which is my point. I'm going to sit here and deny it all day long. Nothing you can do about it with a cop watching."

"Maybe she'll leave."

"She won't. She sits there all day. We'll be gone before she is. Then what are you going to do? Run after us? Which is my other point. Good luck with your night in town. You won't get a meal anywhere. You won't get a drink. You won't get a bed. I got more than one network running."

"I'm sure you're a regular Al Capone," Reacher said. "Except you got the worst piece-of-shit car in the world."

"Get lost. You're wasting everyone's time. Nothing you can do. Not with a cop watching. Code or no code. Which is bullshit anyway. This is America."

"We could run a test," Reacher said. "I could punch you in the mouth, and we could time how long she took to get in here."

The two sentries stepped in closer. No guns. No pushing or shoving. They couldn't. Nakamura was watching. They put themselves one each side of Scorpio's lawn chair, a step ahead of it, overlapping it a little. Closing it off. Reacher was facing them, not more than an arm's length away, in a flat little triangle.

He said, "Is she still watching?"

Scorpio said, "Harder than ever."

"Are you going to answer my question?"

"You got the wrong person altogether."

"OK," Reacher said. "I get it." He patted the air, a placatory gesture, as if defeated, as if requesting a time out, or a reset, or a reboot, or whatever else might help him. He said, "What if," in a speculative way, but he didn't finish the question. Instead he cupped his hand on his brow, and rubbed, as if easing a headache or searching for a word, and then he raised his other hand, too, and ran his fingers through his hair, back and forth fast, like a mental rinse, and then he moved his hands down and put his fingers flat over his mouth, almost steepled, over pursed lips, a meditative gesture, and then he rubbed his eyes, and then he pressed his fingers hard on his temples, like a person just one thought away from a solution.

All of which got his hands up at eye level, with no one suspecting a thing.

He flicked his right hand out and back real fast, a blur, like a snake's tongue, his fingers closing into a fist as it went, and he hit the right-hand guy in the face. Not much force behind it. A busted nose, maybe. Nothing more. But nothing more was required. The idea was to freeze the guy for a split second. That was all. While the same right hand on its way back pivoted into a full-blown right hook, with a violent twist at the waist and the shoulders, which hit the left-hand guy smack in the throat. Better than the face. No bones.

The left-hand guy went down like a slammed door.

Meanwhile Reacher was unwinding the twist and turning it into an equal and opposite left hook, and hitting the right-hand guy also in the throat.

Perfectly symmetrical.

Less than three seconds, beginning to end.

Plus style points.

The right-hand guy went down late and slowly, like a street light in an auto wreck. Reacher heard the slap of linoleum, and the thump of bone.

He stood there like nothing had happened.

He said, "Just you and me now."

Scorpio said nothing.

Reacher said, "Is the cop getting out of her car?"

Scorpio didn't answer.

Reacher ducked down, left and right, and took guns out of pockets. Both the same. Smith & Wesson Chief's Specials, both looking older than he was. He put them in his own pockets.

He said, "Is she out of her car yet?"

Scorpio said, "No."

"Is she on the phone?"

"No."

"The radio?"

"No."

"So what's she doing?"

"Just watching."

"Remember what I said about running a test?"

Scorpio didn't answer.

* * *

Nakamura saw the sentries close ranks in front of Scorpio, who was leaning back in his lawn chair, like some kind of emperor on a throne. Reacher was facing the three of them. Up close. An arm's length away. There was some verbal back and forth. Two questions, two answers. Short sentences. Brief and to the point. Then Reacher scratched his head. Then he seemed to have some kind of violent physical spasm, and for no apparent reason the sentries fell over.

He had hit them.

She scrabbled for her door release.

She stopped.

That's good news anyway.

Don't intervene.

She took a deep breath, and watched.

Reacher sat down in the lawn chair next to Scorpio's. He stretched out and got comfortable and stared straight ahead at an inert Maytag. Scorpio was silent beside him. They looked like two old men at a ball game. The sentries stayed on the floor, breathing, but not easily.

Reacher took the West Point ring from his pocket. He balanced it on his palm. He said, "I need to know who you got this from."

"I never saw that before," Scorpio said. "I run a laundromat."

"What have you got in your pockets?"

"Why?"

"You need to take it all out. I'm going to put you in the tumble dryer. Keys or coins might damage the mechanism."

Scorpio glanced at a tumble dryer.

Couldn't help himself.

He said, "I wouldn't fit."

"You would," Reacher said.

"I never saw that ring before."

"You sold it to Jimmy Rat."

"Never heard of him."

"Where I set the temperature dial is up to you. We'll start on delicates. Then we'll turn it up. Someone told me it goes all the way to where it can kill a bedbug."

Scorpio said nothing.

"I understand," Reacher said. "You're Mr. Rapid City. You're the man. You got a bunch of networks running. Which is your problem. Maybe they're all interconnected. In which case, one question might lead to another. The whole thing might unravel. You can't afford for that to happen. Hence the stone wall. I get it. Perfectly understandable. Except you need to remember two very important things. Firstly, I don't care. I'm not a cop. I don't have another question. And secondly, I'll put you in the tumble dryer. So you're between a rock and a hard place here. You need to get creative. You ever read a book?"

"Sure."

"What kind?"

"About the moon landings."

"That's called non-fiction. There's another kind, called fiction. You make stuff up, perhaps to illuminate a greater central truth. In your case, maybe you could tell me a story about a poor homeless man, maybe from out of town, who came in to launder his clothes, except he had no money, nothing at all except a ring, which you reluctantly traded for a couple of hot-wash cycles and a couple of dryer loads, plus enough left over for a square meal and a bed for the night. All out of the kindness of your generous heart. Detective Nakamura couldn't argue with that. It would be a fine story."

"I would have to admit selling the ring to Jimmy Rat."

"Which was perfectly legal. You run a laundromat. You carry quarters to the bank. You don't know what to do with a ring. Fortunately a guy passing by on his motorcycle offered to buy it from you. Not your fault he turned out to be a bad guy. You're not your brother's keeper."

"You think that's a good enough story?"

"I think it's a fine story," Reacher said again. "Just as long as you happen to remember the out-of-towner's name."

"Out of state," Scorpio said. "That's exactly what happened. More or less. Some broke guy came in from Wyoming. I helped him out."

"When?"

"Six weeks ago, maybe."

"From where in Wyoming?"

"I believe a small town called Mule Crossing."

"What was his name?"

"I believe it was Seymour Porterfield. I believe he told me people call him Sy."

Chapter 11

Across the street Nakamura was still watching. Reacher stood up and stepped over the left-hand sentry. He looked at a tumble dryer. Bigger than people had in their homes. Good for comforters and other large items. He might have gotten Scorpio in there.

He said, "You want me to leave through the back door?"

Scorpio shook his head.

"No," he said. "Go out the front."

So Reacher stepped over the right-hand sentry and pushed out to the sidewalk. The air smelled warm and fresh. He turned right and started walking. He heard Nakamura's car start up. He heard the wheeze of its steering, and grit under its tires, and then it pulled alongside him and stopped. The same as Scorpio's, except lower and bluer.

The window came down.

Black hair, dark eyes, a severe expression.

She said, "Get in the car."

"You mad at me now?"

"I told you not to commit a crime inside my jurisdiction."

"We were in the laundromat. Does that even count?"

"That's not fair. We're trying."

Reacher opened the passenger door and slid inside. He racked the seat backward, for leg room. He said, "I apologize. I know you're trying. Scorpio is a tough nut to crack."

"What did he tell you?"

"The ring came in from a guy in Wyoming named Sy Porterfield. About six weeks ago. Scorpio as good as admitted an onward connection to Jimmy Rat in Wisconsin. So he's part of a chain, flowing west to east along the I-90 corridor."

"Can't prove it."

"Also he pays off restaurant workers for information. Which he claims is only one of many networks he's running. Maybe he's the neighborhood bookie. Maybe he lends money."

"Can't prove any of it."

"But I'm not sure how successful he is. His personal vehicle is a piece of crap worth about a hundred dollars, and his goons had guns older than you."

"Did the car work?"

"I guess so."

"Would the guns have worked?"

"Probably. Revolvers are usually pretty reliable."

"This is South Dakota. People are thrifty. I think Arthur Scorpio is plenty successful."

"OK."

"Where are the guns now?"

Reacher took them out of his pockets and dropped them on her rear seat.

She said, "Thank you."

He said, "Also there's something wrong with his back room. It would have made more sense to talk to me in there. Certainly it would have made more sense for me to leave that way. He must have known you would stop me and ask me questions. Better if I went out through the alley. You wouldn't have seen me. But he wouldn't let me. You should check it out."

"We'd need a warrant."

"You've got the tap on his phone. He might say something stupid. A buck gets ten he's calling Porterfield in Wyoming right now."

"Is that where you're going?"

"As soon as I find a map. The town is called Mule Crossing. I never heard of it."

Nakamura took out her phone. She swiped and typed and waited, and then she said, "It's down near Laramie. A wide spot in the road."

She held out the phone to show him.

She said, "That's the I-80 corridor, not I-90."

He said, "Population density drops to nothing west of here. A supply chain would need to branch out, literally. Maybe there are many Porterfields, all over Wyoming and Montana and Idaho. All feeding Scorpio, like a river system. Do you monitor his visitors?"

"We try, from time to time. We've seen cars and bikes in the alley. Some with out-of-state plates. People go in and out his back door."

"You need to get a look in his back room. It ain't full of drums of spare detergent. That's for damn sure. The guy has no customers."

Nakamura was quiet a beat.

Then she said, "Thanks for the report."

He said, "You're welcome."

"Can I give you a ride somewhere?"

"The bus depot, I guess. I'll take whatever heads west on I-90. I'll get out in Buffalo and go south to Laramie."

"That would be the Seattle bus."

"Yes," Reacher said. "I thought it might be."

He got out of Nakamura's car at the depot and said goodbye and wished her luck. He didn't expect to see her again. He bought a ticket as far as Buffalo, and sat down to wait, with about twenty other people. They were the usual mixture. The room had pale inoffensive walls, and fluorescent squares in the ceiling. Out the picture window was an empty asphalt space, where sooner or later the Seattle bus would show up. It was on its way from Sioux Falls.

* * *

Nakamura called her friend the tech, and asked him to check with his pal at the phone company, to see who Scorpio had called in the last hour, with special focus on outgoing attempts to the 307 area code, which was Wyoming.

No need to check, the guy told her. The lieutenant had re-upped electronic surveillance, too. Everything on Scorpio's land line and personal cell was going straight to a hard drive, accessible from her desktop computer.

Only one problem, the guy said.

Scorpio had made no calls at all.

Reacher saw South Dakota change to Wyoming through the bus window. He was in his favorite spot, on the left, over the rear axle. Most people avoided that location, because they feared a bumpy ride. It was everyone else's last choice. Which made it his first.

He liked Wyoming. For its heroic geography, and its heroic climate. And its emptiness. It was the size of the United Kingdom, but it had fewer people in it than Louisville, Kentucky. The Census Bureau called most of it uninhabited. What people there were tended to be straightforward and pleasant. They were happy to leave a person alone.

Reacher country.

The first part of the state was high plains. Fall had already started. He gazed across the immense tawny distances, to the specter of the mountains beyond. The highway was a dark blacktop ribbon, mostly empty. From time to time trucks would pass the bus, slowly, sometimes spending a whole minute alongside, edging ahead imperceptibly. Reacher was eye to eye with their drivers, across their empty cabs. Old men, all of them.

My wife would say you feel guilty about something.

He looked the other way, across the aisle, at the other horizon.

* * *

Nakamura walked the length of the corridor to her lieutenant's corner suite. He looked up, all glittering eyes and restlessness.

"Bigfoot left," she said. "Scorpio answered his question. Next stop Wyoming."

"What's in Wyoming?"

"The ring was supplied to Scorpio by a man named Porterfield from a town named Mule Crossing. About six weeks ago."

"How did Bigfoot make Scorpio tell him all that?"

"He decked the muscle. I suppose Scorpio knew he was next."

"Did you see it happen?"

"Not really," Nakamura said. "It was over very fast. I couldn't swear to exactly what took place. Not precisely enough for a courtroom."

"So we're nowhere," the lieutenant said. "In fact we're back a step. Scorpio's phones have gone quiet. Which means he went to the pharmacy and bought a burner and some pre-paid minutes. Which means from now on we have no idea who or where he's calling."

The lieutenant said nothing more. He returned to his email. Nakamura walked back to her desk, quiet and alone.

More than eight hundred miles east, in an expensive kitchen in a big Tudor house on the Gold Coast north of Chicago, a woman named Tiffany Jane Mackenzie dialed Terry Bramall's cell number. It rang and rang and wasn't picked up. A recorded voice came on and asked her to leave a message.

She said, "Mr. Bramall, this is Mrs. Mackenzie. I'm wondering if you've made any progress. So far, I mean. Or not, I suppose. I would like to hear either way, so please call me back as soon as you can. Thank you. Goodbye."

Then Mrs. Mackenzie used her phone to check her email, and her bookmarked web pages, and her chat rooms, and her message boards. Nothing.

* * *

Reacher got out of the bus at the Buffalo stop. His onward options were limited. There was no direct service to Laramie. There was a departure to nearby Cheyenne, but not until the next day. So he set out walking, following signs to the highway south, with his thumb out, hoping to get a ride before he hit the on-ramp. About fifty-fifty, he figured. Heads or tails. In his favor was a friendly population not given to irrational fears. Against him was almost no traffic at all. The friendly population was thinly spread. Wyoming. Mostly uninhabited.

But even so, he came up heads within half a mile. A dusty pick-up stopped alongside him, and the driver leaned across and said he was going to Casper, which was about halfway to both Cheyenne and Laramie, straight south on I-25. Reacher climbed in and got comfortable. The truck was a Toyota. It was raised up on its suspension and tricked out with all kinds of heavy-duty components. It looked fit for service on the back side of the moon. Certainly it handled I-25 with no trouble at all. It droned along pretty fast. The driver was a rangy guy in work boots and off-brand jeans. A carpenter, he said, busy fixing roof beams before the winter. Also a rock crawler, he said, on the weekends. If he got weekends. Reacher asked him what a rock crawler was. Turned out to mean driving off-road vehicles over extreme boulder-strewn terrain, or along rocky rapids in dried-up mountain streams. Reacher was at best a reluctant driver, so any assessment was necessarily theoretical, but he was inclined to admit it sounded fun, if pointless.

Nakamura drove her Chevy back to Scorpio's block, but on a hunch she stopped short of the laundromat and parked outside the convenience store instead. She went in and looked around. An inventory check. She saw all kinds of canned and packaged foods, and coolers full of soda and juice and beer in bottles, and rolls of paper towels, and potato chips and candy, and a deli counter, and behind the register a wall of small stuff, including over-the-counter medications, and vitamin pills, and batteries, and phone chargers.

And phones.

She saw no-contract cell phones, in plastic bubble packs. Lots of them, in two rows, on two pegs, left and right, next to a faded sign saying pregnant women shouldn't drink too much.

She pointed and asked, "Did Arthur Scorpio just buy one of those?"

The counterman said, "Oh, Jesus."

"No big deal if he did. You're not in trouble. Information is all I need."

The counterman said, "Yes, he bought one. And some painkillers."

"Which one?"

"Which painkiller?"

"Which phone? Left peg or right peg?"

The counterman thought about it. He pointed.

"Right peg," he said. "More convenient for me."

"Give me the next two."

The guy took down two more bubble packs and Nakamura handed over her credit card. When she was back in her car she called her friend in Computer Crimes. She said, "Scorpio bought a burner in the convenience store. I got the next two off the rack. I'm going to bring them to you. I need you to figure out if the numbers run in some kind of predictable sequence. If they do, maybe we can put Scorpio back on the radar."

"I'll try my best," her friend said.

Terry Bramall let himself into his motel room, and hung his suit coat in the closet. He took his phone from his briefcase and set about answering his messages. The first was from some guy he had never heard of named Reacher. *We waited in line together last night for sandwiches and we were briefly in the breakfast place at the same time this morning.* And then something to do with Arthur Scorpio and stolen property.

He hit delete, because he was done with Scorpio.

The second message was from his client Mrs. Mackenzie. Anxious about progress, understandably. *I would like to hear either way, so please call me back as soon as you can.* He didn't. He didn't like talking on the phone, especially with anxious clients. So he texted back instead, slowly and methodically, using only his right forefinger: *Dear Mrs. Mackenzie, progress remains very satisfactory, and I hope to have definitive news very soon. Best wishes, T. Bramall.*

He pressed send.

In Casper, Reacher had a choice. He could stick with I-25 and head south and east to Cheyenne, whereupon Laramie would be a short hop west again on I-80. Or he could go direct on a state road. Two fast sides of a triangle versus one slow side. The hitchhiker's eternal dilemma.

He chose the state road. He was sick of the highway. And he had plenty of time. There was no big hurry. The ring had been out of Wyoming for six weeks. No red-hot trail to follow. He walked west out of town, more than a mile, until the commercial lots left and right petered out into high desert scrub. A hundred yards later he found a head-high sign that said *Laramie 152 miles*. He set up next to it. He felt it told the story. He watched the horizon for oncoming traffic. There wasn't much.

Scorpio gave his sentries twenty bucks and a bottle of Tylenol each, and then sent them home. They went out the front, and he went in the back room. He sat down at a long counter loaded with humming equipment. He tore apart the bubble pack and took out his new phone. He dialed the activation number, and then he dialed a 307 number.

Wyoming.

Ring tone.

No answer.

A voice invited him to leave a message.

He said, "Billy, this is Arthur. We got some weird shit going on. Nothing real serious. Just a strange piece of bad luck. Some guy showed up chasing a ring. He wasn't a cop. He knew nothing at all. He was just a random passerby, interested in the wrong thing at the wrong time. Turned out he was kind of tough to get rid of, so in the end I gave him Sy Porterfield's name. Which means sooner or later he's likely to arrive in your neck of the woods. Don't mess with him. Use a deer rifle from behind a tree. I'm not kidding about that. He's like the Incredible Hulk. Don't even let him see you. But get on it, OK? He's got to go, because he's a random loose end. Easier for you to deal with out there than it would be for me here. So get it done."

Then he added, "Your privileges are suspended till I hear back from you."

He clicked off and dropped the phone in the trash basket.

Chapter 12

Reacher arrived in downtown Laramie at six o'clock in the evening, after 152 miles in the passenger seat of an ancient Ford Bronco, driven by a guy who made his living turning logs into sculptures with a chainsaw. He let Reacher out on the corner of Third Street and Grand Avenue, which the guy seemed to regard as some kind of an exact geographic center. Which it might have been. But it was quiet. Everything had closed at five, except the bars and the restaurants, and it was still early for them.

Reacher turned a full circle and got his bearings. The railroad tracks lay to the west. The university was east. South was a straight shot to Colorado, and north was back toward Casper. He headed west for the tracks and stopped in at the first bar he liked the look of. It had a mirror on the wall with a bullet hole in it. As if some old desperado had come in mad about something. Maybe faked, maybe real. It was all the same to the mirror.

The room was quiet and the crowd was thin, and the barman had time on his hands. Reacher asked him directions to Mule Crossing. The guy said he had never heard of it.

"Where are you looking for?" some other guy called out. He had foam on his lip, from a long hard pull on a long-neck bottle. Maybe a helpful guy, maybe a busybody into everyone's business, maybe a local expert eager to show off his specialist knowledge.

Or a mixture of all three.

"Mule Crossing," Reacher said.

"Nothing there," the guy said. "Except a firework store."

"I heard it was a small town."

"This is a small town. Mule Crossing is a wide spot in the road. There was a post office, but it closed twenty years ago. I think there's a flea market in there now. Maybe you can get soda and potato chips. No gas, that's for sure."

"How many people live there?"

The guy took another pull on his bottle.

He said, "Five or six, maybe."

"That all?"

"The flea market guy, for sure. Probably not the firework guy. Who would live above a firework store? Probably wouldn't sleep a wink. I bet he drives in from somewhere else. But there's a dirt road into the hills. People have cabins. Maybe four or five of them. According to the postal service it's all officially Mule Crossing. Which is why they had a post office there, I guess. The Zip Code is about the size of Chicago. With five people. But hey, welcome to Wyoming."

"Where is it exactly?"

"Forty minutes south. Take the state road out toward Colorado. Look for a billboard about bottle rockets."

Reacher walked back to the corner of Third and Grand. He was optimistic about getting a ride. To his left was a university and straight ahead an hour away was legal weed. But it was getting dark. Might not be much to see. Clearly Mule Crossing was no kind of a bustling metropolis.

On the other hand, the flea market guy lived there.

He probably had a doorbell.

No time like the present.

Reacher walked south on Third Street, in the gutter, with his thumb out.

Gloria Nakamura rode the elevator two floors down to Computer Crimes, where she found her friend in his cubicle. He had torn her two phones out of their packaging. Now they were side by side on his desk above his keyboard. Their screens were blank.

"Sleep mode," he said. "All is well."

"You got the number?"

"You have to act it out. Pretend you're a Chinese assembly worker. In fact don't, because your job was just automated and now you're not there at all. Pretend you're a machine instead. The phone numbers are carried on the SIM cards, bought in bulk from the service providers, and installed fairly late in the process, I would think. Then the heat-sealed packaging goes on, with the cardboard insert, and the packages slide off the line one after the other into shipping cartons, which are taken away by another conveyor belt. How many in a box, do you think?"

Nakamura thought about it, and said, "Ten, probably. A place like that convenience store wouldn't want more than ten at a time. Mom-and-pop pharmacies would be the same. The manufacturers must know their market. So it's a small box. Bigger than a shoebox, but not by much."

"And are the phone numbers sequential?"

"It would help."

"Let's assume they are. Why wouldn't they be? There are plenty of new numbers to go around. So they fall off the line and go into the box in numerical order, one, two, three, all the way up to ten. So far so good. But we don't know what happens when they're unpacked. This is where you need to act it out. You slit the tape and you rest the box on the counter, and then you hang the contents on two pegs on a board behind the register. Talk me through it."

Nakamura glanced at an imaginary counter, and then over her shoulder at a pair of imaginary pegs. She said, "First I would rotate the box so the plastic blisters were facing toward me. So that I could pick them up, and turn a 180, and place them on the pegs face-out. Any other way would be a contortion."

The tech said, "And presumably they rode the conveyor belt with the blister upward and the flat side down, for stability. So if you have the blisters toward you, number one is nearest and number ten is farthest away. How many would you pick up at once?"

"I would do them one at a time. Those pegs are awkward."

"Starting where? Front or back of the box?"

"Front," she said.

"Which peg first?"

"The further one. More satisfying to fill that first. The nearer one is easier. Like a reward."

"So what do you get on the right-hand peg?"

"Numbers six through ten, in reverse order. Number ten will get bought first. Then nine, then eight, and so on. What were my numbers?"

"They weren't sequential," the tech said. "There was a two-digit gap. You gave me a seven and a four, essentially. Or a four and a seven. I don't know which came off the peg first."

"I'm sorry," Nakamura said. "I should have marked the order."

"Don't worry. Let's make another assumption. Let's say the convenience store guy gets his satisfaction a different way than you. Maybe he fills the pegs left, right, left, right. Perhaps he likes that better."

"Then numbers four and seven couldn't be together on the same peg."

"So let's make another assumption, based on the fact that you have the smallest hands in the world, and the convenience store guy is reasonably dexterous, working as he does with knives and what-not, so perhaps he hung them two at a time."

"Yes," she said. "That would put three and four on the right, immediately behind seven and eight. If I bought seven and four, then Scorpio bought eight. His phone number is one higher than mine."

"And listen to what my buddy at the phone company found," her friend said. He shuffled his mouse and his screen lit up. He clicked on an email, and then on an audio file, and jagged green bandwidth spiked on the screen, and Scorpio said, "Billy, this is Arthur. We got some weird shit going on."

Reacher got a ride from two kids pulling out of a gas station on the southern edge of town. A boy and a girl. Grad students, probably, or undergrads with great ID. They said they were headed to Fort Collins, across the state line. Shopping, they said, but not for what. Their car was a tidy little sedan. Unlikely to attract a trooper's attention. Safe enough, for the return leg of their journey.

They said they knew the bottle rocket billboard. And sure enough, after forty minutes on a gentle two-lane road, there it was, on the right shoulder, caught square in the high beams. It was bright yellow, half urgent, and half quaint. The students pulled over, and Reacher got out. The students drove away, and Reacher stood alone in the silence. The firework store itself was dark and closed up tight. Beyond it fifty yards south was a ramshackle building with a light in a small square upstairs window. The flea market, presumably. The former post office.

Reacher walked toward it.

Nakamura carried her laptop to her lieutenant's office, and played him the voicemail. *Use a deer rifle from behind a tree. Your privileges are suspended till I hear back from you.*

"He's ordering a homicide," she said.

Her lieutenant said, "His lawyer will say talk is cheap. And he'll point out we don't have a warrant. Not for the new number."

Nakamura said nothing.

Her lieutenant said, "Anything else?"

"Scorpio mentioned privileges. I don't know what that means."

"A business relationship of some kind, I suppose. Discount, priority, or access."

"To what? Soap powder?"

"Surveillance should tell us."

"We've never seen anything that looks like privileged access to something. Never. Nothing goes in or out."

"Billy might not agree. Whoever Billy is."

"Bigfoot is going to walk right into trouble. We should call someone."

Her lieutenant said, "Play the voicemail again."

She did. *He's got to go, because he's a random loose end. Easier for you to deal with out there than it would be for me here. So get it done.*

"He's ordering a homicide," she said again.

Her lieutenant said, "Can we ID Billy from his phone number?"

Nakamura shook her head. "Another drugstore burner."

"Where is Mule Crossing exactly?"

"In a county measuring seven thousand square miles. Which is run by a sheriff's department likely no bigger than two men and a dog."

"You think we should play the Good Samaritan?"

"I think we have a duty."

"OK, call them in the morning. Fingers crossed the men answer, not the dog. Tell them the story. Ask them if they know a guy named Billy, with a deer rifle and a tree."

The ramshackle building looked like a post office. Something about the shape, and the size. It was plain and bureaucratic, but also prideful. As if it was saying the mail could be carried anywhere, even into empty and inhospitable regions. *Neither snow nor rain nor heat nor gloom of night stays these couriers from the swift completion of their appointed rounds.* All that good stuff. But not anymore. A car passed by on the road and in the wash of its lights Reacher saw less-faded wood where twenty years before stern metal letters had been pried out of the siding: *United States Post Office, Mule Crossing,*

Wyo. Below that was a replacement message, hand-painted in gaudy multicolored foot-high letters: *Flea Market.*

The market itself had a sign in the window saying it was closed. It was dark inside. The door was locked. No knocker, no bell. Reacher walked back to where he could see the lit-up window. Below it in the end wall of the building was a door, with a shallow stoop, which had a boot scraper on one side and a garbage can on the other. All very domestic. The entrance to the residence, presumably. To the foot of a staircase direct to the second floor. Where the lit window was. Living above the store, literally.

There was no doorbell.

Reacher knocked, hard and loud. Then waited. No response. He knocked again, harder and louder. He heard a voice.

It roared, "What?"

A man, not young, not delighted at being disturbed.

"I want to talk to you," Reacher called back.

"What?"

"I need to ask you a question."

"What?"

Reacher said nothing. He just waited. He knew the guy would come down. He had been an MP for thirteen years. He had knocked on a lot of doors.

The guy came down. He opened the door. He was a white man, maybe seventy years old, tall but stooping, with not much flesh over a solid frame.

He said, "What?"

Reacher said, "I was told only five or six people live here. I'm looking for one of them. Which makes it about an eighteen percent chance that person is you."

"Who are you looking for?"

"Tell me your name first."

"Why?"

"Because if you're the guy, you'll deny it. You'll pretend you're someone else and send me on a wild goose chase."

"You think I would do that?"

"If you're the guy," Reacher said again. "It's been known to happen."

"You a cop?"

"Once upon a time. In the army."

The guy went quiet.

He said, "My son was in the army."

"What branch?"

"Rangers. He was killed in Afghanistan."

"I'm sorry."

"Not as much as I am. So remind me again, how may I help the army tonight?"

"I'm not here for the army," Reacher said. "I've been out a long time. This is a purely private matter. Purely personal. I'm looking for a man I was told was from Mule Crossing, Wyoming."

"But you won't tell me his name till I tell you mine. Because if I'm him, I'll lie about it. Have I got that straight?"

"Hope for the best, plan for the worst."

"If I was the sort of guy other guys came looking for, wouldn't I lie anyway?"

Reacher nodded.

He said, "This whole thing would go better if I saw ID."

"You got some nerve, you know that?"

"Nothing ventured, nothing gained."

The guy stood still for a second, deciding, and then he shook his head and smiled and hauled a wallet out of his back pants pocket. He flipped it open and held it out. There was a Wyoming driver's license behind a scratched plastic window. The photograph was right. The address was right. The name was John Ryan Headley.

Reacher said, "Thank you, Mr. Headley. My name is Reacher. I'm pleased to meet you."

The guy clapped his wallet shut and put it back in his pocket.

He said, "Am I the man you're looking for, Mr. Reacher?"

"No," Reacher said.

"I thought not. Why would anyone look for me?"

"I'm looking for a guy named Seymour Porterfield. Apparently people call him Sy."

"You're a little late for Sy, I'm afraid."

"Why's that?"

"He's dead."

"Since when?"

"About eighteen months ago, I guess. Around the start of spring last year."

"Someone told me he was seen in South Dakota six weeks ago."

"Then someone was lying to you. There's no doubt about it. It was a big sensation. He was found in the hills, mostly eaten up. Killed by a bear, they thought. Maybe waking up after hibernation. They're hungry then. Other folks thought a mountain lion. His guts were all ripped out, which is what mountain lions do. Then the ravens came, and the crows, and the raccoons. He was scattered all over the place. They made the ID with his teeth. And the keys in his pocket. April, I think. April last year."

"How old was he?"

"He could have been forty."

"What did he do for a living?"

"Come on in," Headley said. "I've got coffee brewing."

Reacher followed him up a narrow stair, to a long A-shaped attic that had been paneled with pine boards, and boxed off into separate rooms. There was an aluminum percolator thumping away on the stove. All the furniture was small. No sofas. The staircase was too narrow and the turns too tight to get them in. Headley poured two cups and handed one over. The coffee was thick and inky and smelled a little scorched.

"What did Porterfield do for a living?" Reacher asked again.

"No one knew for sure," Headley said. "But he always had money in his pocket. Not a whole lot, but a little more than made any kind of sense."

"Where did he live?"

"He had a log house up in the hills," Headley said. "Twenty miles away, maybe, on one of the old ranches. All by himself. He was pretty much a loner."

"West of here?"

Headley nodded. "Follow the dirt road. I guess his place is empty now."

"Who else lives out in that direction?"

"Not sure. I see folks driving by. I don't necessarily know who they are. This ain't the post office anymore."

"Were you here when it was?"

"Man and boy."

"How many folks do you see driving by?"

"Could be ten or twenty total."

"I was told four or five."

"Who pay their taxes and sign their names. But there are plenty of abandoned places. Plenty of unofficial residents."

Reacher said, "You know a woman, also ex-army, very small, name of Serena Sanderson?"

Headley said, "No."

"You sure?"

"Pretty much."

"Maybe she got married. You know any kind of a Serena?"

"No."

"What about Rose? Maybe she goes by her middle name."

"No."

"OK," Reacher said.

"What is this about exactly?"

Reacher took the ring out of his pocket. The gold filigree, the black stone, the tiny size. *West Point 2005.* He said, "This is hers. I want to return it. I was told Sy Porterfield sold it in Rapid City six weeks ago."

"He didn't."

"Evidently."

"What's the big deal?"

"Would your boy have given up his Ranger tab?"

"Not after what he went through to get it."

"Exactly."

"I can't help you," Headley said. "Except I can promise you Sy Porterfield didn't sell that ring in Rapid City six weeks ago, on account of getting ate up by a bear or a mountain lion more than a year before in another state entirely."

"So someone else sold it."

"From here?"

"Possibly. Fifty-fifty maybe. Mule Crossing was mentioned. Either true or false."

"I see folks drive by. I don't know who they are."

"Who would?"

Headley squirmed around in his chair, as if gazing west through the wall, as if picturing the dirt road rolling away into the darkness. He turned back and said, "The guy who runs the snowplow in the winter lives in the first place on the left. About two miles in. I guess he knows who lives where, from seeing their tire tracks, and maybe towing them out from time to time."

"Two real miles in, or two Wyoming miles?"

"It's about a five minute drive."

Which even on a dirt road could be more than two real miles. At an average speed of thirty, it would be two and a half. At forty, it would be more than three. And then back again.

"You got a car?" Reacher asked.

"I got a truck."

"Can I borrow it?"

"No, you can't."

"OK," Reacher said. "What's the guy's name, with the snowplow?"

"I don't know his second name. Not sure I ever heard it. But I know his first name is Billy."

Chapter 13

Reacher let himself out and walked down to where the dirt road met the two-lane. In the pitch dark there was nothing to see. No lights in the distance. Underfoot the surface felt like sand and fine gravel. Not hard to walk on. Except for the darkness. There was no clue at all as to direction, or curves, or turns, or camber, or gradient, or anything. He would be like a blind man, staggering slowly, blundering into fences, falling into ditches. Two miles was too far, in the gloom of night. He would have been a severe disappointment as a mail carrier.

He turned around. He crossed the two-lane and waited on the shoulder going north. Back to Laramie. Too soon to get the same students coming home again. But there would be others. Earlier birds, or regular folk coming back from shopping or a blue-plate special. He waited. The first two cars blew by without slowing, five minutes apart. The third stopped. It was a battered sedan with the hubcaps missing. The driver was a guy about forty, wearing a denim jacket. He said he was going to Laramie. Reacher asked him what he knew about motels in town. The guy said there were three types of place. Chain hotels south of the highway, or the same thing near the university, where people stayed for the football games, or dumpy mom-and-pop fleapits on the main drag north of the center. All Reacher wanted was a bed and a pay phone, so he said the guy should let him out wherever was the most convenient. Which turned out to be the chains south of the highway. They were right there, on a service road parallel with the two-lane, across a grassy strip.

He paid for a room, and found a phone in an alcove off the lobby. He dug in his pocket and took out Nakamura's business card. *Those are my numbers. Office and cell. Call me if you need to talk. Scorpio is a dangerous man.*

He dialed her cell.

She answered.

He said, "This is Reacher."

She said, "Are you OK?"

She sounded worried.

"I'm fine," he said. "Why?"

"Where are you?"

"Laramie, Wyoming."

"Don't go to Mule Crossing."

"I just did."

"Scorpio made a call. He set you up."

"I already know he lied to me about Seymour Porterfield. The guy died a year and a half ago. So I want you to give Scorpio a message. If you get the chance. Tell him one day I'm going to come back to Rapid City and pay him a visit."

"I'm serious, Reacher."

"So am I."

"He told a man named Billy to shoot you on sight. From behind a tree with a deer rifle."

"A man named what?"

"Billy."

Reacher said, "I just heard that name."

"Don't go to Mule Crossing," Nakamura said again. "No point going there anyway, if he lied about it."

"He lied about Porterfield. I don't know if he lied about Mule Crossing, too. Depends how fast he was thinking. He was under pressure at the time. I was going to put him in a tumble dryer. How would he even know the name Mule Crossing? It's not a famous place. It's nothing but a flea market and a firework store on a two-lane road in the middle of nowhere. It's possible Scorpio told me the wrong person but the right place. Maybe Porterfield used to be in business with him. Maybe this guy Billy took over."

"Scorpio's call implied Billy gets privileges of some kind. So they might be in business together."

"What sort of business?"

"I don't know. But the threat to you was very clear. In my opinion he was ordering a homicide. I'm going to call the local sheriff in the morning."

"Don't," Reacher said. "That would only complicate things."

"I'm a police officer. I have to."

"What exactly did Scorpio say on the phone?"

"It was a voicemail again. He called it weird shit going on. He said you were a strange piece of bad luck. The implication was there was something taking place on an ongoing basis, but you knew nothing about it, because you were just a random passerby. He said he gave you Porterfield's name to get rid of you. Then he told Billy to kill you. He said not to mess with you, because you're like the Incredible Hulk. He said to use a deer rifle from behind a tree. He was ordering a homicide, Reacher. Clear as day. I have to put it in the system."

"The Incredible Hulk? I thought I was Bigfoot. These guys need to make up their minds."

"This isn't funny."

"Did he mention Mule Crossing?"

"Not in the voicemail. Not specifically."

"Was it a Mule Crossing number he called?"

"No, it was another drugstore burner. We can't trace it."

"Then wait a day, OK? Wouldn't mean much to the sheriff without an exact location. Wyoming is a big state. I wouldn't want to waste anyone's time."

"What are you going to do?"

"Nothing," Reacher said. "I want to know where the ring came from. That's all."

Nakamura didn't reply to that, and they hung up. Room service was nothing more than a Xeroxed sheet of paper with a phone number for pizza delivery, so Reacher dialed again and ordered a large pie with extra pepperoni and anchovies. He waited for it in the lobby. An old habit. He didn't like people to know which room was his.

He woke the next morning with the sunrise, and went out in search of coffee. Which meant walking through the hotel's parking lot to get back to the two-lane. There was a black SUV parked near the door. It was a Toyota Land Cruiser. A serious vehicle. He had seen them in dusty and rugged parts of the world. The United Nations used them. This particular example was fairly new, and basically clean, but a little travel-stained.

It had Illinois plates.

He ducked back to the phone in the lobby and dialed Terry Bramall's cell number from memory. The private eye from Chicago. Last seen leaving Rapid City in a black SUV with Illinois plates. There was a ring tone, but no answer. A voice came on and invited him to leave a message. He didn't. He just shrugged and set out again for coffee.

He found coffee along with breakfast in a diner on Third Street. He asked the waitress where the county sheriff was based. She said right there in town, about half a mile away. Not hard to find. The sky was blue and the sun was shining but the air was cool. He stopped in at a clothing store. In his experience the West was better than the East for tall guys. He found jeans the right length, and a flannel shirt, and a thin canvas jacket. As always he changed in the cubicle and had the clerk dump his old stuff in the trash. Then he walked onward to the spot the waitress had told him, and found the sheriff's office. It was a single-wide storefront, with the bottom part of the window painted over. Above that was a gold pinstripe, and above that was a gold star about two feet wide and two feet high, with the county's name in a curve above, and *Sheriff's Department* in a curve below. The design looked a little bit like the West Point ring.

He went in. There was a woman in civilian clothes at the reception desk. He asked to see the sheriff, and she asked why he wanted to. He said he had a question about an old case. She asked his name, and he told her. She asked if his visit was in some way official. Whether he worked in law enforcement. He said not currently, but he had been an MP in the army for thirteen years. She told him to go ahead upstairs to the sheriff's office, which was the last door on the left. No hesitation. In his experience the West was better than the East for veterans.

He went upstairs. According to gold writing on the last door on the left the sheriff's name was Connelly. Reacher knocked and entered. The office was a dusty wood-framed room gone a golden hue with age, and Sheriff Connelly himself turned out to be a solid leathery guy of about fifty. He was wearing blue jeans and a tan shirt and a Stetson hat. Clearly the woman at the desk had called ahead, because Connelly already knew his name. He said, "How can I help you, Mr. Reacher?"

Reacher said, "I came to Wyoming to look up a guy named Seymour Porterfield, but I'm told he got eaten up by a bear a year and a half ago. I was hoping you could tell me what you know about that."

Connelly said, "Take a seat, Mr. Reacher."

Reacher sat down, on an old-fashioned wooden visitor chair polished to a high shine by a thousand pairs of pants. Connelly looked at him without speaking. A level gaze, equal parts suspicion and the benefit of the doubt. He said, "What was your connection with Seymour Porterfield?"

"None at all," Reacher said. "I'm looking for someone else, and I was told Porterfield might be able to point me in the right direction."

"Who told you that?"

"A guy in South Dakota."

"Who is the someone else you're looking for?"

Reacher took the ring out of his new pants pocket, and said, "I want to return this to its rightful owner."

"A woman," Connelly said.

"Name of Serena Rose Sanderson. You know her?"

The guy shook his head. "She a friend of yours?"

"Never met her. But we look after our own."

"You a West Pointer, too?"

"A long time ago."

"Where did you find the ring?"

"In a pawn shop in Wisconsin. I traced it back to Rapid City, South Dakota. I was told it was brought there from Wyoming by Porterfield."

"When?"

"After he was dead."

"So how can I help you?"

"You can't," Reacher said. "But I'm curious. Getting eaten by a bear seems a little extreme."

"Could have been a mountain lion."

"How likely is that?"

"Not very," Connelly said. "Either thing would be rare."

"So what do you think happened?"

"A practical man would say the guy was gut shot or knifed in the stomach and then dumped in the woods. It was the end of winter. Bears or mountain lions might have been hungry enough to scavenge the corpse. Birds would have, for sure. Also raccoons and what-not. But there was zero evidence either way. We confirmed all the parts were Porterfield, but he was real torn up. We didn't find a bullet. Didn't find a knife. There were marks on the bones, but they were all animal teeth. I had folks at the university take a good long look. All inconclusive. We called it an accident, and maybe it was."

Reacher said, "What do you know about the guy himself?"

"Very little. This is Wyoming. We leave people alone. No one inquires into other people's business. He lived by himself. He had a fairly new car with a lot of miles on it. So he got around some. He had cash in a shoebox in the back of his closet. That's all we found out."

"How much cash?"

"Nearly ten grand."

"Not bad."

"I agree. I wish I had ten grand in the back of my closet. But it wasn't enough to get all excited about."

"Except you formed the impression he was the type of guy who could get gut shot or knifed in the stomach."

"I try to keep an open mind, both ways around."

"No friends or relatives showing up asking questions?"

"Not a peep."

"OK," Reacher said. "Thanks."

"You're welcome," Connelly said. "I hope you find who you're looking for."

"I plan to," Reacher said.

Chapter 14

Reacher walked east the best part of a mile, to where the university buildings started. He stopped in at what looked like a general office and asked for the geography department. The kid at the desk looked like a student. He was half asleep. But eventually he understood the question. He said, "What do you need there?"

"I want to look at a map," Reacher said.

"Use your phone, man."

"I don't have a phone."

"Really?"

"And I want to see detail."

"Use satellite view."

"All I would see is trees. Plus like I told you, I don't have a phone."

"Really?"

"Where's the geography department?"

The kid pointed and said further on down the road, so Reacher went back to walking. Five minutes later he was in the right place, in front of another kid at another desk. This one was a girl, and she was wider awake. Reacher told her what he needed, and she went away and then came back laboring under the weight of a hardbound Wyoming topographical atlas about the size of a sidewalk paving slab. Reacher took it from her and hefted it to a table under a window. He opened it up and found the southeast corner of the state. Found Laramie, and the two-lane south toward Colorado, and the dirt-road turnoff at Mule Crossing.

Reacher had been at West Point when reading paper maps was still taught as a serious lifesaving skill. Terrain was important to an army. Understanding it was the difference between winning and getting wiped out. What he saw west of the old post office was an unimproved road of reasonable width, never quite straight, following the gentle contours of the surrounding land, flanked on both sides by empty plains, which broke up after a mile or so into the faintest first foothills of the Snowy Range mountains fifty miles further on. There were fence lines here and there, engraved as fine as the detail on a hundred dollar bill. There were thin streams colored blue, and forests colored green, and orange contour lines rising and falling. Left and right along a twenty-mile distance were occasional ranch roads, leading to faraway buildings drawn as tiny brown squares. The first such track on the left was almost exactly two and a half miles from the old post office. It ran south for a spell, through patchy conifer woods, and then it curved west, and then snaked east, and then west again, up a shallow rise onto a knoll cradled by a higher U-shaped ridge to the south. On the knoll were shown two tiny brown squares. A house and a barn, maybe.

Billy's place.

The next track on the left was almost three miles further west. Same kind of situation. A meandering dirt track, squirming right and left through the early hills and the thickening forest, leading to some kind of an inhabited dwelling. Obviously Reacher could use that second track and loop back to Billy's place through the trees on the blind side. Which would be an advantage. Except that to get there in the first place he would have to walk the unimproved road all the way from the old post office. He would be visible from Billy's house for the best part of forty minutes. The knoll was at least a hundred feet higher than the road. He would be a speck in the far distance, for sure, but the guy had been warned. Maybe he had binoculars. Or a scope on his deer rifle.

A problem.

The girl at the desk said, "You OK, sir?"

"Doing well," Reacher said.

He turned the page.

Much more interesting was what lay further to the south. The next right off the two-lane after Mule Crossing came three miles later. It was a forest service track into a nature preserve labeled *Roosevelt National* something. It was right at the bottom of the map. Right on the state line. The third word would be on the first Colorado sheet. *Forest,* presumably. Teddy Roosevelt, Reacher supposed, not Franklin. The great naturalist, except for when he was shooting things like tigers and elephants. People were complicated. The service track fed a spider web of more service tracks, one of which curved around north and came out on the back slope of the U-shaped ridge right behind Billy's house. The contour lines showed the ridge was more than a hundred feet higher than the knoll. A person could get within fifty yards completely unobserved, no matter how many binoculars or rifle scopes the guy was using.

Map reading. The difference between winning and getting wiped out.

Reacher heaved the giant book shut, like closing a heavy door. The girl at the desk told him to leave it right there on the table. Maybe she felt she had done enough bicep curls for one day. He thanked her and stepped out to the sidewalk and headed back west to town, in the right-side gutter, with his left thumb out. He got a ride within a minute, with a friendly wild-haired bearded character, maybe an eccentric professor, but the guy was going only as far as the supermarket, so Reacher got out on the corner of Third Street and started over, walking south like he had the night before. A ratty old pick-up truck stopped before he got to the edge of town, and he climbed in and asked for a spot three miles south of the bottle rocket billboard. The driver looked a little puzzled, as if wondering what the hell was there, but he didn't ask. He just drove. *This is Wyoming. No one inquires into other people's business.* They passed under the highway bridge and Reacher glanced left, across the grassy strip, at the lot in front of his hotel. The black SUV was gone.

Chapter 15

Forty minutes later Reacher was alone on the two-lane's shoulder, watching the pick-up truck drive away. The mouth of the forest road was overgrown with sagebrush, and it had a heavy chain slung across it, dipping low between two weathered posts. He stepped over it and set out hiking. The altitude was more than eight thousand feet above sea level, and the air was thin. The effort made him breathe hard, and left him light-headed. The forest was mostly fir and pine, dappled with sun, blazing here and there with bright yellow groves of aspen. His normal rule of thumb for walking north through a wood was to look for moss on the tree trunks. Less of it would be facing east, south and west. Regular daylight would see to that. But the mountain air was bone dry and there was no moss at all. So he navigated by the sun. It was mid-morning, so he kept it forty-five degrees behind his right shoulder. He kept his shadow ahead and to the left. He angled west where he could, and felt the ground rise under his feet. An hour or less, he figured, before he got to the back side of the U-shaped ridge. He pictured Billy, watching the wrong horizon. He trudged on, panting.

*   *   *

Nakamura walked the corridor to her lieutenant's corner suite, and said, "Reacher called me last night."

Her lieutenant said, "Who?"

"Bigfoot," she said. "The Incredible Hulk."

"And?"

"He asked me to hold off a day before calling the sheriff in Wyoming."

"Why would he?"

"He pointed out there was no specific location mentioned in Scorpio's voicemail, and therefore he felt a warning wouldn't mean much to law enforcement out there. He didn't want to waste anyone's time."

"That's very scrupulous of him."

"I got the impression he wants freedom of action."

"Do you think he should have it?"

"That's not for me to say. Or him, either."

"We work for the people of Rapid City, and no one else. Certainly not a bunch of cowboys out west."

"Yes, sir."

"Therefore, on that basis, what helps Rapid City most?"

Nakamura said nothing.

"Well?"

"I checked him out," Nakamura said. "I made some calls. He was an elite MP. He has medals. He's possibly better prepared than the average person."

"Can he help us with Scorpio?"

You could put him in a zoo.

She said, "I really don't see how he could hurt."

"OK then," the lieutenant said. "Wait a day."

Then he said, "No, wait two days."

Reacher found what had to be the lower back slope of the U-shaped ridge after fifty minutes of hiking. The dirt underfoot was thin and gritty. There were pine cones everywhere, some of them the size of softballs. He climbed slowly, with short choppy steps, kicking his toes into the dirt for grip. He got close to the top and found what might have been a fox trail that led him the rest of the way to the summit. He dropped to his knees and took a look.

He was a couple hundred yards east of where he needed to be. He dropped back to the fox trail and went west, three minutes at a slow pace, arms out for balance.

He took another look.

Now Billy's place was directly below him, fifty yards away.

It was a log house, stained dull brown, with a log barn, both structures surrounded by beaten-down brush and dusty red dirt. A rutted driveway ran away through the woods, appearing and reappearing in the gaps between the trees. On the right the land fell away and flattened into wide empty plains. The old post office was visible in the far distance, and the firework store, and the two-lane road. There was a grazing herd of pronghorns about a mile away. The dirt road was vivid ochre, neatly scraped, nicely cambered. On the left the land rose into low jagged peaks, like miniature mountain ranges, like premonitions of what would come for real a hundred miles farther west. The air was still and unnaturally clear. The sky was deep blue. There was absolute silence.

Billy's house had a green metal roof, and small windows with no light inside. Not a trophy cabin. Not a weekend place. But not a mess, either. No junk in the yard. No rusted washing machines. No cars up on blocks. No pit bull on a chain. Just a workaday house.

No people.

Reacher eased down the near slope, slowly, from tree to tree. Forty yards away. Thirty. A pine cone rolled ahead of him and hit a bump and kicked up in the air.

He froze.

No reaction.

He kept on going, stepping sideways for grip, staying where the trees were thickest. Twenty yards away. Ten. He could see Billy's back door. Footsteps had beaten a path from it to a similar door in the back of the barn.

He stopped five yards inside the tree line. Safe enough. All was quiet. He waited. He figured Billy wouldn't have taken Scorpio's voicemail literally. The guy wouldn't be hiding behind an actual tree with his rifle at his shoulder. He was more likely sitting in a chair on his front porch. With his rifle on the boards beside him. He could see twenty miles. He would figure he would get plenty of early warning.

Reacher moved east through the trees and lined up with the back of the barn. His first port of call. He took a breath and stepped out.

No reaction.

He crossed the open space, controlled, not fast, not slow, with tiny slaps and crunches from his feet on the grit and the gravel.

No reaction.

He pressed up against the back of the barn. There were no windows. The personnel door was ten feet to his left. He crabbed sideways and tried the handle. Locked. Which was a pity. Barns were usually good for useful stuff. Hammers, hatchets, wrenches, knives. He crabbed back to where he started, and onward to the corner. The house was twenty feet away. Still quiet. The side facing him was made of heavy logs, and it had two small windows on the first floor and two on the second. All four were backed by half-closed sun-faded drapes.

He took another breath and crossed the open space. He pressed his back hard against the logs. The first-floor window sills were about level with his shoulder. He inched closer and risked a one-eyed look inside. He saw a powder room, with a closed door. He moved on. Checked the second window. Saw a small alcove at the foot of a staircase. Beyond it was the front half of a living room. Two more windows, a front door, a stone fireplace, well-worn armchairs. Log walls, stained dark.

No people.

The front door would lead to a front porch.

Which would be around the next exterior corner.

He moved on, slow and cautious. He stopped a foot short of the corner and listened hard. Heard nothing except silence, and the tiniest eddy of breeze through the trees, and the caw of a rook far in the distance. No breathing, no movement, no creak of wood. Nothing at all.

One more half step.

He peered around the corner. Saw a covered porch, with a railing, and two heavy wooden chairs, and a swing seat hanging motionless on four thick chains.

No people.

No rifle resting on the boards.

No Billy.

Reacher shuffled sideways to the rear corner of the house. He paused a beat, and slid around, and moved along the back wall. He checked the first window he came to. A kitchen. Still and quiet and no one in it. Next to the kitchen window was a kitchen door. Solid wood. No glass. He passed it by and checked a second window. A small back parlor. A desk, a chair. Still and quiet and no one in it.

Silence.

He crept back to the kitchen door. Now logic said Billy was upstairs. He had been warned. His view would be marginally better from a second-floor window. He would see a mile or more of the two-lane beyond the old post office. He would get six or seven minutes, even if an incoming vehicle was driving fast.

Reacher tried the door handle.

It turned.

The door opened.

He pushed it gently, with spread fingers. The kitchen air smelled still and stale. There were dark wood cabinets and a cold stove. Yesterday's dishes were in the sink. There was tile on the floor. The inside door was open to the living room. No people. Last winter's ash was still in the fireplace. A poker and a brush and a long-handled shovel were propped together in a stand on the hearth stones.

Slowly, carefully, he eased the poker out of the stand. It was iron, about a yard long, and it had a vicious hook at the end, jutting out like a hitchhiker's thumb.

Better than nothing.

He crept to the foot of the stairs. Listened hard. The log construction was massive and solid. No sound. Nothing at all.

He started up the stairs. The moment of maximum vulnerability. Nothing to be done if Billy showed up shooting in the upstairs hallway. Short of swinging the poker at the bullet like a slugger going after a high fastball. Unlikely to work. But, nothing ventured, nothing gained. The stairs were sawn half-logs about ten inches thick. No danger of creaking. He held his breath.

He made it to the top. Directly ahead of him was a half-open door to a bathroom, directly above the kitchen. No one in it. Ahead and to his right was a half-open door to a back bedroom, above the back parlor. No one in it. He turned in the hallway and faced two front bedrooms. One had a wide-open door. No one in it.

One had a closed door.

Reacher held the poker across his body, at port arms.

You and me, Billy, he thought.

There was a rag rug in the upstairs hallway. He stepped onto it and walked slowly, carefully, silently. He stopped four feet short of the door. He was a big believer in shock and awe and surprise and overwhelming force. What used to be called common sense, before the Pentagon pointy-heads started dreaming up fancy names for simple concepts. He set his feet and rocked back and forth, back and forth, like a high-jumper going for a record, and then he smashed through the door with the sole of his boot and exploded into the room with the poker scything through the air in front of him.

The room was empty.

No Billy.

Just an unmade bed, and the sour smell of sleep, and a three-pane window with a perfect view to the horizon. Nothing out there except the herd of pronghorns, grazing unconcerned a mile away.

Reacher had searched a lot of houses, and he found the barn keys in the first place he looked, on a nail in the wall near the kitchen door.

The barn was a big one-story space that smelled of dust and wood stain and cold motor oil. There were bald tires and all kinds of mechanical junk and a detached snowplow blade stacked on the floor. No actual vehicles. Nothing else of interest. He went back to the house and stood on the front porch and checked the view. He traced the route, along the driveway, along the dirt road, bit by bit, his eyes moving like a finger on a map, all the way out past the old post office and the firework store.

Nothing coming.

No dust on the dirt road.

He started downstairs and searched the house methodically, running a clock in his head, returning to the porch every sixty seconds to check the horizon. There was nothing of significance in the kitchen. Nothing in the living room. Billy seemed to be a guy with neat but not obsessive habits. The place was reasonably tidy and reasonably clean. The stuff in it was neither obviously expensive nor obviously cheap. It was clear he lived alone.

The back parlor was set up as an office. A desk, a chair, a file cabinet. On the desk was a cell phone. A simple thing. Old fashioned but not old. It was plugged in to a charger. The battery icon said a hundred percent. The screen said *New Message.*

Sixty seconds. Reacher slipped out to the porch and checked the view. Nothing coming. He went back to the office. He had never owned a cell phone, but he had used one from time to time. He knew how they worked. At the bottom of the screen were the words *Menu* and *Play,* and below them were two slim bar-shaped buttons. He pressed the bar below *Play.*

He heard a nervous breath and a throat being cleared.

Then he heard Scorpio's voice.

It said, "Billy, this is Arthur. We got some weird shit going on. Nothing real serious. Just a strange piece of bad luck. Some guy showed up chasing a ring."

*   *   *

Sixty seconds. Reacher stepped out to the front porch again and checked the view. Still nothing coming. He went back in and up the stairs to the slept-in bedroom. First thing he looked at was the closet. Just for fun. Against the back wall behind a rail of hanging pants he found four shoeboxes. They were neatly stacked two on two. The top two held shoes. White athletic sneakers on the left, and rubber soled black leather dress items on the right. The kind of thing a country boy might wear to a wedding or a funeral or a visit with the loan officer at the bank. Both pairs had been worn, but not often. Both pairs were size eight and a half. The hanging pants were all thirty-two waist and thirty leg.

Billy was a small guy.

Sixty seconds. He checked out the window.

There was a long dust plume on the dirt road.

A hanging ochre cloud, long, spiraling, and drifting. A vehicle, coming on fast. Still just a tiny dot in the distance. Too far away to see what it was.

Six minutes, maybe.

He went back in the closet. Checked the bottom pair of boxes.

One was full of money.

Tens and twenties and fifties, used and creased, sour and greasy, done up in inch-thick bricks with rubber bands. Maybe ten grand in total. Maybe more.

The other box was full of trinkets. Mostly gold. Gold crosses on thin tangled chains, gold earrings, gold bracelets, gold charms, gold chokers.

And gold rings.

Some were wedding rings.

Some were class rings.

Reacher stepped back to the window and watched. The dust plume was a mile long, hanging in the motionless air. At the head of it was a tiny dark dot, quivering, bobbing, bouncing. The pronghorn herd rippled, uneasy.

The tiny dot looked black.

It was hammering and juddering right to left in front of him. It was doing maybe forty miles an hour. Maybe more. Some kind of familiarity with the terrain, or some kind of urgency, or some kind of both.

He waited.

It slowed.

The dust cloud caught up with it.

It turned in at the driveway.

Billy's ride would be a pick-up truck, Reacher figured. Snowplows usually were. Winter tires, chains, a hydraulic mechanism for the blade, extra spotlights mounted high. All detached in the summer, leaving a familiar silhouette. Hood, cab, bed.

Which Reacher didn't see.

It wasn't a pick-up truck.

It was big and square and boxy. An SUV. A black SUV. Travel stained and dusty. It flashed in and out of sight through the trees. Then it pulled clear and drove the last hundred yards over the beaten red dirt.

It slowed and turned and came to a stop.

It was a Toyota Land Cruiser.

It had Illinois plates.

Chapter 16

Reacher watched from the upstairs window. The black SUV parked a respectful distance from the house. The driver's door opened. A man stepped down. A small guy, neat and compact, in a dark suit and a shirt and a tie. Terry Bramall. From Chicago. Retired FBI. The missing persons specialist. Last seen the day before, in Rapid City, in the breakfast place opposite Arthur Scorpio's laundromat.

The guy stood still for a long moment, and then he set out walking toward the house, with a purposeful stride.

Reacher went down the stairs. He made it to the bottom and heard a knock on the door. He opened up. Bramall was standing on the porch. He had taken a polite step back. His hair was brushed. His suit was the same, but his shirt and his tie were different. He had the kind of look on his face that Reacher recognized. The kind of look he had used himself, many times. Open, inquisitive, inoffensive, faintly apologetic for the interruption, but no-nonsense all the same. An experienced investigator's look. Which changed for a split second, first to surprise, then to puzzlement, and then finally it came back the same as before.

"Mr. Bramall," Reacher said.

"Mr. Reacher," Bramall said. "I saw you yesterday in the coffee shop in Rapid City. And the night before in the convenience store. You called me and left a message."

"Correct."

"I assume your first name isn't Billy."

"You assume right."

"Then may I ask what you're doing here?"

"I could ask you the same question."

"May I come in?"

"Not my house. Not for me to say."

"Yet you seem to be making yourself at home."

Reacher looked beyond Bramall's shoulder at the view. The dust cloud over the dirt road had settled. The pronghorn herd had gone back to placid grazing. Nothing was moving. No one was coming.

He said, "What do you want from Billy?"

"Information," Bramall said.

"He's not here. Probably been gone about twenty-four hours. Or more. Scorpio left him a voicemail around this time yesterday and it was still showing on his phone as a new message. It hadn't been picked up yet."

"He went out without his phone?"

"It was charging. Maybe it's not his main phone. It looks like a burner. Maybe it's for special purposes only."

"Did you listen to the message?"

"Yes."

"What did it say?"

"Scorpio asked Billy to shoot me with a deer rifle from behind a tree."

"To shoot you?"

"He included a description."

"That's not very nice."

"I agree."

Bramall said, "We should talk."

"On the porch," Reacher said. "In case Billy comes back."

* * *

Four eyes were better than two. They sat side by side in Billy's wooden chairs, with Bramall gazing west of dead ahead, and Reacher gazing east. They talked into the void in front of them, not looking at each other, which made the conversation easier in some respects, and harder in others.

Bramall said, "Tell me what you know."

Reacher said, "You're retired."

"That's what you know? Hardly relevant. Or even true. I'm pursuing a second career."

"I mean you're retired FBI. Which means you don't get to use FBI bullshit anymore. As in, you don't get to ask all the questions and then walk away. You get to give as well as take."

"How do you know I was FBI?"

"A police detective in Rapid City told me. Name of Nakamura."

"She must have done some research."

"That's what detectives do."

"What do you want to know?"

"Who are you looking for?"

"I'm afraid I'm bound by a certain degree of confidentiality."

Reacher said nothing.

Bramall said, "I don't even know who you are."

"Jack Reacher. No middle name. Retired military police. Some of your guys came to us for training."

"And some of yours came to us."

"So we're on an equal footing. Give and take, Mr. Bramall."

"Rank?"

"Does it matter?"

"You know it does."

"Terminal at major."

"Unit?"

"Mostly the 110th MP."

"Which was?"

"Like the FBI, but with better haircuts."

"Is the military connection why you're here?"

"Should it be?"

"I'm serious," Bramall said. "Clients like discretion. Most of the time I make my living by keeping things quiet. For all I know, you work for a website now."

"I don't. Whatever that means."

"Who do you work for?"

"I don't work."

"Then why are you here?"

"Tell me about your client, Mr. Bramall. Broad strokes, if you like. No names at this point. No identifying details."

"You can call me Terry."

"And you can call me Reacher. And you can quit stalling."

"My client is someone in the Chicago area worried about a family member."

"Worried why?"

"No contact for a year and a half."

"What took you to Rapid City?"

"Land line calls in old phone records."

"What brought you here?"

"The same."

"Was the family with the missing member originally a Wyoming family?"

Bramall said nothing.

"There are hundreds of families in Wyoming," Reacher said. "Maybe even thousands. You won't be giving anything away."

"Yes," Bramall said. "Originally it was a Wyoming family. From the other side of the Snowy Range. About sixty miles from here. Maybe seventy. That's about two blocks away, by Wyoming standards."

Reacher said, "Had the family member in question spent time overseas?"

"Give and take, Mr. Reacher. You're retired, too."

Reacher checked his part of the horizon, from the dirt road out past Mule Crossing's forlorn buildings, to the two-lane. No movement. Nothing coming. He checked Bramall's part, too, tracing the dirt road west until it disappeared in the hills. No dust. No movement. Nothing coming.

He took the ring out of his pocket. He balanced it on his palm. He held out his hand. Bramall took the ring from him. He looked at it. He took out a pair of tortoiseshell reading glasses from an inside pocket. He read the engraving on the inner face.

S.R.S. 2005.

He said, "Now we really need to talk."

Reacher told him the story. The bus out of Milwaukee, and the comfort stop, and the pawn shop, and Jimmy Rat in the biker bar, and Arthur Scorpio in the Rapid City laundromat, and the tale about how a guy named Porterfield brought him the ring, which had proved to be a lie, because of the big sensation with either the bear or the mountain lion, or both.

Bramall said, "That was a year and a half ago?"

Reacher nodded. "The start of spring last year."

"Which was when my client got worried."

"If you say so."

"And you're here in his house because you think Billy replaced Porterfield in the ring-transportation business?"

"I think it's likely."

"Why?"

"I'll show you," Reacher said. He checked the view again, both ways, and saw no one coming. He led Bramall into the house, and up the stairs, and to Billy's bedroom. To the closet. He showed him the shoeboxes, one crammed with cash, the other rattling and tinkling with cheap gold jewelry.

"Drug dealers," Bramall said. "Don't you think? Small time. Home-cooked meth or cheap heroin up from Mexico. Twenty bucks sees you right, and if you can't pay you trade your rings and your necklaces. Or you steal someone else's."

"I thought it was all pain pills now," Reacher said.

"That boom is over," Bramall said. "Now it's back to how it used to be. Scorpio is the wholesaler, employing first Porterfield and now Billy as his local retailer, using the first guy as a decoy and secretly telling the second guy to get rid of you. He doesn't like scrutiny."

"Possible," Reacher said.

"You got another coherent explanation?"

"Who's your client?"

"A woman in Lake Forest named Tiffany Jane Mackenzie. Serena Rose Sanderson's twin sister. Married, hence the different name. They were close as children, but pretty soon went their separate ways. Mackenzie's living the dream. Big house, rich husband. She didn't altogether approve of her sister's career choice. But blood is thicker than water. There was occasional contact. Until the start of spring last year. How thorough was the investigation about the bear and the mountain lion?"

"Very," Reacher said. "By rural standards, anyway. The sheriff looks solid. There was only one body, and it was all Porterfield. They knew from his dental records and the keys in his pocket."

"So you think Sanderson is still alive?"

"Probably. The ring showed up in Rapid City about six weeks ago, and in Wisconsin about two weeks later. I'm guessing they move stuff along pretty quickly. The sheriff said Porterfield's car had a lot of miles. He was probably running back and forth pretty regularly. I imagine Billy is, too. What we've got here in the shoebox is probably just a few weeks' worth. The sheriff said Porterfield had cash in his closet, too. A similar amount. Small time, maybe, but it seems to add up."

"So where is Billy now?"

Reacher stepped to the window and checked the view. No one coming, either east or west. He said, "I have no idea where Billy is. There are dishes in the sink. Feels like he stepped out for a minute."

"Show me the phone."

Reacher led Bramall down the stairs, to the small parlor in back. To the phone on the desk. Bramall stabbed at buttons and played the message again. *He's like the Incredible Hulk. Don't even let him see you. But get on it, OK? He's got to go, because he's a random loose end.*

Bramall said, "You took a risk coming here."

"Getting up in the morning is a risk. Anything could happen."

"Did you know Sanderson?"

"No," Reacher said. "I was already out eight years before 2005."

"Then what's your interest?"

"You wouldn't understand."

"Why not?"

"I'm not sure I understand."

"Try me."

"I felt sad when I saw the ring. Simple as that. It wasn't right."

"You a West Pointer, too?"

"Long time ago."

"Where's your ring?"

"I didn't buy one."

Bramall pressed more buttons. Checked the call log, looked for old voicemails. Didn't find any. He went to another menu and chose a keep-as-new option. The screen went back to announcing one new message, the way it was when Reacher found it. Deniability. Score one for the Bureau.

Bramall said, "Leaving dishes in his sink doesn't mean much. Maybe he's just a slob. Leaving the phone at home doesn't necessarily mean much either. Probably doesn't work in the hills. No signal. Right here he's got a direct line of sight to the tower in Laramie. Maybe he never carries a phone with him."

Reacher said, "Scorpio seems to have expected some kind of an instant response."

"Do you believe the story about the bears and the mountain lions?"

"The sheriff has his doubts. He thinks maybe Porterfield was stabbed or gut shot and dumped in the woods to let nature take its course."

"Maybe Billy did it. Maybe he took over from Porterfield by force. Like an armed coup. Now maybe someone else has done the same thing to Billy. Live by the sword, die by the sword. What goes around comes around."

"I don't care," Reacher said. "I'm here to find Sanderson. That's all."

"Might not be a happy ending. Not if she traded her ring to a two-bit dope dealer. You might not like what you find."

"Someone else might have stolen it. You said so yourself."

"I sure hope so," Bramall said. "Because sooner or later I'll have to give the sister the news. And then give her my invoice. Sometimes that doesn't go down so well."

"How big of an invoice?"

"She has a house on the lake. She can afford it."

"You worth it?"

"Usually."

"So what's your next move?"

"I think she's close by. This feels like the end of the line. I think Billy is the final interface with the public. We're down to one degree of separation. Either she gave the ring to him herself or a neighbor stole it and gave it to him."

"Not bad for the FBI," Reacher said. "Plus Billy drives the snow-plow. He knows all the local roads. Ideal cover for getting around and supplying his customers. Never held up by the weather, either. But his retail territory must be huge. Like you said, two blocks is seventy miles out here. All the way to Sanderson's childhood home, as a matter of fact. I assume you've already looked there?"

"The assumption is Sanderson won't go back. Her sister was sure of it."

"Why?"

"She didn't explain. So knowing that, where would you start?"

"I could tell you, but then I'd have to bill you."

Bramall said, "Did you park your car in the barn?"

Reacher said, "I don't have a car."

"Then how did you get all the way out here?"

"Hitchhiked and walked."

"Suppose I let you ride in my truck?"

"That would be nice."

"Suppose you shut up about a bill?"

"Deal," Reacher said.

"So where?"

"What other information did the sister give you? Any names or places?"

"She says Sanderson was always very cagey. Maybe embarrassed, maybe upset. She never mentioned locations. She never said what she was doing. They could go three months without talking."

"Is that usual for twins?"

"Twins are siblings, same as anyone else."

"She got nothing at all?"

"The last time they spoke she got the impression Sanderson had a friend called Cyrus. She heard her say that name."

"Cyrus?"

"Well, Cy, at least. As if he was in the room with her. Like, shut up, Cy, I'm on the phone. Said in a friendly way. Like she was comfortable with him. The sister says for a second she sounded happy."

"Was that rare?"

"Very."

"When was this?"

"A couple of years ago, she thinks. Maybe a bit less."

"Is that all she got?"

"She said their conversations were usually very stiff. Are you OK, yes I'm OK. That kind of thing."

"Maybe it wasn't Cy for Cyrus," Reacher said. "Maybe it was Sy for Seymour. Which was Porterfield's first name. Scorpio told me he went by Sy. Let's go find where he lived. That would be my first move. There might still be something there. Or neighbors we can talk to."

Chapter 17

The old guy in the old post office had said Porterfield had lived in a log house up in the hills, maybe twenty miles down the dirt road, on one of the old ranches Reacher had seen on the university's map, behind fence lines as fine as the engraving on a hundred dollar bill. Bramall's Land Cruiser had a navigation screen that showed the dirt road, but not much else. So they watched the trip meter and drove west and counted the miles as they clicked by. The truck was as neat and competent as Bramall himself. It floated over the rough surface and felt like it could run forever.

Reacher asked, "When was the last time the sisters met face to face?"

Bramall said, "Seven years ago. After Sanderson's third deployment. The visit didn't go so well. I guess they decided not to repeat it. After that it was all on the phone."

"Sanderson was wounded at some point."

"I didn't know that. Mrs. Mackenzie never mentioned it."

"She might not have known about it. Sanderson might not have told her."

"Why wouldn't she?"

"It happens a lot. It's a complex dynamic. Maybe she didn't want to upset her family. Or appear diminished in any way. Or weak. Or to appear to be asking for sympathy. Or help. Or to avoid a told-you-so moment. Sounds like her sister didn't like the army."

"Wounded how bad?"

"I don't know," Reacher said. "All I know is she got a Purple Heart. Which can be anything from a scratch to losing a limb. Or all of them. Some of those people came home in a hell of a mess."

The mileage counter showed eight miles gone. Bramall was quiet for a long moment. Then he said, "You sure you want to do this? I don't see how the outcome can be good. She's either all messed up or a junkie or both. She might not want to be found."

"In which case I'll leave her alone. I'm not trying to save the world. I just want to know."

Ten miles gone. Either side of the road the high plains were getting higher. The mountain foothills rippled and folded, and tongues of conifer forest came and went. The sky was huge and high and impossibly blue, like a sapphire on the horizon, shading to deep navy way overhead. Like a Kodak photograph. Like the edge of outer space. The wind was getting up. The dust plume behind them was pulling south off the road.

"PTSD, too," Bramall said. "I guess they all have that."

"I guess they do," Reacher said.

Fourteen miles. Aspen groves blazed like flares on the slopes. Whole copses of hundreds of separate trees, but all joined together underground by a single root. An aspen wood was all one organism. The largest living thing on earth.

Bramall said, "Did the guy mean twenty miles to the house itself, or twenty miles to the end of the driveway?"

"The driveway," Reacher said. "I guess. That's how it worked with Billy's place. Except the guy underestimated. He called it about twenty percent short."

"So his twenty miles could be twenty-five."

"Unless sometimes he overestimates also. Maybe he's an all-around inaccurate guy, on a number of levels and a random basis. Which could make his twenty miles sixteen. Which would give us a nine-mile window."

"Then logically we should take the next track we see. Unlikely to be two in a nine-mile distance. This is Wyoming. Therefore the first track is our track, however sooner or later it comes."

"Not bad for the FBI," Reacher said.

The track came bang in the middle of the nine-mile stretch, at twenty miles from the post office exactly. Score one for the old guy. It was a right turn off the dirt road, under a high ranch gate, which had a name on it, spelled out in letters so weathered Reacher couldn't read them. Then the track ran straight north for close to a mile, before rising and curving west through the trees, out of sight, toward an unseen destination.

Bramall stopped the truck.

He said, "From my point of view this kind of thing is perfectly normal. I drive up to hundreds of houses. Sometimes there's yelling and sometimes there are dogs, but no one has ever discharged a weapon in my direction. We should talk about how you think those odds might change, with you in the car right next to me."

"You want me to get out and walk?" Reacher said. "Feel safer that way?"

"It's a tactical discussion. Worst case, Billy took over Porterfield's house as well as his business, and he's in there now. He wasn't in his other place, after all."

"Why would he want two places?"

"Some people do."

"Not twenty miles apart. They have a house on the lake."

"There were no heirs or relatives. Why wouldn't Billy take it?"

"Doesn't matter if he did. Doesn't matter if he's in there now. He never got the phone message. He doesn't know me from Adam. He'll think we're Mormons."

"You're not dressed like a Mormon."

"So you go knock on the door. Just in case. If he's there, tell him you're a Mormon who is coincidentally also in the snowplow business, and you want to talk to him about insurance against global warming."

The truck moved on. The track ran through the wooded slopes five more miles, always rough, with deep baked ruts in places, and worn gravel, and flat rocks the size of tables. The Land Cruiser nodded from side to side, and soldiered on. All the way through a final curve, and up a sudden sharp rise, to a stadium-sized plateau, full of trees, except for a home site set about a third of the way in. It had a long low log house, with wide porches all around, all in the center of a slightly tended acre, behind an informal fence made up of posts and rails twisted and grayed by the wind and the weather. Bramall drove in, and parked a respectful distance from the house. There were tatters of crime scene tape on the porch rails either side of the entrance. As if at one time the house was roped off.

"This wasn't the crime scene," Bramall said. "The guy died in the woods."

"He was found in the woods," Reacher said. "Maybe the sheriff thought that was a whole different thing entirely. We know he searched here. He found a car with a lot of miles, and ten grand in the closet."

"Where is Billy right now?"

"Why worry about him?"

"I'm not. But you should. Scorpio was ordering a homicide."

"Billy's not here. What are the odds? Plus he didn't get the message. He doesn't know Scorpio gave me Porterfield's name. So why would he come here to Porterfield's house? What were the odds we would ever find it anyway? Who knew the old post office guy was so good at guessing distances? Billy is somewhere else and this place is empty."

"OK," Bramall said.

He got out of the car and went to knock on the door.

A purposeful stride.

Reacher saw him knock, and he heard the sound, loud and clear, a fraction delayed by the distance, like a mismatched movie soundtrack.

He saw Bramall step back politely.

No one came to the door.

No movement anywhere.

Bramall knocked again.

The same no reaction.

He walked back and got in the truck, and said, "This place is empty."

Reacher said, "How do you feel about going in?"

"It's all closed up."

"We could break a window."

"Legally we have to ask ourselves if the county owns it now. Which it might, officially. Because of the unpaid taxes. Breaking into county property is a big step. You can't fight city hall."

"Maybe you smelled a suspicious smell, or thought you heard something. Like a despairing cry. The kind of thing that would justify a warrantless search. Did you?"

"No," Bramall said.

"You're retired," Reacher said. "You don't have to stick to FBI bullshit anymore."

"What would be the army approach? Set the place on fire?"

"No, that would be the Marine Corps approach. The army would conduct a careful survey of the exterior, and by great good fortune would discover a pane of glass previously broken by persons unknown, at a previous time, maybe long ago, or even just recently, which if true would reasonably suggest an ongoing emergency inside, which in turn would justify a good look around. I don't think the Supreme Court could argue with that."

"Previously broken either recently or a long time ago?"

"Obviously any sounds you hear in real time will be me, accidentally stepping on previously broken glass left lying on the porch ever since the unknown previous incident. That can sound very like a freshly breaking window. It's a common illusion."

"That's a standard FBI trick, too. We weren't all bullshit."

"Some of you came to us for training."

"And some of you came to us."

"I'm going to conduct a careful survey," Reacher said.

He got out of the car.

Chapter 18

It was a big house, but an easy survey, because the porch ran all the way around the structure, flat and level and true, and it served up all the first-floor doors and windows at a convenient height for inspection. Reacher started at the front, with the door Bramall had knocked on, which was a solid wooden affair, locked tight, and way too much effort to break down. So he moved on, to a hallway window, which would have taken no effort at all to get through, except it was on the front of the house, and even in the uninhabited middle of nowhere some ancient part of his brain sounded a warning. The front was never good. Not during, and not even afterward. Why leave after-action evidence in plain view? Not that there would be much. A discreet punched-out hole in the glass, about the size of a big man's elbow, and a slit insect screen rippling in the breeze. That would be all. Not much. But maybe enough to catch a passerby's eye. Always safer if that kind of thing happened later, not sooner, for all kinds of reasons.

The back was better.

Reacher walked down the side of the house, past five more windows all the same as the front. Which made it likely the windows in back would be all the same, too. Some kind of a unifying design theme. Or some kind of a big discount for a bulk purchase. But either way was good news. Windows like that were easy.

He turned the corner, and the first window he came to was broken.

It had a hole punched through it, about the size of a big man's elbow.

The insect screen was slit.

The broken glass was dirty, and the screen was mildewed. A year, maybe more. At least four seasons of wind and weather. Inside was a kitchen. Countertops that should have been shiny were dull with dust. Beyond the kitchen was a dining area, all gloom and shadows.

He walked the long way around the porches, and back to the car. Bramall had gotten out again. He was standing in a no-man's-land patch of dirt about thirty feet from the house.

Reacher said, "I found a busted window."

"Nicely done," Bramall said. "I didn't hear a thing."

"For real. An actual busted window. Previously broken by persons unknown. A year or more ago, by the look of it. Exactly how we would have done it."

"Show me," Bramall said.

Reacher led him along the front porch, and the side porch, and around the corner to the back. Bramall took a good long look. He seemed impressed by the mildew. He said, "A year at least. Let's say a year and a half. Why not? Let's say this happened right after Porterfield died. Was it the sheriff? You told me he searched the place."

"The sheriff had the keys," Reacher said. "He found them in Porterfield's pocket. That's how they identified him, along with his teeth. So the sheriff didn't need to break in. This was someone else, who didn't have the keys."

"Squatters, maybe."

"They wouldn't bust the kitchen window. The kitchen is a room they would want to use. They would have busted a window somewhere else."

"Ordinary burglars, then."

"Possible. We'll know by how much mess they made."

"We're still going inside?"

"We were before," Reacher said. "I don't see why we shouldn't now. This is practically an open invitation. We have a duty as citizens."

"To call the sheriff, technically."

"It's a gray area. The owner is dead. There are no heirs. It's a different situation. People read whole books about this kind of thing in law school. I'm sure the sheriff doesn't want to get in a big long discussion. Plus this could be where she called her sister. Right here. When she said, shut up, Sy, I'm on the phone. Had to be his place or hers. Either way she spent time here. So you know we're going in."

"I know I am," Bramall said. "But you're under no obligation."

"You looking out for me now?"

"I feel I ought to point out the legal downside."

"I get it. You want me to go first. So you can say to yourself the worst thing you ever did was get all swept up. You want me to be the bad guy. Because you have scruples."

"Not as such. What I have is a license from the state of Illinois. Which I would like to keep. Doesn't matter who goes first. What matters is, it would count against me if I didn't explicitly caution a junior partner against potential legal jeopardy."

"Are we partners?"

"Effectively."

"Junior and senior?"

"By age and experience."

"Do you have to explicitly caution me every step of the way?"

"Technically, yes."

"Let's not do that part, OK? Let's take it as read. More fun that way."

"OK," Bramall said. "You want fun, you go first."

*　　*　　*

Bramall's contribution was to stick his arm in through the hole in the glass and wind the window open with the inside handle. Reacher's jacket was new, and his shirt was new. He didn't want to smear either one of them with mildew, which he would if he pushed through the slit in the screen, like the original intruder or intruders must have, a year or more ago, back when the screen was clean. So he tore it out of its frame, all the way around, and folded it in a ragged square, and dropped it on the porch.

Best way into a kitchen was face down and feet first. Because of the countertop. You stood a chance of ending the maneuver standing on your feet, not your hands. But it was hard to set up. It required a contortion. Worse if there was a sink under the window, with a tap. Which could get to the wrong place at the wrong time. But Porterfield's sink was on a different wall. Which helped. A little.

Reacher felt his legs swim free, and he jackknifed at the waist, and planted his feet, and pushed himself upright. Inside, looking out. The kitchen was a little weather-beaten, because of the hole in the glass, but it had started out expensive. That was clear. The wood was thick, and the granite was thicker. There were appliances made out of stainless steel. They all had clock screens, dark and blank. There was absolute silence. No subliminal hum, no rustle in the pipes. No power, no water. No one paying the bills. All closed up.

He moved on through the gloom, out of the kitchen, into the dining area. From where he saw the living room, all open plan, with a complicated cathedral ceiling, and a full-height rock fireplace, made out of stones the size of tractor tires.

A trophy cabin. Authentic designs didn't have fireplaces built with forklift trucks and hydraulic cranes. They used smaller rocks. And why make a weird ceiling, where a flat one would fit?

But it was a lived-in trophy cabin. Reacher didn't hate it. The log walls were stained a light honey shade. The furniture looked comfortable but unobtrusive. There were weird collections on shelves. Animal skulls, interesting stones, interesting pine cones. Almost a family feel. A rich-family feel.

He walked back to the kitchen. To the broken window. Bramall was looking in at him.

Reacher said, "Nothing to worry about. It's like a time capsule. Which rules out a burglary. Because nothing is out of place. The dust is a uniform thickness everywhere. There's no mess at all. Which I guess rules out squatters, too."

"I'm coming in," Bramall said.

He was stiffer in the joints than Reacher, but those joints started out much closer together, because he was smaller, so overall his maneuver was easier. He pushed himself upright, and looked around the same way Reacher had. Kitchen, dining area, living room.

Undisturbed.

Bramall said, "Not what I expected."

"In what way?" Reacher said.

"If I had a cabin it might look like this."

"Dope dealers don't have taste?"

"Not usually."

Reacher checked the hallway.

He said, "There are bedrooms at both ends."

Bramall said, "If it wasn't burglars or squatters, who broke the window?"

"Not the sheriff," Reacher said. "But like the sheriff. A pro with a reason to search."

"But where's the mess? Pro searchers tear a place apart."

"Maybe they found what they wanted the first place they looked. Maybe that's what it means to be a pro. Or maybe they knew where it was all along. Maybe they came to get something back."

"Get what back?"

"I don't care," Reacher said. "All I want to do is find Sanderson."

"You think she was here. Back when she was dating a dope dealer worth getting gut shot or stabbed in the stomach."

"You're her older brother now?"

"I doubt the relationship would have happened. She would have done better for herself."

"She said, shut up, Sy, I'm on the phone. Even the uptight twin called it friendly and comfortable and happy. Best case, they were real good friends."

"Even worse," Bramall said. "You choose your friends."

"Either way, they spent time together. Here, and her place. Wherever that is."

"A year and a half ago."

"Better than nothing."

"If your Sy is the right Sy."

"Fifty-fifty right or wrong. Not bad odds."

Bramall took out his phone.

"Two bars," he said. "She could have called from here."

"What did the cell records say?"

"You need three masts to triangulate. There's only one here. Omni-directional. She was calling from somewhere inside a giant circular area about the size of New Jersey. That's all we know."

"Could have been here. No reason why not."

Bramall moved to the center of the living room. He said, "It was a year and a half ago and this place has been searched twice since then. And if you're right about someone getting something back, then the most important thing we could have found is already gone. So this is about looking for what two other parties missed. Which is slow work. How long have we got?"

"Out here, about a hundred years, I would think," Reacher said. "Pull your car around the back, and we could move in and live here forever. No one would ever know."

"OK, we'll search together. No look-out. Two heads are better than one."

They found the first missed item in less than a minute.

Chapter 19

It was in a mud room near the back door. In a closet where snow clothes were kept. A pair of snow pants had slipped off a hanger. Some kind of stiff nylon. They had hit the floor like spears, and then half crumpled and half stayed rigid, like wobbly legs, like a cartoon picture of a guy who just received a nasty shock. They had toppled backward and had ended up half propped in the corner. Reacher moved them, purely out of habit, and behind them he found a pair of women's snow boots. A technical product, with hooks and loops. A woman's size six. Which was small.

He said, "Boots in the closet is a thing, right? She spent quality time here."

"If it was her. Could have been anybody."

"I agree. But it's evidence a guy two separate people described as a loner living alone actually had a companion in his house. Which should have tilted the investigation a little, when such a guy shows up dead. Maybe we can forgive the sheriff. He had a preconceived notion. And I bet everyone in Wyoming has a closet like that. Hard to see what you always see. But whoever came along afterward should have seen it. They should have had fresh eyes. Makes me wonder who they were. And what they were doing. Maybe they didn't really look at anything. Maybe it really was a fast in-and-out, to get something back. Has to be. Nothing else has been touched."

Bramall said, "We should check the other closets."

They did, but there was nothing in them, except Porterfield's own stuff. Apparently he had been a guy who liked blue jeans, and saw no problem at all with laundering things until they went threadbare.

No women's clothing.

No dresses, no blouses, no pants.

Bramall said, "Why would she leave only her boots behind?"

"She left at the start of spring. She hadn't used them for a month. She forgot them. Or maybe they were uncomfortable. Maybe she left them on purpose. Maybe she was fixing to buy new. But she was here. Or someone was. Porterfield didn't live alone. Not all the time."

"That's a lot to read into a pair of boots."

"I bet we find more."

They did. But not much more. After two hours they had a very modest haul. More persuasive than conclusive. They saved time by ignoring what was on open view. Instead they looked inside things, and under things, and behind things.

They found a woman's comb between the sofa cushions. It was made of pink plastic. All the teeth were widely spaced. Not half and half, like a regular comb. In the master bathroom they found two sinks, each with a soap dish, one with a dried-out cake of scented soap, and one with a dried-out cake of plain. Also in the bathroom they found two sets of towels laid out. In the laundry room behind the dryer they found a pair of women's athletic socks. Some kind of miracle fiber, small in size, pink in color, stuck all over with dust bunnies.

That was it.

Not enough for a courtroom. But suggestive. Reacher said, "She was here. Or someone was. At least some of the time. Maybe just a casual on-again, off-again type of thing. But she was here long enough to get somewhat ingrained. When she left, she did it in style. She made a clean break. Some kind of statement. She scoured the place and packed up everything of hers she could see, leaving behind only the few things she couldn't. Like her lost comb. She couldn't take her soap anyway. At the time it was all wet and slimy. Couldn't just toss it in a bag with her clothes. She didn't count the towels. Who would? She forgot her snow boots. But it's the socks I like best."

"Why?"

"They prove she still has two legs. The Purple Heart might not be as bad as it could be."

"If it's her."

"Suppose it was. Porterfield must have gone to her place from time to time. Where would that be? How far from here? Suppose you were a guy like Porterfield. How far would you drive to get laid?"

"Depends."

"On what?"

"A number of things."

"Look on the bright side. Maybe not Miss America exactly, but assume she's a nice-looking person."

"This is Wyoming. They drive epic distances for a loaf of bread. For a girlfriend, two hours, maybe. A hundred miles."

"Which doesn't help us," Reacher said. "That's too big of an area to contemplate."

Bramall nodded. "I was going to say our next move should be go talk to Porterfield's neighbors. But I don't know exactly what that means out here. Everyone lives twenty miles from everyone else. I bet they never see each other."

"But I guess they depend on each other. Suppose they get a sudden emergency. Who are they going to call? The police department or the fire department two hours away? Or their nearest neighbor, who could be there in fifteen minutes? Maybe that's the country way. Maybe country neighbors are closer than you suspect. Maybe they're always into each other's business and have plenty to tell us."

"You're very cheerful."

Reacher didn't answer. He was alone in the kitchen, perhaps subconsciously needing to keep his exit in view. The open window, with the broken glass and the torn-out screen. A cool breeze came in. And borne on it, sounds. Most of them were inoffensive. Wind in the trees, the beat of a heavy bird's wing, a bee flying by, and pausing, and flying on.

One sound was different.

Very brief, and very distant. Barely audible. A fragment only. A tiny scratch, or a tiny crunch, or a tiny squelch. A small part of a familiar local sound. A Wyoming sound. Like all sounds, made from a mix of different components. Like DNA.

Grit was involved.

And rock.

And rubber.

"We need to get out," he said. "There's a car on the driveway."

Bramall went first. Less likely to get stuck. Reacher followed him successfully, and Bramall put his arm back in and wound the handle to close the window. Then they hustled to the front.

Nothing yet.

"We should get in the car," Bramall said. "Just in case."

Reacher said, "If in doubt, run them over."

They climbed in the Toyota and Bramall started the motor.

A truck came up over the final rise and started across the plateau.

It was a Ford pick-up truck, loaded with a police-department version of a camper shell. Its paint was clean and shiny. All white, except for the doors, which had gold stars about two feet wide and two feet high, with the county's name in a curve above, and *Sheriff's Department* in a curve below. A little like a West Point ring.

Sheriff Connelly.

Connelly parked close by the Toyota, at a casual angle, partly to look nonchalant and unworried and therefore unthreatening, but mostly, Reacher thought, to subtly block off the Toyota's forward path. The guy had judged it well. Not obvious, but the Toyota would have to back up and loop around.

Connelly buzzed his window down. He was wearing his hat in the car. Plenty of room. It was a tall truck.

Reacher buzzed his window down. He was closest.

Connelly said, "You told me you had no connections to Porter-field."

Reacher said, "I don't."

"Yet here you are at his house."

"The woman I'm looking for was here, at least for a few months. I'm trying to figure out where she went next."

"Porterfield lived alone."

"Not always."

Connelly said, "Have you been inside the house?"

"Yes," Reacher said.

"How?"

"There was a previous break-in here, a year or more ago. We went in the same hole."

"What break-in?"

"You searched this place when he died. You found what you found, and you locked up and drove away. Then someone else came by and went in the window."

"Show me," Connelly said.

They got out of their cars and trooped back to the far corner of the house. Connelly took a good long look. He unfolded the torn-out insect screen and held it in place, as if re-creating the original scene. He rubbed the mildew between finger and thumb, and sniffed it.

He said, "Could be a year and a half."

Then he said, "How are things inside?"

Reacher said, "No mess, no damage, nothing pulled out or over-turned. This wasn't a burglary, or squatters."

Connelly said, "Why do you think there was a woman living up here?"

They moved to the porch rail, facing the rear view, all lined up, looking straight ahead at trees and mountains. Bramall talked through the boots, and the comb, and the soap, and the towels, and the small pink socks.

Connelly said, "The boots don't mean much, or the comb or the socks. They could be historic. Twenty years ago there could have been nieces and cousins here every summer and winter. That kind of stuff stays lost a long time."

"But?" Reacher said.

"I'm prepared to admit when I make a mistake. I like the soap and the towels. Two sinks in use always means a couple, and if one soap is smelly, it's a man and a woman. And soap and towels is real-time evidence. That's exactly how the room looked the morning Porterfield died. I guess I missed it. But no one came forward at the time. No one ever has. All the evidence said Porterfield was a loner and no one else had barely even met him. So where was the woman then, and where is she now?"

"That's what we're trying to figure out."

"If it's the same woman."

"Nothing says it isn't."

Connelly said, "The ring you showed me was pretty small."

"Yes, it was," Reacher said.

"Are you judging this thing by the size of the socks? Because maybe they shrunk."

"The boots didn't. They're small, too."

"Where did she serve?"

"Iraq and Afghanistan, five times."

"A tough character."

"Like you wouldn't believe."

"If it's the same woman."

"It might be."

"Would such a woman come home and use smelly soap and wear pink socks?"

"I'm sure she would do exactly that. Stuff like that is the whole point of coming home."

Connelly turned around and looked back at the house.

At the broken window.

Reacher said, "I know."

"You know what?"

"We can't figure out who would have done that either. It's good clean professional work. A neat break-in, and nothing disturbed inside. Feels like training and experience were involved. Feels like government work. Except that's ridiculous."

Connelly said, "Mostly because what would the government want with Porterfield? Whatever he was, he was small-time. And a government agency would have called me first. As a courtesy, at least, and for practical assistance, too. Which I could have given them in this case. I had the keys."

"Then regular petty criminals are getting neater these days."

"That hasn't been my experience."

"Then who was it?"

"Fancy criminals, maybe. The kind who can afford the best."

"What would they want with small-time Porterfield?"

Connelly didn't answer.

Bramall said, "We apologize for trespassing. We intended no disrespect to the laws of the county."

Connelly said, "I can't help you with the woman. There's no evidence of a crime. I can't take soap and towels to a county board budget hearing. I'm sorry. I have no manpower."

"Who could help us?" Bramall said. "Neighbors?"

"They might. I'm their sheriff, but I don't know any of them. In fact this is only the second time I've ever been out here. It's a quiet corner. The squeaky wheels get all my attention."

"We should get going," Bramall said. "Sheriff, thank you for your time."

At that moment three hundred miles away in Rapid City, South Dakota, Gloria Nakamura was sitting in her blue car, on the cross street, artfully positioned, this time watching Scorpio's back door, not his front. She had been there close to two hours, and she had seen nothing of interest.

Until.

A Harley with a Montana plate pulled into the alley. The sound beat back off the walls. Then it shut down. The rider got off, and the back door opened, and the rider went in.

Nakamura made a note.

Four minutes on her watch later, the rider came out again. He got on his bike, and started the noise again, and rode away.

Nakamura made a note.

Then she drove back to the station.

Bramall and Reacher drove the ranch track back to the dirt road, and turned west, which was where they thought they would find the bulk of the local neighborhood population, such as it was. Bramall watched the left-hand shoulder, and Reacher watched the right. They agreed they would take the first track they saw, whichever side of the road it was on, because by definition whatever dwelling lay at the end of it was Sy Porterfield's nearest next-door neighbor.

The first track came eleven miles later. On the left. They nearly missed it. It was a plain and inconspicuous entry. After which it twisted and rose through the trees, steep and tight in places, but better maintained than Porterfield's. The Land Cruiser rolled on, implacably, more than three miles, and then all of a sudden the trees opened up and gave out on a flat acre with a long view east. There was a one-story house up on a stone foundation. It was made of brown boards, in places twisted and silvery. It had a front porch, with ancient millwork holding up the rail. On the porch was an old church pew, pressed into service as a place to sit and take the air in the morning sun.

Bramall parked a respectful distance from the house.

He checked his phone.

"Two bars," he said. "Coverage is actually pretty good here. She could have called from anywhere."

They made to get out of the car, but before they could the house door opened and a woman stepped out. She must have heard their tires. She looked lean and strong and tanned by wind and sun. She was wearing a faded red dress, over bare legs and cowboy boots. She was maybe forty, but it was hard to tell. Reacher would not have ventured an opinion. If forced, he would have said thirty, just to be safe, and wouldn't have been surprised if the truth was fifty. She stood there, hands on hips, just watching. Not hostile. Not yet.

Bramall said, "She thinks we're Mormons."

Reacher got out. He raised his hand. A universal gesture. Unarmed. Friendly. She moved her head, part responsive, part inquiring. Bramall got out. He and Reacher walked together and stopped a polite distance short of the porch.

Reacher said, "Ma'am, we're looking for a missing woman, who we think once stayed a spell with your neighbor Sy Porterfield. We wonder if you could tell us about that."

"You should come in," the woman said. "I have lemonade in a jug."

Chapter 20

Reacher and Bramall followed the woman inside. The walls were made of the same boards as the outside, but stained and polished, not weather-beaten. The kitchen was a low dark room. The woman poured lemonade into glasses. They sat down at her table.

"Are you private detectives?" she asked.

"I am," Bramall said.

She looked at Reacher.

He said, "Military investigator."

Which was true, in a historic sense.

She said, "Was it last year Sy died, or the year before?"

"Last year," Reacher said. "The start of spring."

"I didn't know him very well. Never really met him, except for once or twice. Seemed to be a solitary type of guy, always coming and going."

"What did he do for a living?"

"None of us knew."

"Us? Did you talk about him with other people?"

"That's what neighbors do. You don't like it, mister, go live on the moon."

"What was the consensus opinion?"

"We all thought he was a solitary guy, always coming and going."

"No one saw any sign of a woman living there?"

"Never," she said.

Which sounded definitive.

Reacher said, "You ever heard the name Serena?"

"In my life?"

"Around here."

"No," she said.

"Or Rose?"

"No."

"Or Sanderson?"

"No."

Reacher said, "We found stuff in Porterfield's house."

"What kind?"

"Random items of women's apparel and toiletries. Not much. Like very faint clues."

The woman said nothing.

Then she said, "How faint?"

"We know the bathroom was used by two people," Reacher said.

The woman said, "Huh."

"What does that mean?"

"It means I guess one time I wondered something. In the end I figured I made a mistake."

"Wondered what?"

"I was on the dirt road, heading out to the turn at Mule Crossing. He was driving the other way. From the turn, heading home. It's rare to see another car. It kind of perks you up. It makes you get in your own lane, and so forth. You don't want to get in a collision. So we passed each other by. We kind of waved, I guess. No big deal. Except I was sure he had someone in the passenger seat beside him. I thought it was a girl. Just a glimpse. She was hunched down low, turned away from him, kind of pressing herself into the side of the seat. I couldn't see her face."

"How old?"

"Not young. Not a kid. But quite small, and agile, I guess. She was all twisted around, hiding her face from him."

"Weird."

"And silvery, somehow. That's what I remember. A silvery color."

"Also weird."

"I thought so, too. It stayed on my mind. So the next day I went over there. I took him a pie. Said I had one extra. But really to check. Back then there were all kinds of stories. Human trafficking, and custody disputes. Maybe he was into that kind of stuff. Or maybe she really was a genuine girlfriend. Who knew? Maybe they had been having a fight in the car. I figured they might be over it by then and he would introduce me."

"What happened?"

"He acted weird. He was pleased about the pie. Very polite. But he wouldn't let me in the house. We talked on the porch. He pulled the door almost shut behind him and stood where I couldn't see through the gap. He didn't say much. I tried to introduce the subject. I said I was sorry the pie was too big for one. It was a natural opening. It gave him a chance to tell me he was planning to share it with his girlfriend. But he didn't. He said he would wrap the second slice in aluminum foil and eat it in a couple days."

"What kind of pie was it?"

"Strawberry," the woman said. "They had some nice ones at the market. Where I was going when I passed him on the road."

"What happened next?"

"Nothing. That was it. It was kind of awkward, just standing there, so I said, OK, I guess I'll get going, and he said thanks again for the pie, and then he practically rushed me off his property."

"What was your conclusion?"

"It was in the way he was standing. He was screening me off from the house. He was hiding something in there. Or someone. Then I got to wondering about when I saw them in the car. Maybe she was hiding her face from me, not him. Maybe he told her to. Like she was his secret."

"But you never found out for sure?"

"I never saw him again. He was dead a month later. No one ever said anything about a widow or a partner or a girlfriend. Or a sex slave or a hostage. So in the end I figured I must have been wrong. Then I guess I forgot all about it. Time passes."

"How long had he lived there?"

"Five years, maybe."

"Did any of the neighbors ever take a wild-ass guess about what he did for money?"

"That would enter the realm of gossip."

"I guess it would, technically."

"We figured he already had plenty. We figured he was a rich guy from out of state, come to find himself. We get those, from time to time. Maybe they're writing a novel."

At that moment three hundred miles away in Rapid City, South Dakota, the clerk behind the deli counter in the convenience store was finishing up making change for a BLT and a diet soda, and then picking up the phone, and dialing the police department.

He said, "Excuse me, I think you have a woman detective working for you. An Oriental person. Or Japanese-American. Or Asian, or whatever it's supposed to be now. I need to speak with her."

The call was transferred, and a voice said, "Property, Nakamura."

"This is the guy from the convenience store. On the corner by Arthur Scorpio's laundromat. I got something I figure I need to tell you before you find out for yourself and get mad at me."

"What kind of something?"

"Arthur Scorpio just came in."

"And?"

"He bought another phone."

"How long ago?"

"Five minutes."

"Which phone?"

"First one off the left peg."

Also at that moment, Arthur Scorpio was dialing Billy in Wyoming again. Again there was no answer. Just voicemail.

Scorpio said, "Billy, this is Arthur. I need to hear from you. You're making me worried now. What's with not answering your phone all the time? And you got that guy coming. Plus maybe another guy. We just got a message from Montana. They sent a rider down especially. They have a Fed up there asking questions. He just left Billings. We don't know where he's headed next. Eyes open, OK? And call me back. Don't make me worried, Billy."

He clicked off and dropped the phone in the trash basket.

Bramall's phone dinged. Reacher figured it was a text message. He was getting to where he could tell the difference. The woman in the faded red dress got up and started to gather the empty lemonade glasses.

Bramall read his message.

Twice.

He said, "Ma'am, the lemonade was delicious, but I'm afraid we really have to get going now."

Then he just stood up and hustled out the door. Reacher shrugged at the woman, palms up, as if in puzzlement. Another universal gesture. *Yeah, I know, but I better go with my crazy friend.* He followed Bramall outside, and across the dirt, to the car.

He said, "What's up?"

Bramall said, "Mrs. Mackenzie is dissatisfied with progress so far, and informs me she's going to Wyoming to search certain places near the old family homestead herself. Apparently she's reconsidering her opinion her sister would never go back there."

"Doesn't she know you're only sixty miles away?"

"No," Bramall said. "I never tell clients where I am."

"Why not?"

"I like to build up the mystery."

"You can take the boy out of the FBI."

"We need to get there first."

"When is she leaving Chicago?"

"She'll charter a plane. She has a card. We should go there now. We should have gone there first. But I was told Sanderson would never return. Now we're saying maybe she did? Terrific. Maybe she's been there all along. It's a two-hour drive. Nothing for Porterfield to complain about."

Sheriff Connelly had said a government agency would call him first, before entering on his territory. At least as a courtesy. Which is exactly what happened. He got back from his impromptu trip out to the old Porterfield place, and two minutes later his phone rang with a field agent from the federal DEA. The guy said he was heading south from Montana, and sooner or later was going to be passing through the county, nothing much in mind, maybe stopping in one or two places, but overall nothing for anyone to get concerned about. He said he didn't require assistance or any other courtesies, but thank you very much for asking. Then he hung up.

There was a big difference between crows flying and cars driving. To get across the Snowy Range, first they had to go back to the dirt road, and then back to Mule Crossing itself, and past the old post office and the bottle rocket store, and all the way back to Laramie, all in order to pick up a different westward route, which started with a left turn about four blocks north of the bar with the bullet hole in the mirror. Then the trip started all over again at zero. Still seventy miles to go. Reacher told Bramall to look on the bright side. More hours on the invoice. Bramall told a joke about a lawyer who died and got to the pearly gates. Not fair, he said. I'm only forty-five. Saint Pete said no, we got a new system. Now we do it by billable hours. According to our records you're 153.

They passed a sign that said the road would close pretty soon for the winter. And then it started to rise, into the mountains, up over ten thousand feet, into thin and glittering air. The Toyota slowed a little, but it kept on going, winding through rocky gaps and around sparse copses of wind-stunted trees, across what already felt like the roof of the world. Then the road held level through a wide half-mile curve, and started to fall again, through the same type of gaps and around the same type of trees, and the Toyota started rolling faster and faster, under its own weight, with no gas at all.

Thirty miles later the navigation screen showed a thin tracery of ranch roads, two on the north side, and two on the south. Beyond them was blank.

"Is that it?" Reacher asked.

"I think so," Bramall said. "Apparently one of the ranches is bigger than the other three. That's the old homestead. The others came later."

"Did the sisters inherit?"

"No, the place was sold when they were in college. The parents moved out. New owners moved in. And so on. The same with the other three places, I'm sure."

"You think she's squatting in one of them?"

"I doubt a person who has to pawn her ring is paying rent."

"Why would they be empty?"

"Rural real estate often is. Places shrivel and die. Especially when the neighborhood royalty moves out."

"Is that your description, or Mrs. Mackenzie's?"

"A little of both. Their father was a judge, which back then in a place like this made him the most important man in the county. Everything came through the courts eventually. Mrs. Mackenzie seems aware of that."

"Why did the parents move out?"

"Mrs. Mackenzie had a hard time explaining. I'm sure we could speculate. I'm sure as kids they both had ponies. On a judge's salary."

"I'm sure all Wyoming kids have ponies. There are more ponies than kids."

"It was a metaphor. For little arrangements that work great, until they don't. Then sometimes you need to get out of town and start over."

"Is that how Mrs. Mackenzie remembers it?"

"She was in college at the time. In the end she credits George W. Bush. She claims it was an entrepreneurial thing. The old man was moving from the public sector to the private."

"To do what exactly?"

"No one knew exactly, except they noticed it stopped the day after the banks crashed."

"Where is the old boy now?"

"Dead soon after."

"Mom?"

"Also dead. But much more recently. Still raw."

"Hence the sudden worry about her semi-estranged twin."

"Exactly," Bramall said. "Now her semi-estranged twin is all she's got."

They had no way of knowing which of the tracks led to the largest ranch, because they all ran far out of sight into the invisible distance, so they tried to judge by width or construction or other hint of architectural grandeur. In the end they agreed one track was wider than the others. Possibly the surface was better. There were piles of rocks that might once have been ceremonial gateposts. Like the archaeological remains of a once-mighty palace.

The Toyota turned in, and started climbing.

Chapter 21

The old homestead was both old and a homestead. It was a classic piece of western real estate, with wide tawny pastures, and dark green conifer trees, and outcrops of rock, and bubbling blue water in streams through the bottoms. Way in the distance were the Rocky Mountains, just hints in the mist. The main house was a spreading log construction with all kinds of extra wings built out. There were log barns and log garages. A lot of logs, Reacher thought, and all of them old-school, huge and heavy, hard as a rock, smoothed by axes and joined by pegs.

Like an old-time travel poster on an airport wall.

Except for a new-model rental sedan parked at an angle, and a woman standing next to it.

The sedan was a handsome item with a Chevrolet grille, basic red, with barcodes in all the back windows. The woman was small and slender. Maybe five-two and a hundred pounds. She was wearing boots, and boot-cut blue jeans, and a gauzy white shirt under an open leather jacket. She had a purse on her shoulder. She had long thick hair, heaped and wild and tangled, most of it pale red, some of it bleached by the sun. Her face was like a picture in a book. Pale flawless skin, perfect bones, delicate features. Green eyes, frank and open. A red mouth, confident, in control, almost smiling. Radiant. Composed. She had to be thirty-something. But she looked brand new.

Like a movie star.

"Shit," Bramall said. "That's Mrs. Mackenzie."

The twin sister. An exact replica. Army minimum for women was four-ten and ninety-one pounds. Sanderson would have gotten in comfortably. But everything else would have been twice as hard. From that point onward. Especially with the face. It was drop-dead spectacular.

Bramall got out of the car. He took a couple of steps, and stopped. So did she. Then Reacher got out. He heard Bramall say, "Mrs. Mackenzie, I didn't expect to see you so soon."

She said, "One of those things. The text didn't send till we landed. You thought I was leaving Chicago. Actually I was leaving the Hertz office in Laramie."

"I was close by."

"Of course you were. For which I apologize most sincerely. Fact and logic brought you to Wyoming, but I wouldn't let you get all the way here. I told you it was impossible she would come back."

"What changed?"

"You should introduce me to your friend."

Reacher stepped up and said his name and shook her hand. It felt like a dove's wing in a gorilla's paw.

"What changed?" Bramall said again.

"Now I'm afraid nothing has changed," Mackenzie said. "This place is empty. I think I made a mistake. I wasted a day. I apologize."

"Why would she come back here?"

"Suddenly I thought familiarity might be important to her. I try to think like her. We had some good times here. Eighteen years of stability. Since then she's had none. I thought it might be something she's craving."

Reacher looked up at the house.

He asked, "How long has it been empty?"

She said, "I think it's just someone's summer house now."

"It's still summer."

"They must have skipped this year."

"Do you remember who bought it?"

Mackenzie shook her head. "I'm not sure we ever knew. I was away in school, and Rose was at West Point."

"You call her Rose?"

"We insisted. Jane and Rose."

"How did you feel when you found out your folks had sold the place?"

"May I know the root of your interest in my family's affairs?"

So Reacher ran through the story one more time, from the bus out of Milwaukee all the way to the there and then across the Snowy Range. But some kind of instinct made him smooth it out as he went. He stayed strictly on the poignant pawned-ring track, and didn't mention either Scorpio or Billy, or speculate about anyone's specific occupation. He ended with the meager trove of evidence from Sy Porterfield's hall closet, and his living room sofa, and his master bathroom, and his laundry room.

Mackenzie was quiet a beat.

Then she said, "What size were the boots?"

"Six," Reacher said.

"OK."

He looked at her hair. Heaped, wild, tangled. Untamed was the word. Must take forever to wash.

An exact replica.

He said, "Show me your comb."

She paused again.

Then she said, "Yes, I see."

She dug in her bag and came out with a pink plastic comb. All the teeth were widely spaced. Not half and half, like a regular comb.

Reacher said, "Have you always used that brand?"

"It's the only kind that works."

"It's the same."

"The boots fit, too."

He took the ring from his pocket and balanced it on his palm. She picked it up, carefully, between delicate fingers.

West Point 2005.

The gold filigree, the black stone, the tiny size.

She read the engraving.

She selected a finger and pulled off a designer bauble as thick and gold as a false tooth. In its place she slipped her sister's trophy. Fourth finger, right hand. It sat there like it should. The perfect fit. The perfect size. Prominent, like it should be, and proud, like it should be, but not as big as a carnival prize. Reacher pictured the same hand, but maybe worn down a bit leaner, with a darker tan, and a couple of nicks and cuts healed white.

He pictured the same face, the same way.

Mackenzie said, "You mentioned that you bought the ring."

"Correct," Reacher said.

"May I buy it back from you?"

"It's not for sale. It's a gift for your sister."

"I could give it to her."

"So could the lady at West Point. Eventually."

"You feel a need to hand it over personally?"

"I need to know she's OK."

"You never met her."

"Makes no difference. Should it? I don't know. You tell me."

Mackenzie took the ring off. She handed it back.

Some kind of look on her perfect face.

Reacher said, "I know."

"You know what?"

"I know what you're thinking. You're here because it's family, and Mr. Bramall is here because he's getting paid. Why am I here? I'm giving you the impression I'm some kind of a weird obsessive. Maybe a couple soldiers short of a squad. I don't mean to. But I get it. I'm making you feel uncomfortable."

"Not at all."

"You're very polite."

"I assume it's an honor thing. Rose was in a world I didn't understand."

"What we need now is solid information. Are you confident this place is empty?"

"There are dust sheets everywhere and the water is off."

"So where would Rose go, if not here?"

"This is ridiculous."

"What is?" Reacher said.

"I should be on a psychiatrist's couch to answer these questions."

"Why?"

"We participated in a fantasy. OK? We were required to. As if we were lords of the manor and owned the whole valley. As if when the neighbors built, we were practically giving them almshouses out of sheer benevolence. Obviously later on we discovered Father had to sell some acres. But it was like we still owned them. Like slave quarters. We lorded it over the poor people. We were in and out anytime we wanted."

"Which of the three would she go to now?"

"Any of them."

"You want a ride? In the front, if you like. You're paying the bills, after all."

Reacher got in the back, and got comfortable. Mackenzie took his place in the passenger seat. Bramall drove, but not back to the road. Mackenzie showed him different tracks. The ways they went as kids. Easy enough for a slip of a girl to skip along. Harder for the car. But it made it, bending saplings, all four tires grabbing, like a ponderous cat. The nearest neighbor slid into view. Not a trophy cabin. Built before the word existed. The product of a more innocent age, when a vacation house could be a plain and simple thing. The view was a picture postcard.

Bramall and Mackenzie went to the door.

They knocked.

It opened.

A guy stood there. Same kind of age as the guy in the Mule Crossing post office. Same kind of tired-out stoop. Bramall said something to him, then Mackenzie, and the old guy nodded and made to let them in. Bramall turned and waved to Reacher, and Reacher got out of the car, and walked over to join them. They went inside, and the old guy said yes, all those years ago he had bought the land and built the house. For family vacations. Now he came alone. Which was borne out by the evidence. Reacher looked around and saw one of everything, and felt the quiet patient air of a lonely place.

The guy said he remembered the twins coming by. Way back they were wild-haired little girls in country dresses. They visited all the time, until they were ten or twelve, then not so much, until they were fifteen or so, and then hardly at all after that.

Mackenzie said, "Have you seen Rose recently?"

The old guy said, "Where would I see her?"

"Around here, maybe."

"I guess it's a dumb question to ask what she looks like now."

Mackenzie smiled. "Maybe a bit more tan than me. Maybe a bit more toned. She would claim she's been working harder. She might have cut her hair. Or dyed it. She might have gotten tattoos." She looked a question at Bramall. "Anything else we should consider?"

Bramall looked a question at Reacher.

Is this where we tell her she was wounded?

"No," Reacher said. "I'm sure the gentleman knows what she looks like."

"I haven't seen her," the old guy said.

They used the old guy's driveway, and crossed the road, and took the driveway opposite. It came out on another idyllic scene, but smaller, a quarter-sized version of the old homestead, with a newer house and no active stream.

The house was closed up and empty. Locked doors, shaded windows, no broken glass. No burglars, no squatters. No feral Rose Sanderson, going to earth in a place she remembered.

They moved off again, on another rough trail Mackenzie seemed half to know and half to imagine. The Toyota squeezed between trees, and rode up and down dips and hollows, and bucked and nodded. Bramall stayed calm behind the wheel. He drove most of the way one-handed.

The last house came into view.

It was the same kind of thing as before, an unpretentious A-framed cabin, with a lot of glass on a spectacular view. Bramall looped around to the driveway, as if he had been on it all along, and he parked a respectful distance from the house.

The front door opened.

A woman stood in the shadow.

She must have heard their tires.

She took a hopeful step forward, into the sun.

She looked like Porterfield's neighbor, but wound up way tighter. Upset about something. She was staring all around, and then staring at the car.

Bramall got out.

She watched him.

Mackenzie got out.

She watched her.

Reacher got out.

She watched him.

No one else got out.

She staggered back, like she had been hit in the head. She leaned on the frame of the door.

She said, "Have you guys seen Billy?"

Bramall didn't answer.

The woman said, "I thought maybe you were him. Maybe he got a new car. He's supposed to be coming."

"For what?" Reacher said.

"Have you seen him?"

Mackenzie said, "Who is Billy?"

Reacher said, "We'll get to that."

To the woman in the doorway he said, "I got a question for you first, and then I'll tell you about Billy."

"What's the question?"

"Tell me about the other woman, who looks just like my friend here. Like her twin sister."

"What other woman?"

"I just told you. Pay attention. Like my friend here. In this neighborhood."

"Never seen her."

"She might be Billy's friend, too."

"Don't know her."

"You sure?"

"A woman who looks like her? Never seen one."

"You ever heard the name Rose?"

"Never ever. Now tell me about Billy."

"I haven't met him yet," Reacher said. "But I hear his privileges were suspended. His cupboard is bare. Until he takes care of a local problem. Which he hasn't yet. I know that, because I'm the local problem. And here I still am. So if he happens to drop by, tell him I'm looking for him. The Incredible Hulk. Tell him I plan to stop by and pay him a visit. Give him a good description. That might be worth twenty bucks to him. You could get a freebie."

"Billy never gives freebies," the woman said.

"Who is Billy?" Mackenzie asked again.

They told her in the car. Not the whole story. Still they kept him separate. As if he was an accidental discovery, off to one side. They told her about the shoebox of cash, but not the shoebox of jewelry.

But Mackenzie was a smart woman.

She said, "Then why were you in his home in the first place?"

Which under her critical gaze led to the whole soup-to-nuts narrative, involving Scorpio, and Porterfield, and Billy, and Bramall's old phone records, and Nakamura's overheard voicemails.

Mackenzie said, "In other words for at least two years Rose has been involved with drug dealers and drug users. Meth and heroin. With all that entails. Such as shacking up with one who got eaten by a bear."

They didn't answer.

Mackenzie asked, quietly, "Is she an addict?"

They told her about the shoebox of jewelry.

She started to cry.

Chapter 22

They drove back to the old homestead, where Mackenzie's rental was parked, at an angle, like a garish red blot on the old-timey landscape.

She said, "Now I'm worried about the timescale. Her comb was lost at least a year and a half ago. We know that. Possibly months before. This is likely a two-year thing. Or more. But her ring left Wyoming just six weeks ago. Doesn't that feel like a final threshold? Like some kind of end stage?"

Reacher said, "Did you call the army during your search?"

"They told me nothing. They had privacy concerns. Any other time, I would have been cheering them on."

"I called a place I know. I pulled some strings. They didn't have much. They had a list of her West Point scores. She did very well."

"I remember."

"They had a list of her deployments. Iraq and Afghanistan. Five tours and out."

"OK."

"They had a list of her medals."

"I didn't know she won any."

"She won a Bronze Star."

"For what?"

"The regulation says the Bronze Star medal is awarded to individuals who distinguish themselves in a combat theater by heroism, outstanding achievement, or meritorious service."

"I didn't know," Mackenzie said again.

"She also won a Purple Heart."

Mackenzie was quiet a long moment.

First she said, "I didn't know."

Then she said, "What for?"

Last she said, "Oh, no."

Reacher didn't recite the regulation. Not happy listening. *Awarded to any member of the armed forces who has been wounded, killed, or who has died or may die of wounds.*

Mackenzie said, "How bad?"

"Can't tell," Reacher said. "Right now it's just the name of a medal. Lots of people have them. As a matter of fact I have one. Truth is none of them come cheap. Most of them leave a mark. But you heal up and you walk away. Almost always. Certainly a big percentage. Doesn't have to be bad news."

Mackenzie said, "Iraq and Afghanistan were all bad news."

She looked ahead at her sleek red car.

She said, "I'm not going home. I'm staying here. She's close. You said so yourself. She's in trouble. Maybe she lost an arm. Maybe she's a disabled veteran with nowhere to live and nothing to eat."

She told them to follow her back to the Hertz office, and then take her to see Billy's place.

Nakamura carried her laptop down the corridor to her lieutenant's corner suite. She played the captured voicemail. *We just got a message from Montana. They sent a rider down especially. They have a Fed up there asking questions. He just left Billings.*

She said, "I saw the rider from Montana. He was there four minutes."

Her lieutenant said, "Does this get us anywhere?"

"My friend in the lab is doing great work with predicting the phone numbers."

"What does he want, the Medal of Honor?"

"A pat on the back would be good. You know, stick your head in, say hi."

"What do you want?"

"It would be good to know what kind of Fed they had up there in Billings. And it would be good to know who sent the warning. Was it a subsidiary, an affiliate, a franchise, or just a friendly bunch of guys all loosely in the same boat?"

"What do you want me to do about it?"

"Call the Billings PD and ask them who was in town last night. They'll know, because they'll have gotten a courtesy call ahead of time."

"And this guy is going to Wyoming next? Remind me again, why should I care?"

"Because Scorpio got one of his tentacles trodden on. If we knew exactly who he's scared of, maybe we could work out exactly what he's doing."

The lieutenant called through a closed hutch to his secretary, and told her to get a number for whatever captain or commissioner or other fancy rank was top boy in the Billings PD, over in Montana. And then to dial it, and put it on line one.

They got to Billy's place in the late afternoon. The sun was over the distant mountains. The pronghorns were throwing shadows taller than they were. The colors were different.

The place was still empty.

They went in the kitchen door, and up to the slept-in bedroom. To the closet. Reacher put the shoeboxes on the bed. Mackenzie whirred her finger down the wadded cash, and then poked through the jewelry, pushing her nail through the inch of clinking metal, gathering necklace chains as fine as hair, tumbling high school rings aside, and brassy wise-guy pinkie-finger signet rings, with black onyx faces and tiny off-center chips of diamond.

She said, "Was the pawn shop window like this?"

"Exactly like that," Reacher said.

"Poor Rose."

"Do you know this area?"

"I know Laramie. Or I used to. Down here was all railroad land. Before the track was laid they used mules. Hence the name, probably."

"No old friends or relatives?"

"Seven months of the year the road is closed. This was the other side of the world to us."

"Nowhere she would remember?"

"From later on, probably bars and restaurants downtown. Some stores, possibly. Sometimes we went out to the university. For music, or whatever. But I don't think she would want to live out there now. We're thirty-five years old."

"So where?"

"Forget what I said. Ignore familiarity. I was wrong. I was desperate. Every idea looked like a good idea. Maybe she chose unfamiliarity instead. Somewhere she didn't know at all."

"She knows Wyoming."

"Exactly. To have both is just right. Familiarity and unfamiliarity."

Reacher checked the view from the bedroom window. There was dust on the dirt road. A long cloud, vivid red in the softening light, spiraling and drifting. A tiny dot at its head, winking in the low sun.

Six minutes, maybe.

"Coming here?" Bramall said.

"Maybe," Reacher said. "Maybe not. But I hope so. I hope it's Billy.

He knows where Rose lives. From plowing her driveway, if nothing else."

"He might have his deer rifle."

"Has he listened to his voicemail yet?"

"We didn't check. I guess he could have snuck home at some point. A fast in-and-out. We've been gone for hours."

"OK," Reacher said.

"How do you want to do this?"

"Inside, obviously. Downstairs would be best. There's a poker on the fireplace. I'll head in that direction. You take the other side. Find what you can. Look for steak knives. Often in a sideboard drawer."

Mackenzie said, "What should I do?"

"You go check if the phone is still there. On the desk in the back parlor. If it is, it should say one new message. That's how Mr. Bramall left it. If it's there but it's showing a regular screen, that means Billy came back and listened to it, but left the phone home again for whatever reason. So check it out and tell us which. Shout it out good and loud. Then we'll know what we're dealing with here. We'll know how hard to hit the guy."

"If it's Billy," Bramall said.

"Hope for the best," Reacher said.

They went down the stairs, Reacher first, heading left, then Bramall, heading right, and last Mackenzie, looping back toward the parlor. Reacher took a look out the front window. The dust was closer. It was lit up from within by the setting sun. Four minutes, maybe. He moved on to the fireplace and picked up the poker. The yard of iron, with the hook at the end, like a hitchhiker's thumb.

Mackenzie called out, "The phone is still here and now it says two new messages."

Reacher paused a beat.

Then he called back, "Listen to the second one."

He heard a static whisper from the distant earpiece as the first message was skipped, and then more as the second was played. He figured there might be some kind of urgency behind the faint breathy cadence.

Mackenzie called out, "It's Arthur Scorpio leaving another voice-mail for Billy. They got a warning about a federal agent leaving Montana for parts unknown. And Scorpio wants Billy to call him back. He sounds mad. He said, don't make me worried, Billy. Not in a nice way."

Bramall said, "Got to be either ATF or DEA in Montana. They both have western task forces."

Reacher said, "I don't care."

They waited.

From the shadows deep in the room Reacher saw a truck nose through the trees and come out at the top of the driveway. Not a pick-up truck. It was a Chevy Suburban SUV, the large size. Black in color, but caked red from the road. A basic specification. Cheap wheels, not much chrome. An aftermarket antenna, mounted in the center of the roof.

It crunched over the dirt and came to a stop not far from Bramall's Toyota. A guy got out. He was broad but not tall, maybe fifty-something, with a lot of hard miles on his clock. He was dressed in gray flannel pants and a tweed sport coat. He moved with a certain amount of grace. Maybe once an athlete. Given his shape, probably field not track. Maybe he had put the shot, or thrown the discus.

Now he worked for the government.

The pants and the coat and the truck made that clear.

"Relax, guys," Reacher called. "Step down to Defcon Two."

Mackenzie called back, "What does that mean?"

"We'll try talking to this guy. Before we do anything else."

"Is it Billy?"

"I'm pretty sure not," Reacher said.

Out on the dirt the guy tweaked the tails of his coat and squared up his shoulders and headed for the porch. On the way he took out an ID wallet and held it ready. Reacher saw straps under his coat, for a shoulder holster.

They heard footsteps on the porch boards, and then a knock at the door.

Chapter 23

Bramall opened up. Reacher and Mackenzie stood be-hind him. The guy from the government car held up a federal ID. A worn gold badge, with a shield and an eagle, and a plastic card like a driver's license, except it said *United States Department of Justice, Drug Enforcement Administration.* The photograph was the right guy, a little younger, with his hair brushed better and his tie knotted tighter. The writing said his name was Kirk Noble, and his rank was Special Agent.

Reacher couldn't help it.

He said, "Sounds like a comic book. Kirk Noble, Boy Detective."

No response.

"I guess you never heard that before."

Noble said, "Who are you?"

They all introduced themselves, names only.

Noble said, "What are you doing here?"

Reacher said, "We're waiting for a guy named Billy. He lives here. We want to ask him a question."

"What question?"

"We're looking for a missing woman. We think he knows where she is."

"What woman?"

Reacher had no real sense that Noble could help. But he knew for sure he could hinder. If he wanted to. He worked for the government. He had a shield with an eagle. He had a thick book of rules.

So Reacher told the story fair and square. Maybe somewhat aware of his federal audience. Maybe nudging a little ways toward a certain kind of circular argument, in which the participants' professional backgrounds not only justified but actually required their involvement, while simultaneously absolving them of any kind of blame. Because of their status. As in, a retired military major, with a Silver Star and a Purple Heart, joined a near-forty-year veteran of the FBI, now a properly licensed private investigator in a populous state, to search for another retired military major, this one with a Bronze Star and a Purple Heart all her own. Feds couldn't argue with stuff like that. Not without saying yeah, all our lives are bullshit.

And even if they did, there was the *twin sister*, right there, a connection so spectrally close it legitimized everything, in a blinding flash, like bleach thrown on a crime scene. Especially with the face and the hair. Noble was a guy. Deep down he wasn't thinking legal technicalities. He was thinking: *There are two like that?*

Reacher kept it as subtle as he could.

Eventually he finished up.

Noble said, "You won't get an answer to your question."

"Why not?"

"Because Billy ain't coming back."

"Why not?"

"Long story."

The guy moved in through the hallway and glanced up the stairs. He looked at the ceiling. He looked at the walls. He turned this way and that, craning his neck, like a contractor about to ballpark an estimate.

He said, "Did you check the refrigerator?"

Reacher said, "For what?"

"Food."

"No."

Noble moved to the kitchen. He looked at the dishes in the sink. He opened the refrigerator. He glanced back, as if counting heads.

He said, "We could share bacon and eggs. There's beer to drink."

Mackenzie said, "You're going to eat Billy's food?"

"First of all, it ain't Billy's anymore, and second of all, I have to. I can't claim expenses if there's food in the house."

"Expenses from who?"

"You, in the end," Noble said. "The taxpayer. We're saving you money."

"We make you eat dinner from the suspect's refrigerator?"

"It's your refrigerator. And mine. This place became federal property at two o'clock this afternoon. Seized by the government."

"So where's Billy?"

"That's the long part of the story," Noble said. "We should eat."

At his age, after the things he'd done, Reacher would have said there wasn't much coming, in terms of new and delightful experiences in his life. But strangely the bacon-and-egg dinner in Billy's kitchen was one of them. They felt like conspirators. Or castaways. Like a random group, stranded overnight at the airport. They didn't really know each other. Maybe the first-class cabin, taken by taxi to a country hotel. Mackenzie found candles and lit them. Which then made it feel like the start of a movie. The opening scenes. An innocent group gathers. Little do they know.

Noble cooked, and talked about heroin. It was both his paycheck and his passion. He knew its history. Once upon a time it was a legal ingredient. It was in all kinds of stuff, branded with famous names still known today. There was heroin cough syrup. There was heroin cough syrup for children. Stronger, not weaker. Doctors prescribed heroin for fussy babies and bronchitis and insomnia and nerves and hysteria and all kinds of other vapors. The patients loved it. Best health care ever. Millions got addicted. Corporations made a lot of easy money. Then folks got wise, and by the start of World War One, legal heroin was history.

But the corporations never forgot. About the easy money. At that point in the story Noble was melting butter in the egg pan, and he paused the spoon mid-air, as if to emphasize his point. He said remember, this is an active-duty DEA agent saying this stuff. We know who causes our problems.

The corporations took eighty years to get back in the heroin business. They came in the side door. By that time in history heroin itself had negative PR. Nothing more than underworld squalor and a bunch of dead rock singers. Kind of sordid. So they made a synthetic version. A chemical copy. Like an identical twin, Noble said, looking at Mackenzie. Exactly the same, but now it had a long clean name. All bright and shiny. It could have been a toothpaste. They put it in neat white pills. What were they for? Getting high, baby. Whatever you want. Except they couldn't put that on the pack. So they said they were for pain. Everyone has pain, right?

Not really. Not at first. Pain was not yet a thing. Institutes had to be funded, and scholarships endowed. Doctors had to be persuaded. Patients had to be empowered. Which all worked in the end. Pain became a thing. Self-reported and untestable, but suddenly a symptom as valid and meaningful as any other. As a result, America was flooded with hundreds of tons of heroin, in purse-size blister packs, backed with foil.

By that point of the story they were eating, and Noble was in full flow. Like he was teaching a class at the academy. He paused again, with his fork mid-air, and he said, "Let me emphasize two very important things. First up, most of this stuff goes to the right people for the right reasons. No one could deny that. It does a lot of good. But equally, no one could deny enough has fallen out around the edges to also cause a lot of harm. Because second up, no one should ever underestimate the appeal of an opiate high. Far as I can tell, it's a beautiful thing. The way they talk about it, it's the best thing ever. For some folks it hits the spot so hard it reboots their lives."

He paused to drink some of Billy's beer.

He said, "These are regular folk I'm talking about. American as apple pie. They like the ball game on the radio, and country music. Not the Grateful Dead. They were seduced by the clean white pill. It made them feel real good. Maybe for the first time in their lives. These are plain people. But smart. They soon figured out ways it could make them feel even better. They got the time-release version, and broke it up, so they got the whole hit at once. Couple times a day. Maybe three. Then they discovered the patches. You stick them on your skin. Like when you're quitting smoking. A long clean name on the pack, but it's the same stuff your great-great-grandma lined up for. A nice little maintenance dose, all day long. You could wear two, if you like. Or three. But licking them was better. Or sucking them, or wadding them up and chewing them like gum. So much better, in fact, it got easy to want more than the doctor gave you. It got to where you're prepared to drop ten bucks here and there, now and then, for a couple extras. Then a hundred bucks for a whole pack, if need be. Every day, if need be. There are ways to get a hundred bucks every day, right? By that point these folks are already hopeless addicts. But not in their own minds. It's partly a pride thing. Addicts are other people, with a dirty needle in a toilet stall. What they have is a pharmaceutical product, made in a lab, by pretty girls in masks who hold test tubes up to the light, with wondrous concern radiating from their clear blue eyes. They've seen it on the television, in the breaks between innings. But in fact they're running worse risks. Those patches ain't made for licking. Fifty thousand people died last year. Regular folk. Four times as many as got killed in gun crimes."

He paused again, to eat an egg.

He said, "But we're winning. I would say we've already won, in my region, at least. We can track prescription pain medication from start to finish. We can take out the bent doctors, and we can train the rest to be cautious about how many days they dispense, and we can eliminate pilferage in the factories and along the transportation vectors. So right now the black market is virtually dead, and the medical market is heavily scrutinized. Total success. Except the previous bonanza left us with millions of addicts. Regular folk, remember. They thought a dirty needle in a toilet stall was not their fate. But it's a free market. When we bit down, the price of pills went up, because of supply and demand. What used to be ten bucks was suddenly fifty. It was a crisis. Suddenly regular cartel powder up from Mexico looked like an irresistible bargain. Remember, deep down it's the same chemical. These folks are canny shoppers. None of them ever paid sticker for a car. And numbers don't lie. Even when they factored in the cost to their dignity, with the dirty needles and the toilet stalls and all, hey, the powder was still a bargain. We swapped one problem for another."

He paused again, to put his silverware together, and push his plate away. He took a long drink from his bottle.

He said, "But overall it was good news for us. We like the new problem better. The regular cartel powder is harder to hide. We can follow it better. From our point of view it was like the system had just swallowed a barium meal. Whole networks lit up like neon. Standards got less precise. Our job got easier. But not everywhere. A certain part of Montana, for instance. Nothing lit up at all. We couldn't see incoming product. No cartel powder going there. So what happened to their addicts? Did they all cold turkey? Or die? Or is someone else supplying? That's something I would want to know. So I went out to check. I discovered nothing of value. Except one trivial thing. Anecdotally along the way, I discovered I had spooked a low-level operative, who triggered a long-standing pact with a friend, who was also a low-level operative, but in another network. The pact was both of them would immediately get the hell out the very first time either one of them heard a whisper of trouble. Which was the smart play, no question. I'm guessing this wasn't their first rodeo. These things always fall apart in the end, and they always fall hardest on the lowest-level guys. Better to get out early. Which is why Billy ain't coming home. Billy was the friend. From Mule Crossing, Wyoming. He's in the wind, with his pal from Billings, Montana."

Mackenzie said, "Where have they gone, do you think?"

"A new hustle," Noble said. "Someplace else."

"Are you looking for them?"

"We're not about to call out the National Guard. We'll put their names and their faces in the system."

Reacher said, "Surely the pact implies they worked for the same network, not different. One whisper made two guys run. Maybe what looked like two different networks were really two parts of the same thing."

"Maybe," Noble said. "I don't know much about them. It's an opaque network, remember. That's why I went. Odds are the guy in Montana was just a street-corner dealer. Or the rural equivalent. Odds are Billy was, too. Business schools call it customer-facing. And some of those guys have been to business school. Not guys like Billy and his pal. People who own guys like Billy and his pal."

"So what next for you?"

"I'm going to find clean sheets and make up a bed. I can't claim lodging expenses if there's a bed in the house."

"Then what?"

"Back to some real work. This all was a waste of time."

"The government got a house."

"Two houses," Noble said. "Don't forget Billings, Montana. I bet we won't be able to sell either one of them."

Mackenzie said, "Is there any way you could let us know if you find Billy?"

Noble shook his head.

He said, "I can't help with your sister. I'm sorry, ma'am. But what have you got? A lot of guesswork and hope for the best. A federal manhunt costs a million dollars a day. They need a very good reason. Which you can't give them. You got a lot of probable and not much cause."

Mackenzie didn't answer.

Noble said, "But I wish you the best of luck."

Chapter 24

They left Noble in the house, and drove back to Laramie, with Reacher sprawled across the rear seat, and Mackenzie upright in the front, and Bramall at the wheel, one-handed. They agreed on the chain hotel Reacher and Bramall had used the night before. It had proved adequate, except for no coffee. Reacher said the diner he had found was a good substitute. Bramall agreed. He had found it, too. He said breakfast there was excellent.

"But then what?" Mackenzie said. "What do we do after breakfast? What's our next move? We have nothing now."

"Thanks to the DEA," Bramall said. "Trust them to start a stampede."

"We have more than some folks," Reacher said. "I agree, losing Billy is an inconvenience. But it's worse for others. Like that lady up near the old homestead. Even all the way out there. She needed something bad today. She was getting scratchy. She was waiting for Billy. But he isn't coming. So what next for her? Tomorrow she'll be desperate. She'll come looking, surely. She'll come to town. They all will. If Rose is an addict, she'll come to us."

* * *

They met in the lobby at eight in the morning. Bramall was in a fresh shirt and Mackenzie was in a fresh blouse. Reacher's clothes were a day old, but he felt OK in their company. He had used a whole bar of soap in the shower. They walked up to the diner and got a table. Mackenzie was OK with it.

She said, "Maybe six weeks ago the price of pills had gone especially high, and that's why she had to sell her ring. To afford them."

"Maybe," Reacher said.

"I want it to be pills," she said. "Not needles in a toilet stall."

"Of course."

"I'm sure Special Agent Noble was speaking broadly when he said there are no pills on the black market anymore. There must be some."

Reacher said nothing.

Mackenzie said, "Before this is over, I'll want to know why it happened."

"Probably our fault," Reacher said. "Depends on the wound she got. Could have been a scratch, but if it was something serious on the battlefield, with the medics under fire and so on, then she'll have gotten a morphine jab ahead of a rough evacuation. Then maybe another morphine jab ahead of triage, and another while she was waiting for surgery. And then she got two weeks in a recovery room with a big tub of opioid pain medication by the bed. She was probably an addict before she left the hospital."

"Depending on the wound. Maybe it's still painful. Maybe that's why she needs the pills. Or the powder, now. With the needles in the toilet stall. If Agent Noble is right."

"Did your sister wear silver clothes?"

"Why?"

"Porterfield's neighbor might have seen her in his car. She remembers a silvery color."

"Was it winter?"

"A month before the start of spring."

"You can get winter coats in silver. Almost like foil. Like a high-tech material."

"Would she wear that color?"

"I might," Mackenzie said.

Reacher thought about it. The hair, the eyes, the face, with a silver foil coat. She would look like the picture on the back of a shiny magazine.

An exact replica.

They drove to the university geography department and took another look at the giant book of maps. They traced the settlements westward, from the Mule Crossing turn. First came Billy's place, south of the dirt road, and then Porterfield's, north of it, and then his neighbor's, south again. They had seen all of those. Beyond them lay twelve more places. Six each side of the road, altogether stretching forty long miles into the mountains. Then the dirt road ended. No way out, except to turn around. Not really a bowl, not really a valley. Just a chain of rising foothills, with a road that quit when the mountains came.

Mackenzie said, "You think she's in there somewhere."

Reacher said, "She was either living with Porterfield, or she was visiting with him on a regular basis, yet no one ever saw her, except maybe one occasion. If she lived anywhere else, she would have to drive in and out through Mule Crossing every single time. More people would have seen her, surely. Maybe even the old guy in the post office. But no one ever did. She must have been driving there and back the other way. Deeper into the hills. A buck gets ten she's there right now. Where else would she go?"

"She doesn't own a car," Bramall said. "Not according to the Wyoming DMV. Or any other state."

"She camps out in abandoned ranch houses. Either she finds cars or steals them. She doesn't care whose name is on the title. All a car has to do is start up when she needs it."

"I want to go there," Mackenzie said. "Back to Mule Crossing. It's like the neck of a funnel. If she's in there, she's got to come out sooner or later. I want to be there when she does."

"If I'm right," Reacher said.

"If you're wrong, we'll find her in town tonight. Or tomorrow."

They pulled over and sat in the car, near the old post office, in a spot where they would get a good head-on view of anything coming down the dirt road. Just before the turn, where everyone would slow right down, and look first one way, and then the other, carefully, before making the left or the right on the pavement. Close enough for faces. At first it was awkward. Reacher figured they were all having the same trouble, picturing exactly what it was they expected to see. They knew the theory. The lack of Billy would draw the addicts out. But what would that look like? Reacher had seen his share of movie trailers. The walking dead. All kinds of zombies. He realized he was expecting some kind of apocalyptic vision.

The first candidate approached out of the west in an ancient pick-up truck that was lurching and bouncing and trailing a dust cloud a mile long. Not Rose Sanderson. The driver turned out to be a thin-faced man, with a turned-down mouth, as disapproving as an old-time preacher. Maybe an addict, maybe not. He looked left and right and turned toward Colorado.

The dust cloud settled.

They waited.

From the back seat, Reacher asked Mackenzie, "Where were you, when Rose was at West Point?"

She turned around.

"University of Chicago," she said. "Then Princeton, for postgrad."

"Studying what?"

"English literature. Different, I know."

"Not so different. Some of them can read at West Point now. If you take it slow and point to the letters."

She smiled.

"I didn't mean it like that," she said. "I know Rose is as smart as I am. Obviously. It's a scientific fact. I meant she was prepared to kill people, and I wasn't."

"That was the big dispute?"

"It was never a big dispute. We never fell out. But things happened so fast back then. All of a sudden Rose was in the army. And that was a serious thing. Our resources were stretched thin. She was hardly ever home for nine years. I was never told where she was. I couldn't go visit. Most of the time I couldn't even call. Meanwhile I was working. I got married. That's how it was. We had real lives. Like everyone else with a sibling."

"Except she was prepared to kill people, and you weren't."

"I don't mean she wanted to, or planned to. It was an ethical discussion. That's all. We were eighteen. I wasn't saying it had to be all or nothing. In fact it never is. No one says always or never. Everyone says sometimes. But her sometimes were not the same as mine. She would pull the trigger before I would. Which was OK. Maybe I was wrong. Maybe I was naïve. It wasn't the difference of opinion that bothered me. We always had different opinions. It was that she had thought about it, seriously, carefully, and decided yes, she could do it. For real. Which changed her a little. She changed herself, by deciding it. For the first time ever I felt not the same as her."

Reacher said nothing.

She turned back.

They waited.

The second candidate for the apocalypse was the woman who had given the strawberry pie to Sy Porterfield. His neighbor. Second place on the left. She was in a battered Jeep SUV. She looked left and right and turned toward Laramie. Maybe heading to the market. Maybe planning to spend time in the fruit aisle.

The third vehicle they saw came from behind them. It turned in off the two-lane, and passed them by, and set out down the dirt road west.

It was a pick-up truck.

On the front it had snowplow pistons, bolted to the frame.

Chapter 25

Bramall looked a question, and Mackenzie and Reacher both nodded, so he started the engine and bumped up on the dirt road. A unanimous decision. The obvious play. It cost them nothing to follow the pick-up at least as far as Billy's place. Their eyes would be on the neck of the funnel throughout. Any random driving dead would pass right by, close enough to touch. Certainly close enough to eyeball in great detail. Then in the end if the pick-up kept on going, they could coast to a stop and turn around, and call the snowplow pistons a weird coincidence.

"What if it turns in?" Mackenzie said.

"Maybe it's a competitor just heard the news," Reacher said. "Maybe he wants Billy's Rolodex. Maybe snowplowing is a very competitive business."

"Suppose it's Billy himself."

"I'm sure the Boy Detective changed the locks. Or glued them up, or whatever they do now. Either one of which will make our boy good and mad. He'll get all cross and frustrated. He'll go get his deer rifle from his truck, to shoot the locks. He'll be standing right there on the porch with it when we show up. Finger on the trigger."

"Only if we turn in, too."

"He hasn't heard the phone message. He'll think we're Mormons. Or whichever it is let women join in now."

By that point they had caught up to about a hundred yards behind the pick-up. Which would be considered a very close pursuit, in such a vast landscape, but they were invisible, because of the dust cloud. The pick-up's mirrors couldn't see them.

They rolled on, in secret convoy. The pronghorn herd was grazing a new patch of pasture. Two miles gone. Less than a minute remaining, at their current speed.

The pick-up slowed. They saw it loom large and ghostlike in the cloud ahead. Bramall backed off. The pick-up braked, lights flaring, all the way down to walking speed, and then it turned a wide slow left into the mouth of Billy's driveway.

"Go for it," Reacher said. "Go after him."

Bramall looked at Mackenzie.

She hesitated.

Reacher said, "He hasn't heard the phone message. He doesn't know who we are. We're just three random people."

Mackenzie said, "He knows where Rose is."

Bramall turned in. No dust on the driveway. It was a forest track, all rock and grit and gravel. Now the Toyota was plainly visible. They hung back. They saw the pick-up through the trees. Two hundred yards ahead of them, flashing through the sun and the shadows.

"Stupid to run and come right back," Reacher said.

"Maybe he wants his money," Mackenzie said.

They rolled on, keeping pace. The pick-up drove through the final curve and out of sight. Another fifty yards it would be out of the woods. Then the last hundred, over the beaten red dirt, to the house.

"Let me out here," Reacher said. "I'll walk the rest of the way, in the trees. I can cut the corner. I can get there faster."

"Is that smart?" Bramall said.

"It's smarter than sticking together. A good squad never bunches up. Too big of a target."

Bramall stopped the car and Reacher slid out. Bramall drove on. Reacher watched him go, and then he threaded his way into the woods, and set out on what he hoped was a straight line to the last tree before the house. He got close just in time to see the pick-up drive across the last of the dirt, and park near the house.

He waited.

A hundred yards away in the mouth of the driveway he saw Bramall roll to a stop. His Toyota was well hidden. No glint of paint, no gleam of chrome. All completely covered with thick red dust. Better than desert camouflage.

He waited.

The pick-up's engine turned off.

The driver's door opened.

A guy got out. He was young. Early twenties, maybe. Six feet tall. Couple hundred pounds. Maybe more. Most of it fat. He was a big shapeless guy. He looked slow and clumsy.

Not Billy.

Billy wore a thirty-two waist, and a thirty leg, and an eight and a half shoe.

The big guy took a ring of keys from his pocket, and stared at it like he had never seen one before. He carried it up on the porch, and walked to the door. He chose a key and bent down to the hole.

He looked puzzled.

He touched the keyhole with his fingertip.

Then he straightened up and spun around, as if he was suddenly certain someone was behind him. With a camera, maybe. For kids to watch on their phones. And laugh.

Reacher stepped out of the trees.

He walked across the dirt, and waved a come-on to Bramall. The guy by the door watched him all the way. Not reacting. Still looking puzzled. Reacher stepped up on the porch. Up close the guy looked harmless. His shape made his clothes tight and smooth. There were no unexplained lumps or bumps in his pockets. He was unarmed. He was very young. He was no kind of a physical threat.

Maybe not the smartest kid, either.

Not a whole lot going on behind his eyes.

Reacher said, "Who are you?"

The kid said, "I came by to get something."

Which was technically non-responsive, but Reacher let it go. Bramall and Mackenzie stepped up on the porch. The kid looked at them. Still puzzled. Reacher looked at the keyhole. There was a bead of glue in it. The Boy Detective had changed one lock, maybe at the back, and glued all the others. Efficiency. Saving taxpayer money.

The kid said, "Who are you?"

Reacher said, "I asked first."

"I'm doing nothing wrong."

"Just tell me your first name."

"It's Mason."

"OK, Mason, it's good to meet you. Why are you here?"

"I came by to get something."

"For who?"

"For me. Billy said I could have it."

"Who is Billy?"

The kid said, "He's my brother."

"Is he?"

"Well, half."

"Where is he now?"

"I don't know. He ran off again."

"Has he done that before?"

"Two times that I can remember. This time he called me and told me where he left his truck. He said I could have it. And something in his house, too."

"Where was the truck?"

"Up near Casper."

Reacher nodded. Nearer Mule Crossing than Billings, Montana. The other guy had driven more miles than Billy. Why? Must have been their agreed-upon vector. They were planning to head southeast. Through Nebraska, and away.

He said, "What kind of something did he leave in the house?"

"I'm not sure I should tell you."

"Was it money in a box?"

The kid looked surprised.

"Yes," he said. "In a shoebox."

"Did he want you to bring it to him?"

"No, sir, it's for me. He said he's already with a guy who has plenty."

"Where?"

"He didn't tell me. He wouldn't. No way. He used to say to me, Mason, if you ever have to run, you tell no one where you're going, not even me."

"You completely sure he didn't tell you?"

"Yes, sir."

"What does Billy do for a living?"

"He works the snowplow."

"What about the summer?"

"I think he buys and sells things."

"What kind of things does he sell?"

"Just things. Like flea-market things."

"Where does he sell them?"

"I think all around. Wherever people are who want to buy them."

"Do you know any of his customers?"

"No."

"Have you ever seen a woman who looks like my friend here?"

"No."

"Do you know what an accessory is?"

"Something you put on your truck."

"Also a legal word," Reacher said. "It means if you know a secret, and you don't tell, then you go to jail, too. Billy has strayed far from the narrow path of righteousness, I'm afraid. He has made some poor choices in his life. The government seized this house yesterday. A federal agent put glue in the lock. That's what they do now. So this is our last chance to help you, Mason. If you know where Billy is, you better tell us, right now."

"I don't know where Billy is," the brother said, kind of happily. "But don't worry. He'll be back in a year or two. That's what happened the last two times."

Reacher looked at Bramall, who shrugged. Then at Mackenzie, who nodded. She believed the kid.

Who said, "How do I get in the house?"

"You don't," Reacher said. "No point. The money is long gone. It was in a federal evidence locker before you woke up this morning. But you can keep the truck. Get a blade for the plow, and you could set up in business."

They watched the kid drive away. Mackenzie stayed on the porch and looked at the view. The wide empty plains on the right. The old post office, and the firework store. The pronghorns, about a mile away. The red road, still neatly scraped, still nicely cambered. On the left, the low jagged peaks, like miniature mountain ranges.

She said, "Logically we should keep on going. She's not here. She's not at Porterfield's place, which is next. She's not at the pie lady's place, which comes after that. So logically we could just keep on going, and then stop before the fourth place. We'd be closer. Nothing could happen behind us. It would still all be ahead of us."

"If Reacher is right," Bramall said. "Which he might not be."

"Then why has no one seen her?"

Bramall didn't answer.

Reacher said, "I guess the gift of the truck was a cowboy kind of thing. Billy was making sure someone looked after his best horse, so to speak, come what may. All that kind of good stuff. But ten grand in a box is different. That's a lot of money to give away. I don't think he wanted to. I think he was out on the road when he got the call from Montana. Too far from home to come back and get it. The pact meant he had no time. He had to go to Casper immediately. And given the direction the other guy was driving from Billings, we have to assume they carried on east through Nebraska. And if we time it from Scorpio's first voicemail, this all was at least forty-eight hours ago. They're in Chicago by now. Except I don't think they went to Chicago. I don't think they would have felt at home there. My guess is they turned south for Oklahoma. They could make some kind of living there. Or the same kind of living."

"Possible," Bramall said.

Mackenzie said, "But Special Agent Noble will never be able to figure that out, because he'll never know where the truck was found, because of our decision to give it to the brother."

Bramall said, "Our?"

"Nothing to be ashamed of. I'm sure it was done with the best of intentions. Job creation is a wonderful thing. But I want Special Agent Noble to have a shot at finding Billy. Because I think he would tell us if he does. Why wouldn't he? I think we should call him. I think we should tell him about Oklahoma."

"It was only a guess," Bramall said.

"Based on a fact," she said. "Which Noble hasn't got."

"He might guess different."

"At least he'll get a chance to."

"You really want me to call him?"

"I think we should."

Bramall looked at Reacher.

Reacher said, "He cooked, after all. Normally we would send a note of some kind."

Bramall took out his tortoiseshell reading glasses, and a small notebook. He opened it with his thumb.

Reacher said, "You have Noble's number in there?"

Bramall said, "Just the western division's switchboard."

He dialed and played phone tag for a long minute, saying the name over and over again, with variations, Special Agent Kirk Noble, Special Agent Noble, Kirk Noble. Eventually the guy himself must have come on the line, because Bramall reminded him who he was, in terms of the bacon-and-egg dinner, and then he said now there was very strong reason to believe the fugitives had gone to Oklahoma.

Evidently Noble asked to speak to Reacher.

Bramall passed the phone.

Noble said, "There's a problem with Porterfield."

Chapter 26

Noble said, "I typed it up, word for word based on what you told me, and then I ran it through some software we have, which automatically checks against our existing databases, to see if we know the names already, for other reasons. And Seymour Porterfield came up blocked. I dug around and found three separate files on the guy, all locked, all needing high-level passwords."

Reacher said, "What kind of a guy would get a file like that?"

"A source of information," Noble said. "It's a security measure."

"Interesting."

"I need to know who Porterfield was."

"He had an expensive kitchen."

"I need you to tell me what you know."

"I don't know anything about Porterfield. He wore blue jeans a lot and had an eye for décor. But I don't really care. He's not why I'm here."

"One of the files was about Porterfield and a second person. Judging by the codes, the second person was a woman. I can't read the date on the file but the sequencing suggests it was first opened about two years ago and last looked at by someone not long before Porter-field died."

"Interesting," Reacher said again. "How deep in your system are these files?"

"Very deep. But I don't think they're DEA originals. I think we got copied in as a courtesy, by someone else."

"Who?"

"It's a weird code. Not the FBI or the ATF. It's like what we used to get when we had Special Forces deployed in Colombia. Not a remote source, you understand. Somewhere fairly near our main office."

"OK," Reacher said. "I understand. Don't forget to call Okla-homa."

He clicked off. Told the others.

Mackenzie said, "Does this help us?"

"I don't know," Reacher said. "Who Porterfield was two years ago doesn't necessarily tell us where Rose is now. We shouldn't invest too much time in it. I guess we could go pull off the road ahead of the fourth place, and I could make a call from there, while we were wait-ing."

They parked on the slope of the shoulder, at an angle, like a cop with a radar gun. Ahead of them were twelve more homesteads, all widely separated and out of sight, all along forty more miles of the dirt road. And then nothing. No one was coming. Reacher borrowed Bramall's phone and dialed the same ancient number from memory.

The same woman answered.

"West Point," she said. "Superintendent's office. How may I help you?"

"This is Reacher."

"Hello, major."

"I need to speak with the supe."

"You don't know his name, do you?"

"I guess not currently."

"It's General Simpson. He'll be happy you called. He has information for you. Wait one, major."

There were clicks and dead air, and then the supe's voice came on the line.

It said, "Major."

Reacher said, "General."

He didn't use the name Simpson. Just in case it wasn't. West Point culture was full of practical jokes, and although he very much doubted the woman who answered the phone would set him up, he couldn't be sure.

The supe said, "What progress are you making?"

"Some," Reacher said. "I think I'm close to the right location."

"Which is where?"

"Bottom right-hand corner of Wyoming."

"So she went home."

"Not exactly, but not far away. I found trace evidence in a house in a place called Mule Crossing. She was there about a year and a half ago. My sense is she's still in the general neighborhood."

The supe said, "There's something you need to know. It might be important. Out of curiosity I tried to take a look at Sanderson's service record and medical file. I couldn't get in. They're sealed tighter than a duck's butt on a choppy day. I think your people did it."

"My people?"

"Military police."

"When?"

"Hard to tell exactly. Not recently. But after she left the service, almost certainly. Two years ago, possibly."

"OK," Reacher said. "Now guess what I was calling about?"

"How could I?"

"The house where I found evidence was owned by a guy who also has a sealed file in a government database. Three sealed files, in fact. One of which was first opened around two years ago, and features the guy with a woman. Apparently they are not native files. The folks at the database think the agency in question was copied in as a courtesy, by another agency."

"Do they know which one?"

"They hinted at the Pentagon."

"I find that interesting," the supe said. "As you knew I would. But you didn't call just to entertain me. You want me to do something."

"Who do you know down there?"

"A couple of people."

"Do they owe you?"

"How big of a risk would they be taking?"

"Not much. This thing went cold a year and a half ago. It's ancient history now. And they don't have to give us chapter and verse. Just confirm or deny if Sanderson is the woman in the file with the guy who owned the house. His name was Seymour Porterfield. Social Security should show a county sheriff's notification of death around the start of spring last year."

"He's dead?"

"It's Wyoming. He was eaten by a bear."

Reacher spelled Porterfield's names, first and last.

The supe repeated them back.

"Thank you, general," Reacher said. "You can call me back on this number. My partner Mr. Bramall will answer."

"Thank you, major."

Reacher said, "Sir, is your name Simpson?"

"Correct," the supe said. "Sean Simpson."

"Yes, sir," Reacher said, purely out of habit.

He clicked off, and gave the phone back to Bramall, who plugged it in to charge.

They waited an hour on the shoulder, and saw no one coming, except a small herd of elk, who came out of the trees on one side of a gulch, and into the trees on the other. Overhead, black birds of prey hovered motionless, high in the sky.

The road stayed empty.

"I'm sorry," Mackenzie said. "I did it again. Every idea looks like a good idea. Until it turns out wrong."

"Neither of us had a better idea," Reacher said.

"Maybe it's a good thing if we don't see her. It would mean she doesn't need what Billy was selling. It would mean she's OK. Someone stole her ring. You said so yourself."

"Best case."

"Which sometimes happens."

"Sometimes," Reacher said.

"How often?"

"More than never. Less than always."

"Wait," Bramall said.

He pointed.

There was a dust cloud on the road ahead. In the west, way far in the distance, on the rising horizon. There was a tiny dot at its head, smoothed by the haze, but coming on fast.

They waited. The dot grew bigger and the cloud spun and howled behind it, furiously and endlessly generating itself anew, exactly the shape of a parachute, but infinitely long, hanging together with some kind of internal aerodynamic constraint, before finally going limp, and succumbing to wind and gravity, and drifting back to earth.

"Stand by," Bramall said.

He pulled his phone off the charger, ready to take a photograph.

They waited.

An SUV flashed by, moving fast, an ancient model, boxy and battered and square, covered with rust and red dust so thick it looked baked on. The window glass was just as bad, except the front windshield, which had two smeared arcs from the wipers, where the dust was thinner. Through them they got a fractured split-second glimpse inside.

Just a dull and hazy impression.

A small figure, flinching away.

A silvery color.

Chapter 27

Bramall swung off the shoulder and took off in pursuit
like the highway patrol. The truck up ahead was still moving fast. The
road ran straight for long stretches, then dipped through hollows, and
rose over knolls, and curved out of sight, but the dust cloud was always there, showing the way. The big Toyota growled along, pattering
hard over the rough surface, going plenty fast itself, but their quarry
wasn't slowing any. In fact it was speeding up. At times the cloud
between them grew half a mile long.

And then it was gone.

The Toyota came leaning out of a long fast curve, through the
last of the dust, into clear air, pure and bright and empty for miles
ahead.

No truck. Nothing there.

Behind them the severed cloud swayed in the wind, and pulled off
the road, and died in the scrub.

Bramall stopped.

"She turned off," Reacher said. "There's no dust on the ranch
roads. What's back there?"

Bramall made a U-turn, shoulder to shoulder, and went back to see.

"Driveway on the left," Mackenzie said. "I think. It's hard to be sure."

"The pie lady," Reacher said. "Porterfield's neighbor. We were here yesterday. We almost missed it then."

"But the pie lady is out. We saw her go."

Bramall turned in on the track and drove, the same way as the day before, but faster, twisting and rising through the trees, more than three miles, during which distance they saw nothing and no one, and then as before all of a sudden the trees opened up and the Toyota burst out on the flat acre with the long view east, and the one-story house, with its brown boards, and its ancient millwork, and its old church pew.

Nothing there.

No battered old SUV, caked with dust.

Nothing moving.

No sound.

Mackenzie said, "There must be other ways out of here. Like the places I showed you yesterday."

Bramall drove on, in a wide bumpy circle, all the way around the house, around the outbuildings, always tight to the tree line. They saw three separate forest tracks running onward through the trees. One went due west, one went south, and one split the difference between. They were like trails for hikers or hunters, all worn and beaten down, all gnarled with roots and rocks, all dappled with gentle sunlight, all curving out of sight.

All narrow.

But good enough for a boxy old SUV.

It was impossible to say which one had just been used. The ground was bone dry. There were tire tracks everywhere, sharp in the dust.

"Want to gamble?" Bramall said.

"Waste of time," Reacher said. "These trails have too many turns. The odds would get impossible. Plus your truck is bigger than hers. We'd get stuck."

"If it was her," Bramall said.

"Suppose it was."

"Doesn't matter which way she went," Mackenzie said. "The question is why she went. What happened?"

"We scared her," Reacher said. "We were waiting on the shoulder. We could have been state police. She didn't want us to catch her. So she pulled off the road and tracked back on some weird forest service route only she knows. Now she's laying low someplace, trying to figure out what she wants to do next."

"Where?"

"Within about a thousand square miles of right here. In a spot we'll never find."

Mackenzie was quiet a beat.

Then she said, "Did you see the silver?"

Bramall said, "An impression."

"What did you make of it?"

"A coat," Bramall said. "With a hood."

"But tight," Reacher said. "I thought like athletic wear. The kind of thing they peel off before the race."

"Did it look like foil?"

"Partly," Bramall said. "Maybe the trim."

Mackenzie said, "Why didn't she want us to catch her?"

"She didn't know it was you," Reacher said. "She didn't see your face. Her windows were dusty, and so were ours, and when she came by head-on, she was looking the other way. It wasn't an emotional decision. It was practical. She thought we were cops. Maybe she's the kind of person who can't let a cop see the inside of her car."

"If it was her," Bramall said.

"Because she's an addict," Mackenzie said.

"Worst case," Reacher said.

"Which happens."

"More than never, less than always."

"Which way are you leaning?"

"Hope for the best, plan for the worst."

"Seriously."

"I'm thinking about Seymour Porterfield," Reacher said. "We're assuming Billy took over his business, whereupon that kind of thing usually triggers some kind of vigorous expansion afterward, which seems to be the whole reason businesses get taken over in the first place, all because someone else sees missed opportunities. And this is not a type of business that ever gets smaller anyway. It only gets bigger. Therefore, long story short, on a theoretical basis, for a number of reasons, we could expect law enforcement to see Billy as a bigger proposition now than Porterfield ever was. But the Boy Detective as good as told us he isn't even interested in a person like Billy. He said he was going to put his face in the system. That's code for letting him walk away. Because he's too boring to talk to. Whereas on the other hand, the even less interesting Seymour Porterfield has his own sealed file at the Pentagon."

Bramall said, "Could be nothing. He might once have had small-time connections in Central America. The military wrote everything down. His file might be one word long. You know what that stuff was like. You were probably there."

"Why would a one-word file be sealed?"

Bramall said, "I don't know."

"What do we actually know for sure about Porterfield?"

"Very little."

"What impression did you get?"

"Like the neighbor said. A rich guy from out of state, come to find himself, maybe writing a novel."

"Nice life."

"You bet."

"You liked his house."

"I could live there."

"He had everything a person could need," Reacher said. "Including granite countertops and his very own file at the Pentagon. In fact he had three files at the Pentagon. One of which seems to cover some kind of a joint enterprise with an unspecified woman, during the last six months of his life. On top of which is the broken window in his house. Which looked like government work. Which is ridiculous. Until it isn't. Plus the guy got eaten by a bear. Or a mountain lion. Either of which is highly unlikely. And all of which lead to wild speculations about what exactly happened during those last six months. Especially toward the end. Maybe Rose ran just now because a year and a half ago she learned not to trust expensive black vehicles full of people. So to answer Mrs. Mackenzie's original question, I guess right now I'm leaning slightly away from the worst case. Worst cases are usually very banal. This thing feels more complex than that."

Mackenzie said, "You think Porterfield wasn't the man you thought he was?"

"He could have been ten times worse. Now I don't know for sure. Which is the interesting part. It makes it equally possible he was ten times better."

Bramall said, "If he was, how would Arthur Scorpio know his name?"

"Through Billy, maybe. Billy was Porterfield's neighbor, just as much as the pie lady. They all talk. Maybe Scorpio liked to hear neighborhood gossip."

"He had ten grand in a shoebox."

"Maybe to live on while he wrote his novel."

Bramall didn't answer. His phone rang. He answered, and listened, and gave the phone to Reacher.

"It's General Simpson," he said. "For you."

Reacher put the phone to his ear.

The supe said, "Porterfield was a U.S. Marine."

Chapter 28

The supe said, "Anything below the surface is locked down tight, but we know from Social Security and other unclassified sources that the Seymour Porterfield who died in Wyoming last year was an Ivy League postgrad who joined the Marine Corps the day after 9/11. He was the perfect recruit. A real poster boy. He went to Iraq in the first wave as a lieutenant in a rifle company. He didn't last more than a month. He was an early casualty. The injury is unspecified. He was honorably discharged, and he returned to civilian life. Back then the Marines could still afford mental-health counseling during that type of separation. There's a note that says Porterfield seemed happy to resume academic pursuits, and had realistic expectations of a future inheritance, both cash and real estate, such that no one had to worry very much, least of all the Marine Corps. Then he dropped off the government radar for a very long time."

"Until?" Reacher said.

"Two years ago. Some office deep in the Pentagon got a brand new case. Something to do with Porterfield. We don't know what. We think they dug up his original service file for background, and then sealed it. Which usually means something. Meanwhile they were also opening a second new file, about Porterfield and a woman. That's what we can see so far. Three files, like you said."

"Was Sanderson the woman?"

"We don't know yet. That's below the surface."

"Are you still looking?"

"Discreetly," the supe said. "I'll be in touch."

The phone went dead. Reacher passed it back to Bramall, who plugged it in to charge.

Mackenzie said, "Does this help us?"

Reacher said, "It might not be her."

"Suppose it is."

"It gives us a wounded Marine officer and a wounded army officer in the same place for six months. Such a thing could go either way. They could have been the worst addicts in the history of the world. Or they could have been doing better, with each other's moral support. Or maybe they were never users at all. They were very impressive people, after all. Porterfield quit school and rushed to sign up. Rose was top ten at West Point and did five tours. Maybe they got together for peace and quiet with someone who understood."

"Then where is she now?"

"That's the problem. That question is also an answer."

"Sadly," she said. "It forces us to conclude that these days she's more likely to be an addict than very impressive. Or she'd still be calling me."

"Worst case."

"You were leaning away."

"Still am," Reacher said. "Still hoping for the best. May I ask you a personal question?"

"I suppose," she said.

"What kind of twins are you and Rose? Do you look exactly alike?"

She nodded. "We're identical twins. Literally. More so than most."

"Then we should stop by the hospital."

"Why?"

"By now people are hurting. I guess some of them might have

friends, who might be willing to share. I guess some of them will try to score in town. The rest will go to the emergency room. They'll claim a raging toothache. Or a crippling backache. Whatever can't be tested. But pain is a thing now, so the doctor has to take their word for it. He has to write a prescription for the good stuff. We should check if she's been there. You'll remind them of her. Like a human missing persons billboard."

"I feel like I'm betraying her. I'm accepting she's a junkie."

"It's a percentage game. We have to start somewhere."

She was quiet a long moment.

Then she said, "OK, let's go."

Bramall started the big V8 motor, and steered a wide circle toward the head of the driveway. They turned their backs on the flat acre with the long view east, and the brown board house, with the ancient millwork and the old church pew. They settled in for three rough miles, and then the dirt road again.

But coming the other way out of the driveway right at that moment was the woman who had baked the strawberry pie. The woman who lived there. Home from the market, in her Jeep SUV. Bramall stopped and backed up to let her by. But she stopped, too, side by side, and buzzed her window down.

Bramall buzzed his window down.

So did Reacher.

The woman recognized them, from the day before, and she nodded cautiously, and then she peered beyond them at Mackenzie. Who she didn't recognize. No sign at all. Nothing there. The exact replica. The human billboard.

A stranger.

The woman said, "Can I help you folks?"

Reacher said, "We came by to check a couple of things, connected to what we spoke about yesterday. We didn't know you were out."

"Yes you did. I passed you at the turn."

"Perhaps we didn't notice."

"You're private detectives. You're supposed to notice."

"We're looking for a missing woman," Reacher said. "Maybe we were preoccupied."

"What things do you want to check?"

"About when you saw Porterfield," Reacher said. "Was he disabled in any way?"

"I don't think so."

"Two arms and two legs?"

"Sure."

"Was he limping at all?"

"I don't think so."

"Talking well and thinking straight?"

"He was very courteous and polite."

"OK," Reacher said. "Now about that one time on the dirt road, and what you saw in Porterfield's car. Can you tell us about that again?"

"There was nothing in the car. I was wrong."

"Suppose you were right. What did you see?"

She paused a beat.

"It was real quick," she said. "Two cars passing, that's all. The wind was up, like a dust storm."

"Even so," Reacher said. "What did you see?"

She paused again.

"A girl turning away," she said. "And a silvery color."

"It stuck in your mind."

"It was weird."

"Had you ever seen such a thing before?"

"Never."

"Did you ever see such a thing again?"

"Never."

"Are you absolutely sure?" Reacher said. "How about in a different car? All alone. Maybe driving in from west of here."

"Never," the woman said again. "Are you making fun of me?"

"No, I promise. Now here's a different question. Do you let people use your driveway any old time they want to?"

"Apart from you?"

"Point taken," Reacher said. "But is it generally OK for folks to drive in and use your forest trails?"

"No it is not."

"You never allow that?"

"Why would I?"

"You ever see it happen nonetheless? By trespassers, maybe?"

"Never," she said for the fourth time. "What's going on?"

"The real reason we're here is we followed a truck. It was kind of escaping. It drove up your driveway and out again on one of your trails. We don't know which one."

The woman looked all around.

She said, "It escaped through here?"

"You ever had that kind of a thing happen before?"

"Never," the woman said again. "How could it happen? How would anyone know where my trails go anyway?"

West Point, Reacher thought. Back when reading maps was a life-saving skill.

He said, "Where do your trails go, in fact?"

"All over," she said. "You can get to Colorado if you want. Who were you chasing? They must have been panicking, to come through here."

"We think the driver was a woman."

"OK."

"She looked kind of small, and she was turning away. We didn't see her face."

The woman said nothing.

"There was a silvery color."

"Oh my god."

"The same as you saw before."

"Here?"

"We followed the truck right in."

"You're going to give me nightmares."

* * *

They left her there, and drove back down the driveway, to the dirt road, and the two-lane, and Laramie. The hospital was out by the university. Perhaps it was connected. The emergency room had seven patients waiting. Two of them could have been suffering from Billy's absence. They looked shaky and damp. A likely diagnosis. The other five could have been students. All seven looked up, like people do in waiting rooms. They checked out the new arrivals.

Including Mackenzie.

No hint of recognition.

Nor was there at the desk. Mackenzie asked after a patient named Rose Sanderson, and a helpful woman checked a screen, and smiled an encouraging smile, and said they had seen no one with that name, while all the time looking Mackenzie straight in the eye, in an open and frank and perfectly compassionate way.

Without a hint of recognition.

Mackenzie stepped away from the desk and said, "OK, either she's got friends willing to share, or she's in town right now, trying to score."

They drove to the corner of Third and Grand, and checked block by block for the combination they wanted, which was two bad bars and a decent place to eat, all within sight of each other. They needed a meal, but Mackenzie didn't want to burn surveillance time. She wanted to watch while she ate, at least two plausible places. So they found a café across the street from two cowboy bars, both with neon beer signs behind unwashed windows. They figured there might be business transacted in such places. Cowboys liked pain pills, the same as anyone else. Maybe more so. Because of rodeo accidents, and roping injuries, and other random falls off horses.

The café was a new-age place, with all kinds of healing juices, and sandwiches Reacher figured had been put together by a blind man.

All kinds of random ingredients. Huge seeds in the bread. Like sawdust mixed with ball bearings.

Bramall went to wash up, leaving Mackenzie and Reacher alone at the table. She took off her jacket, and turned left and right to hang it on the frame of her chair. She looked back at him. Pale flawless skin, perfect bones, delicate features. Green eyes, full of sorrow.

She said, "I apologize."

He said, "For what?"

"When we first met. I said you were a weird obsessive, two soldiers short of a squad."

"I think it was me who said that."

"Only because you knew I was thinking it."

"You had a good reason."

"Maybe," she said. "But now I'm glad you're here."

"I'm glad to hear it."

"I should pay you what I pay Mr. Bramall. The same daily rate."

"I don't want to be paid," Reacher said.

"You think virtue is its own reward?"

"I don't know much about virtue. I just want to find out what happened. I can't charge money for a private satisfaction."

Bramall came back, and they ate, and they watched out the window.

They saw nothing.

Mackenzie paid.

Reacher said, "There's another bar we could look at."

"Like these?" Bramall said.

"A little better, maybe. There might be a guy we could talk to."

He led them a block over, toward the railroad tracks, and two blocks down, to the bar with the bullet hole in the mirror. The same guy was at the same table, with the same kind of long-neck bottle. The helpful guy, or the busybody into everyone's business, or the local expert full of specialist knowledge, or the mixture of all three. His table was only a two-top, so Mackenzie sat down across from him, and Bramall and Reacher stood behind her.

The guy said, "You're the gentleman who asked me about Mule Crossing."

"Correct," Reacher said.

"Did you find it? Or did you blink and miss it?"

He was talking to Reacher, but he was looking at Mackenzie. Hard not to. The mass of hair, and the face, and the eyes, and the small slender form under the thin white blouse.

No hint of recognition.

"I found it," Reacher said. "In fact I heard a story down there. A year and a half ago someone got eaten by a bear."

The guy took a long pull on his bottle.

He wiped foam off his lip.

He said, "Seymour Porterfield."

"You knew him?"

"My buddy's friend was the guy who fixed his roof when it leaked. Which was about every winter, because it was built all wrong. So I heard things. I know about the land from way back. Those were railroad acres, even though the track was nowhere near. Some old scam, more than a hundred years ago. Every once in a while some rich guy back east would inherit a deed, and come on out and build a cabin. In Porterfield's case it was his father. He built a modern style, which I guess is why the roof was leaking. Then later he died and Porterfield got the title in his will. I guess he decided he liked the simple life, because he moved in full-time."

"What did he do for a living?"

"He was on the phone all the time, and he drove around a lot. Doing what, no one seemed to know exactly. Maybe a hobby. He had all his daddy's money. Some kind of old fortune back east. Maybe ironworks, hence the railroad connection."

"What kind of a guy was he?"

"He was a college boy and a former Marine. But the old-money kind of both."

"How was his health?"

The guy paused a beat.

He said, "Weird you should ask that."

"Why?"

"His health looked fine from the outside. You could have put him on a movie poster. But he had economy packs of surgical dressings in his house, and also his medicine cabinet was jammed with pills."

"Your buddy's friend would check a thing like that?"

"You know, in passing."

"Was there ever any trouble there? Any strangers showing up un-announced? Any kind of weird shit going on?"

The guy shook his head.

"No strangers," he said. "No trouble, either. And nothing weird, until the secret girlfriend showed up."

Chapter 29

The guy with the long-neck bottle said, "I guess it was the start of the winter before the last one. Porterfield's roof was leaking bad again. My buddy's friend was out there all the time. Sometimes he would get a look in through a window. He started seeing her stuff. More and more of it. But he never saw her. If he had to do inside work, sometimes she wasn't there, and if she was, she would hide in the bedroom. He was sure of it."

"She wasn't always there?" Reacher said.

"Neither was he sometimes. She must have had a place of her own. I guess they were back and forth."

"But when she was there, she didn't hide her stuff," Reacher said.

"No, it was right out in the open."

"Any chance of confusion? Maybe it was all Porterfield's stuff."

The guy shook his head. He said, "I don't think so, especially the nightwear. And you can tell by the look of a place. Men and women make a mess two different ways. This was both ways at once, let me tell you, right there. Two of everything. Two people. Two plates in the sink, two books by the sofa, both sides of the bed with a dent."

"Clearly your buddy's friend undertook an extensive investigation."

"A roof covers the whole house, man. Supposed to, anyway."

"But your buddy's friend never actually met her."

"Which is why he called her the secret girlfriend."

"Never saw her coming and going, or out on the road?"

"Never."

"Did Porterfield ever say anything about her?"

The guy drained his bottle and set it down on the table.

He said, "He never denied it. He never came right out and said some weird thing like hey, by the way, I don't have a girlfriend. But equally he never said, by the way, my girlfriend is taking a nap, so don't go in the bedroom. All he ever said was don't go in. Period. He never said why. All in all my buddy's friend said being there was a weird experience. Like Porterfield was hiding her away, and denying her existence, so no one would ever come looking for her. Except that made no sense, because her stuff was everywhere. I think a man with bad intentions would have taken better precautions."

Reacher said, "Did you believe the story about the bear?"

"The sheriff did," the guy said. "That's about all that matters."

"You got doubts?"

"I wasn't there. But everyone had the same private reaction. It was automatic. Once or twice in your life you find yourself wondering what you would do, if there truly was a guy who had to go. Or you wonder what you would do if something got way out of hand, and someone ended up dead, when he wasn't supposed to. Either way, you would dump him in the high woods. Exactly the kind of place where Porterfield was found. It's a total no-brainer. Maybe you would smear him with honey. Or nick another couple of veins, to keep the smell fresh. Maybe you would get lucky with the big animals, and maybe you wouldn't, but either way you don't need them. You got hundreds of other species already lining up and licking their lips. So what I'm saying is, I promise you every guy who heard the news about Porterfield was thinking hell yeah, that's how I would do it. I know I was."

"You think the sheriff was really?"

"Privately, sure."

"But publicly he called it an accident."

"No proof," the guy said. "That's the whole beauty of it."

"Did Porterfield have enemies?"

"He was a rich guy from back east. I'm sure they all have enemies."

"What happened to the woman?"

"Rumor was she stuck around. No one knew exactly where. No one knew who they were looking for, because no one knew what she looked like in the first place."

"What happened to Porterfield's roof?"

"The sheriff told my buddy's friend to fix it good, once and for all. So he put new metal over the bad part. Which is what he had wanted to do all along, except Porterfield would never let him, because it wasn't that way in the architect's drawing."

They bought the guy another bottle of his favorite beer, and left him there. They walked back to the Toyota, which was parked across the street from the new-age café, on the far curb about halfway between the two bars, with their beer signs and their dirty windows. By that point the street lights were on. The sky was dark. The café was closed. There was noise in the bars, but their doors were shut.

There were three guys fanned out around the Toyota. Out in the street, casting shadows, as if ready to repel a hostile attack. They were all wiry, but also tall. They all had big blunt hands. They were all wearing denim and boots, one of them lizard.

Bramall stopped in the shadows.

Reacher and Mackenzie stopped behind him.

Mackenzie said, "Who are they?"

"Cowboys," Reacher said. "Weaned on beef jerky and fried rattle-snake."

"What do they want?"

"My guess is to scare us off. This kind of choreography usually involves that kind of thing."

"Scare us off what? What are we doing?"

"We're poking around. We're asking questions about a woman who may be involved in some kind of unsavory local business. We're making them nervous."

"What do we do?"

"I need to consult with my senior partner about who goes first." Bramall said, "Do you have a preference?"

"I think we should all go together. Maybe me one step ahead. But I want you to see their faces."

"Why?"

"If I lose you can give the cops a description, from my hospital bedside."

"Lose what?" Mackenzie said. "I'm sure all they want to do is talk to us. I'm sure they'll be aggressive and unpleasant and so on, but I don't see how it necessarily becomes a fight. Unless we choose to make it one."

"Where do you live?"

"Lake Forest, Illinois."

"OK."

"What does that mean?"

"This is already a fight. You can tell by the way they're standing. It's win or go home."

"Did Scorpio send them?"

"That would be a logical assumption," Reacher said. "Technically the unsavory local business is his. All the way up to Montana, apparently. But it's also the opposite of logical. If Scorpio can whistle up three good-looking cowboys at the drop of a hat, why would he have told a half-assed punk like Billy to shoot me from behind a tree? He would have told these guys instead. Maybe this is some kind of distant local subcommittee. Some kind of spontaneous democracy, that Scorpio knows nothing about."

"You worried about them?" Bramall said. "You mentioned losing."

"Cowboys are the worst," Reacher said. "Not much I can do to them, that a horse already hasn't."

He stepped out of the shadows and walked ahead through the evening gloom. His heels were loud on the concrete. Behind him Bramall and Mackenzie caught up and closed the gap. They stepped off the sidewalk and crossed the street at an angle. They headed straight for the car.

The three guys moved, flowing outward to meet them, bunching up, one guy ahead and two behind, like a mirror image. Reacher was wrestling with the brawler's eternal dilemma, which was why not just take out the point man immediately? A surprise head-butt. Don't even stop walking.

Often the smart play.

But not always.

Reacher stopped and the cowboys stopped and they ended up about eight feet apart. That close Reacher thought they looked like three useful characters. Two could have been in their early forties, and the third could have been ten years younger. He was the point man. He had the lizard boots.

"Let me guess," Reacher said. "You're here to give us a message. That's fine. Everyone has the right to be heard. We'll give you thirty seconds. Start now, if you like. Speak clearly. Translate any local words or phrases."

The guy with the lizard boots said, "The message is go back where you came from. Ain't nothing for you here."

Reacher shook his head.

"That can't be right," he said. "Are you sure you heard the message correctly? Generally speaking, folks out here like to welcome a stranger."

The guy said, "I got the message right."

Nothing more.

Reacher said, "Tell me when we get to the part where you say you'll kick our ass if we don't get going."

The guy didn't answer.

Reacher watched him. Watched all of them. They weren't backing off. But they weren't coming on forward either. They were static. They were like a rookie squad when the plan stops working. Something had derailed them. Not Mackenzie. They were looking at her way more than they should, in the middle of a tense get-out-of-town showdown, but the looking was pure animal biology. Not recognition. Mostly it showed in their mouths.

The guy with the boots said, "No one's ass needs to get kicked."

"I agree," Reacher said. "Least of all mine."

"But you should give it up."

"Here's a counteroffer," Reacher said. "You don't mess with me, I won't mess with you."

The guy nodded. Not like he agreed, but like he understood the sentence. Reacher said, "Look, kid," and beckoned the guy close, as if for a private word, like two world leaders sharing a confidence.

Reacher put his hand on the guy's elbow. A friendly gesture, inclusive, intimate, maybe even conspiratorial.

He squeezed.

He whispered, "Tell whoever sent you this won't be like the FBI or the DEA or the ATF. Tell whoever sent you this time it's the U.S. Army."

The guy reacted. Reacher felt it in his elbow. Then he let him go, and the eight-foot gap opened up again. Reacher stood square on and up straight. His old professional pose. Sooner or later everyone's thoughts turned to violence. Better to deal with that upfront. Better to say, you have got to be kidding me. So he stood chin up, his full height, shoulders back, hands loose, not a circus freak, but a little bigger all around than a normal big guy, enough so they noticed. Plus the eyes, which he found most people liked, except he could blink and come back different, like changing the channel, from a happy show to some bleak documentary about prehistoric survival a million years ago.

Then suddenly he changed the channel again and smiled and nodded, in a shared, self-deprecating kind of a way, as if obviously two guys such as them could only be kidding around, and the other four would catch on eventually.

Always offer the other guy a graceful exit.

The guy in the boots took it. He smiled back, like they were just two old boys horsing around, which could happen anytime, and especially in the presence of such a pretty lady. Then he turned around and led his guys away. Reacher crossed to the opposite sidewalk and watched them around the corner. They climbed in a huge crew-cab pick-up parked head-in by a fence. It backed out and took off. It turned left at the first four-way, and was lost to sight.

"See?" Mackenzie said. "It didn't have to be a fight."

Reacher said nothing. He stared at her. Then he stared at the corner, where the pick-up had turned.

Something wrong.

With the wrong thing.

He said to Bramall, "Did you take interrogation classes with us?"

Bramall said, "Only the semester with the rubber hoses."

"We were taught the art of interrogation is mostly about listening. His language was weird. His choice of phrase. At the end he said we should give it up. What did that mean? Give what up?"

"Our quest," Mackenzie said. "Our search for Rose. Obviously. I mean, to give something up, you have to be doing it in the first place, and that's about all we've been doing. There's nothing else we could give up."

"What category of person would care either way about our search for Rose?"

"All kinds. We could be treading on a lot of different toes."

"What category of person might care most of all?"

Mackenzie didn't answer.

Tell whoever sent you.

In his mind Reacher heard General Simpson's voice, on the phone from West Point: *She might not want to be found.*

Then he thought no, that can't be right.

Chapter 30

Reacher said, "At the beginning the guy said there's nothing for us here. Then at the end he said the thing about giving it up. It was a politely threatening opening statement, and a politely threatening closing statement. But in the middle he declined to fight. I think for one particular reason. He was unsettled. There was a new factor he hadn't been briefed on. He was still getting used to it. He had been sent to kick ass, but all of a sudden he realized we were the kind of people who might kick back. He hadn't been warned about that. Which is weird, because every question we ever asked in this town, we asked it standing up. We weren't hiding. Who would send a guy with a message without giving him our descriptions?"

Mackenzie said, "I don't know."

"Maybe someone who never saw us standing up. Maybe someone who never really saw us at all, except as vague shapes slumped down in a car, as she sped past on the dirt road. Hypothetically. It would be the car she remembered, not us. A black Toyota Land Cruiser, with Illinois plates. Maybe she asked three loyal friends to track it down, and run off whoever was in it. Because she doesn't want to be found."

Mackenzie said, "Do you think that's who they were?"

"I did for a moment. I told him the U.S. Army was coming, and he reacted. At first I thought he was impressed. Then later I thought no, his reaction might be because the person who sent him was also U.S. Army. He might have been surprised about the weird connection. He might not have known what it meant. He might have wanted to get away and report back."

"To Rose," Mackenzie said. "Those were her friends."

"Except they weren't," Reacher said. "They were nothing to do with Rose. We know for sure they never even met her. We know that because they didn't recognize you. How could they be friends with your twin without knowing who you were? That's why I wanted you close enough to see their faces. So they could see yours. They would have been staring at you, full of confusion. But they weren't."

"So who were they?"

"I don't know," Reacher said.

They drove back to the hotel. Bramall went straight upstairs. Reacher stayed out in the parking lot. He looked up at the night sky. It was black and huge and dusted with stars. They were very bright, and there were millions of them.

The American West.

Mackenzie came out and stood beside him.

She said, "We could be in the wrong place entirely."

Reacher was still looking at the sky.

"In the universe?" he said.

"In this state. No one recognizes me, which means no one has seen her. All we know is six weeks ago she was in some part of Billy's very large territory. When she traded her ring. Why conclude it was this part?"

"Porterfield's house. She wasn't there full-time. The roofer said so. Yet no one ever saw her heading for the turn. Which means she came and went from the other direction."

"Two years ago."

"Why would she move?"

"Her boyfriend died. People move, after a thing like that. It's a shock."

"She did five tours in Iraq and Afghanistan. She's had worse shocks. She would have assessed the situation tactically. No one had ever seen her. There was no realistic threat vector against her current billet. Presumably it was a decent place. It had been good enough for Porterfield to come over. Why give it up? Replacing it would be tough."

"I would move."

"She would stay."

"You know her better?"

"I know how a person lives through five tours."

"I hope you're right."

"We'll find out tomorrow," he said. "We know roughly where she is. She can't hide forever."

"I wanted to buy you a drink," she said. "To thank you. Since you won't let me pay you. But there's no bar in this hotel."

"No need to thank me either," Reacher said.

"I would have enjoyed it."

"Me, too, I guess."

She moved away a couple of steps, and sat down on a concrete bench.

He sat down beside her.

She said, "Are you married?"

"No," he said. "But you are."

She laughed, short but soft.

She said, "It was an unconnected question. Just purely out of interest. It wasn't a Freudian slip."

"Tell me about Mr. Mackenzie."

"He's a nice man. We're a good match."

"Do you have children?"

"Not yet."

"Can I ask an unconnected question of my own? Just purely out of interest?"

She said, "I suppose."

"It's kind of weird, and I don't want you to take it the wrong way."

"I'll try."

"How does it feel to be so good looking?"

"Yes, that's weird."

"I'm sorry."

"How did it feel when those guys wouldn't fight you?"

"Useful."

"For us it felt like a minimum requirement. Our father had grandiose ideas."

"The judge."

"He thought he was living in a storybook. Everything had to be picturesque. On sunny days we ran around the woods in white cotton dresses. At first it was mostly about the hair. All sticking out. We looked like nymphs or fairies. We got the faces later. Then he started dreaming about who we would marry. We thought it was all pretty stupid. It was almost the twenty-first century, and we lived in Wyoming. We ignored it, mostly. But if I'm truly honest, deep down it made an impression. I was aware of it. It came to be part of who I am. Deep down I guess I believe being pretty is better than being ugly. Deep down I know I would choose to look like this again. I worry all that deep down stuff makes me shallow. To answer your question, that's how it feels."

"Did Rose feel the same way?"

Mackenzie nodded.

She said, "Rose liked things to be perfect. She was smart, and she worked hard, and mostly she made it happen that way. How she looked was the one thing she couldn't control. But happily she turned out OK in that department. I think deep down she took a lot of satisfaction from it. She wanted to be the absolute best, from any angle. She wanted to be the total package. And she was."

"Why did she join the army?"

"I told you."

"You told me she would shoot a guy even before he set a foot on her porch, whereas you would wait a moment longer. She could have stayed home and done that."

"I feel like I'm on a psychiatrist's couch."

"Lie back and pretend you're an actress in a movie. Suppose the hotel had a bar. By now you'd have bought me a cup of coffee. Black, no sugar. Or a beer, if they didn't have coffee. Domestic, in a bottle. You would have gotten some weird kind of white wine. Because of Lake Forest, Illinois. Right now we'd be at a table, talking. I would be asking why Rose joined the army, and you would be telling me."

"She was looking for something worth it. It turned out the storybook was a lie. He wasn't the wise man of the county. At first we told ourselves certain practices were almost traditional. He was a lawyer, after all, and lawyers always get paid something. For an opinion, perhaps, prior to the filing. But there were whispers. If they were true, it was something worse. We never found out. Rose and I went to college. They sold the place and moved out of state. We were happy about it. It was a weird place for us. We always knew we were acting in someone else's play. And then the playwright himself turned out to be made up, too. We reacted in slightly different ways. It left Rose needing something real, and me needing a real storybook. And we got both of them, I guess."

Reacher said nothing.

"I'm going to bed now," she said. "Thanks for talking."

She left him there, alone in the dark, leaning back on the concrete bench, looking at the stars.

At that moment, three hundred miles away at an I-90 truck stop not far from Rapid City, South Dakota, a guy in a beat-up old pick-up truck with Wyoming plates and a vinyl camper shell on the back turned into a service road he had been told led to a covered garage. His name was Stackley, and he was thirty-eight years old, a hard worker, maybe not where he should be in life, but always willing to try his best. He had been told the covered garage was half full with idle snowplows and other winter equipment. He had been told the other half was empty. Plenty of space. He had been told they had it all to themselves.

He had been told there would be a guard at the door.

There was.

He slowed to a stop and wound down his window.

He said, "I'm Stackley. You should have gotten a call from Mr. Scorpio. I'm taking over from Billy."

The guard said, "You're the new Billy?"

"As of tonight."

"Congratulations, Stackley. Drive in and park in slot number five. Forward, on a diagonal. Get out of the truck and open the tailgate."

Stackley did what he was told. He drove in, to an echoing corrugated space the size of an aircraft hangar. On the left were ranks of giant yellow machines, mothballed for the summer. On the right was empty space. Someone had chalked diagonal parking bays on the concrete floor. They were numbered one through ten. One was at the far end, and ten was closest. Seven and three were already occupied. Seven had an old Dodge Durango with its rear door up. Three had a rusted Silverado with a roll-up cover on the bed. Stackley stopped his own truck short of it, and nosed into slot number five. He got out and lowered his tailgate.

Then he checked his watch and waited for midnight. No way to get there faster. The drivers in three and seven were waiting just like him. They nodded, not exactly friendly, not exactly wary. More like a simple same-boat acknowledgment of life's ups and downs. They were guys not unlike himself. Then an old black four-wheel-drive rolled in, and parked in the number six slot. The driver got out, and nodded all around, and opened his rear hatch door. Then he stood next to it, and waited. He looked just like the others. Late thirties, maybe not where he should be in life.

Five minutes later all ten slots were full. Ten vehicles, all in a line, ten tailgates raised or lowered, ten drivers waiting. The guard watched from the doorway. Stackley checked the time again. It was close to the top of the hour. He saw the guard take a call on his cell, saw him listen, saw him click off, and heard him call out, "Two minutes, guys. It's nearly here."

Two minutes later a white panel van drove in a door at the far end of the shed. It looked fresh off the highway. Stackley was reminded of a horse, hot and blowing after a long fast gallop. It nosed in and stopped almost at once, with its rear door level with the truck in slot number one. The driver got out and walked around and opened up. He pulled crisp white boxes from the back of his van, and the driver from slot number one took them from him, and twisted away to slide them in the bed of his pick-up.

The driver got back in the panel van and rolled it forward six or eight feet and stopped again. He repeated the unloading procedure with the driver from slot number two, stacking a teetering pile of crisp white boxes in the guy's arms, who then rotated away and dumped them in his own truck. Then the van moved on to the guy in slot number three, which gave the guy from slot number one the space to back out, and get straight, and drive out the same door the van had come in through.

A slick operation, Stackley thought. And very well supplied. From where he was standing he could see what the guy was getting in slot number four. High-dose time-release oxycodone, and transdermal fentanyl patches, the latter in three different strengths. The boxes were made of high-gloss card, antiseptic white, pharmaceutical grade. They had brand names. They were the real thing. Made in America, straight from the factory.

Solid gold.

The panel van moved on, and Stackley stepped up. He got what Scorpio had told him he would get, which was the same volume Billy had been moving. Which was a decent quantity, for a rural area with not many people. He put his boxes in the camper shell. He put a blanket over them. Not that anyone could see in his windows. They were vinyl, all cracked and yellow. Better than a tint from a body shop.

He waited until the panel van was serving the guy in slot number seven, and then he backed up, and got straight, and drove out the door.

At that moment Gloria Nakamura was sitting in her dark and silent car, watching the alley that ran behind Arthur Scorpio's laundromat. She could see his back door. It had a rim of light, as if it was standing open an inch. It was a warm night, but not excessive. She had approached on foot, quietly, and looked through the gap, one eye, but she had seen nothing. The angle was too extreme. She walked back to her car. She tried to list the kinds of things that could make a room warm enough to want to open the door for extra ventilation. Tumble dryers, obviously, but not at midnight, and not in the back office.

Her cell phone rang.

Her friend in Computer Crimes.

Who said, "We've lost Scorpio again. He must have gone to a big box store and bought up a different batch of phones."

Nakamura said, "He's in his office. Probably making calls. I'm watching him right now."

"We caught something that might have been him. You can kind of work out the triangulation backward. You can make a guess about what a signal would look like, if it was coming from his place. In which case he made a call to somewhere north of here, but not very far north. He just got a text back from the same number. It says, all good tonight including the new Billy."

"When was this?"

"Right now. A minute ago."

"Wait," she said.

The rim of light around the door grew wider. Then died altogether. Arthur Scorpio stepped out into the nighttime gloom. He turned back and locked the door. Then he walked to his car.

She said, "Should I follow him?"

"Waste of gas," her friend said. "He's going home. He goes home every time."

"What did it mean, the new Billy?"

"I guess something happened to the old Billy."

Reacher, she thought.

Billy hadn't found a big enough tree.

Reacher was not a superstitious man. Not given to flights of fancy, or sudden forebodings, or existential dread of any kind. But he woke with the dawn, and he stayed in bed. He felt unwilling to move. He propped himself on the pillow and watched his reflection in the mirror on the opposite wall. A distant figure. One of those days. Not just a military thing. Plenty of other professions felt the same way. Sometimes you woke up, and you knew for sure, from history and experience and weary intuition, that the brand new day would bring nothing good at all.

Chapter 31

They met in the lobby, at eight, the same as the day before. Bramall was in another new shirt, and Mackenzie was in another new blouse. By that point Reacher's clothes were two days old, but once again he had used a whole bar of soap in the shower. They walked up to the same diner, and got the same table. They ordered, and Bramall opened the subsequent conversation by asking for a consensus on a certain legal issue, which was that if they accepted Reacher's hypothesis, then by definition they would be looking exclusively at the old ranches off the dirt road west of Porterfield's place. Which was a very specific area of investigation. It was precise enough to put in a warrant. Normally a local law enforcement official would be notified. Not required, but expected. A professional courtesy.

"Are you cautioning me again?" Reacher said. "Explicitly and every step of the way?"

"Sometimes things bear repeating."

"Sheriff Connelly will claim Rose's place is a potential crime scene. He'll keep us out. Better not tell him. He still wants to know where Porterfield died. He'll chase any connection."

"Rose's place is a crime scene," Mackenzie said. "No potential about it. Trespass, at least. Or illegal occupation of someone else's land. Wyoming has laws about that. Plus a stolen car, it seems. Plus narcotics, we assume. Plus however she's paying for them. I don't want the sheriff to be the one to find her. I can't let him put her in the system. I might never get her out again. We have to get to her first."

"OK," Bramall said.

They drove south to Mule Crossing, and turned at the bottle rocket billboard, and headed west on the dirt road. The first three miles were solitary. Then not long after they passed Billy's place they saw a tiny worm of dust on the far horizon. A vehicle on the road, coming toward them. Two miles away, maybe.

It's rare to see another car.

Like the neighbor told them.

"Pull over," Reacher said. "Park on the shoulder. If it's her, we'll want to follow. Or her friends. If it isn't, no harm, no foul."

Bramall made the same maneuver he had made the day before, which was to stop dead in the traffic lane, and then back up carefully, like he was in a city garage. He ended up at ninety degrees exactly, which put the westward view through Mackenzie's window. She buzzed it down and buzzed it up, to wipe the dust away.

The cloud got closer. It was still early in the day. The air was still cool. No thermals yet. No haze, no shimmer. They could see the oncoming vehicle clearly. It was tiny in the distance. Dark in color. Too far away to say more. Bramall kept the engine running. Transmission in gear, foot on the brake. Ready to go, either left or right.

The cloud got closer. The vehicle got clearer. It was old or dull or both. No flash of chrome against the morning sun. No gleam of paint.

"It's not the friends," Bramall said. "It's too small. Their truck was a huge thing."

The cloud got closer. The vehicle was brown. Rust or dust or sun-baked paint. Hard to say. It was hugging the road. It looked wider than it was tall.

"It's not her," Mackenzie said. "It's too low. Hers was way more square."

A minute later it blew on by, juddering and bouncing. No one they had seen before. Just a beat-up old pick-up truck, with Wyoming plates and a vinyl camper shell on the back. A guy at the wheel, late thirties maybe, looking straight ahead, paying no attention.

Nothing.

"Onward," Reacher said.

They drove on west, past Porterfield's driveway. Then eleven miles later past his neighbor's, as inconspicuous as ever. They had six more places ahead, three on the left, three on the right. The plan was to look at them all, one by one. Simple in principle. Maybe not in practice. The big book of maps had shown neat brown rectangles for houses and barns, but Mackenzie said over the years such places could have built way more than that. Maybe with the proper permissions, maybe not. There could be garages, and smaller barns, and tractor barns, and wood stores, and generator huts, and hobby huts, and staff cottages, and guest cottages, and in-law cottages. Maybe even summer houses deep in the woods. A hundred places for Rose to hide, Reacher thought. But she would have chosen somewhere civilized. Not a cellar or an attic. Reasonably big. Not up a tree. Porterfield had come by from time to time.

Hope for the best.

The first driveway opening was on the left. They took it. It led to a track like the others they had seen, uneven, full of roots and rocks and gravel. The Toyota clawed onward, but slowly, like an overweight goat. There were more conifer trees than before, and aspen, because the elevation was greater, and the terrain more mountainous. The track stayed in the woods all the way, except one bare spot on the shoulder of a hairpin turn, looking east. The pie lady's place was too far away to see. The nearest neighbor. The curvature of the earth was in the way. Then the track swung back into the woods, and wound ever onward and upward.

Six miles later they came out on a scruffy five-acre compound full of the kind of buildings Mackenzie had mentioned.

There was a main house, all log, old, modest in size, nearly matched in its dimensions by a separate log cottage, newer, some distance away. In between were log barns and wood stores and storage structures, some of them big enough for a decent truck, some of them as small as garden sheds or dog houses.

First thing they did was knock on the door. No one was home. Not a surprise. Reacher figured no one had been home for a couple of years. Maybe more. Every step on the porch raised a puff of dust, from the red sand, blown as fine as talcum.

Second thing they did was check the surrounding terrain. It was crusted smooth by wind and snowmelt. Undisturbed. Certainly there were no new tire tracks. The Toyota's own stood out crisp and fresh and vivid. A total contrast. Mackenzie felt that was game over right there. She felt it was impossible to live in Wyoming without a vehicle. Therefore no sign of a vehicle meant no sign of life. Rose wasn't there. Not camped out in any of the various buildings. Reacher agreed. Bramall agreed.

They moved on.

They drove the six miles back down the track, and turned on the dirt road, and headed west again. One down, five to go. The next driveway would most likely be on the right.

"Look," Bramall said.

He pointed.

Up ahead, still far away, another worm of dust. At its head, another vehicle coming toward them. It was rare to see another car? Not really. It was getting like Times Square.

They drove on, closing the gap.

It was a big vehicle coming.

"That could be her friends," Mackenzie said. "Same size of truck."

"Block the road," Reacher said. "Make them stop."

Bramall took his foot off the gas, and steered left, and straddled the crown of the road. He put his hazard flashers on, and blinked his high beams, and coasted on slowly to a hundred-yard stretch that had a knee-high rock ledge on one side, and a drainage ditch on the other.

He came to a stop halfway between them. No way around. The engine idled. The hazard flashers clicked urgently. He pulsed the headlights, fast, slow, randomly, like Morse code.

Up ahead the big truck slowed. Behind it the dust cloud caught up momentarily, and then thinned out and fell away. The truck stopped three hundred yards west, in the middle of the road itself, like a long-distance showdown.

"More than one person," Reacher said. "They can't agree what to do. They stopped to talk it out."

They waited.

Up ahead the truck moved forward. Slowly. Like cruising a parking lot. It rolled on. Two hundred yards away. One hundred. Fifty yards away.

It was the same crew-cab they had seen the night before. Huge size, a rumbling exhaust. Three people in it. The same guys. Reacher was sure of it. They came to a stop fifty feet away. Bramall turned off his hazard lights. For a second the tableau was frozen, two trucks facing off, close together, engines idling, on a narrow red ribbon in the middle of a vast version of nowhere.

Mackenzie got out of the Toyota.

Bramall moved to do the same, but Reacher put a hand on his shoulder.

"We need to talk," he said.

"About what?"

"Your client. She's got a tough day ahead."

"You know what's going to happen?"

"Unfortunately," Reacher said. "It's the only thing that fits."

But Mackenzie was already turned around, miming impatience, so Bramall slid out to join her, followed by Reacher, three steps behind. From the crew-cab came the guy with the lizard boots, and his two companions. Six people altogether, in two groups of three, all of them eyeing the no-man's-land between their radiator grilles, their postures subject to ancient instincts. They met in the middle, five polite feet apart, safely longer than a dagger's thrust, another ancient instinct.

The guy in the boots said, "The message hasn't changed."

"I thought about that," Reacher said. "Seemed to me, if you boiled it right down, the main takeaway from the message was we should go back where we came from. Which makes it more of a suggestion, don't you think? Call it a request, to assume good manners on your part. And hey, plenty of requests are perfectly reasonable. We all know that. I would like to request a million dollars and a dinner date with Miss Wyoming. But the point of a request is that it can be declined. Respectfully, with great regret, and so on. But declined nonetheless. Which is what is happening here."

"Unacceptable."

"Get used to it. We're going to stick around, and if any of the actual landowners out here have a problem with it, I'm sure the state has laws that would allow them to seek a remedy."

The guy said, "Right now we're being nice about it."

"My advice, you should keep on being nice about it. Even if we lose, we'll do some damage. Two of you will go to the hospital. Best case. But from what I've seen, I have to say, the best case looks unlikely. I don't think we'll lose. I think all three of you will go to the hospital."

The guy paused a beat.

Then he said, "OK, it was a request."

Reacher said, "I'm glad we got that cleared up."

"There's nothing for you here."

"Who made the request?"

"I'm not going to tell you. This whole thing is about privacy. You don't get it, do you?"

Reacher said, "You got a phone?"

"Who do you want to call?"

"Take a picture. Video would be better. You got video on your phone?"

The guy said, "I guess."

"All we'll do is say our names. Maybe add a line of background. On your phone. Then you can take it back and show it to whoever it was who made the request. That would be fair to all concerned."

"You might follow us there."

"We promise we won't."

"Why would we trust you?"

"You live in there somewhere. We know that. By now it's a one-in-five chance. We'll find you sooner or later. It's only a matter of time."

The guy didn't answer.

"But I'd rather do it this way," Reacher said. "This way is better."

The guy didn't answer. But eventually he nodded. One of the back-row guys stepped up with a phone. He held it horizontal between splayed fingers, and crossed his eyes, and said, "Go."

Mackenzie said, "Jane Mackenzie."

Bramall said, "Terry Bramall, private detective from Chicago."

Reacher said, "Jack Reacher, ex-army, once upon a time CO of the 110th MP."

The back-row guy lowered the phone.

Reacher said, "We'll wait here."

"Could be a couple hours," the guy with the boots said. "You got water?"

The other back-row guy carried bottles of water from their truck to the Toyota. Then they backed up and turned around and drove away. The dust cloud picked up behind them, turning, rising, falling, hanging in the air like evidence, showing the way they had gone, like a *whoosh* in a cartoon strip.

Bramall said, "Do we follow?"

"No," Reacher said. "A professional courtesy. Not required, but expected."

Mackenzie said, "You know, don't you?"

"I know two things," Reacher said. "She lives here, and no one recognizes you."

Chapter 32

Bramall backed up to where the rock ledge petered out and the ditch filled in. He parked on the shoulder, a little tilted, facing west. Reacher drank a bottle of donated water, and walked back to the ledge, and sat in the sun. The last of summer. No one talked. Mostly Bramall sat in the car, nothing on his face, a man life had taught to be patient. Mostly Mackenzie stood alone, as far from the car as Reacher, but in the other direction. High overhead ravens circled, and looked, and thought not yet, and soared away.

In the end it was less than two hours. It was ninety-three minutes, which was an hour and a half and change. Far in the distance a smudge of dust kicked up, with a black dot in front of it, which grew larger, until they could see who it was. It was the three guys in their crew-cab. Back again. Like before, they stopped fifty feet out, and they climbed down, and they walked forward.

Reacher and Bramall and Mackenzie went to meet them. They all stopped, six people, groups of three, five polite feet apart.

The guy in the boots said, "Just Mrs. Mackenzie."

Reacher waited.

Mackenzie said, "No, all three of us."

The guy said nothing.

Reacher waited again. For their plan B. He knew they had one. Stupid to come without.

The guy said, "OK."

He turned and walked back and the three of them climbed in their crew-cab again. Bramall and Mackenzie and Reacher climbed in the Toyota. The crew-cab backed up and turned, and drove away west. Bramall followed, hanging back, drifting left, drifting right, trying to miss the worst of the dust.

The crew-cab turned in on the second track on the right. Bramall followed. The track was wide, but the surface was bad. Roots, rocks, gravel. Up ahead the crew-cab bucked and bounced. Its tires chirped and slid on stones worn smooth by time. There were trees left and right, mostly conifers, some gnarled by the wind, some stately. There were distant blazes of gold, mostly in the gulches and the gullies, where the aspen was happiest. The track went left and right, around trees, around rocks the size of cars, some of them piled high on top of each other, some of them overhanging.

After more than four slow miles the track came to a building. It was made of logs, and looked like a vacation cabin. Livable, but not for long. Not a permanent home. Dusty windows. Unoccupied. Maybe abandoned. The crew-cab didn't stop. It churned on by, all four wheels working, and half a mile later it passed another cabin just the same. Dusty windows, unoccupied. Maybe abandoned. Reacher figured they were in a compound, laid out like an old-fashioned vacation camp, with isolated accommodations in separate woodland clearings, all connected together by winding tracks like the one they were on, which in theory might sooner or later lead to some kind of central destination.

It did. The track came around the base of a wooded slope, and opened up on what looked at first like empty blue sky, but turned out to be a small plateau on the low slopes of a mountain, with infinite views north and east. There was a sprawling log house made of massive timbers. Not a commercial enterprise. Not an office or a camp clubhouse. Just the main family home. Maybe the cabins had been for their guests. Or for children and grandchildren. Maybe great-grandchildren. Some kind of patriarch's dream. Maybe the owner had been a big man in the county.

The crew-cab didn't stop.

They followed it onward, away from the big house, along another winding track, around a long artful curve through the trees, and then another in the other direction, and finally they came out in another clearing, which had a cabin set high on a rock foundation, at the head of a small fissure or ravine, which crumbled away in a southwesterly direction, and which thinned the trees enough to show a narrow view of the empty plains and the distant horizon. From the front porch the magic hour before sunset would be spectacular. The house itself was made of logs, neat and plain, like a child's drawing, with a door in the middle, and a window on the left, and a window on the right, with a green metal roof and a chimney. Civilized, Reacher thought. Reasonably big. Not up a tree. Plus far from anywhere, comfortably concealed, as secret as could be, but with a view from the porch.

Why give it up?

Next to the house was a barn, with an open door.

Parked in the barn was an old SUV, an ancient model, boxy and battered and square, covered with rust and red dust so thick it looked baked on.

Up ahead the crew-cab stopped.

Bramall stopped.

The guy with the boots got out. He walked around to the Toyota's front passenger door, and he pulled it open.

He said, "Mrs. Mackenzie first."

She got out. The guy led her down a beaten-earth path, and up the porch steps, to the door. He knocked, and she waited. A small figure, her face set, her hair tumbling everywhere.

The guy got a response from inside, and he opened the door, and held it, like a bellboy in a hotel. Mackenzie stood still for a second, and then she walked past him, and into the house. The guy closed the door after her, and came down off the porch, and walked back to his truck.

No sound.

No movement.

"Rose Sanderson is in there?" Bramall said.

"Yes," Reacher said.

"You know this because you know two things."

"Three altogether," Reacher said. "I didn't mention the extra one."

"You know Rose lives here, and you know no one in town recognizes her sister."

"And I know she won a Purple Heart."

Bramall was quiet a long moment.

"It was a facial wound," he said.

Reacher nodded.

"Had to be," he said.

"How bad?"

"Bad enough that no one recognizes her sister. Bad enough she hides all the time. Bad enough she turns her face away. Bad enough she holes up in the bedroom when the roofer works inside."

Bramall sat in the car, but Reacher was stiff from sitting. He got out to take a stroll. To loosen up, like he had at the comfort stop in Wisconsin. He took the ring out of his pocket. The gold filigree, the black stone, the tiny size. *S.R.S. 2005.* Against the vast wilderness all around it looked impossibly delicate, and intricate, and finely wrought.

He walked to the lip of the ravine, and looked at the view. He could see fifty miles. A slice of Colorado, but mostly Wyoming. Thin clear air, immense tawny plains, spiky trees, rocky outcrops, hazy mountains. Nothing moving. He felt all alone on an empty planet. He could imagine hiding out there. Seeing no one. No one seeing him. Nowhere better.

She might not want to be found.

He turned away, and walked up to the garage, and took a look at the old SUV. It was an ancient Ford Bronco, the same make and model he rode in from Casper to Laramie, with the guy who turned logs into sculptures with chainsaws. That had been a basic vehicle, but Rose Sanderson's was plainer still. It was scoured back to bare metal by wind and sand. The metal looked like it had returned to some kind of primitive ore. It was scabbed and pitted, and dented here and there by minor collisions. No panel was straight. The tires were worn. The front end smelled of gasoline.

He walked back to the Toyota. By that point Mackenzie had been in the house an hour. Bramall had his window down. For the air, presumably. Thin and clear, warm in the sun, cold in the shadows.

Bramall said, "One of those days."

"I woke up knowing," Reacher said.

"A hands-on client is always a problem. I could have prepared her. I could have cleaned things up a bit."

"I suppose your job is done now. Don't leave without me. I need a ride back to town."

"After you give her the ring."

"Not important anymore. Not in the scheme of things. Mrs. Mackenzie can pass it on."

"I won't leave right away," Bramall said. "Partly because I think Mrs. Mackenzie is about to request an extension to my contract. She's going to need some kind of help. If not from me, then at least she'll expect a ride to the hotel. Or the airport."

"Does your phone work from here?"

"Two bars, if you face the ravine."

"Which the house does. She could have called from here. When she said, shut up, Sy, I'm on the phone. It was either here or Porterfield's place. Had to be one or the other."

"You plan on asking her much about Porterfield? I'm with the majority here. The thing with the bear is most likely bullshit."

"That plan has changed. Because of the hands-on client. The story skipped straight to the big reunion. Rose won't talk to us now. It won't occur to her. Why would it? When your long-lost twin sister shows up at your door, you don't necessarily invite the cab driver in the house. You don't make small talk."

"You wanted to know the story."

"I got most of it," Reacher said. "I got to the part where it ends about twenty miles before the road runs out."

Twenty minutes later the front door opened and Mackenzie stepped out on the porch. She turned and closed the door. She stood still, more than a minute, visibly breathing, deep and slow, in and out. Then she stepped down on the scrub path. She started walking. Bramall and Reacher got out of the car to meet her. She had been crying. That was clear.

At first she said nothing. It was as if she had lost the power of speech. Her lips moved and she made sounds, but no words came out.

"Take it easy," Bramall said.

She took a breath.

She said, "My sister would like to speak with Mr. Reacher now."

Reacher looked at her, first in surprise, then as if about to ask a question, which he didn't, because what could he say? Is she a mess? Was it worse than you expected?

She looked back at him, defeated, and she half shrugged and half nodded, as if saying yes and no to everything.

He walked down the scrub path and stepped up on the porch.

Chapter 33

Reacher turned the knob, and opened the door, and stepped inside. He realized in his mind he was expecting some kind of an elaborate gothic vision, involving shrouded windows and darkness, with maybe a lone candle burning somewhere, and a vague figure talking softly behind a heavy veil. The reality was a bright sun-filled house made of shiny logs the color of wildflower honey. The front door opened directly into the living room. It was small and neat and clean, but mostly empty. Nothing in it but two large armchairs, placed on either side of the fireplace, at comfortable and companionable angles.

Rose Sanderson was in the left-hand chair.

Below the neck she was her sister's double. No mistake. She sat in a chair the exact same way. Her resting posture was identical. The angle of her wrist. The spread of her fingers. The tilt of her waist. A replica.

Above the neck, not so much. Not anymore. She was wearing a silver track suit top, with a tight hood, which was pulled up around her head. She had tightened the drawstring in front until only an oval of face was showing. On the left was a web of scar tissue, random and uneven, and on the right was a sheet of aluminum foil, oozing with some kind of thick ointment. She had pressed the foil to the shape of her head. Like half a mask.

A silvery color.

She wasn't sweating. She wasn't trembling. Her eyes looked OK. Better than OK. Her eyes were the eyes of a person who felt deeply serene and contented.

She said, "I want to ask you about something my sister said."

Her voice was the same. Same note, same pitch, same volume. Reacher shook her hand and sat down in the empty chair. Up close he could see the left-hand part of her face was somehow reconstructed. It was stitched together from small fragments. The right-hand part was hidden under the home-made tinfoil poultice.

He said, "What do you want to ask me?"

"My sister says you found my class ring in a pawn shop."

"I did."

"Therefore your involvement here was completely accidental."

"It was."

"But it strikes me you would say that anyway, whether or not it was true. And it strikes me my sister is the type of person who might believe it."

"Where else would I find your ring?"

"A police evidence locker, maybe."

"Who do you think I am really?"

"Maybe still the 110th MP."

"That was a long time ago."

"Then why did you mention it on the video?"

"So you would know I wasn't bullshitting about being in the army. No one would claim the 110th if they didn't have to."

She nodded inside her hood. The foil on her face rustled and clicked.

Reacher said, "Are you expecting a visit from the 110th MP?"

"Not specifically," she said. "Maybe someone like that."

"Why?"

"A number of things."

"Not me," Reacher said. "I'm just a guy, passing through. Nothing more."

"You sure?"

"Promise."

She nodded again, as if the matter was settled.

He took the ring from his pocket, one last time, and he handed it over. She rolled it in her palm, and looked at it from every direction. She smiled. The foil clicked, and a jagged hollow crease appeared in her left cheek, as if the structure of her face had collapsed. Maybe a weak suture.

She said, "Thank you."

He said, "You're welcome."

She said, "I honestly thought I would never see it again."

Then she gave it back.

"I would owe you forty dollars," she said. "Haven't got it right now."

"It's a gift," he said.

"Then I accept. Thank you. But not now. Would you hold it for me? Just a month or so. I could call when I'm ready."

"You're worried you'll trade it away again."

"Just recently everything has gotten so damn expensive."

"Must be difficult making ends meet."

"It is."

"Is that why you're worried about meeting someone like the 110th MP?"

She shook her head.

"I'm not worried about what I do," she said. "No one is interested in my situation. They've given up on people like me."

"Then why expect a visit?"

"Something different. I had a friend whose case is still open. Back burner I'm sure, but some work must get done. One day they'll have enough."

"For what?"

"To take another look, I suppose. My working assumption is one day they'll send a guy. For a moment I hoped you were him, equipped with my ring as a stage prop. But apparently you're not him. That's OK. I just wanted to check. Would you ask my sister to come by again?"

Mackenzie was in the front seat of the Toyota. Her skin was pale. Her flawless face looked hyper-vivid, impossibly smooth, impossibly perfect. Reacher told her Rose wanted to see her again. She looked a question at him. He didn't know what she was asking. Maybe she was looking for some kind of general agreement it could have been worse. Some kind of optimistic thinking. Or not. He couldn't tell. He made an all-purpose don't-know expression, and she nodded, as if she understood. She got out of the car and walked up the path to the house. She went inside again.

She closed the door.

Reacher took her place in the car.

He closed the door.

Bramall said, "How was it?"

"Pretty bad," he said. "It hasn't healed."

"What state was she in?"

"High as a kite."

"On what?"

"Something she claims has just gotten very expensive. I guess she's still holding out for the good stuff. She's not in the toilet stall yet."

"Agent Noble implied she would have to be by now. He claims he tracks every shipment."

"Maybe he was out sick the day they taught real life. Nothing works a hundred percent."

"What did she want to speak with you about?"

"She's expecting some kind of investigator to show up one day, asking questions about Porterfield. She was disappointed I wasn't him. She thinks it's still an open case."

Bramall didn't reply.

Reacher asked him, "What did Mrs. Mackenzie have to say?"

"Nothing good."

"I woke up knowing."

"Rose Sanderson got hit in the face by five pieces of shrapnel from an improvised explosive device concealed at the side of a road outside a small town in Afghanistan. The shrapnel appeared to be mostly small fragments of metal, probably off-cuts from a village-style engineering shop. The five pieces that hit her peeled her face off in chunks, and what stayed on was then badly abraded by smaller particles in the blast. But these days battlefield medicine is a miracle. They found most of the missing parts in her helmet and they sewed her back together again. Big name plastic surgeons, the whole nine yards."

"But?" Reacher said.

"Two main problems," Bramall said. "I mean, OK, this was amazing work, no question. This was a definite KIA in Vietnam, and probably any other time in history, until the last few years. It was a virtuoso performance by the doctors. But great as it was, it was actually pretty lousy. It just can't be done. She was left with scars like a jigsaw puzzle. Nothing fits right. Nothing works right. She looks like a horror movie. And that's the good news."

"What's the bad news?"

"The concealed explosive device was concealed in a dead dog. That's something they do out there. This one was maybe four days old. Getting ripe. The weather was hot. The blast drove rotting tissue and necrotic pathogens and all kinds of bad bacteria deep under the skin of her head. This all was four years ago, and she still can't get rid of the infection. She leaks pus. She looks like a monster twice over. She's in pain all the time."

Reacher was quiet a long moment.

Then he said, "No wonder she didn't tell her sister."

"It's a subject they plan to discuss."

"Why did she stop calling a year and a half ago?"

"They haven't gotten to that yet. But something to do with Porterfield, surely. What else could it be?"

Reacher got out of the car again. He wanted the air. He walked back to the edge of the ravine, and watched the distant view. It was like looking out through a narrow window. Behind him the house was cradled by wooded hills. He wondered who it belonged to.

He walked back to the crew-cab truck. All the windows were down. The three guys inside were laying back. Patient. Saving energy. They knew it was all going to take as long as it took. Maybe a cowboy thing.

The guy in the boots looked up.

Reacher said, "You told me you were being nice about it. I agree. You're being very nice about the whole thing. That should be placed in the record."

The guy moved his head, as if accepting the compliment.

Reacher said, "How did it start?"

"We needed a place to live. We stumbled on this compound. Rose had already claimed it. But she let us stay. She helped us settle in. We helped her with a couple of things. We got kind of protective, I guess. She doesn't like people to see her."

"How long ago was this?"

"Three years. Rose was just out of the army. She was just moving in."

"Who owns this place?"

"Someone who hasn't cared to visit in three years at least."

"You must have known Sy Porterfield."

"I guess we met him a bunch of times."

"What did you make of the story with the bear?"

"I guess we thought it was what anyone would do."

"What did Porterfield do for a living?"

"We never inquired. All we knew is he seemed to make her happy."

"She's high as a kite right now."

"Do you blame her?"

"Not one little bit. But I worry about her supplies holding up."

"We can't discuss that with you. We don't know who you are."

"I'm with her sister."

"Not really. The other guy is the detective she hired. No one understands who you are."

"I'm not a cop," Reacher said. "That's all that matters. I don't care about that stuff. But she could have a problem, now Billy is gone. That's all I'm thinking."

"You know who Billy was?"

"Snowplow driver. Especially good in powdery conditions."

"You were a cop back in the day."

"Everyone was something back in the day. I'm sure you can walk past a cow without feeling the need to drive it to the railhead. Billy ain't coming back. I hope Rose will be OK. That's all I'm saying."

The guy said, "They already got a replacement for Billy. He was by here this morning. His name is Stackley. Seemed like a nice enough guy. Reminded me of a cousin I got in insurance. So all is right with the world again. It's back to business as usual."

Reacher said, "What is she buying?"

"Oxy and fentanyl patches."

"We talked to a guy who said that's a thing of the past."

"It's getting expensive."

"He said it should be getting impossible. Where is it coming from?"

"It's the regular stuff. Same as always. In the white boxes, with the brand names. Made in America, right out the factory door. You get to where you can tell the difference."

"You guys like it, too?"

"A little bit, now and then. To take the edge off, time to time."

"I heard that kind of thing was hard to get now. Maybe I was misinformed."

"You weren't," the guy said. "Matter of fact it is hard to get now. Most places very hard. But not here. Which gives you all a big problem. I don't know what your plans are now, but you need to get one thing straight from the get-go. Rose won't move from here. Not an inch, not in a million years. How could she? She's hooked up here. You don't know what that means to a person. Look at it from her point of view."

Chapter 34

The magic hour was the last part of the sun's daily travel, like a sixty-minute farewell performance, when it was low in the sky, shining sideways through the atmosphere, which reddened its colors and lengthened its shadows. Reacher sat on the porch step and watched the tawny plain go gold, then ochre, then chili-pepper red. Bramall was below him, on a rock at the edge of the ravine. The guys from the crew-cab were sitting in the dirt, leaning their backs on trees.

The door opened and Mackenzie stepped out.

Reacher stood up, and she came down the steps past him, onto the path through the scrub. Meanwhile the guys from the crew-cab all got up and dusted themselves off. Mackenzie met them at the end of the path. She shook their hands, one by one, and thanked them for caring about her sister.

Then she said to Bramall, "Back to the hotel."

Mackenzie felt weird, she said, leaving her sister where she was, but Rose would have it no other way. She liked it there, she said, and she had everything she needed. She refused to leave, categorically, even for one night, even to see a doctor. She refused even to consider going to the hospital, or the Veterans Administration, or looking at a clinic, or a rehab center, or living in Lake Forest, Illinois.

"Give her time," Bramall said.

They made the turn at the old Mule Crossing post office, and drove back to Laramie on the two-lane. They ate in town, and drove back out to the hotel, where Bramall parked and said good night. Reacher stayed out in the lot again. The night sky was still there. Still huge and black and dusted with millions of bright stars. Microscopically changed, he supposed, since the night before. But not because of his tiny dramas. It was completely indifferent.

Mackenzie came out and sat down on the bench.

He sat down beside her.

She said, "She's only halfway addicted."

He said, "I had a brother. Not a twin, but we were close growing up. Now I'm asking myself, if this was him, what would I want from people? Something polite, or something uncomfortable? I'm not making a point here. I really don't know. Help me out."

"I want the truth," she said.

"She looked a lot more than halfway addicted to me."

"I meant her reasons. She's in pain. Partly she needs it. She's not doing it just for fun."

"What's with the aluminum foil?"

"The infection. She scrounges up antibiotics if she can, and grinds them down, and mixes them with antiseptic salve from the first-aid aisle. She spreads it on the foil like butter. If she can spare one, she mixes in an oxycodone pill."

"Not the life she expected."

"You knew last night. When you asked how we felt about being pretty."

"It was the only thing that fit."

"She's doing OK, I think."

"Me, too."

"I even liked the house, in a way. I was surprised. For some reason I thought it would be dark inside."

"Me, too," he said again.

"Now tell me what happens next."

"I wish I knew."

"Seriously," she said. "I need to figure out how to handle this."

"She's doing OK because she gets high every day. You could give her money, I suppose, and most likely she would continue to do OK, as long as this new guy Stackley keeps on showing up on time, and as long as the Boy Detective doesn't plug the last leak and put everyone out of business."

"Which could happen."

"Nothing lasts forever," Reacher said. "Her situation out there is not as secure as she thinks it is."

"Even if it was, I couldn't leave her there."

"How are you going to move her out?"

"That's what I'm asking. I'm open to ideas."

Reacher said, "Is she getting no treatment at all?"

"At the beginning she was in the hospital a whole year. She ran out of patience. She hasn't seen anyone since. She won't. She refuses to."

"Instead she lives quietly and self-medicates. She does it well enough we both just agreed she's doing OK. We should respect that. The only way to get her out of there is promise her the exact same thing someplace else. Or even better. As many pills and patches as she wants. You would have to find the right kind of doctor. You would have to find her a quiet place to live. You would have to promise her no hassle. And you would have to mean it. Nothing for a year at least. Which is OK. This kind of thing is a very long game."

"She doesn't like people to see her."

"Then she's better off here than Illinois."

"They don't have the right kind of doctors here."

"How big is your yard?"

"I think six acres."

"You could build her a cabin. With a high fence. You could throw her prescriptions over. Leave her alone for a year. See what happens."

"So the only way to help her is to be a better pusher."

"The Boy Detective said we shouldn't underestimate the appeal of an opiate high. I'm sure she's real pleased to see you, but you should assume getting what she needs right now feels more important to her."

"That's tough to accept. Not about me. That she's so far gone."

"She needs you on her side right now. Proving that is your job one. Don't disapprove of her. What choice does she have? Just bite your lip and shovel pills down her throat. Don't forget she's tough underneath. She's a combat veteran. Sooner or later she'll realize she needs to shape up or ship out, and then she'll want to talk. To you especially, because you were the one who treated her right. That's when you can help her."

"I hope I can."

"There are books about it. You can spend the first year reading."

"Did you take classes?"

"Not enough curriculum time," Reacher said. "In the MPs it was all rubber hoses and nightsticks. But the medics had good people. Psychiatrists in uniform. The weirdest thing you ever saw. Always some inflated rank. I knew a couple. They would tell you a bunch of things."

"Like what?"

"They would tell you to figure out what's upsetting her deep down."

"That's obvious, surely."

"But they're shrinks, and they're in the army. They would say a person can have two things wrong at once. They would say they know what infantry officers are like. They would want more detail on the incident with the roadside bomb."

"Why?"

"Specifically they would want to know if there were other American casualties. If so, they would assume Rose is taking it hard. She was an infantry officer. She got her people killed. The facts don't count. She could have been already wounded and unconscious before anything else even happened. Doesn't matter. They're her people. It's her fault. That's how infantry officers think. Small words, but they mean a lot to those guys. The top boy at West Point said she led her soldiers well. That's the hall of fame right there. You could put that on your tombstone. She led her soldiers well. An infantry officer couldn't hear finer words than those. Because it's hard to do. Ultimately it works because you make an unspoken promise not to get them killed. It becomes a thing in your head."

Mackenzie said, "She won't talk about it."

Reacher said, "The shrinks would also want to know the status of the mission. Was it a routine kind of thing ordered from above? Or was there an element of initiative involved? In which case, they would assume she was taking it even harder. She led her soldiers into harm's way, literally."

"They're shrinks. You said so yourself. They overcomplicate things. If you hear hoof beats, you look for horses, not zebras. Rose is upset deep down because someone stuck her face in a blender and smeared it with dog shit."

Reacher said nothing.

Mackenzie said, "What?"

"I'm sure that's most of it. How could it not be?"

"But?"

"I think like a cop. I can't help it. Her final rank was major. The guy at West Point told me on her last tour she was doing a pretty big job. Which for a major means desk time and briefings. She had limited opportunities to get out and about. Why would she choose to go look at the side of a road outside a small town? She wouldn't. She was bored with that kind of stuff four tours ago. She went because her command presence was required. She had some kind of operation running. She had captains below her, and lieutenants below them, all covering their own ass, so we can be certain the protective detail around her was thick on the ground. We can be certain lots of people were involved. Was she the only one hurt? Unlikely, but we don't know for sure. The files are sealed. Which means most likely her operation was a failure. Perhaps with multiple U.S. casualties. So her face may not be all of it."

Mackenzie said, "I don't know if you're trying to cheer me up, or bring me down."

"It's all bad," Reacher said. "Whichever way around. Let's not be Pollyanna. But she had a boyfriend. Sy Porterfield. There were two dents in the bed. That says something about how she sees herself. It's a glimmer of what might be possible."

"She won't talk about him. I told her about the comb you found, and she didn't deny it. She said it was safer I didn't know. Whatever that means."

"She thought I was an investigator come to ask questions about him."

"No one believes the bear story."

"Which could be an additional traumatizing factor. She really doesn't know what happened to her boyfriend. She really isn't sure which would be worse, the bear or not. The shrinks would throw a party. They would tell you it's a whole big mixture of things."

"In other words it could be worse than just her face."

"That would be a glass half empty type of interpretation. But it's why I asked if you wanted polite or uncomfortable."

"I said truth. You're speculating."

"Agreed," Reacher said. "And I sincerely hope I'm wrong about all of it."

She was quiet a beat.

Then she said, "You're a kind man."

"Not a word that gets used often."

"Thank you for being here."

"My pleasure," he said, and it was. It was a concrete bench in a blacktop lot, but a yard above the ground it was spectacular. The stars were better than he had ever seen. The air was cool and soft and hummed with silence. Beside him on the bench was a woman who looked like the back of a shiny magazine. He figured she would feel firm and lithe and cool to the touch, except maybe the small of her back, which might be damp.

She asked him, "Do you remember what I said about my husband?"

"You said he's a nice man and you're a good match."

"You have a very precise memory."

"It was yesterday."

"I should have told you he keeps a mistress and ignores me."

Reacher smiled.

He said, "Good night, Mrs. Mackenzie."

She left him there, the same as the night before, alone in the dark, on the concrete bench, looking at the stars.

At that moment a mile away, Stackley clicked off a phone call and parked his beat-up old pick-up truck in a lot behind an out-of-business retail enterprise three blocks from the center of town. Earlier in his life he had favored expensive haircuts, and one time when waiting in the salon he had read a magazine that said success in business depended entirely on ruthless control of costs. Thus wherever possible he slept in his truck. Hence the camper shell. A motel would take what he made on two pills. Why give it away?

The old gal across the Snowy Range had bought a box of fentanyl patches, but he had given her one he had already opened, an hour before, very carefully, so he could skim out a patch all his own, for his pocket, for later. The old gal would never notice. If she did, she would assume she was too stoned to count right. A natural reaction. Addicts learned to blame themselves. The same the world over.

He took scissors from his glove box, and he cut a quarter-inch strip off the patch, and he slipped it under his tongue. Sublingual, it was called. Another magazine in the same salon said it was the best method of all.

Stackley couldn't argue.

* * *

At that moment sixty miles away, in the low hills west of town, Rose Sanderson was putting herself to bed. She had pulled down her hood, and taken off her silver track suit top. Under it was a T-shirt, which she took off, and a bra, likewise. She peeled the foil off her face. She used her toothbrush handle to scrape excess ointment off her skin. She buttered it back on the foil. With luck she might get one more day out of it.

She ran her sink full of cool water. She took a breath, and held her face under the surface. Her record was four minutes. She came up and shook her head. Her hair had grown back in. She had cut it the week before West Point. She had to get a hat on. There were regulations. She had kept it short for thirteen years. Now it was back. With coarse threads of gray. Like barbed wire in a hay bale.

The least of her problems.

She took scissors from her cabinet, and she cut a quarter-inch strip off her patch, and she stuck it behind her bottom lip. A maintenance dose. It would keep her asleep all night. It would keep her warm, and gentle, and relaxed, and at peace, and cradled, and happy.

At that moment three hundred miles away, in Rapid City, South Dakota, Gloria Nakamura was sitting in her car, watching Arthur Scorpio's back door. Once again it was showing a rim of light. It was propped open an inch. Another warm night. He had been in there more than two hours. She had been working on her list of what might make a room hot enough for extra ventilation. Electronic equipment, maybe. She knew a guy with a home cinema. He had a closet full of black boxes, that gave out a penetrating kind of heat. It was thin and fierce and smelled faintly of grease and silicon. The guy had a fan in there, whirring all the time.

Her cell phone rang.

Her friend in Computer Crimes.

Who said, "Give me a yes or no answer. Do we assume it was Scorpio who got the text message about the new Billy?"

She said, "We couldn't take it to court."

"That wasn't a yes or no answer."

"Yes, we can assume it was Scorpio."

"The same signal just got a voicemail from a tower in Laramie, Wyoming. From someone by the name of Stackley. He called Scorpio Mr. Scorpio. He said all was well, but there were stories about two men and a woman poking around, asking questions. One of the men was a very big guy and they were in a black Toyota."

Reacher, she thought.

Her friend said, "Then Scorpio called back and left a voicemail in return. He told this guy Stackley the same thing he told Billy. He wants the big guy out of the picture. He was ordering a homicide again."

"Wait," Nakamura said.

Scorpio's door was opening. He stepped out to the alley and turned back and locked up. Then he headed for his car.

"I'm going to follow him," she said.

"Waste of gas," her friend said.

She clicked off and started her motor.

Scorpio went home.

He went home every time.

At that moment six hundred miles away, in a small town named Sullivan, in the Oklahoma panhandle, Billy ran a red light. He was in a six-hundred-dollar Ford Ranger pick-up truck, more than twenty years old. He was out to get a second six-pack. He was mildly buzzed from the first. His pal from Montana was back at the motel, waiting in the room. The next day in the afternoon they were due to meet a guy who had connections in Amarillo, Texas. The employment situation was looking good.

The light he ran had a cop parked on it. The guy lit up his roof bar and yelped his siren once. Billy froze and kept on rolling. Dumb. He had nothing to hide. The buzz, maybe, but hey, this was the panhandle. A couple of beers was probably a minimum requirement to get behind the wheel. Apart from that he was respectable. He couldn't run anyway. Not in a six-hundred-dollar piece of shit.

He hit the brake and pulled in at the curb.

Like all humans the cop was prey to small subliminal emotions. Billy's failure to stop right away kind of pissed him off. He found it cocky and disrespectful. Normally he might just have pulled alongside and dropped his far window and told the guy to take it easy. But now he felt a hot bite of annoyance, and it kind of puffed him up and set his jaw, and he found himself launching into the whole big performance.

He pulled up behind the pick-up, and left his lights flashing. He put on his hat. He counted to twenty and got out of the car. He unlatched his holster and put his hand on his gun. He walked forward slowly, and stopped level with the old Ford's load bed, and he called out loud and clear, "Sir, please step out of the vehicle."

The door opened.

Billy got out.

"I'm sorry, sir," he said. "I guess I was daydreaming. I guess it was a good thing no one else was around."

The cop was pretty sure the air coming off the guy smelled like beer.

He said, "License."

Billy dug in his pocket and handed it over.

The cop said, "Sir, please wait there."

He walked back to his car, as slowly as he could. He got in. He had a computer terminal on a swan neck, bolted to the tunnel near the shifter. Courtesy of the last new mayor. All kinds of budget promises.

He typed in Billy's details.

Up came a code from the western division of the federal DEA.

He got out of the car again. He walked back to Billy, as slowly as he could, and when he got there he spun him around, and banged his head on the old Ford's roof, and cuffed his hands behind his back.

Chapter 35

They met in the lobby at eight in the morning. After the diner they drove to the grocery store, where they bought stuff for Rose. Food, mostly, some of it wholesome, some of it not, but also soap, and a pair of pink socks, and a new comb with wide-spaced teeth, and a paperback book. The kind of little thing that got left out, when a household budget came under pressure.

They bought two of every type of antiseptic cream.

Bramall's phone rang in the checkout line. He looked at the screen and said, "It's Special Agent Noble, from the DEA." He answered and listened, and made appreciative but noncommittal noises. At one point he left a split second gap, as if he should be saying something, but wasn't. As if he was choosing not to. One federal guy playing chess with another. Reacher knew the signs.

Bramall clicked off and said, "Billy was arrested last night in a small town in Oklahoma. Noble questioned him by phone. So far he's denying everything. Including he claims he doesn't know anyone named Rose Sanderson, or where she's located."

"Yesterday's news," Mackenzie said. "We don't need Billy anymore."

* * *

The drive back to Rose's place was a typical Wyoming time warp journey. In their minds they didn't have far to go. It was a purely local trip. Mule Crossing was just down the road, and Rose lived just west of the turn. But in reality it took two whole hours to get there. The long, long two-lane, and then the dirt road, slower than they wanted through the infinite space, and then the rutted four-mile driveway. The sky was the color of steel. Not a threat, but a reminder. Winter was on its way.

The three cowboys met them where the track came out of the woods in the final clearing. They were doing nothing. Just waiting and watching, strung out in a ragged line thirty yards short of the house. Like a defensive perimeter. *We got kind of protective.* Bramall slowed down, in a no-threat kind of way, and eased around to where he had parked before. Reacher unloaded the groceries and stacked them on the porch. Mackenzie carried them into the house. She closed the door behind her.

The clearing went quiet.

Reacher saw Bramall at the edge of the ravine. A small neat man, in a dark suit, with a collar and a tie. He should have looked out of place in the wilderness. But he didn't. He looked perfectly at home. He was that kind of guy. He was thinking about something. Reacher could see it in his face. A problem. A struggle. Some kind of an ethical dilemma.

Reacher was pretty sure what it was.

Billy.

Not yesterday's news.

Tomorrow's news.

Reacher walked over to where Bramall was standing.

He said, "I know," in what he hoped was a sympathetic way.

"You know what?" Bramall said back.

"You feel bad you didn't tell the Boy Detective we found Rose without Billy's help."

"Would you have?"

"No," Reacher said. "Too much information. What happened in Oklahoma?"

"He ran a red light. The system kicked out his name and his face. Noble called him and tried to get some answers out of him. The question is why he did that. It could have been purely a courtesy on our behalf, because he was sympathetic to Mrs. Mackenzie's situation. She asked him to let her know, after all. Maybe he was just going through the motions for her. Or maybe not. Maybe he was getting real. Maybe he figured since he got handed Billy on a plate anyway, he might as well write up a comprehensive report. It would scratch an itch, after all. He doesn't like the ghost network. In which case, if he knew where Rose was, the book says his first logical move should be question her as a witness, or arrest her for buying illegal narcotics, or both. This is not the time for me to risk either outcome. Not right now. For many reasons. One of which is my client's stated preference to keep her sister out of the system. So I didn't tell him. And yes, I feel a little bad about it. I prefer not to conceal things from people like him."

"Was your contract extended?"

"For the duration of the current crisis."

"How long will that be?"

Bramall glanced up at the house.

He said, "I'm not an expert."

"How long will Billy hold out?"

"If Noble gets real?"

"Even if he doesn't, I guess. Billy could say something stupid at any time. Some little slip. The Boy Detective might prick up his ears. There's a big prize, don't forget. Folks who can tell the difference say what they're getting out here is the real deal. Made in America. Straight out the factory door. Whole shipments of it, in the proper boxes. Which the Boy Detective thinks is impossible. He'll take it personally. He'll hunt it down. He'll plug the last leak. This is not the time to risk cold turkey either. I'm sure your client's other stated preference is to keep her sister out of the locked ward in the hospital."

Bramall glanced up at the house again.

He said, "I assume the kind of decisions they're making can't be made fast."

"Normally I guess not," Reacher said. "But this time they can't be made slow, either."

"How long have we got?"

"My instinct would be get out of here within two or three days."

"Until then we should say nothing to Noble."

"Easy for me," Reacher said. "But you have a license from the state of Illinois."

"Tell me about it. While simultaneously having credible evidence a man named Arthur Scorpio, in Rapid City, South Dakota, which is presumably comfortably inside the western division, is currently coordinating a network invisible to the DEA, but that extends at least into Wyoming and Montana, and that uses some kind of last-surviving loophole source, like El Dorado, the discovery of which would be hailed as a major triumph and the capstone of an outstanding regional success story. I could hand it over on a plate. In fact I have a professional obligation to do exactly that. If and when I believe a crime has been or is about to be committed. And on top of all that I have obvious ethical obligations. I should tell Noble everything I know."

"But not yet," Reacher said.

"Because the illegal supply must be allowed to continue. At least until my client arranges an alternative semi-legal supply somewhere else."

"Relax," Reacher said. "You're retired."

"Second career."

"Fewer rules than the first."

"But more rules than you."

"I have rules," Reacher said. "I have plenty of rules. One of which says a wounded veteran gets the benefit of the doubt. But another of which says always be gone before the government arrives. So I agree. We need to thread the needle."

* * *

The house stayed quiet and the door stayed closed. Reacher borrowed Bramall's phone, and carried it to the head of the ravine, where it could soak up maximum signal.

He dialed the number he remembered.

The same woman answered.

"West Point," she said. "Superintendent's office. How may I help you?"

"This is Reacher," he said.

"Hello, major."

"I need to speak with General Simpson."

"Wait one, major."

The supe came on and said, "Developments?"

"We found her," Reacher said.

"Condition?"

"We have concerns," Reacher said. "The Purple Heart was a severe facial wound. She has dependency issues with the painkillers we gave her in the hospital. She has no visible means of support."

"Can I help?"

"At this point only with information. I need to know which boxes she checks. In terms of her mental state. Might help us with what happens next."

"What information?"

"It was a roadside IED. I want to know more about it. Specifically why she was there, and who else was hurt or killed."

"I'll try."

"And I want to know more about Porterfield. She said it's safer if we don't. I'm not sure what that means. Who was this guy? All we know is fourteen years ago he was a brand new butter-bar lieutenant who didn't make the first cut. What part of that twelve years later got him so much attention?"

"Sanderson must know."

"I can't push for an answer. The emotional situation here is delicate."

"Did you give back the ring?"

"She asked for a layaway. Until happier times ahead."

"Will they come?"

"Maybe," Reacher said. "The first part will be hardest."

He gave the phone back to Bramall. Then they waited, ending up in the same places as the day before, Reacher on the porch step, Bramall on a rock at the edge of the ravine. The cowboys were all grouped together in the mouth of the track, standing around, as if they were expecting someone to show up, sometime soon.

Stackley was a man who believed data and information should be put to work at once. It was rule one in the modern business environment. Or maybe rule two, after ruthless control of costs. Different magazines didn't always agree. He played it safe by working both ends. Every morning, right there in his truck, before he got up, he read his overnight texts and played his voicemails. Therefore right away that day he knew the big guy was supposed to exit the picture. He spent his early calls working out how to do it. He was a man who believed delegation was the hallmark of a successful executive. It was rule one in the modern environment. Or two, or three. Or whatever. But it was definitely up there.

By the time he turned at Mule Crossing, Stackley had decided on his strategy. By the time he passed what he had learned was his predecessor Billy's place, he had decided on the bait. By the time he passed what he had learned used to be a guy named Porterfield's place, he had decided on exactly where to offer it.

He drove on, many miles, and turned in on the next-but-one track on the right, ahead of what he knew from the morning before was a slow four miles over roots and rocks. Not good for his truck. But he was a man who believed productivity depended on the maximum use of all fixed assets. It was the number one rule in the new environment.

* * *

Behind him Reacher heard the front door open, and he stood up and turned in time to see Mackenzie step out of the house. In the shadows behind her was a small vague figure. A silvery color. Mackenzie closed the door on it and came down the path. She glanced at the cowboys, still all the way over at the mouth of the track. She headed for Bramall, and Reacher followed. She chose a rock and sat down on it. Reacher chose one six feet away. Bramall used the one he had used before. They looked like three castaways on a rocky shore, making a plan. The endless plain behind them looked as wide as an ocean.

Mackenzie said, "We're making progress, I think. More than I thought we would so soon. That is, if in fact she means what she's saying. Sometimes I think she's agreeing to things far too easily. Because they're about the future. She knows nothing will change today. That seems to be the limit of her horizon. But every day becomes today when you get there. She needs to take this seriously. She needs to understand the day will come when I have to move her."

"When will that be?" Bramall asked.

"New accommodations and the right kind of doctor are the essential components. We can get those searches started immediately, while we're still waiting here. As soon as tomorrow, if we want. By the way, I decided to move in. I think we all should. There are empty houses here. The drive back and forth to the hotel is ridiculous."

Bramall said, "Move in?"

"More efficient, don't you think? If I'm close by all the time, I can look after her all the time. Maybe in the end we might get this done faster."

Bramall said, "We don't know who owns this place."

"Someone who hasn't shown up for three years. Why would they show up now? We won't be here very long."

Bramall said, "How long, do you think?"

"Depends entirely on the accommodations and the doctor."

"Best guess?"

"Mentally I'm allowing a month," she said. "Worst case two."

Up at the head of the driveway there was engine noise and tire scrub and the cowboys stood back. Reacher saw a beat-up old pick-up truck drive out of the woods. It had a plastic camper shell in the bed. He had seen it before. On the dirt road. Driving by, with a guy at the wheel, late thirties maybe, looking straight ahead, paying no attention.

Mackenzie turned to see.

"This must be Stackley," she said. "Rose hoped he would come by again today."

Chapter 36

Stackley saw the cowboys step back. He recognized them from the day before. The same three guys. Partly they were moving to get out of his way, and partly to form up like a welcoming committee. Or like a guard of honor. Deep down Stackley enjoyed dealing dope. Customers were so grateful and enthusiastic. Not like some jobs he had worked.

Then beyond the cowboys he saw the dusty black Toyota. Right there. The actual truck he had called Scorpio about. He had described it, parked on the shoulder of the dirt road, like a cop, with the two men and the woman in it, who folks said had been asking questions. One of the men was big.

Stackley had called it in, and had gotten his reply.

He looked at the house. All quiet. The door was closed.

He looked right, at the far tree line.

Nothing there.

He looked left, at the rocks near the edge of the ravine.

Three people sitting on them.

An old man in a suit.

A pretty woman.

And a very big guy.

Stackley stopped his truck in the mouth of the driveway. He paused a second, and then shut it down. He got out and led the eager cowboys back to the camper door. Where he did something he never did. He let them see inside. He pulled back his blanket a little too far, as if carelessly, and he exposed the boxes, dozens of them, most still shrink-wrapped, some opened but still mostly full, all white and clean and printed with American writing. Behind his shoulder he felt the hum of desire. Which was good. He needed his new pals to feel what he had to offer.

He huddled them close, and he told them what they could do for him, and what he could do for them. Delegation. Rule one in the modern environment. Especially against a guy so big.

Reacher saw them cluster at the back of the truck. They all looked inside. Inspecting the merchandise, maybe. They seemed happy with the quality, or the quantity, or both. They reminded Reacher of his mother, a lifetime ago, on a foreign base somewhere, huddling on the curb with the other army wives, when the fish truck came to call. Then Stackley moved in close, and started on a big discussion. The price, maybe. Important to them all, in different ways.

Mackenzie said, "Rose isn't coming out of the house. I guess her friends are buying for her. Maybe they always do. Which would mean Billy never saw her. He couldn't have helped us anyway."

Reacher said, "We need to talk about Billy."

"Why?"

"He's in the system now. The Boy Detective has already talked to him once."

"He's denying everything."

"Will he forever?"

"I assume you guys were kidding about the rubber hoses and the nightsticks."

"He'll take a deal. Or he'll cough it up by accident. He doesn't know which pieces they're missing. Sooner or later he'll say the wrong thing. It would be prudent to assume the clock is already ticking. We might want to revisit the timescale for getting out of here. No point still being around when the supply cuts off. Definitely no point still being around when the Feds show up. I know how hard this is for both of you, but those kind of problems would make it much worse."

"You don't think a month is possible?"

Reacher saw money change hands, behind the truck at the mouth of the driveway.

He said, "I think we should aim for a little faster."

He saw small white boxes change hands in the other direction.

"How much faster?" Mackenzie asked.

"I told Mr. Bramall my instinct would be get out of here within two or three days."

"Impossible."

"How fast can you do it?"

The truck started up and turned around, and headed back down the driveway. The cowboys carried the small white boxes toward the house. They stacked half of them on the porch, outside the front door, and they took the rest away with them, down a path that curved through the trees, and out of sight.

"It's about finding the right doctor," Mackenzie said. "She can't live without this stuff."

"Ask your neighbors back home."

"They go to rehab. We need a pusher."

"We're sitting ducks here," Reacher said. "Some kind of trouble is coming."

Mackenzie spent another hour with her sister, and then she came out and said she was ready to go check out of the hotel. Back in four hours, she had promised. With her bags. Ready to stay as long as it took. Bramall shrugged, and finally agreed to do the same. Outside his comfort zone, but hey, second career. Reacher said he was already checked out. He never paid for more than a night at a time. His tooth-brush was in his pocket. He had no other luggage. All in all he would prefer to stay in the peace and quiet, and see them later. Mackenzie went back in to tell her sister the updated arrangement, and then she and Bramall drove away.

Reacher sat on the porch step. Already his accustomed spot. Ahead of him the ravine widened and fell away. Beyond it the horizon was dusty orange, with ghostly blue mountains behind it. The air was clear and silent. He watched birds of prey riding thermals, and condensation trails eight miles up, and a chipmunk on a rock ten feet away.

Then behind him the front door opened.

The chipmunk disappeared.

The shared voice said, "Major Reacher?"

He stood up and turned around. She was in the doorway, in her silver track suit top. The hood was pulled forward. She was peering out from deep inside. Shadowy scars, and aluminum foil. Steady eyes.

She said, "I would like to continue yesterday's conversation."

"Which part?"

"When I thought you were here on business."

"I'm not."

"I accept that. All I want is your opinion. You might know things I don't."

"Come sit down here," he said. "It's a beautiful day."

She paused a beat, and then stepped out and crossed the porch. She was lithe and petite and moved like an athlete. Which she was. The infantry was an athletic discipline. She sat on the same step as Reacher, maybe a yard apart. She smelled of soap, and something astringent. The stuff on her face, he figured. Under the foil. Sideways on all he could see was the hood, pulled forward like a tunnel.

The chipmunk came out again.

She said, "I told you I had a friend whose case is still open."

"Sy Porterfield," he said.

"You are here on business."

"No, but I picked things up along the way."

"How much do you know about him?"

"Very little," Reacher said. "Except he was your friend for a spell, and a rich Ivy Leaguer, and a Marine, and wounded, and he liked authenticity so much he would rather catch drips in a bucket than replace his leaky roof."

"That's a fair summary."

"Also he had three sealed files in the Pentagon."

"I can't talk about those."

"Then how can I give an opinion?"

"In theory," she said. "Why would an investigation just die away?"

"All kinds of reasons. Maybe it wasn't what they hoped it was. Maybe it dead-ended. Maybe it was too hard all along. I would need to know more."

"I can't tell you."

"Then let me make an educated guess. Maybe it fell between two stools. The Pentagon seems to have the original file. Let's say two years ago Porterfield had something on his mind. Why would he call the Pentagon? That was not a natural reflex. Twelve years before he had been a combat lieutenant in the Marines. The Pentagon was never a part of his life. I bet he never even saw the place. I bet he didn't have the phone number. But he found it out and dropped a dime. Which means the thing on his mind must have had some kind of high-level military aspect. Then the Pentagon copied in the DEA, which means it must also have had some kind of high-level narcotics aspect. Maybe there was miscommunication. Maybe the Pentagon thought the DEA was dealing with it, and the DEA thought the Pentagon was dealing with it. So in the end no one dealt with it."

"I can't talk about the details."

"We know his house was broken into after he died."

"Yes, I saw that. I went back a few times, just to walk around."

"Looked like an old-fashioned black-bag job to me."

"I agree it was neat."

"You know who it was."

"I can't talk about it."
"You know what was taken."
"Yes."
"Will you answer one question?"
"Depends what it is."
"Just a yes or no answer. That's all I need. No details, no background. Nothing more than you want to say."
"Promise?"
"Just a yes or no. To put my mind at rest about something."
"About what?"
"Do you know how Porterfield died?"
"Yes," she said. "I was there."

Special Agent Kirk Noble's division was based in Denver, Colorado. His office was a bland beige space temporarily brightened up by the gold from the shoebox he had taken from Billy's house in Wyoming. It was all laid out on his desk, all in an orderly fashion. All the gold trinkets. The crosses on the chains, the earrings, the bracelets, the charms, the chokers, the fashion rings, the wedding rings, the class rings. He had to fill out an inventory form. Description and value.

Some of it was junk. Some of it was pressed out of thin alloys no jeweler would have recognized. Twenty cents, literally, for some of the items. Others were merely mediocre. Seven bucks by weight for this, nine if you were lucky for that. Other items were better. There was an eighteen-carat wedding band, thick and heavy. A handsome piece. Fifty bucks in a pawn shop, easy. Same for a pair of earrings. Eighteen carat, solid and heavy. Two of them. Maybe sixty bucks together.

When he was finished he looked at his list. The right-hand column. The values. They made no sense. They were completely random. From practically zero all the way to a decent wad of cash. Stopping, crucially, at every price point along the way. Two bucks, three bucks, four bucks, all the way to more than sixty. Which was not how the business worked. It was not like a boutique delicatessen, where you bought a pinch of this and a twist of that. You bought a ten-dollar bag of brown powder for ten dollars. Or you didn't. Or you bought two for twenty dollars. Or three for thirty. What an economist would have called stair-step pricing.

Whereas Billy's pricing was notably granular. As if he was selling five-dollar bags, and six-dollar bags, and thirteen-dollar bags, and seventeen-dollar, and nine-dollar. Full service. Whatever the customer wanted. Filled there and then, and weighed on a scale.

Highly unlikely.

Therefore perhaps he wasn't selling bags of powder at all. Perhaps his product came in bulk. Perhaps for retail purposes the large quantities could be broken down, all the way to individual items if necessary, for folks with limited resources. Or cut with scissors into halves and quarters, for the truly broke.

Just like the old days.

Impossible.

He picked up his desk phone and called down to the jail.

He said, "I'm expecting a transfer from Oklahoma. Name of Billy something."

The voice on the phone said, "We just processed him in."

"Take him straight to an interview room. Tell him I have questions. I'll come down in a couple hours. Let him sweat till then."

Nothing more than you want to say, Reacher had promised, and it turned out Rose Sanderson wanted to say nothing more. Not on the subject of Porterfield, at least. She just nodded to herself, inside her hood, as if the matter was settled.

Then she said, "My sister told me you asked how it felt to be pretty."

"Yes," he said.

"You knew about me by then."

"It made sense."

"I'm sure she gave a conflicted answer. She's still pretty. Deep down pretty people know other people feel they're getting something for nothing. They have to be aw-shucks about it. They have to say it makes them feel shallow. But now I can tell you. It makes them feel great. It's like bringing a gun to a knife fight. Sometimes I would dial it up and just mow them down, one by one, bam, bam, bam. It's a superpower. Like clicking the phasers from stun to kill. There's no point denying it. It's a significant evolutionary advantage. Like being as big as you are."

"We should have children," he said.

He heard a click of foil inside the hood. A smile, he hoped.

She said, "Those days are over."

"Apparently Porterfield didn't agree."

"We were friends, that's all."

"There were two dents in the bed."

"How do you know?"

"The guy who fixed his roof told a guy who told a guy who told us in a bar."

"The roofer was looking at my bed?"

"Your bed? Sounds like you agree with him."

She said, "Sy was different."

He said, "What would it take to fix the infection?"

"A long course of IV antibiotics. It's a common thing. Most wounds get infected. The bacteria wall themselves off. It's hard to get rid of."

"And you don't want to go to the hospital."

"I didn't like it. I was an embarrassment. I was every soldier's worst fear. A disfiguring wound. The glamour was with the arms and legs. All that scientific technology. Titanium and carbon fiber. Some of those legs cost a million bucks. They looked better than new. Guys would wear shorts to show them off. Not me. I would have been a PR disaster."

"You can get IVs at home," Reacher said. "With a certain kind of doctor. Your sister will find one. The kind who will also advocate a very long slow glide path, when it comes to dependency issues. The kind who might want to maintain your current habit for at least another year, while you settle in."

"I don't believe her."

"That she wants to?"

"That she can."

"She has money. This is the civilian healthcare system we're talking about here. She can get what she wants."

"People will see me. It's a suburb."

"It's Lake Forest, Illinois. You could wear a bag on your head. They'll think it's performance art. A year from now you'll have your own show."

"I like it here better."

"Because of what Stackley brings. Before that what Billy brought. Which is a freak aberration. That trade was closed down. You're on the end of the very last leak. They're hunting for it right now. They have Billy in a cell. They're two steps away from cutting you off. Think about it tactically. We need immediate action."

She didn't reply. She just breathed a bit harder, and stiffened. He felt it from a yard away. A low vibration, through the wood of the step.

She said, "I'm going inside now."

He said, "I'm sorry I upset you."

"I'll be fine ten minutes from now."

She stood up, and stepped up on the porch, and then he heard her turn around again and wait. He looked up at her. She looked back at him from deep inside the hood. In the movies her eyes would have lit up red.

She said, "This is the problem. It will need to be seamless. Unfortunately I find I need this stuff. Like right now the most important thing in the world to me is a new fentanyl patch. Right now that's worth a hundred rings or a dozen sisters. But fortunately I have a new fentanyl patch. I already decided to lick it. I already made that choice. Does all that upset you?"

"Yes," Reacher said. "A little bit."

"Me, too," she said.

He waited ten minutes for the hit to click in, but she didn't come out again. So he took a walk, around the tree line, until he saw the cowboys coming along their path toward him. The three guys, as always with the one in the lizard skin boots a step in front. They said hello to Reacher in a way that made him feel they were surprised to see him. He told them he had stayed behind.

The guy in the boots said, "The others aren't here?"

"For a couple more hours," Reacher said.

"Were you talking to Rose?"

"I was," Reacher said. "As a matter of fact."

"How's she doing?"

"She said she was there when Porterfield died."

"I believe that's true."

"Where were you?"

"We were in Colorado. Spring was late down there. We got work hauling hay."

"What did she say about it when you got back?"

"She never talks about things like that."

Reacher said nothing. The three guys looked at one another, a little hesitant, a little momentous, as if they had just gotten a weird idea.

The guy in the boots said, "We could show you the place where he was found, if you want."

"Is it near here?" Reacher said.

"About an hour on foot. Mostly uphill."

"Is it interesting?"

"The walk is interesting. As far as the argument goes. You get to judge what kind of person could have carried a body that far."

"You said anyone could have."

"I said anyone would have. There's a difference. The people who could have are a subset of the population."

"OK," Reacher said. "Show me."

They crossed the clearing near the corner of the house, and headed toward another gap in the trees, but first the guy in the boots detoured to the crew-cab, and came back with a rifle. He said right or wrong, remember why they were going. It was bear country.

Chapter 37

The path rose through the woods, which thinned a little as the slope got steeper. Some trunks were scored by elk antlers. There were moose prints on the ground. No sign of bear. Not yet. Which Reacher was happy about. The guy's rifle was an ancient M14 Garand. A U.S. soldier's main squeeze sixty years before. A clumsy weapon. But competent. Except it was chambered for the NATO round. Which was a slim little thing compared to a bear. Maybe it was all the guy had left. Maybe he had traded the rest away, to pay for something that had suddenly gotten expensive.

Better than nothing, Reacher thought.

They walked on. The air felt thin. Reacher felt he was breathing hard. Not the three cowboys. They looked normal. They were used to it. At sea level they would be dizzy with excess oxygen. Maybe better than licking a patch. The hike itself was no big deal. Roots and rocks and gravel, the same as the tracks they had been driving, but narrower. The gradient was modest. Occasionally there were big steps up. Carrying a heavy weight would have been slow and awkward, but possible. For a subset of the population. Like the guy had said.

Five minutes later they came out on an open area where a young tree had been pushed down by a moose. There were animal tracks in and out, some of them large.

The guy with the rifle said, "It was a place like this."

"Like this?" Reacher said. "Or this place?"

"It's further on. But you get the picture. In case you want to turn back now."

Reacher looked left and right and onward, into the trees. He wasn't sure what he expected to see. He felt a bear was unlikely. What were the odds?

"I'm OK," he said. "Let's keep going."

They did. The woods changed around them as they walked. The clearings stopped coming, because the trees themselves thinned out, to the point where the whole vista became a kind of low-density mixed-up half-woods, half-clearing type of landscape. Low scrub on the ground. Access lanes were clear and straight. Lines of sight were long. It was good predator country.

The guy with the rifle said, "Still OK?"

Reacher looked all around. The back part of his brain was stirring. It was telling him that kind of terrain was best gotten out of, and quickly. Some kind of a primitive instinct. The front part was thinking about bears. Unlikely, it was telling him. But a reality at some low level of probability. A factor. Worth taking into account. Worth preparing for.

In his mind he heard General Simpson's voice, on the phone from West Point: *Off post she would have been armed at all times.*

He looked all around again.

There were no bears.

Not there.

He said, "Let's go back."

The guy said, "Why?"

Because I want to get back in the trees, he thought.

Out loud he said, "I get the picture now."

And he felt he did. Stackley was the new Billy. Inheritor of the whole local empire. Including the periodic voicemail instructions.

Stackley must have gotten a new one. Shoot the Incredible Hulk from behind a tree. All over again. Or whichever cartoon character he was by then. Message received and understood. Except Stackley hadn't tried to execute the mission himself. He had brought in mercenary services from the outside. During the big discussion behind the camper shell. The pitch, the offer, the bait, the acceptance. Maybe handshakes.

He knew because of the weapon. And culture, and habit, and plain common sense. How likely was it a Wyoming cowboy would venture into legitimate bear territory without a rifle capable of shooting a bear? It was like getting dressed in the morning. Therefore it became a logical sequence. The wrong gun meant there were no bears, which meant they were not close to where Porterfield had been found, where bears had been plausible, which meant the three guys had brought him to the wrong place for a completely different purpose. With an M14, which for sure was capable of shooting a person. Or gut-shooting a person. After that they wouldn't need bears. What had the guy said, in the bar, with the long-neck bottle? *You got hundreds of other species already lining up and licking their lips.*

He looked all around. Not good. Wide gaps, slender trunks.

The middle of nowhere.

No witnesses.

No proof. That's the whole beauty of it.

For a second he wondered how much they were getting paid, but then he dismissed the question, partly because it was inherently vain, and partly because the answer was obvious. *Far as I can tell, it's a beautiful thing. The way they talk about it, it's the best thing ever.* They were getting a couple boxes of oxycodone and fentanyl patches. Like getting offed in prison for a carton of cigarettes. Life was cheap. Then for another second he felt betrayed. He felt they had gotten along well so far. He had made an effort. He had been polite. Then he got real. He looked at it from their point of view. Some things were more important to a person. More important than family and friends and any kind of a regular trustworthy life.

No one should ever underestimate the appeal of an opiate high.

He hoped they were getting a couple boxes each.

They would have to earn them.

He turned and walked back, keeping the guy in the corner of his eye. He wasn't too worried about the first cold shot. It would miss. Snatched at, unaimed. The second shot might get complicated. And the third. And the rest. There were twenty rounds in an M14 magazine. He slowed down, to keep the guy in front of him. He intended to keep him there all the way. A shot low in the back would work just as well. The round would go through and through, and bury its smeared and bloody self deep in the grit ten feet away. It would never be found. How could it? The round that killed him would be a random singularity a quarter-inch wide in an uninhabited state bigger than some foreign nations.

No proof. That's the whole beauty of it.

He slowed again, a wordless shepherding, a polite *after you*. The guy with the rifle walked on ahead. He could afford to. They were heading back to the first clearing they had seen. Where the young tree had been pushed down by the moose. *It was a place like this.* Their preferred location, presumably. Why else had they stopped there?

They walked a minute downhill, some places single file, as the trees thickened up again. Reacher stayed last in line. Where he wanted to be.

He scanned ahead, and picked a spot.

Just in case.

He said, "Let's go back a different route. I already saw this view."

Which was a tactical risk. They didn't know he knew. Not yet. The time for making waves came later, not sooner. But it was a much smaller risk than arriving exactly where they wanted him. That was for damn sure. Open ground, that they knew, and he didn't.

The guy with the rifle stopped and turned around.

He said, "I don't think there is another route."

"Must be," Reacher said.

"You wouldn't want to get lost out here."

"I have a pretty good sense of direction. Most days I can tell which way is up."

The guy took a step. Now he was maybe ten feet from Reacher, face to face on a narrow section of path, with the rifle held easy down by his side. The other two guys were closer, maybe five feet away, standing apart, so the guy with the rifle could see through the gap between. Underfoot were roots and rocks and gravel. Either side were trees.

As good a place as any.

Reacher took a step.

He said, "This land is not where Porterfield was found."

"You're the big expert now?" the guy with the rifle said.

"Sheriff Connelly conducted a thorough investigation. At a minimum we can expect he searched every building on the land where the corpse was found. As it turns out the only building he searched was Porterfield's. Therefore Porterfield was found on his own land. Which is about forty miles from here. With some kind of different ecology. They have bears there."

The M14's safety was a small manual catch tight in front of the trigger guard. Clicked back, it was set to safe. Flicked forward, it was set to fire.

Reacher watched it carefully.

So far it was set to safe.

But all four of the guy's fingers were near it.

Reacher said, "Put the weapon down, and we'll talk about it. It doesn't have to be like this. Maybe we can all find a way out together."

The guy said, "How?"

"Put the weapon down, and we'll talk about it."

The guy didn't.

Reacher said, "You need to look ahead. Stackley is your best friend today, but tomorrow he could be out of business. Rose's sister is taking her to Chicago. A suburb, not the city. A nice place. She could make it a charitable foundation. You could go with her."

"We're fine here."

"They have Billy in a cell," Reacher said. "They're two steps from cutting you off."

As soon as he said it he knew it was dumb. They reacted like Rose Sanderson had. Sudden breathing, and stiffened postures. The low hum of instant panic. Plus in their case some kind of instant urgency, about what to do next. As if the glittering payday they had been promised could be snatched away. Reacher saw in their faces his words *cutting you off* translate instantly into a howling voice in their heads screaming *get more now now now*.

The guy raised the rifle, right hand to left hand to right hand, a clumsy old thing, nearly twelve pounds in weight, nearly four feet long.

His trigger finger detoured ahead of the guard.

It flicked the safety catch forward.

Reacher crashed into the guy nearest him and used the bounce to hurl himself against a tree. Not really diving out of the way of a bullet, for such a thing was surely impossible, but it was easy enough to estimate a bullet's likely future trajectory comparatively far ahead of time, and then avoid it, not forgetting that Newton's Laws of Motion said the same bounce that helped him also helped the other guy, but in the opposite direction, toward the gun, action and reaction, which in his case got him killed. The rifle fired and the guy got hit and went down like he had walked into a clothesline. The roar of the shot died away to an immense cracking mountain echo, then a whisper, then nothing. The guy with the rifle stared. Reacher peeled off his tree and smacked him in the head and took his rifle away.

The guy staggered and dropped to his knees.

The third guy was frozen in place.

Reacher said, "Check your friend."

But even from there he could see it was hopeless. The guy had fired high and the round had gone through his buddy's throat. Just as good as a gut shot, from the point of view of the prevailing theory. Maybe even better. The bullet would fall to earth a hundred yards away. The soft tissue of the neck would be quickly consumed. Damaged vertebrae would be carried away and crushed, for the spinal cord inside. No proof at all.

The guy kneeling down looked up and shook his head. Reacher pointed the rifle at him, and then at where he wanted him to go. Which was next to the guy with the boots, who was struggling to his feet, steadying himself with a palm on the ground, then finally making it.

"Lead on," Reacher said. "We'll go this way after all."

They stumbled ahead of him, and he followed behind, carrying the rifle one-handed. They offered no resistance. They were completely passive, as if resigned to their fate. Maybe in shock. Maybe an addict thing. Maybe a cowboy thing.

They got back two minutes after Bramall and Mackenzie got back from checking out of the hotel. Rose Sanderson was out on the porch, greeting her sister. Bramall was over by his car, giving them space. The two guys and Reacher came out of the woods right in the middle. And stopped. Center stage. No need to tell the story. It was all right there. Two guys, not three, both of them sheepish and beaten, driven from behind by Reacher with a rifle.

Rose Sanderson seemed to recognize the rifle. Her head turned. The cuff of her hood traversed like a periscope. She stared at the scene. At the two guys. At the rifle. At Reacher. He knew she was thinking. Like an infantry officer. She was running war games through her head, like a chess computer. Like a West Point graduate.

She found one that fit.

She said, "Was it freebies from Stackley?"

He said, "Yes."

"I guess that's really bad."

"I'm not loving it so far."

"What does Stackley have against you?"

"His boss doesn't like me."

"But you're not here on business."

"I picked things up along the way."

"What happened up there?"

"One KIA," he said. "Friendly fire. Hasty aim, a moving target, confusion in front of him."

"Let them go," she said. "Keep the rifle. It's their only remaining weapon."

The two guys shuffled off down their own path, and the sisters moved to meet Reacher and Bramall at the porch step, where they all sat down to talk. Sanderson had her hood pulled forward again. It was molded into a narrow vertical aperture. It turned and lined up with Reacher's face, and she said, "I apologize for them."

"No need," he said. "No harm, no foul. Tactical sophistication and superior skill in maneuvering overcame an initial material deficit."

"When did you know?"

"First sign was we stopped in a clearing and they got a bit weird. But I guess the guy couldn't pull the trigger. I guess he had never done it before."

"I apologize for them," she said again. "They were my friends."

"No need," he said again.

"But I can't condemn them. You have no idea of the magnitude of what they were offered."

"I'm getting an idea. From cause and effect alone. I'm taking it seriously, believe me. I'm not judging it, either. It is what it is. You got to do what you got to do. Right?"

"Yes."

"Right now what you got to do is go inside and get a brand new patch, because after that the next thing you got to do is make a choice."

"Between what?"

"You can have a sensible conversation about what comes next."

"Or?"

"I'm moving on without you."

Chapter 38

Rose Sanderson went inside to get a brand new patch, and as the door closed behind her Bramall's cell phone rang. He checked the screen and said, "It's Special Agent Noble, from his office in Denver."

"Don't answer," Reacher said. "He's going to ask if you found Rose. Either as a pleasantry in passing, or because he wants her for a witness. You can't tell him where she is. Not now. You'll feel bad holding out on him."

"He might have something for us."

"He hasn't retired yet. He's all take and no give. Don't answer."

Bramall didn't. The call timed out and voicemail clicked in. Bramall retrieved it immediately. He listened, and he said, "He wants to know if we found Rose."

Behind them the door opened again and Rose stepped out. Small, lithe, graceful. With the hem of her hood leading the way. She sat down on the step.

She turned her hood Reacher's way.

She said, "Obviously it's your own decision when to move on."

He said, "I'm not looking to save the world. All I wanted was to know the story. Which I do now. Not a happy ending. I don't want to be here when it turns even worse. I don't want to be here while you go cold turkey in federal lock-up. With no medical supervision. Not even antiseptic cream. While your sister gets busted as some kind of an accessory, all because the Boy Detective thinks a rich white woman would balance the books on the TV news. While she goes bankrupt, fighting the bullshit charges. While Mr. Bramall loses his license and has to find a third career. I want to be gone before all that happens."

She said, "You make it sound certain to happen."

"They have Billy in a cell. And you have a dead cowboy on your land. Someone will find him, like someone found Porterfield. Sheriff Connelly will search your place. Unless the Boy Detective has already gotten here first, thanks to Billy drawing a hand-lettered map. Unless the supply cuts off before either one of them arrives, in which case you'll be in the ER five times a day with a toothache. One of those things is certain to happen."

"How long before the supply cuts off, do you think?"

The thing that mattered most.

"That's a circular argument," Reacher said. "If I move on without you, my first stop will be Rapid City, South Dakota. I need to pay Arthur Scorpio a visit. He lied to me about Porterfield, and he told two separate people to shoot me from behind a tree. He crossed the line. It's not going to end well for him. He's going in the tumble dryer. Two days for me to get there, and one day to do it. I would say the supply cuts off about three days from now."

"You're forcing my hand. Either I agree to go now, or you'll make me go anyway. It's a unilateral three-day deadline."

"It's an unintended consequence. Look at it from my point of view. Obviously I don't want to be here when it goes from bad to worse. And obviously when I leave here I have no choice except go straight to Rapid City. What else could I do? The guy is messing with me. What would you do if you were taking rounds from a distant building?"

"I would call in an air strike."

"This is my version."

"So I have three more days here."

"But only as an unintended consequence. I'm not looking to save the world."

She didn't reply.

Jane Mackenzie said, "Reacher, three days is not possible."

"Let's challenge that assumption," he said. "Let's make it possible."

They moved inside. Bramall took a chair, and Mackenzie took the other. Sanderson said she was happy sitting cross-legged on the floor. Reacher laid out on his back, with his arm behind his head, and he stared at the ceiling, and listened. They started out by making a list of what Rose would need, which was easiest done by making a list of what she already had, which was quiet and isolated accommodations, and access to pharmaceutical-grade opioid medications in daily doses wildly in excess of what any responsible physician could even contemplate.

Mackenzie said in the long term the accommodations were no problem at all. But in the short term they didn't exist yet. She and her husband owned no beach houses or hunting cabins. There was an original staff apartment over their stable block, but it would need new heat and a new bathroom.

Reacher said, "Do you have a guest suite?"

"Two, but they're in the house."

"With you and Mr. Mackenzie, a nice man and a good match. Is he going to be a problem with all of this?"

"No, he's going to be totally on board."

"Are you sure?"

"Completely."

"OK," Reacher said. "How about Rose lives in a guest suite until further notice. Put her in the east wing, facing the lake. You got a six-acre yard and I'm sure it's a quiet leafy street. Not like living in the middle of Times Square. We need to make fast decisions here. We can't let the perfect be the enemy of the good."

Mackenzie looked at Rose, who nodded. She agreed. She could afford to. It was about the future. Which wasn't coming. The second item on the list meant they could never get there.

Mackenzie said, "We need to be realistic about the doctor. We haven't even started looking yet. I'm sure they're thin on the ground. I suppose the internet will help. But we might have to wait for an appointment. And I'm sure they at least go through the motions. They'll want an initial consultation. Or else right now the right guy is on Anguilla playing golf. You know what this crap is like."

"I don't," Reacher said.

"Two weeks," she said. "I live in that world. Trust me. This feels like a two-week thing, absolute bare minimum."

No one answered.

From deep in her hood Rose said, "You're all very polite people. So I'll say it myself. I'm the big problem. How are you going to bridge the gap? How are you going to hook me up every day for two weeks? Some of which will be spent on the road. A different town every night. You can't do it."

Again no one answered. The questions hung in the air. *How are you going to bridge the gap? How are you going to hook me up?* It was the snag in every plan. Like a splinter in a banister rail. The rest was easy. Reacher could picture it all. Except for that. The quantities were staggering. It would be a full-time job.

To fill the silence Mackenzie talked for a spell about Lake Forest, Illinois. It sounded like a very nice place. Their house was a grand old Tudor, with ancient bricks and leaded windows, and a long sloping lawn, and a stone dock, with a small boat, and the glittering lake beyond, as big as an ocean. Then Reacher realized she wasn't just filling the silence. Or bragging on her real estate. She was spinning some kind of shared twin fantasy from long ago, about the lives they were going to have, and what would be in them, like an ideal dream. He could understand how girls in landlocked Wyoming would want a waterfront. Now Mackenzie was saying she had made it happen. It was right there for the taking. She was saying come live in your dream for the rest of your life. With its damp lawns and its mossy bricks. It was a masterpiece of gauzy seduction. Reacher could only imagine how much more power it had, from one twin to another, down on some unknown level of intimacy. It was enticing. Irresistible. Worth sacrificing for. Great psy-ops. Except he was left with a couple of questions.

How are you going to bridge the gap? How are you going to hook her up?

Down in Denver Kirk Noble had gotten caught up in some other thing, and then he had gotten dragged into a meeting about something else entirely, so in the end he left Billy to sweat way longer than two hours. Closer to four. He stopped and looked in the one-way window. Good and carefully. He prided himself on reading the signs. Right away he saw Billy was a hardscrabble country boy, maybe forty years old, lean and furtive, like a fox and a squirrel had a kid, and spent half the time baking it in the sun, and the other half beating it with a stick. He wasn't sweating and he wasn't shaking. He wasn't drumming his toe or picking a nail. Not a user. Not even a smoker.

Such a guy would give nothing up. Except by accident. Foxes and squirrels had numerous admirable qualities, but they didn't get college degrees. There would be some kind of side door. Some kind of trigger. Maybe approval. Billy was the type of guy who most likely never had much. Maybe he could be stroked into prideful reminiscences, about the deals he had done. Maybe using the granular-priced jewelry as a show-and-tell example. He could recall how he came by each item. He could say, yeah, some chick had no money so she gave me this.

In exchange for what, Billy?

Noble sent a runner to his office for the shoebox of jewelry.

* * *

The impromptu conference broke up, and Reacher went out on the porch. Then Bramall came out. Reacher imagined Sanderson would replace him in the armchair. He imagined the sisters would talk. Not too long, he hoped.

Bramall said, "We can't fix this."

"There must be a way," Reacher said.

"When you figure it out, be sure to let me know."

"You sure you want me to? You have more rules than me."

"One of which makes me delinquent if I don't prepare a plan B on behalf of my client. At least a mental sketch. In this case it would have to start with hospitalization privileges for Rose. No federal lock-up. A private facility of our own choice. Secured, if they want, at our expense. Obviously the guy to talk to would be Noble, down in Denver. He has the discretion. We already have a relationship. I should maintain it. I should have answered his call. I'll have to answer the next one. I might need him in the future."

"We don't need plan B yet."

"Better to lay the ground."

"If you answer the phone to him now, you'll have to tell him where Rose is. Which will lead straight to plan C, which is the whole thing falls apart. Or you'll have to lie to him, which is technically a felony."

Bramall didn't answer.

Reacher said, "Will you do me a favor?"

"Depends what it is."

"Go ask Mrs. Mackenzie if her sister mentioned whether Stackley is coming by again tomorrow."

"Why?"

"I want to know."

Bramall went in, but a minute later it was Rose Sanderson herself who came out. She sat where she had before, on the step, hooded, a yard away.

She said, "My sister gave me money. I told Stackley to come back every day until it's gone. Or until he runs out of product."

Reacher said, "What happens when he does?"

"Sometimes they miss a day. I guess they go somewhere and get more. We're real happy to see them come back."

"I can imagine."

"I'm sorry."

"Don't be. We both took the same history class."

She nodded, inside her hood.

She said, "Morphine dates from 1805. The hypodermic syringe dates from 1851. A great combination, just in time for the Civil War, which left hundreds of thousands of addicts. Then World War One, same thing. Literally millions of addicts in the 1920s."

"The army likes tradition."

"World War One was also the start of large-scale facial injuries. Millions of them, by the end. The French called them the *mutilés*. The mutilated. Which is a good word, because that's how it feels, and because it sounds like mutated, which is also how it feels. You feel yourself become a different person. There was an early type of plastic surgery back then, but mostly they wore tin masks. Artists would match them to their skin color. But nothing really worked. City parks had benches painted blue, where the public was trained to look away. That's where they sat. But most of them never went out. Most of them never saw daylight, ever again. Most of them died of infections or killed themselves."

"You don't have to convince me," Reacher said. "I don't care what you chew."

"But you can't get it for me. Not fourteen days straight."

"Suppose I could. Suppose you could get it forever. What would you do?"

"Seriously?"

"Give me an honest analysis. You like the truth."

She paused a beat.

"I would party at first," she said. "Big time. No more rationing. No more cutting patches. I would bathe in the stuff."

"Dangerous."

"God, I hope so. It's a world you don't understand until you're in it. There is no feeling better than tiptoeing all the way up to the gates of death. All the way up to the big black door, and then knocking on it. It's a whole different zone. If I hear a news story about some other user dying, due to some batch of something showing up unexpectedly strong, I'm not feeling sorry for the guy. I'm thinking, where can I get some of *that* good stuff? Not because I want to kill myself. Far from it. I want the exact opposite. I want to live forever, so I can get high every day. I'm sorry, Reacher. I'm not the person I was. I mutated. You should have found someone else's ring."

"What next, after you're done partying?"

"Eventually I guess I would have to tone it down. Probably get the IV, if I can have it at home."

"You think you can tone it down?"

She nodded, inside her hood. "I love it like crazy, but there's enough of the old me still in there. I know that. I made it through West Point and nine years in the infantry. I could make it through this. As long as I knew I didn't have to quit entirely. As long as I knew the promise was always there. Maybe Saturday night, if I was good all week. I think I could get myself to that level."

"And then what?"

"Then I'll hide out in my sister's house until I'm a hundred years old. By which time we'll all be ugly and I won't stand out so much. Until then let's not be Pollyanna. There won't be any then-what going on. I don't see how it could."

"You could get a job."

"You must have missed that memo."

He smiled.

"I work now and then," he said. "Laboring, or nightclub bouncer. One time I dug a swimming pool in Key West, Florida. By hand. I bet it's still there."

"The psychiatrists came to see me in the hospital. There was a new school of thought, about confronting issues head-on. No false comfort. I was an O-4, don't forget. All grown up. I was supposed to be able to take it. They showed me the data. Employees with facial disfigurements upset customers and co-workers so badly that virtually a hundred percent of them end up working alone in a back office."

"OK, don't get a job."

"Then we had long conversations about how much our personalities are tied up with our faces. About subliminal cues and nuances. Something very fundamental. Later I realized the head-on stuff went only so far. Now they were being subtle. They were dropping hints. They were telling me my romantic life was over."

"Porterfield didn't agree."

"He was different."

"Was he blind?"

"He had problems of his own."

Behind them the door opened, and Mackenzie came out on the porch, followed by Bramall. Mackenzie looked like she had something to say, but Bramall's cell phone rang. He took it out and checked the screen.

He said, "It's Special Agent Noble, from his office in Denver."

He looked at Rose.

Then he looked at Reacher.

Asking for something.

Reacher said, "You want me to be the bad guy?"

He took the phone. He hit the green button. He put the phone to his ear.

He said, "Hello?"

Chapter 39

Noble asked why Reacher was answering Bramall's phone, and Reacher gave him a vague reply, about Bramall taking a walk, maybe out of range, therefore leaving his phone behind.

Noble said, "Mrs. Mackenzie hired Bramall, right? For actual money."

Reacher said, "Yes."

"But not you."

"No."

"Then it's better I talk to you anyway. Can Mrs. Mackenzie hear what you're saying right now?"

"Yes."

"Move away."

Reacher held the phone up toward the ravine, and mimed heading that way for better reception. When he got there he stood on a rock, and said, "What's going on?"

In his ear Noble said, "I think you found the sister."

"Why?"

"Are you saying you didn't?"

"I'm asking how you think we could have."

"How hard could it be? She was in there somewhere."

"It's a very large area."

"That's a description," Noble said. "Not a denial."

"Finding an entrenched individual in an unlimited acreage of forested land peppered with abandoned cabins is virtually impossible."

"That's also a description."

"I can do this all day long," Reacher said. "I was in the army."

Noble said, "I need Rose Sanderson."

"Why?"

"For information. I need to close a file."

"You have Billy for that."

"Billy is why I need Sanderson now. I think Billy is lying to me. He's boasting. Either for fun, to tempt me into wasting time chasing rainbows, or just for the sake of his ego. Some dealers love to lie about how they can get the good stuff. It makes them look cool. They're the man, and so on. But before I can close the file I need corroborating testimony from a customer. Just in case. It's a cover-your-ass thing."

"What did Billy tell you?"

"That he was still selling what he always sold. Domestic oxycodone and fentanyl, branded and packaged inside the United States."

"Obviously that's a boast," Reacher said. "You told us it's impossible."

"It is impossible. I can prove it. Literally everything is barcoded every step of the way. Literally every pill. We have access to their data. There is zero leakage now."

"So he's boasting."

"Except he knows things he shouldn't. There have been packaging changes. He knows the new promotional message on the inside of the hospital pack. No one ever sees that."

"So he's not boasting."

"Of course he's boasting. They track every conveyor belt, and every package, and every carton as it goes out the door, and they have GPS on the trucks, and they match the orders with the payments received, and if there's a mismatch anywhere all kind of red lights start flashing. Which isn't happening. Nothing is going astray."

"So which is it? Boasting or not?"

"I would like to put my mind at rest. Either way I need to ask Rose Sanderson exactly what she was buying."

"Why not go up the chain? Surely a wholesaler's testimony would carry more weight than a customer's."

"I don't know these people. It's an opaque network."

"Won't Billy name names?"

"So far he's playing the good soldier. I only got what I got by tricking it out of him sideways. I would need to start a whole new investigation. I don't have time. We can do it quicker this way. We don't need much. We're only closing a file. All she has to say is Billy is a lying asshole and he was selling regular Mexican powder all along."

Up at the house Sanderson and her sister and Bramall were still on the porch. They were talking a lot. Some kind of a big discussion.

Reacher said, "OK, if I ever get the opportunity, I'll be sure to tell her what you need."

Noble said, "Where are you now?"

"It's a very large area."

"Are you at her place?"

"It's hard to pin down an exact spot."

"You're talking on a cell phone."

"On an omnidirectional antenna somewhere inside a giant circle the size of New Jersey."

Noble said, "Certain laws apply when a citizen talks to a federal agent."

Reacher said, "Sorry, I was waiting for the dramatic music."

"Do you know Rose Sanderson's current location?"

"Certain other laws apply when this citizen talks to a federal agent. Mostly the ones about saving breath by skipping bullshit. I know how these things go. And I know you know. Usually worse than expected. Therefore you always have a plan B, so the main office sees a notch on your bedpost anyway. Anyone will do. You want Rose Sanderson on the record buying Mexican powder. Just in case. She's your plan B."

"She breaks the law every day."

"You should forget her right now. Seriously. She would be a very serious blunder on your part. She was wounded in the face in Afghanistan. You met her twin sister. Think about it. Their photographs will be printed side by side in every newspaper in the world. The movie star and the monster. Before and after serving her country. Now you're busting her for pain medication? The backlash would be ferocious. The DEA would be ridiculed. I'm saving you from a PR disaster."

"Do you know where she is?"

"In the state of Wyoming."

"Are you refusing to answer my question?"

"No," Reacher said. "I'll answer all your questions. Including the ones you haven't thought of yet. Let's set up a call about three days from now. On two conditions. You butt out till then, and you forget you ever heard Rose Sanderson's name."

"Why three days?"

"That kind of question would fall under the butting-out part of the deal."

"I'm not going to negotiate with you."

"Then suggest an alternative approach. Oh yeah, there isn't one. So let's try to get along. I was an MP, remember. The same as you, except different clothes. I'm not out to screw you. I'm trying to do you a favor. This is one of those lucky things that happen from time to time. I take the tiny slice I want, which is Rose Sanderson, and you get all the rest. It's a big deal, I promise you. It will win you a medal and make you a hero. Even Mr. Bramall thinks it will be hailed as a major triumph and the capstone of an outstanding regional success story. It's something for nothing, Noble. The opposite of collateral damage. The Boy Detective would take that offer, I think, in the comic books. He knows it's how government business gets done."

"You're not the government."

"You never really leave," Reacher said. "Not if you're the right kind of person."

Noble said nothing. Checkmate again. He couldn't argue. Not without saying yeah, all our lives are bullshit.

"Three days," Reacher said. "Relax. Maybe take in a show."

He clicked off the phone. He walked back to the house. Bramall met him halfway. Reacher gave back the phone.

"Three days," he said. "Plus he forgets about Rose."

"Nice work."

"Thank you."

"In exchange for what?"

"We let him pick up the pieces."

"What pieces?"

"I'm sure there will be pieces."

"You saying you got an idea now?"

"More like a mental sketch," Reacher said. "I need to ask you a question."

"What question?"

"When you were in Rapid City, why were you eyeballing Scorpio's laundromat? What did you expect to see there?"

"Customers, initially. According to phone records Rose called there once. Who else would call a laundromat? Only a customer, surely. Maybe she lost something there. Maybe she wanted to know the opening time. I wondered if it meant she lived nearby. Or had, at one time."

"But there were no customers."

"Only one or two."

"Any other traffic?"

"None at all."

"Did you watch the back?"

"A couple of bikes."

"But no loading or unloading."

"None at all," Bramall said again. "It's not a loading dock. Just a regular door."

"OK," Reacher said.

Then Mackenzie came by, and said she wanted to go find the cabins they would be sleeping in that night. Apparently Rose had told her there was a nearby clearing with four small houses all in a square. They were aired out and habitable. Apparently Rose kept them like that all the time, because she felt it was a shame to see good things go to ruin.

They found the right path, which was like all the other paths Reacher had seen, including most recently the path where the guy with the boots had aimed the rifle. Apart from that it was easy going. After a hundred yards they came out on a clearing, exactly as promised, with four one-room houses built around a space about the size of a tennis court. Like a tiny village. The houses were made of log, each one different, each one built like a serious structure, each one no bigger than a single-car garage. All four doors were unlocked. Bramall claimed one at random. Mackenzie moved in opposite. Reacher split the difference, facing south.

In a city the place would have been called a studio apartment. A living room with a bed in it, or a bedroom with a sofa in it, plus a token kitchenette, and a tiny bathroom. Overspill accommodation for house parties, he figured. They ate and drank and made merry at the big house, but came out there to sleep. Maybe four couples, who all knew one another.

He put his toothbrush in the bathroom glass and came out to find Mackenzie watching him from the doorway.

She said, "My husband has started the search for a doctor. He's taking vacation days from work. He understands the parameters. Our housekeeper is preparing the suite. Mr. Bramall is ready to drive us all to Illinois. I'm sure his vehicle will be comfortable."

"I agree," Reacher said. "It's a fine truck."

"I guess what I'm saying is the rest is up to you now."

"The rest?"

"Bridging the gap."

"OK," Reacher said. "That seems fair."

"If you can."

"I'm working on it."

"Will it be possible?"

"Rose will need to hang tough. I hope she can. She told me there's some of her old self still in there. She was smart enough to ask me to hold her ring. Or self aware enough. To some extent she knows what she's doing. She can still think the old way. At some point she'll have to trust us and we'll have to trust her."

"When will we leave?"

"Tomorrow," he said.

They ate dinner together, out of what they had brought from the grocery store. Rose was high as a kite and happy. She was mobile and animated. Under her hood and her foil she laughed and smiled and turned from person to person, and talked and listened and answered. Mackenzie laughed with her, half the time projecting boundless energy and support, like a tractor beam in a science fiction movie, something solid for her sister to lean on, and the other half of the time projecting hopeless bewilderment at her new situation. She was adrift. There were old-time fairy tales where the beautiful sister came home scarred, and all kinds of hidden anger and resentment were revealed, ahead of a warm and tearful resolution. But this was different. There was no narrative template. They were both the beautiful sister. They started level. There was no anger or resentment. There were no issues. They were the same person. Almost. Reacher saw the air between them ebb and flow, sometimes making them a single organism, like an aspen grove, sometimes making them separate, but never completely. They were a unit. They were a they. Always had been, always would be. But neither one knew how the current version worked. Or even what it looked like, from the outside. How would they describe themselves now? Would it have to be I and she? No longer we? These were not questions they had asked before.

Then Reacher told them how he thought the next day might go.

Bare bones, a rough outline, three steps, plenty of holes still to fill. Mackenzie was horrified. Bramall looked away, as if to say, is that all you've got? Rose quieted down and Reacher felt her eyes on him, under her hood. He felt careful appraisal. She was his main audience. She had the most to lose. She was a professional soldier. She knew no plan survives first contact with the enemy. After that it was about luck, or not. She knew that for sure.

Afterward Reacher asked Bramall to move his truck behind the house, out of sight from the mouth of the driveway. Then he walked up the cowboys' path, to where he figured their quarters must be. He found them on the porch of a low log building made to look like an old-time bunkhouse. Two guys, not three, sipping from cans of beer. He thought they looked uneasy, with shock and guilt, presumably, and a more ancient humbling, the guy in the boots especially, where you fail to kill a man, and then you look up and see him walking toward you. Some kind of an atavistic feeling, deep in the back of your brain, about your place on the ladder, from back when the only ladders were trees.

Reacher said, "We live in crazy times."

Neither guy answered. Perhaps they thought he had earned the right to speak uninterrupted. Like giving a lecture. Maybe a cowboy thing. He wanted to tell them no hard feelings. That he understood the pressure. How it distorted judgment. But in the end he didn't. Too complicated. Instead he told them what they had to do for him. He spelled it out, step by step, and he walked them through it, and he gave them what they needed. He saw it was better than forgiveness. Their heads came up an inch, with new resolve in their eyes, as if they were subject to an older legal system, where through labor or forfeit they could buy back their freedom.

Reacher walked back to Sanderson's place. It had a light on inside. He checked where Bramall had left the Toyota. It was safely out of sight. Not bad for the FBI. He walked back to his one-room cabin. The little village. Mackenzie's place had a light on, and so did Bramall's. All kinds of people, going to bed. All kinds of preparations and rituals. Maybe lengthy. Maybe Bramall brushed his suit, like a valet. No doubt Mackenzie had a complicated routine, involving potions and unguents.

For sure Sanderson did.

Reacher got into bed. Log walls, log ceiling. He understood the appeal. They were solid and massive. They made him feel safe.

Chapter 40

The cowboys were up at dawn, drinking coffee from tin mugs, in rocking chairs, on their bunkhouse porch. The sun came up behind the hills, and threw a flat shadow across the plain. In her house Rose Sanderson slept on. She was not a dawn riser. Fentanyl saw to that. Bramall was up, already showered, and dressed, with his hair brushed, and his necktie knotted. Mackenzie stirred, and woke, and lived a happy oblivious moment where nothing had ever happened. Then she remembered, and half wanted to go back to sleep again, and half wanted to get up and do something, anything, for as long as it felt like progress. In the end going back to sleep won the contest. For a short time. Outside the air was cold. Early on a late summer morning, high in the mountains.

An hour later the cowboys walked down to the mouth of the driveway. They waited there, the same as they had the morning before, and the morning before that, except now they were two, not three. They stood around, not talking, like part of the landscape, infinitely patient. In her house Rose stirred, and woke. She put her hand on her night table. Two patches. Still there. She breathed out and sagged back on her pillow. It was safe to get up. Bramall had made coffee in his token kitchenette, and was out on his porch drinking the last of it. Mackenzie was in the shower, hosing water through her hair.

An hour later the cowboys still waited. The sun climbed higher and came up over the ridge behind them. It dappled the trees where they stood, and warmed the air. In her house Rose was showering. Bramall was still on his porch, his coffee long gone, just passing the time. He was a man life had taught to be patient. Mackenzie was in her cabin, in an armchair, on the phone with her husband, talking about doctors.

An hour later the cowboys were still waiting. Waiting for the man, for their connection, for their hook up. Wasted hours. Part of a user's life. They leaned on trees and breathed the air, soft and piney. In her house Rose Sanderson was dressed, in her silver top, with the hood pulled forward. She had cut a new piece of aluminum foil, and smeared it with new lotion, and smoothed it into place. She was in her living room, with the window open. In position. Ready. As was Bramall, fifty yards away in the woods. He was sitting on a log. Mackenzie was fifty yards the other way, leaning on the trunk of a fir, with filtered sunlight playing in her hair.

A minute later at the mouth of the driveway there was the sound of a straining engine, and the scratch and patter of struggling tires, and the cowboys stood aside. The beat-up old pick-up truck came out of the woods, carrying its camper shell on its back like a turtle. At the wheel Stackley scanned ahead. He saw no black Toyota. No big guy. No one else.

He eased to a stop.

The guy with the boots walked over.

Stackley got out.

He said, "How's it going?"

The guy said, "You owe us."

"For what?"

"The big guy."

"You got it done?"

"Yesterday in the afternoon."

"How did you do it?"

"Lured him in the woods and shot him with a rifle."

"Want to show me?"

"Sure," the guy said. "But he's an hour uphill. We didn't want him found too soon."

"Then how do I know you did it?"

"We're telling you."

"I need proof. This is a very large fee we're talking about here."

"Two boxes each."

"Between you," Stackley said.

Then he looked again and said, "There were three of you yesterday."

The guy said, "Indisposed."

"With what?"

"Sore throat."

"I need proof about the big guy," Stackley said. "This is a business deal we got going here."

The guy with the boots put his hand in his pocket and came out with a slim blue booklet. Silver printing. A passport, maybe three years old, a little curled and bent. He handed it over. Stackley opened it up. The big guy's photo was right there. A face like a stone. His name was Jack Reacher. No middle initial.

"From his pocket," the guy said. "Less messy than his scalp."

Stackley put the passport in his own pocket.

He said, "I'll keep it as a souvenir."

"Sure."

"Nice work."

"We aim to please."

"But you caught me out," Stackley said. "Business is too good. I'm running low."

"What does that mean?"

"You'll have to wait."

"That wasn't the deal."

"What do you want me to do? Say no to someone else, just in case you got it done, which frankly I didn't expect so soon? I can't hold stuff back on a theoretical basis."

"So you got nothing left?"

"Not much."

The guy said, "Want to show me?"

"Sure," Stackley said. He wasn't averse. A dwindling stock was a kind of advertisement all its own. The modern environment. Business was all about velocity now. It was rule one. He turned toward the camper door.

And came face to face with the guy from the passport.

Reacher eased out of the trees, and crept up within a yard of the guy. He was about to tap him in the kidney, but right then the guy turned around toward the camper door, so he tapped him in the stomach instead, just enough to fold him over. He used the same hand on the guy's shoulder to force him face down in the dirt, where he searched him. He came up with his own passport from one coat pocket, and a nine-millimeter from another, and a .22 jammed in one boot, and a switchblade jammed in the other. The nine-mil was an old Smith & Wesson Model 39, with handsome grips made of polished wood. The .22 was a Ruger, not a vest pocket gun, but it fit in the boot. The switchblade was a piece of junk, made in China, maybe in a toy factory.

Stackley was huffing and puffing in the dirt, and squirming a little, which Reacher thought was excessive for a guy barely hurt. He checked the pick-up's cab. Nothing in the glove compartment. But under the lip of the driver's seat there was a mounting clip, where a fire extinguisher might have been, except in this case the clip had been modified, and was currently full of another elderly nine-millimeter with wooden grips, in this case an old Springfield P9. Apart from that there was nothing but drifts of old gas receipts and sandwich wrappers.

Reacher stepped back to where Stackley was lying, and he held the old Smith out at arm's length. He clicked the button and dropped the mag from five feet up. It hit Stackley in the head. Stackley yelped. Reacher dropped the gun itself. Stackley yelped again. Reacher did the same thing with the Ruger, mag and frame, and then the Springfield, mag and frame. A total of six separate yelps.

Reacher said, "Get up now, Stackley."

Stackley forced himself upright, a little bent over, a little pale in the face. All shook up. Rubbing his painful head. Facing the same kind of animal issues the two cowboys had, the night before. You fail to kill a man, and then you look up and see him right there. Does he own you now?

Reacher said, "Open up the back of the truck."

The doors were flimsy plastic. Stackley got them propped wide. Then he stood back. Reacher pulled a blanket aside. One forlorn box, mostly empty. It had just three patches left in it, each one individually wrapped, all of them sliding around in a space made for more.

Not much.

Reacher stepped away.

"Stocks seem to be running low," he said. "What do you do about that, in the normal course of business?"

"I'm sorry, man," Stackley said. "About the other thing. I had no choice. I was told to do it. It wasn't personal."

"We'll discuss it later," Reacher said.

"There's a guy. I have to do what he says. He told me to. It wasn't like I wanted to. You have to believe that."

"Later."

"I really didn't think these guys would do it. I thought I was going through the motions, that's all. So at least I could say I tried. It's their fault really."

"I asked you a question."

"I don't remember what it was."

"Your stock is low," Reacher said. "What happens next?"

Stackley got a look in his eye, like some kind of a thought process

was taking place back there. He looked up, and then down. A junc-
tion, Reacher thought, or a transition. A change from one thing to
another. From winning to losing, from hope to despair.

To surrender.

Stackley breathed out, like a sigh of defeat.

He said, "When I run out I go get more."

"Where from?"

"It's a kind of warehouse, where you drive in and line up. You wait
until midnight."

"Where is the warehouse?"

Stackley paused a beat.

"We have a special burner phone," he said. "We get a text message."

"Where is your special burner phone?"

Stackley pointed at the camper shell.

He said, "In a locker in back."

Reacher said, "Get it for me."

Stackley stepped up and leaned inside. Reacher heard the snap of
a catch. Afterward he recalled a split second of fast chaotic thought,
like his whole life was flashing in front of his eyes, except it wasn't his
whole life, merely his mistakes of the last thirty seconds, explained
and analyzed and ridiculed and exaggerated to a ludicrous degree. To
the point where in his mind he saw his name as a footnote in a psychology textbook about bias confirmation, in a famous case where a
guy saw a movement in another guy's eyes, and took it to mean exactly what he wanted it to mean all along.

Stackley hadn't surrendered. Instead he had thought hard and fast
and seen a way out. A lifeline. The guy was no dummy. The change in
his eyes had been a movement away from losing and back to winning.
From despair back to hope. Reacher had read it completely wrong.
Completely ass-backward. Too optimistic. Too willing to look on the
bright side of life. Which also screwed up his conclusion about the
weapons. He had instinctively assumed once you had taken a Springfield, and a Smith, and a Ruger .22 from a guy, then you were pretty

much done with finding more firearms. Which had made it fun to take them apart and drop them on the guy's head.

Whereas the psychology textbooks would say a guy with three could have four, dead easy. Especially a dope dealer, who took things in trade.

Dumb.

Stackley straightened up and turned around.

He had a gun in his hand.

From the locker in the camper shell.

The gun was an old Colt .45, worn steel, rock steady. Maybe nine feet away. Eight, if Stackley braced forward for the shot. Hard to miss from there. The downside of being a big guy. A sudden evolutionary disadvantage. Too much center mass.

Reacher watched Stackley's eyes. The guy was still thinking hard. Cost, benefit, advantages, disadvantages. All the reels were coming up cherries. In the short term he could solve his immediate this-minute problem. In the long term he could impress Arthur Scorpio as a reliable guy who got things done. All by pulling the trigger. Right there, right then. Just once. The only negative was location. Couldn't leave a corpse in the mouth of the driveway. It would need to be moved a mile into the woods. But he had the cowboys for that. They would trade labor for a free patch. For two, they would carry a corpse to Nebraska.

Reacher said, "Don't point the gun at me."

Stackley said, "Why the hell not?"

"It would be a serious mistake."

"How would it, man?"

Stackley raised the Colt.

Two-handed.

He pointed it at the center of Reacher's chest.

Like aiming at a barn door.

He said, "How exactly is this a mistake?"

"Wait and see," Reacher said. "Nothing personal."

Stackley's head exploded.

There was a wet thump like a watermelon rolling off a table, and then immediately the flat crack of a supersonic NATO round in the air, and the antique bark of an M14 firing. Stackley's head came apart in an instant cloud of red mist, and fragments of it followed his body down, vertically, like a disappearing trick, into a puddle of clothes and limbs and lifeless flesh. Reacher looked back at the house, and saw Rose Sanderson at her window, checking downrange, assessing her aim. Which was pretty damn good, he thought. From a hundred yards out she had put a round through the gap between himself and the cowboys, and she had hit Stackley right above the ear. All with a rifle dumped by the army twenty years before she was born.

Impressive.

She came out of the house and walked down toward them, hood forward, carrying the rifle one-handed. From the right Bramall came hurrying in, and from the left came Mackenzie, who had the most trouble with what she found. Theoretically she might have been happy with what turned out, in pragmatic terms, and maybe even moral terms, but a human head shattered by a high-velocity rifle bullet was far from theoretical. It was a purple mess, steaming slightly in the cold mountain air. She turned and looked at her sister. *She was prepared to kill people, and I wasn't.* One thing to talk about it. A whole different thing to watch it happen.

Reacher said, "Thank you, major."

Rose said, "How much did he have?"

The thing that mattered most.

"Not much," he said.

"Shit."

She stepped around Stackley and looked in the back of the truck. She twitched the blanket aside and poked around. Her shoulders slumped. Not exactly surprise, but certainly disappointment. *No plan survives first contact with the enemy.* She looked back at Reacher, as if to say, *This one went south pretty damn quick, didn't it?*

She said, "Where does he go to get more?"

He said, "The conversation didn't get that far."

"Arthur Scorpio's place, right?"

"No," Reacher said. "There's no traffic at Scorpio's place. No loading or unloading. Whatever Scorpio does, he does it by remote control."

"What exactly did Stackley tell you?"

"He said there's a warehouse, where they drive in and line up and wait until midnight."

"Where?"

"He said he gets a text message on a burner phone. He said the phone is in there."

He heard the click of catches and the muted thump of compartment doors being opened and shut. Maybe twelve of them. The camper shell had lockers all over it. Like living on a boat.

"There's no phone in here," she said.

"There never was," he said. "It was a decoy. It was a way to get to his gun."

"So how do we know where to go?"

"We don't."

She just stood there. Tiny, slumped, defeated. She was a drug addict. She had just shot and killed her dealer. Catastrophe. Like jumping off a building. Right then she was in mid-air, falling fast, the hiss of terror loud in her ears.

She was going to panic.

Reacher said, "Forget the phone. The phone was a trick. He invented it. They couldn't possibly work it that way. A warehouse big enough to drive in and line up can't be a moveable feast. It can't be a last-minute arrangement. It must be a permanent location. Fixed and secure. Hidden away somewhere."

Rose said, "But where?"

Bramall said, "Where is his regular phone?"

He ducked down, a small meticulous figure amid the gore. He dug through Stackley's crumpled pockets. He came out with a Samsung smartphone about the size of a paperback book. It had a cracked screen. No password. Bramall dabbed and swiped.

"He replaced Billy three days ago," he said. "Obviously he would have had to pick up supplies."

There were no text messages from three days before. No emails. But there was a voicemail. Bramall played it, and listened, and narrated as he went.

He said, "There's a service road leading to a covered garage. The covered garage is for snowplows and other winter equipment. There's plenty of space and they have it all to themselves. There will be a guard at the door."

Reacher said, "Where?"

"It doesn't say."

"It must. Stackley was new."

"It doesn't. Maybe it's somewhere he was already familiar with. Maybe they already told him the general area."

"Who left the message?"

"Sounds like a transportation captain. He's all about the details."

"Is there an area code?"

"Blocked number."

"Terrific."

Rose Sanderson went back to the camper shell. She leaned in and came out with the three wrapped patches. She gave one each to the cowboys. For old times' sake, Reacher figured. A parting gift. And like a good officer. Always make sure your men are OK. She kept one patch for herself. She took another from her pocket. The last of yesterday's purchase. She butted them together, and then fanned them out, like a tiny hand of cards. She counted them. One, two. Then again, in case something had magically changed. One, two. Then again, obsessively. Same result.

She said, "This is not good."

Reacher said, "How long?"

"I'll be getting sick by tonight."

"Where would we find snowplows?"

"Are you kidding? Everywhere. Billy had a snowplow."

"At his house. I mean big machines stored in a covered garage."

"An airport?" Bramall said. "Denver, maybe."

Reacher said nothing.

Then he said, "Three days ago."

He stepped over the leaking body and leaned in the pick-up's cab. Sandwich wrappers. Gas receipts. He threw the wrappers on the driver's seat and piled the gas receipts on the passenger seat. He checked the floor and emptied the door cubbies.

He said, "What was the date three days ago?"

Mackenzie told him. He riffed through the flimsy paper, checking dates. Some receipts were a year old. Some were brittle and yellowed. He learned to look at the crisp items first.

Bramall said, "Let me help."

In the end they split the drift of paper four separate ways. They all stood around the pick-up's hood, and licked their thumbs, and sped through the piles, like bank tellers with dollar bills around a counting table.

"Got one," Mackenzie said. "Three days ago, in the evening. Not a gas station. I think it's a diner or a restaurant."

"I got gas here," Bramall said. "Three days ago, also in the evening."

They clipped them under the pick-up's windshield wiper, like parking tickets. They scanned through the rest. They found nothing more.

"OK," Reacher said. "Let's take a look."

The diner check was for thirteen dollars and change, paid in cash at 10:57pm, three days before. The gas receipt was for forty bucks even. Most likely prepaid in cash before lifting the nozzle, two twenties on the greasy counter. At 11:23pm the same night.

Reacher said, "He had a late dinner, and was done by eleven. He drove twenty minutes and got gas. Done by eleven-thirty. Then he drove to the secret warehouse and waited for midnight."

The gas receipt had Exxon Mobil at the top, but no address except a location code. The diner was called Klinger's, and it had a phone number. The area code was 605.

"South Dakota," Bramall said.

He walked away to the head of the ravine, where his cell worked better. He called the number. He came back and said, "It's a mom-and-pop on a four-lane coming north out of Rapid City."

Mackenzie and Bramall and Sanderson went to pack their stuff in the Toyota. Reacher's toothbrush was already in his pocket, and his passport was back where it belonged. He found Stackley's Colt and picked up the other three disassembled guns. He told the cowboys to put Stackley in the camper shell and drive the truck somewhere remote. An abandoned ranch, maybe. He told them to park it in a barn and leave it there. He pictured Stackley ten years from then, all dried up and mummified, discovered by chance with the remains of his head in an empty fentanyl box. The whole story, right there. A cold case that would stay cold forever.

The cowboys drove away, leaving no trace behind except blood and small flecks of bone and brain tissue on the gravel. Reacher figured they would be gone an hour after the clearing went quiet. *You got hundreds of other species already lining up and licking their lips.*

Bramall brought the Toyota around. The women had taken the rear seat. Mackenzie had her traveling bags in the trunk, next to Bramall's. Sanderson had nothing to bring with her except a canvas tote bag. She was looking around, already separated from her home of three years by the thick tinted glass in the Toyota's windows. Not that she cared. Nothing to stay for. Her dealer wouldn't be stopping by anytime soon. That was for sure.

She settled back and faced forward, breathing shallow.

Reacher got in the front next to Bramall, who put the car in gear and set out down the driveway. Four miles of roots and rocks, and then the dirt road out of there.

Chapter 41

Gloria Nakamura walked the length of the corridor to her lieutenant's corner suite. She had been summoned. She didn't know why. When she got there the guy was looking at his computer screen. Not email. A law enforcement database.

He said, "The federal DEA have custody of a guy with the first name Billy and a home address in Mule Crossing, Wyoming. He was arrested in Oklahoma for running a light. He is thought to have fled Wyoming because of a warning from a friend about a DEA operation in Montana. So no need to call the two men or the county dog. Billy's days of shooting people from behind a tree are over."

Not Reacher after all, she thought.

For some reason she felt disappointed.

"But here's the thing," her lieutenant said. "The Feds don't know about Scorpio. The report makes that clear. They're asking us all to cross-check Billy's name against our open files, to help them figure out who's running him. They don't know."

"Are you going to tell them?"

"Hell no. I don't want a bunch of fancy-pants federal agents swooping in here to grab the glory. Scorpio belongs to the Rapid City Police Department. He always has. We're going to get him."

"Yes, sir," Nakamura said. "We know Scorpio already replaced Billy. Inadmissible evidence, but there's a new guy out there."

Her lieutenant said, "There's another DEA request on the system. Looks completely separate, but I don't think it is. It was posted just afterward. They're asking if anyone in the western region is seeing domestic packaged prescription oxycodone or fentanyl. Lots of it, like in the old days."

"I thought that was over."

"It is over. Every truck that leaves the factory is logged in the computer, and followed on GPS, plus they know exactly what was in it to start with, so in theory if they wanted to they could track down every single separate pill."

"So why are they worried?"

"Something must not be working right. Or Scorpio is smarter than we thought. Either way, we can't let the Feds get him first. So whatever you're doing now, I want you to do it ten times harder. Put your other cases on the back burner. I don't want federal agents coming in here."

Bramall's navigation screen showed their best route would be Laramie to Cheyenne on the highway, and then straight north on a state road, all the way. So they turned at Mule Crossing, off the dirt road, onto the two-lane, past the post office, past the firework store, past the bottle rocket billboard, and all the way up to the highway, where they turned east. Mackenzie looked anxious all the way. She had jumped off the same building as her sister. They had jumped hand in hand. They had committed to the same problems, one from the inside and one from the outside. Sanderson herself was sitting with her head turned, watching out her window. Her hands were clasped together. To keep them from shaking, Reacher thought. She was pushing herself hard. She was rationing. Maybe she had set a target. A hundred miles, maybe. Before the next quarter inch. Or five red trucks, or a rest area, or a hybrid car.

Reacher checked the guns. The Smith & Wesson 39, the Ruger .22, the Springfield P9, and the Colt .45. All four were scratched and battered. But they probably all worked. All were only part loaded. The Smith had four Parabellum rounds in it, and the Springfield had five. He liked the Smith better, so he put all nine rounds in it, eight in the mag and one in the chamber. He dumped the empty Springfield in the door cubby. He put the Smith in his coat pocket. The Ruger was an ancient thing, a Standard, maybe dating all the way back to 1949, when it was the company's first product. It had just two rounds in it, .22 Long Rifle rimfires. Not Reacher's favorite caliber, so he dumped it in the door cubby along with the empty Springfield. The Colt was a military M1911, and judging by the style of its engravings and markings it could have been even older than the Ruger. It had three rounds in it. He held it by the barrel and half turned in his seat and offered it to Sanderson.

She was sitting behind Bramall, at that moment turned toward him at an angle where he saw more of the left side of her face than the right. Amazing work, Bramall had said. A virtuoso performance. But actually pretty lousy. Reacher thought all three things were true. She was sewn together from pieces the size of a postage stamp on a regular first-class letter. He could only imagine the immense skill and care employed in the surgery. Hours and hours of precision work. Reattaching nerves and muscles. But some hadn't taken. There were dead spots. And each postage-stamp piece was thickened and scarred at the edges, and lumpy with sutures. There had been some guesswork about what went where. Her nostril was stitched to her cheek at an odd angle. He couldn't compare it to the other side, because of the foil.

She said no to the gun. Not in words, but by unclasping her hands and holding them up. He saw a faint tremor. Nothing terrible. But it was still early. He turned back and offered the gun to Bramall. Who had different problems. More rules than Reacher, and a license from the state of Illinois. He thought for a moment, and then he took the gun, but he put it in the door cubby, not his coat pocket. Some kind of an ethical compromise.

Nakamura saw Scorpio go in his back door just as late morning turned into lunchtime. She was parked on the cross street, at just the right angle. Scorpio left the door open again. Just an inch. Another warm day. A cloudless sky, above the tangle of cables on their leaning poles. Power lines and phone wires. Some thick, some thin. Some old, some new. Some very new. Maybe fiber optics, for the internet.

She took out her phone and dialed her friend.

She said, "Look out for that signal again. Scorpio just went in his office."

Her friend said, "It's not an exact science."

"You got it right last time, about the new Billy. There was a DEA bulletin."

"I saw it."

"Plus another one, posted just afterward, about prescription medication. Which is weird, because they already track that stuff. They log the trucks as they leave the factory, and they log their routes by GPS, and they match invoices to payments. So where's the leakage?"

"That's your job. I'm just a humble tech."

"Which is why I call you all the time. So I don't make a fool of myself."

"What's the wild idea this time?"

"The computer guys at the factory could erase a whole truck, right? They could just delete it completely. They could erase its inventory and its GPS track. Like the departure never existed. Like that particular truck was in the shop that day. Or parked in the lot."

"That suggests corruption among computer guys. I may not be the person to ask."

"Is it possible?" she said.

"They would have to erase the invoice, too. Also the original order. They would have to amend the factory production records, otherwise it would look like they were making more pills than went out the door. If they did all that, then everything would balance. The unrecorded surplus would be a kind of ghost quantity, floating out there somewhere."

"Could they do all that?" she said.

"Of course they could," her friend said. "A computer does what it's told. The result depends on who's doing the telling."

"What about someone not in the factory? Could they do it by remote control?"

"A hacker, you mean? Sure, if they breached security. Which would be tough, since we're talking pharmaceuticals and the DEA. But not impossible. You can buy software from Russia."

"What kind of equipment would he need?"

"In the end nothing more than a laptop. But getting there would involve a lot of high-speed number crunching. There would be a lot of stuff running at once. He would have a couple of racks at least. Like his own server."

"Hot, right?"

"We use max AC down here."

"Thanks," she said.

She clicked off, and looked at the wires overhead, and Scorpio's open door.

Bramall's cell phone rang just north of a place named Defiant, which had a John Deere dealership and not much else. Bramall fumbled the phone up out of his pocket and checked the screen. He offered it to Reacher, the same way Reacher had offered him the Colt.

The screen said West Point Superintendent's Office.

Reacher said, "How does it know?"

"I programmed it," Bramall said. "When he called the first time."

"You can take the boy out of the FBI," Reacher said.

He answered the phone.

The same woman.

She said, "Major Reacher, please."

"Ma'am, this is Reacher."

"Please hold for General Simpson."

The supe came on and said, "Major."

Reacher said, "General."

"Progress report?"

"We're in the car."

"Can she hear what you're saying?"

"Loud and clear."

"Is she OK?"

"So far."

"We're still working on the roadside bomb. Those files are sealed up pretty tight. But we got something new on Porterfield. Through the Marine Corps side. They had a stray copy classified at a lower level."

"What did you get?"

"There was an arrest warrant out on him. Sworn a week before he died."

"By who?"

"Defense Intelligence Agency."

"Have you seen it?"

"No point. The DIA never says why."

"Did it feel like a big deal?"

"It was DIA. That's always a big deal."

"Do you know anyone there?"

"Forget it," Simpson said. "I want to retire in Florida, not Leavenworth."

"Understood," Reacher said. "Thank you, general."

He clicked off and passed the phone back to Bramall. As he turned he saw Sanderson's eyes on him, from under her hood. She knew something was up. He had asked, what did you get? She wasn't dumb. She knew what was out there.

He said nothing.

She said, "Let's talk later."

Then she turned away to look out the window. Reacher faced front. Bramall drove on.

Chapter 42

An hour later they stopped late for lunch in a one-light town. There was a Shell station and a family restaurant. Reacher saw that Sanderson wanted to stay outside, on the smokers' benches, to take care of business. But she forced herself inside, and ate first, fast and dirty, and then she excused herself and ducked back out again.

Reacher went with her. He sat beside her, a yard away. A concrete bench in a blacktop lot. With almost the same person. She had a ready-cut quarter-inch, rolled tight and set to go. The size of a wad of gum. She slipped it in, and chewed a little, and sucked a little. She clicked her neck and leaned back and looked up at the sky.

She said, "I can't believe you talk to the supe on the phone."

He said, "Someone has to."

"What did he tell you?"

"There was an arrest warrant out on Porterfield."

She breathed out, a deep sigh of release and contentment. The fentanyl, Reacher guessed, not memories of her boyfriend's demise.

She said, "Arrest warrants lapse when the suspect dies. Obviously. So that's ancient history now. You should forget all about it. Although I'm sure you won't. My sister says you still think like a cop. You won't let things go. Probably you think I killed him. You have to, really. We were domestic partners at the time. Statistics don't lie."

"Did you kill him?"

"In a way."

"What way?"

"Better that you don't know. Or you'll want to do something about it."

"That's not a smart thing to say to someone who won't let things go."

She didn't answer. She just breathed. Deep, long, slow, in and out. All was well with the world. Reacher had read a report that called it a euphoria users swore had no equal.

She said, "Sy was wounded in the groin."

Reacher said, "I'm sorry."

"Not a glamorous location," she said. "The second most feared, as a matter of fact, after a disfiguring facial wound. But they sewed him back together again. It all worked. He could have sex. Except one of the sutures always leaked. Under certain circumstances. It could get messy."

Reacher said nothing.

"Apparently there's a lot of blood pressure involved," she said.

"I hope," Reacher said.

"And he had an infection. From the day he was wounded. His uniform pants were filthy dirty. He had been wearing them every day since California. The bullet punched tiny shreds of dirty cloth way deep inside. Happened all the time. The bugs take hold, and then you can't move them. They must be smarter than we are."

"That was twelve years before."

"He started out seeing doctors. But he didn't like them. In the end he looked after himself."

"Like you did," he said.

"I was like him," she said. "He showed me how to do it. He showed me how to do everything. He showed me the gates of death. The doctor said the leaky suture was equally likely to burst. Every night he

322 | L E E   C H I L D

could have bled to death. He said he learned to live with it. Then to love it. In the end I did, too. Mostly."

"Sounds like an interesting way to live."

"He told me he felt secure with me. But I was never sure why. Did he think it was because I was a nice person? Or did he think I owed him for his attentions, because I was even more hideous? I couldn't let him think that. Or I would have to think it, too. I would have to accept I needed special favors. Which I never took before. Why should I start now?"

Reacher didn't answer. She was quiet a long moment. She sighed again. A deep low shudder of pure contentment. She spread her arms along the back of the bench. Her right hand came near Reacher's shoulder. She laid back and looked up at the sky.

She said, "How important is a woman's face?"

"To me?"

"For example."

"A little bit, I guess. But for me it's mostly the eyes. Either there's someone home or there isn't. Either you want to knock on that door or you don't."

She sat up and half turned on the bench. To face him, full on. She dropped the zipper on her silver top, maybe three inches down, and she eased her hood back, all the way, and off. Her hair spilled out and down and forward. Like her sister's, but shorter. Maybe grayer. But it fell the same way. It framed her face the same way.

Her eyes were green, and they were warm and liquid with some kind of deep dreamy satisfaction. There was sparkle, muted, like winking sunlight on a woodland stream. And bitter amusement. She was mocking him, and herself, and the whole wide world.

He said, "We're of equal rank, so I'm allowed to say it. Discouraged, but permitted. I would knock on your door."

"That's nice of you."

"For real. I'm sure Porterfield was for real, too. He won't be the only one. People react in different ways."

She pulled her hood back in place and tucked in her hair.

He said, "You should get the IV. It's the foil that looks weird."

"First I have to live through the night."

"Sheriff Connelly found ten grand in a box."

"Sy didn't trust banks. He preferred cash. What was in the box was all he had left. The banks lost the rest, back when I was overseas. Maybe that's why he didn't trust them."

"How long would ten grand have lasted?"

She sighed again, deeply contented.

"Not long," she said. "Not the way we were going at it. And sometimes we had to buy food. And he was forever paying the guy who fixed his roof."

"Why did you stop calling your sister after he died?"

"That's easy," she said. "Reduced circumstances. I had to sell my phone."

"Was it DIA who burgled his house?"

She nodded. "They were late to the party. The circus was over by the time they arrived. But they got what they wanted."

"Which was?"

She didn't answer. She just waved the question away, like it didn't matter.

Nakamura's cell phone rang. Her friend from Computer Crimes. He said, "Scorpio is making calls. Or at least the signal we think is Scorpio. The traffic feels about the same as three days ago. And he called the same number again. The one that texted back about the new Billy."

She said, "He's still in his office."

"He's doing it by remote control. It's happening a little ways north of here. I assume the guy who texted is his man on the spot."

"Can we tap his computer wires?"

"We already are. It's called the internet. But he has a firewall. We could hack him but it would take us days."

She said, "The driver must be his. Of the ghost truck that never leaves the factory. Except it does. The guy must know where to drive it."

Her friend said, "I wonder if they remembered about employment records. They would need to amend the guy's hours and miles. That might be a way in."

"We don't have the records."

"Then there's nothing you can do."

"Maybe there is. Only half of this thing is records and computers. The other half is a physical reality. It's a real truck, driving on a real road, with physical stuff in it. How would it get here?"

"From where?"

"New Jersey, I think."

"I-90."

"And what's a little ways north of here, where the text came from?"

"I-90."

"Where could he stop?"

"Lots of places. A lonely gas station ten miles out from an exit. Or some old industrial park somewhere, full of empty sheds with roll-up doors."

She said, "Scorpio is not going to leave his office tonight, right?"

"He never does," her friend said. "Except to go home."

"OK, I'm heading up to the highway to take a look."

She clicked off and started her motor.

They had already driven as far as New York to Boston, but they were still in Wyoming, and so far barely halfway through their trip. The big Toyota kept on rolling. Mackenzie and Sanderson talked together in the back, in quiet murmurs, in the kind of fast, unfinished shorthand Reacher guessed must be second nature to twins. Sanderson stayed in the good zone for most of an hour. Then she started to fade. Pretty fast. She withdrew into herself, as if she was preparing for a hard internal battle. She seemed to cramp up and get uncomfortable. She stared out the window. Maybe she was setting herself a new target. Different than on the highway. Maybe three herds of antelope, or two of mule deer, or a break in the snow fence.

Nakamura drove north out of town on the four-lane, past Klinger's family restaurant, where she ate sometimes, if work brought her out in that direction. She kept on going, through the empty miles before the I-90 ramps, looking left and right, seeing what there was to see. Which wasn't much. In fact nothing at all, from the truck driver's point of view. Not exactly a stolen vehicle, but hot nonetheless. Or in fact cold. Zero degrees. It wasn't there. It didn't exist. Which put a lot of pressure on the driver. Attention had to be avoided. No speeding tickets, no weird maneuvers, no traffic cameras, no exposure at all. South of the highway felt wrong. He wouldn't go there.

North of the highway was worse. She carried on under the bridge and came out amid no density whatsoever. No cover, no concealment. Mostly open prairie. Flat land. Distant horizons. She drove ten minutes, and pulled over on the shoulder. There was nothing ahead of her.

South of the highway felt wrong.

North of the highway felt wrong.

Therefore the guy stayed on the highway. Had to. No other choice. He never got off. There was a rest area six miles east. It was a big place. She had been there before. Food, fuel, a state trooper building, a motel in back, some highway department stuff. All kinds of nooks and crannies.

She U-turned ditch to ditch and headed back to the highway. She hit the ramp and hit the gas.

They stopped again, at a gas station that had a two-table coffee shop next to the car wash machine. Mackenzie used the bathroom. Sanderson popped another quarter-inch strip. She sat on a bench outside, and nursed a go-cup of coffee, with the smell of unleaded coming from one direction, and auto shampoo from the other. Reacher came out and she scooted over, as if to offer him room, plus a yard of space between.

An invitation.

He sat down.

He said, "You OK?"

"Right now," she said.

"Tell me about the gates of death."

She was quiet a long moment.

Then she said, "You build up a tolerance. You need to use more and more, just to get to the same place. Pretty soon you're taking what is technically a fatal dose. One sniff would kill a straight person stone dead. And then you want more. Now you're taking literally higher than a fatal dose. Are you brave enough for the next step?"

"Were you?"

"I felt the same way when I was overseas. The only way to get through was never back down. Always step up. Always take it on. You had to be scornful. Like, is that all you got? So sure, I took the next step. And the next."

She sighed. The new quarter-inch strip was kicking in.

She said, "That's the beautiful thing about next steps. There's always another one coming."

Reacher said, "Logically there must be a last one."

She didn't answer.

He said, "What did Porterfield do for a living?"

"Didn't the roofer tell you?"

"He said he talked a lot on the phone. Sheriff Connelly said he drove a lot of miles in his car."

"Sy was a disabled veteran. He didn't work."

"Apparently he filled his time somehow. Was it a hobby?"

"Why do you care about Sy so much?"

"Just a professional thing. Either he was killed somewhere else and dumped in the woods, or he got eaten by a bear. I never had a situation where getting eaten by a bear was a genuine possibility."

"There's a third possibility."

"I know. And I know you were there. You told me."

She was quiet another moment.

"I'll make a deal," she said. "I'll tell you the story if we win tonight."

"That's a hard bargain," he said. "Could be tough. Is the story worth it?"

"It's not exciting," she said. "But it's sad."

"Then we need more of a prize. I would want to hear your story, too."

"About the roadside bomb? My sister told me your theories. A failed operation with multiple U.S. casualties."

"Worst case," he said.

She sighed again, long, hard, deeply, happily.

Almost like purring.

She said, "It was way worse than worst case. It was a catastrophe. But it wasn't my operation. I was representing the support effort, but the whole thing was a much bigger deal than that. It was devised at a much higher level. The town was in hilly country, compact in size, not walled but well defended. The road looped in on the right and out on the left. Long story short, we needed to take the town, but the pointy-heads said we had to do it without unprovoked civilian casualties. Which at the time was code for no air strikes. So we planned approaches by armored infantry on the road from both directions at once. But the same pointy-heads had some clever analysis that said the enemy would expect that, and be capable of defending it, so we should mount a third approach up the open hillside, halfway in between, so we could come up in the middle of the town and isolate both sets of defenders at once."

Reacher said, "How bad was the terrain?"

"That was everyone's first question. It was the kind of place you had to get eyes-on. The pointy-heads worked out a spot where we could see the whole rise at once. They said in terms of seeing one contour in particular it was where we had to be. They were very precise. But they said not to worry, because it was outside RPG range. So we went there. The dead dog was on the exact same spot. Three of us died, and eleven were hurt."

"Any of yours?"

"Happily no. Only upward, which isn't the same. But that was the problem. That's why the files were sealed. Some big names went down. It was a failure of intelligence. With a small letter, not a capital. Ours was less than theirs. Once again we underestimated them. These unshaven guys wearing dresses had predicted exactly how we were going to attack, and even exactly where we would stand to plan it out, and exactly when we would show up to do it. A day either way on that, maybe. But four-day dogs are what they like best, and that's what we got. The umpires would have to call it one–zip for them. We had fourteen down. Cost them nothing except a cell phone and someone else's dog."

"OK," Reacher said.

"You were worried I got my people killed."

"I thought it would upset you."

"I wouldn't be here if I had," she said. "I wouldn't have made it through."

Then Mackenzie came out, and next Bramall, and they both stood around in let's-go poses, so eventually Sanderson got up, and Reacher followed her back to the car.

They hit Rapid City's southern limit just as the sun was setting.

Chapter 43

They drove through town, straight south to north in the dark. Reacher recognized some of what he saw. He recognized the street with the chain hotels. He recognized the all-day Chinese restaurant, where Scorpio's guy had picked him up, in the battered old Lincoln. They kept on going and came out the other side of town on what Bramall's phone said was the four-lane that led up to Klinger's diner. And it did, as promised. Klinger's turned out to be more of a family restaurant, all lit up, floating alone in a vast dark parking lot, somehow both faded and majestic all at once.

They went in, and ate, because it was past dinnertime. Eat when you can, Reacher said. You don't know when the next chance will come. Sanderson endorsed the theory. For a small guy Bramall was always hungry. Mackenzie said she didn't really feel like eating, but in the end she ordered a meal. Afterward she said it was good. Reacher agreed.

They asked the waitress if she knew an Exxon station about a twenty-minute drive away. The woman screwed up her face, like she knew, like it was on the tip of her tongue. Then like she knew once, but she didn't know anymore. One of those questions so everyday it couldn't be answered.

Then something came to her.

"The highway gas is Exxon," she said. "Up at the rest area."

Back in the car Bramall looked at his navigation screen. The closest rest area was six miles east of the closest on-ramp. The electronic brain said it was twenty minutes away. Bramall said the pharmaceutical factories were mostly in New Jersey. Trucks would come west. A secret warehouse inside an I-90 rest area would be a very convenient thing to have. It could be stocked and re-stocked at any time of night or day. Equally it could stock and re-stock incoming visitors at any time of night or day.

"But it didn't," Reacher said. "Stackley told us they had to wait until midnight. It sounded like the opposite of a warehouse to me. Nothing was stored there for people to show up and get. It was the other way around. People got in line and waited for stuff to show up. Maybe it arrives there at midnight. So I agree, the rest area is the obvious place. But as a meeting point only. As a rendezvous. With a lot of moving parts. One rogue westbound truck comes in, and six or ten guys like Billy and Stackley load up and move out. It must be a real fast hustle. Right in the middle of an I-90 rest area, but under the cover of a shed half full of snowplows. The voicemail said they've got it all to themselves. I guess that's correct. It's summertime."

Bramall said, "So after eating dinner at Klinger's, Stackley drove twenty minutes to the rest area, where he bought gas, and then he rolled a hundred yards around a corner and waited till midnight. All we have to do is figure out which corner. Which won't be difficult. The rest area is a finite size. We're looking for a service road leading to the snowplows. How many can there be?"

"Is it always this easy?" Mackenzie said.

"Mr. Bramall makes it look easy," Reacher said.

Sanderson said nothing. She was infantry. She knew about pointyheads and their best laid plans.

Bramall started up and headed north on the four-lane, through the nighttime darkness, all the way to the highway ramps, where he made the right to head east toward the rest stop, which the machine told him was just six minutes away.

The machine was correct. Exactly six minutes later Bramall coasted off into a giant central facility. The eastbound and westbound lanes skirted it in mile-wide loops through the prairie. It was like a town all by itself. It had lit-up acres of Exxon gas and diesel, and half a dozen bright neon fast food franchises, and a highway patrol building, and a chain motel, and a highway department office with a weighbridge.

What it didn't have was snowplows. At least not within easy view. Reacher felt red-hot infantry skepticism coming out from under Sanderson's hood. Mackenzie looked disappointed. Maybe not so easy after all.

They gave it one more go-round. After which they were confident there were no snowplows stored anywhere within the bounds of the facility. There were no service roads leading to covered garages half full of any kind of winter equipment.

Which raised an obvious question. If not there, then where? There had to be winter equipment stored somewhere. A lot of it. Winter was a serious issue in South Dakota. Mackenzie said maybe so serious they used a whole separate depot for it. She knew the West.

But where was the depot? Who could they ask? It was a weird question. Do you know where the state stores its snowplows? No one would know. Most folk would take it for some kind of a weird political stunt, to make a point, or to expose their ignorance, like asking if they knew their congressperson's name. The only people who would know the answer were people who were currently somewhere else. Wherever the state stored its snowplows.

Reacher said, "He prepaid his gas at 11:23. Right here, very close to where we're sitting now. Let's say it took him two minutes to walk back from the kiosk and get set. Let's say he started pumping at 11:25. How long does forty bucks last?"

Mackenzie said, "Out here you could fill a big tank."

"So it took a few minutes. It could have been well after 11:30 before he was back on the road. But he was the new boy there. He didn't want to screw up. He needed a big margin of error. He must have been going somewhere real close by. Three-minute maximum, literally. He would want to make sure he got there on time. Or early. He would want to be comfortable."

"What's three minutes from here?"

"Maybe the separate depot. For the snowplows. A central facility. Access from both sides. On the same land as this, before eastbound and westbound narrow down again. Right next door to here, maybe. It's a wedge of wasted space otherwise. There could be an inconspicuous little off-ramp, with a sign, saying highway department only. Plenty of trees all around. No one notices a thing like that."

"Then it could be in either direction. We might have already passed it. There must be wedges of space both sides. We don't know which way to go now."

"We didn't already pass it," Sanderson said. "There were no inconspicuous little ramps. I notice a thing like that. It means for the moment we're trapped on this road. But neither can the enemy reinforce an ambush up ahead. So on balance I'm happy. The tail gunner can relax for a second. If you're right about a separate facility, then it must be east of here. And if Reacher is right about how anxious Stackley was, it must be close by. Close enough to get back on the highway and then get off again immediately. If he's wrong about how nervous Stackley was, it could be further away. But it's within fifteen or twenty miles maximum, because even if the guy was cool as ice, he had to get where he was going by midnight latest. And he couldn't drive a hundred miles an hour to do it. Those guys can't get away with things like that. They must never stand out. So I would recon to the east. If we don't find anything, we still have time to come back and think again."

Bramall looked over his shoulder at Mackenzie.

His employer.

"Want to try it?" he said.

"Yes," Mackenzie said.

Bramall circled the parking lot, under sodium lights high on poles, looking for the way back to the travel lanes. In the corner of his eye Reacher thought he saw a pale blue car, circling the other way. A domestic product. A Chevrolet, possibly. Nothing fancy. A plain specification.

He looked again.

It was gone.

Bramall found the exit and followed the arrow marked Sioux Falls, which was east. He watched the road ahead, like a good driver should. Sanderson and her sister and Reacher all watched the left shoulder. They watched the narrowing space between the eastbound and the westbound lanes.

It turned out Stackley had been anxious, but not quite as anxious as Reacher thought he should be. It was more than three minutes out. Closer to four and a half. They saw an inconspicuous off-ramp. They saw a small bland sign that said *Authorized Personnel Only*.

"Don't take it," Reacher said. "Not yet. We need to make a better plan."

Chapter 44

Gloria Nakamura drove every inch of the rest area.
Night had fallen, but it was all lit up. She pictured a truck pulling in.
Maybe not a semi. Maybe not an eighteen-wheeler. Maybe just a panel
van, loaded with smaller orders from mom-and-pop pharmacies and
suburban clinics. A Ford Econoline, or some such. Probably painted
white. Probably a shiny high-gloss finish, to suggest health and clean-
liness and antiseptic pharmaceutical wholesomeness. Probably a
bland brand name in a friendly font, pale green like grass, or blue like
the sky.

Where would it park?

Nowhere near the state police building, for obvious reasons. Not
near the gas pumps, either. Even in the dark. The oil company had
cameras, in case of drive-away no-pays. Not near the entrance or the
exit either, because the highway department had cameras, too, for
traffic flow. The truck couldn't afford to show up on video. Not in
South Dakota, when the mothership's computer had it idle in a factory lot in New Jersey. There was a big parking area shared between
the restroom block and the fast food franchises. It was lit up bright.
But it had cameras, too. For liability, she supposed. In case someone

got in a fender bender, and blamed it on the burger stand. Probably an insurance requirement.

There was a weighbridge, with a highway department office, all tan brick and metal windows. Closed up and dark. But it was way out in the open. Too exposed. She pictured the panel van, with its rear doors open, feeding a cluster of smaller vehicles. An anxious crowd, waiting. People like Billy, and the new Billy, and all the other guys like Billy, in pick-up trucks and SUVs and old sedans. Loading up, before taking off.

Where would they do that?

Nowhere. The rest area felt wrong.

She circled the parking lot one more time. In the corner of her eye she saw a black SUV, circling the lot the other way. It had blue plates, she thought. Illinois, maybe. She looked again, but it was gone.

Bramall pulled over on the shoulder, in the dark, a mile further on, where the eastbound and the westbound lanes came back together again, either side of a standard grass median. Safe enough. If a trooper came by, they could say they had an engine light, or a worry about a tire. There wasn't much traffic. Cars blew by, one by one. Then a semi truck, in a howl of noise and wind. The Toyota rocked on its springs.

Reacher said, "How far is the next exit?"

Bramall checked his screen.

"About thirty miles," he said.

"Waste of gas. Do a U-turn across the median. Rose and I will get out at the depot ramp. You and Mrs. Mackenzie can go park in the rest area and walk back through the trees from the west. You can meet us there. We can take a look around and figure out how we do it."

"You want me with you?" Sanderson said.

"Why not?"

"I can't," she said. "I don't feel so good."

"You can fix that."

"I can't," she said again. "I only have one strip left."

"We're about to get more."

"We don't know that."

"You have to use your last strip sometime."

"I want to know I still have it."

"Shape up, major. I need you with me, and I need you in good condition at midnight. I'll leave you to work out the timings."

The car went quiet.

Then Mackenzie said, "Let's go."

Bramall waited until he saw no headlights coming either way. He turned the wheel and drove across all three traffic lanes. He bumped down onto the median, which was dished in the middle, like a wide drainage channel. For snowmelt, Reacher figured. The plows had to dump it somewhere. The Toyota drove down one slope and up the other, where it bumped up into the westbound lanes and turned and took off, in the direction it had come from. Now they were heading the same way the truck would be later. Coming west from New Jersey. It was already rolling. It had been rolling for hours. It was somewhere behind them, past Sioux Falls by then, doing the long miles Reacher had done in the huge red truck with the sleeper cab. With the old man at the wheel. *My wife would say you feel guilty about something. She reads books. She thinks about things.* They were seeing what the truck would see later. Which was nothing much for a mile, and then at the edge of the left-hand headlight beam an unannounced off-ramp, and a sign that said *Authorized Personnel Only.*

Bramall stopped on the shoulder a hundred yards later. Reacher got out and walked around to Sanderson's door. She got out. Boots, jeans, silver jacket zipped to the neck. But this time the hem of her hood was folded back. For peripheral vision. For situational awareness. She was ready for action. Her face was exposed from her cheek bones forward. The foil on the right, and the scars on the left. The misshapen mouth. One eyebrow terminated halfway through, for no good reason, except it was sewed to something that wasn't an eyebrow.

"It's dark," she said. "It's OK."

Bramall drove away.

They waited on the shoulder. No traffic came by. She was chewing hard. Not gum, he thought. Her last quarter-inch. Or maybe half of it. She could have torn it in two, thumbnail to thumbnail. *I'll leave you to work out the timings.* He hoped she knew what she was doing. It wasn't working like it had before. She wasn't calm. Maybe the last quarter-inch never was. How could it be? It was like swinging on a trapeze, letting go, flying through the air toward nobody, hoping somebody would get there and catch you before you fell. Maybe the new gold standard for insecurity. An addict with an empty pocket. Suspended above the abyss. Nothing in reserve.

They walked back the hundred yards and stopped level with the sign. *Authorized Personnel Only.* Nothing coming.

Reacher said, "Ready?"

They ran across the traffic lanes, and around the sign, and into the ramp. Where they stopped and got their breath and looked ahead. They were on a heavy-duty engineered road, good for heavy-duty trucks. It was long enough to disappear into the darkness. There were trees planted both sides, to pretty it up, but it was industrial access, nothing more.

Sanderson said, "Do you have a flashlight?"

Reacher said, "No."

"I'm sure Mr. Bramall would have lent us one. I'm sure he has several."

"Do you like him?"

"I think my sister chose well."

They set off walking through the dark. There was enough moon to get by, helped by occasional spill from distant headlights, which flashed on things like camera strobes, so they could be fixed in time and space, and accounted for. Beginning to end the ramp was half a mile long, and it led to a drive-in, drive-out garage big enough for heavy equipment. They stayed in the trees and scoped it out. There were four roads in total, an on-ramp and an off-ramp each side, like four long legs on a skinny insect, all meeting at the garage, which had a door each end. Both of which were closed. There was no one around. No vehicles. No sound. It was a snowplow shed at the end of summer.

Deserted.

"What time is it?" Sanderson asked.

"Ten o'clock," Reacher said. "Two hours to go."

"Is this going to work?"

"It looks right. It's what the voicemail said. There's a service road leading to a covered garage."

"That was then. They might have a different place for tonight."

"As good as this? I doubt it. This place is solid gold."

"There's no sign of life."

"Not yet. I think that's the point. They get in and out real fast. It's a totally hidden location. Who pays attention to these places? Someone drives in here, they're invisible."

He turned and looked back. The truck from Jersey would come in from the east, the same way they had walked. Then it would loop around the garage and head back the other direction, for the empty run home. Stackley would have headed west. The other guys like him could have headed either way. It was a secret rendezvous and a hidden highway interchange all in one. Solid gold.

They walked up to where they thought Bramall and Mackenzie would come through the trees, and found them just arriving. They did the tour again.

Mackenzie said, "Obviously I'm not the person to ask how we play this."

Sanderson said, "Operationally the soundest plan would be ambush the incoming vehicle halfway along the service road. After it leaves the highway but before it gets to the garage. One operation, maximum one round fired, maximum one enemy killed. Focused and efficient."

"How would we ambush the vehicle?"

"I don't know if we should."

"I don't follow."

Reacher said, "We don't know what kind of vehicle it is. But it came out the factory gate, so it's probably an official pharmaceutical truck. I'm sure the Boy Detective discussed the matter with them. Lots of meetings and memos. The truck is probably locked. Maybe only the driver can open it. A combination or a special key. Your sister doesn't want to run the risk of having to beat it out of him."

"Would you?"

"The guy already took money to deliver to the wrong address. Clearly he's open to a negotiation. Fair exchange is no robbery."

"So which?"

Bramall said, "There could be ten or twelve guys picking up here. To get what they got we would have to rob them all, one by one. On their way out of here. Like the ticket booth in a parking lot. Twelve robberies, one after the other. Maybe a minute apart. I don't think we could do it. We have no choice."

"Rose?"

"Like I said, the ambush chooses itself. Let's hope the truck is not locked."

"There's a third way," Reacher said. "The best of both worlds."

Chapter 45

Nakamura returned to the rest area, because she ran out of options. It was a bad location, but maybe better than anywhere else. She pictured a panel van, shiny white. Where would it park, to conduct its business? As far away as possible, surely. Which meant somewhere on the far edges of the lot. Late in the evening there were many empty rows. Folks liked to park as close as possible to the buildings. Why not? Why give themselves an extra walk?

She cruised by, in her pale blue car. She was right. The western edge of the lot was completely deserted. Row after empty row. The eastern edge had just one lone car. It was parked with its grille tight up against the trees.

It was a black SUV, with a blue license plate.

Illinois.

She dialed her phone.

She said, "Expedite a request for an out-of-state plate."

In reply she got a burst of static and a verbal OK.

She read out the number. She kept the phone to her ear, and parked next to the black SUV. It was a Toyota. She got out and checked it over. It was dusty. It had done some miles out west. It was hard to see inside, because the windows were high and she was short. But it looked like folk were traveling. There were bags in the trunk. But why park there?

She looked ahead at the trees and concluded a person could walk through them. But what for? Illicit activity was safe enough in the last row of the parking lot. No one needed to hide out in the woods. There was nothing on the other side, until eventually the trees thinned out and the regular median started up again. Technically a person could walk from there to the next rest area with grass under his feet all the way. Or was there a highway department maintenance depot in the way? She couldn't remember. There was one somewhere. They were the kind of places you never really paid attention to.

There was static in her ear, and a voice on her phone.

It said, "Illinois DMV lists that plate as a black Toyota Land Cruiser, registered to Terrence Bramall, at a Chicago business address. He describes himself as a private detective."

Sanderson walked to her starting position, and Reacher went with her. He wanted to know she was still chewing. Or if not, whether that was a good thing or bad. She was still chewing. Doing OK. He hoped she wasn't peaking too early. She had the Ruger Standard. The .22. Two rounds in it. It was all she would take. Bramall had the Colt .45. Three rounds in it. Mackenzie had the empty Springfield. Better than nothing. Like the man said, ninety percent of everything was striking a pose.

Reacher said, "Get the story ready for me."

Sanderson said, "A hundred things could go wrong."

"Not a hundred," he said. "Couple dozen, maybe."

"The arrest warrant was bullshit. I want you to know that, whatever. They were trying to shut him up."

"You want me to know part of the story, but not all of it?"

"I want you to know that part at least."

"What was he trying to say?"

"Something he shouldn't."

"OK," Reacher said. "Stay on the ball and tell me the rest later. You doing OK?"

"So far."

"Good until when?"

"What time is it now?"

"Close to ten-thirty."

She did the math in her head, and she didn't answer.

Reacher walked back to his own starting position. But before he got there Bramall walked up with his phone, which was glowing green, with what was apparently a call in progress with the West Point Superintendent's Office.

"For you," Bramall said.

Reacher took the phone.

He said, "General."

The supe said, "Major."

"We're currently maneuvering. Success or failure within two hours from now."

"Do I want to know the details?"

"Probably not."

"What are your chances?"

"Uncertain. It's a rules of engagement issue."

"She got more scruples than you?"

"She could hardly have fewer. But there are things I won't do. And we have civilians with us."

"Welcome to the modern army. You could come back and take a class."

"She told me Porterfield's arrest warrant was bullshit."

"What was your reaction to that?"

"She would say that, wouldn't she."

"Mine, too. But she appears to be right. My friends to the south got into the file, and there's nothing in it. It has to be phony. No one knows the guy who swore it out. We looked him up, and the only match on the name was a guy in the press office in a Marine Corps medical battalion."

"The way she talks, I think she feels Porterfield had some kind of a just cause going on. In which case there must be a lot of files. He was an unemployed veteran who had to change a dressing every day. If a guy like that gets a bug up his ass he tells everyone about it. He writes letters to the newspaper and calls his congressman every day. And then the White House and the talk shows and every law enforcement agency he can think of. His name must crop up everywhere. I want to know. She might never tell me."

"How is she doing?"

"Pretty good, all things considered."

"Is her attitude OK?"

"In what way?"

"Are you free to talk?"

"Sure," Reacher said.

"Why I wanted to call. We found a sideways reference to a document in a medical ethics case. An army psychiatrist had published a paper. The charge was he had failed to adequately conceal the identity of his subject. The paper was about a woman officer who had been grievously wounded in the face. During an on-site inspection she wasn't required to attend. She was standing in for another officer. Purely as a personal favor. The operation was nothing to do with her. She was there because some other asshole had another appointment. Which upon investigation turned out to be extremely unworthy. The guy killed himself when the questions started. Turned out he was getting jacked off by some Afghan whore, while the most beautiful woman in the army was getting maimed. The paper was about her psychological struggle to see herself as wounded in the line of duty."

"The woman was Rose Sanderson?"

"It was while she was still in the hospital. She said the publicity upset her."

"She hasn't mentioned it," Reacher said.

"It's a factor," the supe said. "She feels betrayed."

* * *

At eleven o'clock the compound was still pitch dark and silent. Which Reacher expected. His theory allowed for maybe twenty minutes of furtive gathering, and then frantic action at midnight. And then nothing again. So he wasn't worried. Not yet. Not unless he was completely wrong, and a bunch of guys was assembling somewhere else entirely, miles away, right then, slapping each another on the shoulder, opening their trunk lids and their tailgates wide, exposing hungry space inside.

Possible.

He waited.

Eleven-thirty was just the same. Pitch dark and silent. Still OK. Still consistent, still logical, still expected. But getting close. All the well-known sayings. The crunch was coming. The money shot. The rubber was about to meet the road. For the first time in his life he paid close attention to what his body was doing. He felt stress building inside him, and he felt an automatic response, some kind of a primitive biological leftover, that converted it to focus and strength and aggression. He felt his scalp tingle, and an electric flow pass through his hands to his fingers. He felt his eyesight grow vivid. He felt himself get physically larger, and harder, and faster, and stronger.

He knew Sanderson would be feeling the same things. He wondered how they mixed with fentanyl. He hoped she was doing OK.

Then he saw headlights on the service road.

Chapter 46

The headlights were dim and yellow, which meant it was an old vehicle, and they were at a modest height and a regular width apart, which meant the old vehicle was normal size. Not a giant pick-up truck. Not a huge SUV. It drove up to the building and the wash from its lights on the siding showed it to be a sedan maybe twenty years old. Shaped like a slug. Dull paint, an indeterminate dark color. No hubcaps. A snapped-off antenna.

It backed up and parked neatly, out of the way, and a guy got out. He could have been fifty. Thick around the waist, hair plastered to his scalp with oil. He was wearing blue jeans and a gray sweatshirt with a word on it. A brand name, perhaps. He walked over to the roll-up door, and did something with a key. Then he squatted like a weight-lifter and hauled on the bottom lip, and the door came clattering up, getting faster, as if a counterbalance was kicking in.

The guy walked into the garage and a minute later there was a muted repeat of the same noise, as the far door clattered up. Inside on the left were ranks of huge yellow snowplows. On the right was empty space. Someone had chalked diagonal parking bays on the concrete floor. They were numbered one through ten. One was at the far end. Ten was at the near end.

The guy in the sweatshirt walked back to his car. He leaned in and got a clipboard from the passenger seat. It had a pen on a string. Some kind of a list. The guy walked back to the garage and took up station near the entrance.

There will be a guard at the door.

The guy took out a handgun and checked the chamber.

Eleven forty-one in the evening.

Four minutes later there were more headlights on the service road. Higher, wider, and brighter than the guy's old sedan. It was a Dodge Durango SUV. It drove toward the garage door. It stopped next to the guy. The window came down. Something was said. The guy checked his clipboard, and waved the truck inside. It parked at an angle, in a chalked-out bay.

A minute later a rusted Silverado drove up the road. No better condition than Stackley's old thing. But no camper shell. It had a flat vinyl cover on the bed. Then an old black four-wheel-drive showed up. Both parked inside.

By five minutes to midnight nine of the ten chalk bays were occupied. Only number five was empty. The guy in the sweatshirt looked relaxed about it. Rules were rules. The other nine guys waiting next to their trucks looked happy about it. More to go around.

The guy in the sweatshirt checked his watch.

His phone rang.

He listened.

He called out, "Two minutes, guys. It's nearly here."

Two minutes later a white panel van came charging up the road, going fast, then braking hard. It stopped and waited. It had New Jersey plates. The guy in the sweatshirt gave it a sign, and then he ran inside the building. The van turned and drove along the outside of the garage, all the way, front to back. It turned again, tight and awkward, and nosed in through the rear door. The opposite way from everyone else. It stopped level with the truck in bay number one. The guard ran up inside and met it there. The driver got out.

Which all changed the plan. Afterward Reacher was mad he hadn't read more into the chalk numbers on the floor. At first he thought they might represent geographical regions, or length of service. Some tradition or perk of the job. Or nothing at all. Maybe they were there just for the fun of it. You chalk some bays, you might as well chalk some numbers. To make it look professional.

But they were a priority order. Some kind of a status ladder. Maybe number one was the guy with the best volume. Like salesman of the week. Like a prize. Part of which was the right to a fast getaway. First served, first out of there. A decent incentive.

There were a dozen different mechanical ways to make that happen. All kinds of maneuvers. But by far the simplest was to bring the panel van in through the rear door.

Reacher was at the front door.

He had foreseen that the guard and the driver from the panel van would be side by side at the start of the process. The plan was, as soon as the driver opened the van, unsuspectingly, voluntarily, without having been beaten or coerced in any way at all, so that everyone's conscience was entirely clear, then Reacher would fire a nine-millimeter round over their heads, into the booming space beyond, to freeze them, to claim possession of the panel van, whereupon Sanderson would announce her presence from behind, and they would all glance back and see a mysterious figure pointing a handgun, and any spark of early trouble would snuff out right then. Only an expert would spot the Ruger for a .22. Only an expert with X-ray vision would know it was nearly empty. He thought the plan would work. First the guard and the driver, and then the other guys. Two different categories of people. He felt the sequence was important.

He was at the wrong end of the garage.

Everything was turned around.

He was now Sanderson.

She was now him.

With adrenaline, and fight hormones, and fentanyl, or maybe half fentanyl and half withdrawal, and pain and discomfort, and the sweats and the shakes. Right then she would be watching the driver. Waiting for him to open up. A combination or a special key. Or maybe not. Maybe just a regular door. In which case it would all happen faster. The .22 was quiet for a firearm, but still a lot louder than anything else in life. In the echoing space a .22 would do the job just fine.

If she took over.

If she did it.

Nothing yet.

Still nothing. Maybe it was a long combination. Like a computer. All kinds of characters, upper case, lower case. Numbers and symbols.

Nothing.

Then a colossal gunshot explosion, and a brutal *bang* as a bullet hit a beam overhead.

Everyone froze.

Up ahead she stepped out and said, "Stay where you are."

Like he would have.

Behind them he stepped out and said, "Nobody move."

Like she would have.

They glanced his way. He had the Smith aimed low, at their waists. He had learned that angle worried people. Some kind of an old animal instinct.

Up ahead she shook her head. They were turned around. The next lines were his.

He used his MP voice.

He said, "Remove all cell phones and firearms from pockets, holsters, and other places of concealment. Place them on the floor at your feet. Do not get cute with me. In a moment I will search you. If I find a further firearm I will shoot you through the back of the knee with it. If I find a cell phone I will shoot you through the back of the knee with my own firearm. These are promises as solemn as government debt. Please take a moment to think about it. We're not cops or federal agents. This is purely private business. For you, just a temporary nuisance. So weigh it up. You can walk the rest of your life, or you can use a wheelchair. Figure out what works best for you."

Eleven guys, eleven phones, twelve guns. The guard had a small .38 on his ankle. Mackenzie stepped out to collect them. She was pointing the empty Springfield. She looked like an afternoon movie. The beautiful queen of the underworld. They all stared. Reacher told them to kick their guns and their phones toward her. She picked them all up, one by one, and she put them in a bag she found in the panel van. It had a cheerful logo, in greens and blues, like the grass and the sky.

Reacher and Sanderson herded all eleven guys into bay number five. A tight fit. Like on the stairs, getting out of the ball game. Trapped between two slab-sided trucks. Reacher and Sanderson stood off at forty-five-degree angles, face on, guns leveled. Not operationally necessary. Either one of them would have been effective. But two had a calming effect. It kept unwise thoughts to a minimum. And therefore casualties. It was a humanitarian deployment of resources. The modern army.

At first he thought it was working. The eleven guys were unusually subdued. They were stunned, quiet, defeated, somehow shaken. Somehow demoralized.

Somehow sickened.

Then he realized.

Sanderson's hood was still peeled back.

Behind them in the corner of his eye he saw Bramall reverse the Toyota through the same door the van had used, and maneuver it backward straight in line with the panel van, the tailgate close to the van's rear doors. He saw Mackenzie start shoveling boxes across, from one vehicle to the other. White and crisp and shiny. Lots of them. Bramall lent a hand. They worked hard together. Box after box.

Space became an issue. He saw them tossing bags out of the trunk, over into the back seat.

He stepped back a pace and looked left and right along the row of vehicles. He liked the look of the Dodge Durango best. It was a regular shape. It looked like it would have familiar controls.

He pointed at it.

He said, "Whose is that?"

Some guy shuffled.

Reacher said, "Are the keys in it?"

The guy nodded.

"Gas?"

The guy nodded.

"Good to go here," Bramall called out, from behind.

"OK," Reacher said. "We know what we're doing. By the numbers now. One, two, three, and out of here."

Step one was Mackenzie visiting every vehicle except the Durango, including the guard's old car outside, and adding all the keys to her bag. Most of the cars were old enough to hot-wire, but the pharmaceutical van was a brand new Mercedes, with a chip in the key. It was going nowhere. Which was good. The Boy Detective needed to see it, sitting there stranded, inert, caught out and shamefaced. It explained everything, all by itself. It was the master clue.

Step two was Mackenzie and Bramall getting in the Toyota and driving away.

Which they did.

Step three was Reacher coming close and central, with the Smith aimed two-handed, low, at their waists, or lower, and then Sanderson backing off, step by cautious step, toward the Durango, feeling one-handed behind her for the handle, getting in, starting up. She backed out of the angled slot, and then couldn't go forward because of the panel van in the way, so she reversed all the way out through the front door.

And was gone.

Reacher waited. On his own. Eleven guys penned up. He felt them stir. A flicker of anger. At themselves, at first. Eleven to one. Ridiculous. What were they, pussies? Which was a bad kind of thing to think. They were going to make trouble for themselves. He had seen it before. Sooner or later he would have to shoot one of them in the leg. To get their attention. It would be their own fault.

Behind him in the corner of his eye he saw Sanderson back the Durango in through the same door the panel van had used. Now she was on the right side of it, and facing in the right direction. Ten yards from him. He heard the transmission clunk. From reverse back to drive. Engine idling. Foot on the brake. Ready to go.

He backed away, raising his aim a little as he went, but not much, randomly scouting side to side, to the guy on the left, to the guy on the right. Then back to center mass, getting further away, step by backward step, hearing the Durango's passenger door squeal open behind him, no doubt Sanderson leaning across inside. He got there and backed into the seat, still with the Smith held level, but the guys had given up. No weapons, no phones, no transportation. They were already thinking ahead, about how to get the hell out before the hammer came down.

"Go," Reacher said.

Sanderson hit the gas, and she jinked the wheel twice, first right, then left, and she met the start of the westbound ramp doing about sixty miles an hour.

Chapter 47

Sanderson eased off a beat, to let a guy one lane over get well out of the way, and then she merged on the highway, and crept back to sixty. Four and a half minutes to the rest area. The car felt rough and noisy. Not up to Bramall's standards. But possibly better than her ancient Bronco.

She said, "How much did we get?"

The thing that mattered most.

"More than two weeks' worth," he said. "That's for damn sure. You owe me the story now."

"I did all the hard work."

"Doesn't matter. You said you would tell me the story if we won tonight. No difference who did the work."

"When I've seen it," she said. "When I've seen more than two weeks' worth."

"It's way more."

"I want to bathe in it."

"You should. You did well tonight."

"Thank you."

"Are you still doing well?"

"Did you see the way those guys looked at my sister?"

"Yes," Reacher said.

"Did you see the way they looked at me?"

"Yes," Reacher said. "I saw."

"That's how I'm doing."

They pulled off again, just a short hop, into the rest area. They rolled past the gas and the diesel, and the fast food, and the highway patrol, and the highway department weighbridge. All the way to the chain motel. Where Bramall had scouted two main advantages. It had private parking in back, so the Toyota would be hidden from casual view. And it was so absurdly close to the scene of the crime that no one would think to look there. They were in South Dakota. There was infinite space all around. Every instinct would be to search the far end of a radius that was growing by sixty miles every hour. No one would look close to home.

Sanderson drove around the back and found the Toyota waiting. Bramall and Mackenzie were standing one on either side of the tailgate. Which was open. They had been tidying the load.

Which was spectacular.

There were dozens and dozens of boxes. They were stacked in a block a yard high and a yard wide and a yard deep. There were brand names and pictures. There were quantities. There were tens, and twenties, and fifties, and hundreds. Over and over again. One box had twenty packs of twenty patches. Some kind of pharmacy size. Four hundred items right there.

"More than two weeks," Sanderson said.

She leaned in and pulled out a box. She opened it up and took out a foil pack the size of a fat playing card. Twenty patches. She put it in her pocket. The richest woman in the world. The new gold standard for affluence. An addict with more than one hit.

She turned to Reacher and said, "Now I'll tell you the story."

"Later," he said. "First I'm going to pay Arthur Scorpio a visit."

"I'm coming with you," she said. "Scorpio has a place in the story."

* * *

They trawled through Mackenzie's bag and found the phone they had taken from the guard at the door. There was an old batch of text messages from three days before, ending with the guard telling Scorpio *All good tonight including the new Billy.* The current batch was not as happy, and it was very one-sided. Since a quarter past midnight Scorpio had been sending increasingly frequent and urgent demands for information. *What is going on? Must hear back from you immediately.*

Reacher said, "Tell him there was a delay. Tell him the guy will come over to the laundromat and explain in person as soon as he can. Write it so it sounds like him."

Mackenzie did the texting. She seemed most at home with it.

Sanderson traded her last-round Ruger for Bramall's three-round Colt.

Then she got back in the Durango with Reacher, and they drove away.

Gloria Nakamura saw the whole thing through the trees. In the end she had figured the Toyota was parked where it was for the same reason everyone else was parked where they were. *Why give themselves an extra walk?* The folks from the Toyota had wanted to hike the other way. Not toward the restrooms, but into the trees. Toward nothing, unless the maintenance depot was there. Which it had to be, or else who would want to hike in that direction? Circular logic, but it made sense to her.

She followed.

She stopped ten feet short.

She saw Bigfoot. She saw Terrence Bramall from Chicago. The private investigator. Who had taken her table in the breakfast place. Two times. She saw a pretty woman. She saw a second woman, horribly disfigured. Immediately she knew this was the owner of the ring. She sensed it. The ring she had worn herself, just briefly. West Point 2005. The black stone.

She watched. Bramall and the normal woman walked back through the trees. They passed twenty feet from her, but they didn't notice. Then nothing happened for nearly an hour. Then vehicles started to show up, and finally the white panel van, New Jersey plates, fast and furious, just as she had predicted. Running wild, technically not there at all, erased from the record.

Then there was a gunshot, and the black Toyota showed up again, and drove in and drove out, and then a Dodge Durango, and then it all went quiet again, until about a dozen different guys crept out and started milling around.

They looked sheepish.

She stepped out of the trees, with her badge in one hand and her gun in the other.

They ran, hard and fast, in eleven different directions.

She called it in, but she knew it was hopeless. The highway belonged to the state troopers, not the PD's traffic division, plus late at night any number of guys could run across all three lanes undetected, and then they could disappear beyond the shoulder to either the north or the south, into space so big it was effectively infinite.

They were gone.

She looked at the empty panel van, and the eight parked vehicles, and then she walked back through the trees, and drove back to town. She wanted to see what Scorpio was doing.

Sanderson and Reacher took the four-lane south past Klinger's restaurant. She was chewing steadily all the way. Not partying or bathing yet. She was maintaining. She was getting herself where she wanted to be, and she was keeping herself there. He thought the huge quantity they had gotten from the panel van had changed her. He guessed part of being an addict was always being anxious. The next buck, the next hit, the next day, the next hour. She was no longer anxious. She would not be anxious for a very long time. Maybe ever again, if it worked out with the sister. So was she still an addict? Not the same way. Now it was all upside. The highs, literally, and none of the lows.

He could see the highs were worth having. Her face was not expressive. It didn't work that way. But her eyes were alive. And her body. She looked like she was having the best day of her life. Without a near-fatal dose. Once necessary, maybe, to obliterate how bad it was for the other twelve hours of the day. But not anymore. Now she could take it easy. Maybe she would be OK.

Not his area of expertise.

He said, "The supe told me why you were on the road outside the small town."

She said, "I told you."

"You told me you were representing the support operation. Representing is a real five-dollar word. Maybe you could use it, if you were asked to stand in by a senior officer. But you were already a major. We didn't need a colonel to figure out how to haul ass up a hill. So there was no senior officer, which makes it a weird choice of word."

She was quiet for a moment.

Then she said, "How did the supe know?"

"A shrink wrote a paper."

"He saw it?"

"He's been looking for you."

"Bullshit."

"He's calling in favors."

"For me?"

"He said you felt betrayed."

"By the shrink."

"He meant by the situation."

Again she was quiet.

She said, "I was in the hospital a long time, and I got to know a lot of people. Missing an arm or a leg. Believe me, no one had it easy. But

I hated those guys. They wore shorts. They could make the best of it. I would have been OK with a leg. Even for doing a favor. I was overseas five times. Some shit was going to happen. Even an arm. But not my face. You saw how those guys looked at me."

Reacher said nothing.

She said, "They wrote it down wrong. All they did was check a box. I never felt betrayed. Truth is I felt unlucky. Literally for the first time ever. At first I didn't even know what it was. It was new to me. It was like getting a lifetime of bad luck all in one day. Every rotten thing. Of course the guy who asked me to go for him was out catching a disease. He had to be. It was inevitable. I'm surprised he wasn't doing something worse."

He said, "Now tell me Porterfield's story."

She ducked her head and looked up at the street signs.

She said, "Do you know where we are?"

He said, "We make a right up ahead. Then a left somewhere."

"I'm going to pull over."

"Why?"

"To tell you the story. Before we get there."

Nakamura eased to a stop on the cross street, and then rolled forward until her view was perfect. Scorpio's back door was open. She could see the rim of light.

She turned the engine off.

She got out of the car, and walked halfway there. The Supreme Court said if she was reasonably sure a crime was afoot in a public place, then she could intervene without a warrant. But Scorpio's back office was not a public place. The Court said therefore she would need evidence tantamount to an emergency. Gunshots or screams or cries for help.

The alley was silent.

She crept closer.

She heard Scorpio's voice, talking low. A composed sentence. A monologue. He was leaving a message. He sounded worried. He wanted answers. The guard at the gate, no doubt. His man on the spot. Who couldn't answer. Reacher had taken their phones. She had heard him, even in the trees. She had absolutely believed he would shoot them through the back of the knee.

She crept closer.

Now Scorpio was off the phone. There was no discernible sound at all. Maybe a low hum. Maybe the noise of a fan. Certainly no gunshots or screams or cries for help.

She crept closer.

She put her eye to the gap.

No angle.

She put her fingertips on the door and pushed it open.

Sanderson pulled over in a strip mall lot. She put the lever in park, but she kept the engine running. The Durango was full of gas. It was ready for a long trip somewhere. A sales trip. Idaho, maybe, or Washington State.

She said, "Turns out there are a lot of nerves in the groin."

"Who knew?" Reacher said.

"Sy was in pain all the time. Also addicted, of course. At first he got treatment direct from the Marine Corps. Then they stopped prescribing. No reason was given. At first he thought it was medical caution. These were powerful opiates, after all. But he needed them. He argued about it, but it got him nowhere. So he started doctor shopping. He drove all over. Then he started buying. Which was easy enough. Back then there was plenty to go around. Which made him mad. Every other faucet was wide open. Why was the Corps being cautious? He got back to them. They let something slip. Turned out it wasn't caution about prescribing. Their inventory was all screwed up. They were running out."

"Someone was stealing."

"Sy made it his life's work to find out who. On behalf of himself and his brother Marines. He was made for the job. He was already buying, after all. He was already in the network. All he had to do was poke around a little. Eventually he figured it out and wrote it up and sent it to the Defense Intelligence Agency."

"Why them?"

"He had a theory. DIA spanned all the services. Better than sending it direct to the Marine Corps. They might bury it."

"What happened?"

"We waited. We figured five or six days. The mails are slow from here. But he was sure they would get back to us immediately. What actually happened was we heard nothing for six months. Then he got the arrest warrant."

"Someone was covering his ass."

"That's what Sy thought. He gave it up, there and then. You win some, you lose some. You can't fight city hall. We went up to the high woods, because it was the start of spring. The first tiny shoots were out. He was happy as can be. He was an East Coast guy, really, quite reserved in his nature, but he was messing around that day and chewing on a stick and pretending to be a mountain man. We lay down on the ground. We had stuff in our pockets. A day like that, we both knew we were going to chase it. We were going to hit it hard. We were a couple who shared a hobby. We wanted to make it epic together."

"What happened?"

"He died."

Nakamura pushed the door. Six inches, eight, ten, twelve. She leaned in the room. Scorpio had his back to her. He was sitting alone at a long bench covered with humming computers. Tower units, screens, keyboards, mice. The room was hot. A fan was running. She took out her badge and her gun. She pushed the door all the way open.

Scorpio heard it. Or felt the air, or sensed her presence.

He turned around.

"Stay where you are," she said. "Let me see your hands."

He said, "You're trespassing."

"You're committing a crime."

"You're harassing me."

She took a step and raised her gun.

She said, "Face down on the floor."

He said, "You're making a fool of yourself. I'm doing my accounts after a long hard day. So I can pay my taxes to pay your wages. One of the many burdens a small businessman bears."

"You're hacking pharmaceutical industry security. Which is supervised by the federal government. Are they going to find Russian software? In which case you're in a lot of trouble."

"I run a laundromat."

"The laundromat of the future. It looks like IBM in here. But your system just crashed. Check your GPS. Your panel van is stuck in a snowplow shed. Reacher took the key. And everything else."

Scorpio went quiet.

She put her badge away and took out her handcuffs.

Then it all fell apart.

Behind her a guy walked through the open door with two go-cups of coffee from the convenience store. Black coat, black sweater, black pants, black shoes. More than six feet tall. A bruise on his neck. She had seen him before.

Scorpio hit her in the back of her head, and she sprawled on the floor, and her gun went clattering away. She was dazed for a second, and felt herself being mauled and manhandled, and then she came to sitting on the floor, cuffed to a table leg. With her own handcuffs. Her skirt was up. She pulled it down, one-handed. Her bag was gone. With her phone.

Scorpio asked her, "What did you mean, everything else?"

She said, "All of it."

The guy in black said, "Want me to go check it out?"

"We'll both go," Scorpio said.

He looked at the alley door, at the inner door, at Nakamura.

"Bring the car to the front," he said. "I'll go out that way. We'll leave her right here."

The guy in black hustled out. Scorpio locked the alley door. He sat down and stared at a screen.

Nakamura said, "You're out of business."

"No," he said. "I'll never be out of business. It's about moving on, that's all. One door closes, another door opens. Nothing lasts forever. I'll get what I need somewhere else. I always did before."

He left her there, sitting on the floor, handcuffed to the table. He turned out the lights. He stepped through the inner door to the laundromat. He closed the door behind him. The office went pitch dark. She heard the door lock from the other side. Then immediately she heard the street door open. Not Scorpio going out. Too soon. He was still thirty feet away. It was someone else coming in. The guy in black, presumably. With the car.

But then she heard a muffled voice.

Familiar.

She thought it said, "What have you got in your pockets?"

Sanderson said, "Afterward I realized he wasn't chewing on a stick. Or just a stick. It was to hide himself chewing on something else, too. He had started the party early. He was going for the big OD. One fatal dose on the walk up the hill, and another when we got there. He hated his life. The thing with the DIA kept him going. But that was over now. They had closed ranks against him. He gave up. He decided this time, when he knocked on the gates, if they opened for him, he would go in."

Reacher said nothing.

"And why not?" she said. "It was the end of everything. He had no money. Which was different for him. Like me being unlucky. I watched him go. He started out good. He was happy as could be. I guess he knew what was coming. He was lying on his back, with the smell of pine all around. His breathing got slower and slower. Then it stopped. That's how it was."

"I'm sorry."

"I was, too. For myself. For him, I was happy. It was for the best. Like people say. I left him there. He loved those hillsides. He loved the animals there. I packed my stuff and drove home."

"What was the black-bag burglary for?"

"His copy of the report. In the desk drawer. The first place anyone would look."

"What was in the report?"

"Old-fashioned cash at the supply depot door. A colonel in a Marine Corps medical battalion was selling stuff to Arthur Scorpio. That's how Scorpio did it two years ago. Different now. But back then Sy was buying the stuff he should have been getting all along. It was weird. I guess the colonel saw the file and took care of the problem behind the scenes."

"Scorpio knew Sy's name, too," Reacher said. "He gave it to me as a decoy."

"Maybe the colonel told him."

"Or maybe he told the colonel. If the roofer saw things, then Billy did, too. Maybe Billy told Scorpio, and Scorpio told the colonel. The investigation hadn't started yet. Now it never would. The guy shut it down with the phony warrant. I think that's the only way the timing works."

"You're saying Scorpio sold him out."

"We should get going," Reacher said. "Time to pay him a visit."

Chapter 48

Sanderson and Reacher rolled through dark tomb-quiet
streets, slow but never stopping, to the corner with the convenience
store, where up ahead they saw a black sedan slowing at the curb.
Arthur Scorpio's car. The same car that had picked him up outside the
restaurant with the chromium phone. The same guy in it. Last seen
gasping for breath on the laundromat floor.

Sanderson stopped tight behind the Lincoln, and Reacher caught
the guy on the sidewalk, halfway to the laundromat door. He hit him
once, just a loosener, and the guy took a knee on the concrete, and
flapped a hand in surrender. Turned out he had been sent to bring the
car around, ahead of a trip to a highway department maintenance
depot, where there was a problem of some kind. Mr. Scorpio would
be out in a moment.

Reacher put the guy in the Lincoln's trunk, which was big enough
for two of him. The old square design. Then he headed for the laundromat door and got there just as Scorpio came out from the office.
Tall and bony, maybe fifty, gray hair, black suit, white shirt, no tie. He
closed the door behind him, and locked it, and turned back around.

Reacher stepped inside.

He said, "What have you got in your pockets?"

Scorpio stared.

Didn't answer.

"You told Billy to shoot me," Reacher said. "And then the new guy, same thing."

No answer.

"They didn't get the job done," Reacher said. "As you can see. So what happens next?"

Scorpio said, "It was nothing personal."

Then he glanced at the street.

"Your boy ain't coming," Reacher said. "It's just you and me now."

"It was business. What would you have done?"

"You sold out Sy Porterfield, too."

"He was a nuisance. He had to go."

Reacher heard a faint metallic sound. In the office. Maybe a machine, counting quarters.

He said, "What was the colonel's name?"

Scorpio didn't answer.

Reacher went to hit him.

Scorpio yelped, "Bateman."

Like a sneeze.

"Thank you," Reacher said.

Nakamura heard Scorpio say Porterfield was a nuisance and had to go. Which was a confession of some sort. It had legal gravity. She was torn between shouting out and keeping quiet. In the end she compromised by clinking her handcuff against the table leg. To no effect. No one busted down the door. Then Scorpio shrieked what could have been *Bite me,* and then she heard nothing more, except grunts and gasps, and the scrape of heels on the floor.

And then the slow roar of a tumble dryer, growling and droning, around and around, with a heavy load, thumping and bouncing.

* * *

Sanderson parked alongside the black Toyota, to further shield it from view. Her room was next to Reacher's. She said good night and went in. He went in to his. He sat on the bed. He heard her through the wall. Moving around. Then he heard her go out again.

There was a knock at his door.

He opened up.

Her hood was still back.

She said, "I guess things have changed about what I'm likely to do. You could give me my ring now. It would be safe."

"Come in," he said.

She sat on the bed, where he had. He took the ring from his pocket. The gold filigree, the black stone, the tiny size. A long journey, for a small item.

She took it.

She said, "Thank you again."

"You're welcome again."

She was quiet a long moment.

She said, "You know the weirdest thing about this situation?"

He said, "What?"

"I'm on the inside looking out. I can't see myself. Sometimes I forget."

"What did the shrinks say?"

"What would the 110th say?"

"Deal with it," Reacher said. "It happened. It can't un-happen. Most folks aren't going to like it. Deep down humans haven't been modern very long. But some won't care. You'll find them."

"Are you one of them?"

"I told you," Reacher said. "I'm all about the eyes."

She pushed down her hood. Her hair spilled out.

She said, "Would you like to see me with the foil taken off?"

"Honest answer?"

"The truth."

"You sure?"

"Don't be polite."

"I would like to see you with everything taken off."

"Does that line work often?"

"Now and then."

"There's a lot of ointment."

"I hope," he said.

"The best way to get it off is take a shower."

"We could do that. It's a motel. We could use a whole bar of soap. They always bring more."

She closed his door. She stood on the bed to kiss him. She was fifteen inches shorter. Much less than half his weight. She felt impossibly delicate. The foil crinkled and the ointment oozed.

"Shower," she said.

He unzipped her silver coat, and she shrugged it off. He pulled off her T-shirt and unhooked her bra. She felt like he had imagined her sister would feel, firm and lithe and cool to the touch, except the small of her back, which was damp. She peeled off the foil. It slid off her skin. Underneath were different shapes. Entry wounds, maybe, not exit wounds. Easier to stitch. But red with infection.

They spent twenty minutes in the shower. Then four hours in bed. Most of it sleeping. But not all. At first he was cautious. Not because of her face. Because of her size. She was tiny. He thought he might break her. Then he figured hey, she survived the army. How much worse could it be? After that they got in the same groove together. Not better than fentanyl, he was sure. But better than aspirin. He could testify to that.

Before seven the next morning Reacher was carrying coffee back to the room, when Bramall cut him off, with the phone. Another call in progress with the West Point Superintendent's Office.

But first Bramall said, "I already called Special Agent Noble. DEA is on its way to pick up the pieces. We need to get out of here right now."

"Works for me," Reacher said.

He took the phone.

He said, "General."

The supe said, "Major."

"We're about to exfiltrate. The mission succeeded. We resupplied and we're good to go."

"Do I want to know the details?"

"Probably not," Reacher said.

"We found out about Porterfield's crusade. It was a colonel named Bateman who killed it. But DIA didn't like him. They left Porterfield's copy of the report in his house for a month. They hoped the sheriff would find it. Outside pressure would have given them cover. But the guy didn't bite. Eventually they had to go get it back. But they got Bateman later, for something else. He went down hard."

"Thank you, general."

"Thank you, major."

Reacher walked the phone back to Bramall. He was fussing around the Toyota, moving stuff, trying to make more space. Mackenzie was helping him.

Reacher said, "Relax."

He walked back to the room. Sanderson had new foil in place. Her hood was forward, and the drawstring was tight.

He said, "The supe told me Colonel Bateman went down later. So that's two for two. Him and Scorpio."

"Would that make you feel better?"

"A little," he said.

"Me, too, I guess."

"I'm not coming with you."

"I figured you wouldn't."

"Get the IV."

"I will."

"Good luck."

"You, too."

They didn't kiss, because the foil was new. Instead they stepped outside and Sanderson got in the car. Reacher shook hands with Bramall, and Mackenzie, and he watched them drive away. He walked up to the gas and the diesel. He found another homeless guy running another hitchhiking market. A dollar to play. Like Sioux Falls. Maybe a South Dakota thing. There were only three choices. Because of the way the lanes were laid out.

You could bid for south on a state road.

Or east on the highway toward Chicago.

Or west on the highway toward Seattle.

Reacher paid his dollar and chose south on the state road. Ten minutes later he was in a carpenter's truck, with a guy who was heading to Kansas, looking for tornado work.

About the Author

LEE CHILD is the author of twenty-one *New York Times* best-selling Jack Reacher thrillers, twelve of which have reached the #1 position, and the complete Jack Reacher story collection, *No Middle Name*. All his novels have been optioned for major motion pictures—including *Jack Reacher* (based on *One Shot*) and *Jack Reacher: Never Go Back*. Foreign rights to the Reacher series have sold in one hundred territories. A native of England and a former television director, Child lives in New York City.

leechild.com
Facebook.com/LeeChildOfficial
Twitter: @LeeChildReacher

To inquire about booking Lee Child for a speaking engagement, please contact the Penguin Random House Speakers Bureau at speakers@penguinrandomhouse.com.

About the Type

The text of this book was set in Life, a typeface designed by W. Bilz and jointly developed by Ludwig & Mayer and Francesco Simoncini in 1965. This contemporary design is in the transitional style of the eighteenth century. Life is a versatile text face and is a registered trademark of Simoncini S.A.

I pull off the metal frame. *They're hurling their shoulders against the door. It opens a crack. The muzzle of a gun peeks in.* I climb through the hole, wiggling. *You feel gunfire strike the wall around you. A bullet pierces your foot. Extreme pain.* I drop into the library and sprint-limp to the windows. *You hear them running back out into the hall, toward the library. They're on to you.* I open the middle window, the one closest to the oak tree whose branches are just within reach. I climb over the xylophone display and get my feet on the radiator ledge. *One of the gunmen follows your blood trail and sees you between the stacks. He takes aim. You can't jump in time.* I use Simon's glasses again. It's sunny out. I hold the lens, catch the light, and reflect it right into his eyes. *The gunman squints, recoils, and shoots a round into the ceiling.* I stretch my legs over the windowsill. I see the branch. I jump."

It went on like this, on and on and on. We took turns. We improvised weapons and shields and intricate booby traps constructed out of Old Masters paintings or jugs of crab salad. Occasionally we dangled lifesavers, like keys pressed in the hands of the dying or dead (janitors were messiahs with very short lives). Sometimes, maybe one in six, we didn't make it. We died panicking, stung by our wrong choices, on the ice floes of penguins or across our parents' beds or on the unclaimed bags in coat check. I always fared better than Charlie did, either because I proved a wilier strategist or because Charlie didn't enjoy reveling in my murder. But it was Charlie's tendency to make bad decisions, as if attracted to the deadest of ends and yet still expecting to escape without a scratch.

I don't know what Destroyers said about us. I never mentioned the game later to a roommate or a therapist, perhaps embarrassed by its macabre premise, even though such tragedies occurred with almost weekly regularity in real life and the news fixated on the same lurid details bullet by bullet. I often think the whole world was secretly playing the same game. In our defense, our obsession with Destroyers hardly seemed a symptom of psychosis. We were never the killers, never the black-balaclava gunmen of unknown political or personal affiliation savoring the massacre's toll—and if anything, it caused us to be nicer to those who unwittingly supplied cameos, people like Simon McMarnely and his obliging glasses, poor Simon and what he went through in our fantasies in order for us to live.

We didn't much mention Destroyers to each other once it bled out of our free time. Like most childhood games, by the eighth grade it had lost its magical hold. I think it stopped when Charlie started in-sisting on saving girls he liked or when he kept leading the scenario into the more complicated backdrop of locker rooms and swimming pools. ("Ian, the broom is firmly securing the door. Now you say it's steamy, but I'm walking toward the showers. Be specific. What do I see?")

It occurs to me now, almost twenty years later, that Destroyers was teaching us something all along. It wasn't just the thrill of the chase. We were sharpening our instincts, jettisoning attachments. We were honing strategies for survival.

I HAVE NO plan but this one.

The Acropolis is golden in the afternoon sun, but I can't take my eyes off the dogs. The rooftop bar of the Hotel Grande Palace is an oasis of mist machines and tilted umbrellas growing out of warm, black pools of shadow. Music plays on hidden speakers, a slow trem-olo of keys like ice falling softly in a glass. For the past half hour I have been leaning against the railing, staring out over Syntagma Square and the wild dogs that patrol it. They move in a pack, vicious arrow-headed trotters, the color of corroded razor blades, snapping and growling and taunting the tourists whose guidebooks have led them imprudently toward this danger. Pamphlets and burned flags from a dispersed political rally litter the ground like New England leaves. I know I should spend my few free hours climbing around the Parthenon or at least glancing up at it. But in the swampy heat of early August, all of Athens looks like a ruin, sunken and edgeless and blurred spit white. The dogs are thin and frantic.

I shouldn't be here. In Greece. At the Grande Palace. On vacation.

I have been wearing the same clothes for twenty-eight hours, minus a missing pair of underwear. I smell of spilled red wine, duty-free cologne (Texas cedar and Haitian vetiver), quick intercourse, tube-rose hand soap, and human grease. I am only at the Grande Palace at the invitation of the woman I sat next to on the overnight flight from New York. Amy, Ann, Annabel? Neither of us could sleep in the soaring adult nursery full of weighted breathing and fleecy blankets. As I watched the progress of our plane on the miniscreen, she nudged me. I had fallen into the sad, homeless trance of sky travel. We were halfway over the Atlantic.

"What's wrong?" She pulled her headphones from her ears. "Excuse my prying, but you look upset."

"My father just died," I told her.

"Oh," she whispered. "Are you flying over for his funeral?"

"No, I'm flying away from it."

I have no idea what she saw in me. Maybe she held the belief that anyone traveling business class moved through the world on a special pass. Or maybe she spotted, correctly, an easy target. She was ten years older than me, in her late thirties. She had a dancer's skeletal grace, was married according to her finger, and was headed to Athens to attend a telecommunications convention. "God knows why it's in Greece with all the turmoil going on." She spoke the language of acronyms—ATSZ, CLO, a satellite hookup on PBX—which sounded too much like the city we had left. The mention of death only suppressed her urge to talk for a few minutes. "Fly Korean, fly Air India, if you ever get the chance, fly Singapore," she confided in the whisper of trade secrets. "You never get the feeling they're delivering your dinner at gunpoint. Actually, no, you *do* get that feeling, and that's why the service is so strong." She laughed at her joke and cued me with another nudge to the shoulder. The only other insomniac in our cabin, two rows ahead, had spent the last twenty minutes trying to pluck an intractable nose hair; I was growing impatient for the decisive yank of victory. Ann or Amy seemed to appreciate me most when I didn't interrupt her. She told me she traveled *beaucoup trop trop* for work and expounded on her theory that onboard entertainment systems had replaced the need for puke bags—"haven't you noticed no one gets sick anymore because all of their nervousness has been abated by unlimited movie options? That and the extra legroom." She motioned toward the Velcro-shut curtains behind us. "I try not to imagine the favela back there." By the time the plane ticked over the coast of Croatia, the attendants were passing around schizophrenic trays of champagne and coffee, dawn was roaring through the windows, and I didn't have the heart to tell her I'd upgraded from economy on miles. Business class had the only available seats left.

"Do you have a hotel?" she asked as we waited in line at passport control.

"No, but I have a boat at midnight. I guess I'll kill time visiting the Acropolis."

Her hotel had a view of the Acropolis, she said, as well as a sofa in case I needed to sleep. "It's the least I can do after your loss." Room 411. She unlocked the door, tipped the bellboy, and in the early-afternoon curtained darkness, the AC blasting, lifted her pleated skirt and spread herself across the bed. At the time, I felt good for something, and afterward, not for much. Her fingers gouged my hips, but she stared at the door as if waiting for someone more present to enter. We were still two Americans following the standard procedure for arrival. After we finished, I crawled off of her and searched the floor for my clothes.

"I didn't even ask what your father died of," she said, digging her hands underneath the pillows. It seemed less a question than a boast of her impulsiveness. I slid my pants on and went into the bathroom to wash my face. When I returned she was fast asleep, blond hair leaking from a cocoon of blankets.

I am leaning against the railing, putting all of my weight on it. Like much of the fading hotel—a Beaux-Arts mansion littered with flypaper and velvet-flocked rooms named after deposed royalty—the railing is old and in need of a paint job. Cement dust leaks from its rivets. Even if the railing were to give, I'd fall ten feet onto a patio where a man in a red keffiyeh is clipping his toenails. Taxis shoot around the square like dice, and the dogs are fighting by the fountain. I wonder how many of them were kicked out of homes and how many were born behind the Dumpsters of Plaka. Some of the females have teats that droop like the squishy, netted bags old women carry to the markets. Behind me, tourists drift in the pool, nipple-deep, swirling their arms in exaggerated circles—Germans, Italians, Russians, a few lanky Americans with phosphorescent teeth. Every so often, by the clench of a watch or a wave of an itinerary, couples reunite to gather their belongings. The rooftop of the Grande Palace is a waiting station before taking boats to the islands. I think of Charlie in his house on Patmos with a spare bedroom and a locked door.

"Fuck America," a little boy screams, hurtling off a lounge chair. "Fuck going back early! You promised we could stay!" His body is a rack of jutting bones, on the breaking edge before the padding of adolescence. His mother wearily gazes up at him while rotating her bracelets.

"Please don't run by the pool," she says.

"Mister Bledsoe." The waiter taps my shoulder. He is young, doughily handsome, and the curls of his hair are frozen with mousse. Waiters never tap customers on the shoulder in New York; there must be a policy against physical contact. I remember four days ago in my father's bedroom, my stepmother saying, "The dying don't like to be touched."

The waiter hands me back my credit card. "It doesn't work. Maybe you forgot to call your bank?" He's so unwilling to assume the worst I could almost kiss him. "Do you want me to charge it to your room?"

Hotel guests are the only ones allowed up here.

"No." I set my drink down and reach into my pocket. I take my only other card out of my wallet, the one connected to the personal credit history of a twenty-nine-year-old man whose postcollegiate career consists of sporadic but deeply fulfilling charity work. "Try this one." I slap the plastic into his hand and smile to hide my panic.

The family card, my last link to the emergency Bledsoe reservoir, has been deactivated.

The waiter eyes the new card suspiciously. I no longer want to kiss him. I wonder if the dogs bother him when he leaves the hotel at night. I wonder if he lives with his parents. Below us, two officers enter the square toting high-power water rifles. The dogs must know their run is over because they scatter across the bleached cement.

"Which room are you staying in?" he asks me.

"Room four-eleven," I say. "With my girlfriend. She's asleep downstairs." I picture Amy or Annabel waking to a hefty tab, yelling acronyms at the concierge, demanding Singapore service. My underwear must still be tangled somewhere in her bedsheets. "I'll have another." I grab my suitcase and follow him to the bar.

It is cool in the shade of alcohol and awnings. For a second, the stain of the sun lingers on my eyes, purple circles that slowly evaporate. Very few guests settle around the counter. The waiter swipes the card, and that beautiful atonal sound of scrolling receipt paper issues from the machine.

Just get me to Patmos, I think.

On the other side of the bar, a skinny, twitching man chats up an older Russian woman. He looks familiar, the way anyone young and amphetamine-eyed looks vaguely familiar in proximity to a bar. "I'm a traveling vigilante," I hear him say without a hint of sarcasm. The Russian laughs, her burned breasts and chandelier earrings shaking like a minor earthquake.

She holds up her phone. "Let me take picture," she says. "First vigilante on vacation."

He presses his hand over the phone to block the lens.

The guy is so sweaty I can make out the pattern of his chest hair underneath his shirt. A scar runs from the corner of his mouth, and his head is shaved to disguise the twin islets that remain of his hairline. He looks like a gigolo in his last year on the circuit, his flirtation cut with a baffled desperation. His index finger is just a nub, like the end of a pool cue steadying for a shot. He might be my age, he has my accent, but his face is so beaten I can't imagine how the guard in the lobby let him up here without asking to see his room key. He catches me staring, so I turn to the view of the Acropolis. When I look back, he's still watching me, wincing. He snatches his wallet from the counter and stalks off toward the elevator. The Russian woman is too busy gazing into the aurora borealis of her phone.

The waiter pours my second drink. The gin will help the panic. It has already painted the flowers in the planters a softer shade of pink. But I have to be careful from here on with my spending. I only have what's left in my bank account and the small stack of cash, hidden in my suitcase, that I managed to siphon before the reservoir went dry. I once spent a winter after college helping single mothers in the Bronx set up bank accounts. "Five dollars. Let's start your future of financial solvency with five dollars. Surely you can spare that much."

The Russian woman pats the counter, as if she's feeling for weak spots in the wood. She jumps from her stool and kneels on the ground. As I sign my name on the receipt, she begins to wail about missing money, her wallet stolen. "Asshole vigilante. It had my boat ticket. Waiter, fast, call down! Don't let him leave the hotel!"

I take my drink to the railing, trying to remain uninvolved. It's my new tactic, distancing myself from the problems of others. It feels surprisingly liberating, cordoning off worry to the limits of myself.

How do you feel sorry for a rich kid? This was my father's favorite joke when I was little. I'd be midmission in a video game or at the dining room table conjugating French verbs on one of the weekends he was mandated to watch me. He'd ask it like a dare, and, without missing a beat, he'd supply his unfunny punch line. *You don't.*

But I have a better answer.

You make him not rich. I have fallen out of money. It's like falling out of love. Only with money, it's not you that walks away, you're still here, it's the money that goes elsewhere, finds a new home, forgets. It's my fault—not that it matters; you can't talk your way back into money like you can with love, calling it up in the middle of the night, pleading for a second chance. I try to picture Charlie on his yacht in

Patmos, a black-oak sixty-footer agitating waves, the free food and sun and the hours of sleep ahead. But I am sweating and the dogs are gone and the Acropolis is so blurry I wouldn't mind it torn down, and all I can think of is my call to Charlie four days ago, the first time I had spoken to him in years.

"I need to ask a favor. It's urgent."

"Hi, Ian. I'm fine. Can't complain. You missed my birthday by a month."

"I'm serious. And it's more of a proposal than a favor."

"How about asking nicely? How about putting some sweetness in that New York whine of yours?" The phone fell from his ear and after a short scuffle, he was back. "How's volunteer life? How many starving kids did you save from the death camps today?"

"I'm in hot water. I need your help. You always told me I could ask. Well, I'm asking now."

"Hot water?" He paused. I could hear the static in the distance between our voices. "I'm in Greece. The water's freezing. I have an idea. Why don't you come?"

EVERY SUDDEN DEATH is a murder. The incidents surrounding each last breath are analyzed exhaustively for a person to blame. How much morphine did the night nurse add to the IV drip? Was the walk light still white before the taxi rounded the corner? What was the final call on the phone found near the open window? Even a presumably natural death holds the opportunity for a finger to point. My father died in bed at his home in the West Village. Edward Bledsoe, senior vice president of Kitterin Inc., international baby-food manufacturer, twice married, age sixty-seven. I am "also" according to his obituary. "He also had one son from a previous marriage." Lily, my stepmother, was downstairs in the kitchen, lecturing the nurse in her operatic Spanish. I sat by his bed in one of the Amish rockers that Lily spent her free time collecting from antique stores, under one of the modernist prints she wrangled poker-like at night from online art auctions. I hadn't seen my father since the two strokes stalled his face six days earlier. "He's going," Lily had warned me. "At least it feels that way. The doctors say there's a chance he'll pull through. Try not to upset him, okay?" His eyes still worked, flinched, and as I peered down, I got the feeling I had cornered an injured animal, a creature that had no choice but to relent. His gray mouth gaped, and his white hair was combed back in a style that was never his. It must have been the nurse's preference.

"Hi, Dad. How are you feeling? I thought I'd keep you company."

There was only one photo of me in the many framed above his bed—where younger, happier Bledsoes celebrated birthdays and graduations like the repeating pattern of wallpaper. In the photo, I am a toddler in Central Park, tumbling in his lap like a Labrador, while his eyes are fixed on a great concern beyond the red autumn trees and the pond of miniature sailboats. It was the same pond that Charlie and I used to visit after school as teenagers, stoned beyond the ability to tie our shoelaces or wonked out on some of Charlie's mom's funny pills. We were engaged in the great postadolescent pastime of trying to obliterate our innocence as brutally as we could, torching every last place in our minds that it might hide. We'd sit on the benches by Kerbs Boathouse watching the armada of white, spinning sails, our jaws slack, our eyes as glassy as oyster meat, and my head rattling with liquid-fire revelations I wasn't sure I had only imagined or had spoken out loud. "Did I just tell you about terrorists putting piranhas in the pond to devour children?" I'd ask him worryingly, each forgotten second betraying the stability of the current one. Charlie would look over, as if trying to assess how to save a drowning man without getting wet. A round of Destroyers would have lent my brain a focus, but Charlie and I were past that age. Charlie was already deep in his street years, a platinum cap on his left canine, Cyprus by way of Compton, a sudden expert of subways. But Charlie always brought along his velvet bag of chess pieces, and we'd play on the stone tables next to the sleeping homeless as night fell.

I sat and my father lay there, in the silence of minutes and the birds in the backyard birches. The town house was about as accommodating to me as a shotgun in a mouth—no room but to get to the point.

"I couldn't get ahold of Mom," I said to fill the quiet. "She's been traveling in Bangladesh. Did she tell you she's thinking of opening an orphanage in Delhi?" It was a futile question. They never spoke. My mother had been living in India for the past seven years, surviving like a new age maharaja on the meager residue of her divorce settlement. We communicated once a month by Skype, and her damp, midwestern face in the midst of a yellow monsoon diluted my memories of her midtown studio with its bone-dry static that would terrorize me every time I touched a doorknob. "I'm sure she sends her love."

His brown eyes fled to their corners. He could still control his breathing, and air shot spastically out of his nose, as if trying to expel her from his mind.

"Lily says you're going to be fine," I assured him. "The doctors expect a full recovery."

After more silence, I told him the truth of my situation: I had been let go as operations manager of a nonprofit that prided itself on taking in anyone, no matter how deranged or needle tracked or urine scented; my rent was overdue on my Harlem walk-up; I had few friends left in the city to count on. Maybe I told him all this because I was sure he couldn't respond.

"I'm dangerously low on funds," I said.

You never know who will help you, but you can often predict who won't. My father's working hand spread out on the mattress. His eyes shut. He hated me. He always had. But he especially hated me when, upon his insistence, I took a low-level desk job at the Panama City branch of Kitterin Baby Food Inc. and promptly abandoned it to help out in the gang-ridden, red-zone quarters. "You'll find equality is a young man's game," he had said to me on my first visit back, the last pulse of restraint before his lips creased. "And when your father's business relies on the stability of the current Panamanian administration, going in and tampering with that stability, no matter how corrupt, is not a cause for gratitude." He treated my efforts in Panama as an extended vacation, days that didn't add up, and in terms of mere addition he might have been correct. Perhaps he knew one day I'd wash up on the shores of his sickbed asking for a handout.

I sat there for almost an hour with his hatred, rocking back and forth and trying to perfect the next sentence: "A small loan, an advance to me and I promise no more, just some cash, five figures, the price of one fucking sponge-colored modernist print, and I'll leave you and Lily alone for good." I sat and he hated and I felt sure we had both entered the terrible universe of each other's minds.

The doctors were wrong. He was dying. I don't know when he began actually dying, but he did, as I sat pinned to the chair and his hand finally went still. He went right beside me, this thin body I had depended on and feared. "Dad, Dad? Please Dad?" He looked peaceful, as if he'd finally been let go of.

"What did you do?" Lily screamed when she entered the bedroom. Those were her only words to me during an afternoon of doctors and phone calls. I retreated to the greenhouse, trying to keep out of the way, pinching the tears from my eyes. Death and money don't mix. Death frightens money, money dwarfs death. Doctors give way to lawyers, like tired football players sent to the sidelines by overofficious referees. My two half-siblings hurried over as soon as they heard.

Lex, the youngest, stood trembling in the greenhouse doorway. "Ian, what did you do?" she cried before darting back into the kitchen. I could hear her talking to Lily. "Why did you let him up there? *Alone!*" My half-brother, Ross, kept eyeing me nervously through the kitchen window, as if I were a mental patient who had accidentally wandered into their backyard. He, at least, had the courtesy to lower his voice. "It's not right that Ian was the last one with Dad. Can you imagine what he was talking about? Mom, you should have been up there with them. Or even the nurse. What exactly are the doctors saying he died of?"

I was the answer. Every death needs someone to blame.

Lily finally ended her vow of silence at nine o'clock that evening. She was building a fire in the living room on a humid summer night with all the windows onto Perry Street shut. The headlights of cars flared and receded through the panes. I couldn't shake the sense that she was trying to make her home as inhospitable as possible.

"By the way," she said, grasping the mantel, her back bothering her as it often did, tears in her eyes. She had her own children to worry about. "He left you nothing. Just so you know. It wasn't my doing. That was his wish."

I walked out the front door. It was ninety degrees in the darkness. I was cold.

ALL OF ATHENS is purring with light: the green lights of the streetlamps furry with coastal fog; the metallic fluorescents of street-level bars and falafel stands; the boats at sea scattering hurricane yellow across the glossy water. Not New York light, no overbright excess, but an oily, needling, low-to-earth current like mood lighting for quick petty crimes. At night in Athens history dies, and the city spins. Life, I've always thought, is felt more intensely in the dark.

We are racing at high speed, rosaries swinging from the rearview mirror. The taxi smells like a midnight mass. The driver has a picture of the Virgin Mary taped to the underside of his sunshade, just as yesterday on my way to JFK, the driver had a postcard of Jamaica stuck to his. A small glass jar is affixed to the dashboard holding a lit stick of incense. The glass jar might be a repurposed Kitterin baby-food jar—that's how far the shadow of a global conglomerate reaches. The four drinks I had at the hotel have left me in alcoholic limbo, thirsty for another, regretful of the fourth. I roll down the window and let the wind rinse my face. The driver licks his fingers and smothers the incense tip. The smoke flows. "What side are you on?" he asks.

"Side?"

"Side. Dock. Do you have your boat number?"

I flip through my printouts to find my ferry reservation. "Blue Star," I tell him.

"That is ferry company. Which dock? Piraeus is very big port, very crowded this time of year."

There is no dock listed on my printout.

"What island are you going to?" the driver finally asks. His bald spot is a yarmulke of sweat.

"Patmos."

"Holy island," he says. His foot eases on the gas pedal, slowing his mobile church. Tourists fight through waves of touts on the sidewalk and battle their own refractory luggage wheels. "You don't need to worry, I don't think, about the bomb."

"What bomb?"

"You did not hear on the news?" he scolds, as if the least he can expect from a visitor is a basic awareness of current events.

"I've been distracted lately," I respond, which is the truth. Poverty tends to drown out the latest international horror, and, from the distance of Manhattan, one faraway explosion becomes confused with all the others.

"Last month, on Patmos. Bomb blew up in a café. Killed tourists there. French and two Americans. No one has taken responsibility, not even the radical Islamists who take credit for everything. But it is hard time in Greece now. Today is our Great Depression. So there was bomb." He utters this cause-and-effect relationship lightly, his voice a spray of chimes, but I realize he's simply practicing his English.

"Does that happen often? Bombs on islands?"

"No, never. Never before. But we have never been so poor before. Never so desperate because of the sanctions, the"—he lifts his hands from the wheel to strangle his neck—"austerity measures. And now with this new deal we make it's only getting worse. I pay more tax to drive this taxi than I make waiting all day for a fare." He pats the vinyl dash, as if to reassure the vehicle he won't abandon it. "We never should have joined the rest of Europe. No work, people angry, angry at government, angry at the West. Now is the time of bombs. 'Kill the foreigners.' 'Kill Europe.' It is written on every wall." He ducks his head, as if physically struck with a thought. "Problem is all we have is tourism. Maybe not for long. You want to buy an island, soon the government will sell it to you. They will even sell you the people on it. Sell whatever they can. Even the police in Greece are for sale. So bomb blows up on island, kill the foreigners, make you remember Greece has teeth."

He studies me in the rearview mirror, gauging the fear on my face. He doesn't know I've already lived in dangerous countries. I glance out the window where men are lined up on the sidewalk with their backs to the street, each one pressing his nose tightly against a wall. At first I think they're peeing, like men at a urinal, and then I think they're about to be shot. Panama comes back, men at a wall arranged for rapid machine-gun fire—in Panama killing is a chore that everyone wants to finish as quickly as possible, the killers and the killed. Ever since Panama, I can't take my place at a urinal without thinking of executions. But the wall is a window, changing light, and I see the flickers of a soccer match. The men raise their arms when a goal is scored.

"Don't worry," the driver says. "No one wants to blow up the Irish."

It's my red hair. For my entire life, I've been renouncing citizenship to a country I've never visited. I picture Charlie's hair, the brown, stringy *anywhere*-ness of it.

"I'm an American," I tell him. The driver looks in the rearview mirror and makes a turn into the port.

"You stay at a hotel? A cousin of mine has a small—"

"I'm staying with a friend."

Docks stretch into darkness. Mobs collect around enormous, cake-tiered ships. The driver blasts the horn and waves wanderers out of the road. He points to a huge, blue-striped craft that is already releasing returning passengers.

"Twenty-four euro," he says. I pay him the money he wants in the currency he hates and press my bag under my arm.

Food vendors ring chrome bells. Men and women are spilling in all directions, pressing, pulling, oblivious to the American concept of personal space. Only the bright colors of bags and windbreakers stand out in the night. A group of hippie backpackers sits in a circle, singing Jesus hymns and holding hands. I'm knocked off balance by the straw satchel of a heavyset woman pushing her mother in a wheelchair. The taxi driver has implanted the fear of a bomb in my head, and now I'm stuck with it in the midst of this human congestion. I see bombs in backpacks, in cake boxes, in the dirty cooler of the Tunisian grandfather selling bottles of water, a bomb strapped to the chest of a handsome woman reading a romance novel. *Bomb*, I mouth, as if saying it will stop it from happening, as if bombs like surprise birthday parties are foiled by mere expectation. A boy in an olive sweatshirt shoots his arm out in front of me, men's and women's counterfeit watches buckled from wrist to elbow. He looks up and rubs his thumb against his finger. After the smile that must be the oldest human gesture, two fingers rubbing for lucre. He and I wear the same brand of sneakers. I don't know why this detail captures my attention, but it does, our unsimilar lives overlapping only in our allegiance to a leather swoosh. An older man in a brown turban, maybe his father, barks at him in a clipped dialect that must mean, *try harder, get the sale*. I can't control the urge to clutch my pocket to make sure my wallet hasn't been stolen. It's a confusing motion, the thing I'm protecting the very sign of acquiescence. The boy smiles hopefully, a henhouse of raw white teeth. "Here you go," I say in defeat and give him ten euros without asking for a watch.

The guards signal the acceptance of passengers, and I'm swept forward in the tide up the metal ramp. I check my cabin number. Single occupancy, one bed, berth 805. I need to stick to my new austerity measures; general steerage was half the rate. It's a small, beige, plastic-molded room with no window, and I'm asleep on the bare mattress before the ferry pulls out of the harbor.

I WAKE TO the groan of the ship. In a windowless room nothing tells the time. Did I miss the stop at Patmos, headed now for Kos or Rhodes? I check my cell phone. 6:09 A.M. We don't reach the island until eight. My cheek pinned to the pillow, I feel the slightest sense of movement, so faint I have to go completely still to find it—a lurch of riding on water, not just back and forth but side to side. It's like the teetering of a plane without the impending fear of a crash. I suppose we could always sink.

I get up, brush my teeth, swallow down an aspirin, and change into shorts and a button-down. I use wet fingers to straighten my hair, forging a part like an underused forest trail. Do I look the same as I used to? I haven't seen Charlie in five years, and I haven't spent a solid block of time with him since college. In the spring of our senior year of high school, university catalogs littered the hallways like autumn leaves—fall being the preferred seasonal motif of those brick and cable-knit tableaus that practically guaranteed not jobs nor intellectual whetting but a lifetime of nostalgia and days made only to be played back later as a highlight reel of youth. Charlie and I clamped our hands around the same catalog for a small liberal-arts college in Western Massachusetts, intent on leaving everything in the city except each other behind. Charlie managed five semesters before dropping out, and I helped him pack up his dorm room—his plan for his next steps then as disagreeable to outside interference as a wildfire. We met a few times after that in New York, teaming up for long lunches when he was in town visiting his family, and he'd tell me vaguely that he'd put down roots in Cyprus, dating one woman after cheating on another. Charlie was still at the age where cheating seemed more an emblem of a dazzling personal life rather than a moral failing. He gave, as he always did, the conflicting impression of maturity and irresponsibility beneath an out-of-season tan. At the end of our last lunch he looked at me sympathetically, as if he could see something in me that was falling apart—a crack I myself couldn't locate. "Ian, you just tell me when you're ready to quit volunteering and escape this shithole. The only redeeming quality left in a New Yorker is their ability not to take up space. That's nothing to brag about. I think this might be my last visit home." I told him I didn't mind the shithole. "Anyway, I might try a job in Panama City." His voice turned serious without sounding impressed. "You know, I'm always here if you need me. I wouldn't offer that to anyone but you. Just say the word." At the time, I figured he was lonely in Cyprus and that helping me was a convenient way of fixing what he had lost. But I wasn't ready to admit defeat. We were only twenty-four.

I leave the top three buttons of my shirt undone to suggest the relaxed demeanor of a Mediterranean houseguest capable of slack days in the sun. I don't know what Charlie does these days for a job, but I don't want to look like the last five years have bulldozed me under. I put my Dopp kit in my suitcase, where the $9,000 in cash is Ziplocked in a plastic bag; each thin, green stack counting to one thousand is bound in a yellow bank band. I could have withdrawn more from the Bledsoe family account, the in-case-of-emergencies reserve that I had prided myself on never touching. But any larger amount would have been a red flag at customs. And I can't imagine Lily will notice the loss of anything as low as four figures.

I carry my bag out of the cabin and follow the lava-orange carpeting toward the escalators. In the past six hours, the ship has transformed into a state resembling a floating refugee camp. Only the huddled passengers aren't Middle Eastern migrants who have been pouring into Greece all summer on the news, but ticketed vacationers without the luxury of cabins. Every inch of floor has been claimed by unconscious bodies wrapped in blankets and sleeping bags. Whole families cluster in a stairwell under a makeshift tent of beach towels. Old women hug their purses, using their shoes for pillows. Scuba gear and grocery bags mark tense perimeters, and walls have been built out of suitcases to shield sleepers from the overhead lights. I have to jump sideways to cleave a path. The hallway is balmy with sleep, the moist warmth of measured exhales. Eyes open lizard-like, study me, and close.

I walk down the stopped escalator, where the ferry mutates into a bleak casino of shiny surfaces and garish bulb lights. A bearded barman in a tuxedo jacket makes drinks for sloe-eyed insomniacs, and elderly Norwegian tourists, wearing surgical masks and the red T-shirts of their future cruise ship, sit on stools playing the slot machines. A police siren on the top of each machine threatens to wake the ship, but no one seems to win. I follow the hallway toward the outdoor deck, passing rooms of rowed seats glazed in television light. The plastic odor of nuked meat issues from the cafeteria.

Through the water-slick windows, the night is bluing with morning, black burlap wearing to indigo. Right by the deck door emblazoned with warnings about falling overboard, a man sleeps crouching. His elbows are anchored on his knees, and a purple nylon jacket covers most of his head. As I stare down at him, I see the gristle of his scalp and the nub of his finger holding the jacket over his face. I wonder if he still has the Russian woman's wallet in his possession and if I should alert the authorities about a thief on-board. But he already looks so broken I leave him be. I open the door to the deck, where the air is soft with the sea. A few smokers watch the first pinks dilute the sky, the gallop of yellow, and, not long after, the orange gas star fanning out on the horizon. Two young hippies stand at the bow, humming, with their gold crosses lit by the sun; the girl's blond hair runs to her waist, strands lifting like streamers in the wind. We are sailing right toward the eye, and everything in me gives to the simple religion of a sunrise.

Some take pictures; others call home. By the time the island appears, a faint black groove jutting from the water like the pinched, coiled body of a crocodile, the announcement has come over the speakers. First in Greek and then in English: *Please prepare for disembarkation on the island of Patmos. Passengers are asked to proceed to the marked exits.* The ship's horn wails, alarms bleat, and we are spinning around in the harbor, under a churn of gulls and morning bells. The island is white with houses, filling the valleys like snow. I feel ready, lucky, as if already the future has been sworn to me. I am not as good as I was, but maybe I can be better. The ferry readies for its mass exodus, which follows the natural order of pushing and cursing and using children as battering rams. I text Charlie. I'M HERE. HOW DO I FIND YOU?

He writes back. JUST LOOK.

I 've never known the specifics of Charlie's family's wealth. Like pools or country houses or fathers with healthy, poorly hidden porn collections, money was just a condition that some kids had and others didn't. That's not to say I didn't realize early on that the Konstantinou fortune trumped my own—that I was a votive candle set beside a bonfire. Their residence was a labyrinthine, low-ceilinged duplex on the forty-eighth floor of Fifth Avenue and West Fifty-ninth Street, its brown-tinted windows glazing all of Manhattan with a high-desert varnish. The front rooms were rearranged and redecorated with the same seasonal restlessness as their corner view of Central Park: flocked wallpaper gave way to raw muslin; oily Regency chairs lost favor to skeletal Italian minimalism. The only permanent décor was a collection of tiny silver-framed pictures of skinny children and overfed dogs.

Charlie's family had staff—real staff, housekeepers and au pairs and drivers and a Portuguese chef who, for reasons unclear, insisted on buying meat at a certain kosher butcher (Saturday was their night to eat out, and the chef's night to chain-smoke on the balcony). Orders were relayed in subtle, inscrutable eye movements. During my visits, there was always someone dressed in unobtrusive black to provide drinks or snacks or movie times or alibis for Charlie's older brother, Stefan, who was more a constant point of conversation than an actual presence in the house. Meanwhile, my mother and I, living post-divorce in a garden apartment on Riverside Drive, had a pudgy Peruvian cleaner who would come for three hours every Tuesday, begrudgingly paid for by my father. When I phoned Charlie there was very little chance he'd be the one to answer; it was the rare kind of New York home that took five minutes of waiting on the other end for him to be tracked down. When he called me, I was right on the line 90 percent of the time, turning "hello?" into a life-or-death question.

We were all spoiled kids, no question. Whatever dim connection Buckland Academy maintained to its Protestant roots reminded us that we were all born with unfair advantage. Some of us were just more spoiled. I knew even at age nine that Charlie's money was the kind generated from larger reserves than baby food. It was a strange pocket of America in which I was raised: children whose ancestors reached the shores of this country already loaded. The Bledsoes are a Michigan breed, devoutly modest and thrifty, proud of owning their own snow shovels. My family goes back several midwestern generations, but we are first-generation millionaires, and my father despised ostentation wherever he encountered it (especially in his son). He was a New Yorker by trade and not by social observance. The Konstantinous, on the other hand, seemed to revel in their fortune: trips to Biarritz or St. Barts or Greece or Palm Beach were treated as migratory necessities rather than as vacations, something one couldn't not do, and there was always a new cause or artist or wetland they were subsidizing with the giddy thrill of an illicit romance. I grew up alongside Charlie's wealth, I made a second home in it, and, as with anything introduced so young, I never really questioned its source. Both of our fathers were "businessmen focused on the global economy," which was similar to calling them "sharpshooters"—a designation that didn't lend itself to particulars.

Over the years, though, I did learn certain crucial details. Mrs. K was a quiet, stout woman with deep wrinkles running from her eyes like two palm trees blowing in separate directions. She had the curious habit of cracking open little half-and-half creamer containers in her kitchen and knocking them back like whiskey shots. "For calcium," she'd say. She was kind and eloquent and had a tic of rotating the clasp of her earring, and she treated me with the sincere appreciation a mother bestows on a friend who might be a positive influence.

"Now how is your mother?" she'd drawl in concern, without ever re-membering that her name was Helen. Mr. K, at least fifteen years older than his wife, was bald and brown. He had the round, boneless face of a seal, and he sat cross-legged on the sofa, his pant cuff pulled up to reveal the spot where an argyle sock met his hairless leg. He laughed with his shoulders and asked a scatter of questions, which I rarely understood because of his thick Greek-Cypriot accent. Char-lie would quickly intercede. "No, Dad, Ian isn't doing lacrosse this year either. I told you, we're committed to after-school chess club." Occasionally, though, words and sentences did leap out with clarity, and the Konstantinous enjoyed talking about their homeland over dinners of expensive kosher lamb needlessly slaughtered according to Jewish decree. This is the story I managed to piece together: Mr. K and his father had built a construction empire in Cyprus in the late 1960s. When the 1970s oil crisis cut American businesses off from the Middle East, Konstantinou Engineering took full advantage, be-coming the region's premiere construction company, partially due to its ties with the West. I also learned that after the Turkish invasion of Cyprus in 1974, the family abandoned Nicosia for London and then New York. In the 1980s, Mr. and Mrs. K briefly moved back to have their two sons, Stefan and Charalambos, before resettling perma-nently in New York.

"But what does your dad build in the Middle East?" I'd ask Char-lie. He'd shrug. "Things that need building." "But what's their spe-cialty?" Charlie had been taught to be oblique, and he'd dutifully change the subject. He remained oblique even when, once in high school, protesters besieged the lobby of their apartment building, ac-cusing Mr. K of traitorous oil deals and the mistreatment of Burmese laborers. Mr. K could be found forty-eight flights up, cross-legged on the sofa, an argyle sock snug against his calf, and his shoulders shaking in mirth. *"Dehors eastos raskhish anix?"* "No, Dad, Ian can't stay for dinner."

There were threats made and suspicious packages destroyed with-out ever being opened. For a month, Charlie was assigned two bodyguards to shadow him, a cause of bewilderment even in the halls of Buckland (where the sons of disgraced dictators included their familiarity with the political process as campaign planks during student-council elections). I found Charlie sitting on one of the benches in the school locker room, nude and slumped, wiping his face with a towel. The bodyguards were lingering somewhere out of sight, the whole subterranean room as steamy as a prep kitchen in a Chinese restaurant. I couldn't tell if he was crying or just taking a minute to compose himself. But he looked up at me just then, his brown eyes defiant, his naked body so vulnerable and strong. He said in a slow voice worn-out by its own rehearsal, "What's so bad about us really? Is it because we're successful? We built the highways in the Middle East."

That was it, all I knew of the Konstantinou wealth, and maybe, dimly, all that Charlie knew. We never discussed our parents' dealings. When you look for the monsters tearing at the seams of the world, you rarely examine the people who love you. So we went on, teenagers, shoplifting at CVS and attending black tie benefits at the Harvard Club. We wanted our own lives to be pristine, untouched by anyone before we slid across them. We talked about girls and ate microwave pizzas and got into the idling town car and saw a movie. Normal things. My father made baby food, and his father built the highways in the Middle East.

THE CONCRETE DOCK is runny with soap and hose water. Fetid rainbows collect in the puddles. Compact cars and supply trucks lumber out of the ship's hull and disappear like gleaming hammerheads into the crowd. Leather-skinned women hold color photos of rooms for rent and deep-sea shots of tropical fish as reminders that rooms needn't be luxurious. Everyone is in finding mode: the locals studying the new arrivals, and the arrivals scanning the locals and the taxis streaming on the cobblestones and the chalk-white buildings of Skala. Already stretched octopi are drying on the lines. Red bougainvillea cracks from alleys and creeps along the sides of stores, its flowers a fluttering parrot red that jars the sleepless and the slept. I search the street for Charlie. I do what he told me to: I look. But so many people are weaving around the port or filling the seats of outdoor cafés, loud with the clatter of cutlery and lounge music. I read signs for my name and walk up to a woman holding the photo of a yellow room in her hand.

"Good bed. Fresh towels. Free TV."

"Excuse me. Do you know—"

"That hotel no good, has bugs," she says angrily. "My place, new AC!"

"No, I'm trying to find—"

"Bledsoe," a voice yells. "Bled*soe*." It rolls smoothly through the air from someone accustomed to calling it. I see Charlie forty feet away, leaning against the back of a mini truck, its empty flatbed a series of thin wood planks. As I walk toward him, I take in what five years have done. His black hair is longer and wavier than I remember it, curling around his forehead and ears like boiling water, and his shoulders are wider by an inch. The years have dissolved the fat from his face, chiseling out a man of thirty, with high cheekbones and tight brown lips. He wears faded pink shorts, the drawstrings hanging limply, and a loose white T-shirt with the glimmer of a silver chain at the collar. His legs are hairier, scribbles of black, and he holds himself up on the bumper with his ankles crossed. Ratty white boat shoes have been pummeled into slippers. His deep tan whitens his teeth.

If I saw him this way in a photograph, I'd say, *Yeah, that's Charlie, handsome and unhassled, the same as he always was.* But in the sharp sunlight and mounting heat, under the blue blaze of sky, I feel like I'm closing a great distance, that we're strangers meeting on an island who have only some half-forgotten past in common. It hits me that we're men now, still young, but men separated from each other by all the nights and days that make long deserts out of years. I'm nervous and dazed and my throat catches and, for some reason, I can't summon one joke or funny memory to tie us to the kids we were. Before I went to Panama to work for Kitterin, my father advised me always to have my first sentence ready, the clever, crack-shot opener that determines whether you're just another man in the world or whether there's a world inside a man. He also told me to stick my hand out and force others to lunge to shake it. "Like your arm is a sword and they could impale themselves on it." I never shared his bloodlust for the baby-food business.

Charlie remains leaning, stone still, and I can tell he's assessing how much I've changed since he last saw me. He squints like a man studying an orchestra recital for the slightest instrument out of tune. His tongue flickers across his teeth; one of his incisors has a tiny chip in its corner. He waits until the last second to push off from the bumper. He creeps forward, his back bent, taking enormous, goblin-like steps, and springs. He wraps his arms around me and knocks my suitcase to the ground. His palm presses against my cheek. I can feel his heart beating against my chest and catch the faint smell of fish and tobacco on his breath. His eyes are the same, deep and brown, like two pennies dropped in fountain water. His hand moves from my cheek and slides around the back of my neck.

"God, it's good to see you," he whispers, staring directly into my eyes. He squeezes my neck. "I've missed us."

My hands are on his hips like we're slow dancing. I feel as if Charlie is the first person I've touched in weeks, or maybe it's just his way of holding me, like I'm something that belongs to him. One early memory does come to mind, an indecent one—both of us at twelve in his bedroom, Charlie's face glowing with pride, the waistband of his sweatpants pulled down in the front, showing off his first pubic hair; it was a tiny black corkscrew, a hesitant too-early flower, and for some reason I reached toward him in that moment, and Charlie jumped back wincing. "Don't you dare pluck it out." I might have reached out because I wanted him in some way I couldn't have understood at that age, or I needed him to take me along in his teenage ascent, or perhaps I was trying to pull him back. We spent that afternoon applying his father's Rogaine to our crotches and the proceeding weeks providing regular updates on follicle growth. It would be another year before I farmed my own. How many prayers have been sent to heaven over a single wisp of hair? How many mornings have made apostates by their answer? A few years after that, Charlie was responsible for the loss of my virginity. He threw a small party at his place when his parents were out of town and invited a clutch of young models from lonesome tornado states who were in New York on go-sees. I knew her name, but we referred to her later by a promotion on a sign we saw advertising weekend brunch specials: ENDLESS MIMOSA. She took a bizarre, entirely unearned interest in me, the act was accomplished in Stefan's bedroom, and her teeth were caked black from her personal stash of pot brownies. For the next decade, Endless Mimosa haunted me, showing up in retail catalogs and advertisements for better wireless service, and a brief fever of guilt and dread would overwhelm me during those surprise visitations. *Did Charlie pay her to do that?* "Of course not," he said when I confronted him. "You're out of your mind. Christ, what a question! As I recall, you two just liked each other. Give yourself some credit." I never knew whether to hate or love him for that, and, like most first experiences, it grew so vague and abstract in my head it felt intrusive for me to return to it for a cheap moment of pleasure or shame. *My first time*, and still Charlie's fingerprints were all over it.

The sun is leaking down my face. Charlie grimaces. "I'm sorry about your father. Are you all right?"

"Yeah." I step back and wipe my forehead. Holding Charlie while thinking of my father spread out right now in a funeral home brings me too close to the brink. "I'm fine. Really, I am."

"When I lost my mother, it took a few months for it to register that she was gone. It's not the kind of pain you can count in days."

"Your mom? Oh, god, I didn't know." Kind Mrs. K, dead, like a stamp marked over the image of her in my mind, FINAL, PAID, NO FURTHER ACTION REQUIRED. I had spent years speeding past their

Fifth Avenue building, picturing her high up in its glass, guzzling creamer and packing and unpacking between trips. "When?"

"Two years ago. Breast cancer. I didn't write you about it?" I shake my head. "She spent most of her last months in Switzerland for treatment. It was important to be with her at the end. One of the most important experiences you can have, don't you think? Like walking through a door labeled ADULTHOOD, NO REENTRY. We buried her in Nicosia. If we had done it in New York, I would have called you."

"I wish you had called me anyway."

"Yeah, well, now it's just the Konstantinou men. It was good to be around family at the time."

"I couldn't handle the rest of my family. I didn't see the point of the funeral. No one wanted me interrupting their hard-earned grief. I guess I didn't earn it. You know, after Panama, my father and I weren't close. We weren't close before Panama either. You remember how it was."

"Well, you're here now. And I'm family." He smiles like a shot of sun through cloud cover and picks up my suitcase. "*Kalosorisma.* Welcome to Patmos. What do you think?"

I examine the port town again. Already it seems calmer and more navigable. Dry, dirt roads wind through the hills with the haphazard logic of ant tunnels. The sea sways forth and back. Possibilities magnify: the cold drinks and the thin legs of backpackers and the yachts along the dock teeming with hectic crews. It's a loud, greedy paradise hardening white in the morning sun like an egg in a frying pan.

"It's nice."

"It's nice," he huffs. Then he repeats the Athens taxi driver's description. "Holy island. Some people say they can feel it vibrating. We get our share of crazies. They arrive crazy and then they blame it on the island." He drops my bag in the truck bed. "My god, I can't believe you're here. Look at you. You're still so—" He searches for the right word and comes up empty. "You haven't aged at all."

"I feel like I have."

"All you need is some rest. And a swim. We can take the boat out tomorrow. You don't get seasick, do you?" Charlie's accent is different, lighter on the vowels, less drying-concrete American. He chops the edge of his hand against his palm, a gruff Mediterranean gesture to indicate decisiveness or that we're running late. He turns to the white buildings and waves his arm. An old man with silver hair jogs toward the truck, carrying grocery bags and a case of beer. The man is beetle brown from a lifetime roasting in the sun. "That's Christos, my captain. He's been with us forever. You can trust him." He looks over and winks.

"Who can't I trust?" I ask.

Charlie yawns, as if the excitement of our reunion has already subsided and he's feeling his early wake-up.

"You found the red hair," Christos grumbles as he plants the groceries next to my suitcase in the truck bed. "I look but not find."

"I'm used to finding Ian," Charlie replies. The captain offers his hand, and I lunge over the side of the truck to shake it. His stubble and chest hair are the color of Christmas tinsel, but his taupe skin is magically unlined. The hollows of his cheeks suggest missing teeth.

"Where's Helios?" Charlie asks. And to me, "That's Christos's son."

"He down by boat. He working. He remove . . ." But he can't think of the word. Both Charlie and Christos are speaking English for my benefit, and the captain grows frustrated. He finishes in Greek, and he and Charlie continue their conversation in the island vernacular. Charlie ties my bag to the truck bed with a rope, and Christos climbs into the driver's seat. There isn't room for three inside the tiny vehicle.

"You're not too tired, are you?" Charlie asks me.

"No. I need to get back on a normal clock anyway. I should try to stay up."

"Good. Christos is going to take your bag to where you're staying. See, he's even stocking your fridge." Charlie shakes a ball of white cheese and returns it to the grocery bag. He knocks on the truck twice to signal departure. "We can get a taxi to my house."

"I thought I was staying with you." Worry floods in, as much because I don't understand the geography of the island as because I don't want to be separated from my suitcase. I think of the cash in its plastic bag without even a lock on my luggage.

Charlie shakes his head. "Full house, I'm afraid. It's August, high season, and the place is exploding with family. If you'd come any other month, there'd be plenty of room. Sonny wants to boot them into a hotel, but you can't kick out family."

"Who's Sonny?"

"Wow, it *has* been a long time." Charlie grabs my shoulder to lead me from the truck, but I lock my legs, unwilling to leave my bag. "You'll meet her. I also have a surprise guest for you. She's staying out where you are, on the north side of the island, in some cabins I own. It's quiet countryside, away from the tourist surge. You might even say romantic." He grins deviously, an impression enhanced by his chipped tooth.

"Who?"

"I don't organize surprises to blow them just before they're revealed." His hand pulls at my shoulder. The truck engine revs with an up-chuck of diesel, and my poorly tied suitcase lurches away. Charlie notices my panic. "Your bag will make it to the cabin fine. I told you, Christos is trustworthy. What do you have packed in there, your inheritance?"

I'm blushing. I can feel the betrayal of capillaries, and I compensate by walking swiftly toward the taxi stand. Charlie leans in and kisses me on the cheek. "Forever, together, friends make the weather," he sings. "Fair warning. Sonny's going to treat you as competition. I'm in love with both of you, what can I say?"

"Can I trust her?"

"Hell no." He groans. "I often wonder if she'll be here the next morning or the one after that. Every time she says something nice about me, I think she might be eulogizing, softening me up before the final split. I just hope she's staying with me for—" He grows as flustered for the word as Christos did for "barnacles." He flinches briefly and shuts his eyes. Charlie's face has aged to thirty but there's still the boy I knew lurking behind it; a scared kid hoping the goodness in others matches the goodness in him. Charlie can afford to be good. I'm beginning to think that duplicity is a necessity of hardship. "Real reasons," he finally mutters. "Whatever those are."

I've never known Charlie to be worried about someone leaving him. Maybe he has matured. I do what I can to comfort him and pat his chest. Charlie presses his hand against mine, as if forcing me to feel him up. It's another game we played as kids, just before the turn of the century, pretending to be prepubescent lovers, holding hands or fake groping each other on the sidewalk to the shock of the last Upper East Side matriarchs taking their nurses and canes for a walk. It was hilarious in its obnoxiousness then, but now not so much.

Three young men in tie-dye T-shirts, their beards patchy like desiccated shrubbery, squint at Charlie and share bent smiles. Charlie growls as we pass them, a little animal motor through bared teeth.

"Do you know them?" I ask.

"I try not to. Jesus freaks are taking over Patmos. More like Apocalypse freaks, death heads, camping out on the beaches of Armageddon, just hoping to catch the last gnarly wave to the end of the world. Remember when surfers and hippies were all about peace and love? It's a new world, Ian. Poor Jesus isn't even safe in it." He stops for a second in the middle of the road to point to the southern hills of the island. He seems oblivious to the lanes of traffic bowing around us. "Over there is the cave where John wrote Revelation. And up there, that giant gray fortress is the Byzantine monastery that looks after it. It's right by my house. You can visit both of them. You should take . . . Oops, I almost said her name."

I still have no idea who the surprise guest is. I'm too tired and dazed by time zones to figure it out.

We climb into a taxi, and Charlie directs the driver to a town pronounced *H-O-R-A*. A wave of nervousness returns, a wave cresting on the quicksand beach of personal Armageddon. I feel like we're both avoiding mention of the help I asked for when I called him from New York, the desperate pleading that strips this visit of its aimlessness.

Charlie, you're like a brother. I need your help. Please take me in. I'll do anything. Just don't abandon me.

"How have you been?" I ask him.

"I've been fantastic," he replies, flashing a tuning fork of a smile, as if just enough time has elapsed mourning our dead parents to return to his natural ease. "I love living here. It's so good for me. It's rare to find a place in the world that draws an X and tells you *home*, but when you do—"

"It's perfect weather."

"Perfect," he agrees. "Turns red when the winds pull up from Africa. And if there are rings around the sun that means three days of crap weather for sailing. Heavy seas. But no rings today."

The taxi snakes along the waterfront of Skala. At the end of a row of T-shirt shops and shaded tavernas, there's a boarded-up storefront, plywood sheets where windows once hung. The stone around the wood is scorched black, and fresh flowers are clumped on the ground, torn petals skidding in circles in the wind.

"Is that where the bomb went off?" I ask.

"Yeah," he mutters. "Did you see that on the news?"

"I heard about it in Athens."

"Awful," Charlie says flatly. "Killed eight people. They beefed up the police presence for a week or two, even brought in the military, but it could have been any island. I used to go there for coffee every morning."

"Some Americans were killed, right?"

But Charlie isn't listening. He's staring at the boarded-up shell through the rear window, his lips contorted as if hit with a sudden toothache.

"Americans," I say again. "Two died. That's what my taxi driver told me."

"What?" Charlie looks at me with confusion. His cheerfulness has been replaced with something darker and agitated. He tenses the muscles of his forehead, and when he relaxes them the wrinkles go white. When his voice returns, it sounds far away. "Yes. Two American girls. Vacationers. They were about to board the ferry."

"Jesus, that's bad luck."

Charlie opens his mouth and keeps it open, like his expression is stuck.

"Aren't you scared it could happen again?" I ask.

"No, I'm not scared," he says. "It could have happened anywhere. Bad luck for anyone who dies like that." And then he snaps, as if I'm blaming him for the force luck plays on the world, "It has nothing to do with me."

"My driver thought it might be some antigovernment contingent."

Charlie drops his hands in his lap and concentrates on the sea out the window. The taxi is twisting along the coast.

"Skala's a shithole anyway," he mumbles. "Too many tourists tripping over each other and expecting everything to be a postcard. Soulless shithole. It's the hippies that ruined it. I pray I never find religion."

Since the illusion of peace has already been broken, I decide to lay the facts down straight. There is nothing worse than the silence of expectation and all the plotting for the perfect second that never arrives. Plus, with all the August houseguests, I'm not sure when Charlie and I will speak again alone.

"There *is* no inheritance," I tell him, my fingers pinching the seam of the vinyl seat. I don't mean to sound pitiful but the pity is there, trembling in the words. "I went to see my father the day he died. I was going to ask him for a loan. For the first time I was going to beg him for money because that's how bad things have gotten. And you know I've never asked him for a cent. But he died before I could, and he left me nothing. I guess I deserve that."

Charlie doesn't react. He continues gazing out at the blur of blue, here and there interrupted by the contrails of a speedboat.

"I just wanted you to know my situation."

A minute passes, as if I have been talking passionately about breakfast.

"Don't you think we're too old to blame our deficits on our parents?" he murmurs to the glass. It's a punch I'm not expecting, and I hook my fingers around the door handle to steady myself. Charlie, whose whole existence has been paid for by his parents, is lecturing me on financial maturity. In the backseat, I watch the future go dark. He isn't going to help me. And all the money I have is tied to a truck heading in the opposite direction.

"I said a loan. I was going to pay him back. Don't worry, I'm not here to ask you for a handout either. Forget I mentioned it."

Charlie turns, his lips stiff and pained. I've seen that look before, on the corners of the Financial District, on the long sidewalks of Fifth and Madison, on every student of Buckland forced to work in a soup kitchen for volunteer credit. It is privilege encountering the mess of the weak, empathy offset with gratefulness. It isn't pride. Pride is meaner and unguarded, sweeping into rooms rather than shrinking from them. This is the look of self-protection. I might as well be raving on about 9/11 in pajama bottoms while holding a cup for spare change. But Charlie makes a fist and taps it against my knee. He stares at me curiously, as if he only remembers my last outburst and not the entire conversation that preceded it. I have forgotten what a bad gauge Charlie has for censoring his thoughts. But I am still afraid of his eyes.

"Easy," he says, loosening his lips into a smile. "I didn't invite you all the way here so I could shut the door in your face. Things are going to work out. We can talk about it in a day or two. Can't we have a nice time first?"

I nod, and he returns to the view.

"You're planning on staying a while, aren't you?" he asks.

"I'm here." Here for as long as he wants me. For the rest of the ride we sit in silence, pretending to admire the water.

THE ONLY WAY to describe the hilltop town of Chora is that it's fashioned like a wedding cake. A maze of white, curved walls appear built out of slathers of frosting. Paths branch and fork along tilted tiers, each cobblestone surrounded by thick, coagulated rivers of icing. Doors and shutters hang crookedly like fragile ornaments pressed in the whip. Small arched towers ring with matrimonial bells, and couples, lovers I suppose, wander around in the morning sun glare. I follow Charlie, who runs his fingertips along the walls like a boy gathering up a dollop to taste. A few cypress and evergreen trees erupt out of hidden gardens, and, after several narrow passageways, the gray-brown foundation of the monastery tilts upward like the top cake layer, yet to be decorated.

Two monks descend the slanted path we're climbing, their legs moving through their black robes like steady pendulums. Their unkempt beards are the color of bad weather. Charlie nods as we pass them. Their body odor, sweetened by some unidentifiable herb, lingers behind. I give up trying to memorize the path to the house. My breathing is heavy, and my knees ache. I realize how flat New York is, the future conducted sidewalk-square by sidewalk-square, complicated only by the exercise of walk-up apartments. In an open doorway, a Greek family is sitting on a marble bench, and behind them a gold altar glints through the darkness. They seem to be partaking in a religious ceremony that requires candles and blank, passive stares.

"A lot of the homes here come with shrines," Charlie explains. "The owners are required to keep them up. The monks police everything. Don't ever forget who really owns this island." He nods up toward the monastery.

At the next corner, a dozen cats eat from a spill of kibble that someone has poured out for them. Charlie kicks some of the stray kernels out of the path. Soon we're in a tiny square, with two closed restaurants on either side.

"This is the Plateia. At night it's a zoo," Charlie says unhappily. "It's like Mykonos parachute-dropped by party helicopters and sponsored by Grey Goose. Every European with a title and pair of white pants is up here mating. You missed the last baroness going home unlucky by about two hours. The young males of the island do pretty decently around sunrise."

"*Hoo hoo*," owls an old man resting cross-legged on a stone perch. He has long white hair and a magnificent hooked nose, from which his entire face spills back. Sunspots, brown and green, collect like mildew along the corners of his jawline. Charlie waves, and the man returns the gesture, a ruby glinting on his middle finger.

"I've imported a friend," Charlie says, tapping my shoulder.

"In August?" the man replies, laughing. "Haven't you enough?"

"We need more Americans," Charlie answers.

"Oh, dear, I'm not certain we do. How's your brother? Where is my godson?"

"Stefan's working," Charlie says.

The man flutters his eyelids. "He works too much to make any money. Hasn't he learned that yet?"

Charlie smiles and gives a thumbs-up as a good-bye.

"Tell Sonny I expect a visit soon," he shouts after us.

We turn down an alley too tight for the sun to breech.

"Who was that?" I ask.

"Prince Phillip," Charlie says casually.

"Prince, like—"

"Yeah, like Greek royalty. He's a family friend. And very special. *Sensitivo*. A mystic. He sees ghosts." A prince who sees ghosts? Where is the teenage Charlie who stuffed forties of malt liquor down his pants in bodega aisles?

Twenty feet down the alley Charlie stops to open a red door with a brass doll hand for a knocker.

"You still alive?" he asks, noticing my hands on my knees.

Even as a kid, Charlie's taste in décor was hopelessly old-fashioned. Charlie often bragged that he had a separate group of friends—"my downtown friends" he called them, with all of the wasted itinerancy that implied—but I doubted any of them ever visited his childhood bedroom. It was hard to imagine what they'd make of his tiger-skin footstools or the coral-inlaid Chinese screen behind which he stowed his collection of bongs. Still, the Konstantinou house in Patmos predates even his decorative touch. The interior is damp and chilly and every three feet seems to contain a sunken stair. Unfamiliar thieves in the night would surely break their ankles. Smoke-damaged saints peer out from painted wood panels. Miniature marble torsos and large marble heads recline in alcoves like mutant scientific specimens isolated in jars. A cedar chandelier hangs from a rafter beam over a rectangular sitting room. It's furnished with a scarlet threadbare rug, a copper coffee table, a bookshelf, and what looks like a medieval torture chair. Only a puffy IKEA sofa by the bright, open windows gives a nod to the disposable new world.

"My grandfather bought this house," Charlie says. "Built in 1387, remodeled never. Except for the bathrooms and kitchen. I had those redone two years ago." He points to a burrowing staircase. "It goes down and down."

A figure floats from a doorway, the shape of a body in a black sheet. A woman in full burka carries a plastic laundry basket through the sitting room. Her wrists clink with bracelets and her fingernails are as silver as Charlie's neck chain. I am stunned, unable to make sense of her, this shrouded Middle Eastern woman performing an ordinary chore, and there's something frightening about her direct approach. Her bare feet clomp across the rug. She stops in front of me, the basket's wet socks and underwear lifted between us like she's offering a tray of food.

"Hello," a low, oaky voice booms. Her eyes are Gulf-water blue, blinking wildly in the slit of fabric. "I'm Sonny, Charalambos's girlfriend. I've heard so much about you."

"Charlie?" I glance over at him in panic.

His jaw twists to the side, and for a second he's too aggravated to collect an answer.

"Sonny!" he screams. "Take that off!"

Laughter erupts from the burka, shoulders quivering. She lets go of the laundry basket and tugs off the black veil. Blond curly hair, the color of whiskey in sunlight, falls across her tan shoulders. Her face is muscular and paler than her arms with faint freckles pulsing around her eyes. She's exactly how I imagined Charlie's girlfriend: like a hypnotist's watch, impossible not to look at in awe. She breaks down, snorting, her eyes searching not for me but for Charlie. He joins her laughter, holding on to the wall, almost hitting his head against it in hysterics.

"I'm sorry," she manages to gasp. "I couldn't resist. It was *too* good."

"Your face," Charlie says, nodding at me. "Perfect. Horrible. *Sonny!*"

She scoops up the burka, draping it between her arms.

"Isn't it lovely, though?" she says. "We bought it in Cairo last December, and I really have to stop myself from wearing it. I get the whole political thing against it, but honestly it's so freeing to walk around unbothered, no one looking at you, like you can just cancel yourself for a while."

"Sonny's an actress." Charlie stumbles over to gather her around the waist. "She never cancels herself." He fake-bites her neck.

"What kind of roles—" I begin.

"Was," Sonny corrects, holding up her finger. "*Was* an actress. No longer. The only good Charlie's ever done me is save me from California." She slaps his chest. "And by the way, nice one." She slips from his arms and snatches a canvas tote bag from the sofa cushions. She pulls out an ivory letter opener, its crystal handle imbedded with a seahorse. "Look what was in my bag while shopping at the market this morning."

Charlie smiles. "Oh, good, you found it."

"This has to stop," she wheezes, delighting in the fact that whatever game they're playing it's likely not to. She presses the tip of the knife against Charlie's heart. "It started with ashtrays."

"Ten months ago?" Charlie guesses. "The Pera Palace in Istanbul."

"Charlie was obsessed with the onyx ashtrays in the hotel room."

"They were the right weight."

"I told him not to take them. And when we got back here, guess what I find in my suitcase? Two onyx ashtrays."

"But you got me back in Corfu."

"We did need a blow dryer. Then it got worse, maniacal." Sonny is relaying these incidents for my benefit, but she's staring greedily at Charlie, as if he might disappear without her constant supervision—or vice versa. Her silver nails are clenched on her hips. It's strange when someone speaks to you but doesn't take you in. "I get stopped at customs on our way back from Tel Aviv. The officer unzips my luggage on one of those steel morgue tables under fluorescent bulbs, and guess what we both stare down at?"

Charlie's laughing again, his face bloodshot, and he collapses sideways on the couch, burying his eyes in a pillow.

"A lamp," comes his muffled reply.

"You shit," Sonny yells. "A fucking bedside lamp, paisley shade and all, with its cord wrapped around its Ming base. Do you realize how much improvising I had to do to explain that? *Did you pack your own bags, ma'am?*" Sonny does a sound impersonation of a Greek customs agent. "Why, yes I did. And this lamp has been in my family for generations. I take it wherever I go."

Her eyes are running and she wipes them. Finally the humor seems to be purely for her and not for Charlie. She breathes for a minute and glances at me.

"Anyway, now you've seen how awful we are." She examines me matter-of-factly like I'm in need of summing up. "Ian, you have such beautiful brown eyes. Brown eyes and red hair is so uncommon. Charlie never told me how handsome you are." I worry my eyes will be found tomorrow in one of Charlie's suitcases.

Charlie sits upright, snapping his fingers. "The surprise."

"Oh, god, I totally forgot." Sonny moans. "I told her to wait downstairs. I'll go and get her." She darts down the steps, and Charlie shakes his head at me.

"She's not awful. People are hard on her for some reason. She gets nervous around strangers, so she overdoes it a bit."

I understand. We're all salesmen in our introductions, promising all-expenses-paid vacations to places we ourselves have rarely visited.

"She's very pretty," I say. He rolls his eyes at the comment, as if I'm pointing out a quality as obvious as a stutter or the use of a cane.

"Yeah, it becomes quite a show when we're at the beach. Greek men actually line up on the shore to watch her walk out of the sea. The Italians are subtler, or their girlfriends are more vigilant. She hasn't made many friends on Patmos. Now, with our mystery guest, she has one."

The onyx ashtrays must be located in another part of the house. Charlie reaches for a porcelain teacup dish that's littered with pinched, expired butts. He rolls a cigarette on the coffee table. He didn't smoke the last time I saw him. It's a habit picked up somewhere in the last five years.

"It sounds like you've been traveling a lot."

He lights the cigarette—he's rolled it so tightly it looks too delicate in his hands—and leans back on the sofa, relaxing in the exhale of smoke.

"We're here for half the year, and then in the winters we go to Cyprus and take little trips. Sonny's trying to get interested in art history. Right now she's big on rococo." He grunts out a lungful of smoke. "I say that like it's our pattern. We've been together for less than two years. Just so you know, she has a daughter, a seven-year-old named Ducklin."

"Really? She seems too young to have a seven-year-old."

Charlie nods and wipes his nose with his wrist.

"Duck lives with her father in L.A., a director, but she comes for visits. She's here for August. Christos's wife, Therese, looks after her. I told you, it's a packed house."

Voices echo up the stairwell. Sonny returns, pulling behind her an unwilling arm. The hesitant young woman has dark hair cut just below the ears, a mole dotting her chin, wide eyes already apologizing, and she wears a black silk blouse and navy trousers. There's a feral boyishness to her slouched, uneven shoulders.

"Hi, Ian," she says harshly, with a smile either forming or evaporating. It wavers between life and death. "I might be a surprise, but probably not one you hoped for. These two had me locked in their bedroom for the past half hour."

Louise Wheeler. It's her voice, severe where others would have been soft, that gives her away. Louise was my sophomore crush at our very-liberal arts college nestled in the velveteen shadows of the Berkshire Mountains (liberal on its grading system; liberal on drugs; liberal about turning the student body into a harem for visiting faculty; achingly liberal in the conservative tractor town that seemed forever on the verge of dousing its strident nemeses in gasoline). Louise and I dated for two months, had sex exactly six times, and we even did a two-week volunteer trip together rehabbing houses in rural Mississippi for owners who had no clue why we were gleefully tampering with their roofs and basements. Louise was a sociology major from Lexington, Kentucky, on scholarship, and months before I found the courage to ask her out, she appeared mostly as fleeing knees and cheekbones in dark sunglasses and long unbrushed hair, passing along the quad to the library. She was so serious in school she's the last person I'd suspect of spending a summer blowing around the Dodecanese island chain. For at least a week of those two months, we were terribly in love, or terrible at it. Louise threw me aside for a law student at UMass. I struggle to remember if that was before or after Charlie dropped out. Did Charlie know how viciously she dumped me? I look over at him and he's wiping ashes off his shorts. Louise tilts her head, as if she's draining water from her ear.

"Well, it's great to see you," she says.

I can still picture her in the computer room of Stearns Hall telling me succinctly that we're over. It reeked of obligation and imaginary disappointment. But now the present has superimposed itself on the past, and she's telling me we're over in the computer room of Stearns Hall with her hair cut short and her head tilted, draining water from her ear.

Sonny, the only person with whom I don't share a history, is a strange candidate to come to my defense.

"I hate seeing people I once slept with." She claps my shoulder. "Does everyone want a drink? It's not too early?" She slips out of the room, refuting all claims to this deflated surprise, and begins to bang cabinet doors.

Louise steps forward, as if still fulfilling obligations. Her lips open, exposing the familiar collision of her top front teeth. Louise came to beauty by different roads than Sonny, whose overt prettiness was no doubt foretold from blond toddlerhood. Louise once told me that she had weathered hard childhood seasons of awkward and homely, a survivor of tornados of ridicule and thunderheads of rejection, where it was probably safest to take cover in a school hallway with her head between her legs. Those early trials infuse her looks with a toughness and complexity that probably still reads as unattractive in Kentucky. She has the kind of face that changes depending upon the angle. Right now, at a quarter tilt, she studies me in the cautious way one enters a bathroom in a foreign country, unsure of the reliability of basic equipment.

"Can I ask what you're doing here?" I say to her. "I mean, I didn't know you and Charlie were still friends." I'm not angry. It was too long ago. I don't feel more than a little thorn of humiliation, a splinter in the finger that you rub almost to suffer a bit of pain.

"I found her on Facebook," Charlie says, dabbing his cigarette in the dish. He says it like he ordered her off the Internet.

"No, I found you," Louise replies, retreating to the medieval chair. She sits down and tries unsuccessfully to position herself comfortably in its sharp contours. Has anyone since 1387 been able to make a nest out of that torture device? "And we kept in touch. I've been spending the summer in Europe as a break from law school. I was in Paris last month—"

"Sonny went up to Paris at the end of June. Rococo research," Charlie says. "I saw that Louise was in Paris, so I arranged a lunch."

"It wasn't a lunch, it was the Louvre," Sonny corrects him, carrying a bottle of vodka and four red tumblers. "Let's go out on the balcony. Ian's traveled eight thousand miles. I'm sure he'd like to sit outside." She kicks open a glass door, and the three of us follow her. Charlie brings his dish and rolling papers with him.

The white stucco porch overlooks a garden, thistle green and fragrant with jasmine and sage. A tiny, whitewashed shrine, as bright as butcher paper, glimmers far below under the branches. Giant maroon and yellow bees orbit the leaves. In the distance, the island dips down, swerving its coastline like an alcoholic at the wheel, until it disappears into the sea and the dense blue haze of the horizon.

Sonny places the glasses on a metal table. Three matching metal chairs are fitted with emerald cushions. Charlie props himself on the wall of the balcony, holding the dish awkwardly at his chest, as if he's drinking tea. A pot of purple nightshade sits in the corner. Sonny shoves her finger in its soil and tugs on a petal.

"Has Therese been watering?" she asks. A hose lies by the pot, but Sonny doesn't reach for it. She backs away in her tight shorts and begins pouring out equal shots of vodka. "So Louise and I hit it off in Paris, and I convinced her to skip Madrid in August and visit us instead."

"Madrid's way too hot in August," Charlie agrees, setting the plate on the wall.

"Madrid's a dead city," Sonny proclaims. "You can always tell a dead city by one simple rule: Do the young people go where the tourists congregate for fun? If your hotel bar is crammed with nightclubbing locals, you know there's really nothing interesting going on. That's the problem with New York these days, another sad fatality." She shrugs, as if New York were an alley cat that was euthanized before it managed to get adopted, *depressing but what can you do?* "Living cities take work to understand. Although we're crazy about the Prado in Madrid, aren't we, Lamb? The Goyas make me want to kneel on the stone floor and weep."

Charlie, or the Lamb in Charalambos, smirks at me. Sonny is overdoing it again. As an actress, Sonny must have learned the trick of stealing every scene from the other performers. I wonder if the burka routine was orchestrated to outshine the surprise of Louise.

But I recall Charlie's concern about her splitting any day. Sonny must also know when to rein it in. Quietness on her could be a cause for paranoia.

"I think I'm staying where you are," Louise says, glancing over at me. "In Charlie's cabins near Kampos."

"That's right," he says. "But if you two don't get along, I promise the connecting door bolts from both sides."

"You can keep yours bolted," Louise whispers with a repentant grin.

"Cheers." Sonny raises her glass. "*Yamas.* To Ian." We each clink and follow the universal law of direct eye contact. *These faces are too easy, too beautiful,* I think, members of Charlie's kingdom and not mine. The vodka is cold, the first gulp slipping down my throat like a tiny, supple frog.

"Ian was working in Panama for a while. Gangs, wasn't it?" Charlie asks. "Helping the drug cartel?"

"I wasn't helping the drug cartel." I groan. "But you do realize that it isn't so simple as blaming the gangs for drugs. When you're poor and your government aims to keep you that way, sometimes that's your only option. We were trying to foster other alternatives." My attention is on Louise, who listens with eyebrows raised. The vodka has unlocked the horrible need to show off.

"Ian's a professional big heart," Charlie concludes. "And then back in New York, what was it, homeless cokeheads in Brooklyn?"

"Crack addicts in the Bronx."

"Oy." He winces.

"I think that's really impressive," Louise says harshly. For a mathematical second, me plus vodka plus Louise's approval equals resurrected love. She touches my hand on the table, her nails bitten and unvarnished. There's a tiny black cross tattooed on her ring finger, blurred by doses of sun. "I'm sorry to hear about your father," she says.

"Oh, Jesus," Sonny wails, wiping her lips. "I am too. I should have said that right away. And instead I've been making a bunch of crass jokes. Why didn't you remind me?" She gives Charlie a scalding look. "Was your father old? As old as Charlie's father?"

"No. He was only sixty-seven."

"That's too young," Sonny decides. "There should be so much more time. My family has the habit of living well into their hundreds."

"That's an expensive habit," Charlie says.

Sonny picks up the bottle and refills my glass. She goes to refresh Louise's drink but it's still full. Louise has been holding her glass and lifting it to her mouth in esprit de corps, but she was never much of a drinker.

Charlie starts to roll another cigarette but is interrupted by a young man leaning halfway out of the balcony door. He couldn't be older than twenty-five, with dark, joyless eyes and skin the shade of erased pencil. He has on a blue Speedo and rubber water shoes. He is not well made. His legs are as thin as arms and his chest is sunken, a canyon of matted black hair. There's a small mark in the center of his forehead, in the shape of a priest's thumb on Ash Wednesday. He glances disinterestedly at the drinking party around the table.

"Rasym," Charlie says. "This is Ian." I lift my hand, and Rasym looks at it dubiously, as if I'm about to propose a high-five. "Rasym's my cousin from Nicosia."

"Did you have any weird dreams last night?" Sonny asks him delicately.

"No," Rasym says, refusing her bait. "Could I borrow the car to drive to the beach?" It's a stronger voice than his body lets on, and its bluntly dismissive of Sonny and all of her cautious kindness. She takes the wound like a veteran, skirting her eyes to the trees. Charlie pats his pockets, comes up empty, and heads inside to retrieve them. On his way in, he turns to me.

"Can you drive a stick?"

"Badly, but yeah."

"There's a second motorbike at the cabins. You can use that. Louise can take you home tonight on hers."

Louise's ears redden at the prospect of driving me back, my legs and arms wrapped around her in the erotic arrangement of sharing a motorbike. Three puncture holes line her earlobe, but nothing fills them. They're scars of earlier vanities.

"Prepare for crazy dreams," Sonny says to me while fixing the lock on her bracelet. "There's something about Patmos that brings out nightmares. I swear."

"It's true," Louise concurs. "Last night I had an insane one about sharks. I couldn't climb out of the water where a Great White was lurking. I kept getting halfway out and slipping back in. I woke up in a sweat." I like imagining Louise waking up this way.

"There are no sharks in the Aegean," Rasym says with the coldness of a fact-checker.

Sonny ignores him. "Tell Ian about the dream you had two nights ago," she says to Louise.

"Don't mention that! Don't!" But the pressure of telling it is too great and Louise submits. "My arms were cut off and I was sold into sex slavery. I can't believe we're still talking about it! Are you satisfied?"

"Yes, mildly." Sonny laughs and stares at me. "There's a man two houses over who arrived in June, a psychologist from Chicago. Apparently, he had a dream that told him it was his destiny to live on the island of the Apocalypse. Like a divine calling he couldn't shake. So he up and left his wife and rented a house here. Rumor is he's also a pedophile. I won't let Duck get within twenty feet." She consults Louise while chewing on her lip. "Do you think that's true?"

"Which part?" Louise says bluntly, as if imparting useful information.

A figure slides behind Rasym and steps onto the balcony. His hair is white-blond, flame-like even in the shade. He's as skinny as Rasym but inordinately fit, with blue veins protruding down his arms like the fins of old sports cars. He smiles so intensely it's almost hard to look at, like looking in the direction of loud music.

In Charlie's absence, Sonny takes over introductions. "This is

Rasym's boyfriend, Adrian. He's from Kraków. Now that's a city."
Adrian nods, a more benign fact-checker.

"Good to meet you," he says in what sounds less like an accent
than a speech impediment, a freight train of consonants clunking
over a broken track.

Sonny taps the bottle. "If you get a glass from the kitchen, you can
have some."

"No, I have a long swim to the goat island today." He pats his
stomach, never easing out of his smile. I get the feeling he will keep
smiling until someone asks him to stop.

I stand up to use the bathroom. "Downstairs," Sonny directs, in-
tuiting my purpose. The staircase is so dark I brace my hands on
the cool, coarse walls to find my footing. The lower floor is a colony
of austere, dust-mottled bedrooms. The largest one with a gold bed-
spread and a jewelry box upturned on the dresser, earrings and
chains strewn across its surface, must belong to Charlie and Sonny.
The next room is fitted with a lonely row of stuffed animals and pre-
teen romance books for Duck. A child's white caftan hangs on the
door like a doomed snow angel. Across the hall is an explosion site:
suitcases overflowing like clogged sewers; iPods and headphones
knotted together by their cords; swimsuits, fossilized by seawater,
left in clumps on the brick floor. Two maroon passports embossed
with different ideas of an eagle sit on a bookshelf, Polish and Cypriot.

The final room contains just a slender cot with a brown blanket
spread neatly across the mattress. There are no signs of inhabitance.
The luggage rack is empty, as is the open armoire. A monastic hush
fills the space, somber as a sacristy with its treasures packed away or
the first day of summer camp with the gloom of hard trials ahead. I
pass through the room to its adjoining bathroom. Red marble runs
across the floor and rises to scoop out an enormous tub. Three dying
cacti line the sink counter, along with a half-filled vial of medication
made out to Charlie's older brother, Stefan, from four years ago. As
I pee, I wonder if Charlie has purposefully stuck me in the faraway
cabins with Louise, out of some misguided matchmaking scheme;

or maybe the past five years have rendered me an undesirable inter-
loper so close to his bedroom. On my way out, I notice a picture lying
on top of the armoire. It's a photo of two boys in suits standing next
to each other, their arms at their sides, as if lined up for comparison.
Neither smiles. It's Charlie and his brother from the days when cameras still used film and moments seemed both more orchestrated
and more haphazard.

I never really knew Stefan growing up. He was four years older,
boarding-schooled in Pennsylvania, cerebral and humorless—he
endured jokes the way an alcoholic endures sunlight, with a wince
and a short-fused smile. Stefan's only detectable passion was a love
of tennis, if a boy loving a sport can be considered a personality
trait. I remember he attended Princeton and dove instantly into the
Konstantinou family business. I also remember that he and Charlie
never got along. In the photo, their faces and bodies are deceptively
similar, their skin a yellow Mediterranean bruise faded by north-
eastern winters. But they weren't similar. Stefan never had Charlie's
warm-blooded charm, the kind of charm that could seduce an egg
from its shell.

Feet stomp up a flight of steps from the floor below. Charlie races
past the doorway with a jingle of keys, but he stops and reverses. He
rests his arm on the top of the doorframe, black armpit hair flaring
from his T-shirt sleeve.

"What are you doing in here?" he asks lightly.

"I was using the bathroom," I reply. I almost expect him to march
into the bathroom and urinate, like a dominant dog obliterating my
mark with his own. "Hey, why are you exiling me off to northern
Siberia when this bedroom is free?"

"Northern Siberia happens to have the better beaches," Charlie
says, walking over. "And don't tell me you aren't secretly ejaculating
at the prospect of you and Louise stranded in the hills all alone."

"I think you might have already left college, but Louise dumped
me. Like a garbage bag on the curb. It's great seeing her and all, but
I'm not trying that again."

"I hadn't left yet," he says, laughing. "I'm the one you came crying to. You threw up in my bathroom. Ian, that was forever ago. She's right in front of you now. You're welcome."

"Why did you stay friends with her?" I ask.

"Why wouldn't I? And I'm glad I did. She's been great for Sonny."

"Can't I just stay here?"

He shakes his head. "This is Stefan's bedroom. I got the whole house, but he got this bedroom, which he never uses. I think he pays Therese to ensure that no one else does either. Every summer he says he might come for a visit, but he never shows. He lives in Dubai now, handling the regional operations of the family firm. My father's on his last legs, or really his last wheelchair, and Stefan's being groomed as his replacement. Fluffed really. He's still the asshole you barely knew and loved."

"How's his tennis?"

"Ha!" Charlie clucks, rubbing my shoulder. "Exactly. Finally someone who remembers what a robot he was. You know he finally found a girlfriend. Their hobby was learning Finnish together— Finnish in Dubai. And guess what, when it was over they broke up in Finnish. Might as well get some final practice in, right? Even his romances have to double as learning opportunities. Not a minute wasted."

"They finished in Finnish." Charlie doesn't acknowledge my joke. He peers down at the photo on the armoire.

"Look at us, so stiff, like we're being measured for our coffins."

"So you aren't part of the family business. Are you working? Or are you officially retired?"

His thumb digs into my shoulder bone.

"I work," he says defensively. "God, you sound like Stefan. Do you think I'm just sitting around breaking my toys? I work my ass off, actually. Let's go upstairs and you can see for yourself."

He grabs the picture and carries it up with him. At the top of the steps, he tosses Rasym the car keys. Adrian is already lugging their beach gear out the door, and Rasym follows him without a good-bye.

Charlie flaps the photo in his hand and turns, hunting for a place to stow it. He finally yanks a green Bible from the bookshelf and tucks the snapshot into the pages.

"If I die, shake my books," he mutters.

Outside on the balcony, Louise and Sonny are whispering at the table with their heads bent close. "This is becoming one of those centuries," Sonny says, as if she's weathered enough of them to discern a contrast. "Honestly, it was only the twentieth century that was rational. I think the twenty-first will be more like the others. Unreal, cleverer. Although we're only in the shallow end."

Charlie tugs on her ear as he guides me toward the view. He points at the southern tip of the island, to a yellow patch by the sea. "That's a port called Grikos, which most of the private boats use. But a little farther south—" He runs his finger along the coastline, stopping on a dent of land half obstructed by cliffs. "That's a tiny port I've rented from the monastery for my boats."

"What boats?"

"I've built up my own fleet. Refurbished yachts I rent out to tourists for sailing around the Aegean. I know it isn't a construction empire, but it's my own. I'll show you tomorrow when we go out. This house belonged to a captain dynasty. Hundreds of years of men who made their money from the sea."

"Make sure Christos brings fresh towels tomorrow," Sonny warns, leaning her head back to stare up at us.

"Don't invite Miles," Charlie snaps.

"You're being ridiculous," Sonny says softly, pressing her hand against her eyebrows to block the sun. "He's good with Duck."

"He's obsessed with you," Charlie says coldly.

"I really think he is," Louise confirms, shaking her drink.

"He's not," Sonny swears. "Or so what if he is? Competition's getting too tough for you? Afraid I'll run off?"

"He was a pretentious leech when I knew him as a kid, and he's still exactly the same. 'I'm Miles Lyon-Mosley,'" Charlie singsongs, prancing in place. He makes a fey adjustment to the dish on the balcony. "'This must be just so,'" he whines. "'Now, Charles, drinking in the morning simply isn't done in proper London. At my estate in the Cotswolds, we have a saying—'" Charlie mimes aristocracy badly. It's an ugly performance, cruelty showing through, and it's strangely depressing. I want Charlie to be better than that. I've forgotten how flinty his face becomes when he's angry, the wrinkles at his eyes hardening, his nostrils trumpeting.

"I bet he has an estate," Charlie murmurs, easing out of Miles. He slaps me on the back. "Quick, Ian, three gunmen in black balaclavas burst through the front door."

I almost choke from laughing. Sonny turns around in her chair.

"Black baklava?" she says. "What the hell are you talking about?"

"Nothing," Charlie tells her. "An old joke between us." Sonny won't like a game in which she isn't a player. She grabs the bottle of vodka and stands up.

"I'll get a fresh one," she says.

Louise pulls her phone from her pocket and motions for me and Charlie to stand for a photograph. Her phone clicks like an old camera.

"Cute. I'll post it."

Sonny smacks her thigh by the door. "Fucking mosquitoes," she roars. "We need those special candles, Lamb. *Hay bastante espinas del paraiso.*" I'm impressed by her Spanish. Her worldliness seems like a recent acquisition.

Espinas del paraiso. Thorns of paradise.

LOUISE'S YELLOW BIKE spins us through the hills. She guns the motor, and we're dipping and lifting, flying through pink farmland that rushes by us like blurred graffiti, the sea spread out on our right. My hands are hooked on her waist, where I can feel each contraction of her spine. My lips are near her ear, and only the whipping of her short dark hair keeps me from resting my chin against her shoulder. It is eight o'clock, not yet sunset, but the trees cast long shadows across the scrub, and sheep spring from the shade, jumping through the cooling air. I'm drunk.

"Shouldn't we be wearing helmets," I yell so she can hear.

"You should be, yes," she says. "But I didn't bring mine."

Louise doesn't believe in brakes. I can't tell if she's speeding around the lurching turns to impress me or because she wants to end this vehicular spooning session as soon as possible.

"Maybe we should slow down," I advise.

"You know the cause of most accidents," she shouts. "Lack of confidence." My drunkenness prompts me to take everything she says personally, and I try and fail to apply that rule to our former love life. But it does give me an excuse to twist my arm around her stomach, hugging tightly. For this second, and maybe only for this second, I love Charlie for bringing Louise back into my life. I press my cheek against her shoulder and stare out at the island, where a few remote houses in the hills begin to bead with light. It is humanly impossible not to be infatuated with someone driving you on a motorbike.

"You know, when I was a kid I had a vision I'd die at the age of thirty in a car accident," she says. "For years, I was convinced of it."

"Then you should slow down," I call.

"Don't worry. In the vision, I died in a really nice car."

I'm not sure how to respond. When a hill reduces our momentum, I switch subjects.

"It's so beautiful here."

"Isn't it?" Louise replies. "So much simpler than Italy. Like nature hasn't overdecorated. The colors are honest, know what I mean?"

Yes, I do. And I can feel her breathing under the thin membrane of her leather jacket.

The motorbike trembles over cobblestones in a silent square, and soon we're on concrete again, swooping down. A harbor slides up against a rocky beach, and outdoor tavernas streak across the opposite side of the road where waiters bend over tables to light the candles. We're faster than their matches. Louise shakes her shoulders to amputate my jaw from her back. "You're crushing me," she says.

She zooms through the village of Kampos and turns left, hurtling us into the darkening interior, like we're racing nightfall. Eventually, she eases up on the engine.

"You and Sonny," I say. "You've become good friends."

"Yes. She's smart. And I'm not just saying that because I'm staying here on their dime. Why? Does that surprise you?"

"You don't seem very much alike." Louise doesn't speak for a minute. Because I can't see her expression, I worry I've offended her. "I just mean you've always been so together."

"Believe it or not, I'm capable of friendship with a person who's not exactly like me," she retorts. "Sonny's very kind if you give her a chance. Do you get the impression she's happy?"

One source of pride in me is that, even drunk, my loyalty holds. I play on the side of my friend.

"Yeah, she seems happy. She and Charlie are a good match. Why wouldn't she be?"

"No reason."

We steer off the concrete, onto gravel, winding along a thin channel between rock walls. Sheep begin to dissolve in the darkness. Louise throttles the motor to tackle an almost vertical hill, and I'm pitched back, clinging on to her, trying to save myself from falling off. After a minute of cats and wall and a cypress tree whose roots have split through the cement, we float onto a horizontal driveway, the engine reeking of burned gas. Louise finally uses her brake, gliding us under a deck. I hop off and she parks, punching the kickstand with her heel.

The two cabins, or really two distinct sections joined in the center, stand on stilts. We take the stone staircase, and Louise nods to the gray door on the left with a key in its lock.

"That's your cabin," she says. "I wondered who was taking the good view."

From the entryway, the village of Kampos and the shell-shaped harbor glitter far below. The air is chillier in the hills, and somewhere in the dim braid of olive and oleander trees, goat bells clang forlornly, as if by a hand that has given up expecting anyone to answer. The western sun pulls its reds from the dirt.

We both enter through our separate doors and immediately catch sight of each other in the narrow frame that connects our rooms. The interior is spare, with bleached pine floors and a low, made bed. My suitcase sits at the foot of the bed, still zipped. Nothing medieval impedes upon the Lucite folding chairs and the smell of cleaning products and freshly split wood. A stone patio with an outdoor kitchen juts from my bedroom beyond the sliding glass, where Christos has stacked fruit in a bowl. I walk to the nightstand and turn on the lamp. When the bulb brightens the shade, I notice that it's dented and paisley, hanging over a cerulean, dragon-patterned base. Sonny's smuggled hotel plunder. A green onyx ashtray sits beside it.

Just to be sure, I open my suitcase and pull out the plastic bag of cash. I inspect the stacks in the light to make sure they're all accounted for. Paper money always looks so frail with its morose, coiffed patriarchs staring out in eternal disappointment. It's an expression I'd seen on my father, one that says, *Does it have to be this way?* I can't think of anything less current than hard currency, irreplaceable, tactile, as single-minded as missionaries, capable of getting lost. Panama runs on the American dollar, and long before my time there, in the months leading up to the U.S. invasion, the government couldn't refresh its worn-out notes with new ones from the American Reserve. I heard stories of Panamanians carrying around their ripped, crumbling bills in plastic sheaths, like photos of dead relatives protected from careless fingers.

"Ian?" Louise calls from her room. I quickly pull the drawer of the nightstand open, where a Bible and a Henry Miller novel lie inside. I shove the bag in the drawer and slam it shut. Louise stops in the doorway, observing established borders. Her jacket is off and her arms are crossed. She's undone the top two buttons of her blouse. The outline of a white bra gleams in the valley of her shirt. She watches me by the drawer, or me and the drawer, or just me.

"There's a Bible in there," she says. "I guess Charlie wants us brushing up on our Revelation."

"We should read a chapter each morning. A furnace of fire with our coffee. A weeping and gnashing of teeth before we rub sunscreen on our backs."

"That's from Matthew," she says drolly.

"I didn't know you were such a biblical expert."

"Well, I *am* from Kentucky." Her foot taps the wood, and she stares down at it, as if watching her own impatience. "You must be tired."

"I'm pretty exhausted, yeah."

"When you're up for it, I'd like to hear more about Central America, what you were doing down there."

"You don't want to hear about that."

"I'm interested. The things you must have seen." I pray she doesn't Google me. Plug "Ian Bledsoe" and "Panama" into a search engine and nothing pleasant emerges.

"Maybe tomorrow," I tell her, stepping toward the doorway.

"Do you remember the vultures in Mississippi? How they'd sit on the fence posts, just waiting for their chance with us." Louise has several memories to choose from, and she selects the most cheerful one, our volunteer expedition hundreds of miles from the college quad or the Stearns Hall computer room. Death by birds is preferable to our breakup.

"I think the cars saved us. What did they eat before roadkill was invented?"

She nods distantly. "I've thought about you from time to time. Wondering what became of you. Funny that we're here."

"Charlie." I groan. "He makes the world small. Is that a good thing?"

Louise steps forward, as if to kiss my cheek, but she thinks better of it. "Sometimes it's a good thing. I'll wake you for that coffee." She turns and slowly returns to her room, shutting her door behind her.

I close mine and bolt the slide lock. I wait for a minute to hear if she bolts hers too, but the thud doesn't come. We never lied to

each other, Louise and I. Never deceived or struck deep or regretted. There wasn't time to. Just the skirting of painful differences.
But for once I'm glad for the fast end of an old heartbreak. It makes
the future less spoiled. I consider unbolting my door, in case Louise
gets lonely in her cabin. But one night doesn't matter. I strip off my
clothes and climb into bed. What matters is we've begun.

CHAPTER 3

I 'm on vacation.

I didn't come to Patmos for a holiday, but morning brings it on. Dawn erupts, and night shrinks to the scratchy blotches of trees, the trees holding the darkness the longest. The sun blasts out of the sea, and the water beats against the pebbled shore. The whole island spreads out horizontal, a dazzle of land undulating and dripping with spidery dew. I can see the yellow dirt trails and gray roads running down our hillside, already rippling with the day's first beachgoers. The buildings of Kampos are amnesia white, and colored boats rock sleepily in the harbor. It is impossible not to be on vacation here. You are on vacation the way citizens in a bomb-fogged, mortar-scorched city are at war. A place claims you whether it has your consent or not.

My sleep was heavy. Despite Sonny's warning, I didn't dream at all. I put on my only pair of swim trunks, black and boxy for American legs thicker than mine. I feel oxygenated, alive, as if the fear and worry of the past is weather in a different hemisphere. Soon, with luck, the memory of Manhattan will shrink to a little rat-run garbage pile on the other side of the planet. At this point, the only living beings waiting for me at home are the brittle ferns lining the kitchen sill of my Harlem walk-up—almost beggar brown by now, a sad two feet from the faucet.

I slide open the glass door, carrying my phone toward the outdoor kitchen under a pergola strewn in vines. A breeze pours over the deck, trembling the wet tablecloth under the fruit bowl. I check my messages, promising myself I'll only do so once a day. Today is my father's funeral at Holy Redeemer, which I'm not sure increases or decreases the likelihood of family members reaching out. There is only a text from my mother, not even a typed note, just a link to Edward Bledsoe's obituary in the *New York Times* and an emoji of a yellow crying ball. They were married for eleven years, had a son, and her response to his death is a weeping cartoon circle. I don't dare click on the *Times* obituary; I don't want to read it again for fear they've expanded upon my mention as "also." My phone comes equipped with an inventory of emojis and I choose one at random: a beaming police strobe. After I press SEND, I regret the selection. I should have chosen the greedy octopus.

I find coffee in the freezer and fill the metal espresso pot. I rinse a peach and eat it as I wait for the pot to boil. All of these simple activities feel enhanced, hypnotic, in the rising light. I can already feel how time moves in Greece—there's so much of it, floating and fading along the shadow-cracked hills. Words like *now* or *soon* could span decades.

"Meditating?" Rounding the cabins, Louise hops the wall onto my deck. I wonder if she tried the connecting door and found it bolted, an unintentional rebuff after she breeched the doorway effortlessly last night. She wears a blue one-piece swimsuit and gray, high-waisted shorts. Her hair is wet from the shower, stringing down her narrow forehead. Swirls of white cream lather her shoulders, and violet smudges of blood vessels line the skin around her eyes. "Am I interrupting?"

"No, I was thinking about houseplants."

"Depressing," she grunts.

"Where exactly are you living these days?"

"D.C.," she says, helping herself to a peach. "I'm in law school at Georgetown. I know what you're thinking: law school is for those unimaginative souls who've run out of options. You're right. I saw age thirty up ahead on the turnpike, so I panicked and applied. I swear I could be a hairdresser right now if a local beauty college sent me a pamphlet on the right week. I was supposed to intern this summer with a D.A., but instead I ransacked the last of my savings to drift around Europe. I figure everyone should get to do that once. I also figure I'll be so poor by the end of my trip I'll have no choice but to go back. Attendance by lack of means. Or, just maybe, I'll find some reason not to."

She bites sloppily all the way to the pit. I want to be her reason not to, perhaps less than I did last night, but at least I want to be an option. There are two kinds of longing, the spiteful morning erections that search for any target of release and the one drawn from a specific source, a specific body in a blue one-piece that catches stray peach juice because its wearer is gumming the fruit like it contains a chunk of gold. It's 9:00 A.M., and I'm suffering dual longings. I turn to readjust my swimsuit and am struck for the millionth time in my adult life by a hard-won fact: so many desires require the involvement of another participant. I stretch my leg within easy engagement of Louise's hand.

Louise reaches for a mug from the counter, blows into it to clear the dust, and, before I can stop her, grabs the coffeepot on the stove.

"Oww," she cries, releasing the metal handle. I open the freezer to get her ice.

"Not ice. Is there any butter in the fridge?"

I scan the groceries. "Goat cheese?"

She shakes her hand, making a fist. "I'll be fine."

My phone beeps with a message. It's my mother. I DON'T UNDERSTAND??

"Is that Charlie?" Louise uses a towel to muffle the handle. She pours out two coffees. "He texted me an hour ago. We're all meeting at his dock at ten." She adds milk without asking how I take mine and deposits one of the mugs in front of me on the terra-cotta counter.

I could get used to this, to us, shirking our obligations back home, drinking coffee together in our bathing suits. I watch as Louise sips hers, her lips puckered on the rim, her eyes in the direction of the sea like some fish-eating bird scanning her hunting grounds. She looks over at me.

"What?"

"Nothing." I become uncomfortably aware that I'm only wearing shorts. I go inside and grab a black T-shirt, slipping it over my head as I step back out.

"Have you been on Charlie's boat before?" I ask.

"Twice," she replies. "It was my first time on a yacht. I knew Charlie was rich, but I didn't realize the extent of it. Did you?" She waves her hand. "Of course you did. You two grew up together, thick as thieves."

"I'm not rich. Not like that."

She smiles. "You make it sound like a character flaw."

We lean against the counter, staring out at the view for what feels like an hour. It's probably been three minutes. My eyes slip from the sea to her mouth, studying the crash of her upper teeth. I try to remember what it was like to kiss her.

"He's like a boy with a new telescope on that boat," she says. "Do you sail?"

"I took some lessons on the Hudson River when I was a kid. But nothing like Charlie. Those were cheap little skiffs that were allowed to flip over. You didn't flip over because you didn't want to swim in the Hudson."

"Miles can't swim." Louise deserts her coffee halfway through. "The British guy we were talking about yesterday. How does someone have a house here and spend days out on boats, but has never learned to swim?" She glances at me, and in the same harsh monotone that doesn't just level her sentences but also strings stray thoughts together in a deceptive progression, says, "Be careful today. You'll burn."

We return to our cabins to collect our gear. I open the drawer to the nightstand and try to find a better hiding place for the money. The room is uncooperatively bare. I examine the cabinet under the bathroom sink, but it's filled with cleaning supplies, suggesting the presence of a maid who comes when guests are out. I decide to leave the money in the drawer, stuffing it inside a sweater, and take the

Henry Miller novel in case we end up marooned on a beach. I shove my feet into my sneakers and bolt the glass door and window shutters. When I step outside, Louise is already on the driveway, walking her motorbike across it.

"You don't have to lock up," she calls as I slip my key into the hole. "This isn't New York. No one can find this place—thieves, friends, tax collectors." I lock it and put the key in my pocket.

"Are we riding together?" I ask.

She points to a second bike under the deck. "They're faster with one person on them. There's a helmet in your seat." I make the slick, stupid decision not to put it on.

The hill is hellish. Total unidirectional hell. If I had gotten my bearings on a flat surface, I might have cleared it smoothly. But I'm braking and skidding, learning the strength of the throttle as I descend at a sharp, winding slant. In the low, diagonal fields, sheep crowd the shadow of a tree, creating a perfect wool reflection of the sapling. Thirty eyes dully watch me halt and rev and nearly crash into their pasture. My shirt is soaked with sweat by the time I reach the end of the gravel path, where Louise lingers on the cement. She spots me and races on.

We play an embarrassing relay: Louise speeding away, stopping for me to catch up, speeding away again, like fast prey taunting its hapless hunter. "I think you have the better bike," I yell, an excuse neither of us believes.

She's out of sight along the zigzagging hills beyond Kampos and the silent square. Her absence lets me practice, gun hard, brake easy, shift my weight on the seat to guide through the turns, full-metal fury on the straight slices of blacktop. The wind snaps softly around my body, as if locating new erogenous zones along my legs and sides. I can taste the wild oregano pouring from the fields; it tastes like Saturdays in childhood or lost favorite love songs. What is this sensation, this lightness and sure-footedness, this race of the heart over the sea? It's as close as I've been since a teenager to feeling young, raw-egg young, wide awake in careless hours, this newness of a place that I could gather in my arms and still wouldn't have enough. Pleasure is back, unsnapped from its cage.

After five minutes along the road, I sense a car behind me. A white Mercedes station wagon flashes its lights before it plunges into view on my left. There's a priest at the wheel, or a monk, in a dark robe with a black, trimmed beard. In New York, religious drivers are not a miraculous sight: a decent portion of the Manhattan-bound bridge traffic consists of Hassidic rabbis in thunderstorm-colored Toyotas holding their own among the Hindu and Muslim cabs. But this Greek priest, in gold-plated sunglasses with his free arm dangling from the open window, has all of the trappings of an agnostic playboy. He can't even be bothered to glance over at me.

In another second, the car lurches toward me, its side mirror nearly clipping my handlebar. I yank the bike toward the shoulder, braking, wobbling, and the wheels freeze under me. I'm skidding and thrashing for balance. Images of limbs and ambulances mix with the dusty roadside weeds, a hospital helicopter lifting off of Patmos, the Holy Redeemer rebooked for a second Bledsoe funeral. I slow down enough that I manage to catch my foot on solid ground, the rubber sole of my shoe burning against my toes, and quickly throw my other leg over the seat. The bike keeps going, riderless, and slides ten feet to a defeated stop. The white station wagon continues on oblivious, disappearing around the turn.

It's impossible to convince myself that was unintentional. I limp to the bike and lift it off the hot asphalt. The motor works. Besides a few scratches, there isn't any damage. I take the helmet from the seat compartment and clip it under my chin. No Louise for miles, just the occasional hush of expert bikers traveling in the opposite direction. A barefoot woman in a dirty head scarf stumbles along the road, avoiding eye contact; her dark, empty hands are dipped in mud. At the bottom of a gentle slope into the port town, I see Louise rolling out of a gas station.

"What took you so long?" she asks. Her hair has dried in the breeze, and she's wearing aviator sunglasses, reflecting me in duplicate.

I want to tell her I almost died. I want to warn her about a white Mercedes station wagon and a priest with a groomed beard. I want her reassurance that there are proper medical facilities on Patmos that can handle near-fatal collisions.

"Just stopped to look at some of the beaches from the cliffs." I smile underneath my fiberglass hood. "I've never seen anything so peaceful."

"No jellyfish this summer," she says. "We're lucky."

We pass through Skala and its boarded-up taverna. Fresh yellow roses are bundled in front of it. We follow the corniche along the southern mountains. High above us looms the monastery, all wall and no windows like maximum-security devotion. The traffic slows us, blessed traffic, blessed elderly French vacationers who can't master the rental stick. I stay with Louise, calm and in low gear, glancing at the roiling, blue water, with only a dull pain shooting from my foot. Mud-fringed cats cavort in a Dumpster. Eventually we pass the town of Grikos and after another mile we make a turn toward the coast. A concrete garage hangar sits by the dock, alongside a small aluminum-sided trailer with windows the oily chemical purple of soapsuds. Two brine-stained boats are cradled in steel scaffolding in the lot, and a crane hovers above, swaying cables and hooks.

We park our bikes. I need to lie down. After my show of indifference, the shock of near death has returned. I drop my helmet in the seat compartment and tuck the novel under my arm. Three young Greek men in greasy trousers are busy treating one of the dry boats. One rubs sandpaper along its corroded hull. The other two are stealing glances at Sonny, who stands on the dock, holding a straw satchel. Her white bikini peeks out from a short terry cloth robe. The two Greek boys hit each other in the stomach every time one of them looks at her.

Louise and I walk toward the dock, Louise clicking photos of the hangar and shore with her phone. A little girl, topless, with bikini bottoms printed in strawberries, squats next to Sonny. She slams a stick against the dirt, as if punishing the planet for some personal atrocity. Sonny extends her hand, trying to get her to stop. The girl must be Duck, chubbier than I pictured her, with a snub, round fist of a face and frizzled brown hair. Only her large blue eyes give an indication of her mother's genes. I instantly feel sorry for her future self, the blunt, awkward teenage progeny who will always be compared unfavorably to her mother, who will never be able to shake off that cold birthright, especially in Los Angeles. She beats the stick in the dirt with vicious amusement.

Rasym and Adrian take turns chugging on a water bottle, and they share headphones from a device clipped to Rasym's swim trunks. Adrian's body is as efficient as a shark's, each muscle contracting under his pale skin with mechanical purpose. His smile is the only wasteful enterprise, a porch light shining inanely in the daytime. His happiness makes me uncomfortable because I believe it. He's so handsome the world could have been invented simply for his pleasure, every drop and ounce of it, oranges and stars, just for him. Even Louise is staring at the complex corrugation of his pelvic muscles disappearing into spandex.

A tall man, thin and angular, leans against an oil drum. His striped button-down shirt blows open in the wind, and madras shorts are rolled just above two thick hubcap knees. A riptide of premature gray runs through his brown, unruly hair, and he keeps trading the handle of a picnic basket between his palms. He's the first to spot us.

"You must be Ian," he says with a British accent as he bounds forward. He pivots the basket to his left hand and reaches his right hand toward me. "I'm Miles Lyon-Mosely, a friend." He announces himself friend to all, eliding specific allegiances, and his hand is warm and long with friendship. His lips don't close over his teeth, and his hooded eyelids don't seem to touch either when he blinks. He has a blocky, elongated face that might appear imperial if rendered in marble. In white flesh, it sits awkwardly atop a lean neck at a crooked tilt. Miles is a few years older than we are, and age suits him.

Charlie's black-oak sailboat rocks against the dock, longer and wider than it appeared in the photo he texted to me a few days ago. Christos is climbing around the stern, uncoiling ropes and securing tackle. He reaches for Miles's picnic basket, grunting a clipped form of *here, give it to me.* Miles passes it over the gunwale and steers Duck by the shoulders toward the center of the boat. He manages to pull the stick from her while distracting her with a leap onto the deck.

"Where's Charlie?" I ask Sonny.

She removes a jar of cream from her satchel and glides her fingernail around the edges.

"He's just coming out," she says, streaking the cream across her cheeks. "How was your first night?"

"A blackout," I say. "I was exhausted."

"I made a reservation for dinner tonight up in Chora." Sonny braids her hand in Louise's, which stops her from her relentless photo taking. "Charlie hates the restaurant, but if we're not too tired, it's delicious."

"The waiters, though," Louise balks.

"They forget they're waiters," Sonny explains. "You might sit next to one for an hour, thinking he's another guest drinking from your carafe of wine and suddenly he whips out a pen, asking how you like your fish."

Charlie strolls out of the hangar, carrying a cooler. He's wearing red-tinted sunglasses and a maroon T-shirt. It's faded by years of sun and laundry, but I recognize it instantly as our senior year Buckland shirt with its nonsensical crest of swords and interlocking rings. I had that T-shirt once too—all of our names are listed on the back— but like most old clothes, mine vanished before I built up the unsentimentality to throw it out. Charlie pinches the logo on his chest.

"Look familiar?"

"How did you keep it for so long?" I ask.

"Some things just stick around." He turns so that I can inspect the block of names. There are fifty of them, first names in meager italics, last names in bold block letters, like *species* followed by GENUS in an entomology display at a museum. Bledsoe and Konstantinou drift amid the American wasps, South American hornets, rare Japanese moths, rarer Middle Eastern locusts, and Jewish butterflies—all expensive specimens pinned to pilled maroon fabric. Where are these men today, their faces no longer spotted with puberty and hope? Adams, Barington, Craven, Faringer, Frisch, Frost, Herzenstein, Levy, McMarnely, Stamford, Santo Domingo, Yasuda. They're flaking off of Charlie's shirt faster than I can recall them.

"Want to bet most of them have just left their offices in midtown?" Charlie says to me. And then to Louise and Sonny he adds, "Buckland's strength was never the cultivation of independent minds. Its specialty was hatching flightless birds."

Most of those fifty names are now thirty years old and solvent. The familiar fear that I have nothing overtakes me, poor and desperate and tossing my chances behind Charlie and a day cruising around on his sailboat. If you follow the sun all you do is move in circles. I'm already seasick, or homesick, or sick for things I no longer own.

"Do you think we could talk—" I whisper to Charlie, but he doesn't hear me. Christos is yelling to him in Greek from the boat.

"Helios can't come out today," Charlie answers. "He's not feeling well."

A young goateed man slinks from the darkness of the garage. He wears the same blue polo as his father, over a long-sleeve white T-shirt. His face is sweaty and his cheeks a jaundice yellow.

His father shouts at him angrily, and Helios raises an impassive hand, as if to bat his responsibilities away. Even here, sons disappoint fathers. Charlie intervenes to add a few calming words in Greek. It's clear that Christos is annoyed, cursing and shaking his head, but he has a full ship today, and he claps his hands to signal us aboard.

"This is *Domitian*," Charlie tells me. "My boat. The others out here are the ones I was telling you about. We fix up wrecks, make them good as new, and rent them out during tourist season. They're basically small apartments with motors, so I don't have to worry about sailing qualifications. We send them all over the islands, from

Turkey to Athens. Already I have ten rented out at sea for August. Those boys working over there are some of my captains."

"Does Christos help?"

"No," Charlie says firmly. "He's our family man. The business is mine." The word *mine* induces a prideful clench of his teeth. "I keep it separate from the family on purpose."

"Not from the whole family, I hope," Rasym mumbles, staring at his cousin with a bitterness that might be meant as optimism.

Christos yanks me by the hand onto the boat, a rough, whiplashing motion that prevents guests from toppling with timidity into the water. White leather cushions wrap around the deck, and crystal glasses sit on a table next to a basket of folded black towels. The rest of the boat is wood, purple-brown and waxed like a violin. We each take our shoes off and place them in a wicker bin.

"Everyone," Sonny announces, turning in circles. "If you happen to see a diamond ring, please tell me. French-set, four carat, a platinum band."

"Is it something you've lost or just something else you want?" Rasym asks mockingly. The black mark on his forehead hasn't rubbed off.

She looks at him as if silently sentencing him to death by the Old World torture of scaphism.

"Honey," Charlie says. "I don't think you left it here. I'm pretty sure you took it with you to Paris."

"Stop saying that," she yells. "I told you I didn't. I left it here, on *Domitian*. I know I did. Please, if everyone could just look."

Louise and I both dutifully glance around. Miles drops to his knees and begins sweeping his hands under the cushions, gently lifting Duck to scoop the crevices around her. "We'll find it today," he says hopefully. Rasym and Charlie watch his searching with appalled delight.

"Miles," Charlie huffs. "Do you want a life jacket? In case you fall over. We sail under the assumption that all on board can swim." Miles's face reddens as he continues his thorough sweep.

Sonny strips out of her robe and balls the fabric against her face. Her legs are ruby-tinted like overripe fruit. It's possible to see her entire skeleton under the thin sinew of muscle, and whatever cream she's applied to her skin gives it the nacreous varnish of glossy paper. She steps over to Charlie and presses her forehead against his shoulder.

"Lamb, I swear it's here. I didn't lose it." I feel bad for her. She's on the verge of tears. Charlie wraps his arm around her and shoots me an incredulous look.

"We'll get you another one someday."

"I don't want another one. That's not the point."

"Terry," Duck screams, opening her hands. "Terry. *Tchh, tchh, tchh.*" A gray cat darts from the galley and onto her lap. She cradles it in a headlock, stroking its flank. I wasn't previously aware of the existence of boat cats. Rasym climbs over the seats to help Christos untie the mooring ropes.

"Good weather today?" I ask Charlie.

"Perfect," he replies. "Look how clear the sun is, and the wind is blowing from the south. I love it here. I love it, I love it."

Slipping lines, we cast off. The white sails slide and launch, holding the wind. We move quickly out of the harbor, tacking back and forth in the breeze. There is a deft choreography among Christos, Charlie, and Rasym, scrambling and leaning and tugging the ropes, their feet agile and precise as they dance around the rest of us lounging inertly on the cushions. We head north, streaming one hundred feet out from the coast, where the island rises and the monastery shoots into view like a volcanic crater. Every so often I catch Miles inspecting the control panel or the corners of the pinewood floor, still searching for the ring that would win him Sonny's everlasting appreciation. He's a perfect babysitter for Duck, making animal shadows on the cushions out of hand gestures.

Louise grabs a bottle of sunscreen and offers me her back, gathering up her short hair at the nape. I slide my hands around her shoulders, massaging methodically.

Charlie chucks his balled Buckland T-shirt at my head and laughs. He's not as worked-out as Adrian, who lies on the hot wood with his eyes closed like an Olympic swimmer contemplating each stroke of a future race. Charlie has a tiny O-shaped cushion of fat around his navel. Black tufts of hair chimney up his stomach, flaming out in the cleft between his chest muscles. His hairy legs are muscular and thick, perfectly engineered to hold him firmly against the mast. His back is wide and sculpted and chipped with pink, peeling skin, and finer hairs dust the base of his spine. A gold box cross hangs from his silver chain, caught by the light when he bends over. Compared to Rasym, Charlie looks like the family's Odysseus. And there's such a smooth, all-involved rhythm to his sailing, his whole body engaged in its labor, it's hard to recover the friend I knew from New York, surrounded by water but never at one with it.

Louise rotates around and jabs my forearm with her finger. We both watch the point of impact redden.

"I told you," she says. She squeezes out a dollop of lotion and wipes my arms, not unlovingly but with a cook's basting motion.

Rasym takes a break from the jib. He kneels down and kisses Adrian on the lips. Adrian reacts by running his hand along his boyfriend's neck. I don't get what there is to love in Charlie's cousin, but whatever it is, Adrian has found it. The kiss lingers for a minute, tongues rooting.

"Adrian's lucky," I say quietly into Louise's ear. "He gets to come here and stay in such luxury." I suppose I mean to claim him as one of us, the freeloaders.

"Don't feel sorry for Adrian Kromer," Louise replies, matching my low decibel. "Back in Poland, his father owns the power plants. Billions upon billions, apparently. Power plants and copper mines and the nation's entire broadcasting system. Although Adrian doesn't talk about it. I heard that from Miles. Honestly my eyes start crossing every time he brings up someone's net worth."

Adrian's happiness takes on new and disturbing dimensions. His happiness comes easily, like door-to-door car service, but his love for Rasym is entirely self-determined. He's freely at the wheel of that excursion. Why he'd choose Rasym when he could conceivably have anyone is beyond even my supernatural conception of romance.

We tilt and glide along the water, gas-flame blue, the blue of a June sky back home with the prickling sweat of a summer starting up, the pure anxious blue around us, deep and see-through and sliced with fish. We ride the wind, doused in the chop. Hazy islands span the horizon, glitter and fade. Patmos shines hard and brittle. How can I worry when I'm surrounded by such beauty, in Charlie's comfortable grip? As I look over the boat's edge, I half expect to see paper money floating like seaweed on the surface.

Christos disappears into the galley and returns with a magnum of champagne along with a nectarine for Duck. He pops the cork and fills the glasses. His thick, tarry hands make a mockery of the delicate, waiter-like position in which he's been trained to hold the bottle: by its bottom end. I sip from my glass reluctantly, knowing the alcohol could turn the boat's rocking against me. The heat is pouring over us through the white hole of noon.

"Maybe it's in the sea," Sonny says faintly. She bites a sip of champagne and swallows it down. "Maybe it rolled off the boat and is somewhere on the seafloor, and a hundred years from now a snorkeler will find it and it will change their life for good." Sonny seems to be inventing an ending so that her suffering isn't in vain, a Hollywood through line that concludes on an upbeat *fin*. Miles stops making foxes with his hands and touches her knee.

"Look at the hippie camp," Louise says, pointing to the coast. On an indent of beach amid sharp boulders, several tents are staked in the pebbles, with crosses drawn on their sides. Men and women, some naked, with lean, salamander forms, are huddled together. Among the splashing waves, I can barely make out their far-off singing.

"It reminds me of California," Sonny says with a shiver. "Not in my time, but my grandparents'. Grandma and Grandpa Towsend were all about free love in the sixties. Funny, in their memories they never mention venereal diseases."

"These aren't those kind of hippies," Charlie says from the mast. "They're born-agains. Or die-fasters. They're praying for the end of the world. Be careful, Ian, the prettiest ones will come up to you and invite you down to their camp and then try to convert you onto one of the four horses."

Louise pushes her sunglasses down the bridge of her nose to study them. The sockets of her eyes are black grottos in the sun.

"What's the name of their leader?" Miles asks, snapping his fingers. "The heavyset one with the cough."

"Vic," Adrian says, not even tilting his head from the sun. "She was sweet. I spoke to her once in Skala. She invited me to a bonfire."

"Don't go," Rasym commands, stepping around the hatch. "Everyone knows they planted the bomb."

"Is that true?" Sonny asks. Her lips are ghost white from the cream. "I thought it was left-wing radicals. I didn't think we had anything to worry about." She glances at Charlie as she reaches over to fit a cap on Duck's head.

Charlie tacks hard, turning the boat away from the coast, and in the whiplashing spin, I catch a last glimpse of two nude men waving from the shore.

"I'll take the monks anytime over them," Charlie hisses. "At least you know where you stand. At least they don't smile at you hoping every second is your last."

"Now, Charles," Miles interrupts. "You know from when we were kids that there's a rich tradition on the island of—"

"Death cults," Charlie snaps. "And they trespass wherever they want. Can't they pass out their Kool-Aid and be done with it?"

"Wait"—Sonny gasps—"whose blood is that?"

For a second, nobody moves, caught between reality and an actor's line. But I notice congealed red spots sprinkled across the wood deck. Terry, the cat, is licking one, and, conscious that everyone is staring at him, licks faster.

I grab my foot, and that's when I discover the torn nail. It must have happened when I jumped from the bike. Blood fills the entire nail bed and drips over the yellow rind of toe.

"Jesus, Ian." Louise groans.

"I didn't even realize. I must have stubbed it." I decide not to mention the religious maniac with the trimmed beard running me off the road like God's crusader. Half the group already seems fervently on the side of the monks.

"I'll find a bandage," Sonny says. She eyes Duck, who stands on the stern, tossing nectarine peels into the water. "Sweetie, be careful."

"I got her." Miles jumps into action, holding his long hands around the little girl like she's a prize vase in danger of toppling.

Thank you, she mouths to him, and, out loud to Charlie, "Try to control the turns, okay? It would be great if everyone survives the day."

Sonny returns from the galley with a first-aid kit and insists on doing the bandaging job herself. She dabs the wound with a cotton ball. I'm impressed by her nursing skills, infused with a mother's firm handling of cuts, as if she's accustomed to uncooperative feet. Louise avoids my toe entirely until the Band-Aid is in place. In her defense, blood looks more gruesome in direct sunlight.

"Is there a hospital on the island?" I ask.

"Yeah, but not a good one," Sonny answers. "If you need more than stitches, it takes hours to get to a decent facility in Leros or Kos."

"So what happens if you get seriously injured?"

"Oh, that's easy." Sonny squeezes my foot. "You make sure you don't."

Christos drops the sails and gestures toward a speck of rocky island off the coast, mint green and sac-cloth brown, with steep jagged cliffs pitched up at its peak like ram's horns. A tiny unadorned chapel sits halfway up the mountainside.

"Goat Island," he says in his cardboard English. "My family"—he touches his chest and points—"our island. We raise goats."

"Christos's family island," Charlie clarifies. "But the goats are gone now, aren't they?"

Christos chopsticks his giant fingers at his eye, an inch of space between them. "Few now. They are stolen."

"I saw two yesterday," Adrian testifies, propping himself on his elbows. "When I swam over." The island is a mile or two from Patmos, a marathon swim even for someone as fit as Adrian. "Their hair hasn't been shaved."

"Your family should mark them," I volunteer. "A tag on the ear."

Charlie snorts, grabbing onto Christos's shoulder. "Did you hear that?" He mimes a puncture to the ear. "Ian, you know what the local thieves would do? They'd cut the ear off before they carried them off. It would be an island of goat ears. Greek law: it's yours until you can't prove it is."

"Well, a missing ear is an identifying marker too. What about informing the police?"

Now Charlie and Christos both laugh, one mouth full of white teeth, the other a cave of black throat.

Christos drops anchor. The vibration of the chain's unspooling motor causes the glasses on the table to jitter. The captain grabs a plastic bucket, tugs off his shirt, and, without a preamble, dives off the side of the yacht.

"Christos goes deep because he isn't afraid," Charlie says, "of the enormity of the water. I can't stand tourists who swim with one hand latched onto the side of the boat. You've come this far, *let go*."

Louise slips out of her shorts.

"Are you coming?"

"Maybe in a minute," I tell her.

Soon everyone except for Miles and me dives off the boat, as naturally as if they've been trained from the diving boards and docks of their youth. Even Duck, taking fledgling steps to the edge, manages an upside-down launch.

"You don't swim?" Miles asks, resting his head on the cushions.

"No, I do. It's just . . ." I feel dizzy, and the pain in my foot, once identified, has started to sting. Blood has already leaked into the bandage. I can't remember the last time I was on a boat, and the bobbing motion combined with the glare off the water reminds me of the sickness of watching television too long on a hot afternoon—the nauseating claustrophobia of unreal colors and sounds.

"Sonny tells me you were living in Panama?" Miles prompts. I don't respond. "My family had some dealings with a Dutch shipping company that has its headquarters there. My father has a thing for the Panama Canal. The eighth wonder, and, for him, the only improvement Americans ever made on the world." I smile wanly and perform an examination of Goat Island. Nothing moves there, not even the trees. "What were you doing in Panama?" he finally asks.

"Helping out," I say vaguely. *Making mistakes*, I think. I excuse myself to go to the bathroom. I climb down the ladder into the galley, steadying myself on the lacquered wood walls. In the gentle quiet below, the boat's pitching is less severe. A chrome dining area with an entertainment system leads into a square bedroom. A king-size mattress takes up most of the space. The bedroom is littered with Charlie's personal items: books and coins and DVDs and old chess trophies, much like the décor of his dorm room in college, as if the moving boxes were shipped directly from Massachusetts to *Domitian*. I pass back into the main room, where the cat leaps onto the kitchen table. Above the table hangs a framed photo of Charlie and his father in Venice. They smile amid the gray feathers and puddles of Piazza San Marco. I haven't seen Mr. K in nearly a decade. The seal in him has turned walrus, and he grins proudly and sickly from a wheelchair. There's an oxygen tank hooked to his side and a mask in his lap. It won't be too long now before Charlie also loses his father, with one less species listed under the Konstantinou genus. But unlike me, Charlie will bury him alongside his family.

I hobble into the bathroom on my injured foot. When I finish, I wait a few more minutes down below, toying with chess pieces that roll on a cut-wood, opal-inlaid table across from the galley's radio equipment. By the time I return, everyone is toweling off on deck.

Sonny is wringing Duck's hair out, and Louise is rinsing off on the stern with a shower nozzle attached to a rubber hose. I can see her nipples through the blue bathing suit.

Charles winks at me as he lights a cigarette. "It takes a day or two to get used to her." At first I think he means Louise. "After a week, you'll be steering *Domitian*." *After a week.* By then, will I still be drifting through an accidental vacation or will Charlie have given me keys to a brand-new life?

LUNCH IS FRESH urchin, gathered by Christos from the sea and sliced in half with a switchblade on deck. The spiky black stars look like the orbs held by the saints in Charlie's icon paintings. I pick at the slimy brown meat without commitment. I'm thankful when Christos switches to the motor to guide us smoothly toward the coast, a bright blue wake trailing behind us. We anchor again thirty feet out from a quiet, crescent beach on the north side of the island. Rasym and Adrian jump into the water first, holding a pile of towels above their heads as they wade toward shore. Christos unstraps the tender from the boat with irritated effort. If Miles could swim, he wouldn't have to use it, and if his son were here, it wouldn't be his job.

"I can stay on board," Miles says apologetically. "I don't mind. He doesn't have to go to all the trouble."

"It's fine," Sonny replies. "And now we can bring supplies with us." She tosses three water bottles in the inflated dinghy and I place my novel in there too, wrapped in a towel. Sonny guides her daughter by the hand down the ladder. Charlie dives from the bow, reemerging to position Duck on his shoulders so she can ride him to shore. I pull off my shirt and stare down at the soft turquoise. There are two kinds of swimmers, those who jump headfirst without even testing the water, and those who linger at the edge, steeling themselves for the cold jolt, pep-talking themselves into free fall. I've always been the latter, but I believe it's misplaced to call

it cowardice. There's a thrill to the waiting and slow-building resolve, a body beating back its instinct to remain on solid ground.
It's the pleasure of reticence, of the brain sweating, of the notion
that actions have prices, which the fast, careless divers know nothing about. Eventually though—mainly because Miles is staking
his claim to my attention, darting toward me from across the deck
(*wait, is he going to push me in?*)—I jump.

The water is sharp at the surface and instantly giving underneath,
the entire blind hug of it. I take my time, paddling in the stillness,
opening my eyes, sinking under to the soundtrack of my own breath.
I watch Sonny on the beach, marking a spot with the spread of a
towel. Charlie was right. Two beefy Greek men, their stomachs industrial mixing bowls over impressively scant swim trunks, stand
a few feet from her, leering with predatory intention. She ignores
them, and it's only Duck falling against her, whining like an air
horn, that eventually clears them from the vicinity.

I climb onto the brown-pebbled beach, the undersides of my feet
throbbing with each step on the coarse stones. Louise pats a black
towel that has already been opened next to her.

"You need to buy water booties," she says, holding her humor on
her lips. "You can get them in Skala, along with your very own Anti-
Bethlehem T-shirt."

"Anti-Bethlehem?"

"It's the hot Patmos shirt of the summer. You know, Revelation
Island, Anti-Bethlehem, the birthplace of the end of the world. There
are also Anti-Bethlehem bibs and beer mugs. Get your Christmas
presents early."

Charlie is buttering Sonny's back with lotion. Rasym and Adrian
are floating in the shallows, their chins catching the wave crests.

"Now do you miss New York?" Sonny asks me.

"Not for a minute," I say.

"Neither does Charlie."

Charlie picks up a pebble and launches it into the water.

"If the world is a bomb, New York is its fuse," he says gruffly.

"That's where all the bad things start. Not here." Louise wrinkles her nose, as if finding his metaphor a touch too pat.

The sun dries my body in minutes, and for a while all I can do is watch the water's surface, brown and purple like peacock feathers. The tide spreads across the pebbles and pulls back out, each time with a *skeeeeth* like the sound of a rake driven over concrete. All day and night for millennia, for light-years, there has been this sound, this *skeeeeth*-ing, and maybe it will be the last sound too, the world's last sound, one final *skeeeeth* before it's all blown like cartwheels into space.

A few minutes later, the tender cuts through the waves, Miles crouched at the prow with his button-down wrapped around his neck, and Christos in back, directing the motor. Miles's chest hair is long and crinkled, and his doughy nipples poke periscopically from his chest. His chin is raised proudly against the wind, like Christopher Columbus centuries too late for colonization or even a good spot on the beach. He steps into the water and gathers the supplies we've stowed. Charlie greets his arrival by springing up and running into the sea. He takes large, lunar steps before he disappears under the carpet of blue.

Miles drops my book between my legs and sits down beside Sonny in Charlie's perch.

"I'll take a cab back to Chora," he says. "I don't want Christos to bother again."

"I don't know why you don't let me teach you," Sonny says. "I taught Duck."

"Pride," he answers honestly as he twists open a water bottle. "But maybe with your coaching I could try. When I attended Ludgrove I had an uncle who drowned off Borneo, so I was released from swimming instruction."

"That seems like a reason to keep you enrolled," Louise counters. Miles laughs, rubbing his chin. He's not such a bad sport.

Time passes. The heat thickens. An Italian couple argues under their umbrella in a sleepy seesaw rhythm. A fat man smokes nearby while playing Sudoku in a metal folding chair, squares of burned flesh swelling through the metal's weave. Goat bells ring in the hills around the beach. Extended thoughts prove impossible, snatches of concern at most, more their feeling than their source. In the shadow of an olive tree, an older European couple, nudists, crouch with their legs splayed, offering full genital exposure, every labial fold and uncircumcised droop on display. Their nudity is so frank it doesn't read as sexual, as if arousal must find its establishing rhythm in a small degree of shame.

I lie on my towel watching Miles playing a shell game with Duck using actual shells. He moves the three shells around an open magazine, and she studies their crisscrossing intently. "Now which one is the beetle under?" he asks her.

She points to the middle one, the most obvious or the most-clever-for-being-so-obvious choice. Miles turns them all over. There is no beetle. Duck's horrified face approximates the moment she will first learn of the hydrogen bomb.

Miles opens his fist to reveal a crawling black beetle.

"Remember," he advises. "Before you pick, always ask to see the dealer's hands." She nods attentively. "Sometimes the shell hides the hand." I often find childhood lessons are the ones most in need of relearning.

Adrian and Rasym climb barefoot with a mat into the scrub hills above the beach. I wonder if they're going to mess around in the bushes. I try to begin on Henry Miller, a book called *The Colossus of Maroussi*, as Louise dozes next to me, but around the tight black type is an inch of white border, and beyond that border the blue sky and sea, and my eyes slip across sentences into the far margins to find Charlie and Sonny kissing in the water. *A few months before the war broke out I decided to take a long*—Sonny leaning back in Charlie's arms, swaying her brown torso in the current. My eye struggles back to catch the next cliff edge—*vacation.* I give up a few cliff jumps later and flip lethargically through the pages. I assumed the book was new, bought randomly by Charlie's interior decorator as cerebral décor, but someone's initials are penned on the first page. G.F. A few sentences are underlined midway through the novel: *Who are you, what are you now in drugged silence. . . . Are you you? If I should bash your skull in now would all be lost . . . will there come out with the blood a single tangible clue?* The heat gums my brain. This G.F. had more patience for Miller's disquisitions than I do. It's defeating not to connect to passages a previous reader has taken the trouble to mark, like coming across a postcard of buildings long torn down. Sonny climbs dripping out of the water, adjusting her bikini top. The fat, smoking man ignores his numbers game.

"How's the reading?" she asks, worming herself down on her towel.

"Nonabsorbent," I reply. "I found it in the cabin. A G.F. got to it first."

Sonny shrugs. "Here's a confession. I always check that the characters in a novel are older than I am. Ideally they're a minimum of five years older. Otherwise, I have trouble taking their mistakes seriously."

"Was that true for the roles you played?"

"No." She laughs. "Five years younger and deeply tortured was the ideal. I meant it when I said Charlie saved me from the psych ward of Hollywood. It's like my body was broken and he set every bone back into place."

"Have I seen any of your movies?"

"Probably," she says defensively. "Or maybe not. Who cares? I'll never go back. I'm *so* done with it." I wonder how much she was done with it and how much it was done with her. "I always tell Duck, she can be anything she wants except famous."

Duck lounges next to Miles, glaring at an Italian man who emerges from the sea in a snorkel mask holding a bright red starfish in his palm. He places it on his girlfriend's knee a few sunbathers down from us. Duck gets to her feet and storms over to them, her back rigid like the hind of a deer.

"Sir," I hear her say in a loud voice. "Can you put that creature back in the water? You're watching it die."

The young Italian couple exchange uncomfortable looks. Finally the Italian woman manages a response.

"Little girl, it is not your business. Go back to your towel."

"Do you like watching it die?" Duck didn't seem to mind when Christos cracked open the urchins on the yacht.

The Italian woman struggles to answer. "Do you not eat fish?"

"These starfish are endangered. Are you planning on eating it?"

There is no chance for the Italians to win this showdown, no ethical plank they can hold besides the superiority of their age. It is an unfair match. To stand their ground is to appear as jerks in this temporary sun community; to acquiesce and return the starfish to the sea is to show their moral inferiority to a seven-year-old in strawberry bikini bottoms. A certain finesse is required that the afternoon heat has drained from them.

"When you're an adult . . ." The Italian woman begins to lecture. Sonny watches without interrupting. I hadn't noticed before that the default lock of her mouth is a slanted sneer, the kind culled from dark, atonal music collections or adolescent years hanging out in basements with boys. It's a pubescent expression of anger and powerlessness that, on her, seems powerful and persuasive. It breaks the streamlined beauty of her face like a bullet hole in a store window.

"I love Duck's balls," she whispers. "I don't know where she gets it. She's starting to ask the big questions. Yesterday she asked me how many planets there are in outer space. And I felt like an idiot because I couldn't tell her. I know Pluto's been demoted, but haven't they found a bunch of others in nearby solar systems? What are we up to now? And what the hell's a dwarf planet? The things we learned in school, they're not accurate anymore."

I think of the outer space Duck is learning, complicated with so many planets, more crowded and democratic than ours was with its nine foam-core balls rotating on a rusty stand in science class. Sonny's right. It seems impossible that we ever believed, hand on heart, in such an infantile idea of space.

Louise wakes, startled, as if pulling out of a nightmare, but she's quickly reassured by the lap of waves. Pebbles have made red indentions the shape of upward arrows on her thighs. She nudges me with her hip.

"Doesn't it feel strange to be here?" she asks, stretching her arms. Her back muscles dip and clench. "Too lucky, like we've cheated the terms?"

"A little bit. Is this enough of a reason not to go back to Georgetown?"

"Maybe," she says, resting her cheek on her knuckles. "Almost."

"But you *will* go back, won't you?" I have a fantasy of Louise staying on with me in Europe, the two of us building new, purposeful lives and reading everything but Miller to each other at night in bed. "I mean, you've already put in a year."

"It's not the seminary, Ian," she says tiredly. "I didn't have a calling. I could skip out with what I've studied and be satisfied. But don't you think we're getting too old to be wanderers? All this lightness for too long"—she grabs at the sunlight like it's a curtain she can gather in her fist—"and you just disappear, floating away in it." She squints up at me, hunting for my eyes. Her face glows, her chin dented with its mole and dimples, and an invitation I haven't found before offers itself in the steadiness of her eyes.

Duck returns, climbing across her mother's knees. Louise rakes her toes through the pebbles at the end of her towel.

"It's weird that Charlie's the one who has his life together," Louise says. "I wouldn't have predicted that back in college." She stares out at the water. "What about you? What's going to be *your* next step?" I worry Louise has Googled my name and has come to realize the corner I'm in. And like dominoes, one worry knocks against the next, setting a constellation in motion: my father in his casket, a church gone black, and his eldest son baking faraway on a beach towel in paradise. I fix the bloodstained bandage on my foot, buying time in order to change the subject.

"If you do go back to law school, what will be your specialty? I think you'd be a terrific prosecutor."

Louise rolls over. She presses her hands against her chest, patiently exhausted by my mentions of life back in the States.

"God, no. Not that. Civil liberties. Environmental law. Nothing criminal."

"Do environmental," Sonny encourages. "Duck would love that." As if Duck is Louise's mother in Kentucky and should be considered before making any major career decisions.

"Oh, good," she says, laughing. "Who would Duck like for me to marry?"

"Easy," Sonny answers. "Assuming she still believes in marriage, which I doubt she does, that would be Miles." Louise and Miles exchange looks as if they've been incorrectly identified as members of the same crime syndicate.

The Italian man strolls silently toward the water, his head bent away from us. He returns the starfish to the sea. A victory for innocence.

I see Charlie descending a path from the hills. In his hand he holds a pastry from a small taverna nestled high above the rocks, its peach awning flapping in the breeze. It's deep in the afternoon, and now that I'm onshore my appetite has returned. I borrow Miles's flip-flops and cross the beach toward Charlie. Alone, holding his pastry but not eating it, Charlie has worry scored across his face. Trickles of sweat leak from his armpits. He's wrapped his T-shirt around his head, fashioned like a turban on a desert scavenger. As he watches the boats at sea, some anchoring near *Domitian*, his tongue worries the chip in his tooth. He's so lost in thought he doesn't notice my approach.

"What's wrong?" I ask.

He shakes himself into the present and bites into the pastry.

"Nothing," he says, chewing. "Just work. It looks like a vacation, but it's the busiest time of the season for me. I probably should have stayed behind."

Since we're finally alone, I consider making the case about my finances. I don't want to add to his troubles, but how many days of sailing will pass before Charlie takes my silence for contentment, like I've traveled all the way here just to spend a few relaxing days with him?

"Do you want to go for a walk?" I ask. "We could talk about—"

"Your situation," he concludes. "I haven't forgotten. Tomorrow." Realizing it sounds like a dodge, he touches my arm. "Noon. Down at my port. We can play chess like old times."

Men on the two newly moored yachts are arguing and pointing at the water. One flails his arms in the melodramatic fashion that only Europeans manage convincingly.

"Amateurs," Charlie jeers. "Their anchors are tangled. One threw his line too far out." He nods up the hill toward the taverna. "Charge what you want. I have a tab. I'm going to swim back to the boat to make some calls. I have to check in on my captains. Busy day running paradise."

I hike the trail that Rasym and Adrian took. The goat bells ring louder in the hills, but the goats are still invisible. The dirt trail snakes through the scrub, dips, and rambles as if intent on taking its time. Ahead, near a stretch of concrete, a bush shakes. I think I might be intruding upon Rasym and his boyfriend having sex. But as I round the trail, I find Adrian a few feet away, doing knuckle push-ups on the ground. At first I only see the arches of Rasym's feet. But then his body lifts to his knees and he chants in lilting Arabic. He swoops down again, his head striking against the mat. The mark on his forehead isn't ashes or dirt, but a bruise from tapping it in prayer. His head points toward Mecca, his back prone and his hands placed flat by his ears. The beach sways far below, and the late afternoon light strips the water of its depth. The darkened yachts look like flies crawling on raw, blue meat. Rasym hums his verses in obedience. I rush by him, not wanting to interrupt—interrupting prayer seems worse than interrupting sex; it's even more vulnerable and exposed. I honestly didn't know it was possible to be a practicing Muslim and openly have a boyfriend. But maybe Rasym has found a balance in the two virtues religion offers: safety and fear.

The taverna is empty except for a few Spaniards on the porch smoking a joint, and inside there is the cold humming of antique refrigeration. I order a phyllo and take a more direct path down to the beach. From a low bluff I notice Sonny sprinting along the shoreline. I follow her jagged course. She reaches Duck, standing by a clump of motorbikes and talking to a heavyset man in a straw fedora. Sonny scoops up her daughter's hand and leads her away. When I reach our towels, Sonny is gathering up our belongings. Duck slumps on the pebbles, her arms crossed.

"Did you see who she was talking to?" Sonny wheezes. "That's the pedophile."

It takes me a few seconds to locate him. Most of the beachgoers are also packing up their camps. He sits on a foldout stool under the shade of a boulder, molding the brim of his hat. He has a round child's face, although he must be in his fifties, with rash-red legs and brown leather sandals.

"When I ran up, Duck was chatting away about her friends in school." Sonny turns to her daughter. "Never talk to that man, do you hear me?"

"I thought he only liked boys," Louise says.

"Thanks." Sonny grunts. "That makes me feel much better."

"How very 1950s Englishman of him," Miles ventures. "Come to Greece, corrupt the boys. I thought those types had all moved on to Thailand."

Sonny gives him a caustic look. She grabs his button-down and bundles it around Duck's shoulders. "Put this on, sweetie." A network of grooves appears between Sonny's eyes when she's upset. "If he talks to her again, I'll get Charlie to pay a visit."

"I could talk to him." Miles speaks so unthreateningly it cancels out the suggestion.

Sonny waves her arm toward *Domitian*, trying to signal to Christos or Charlie to pick us up in the tender.

"We still have a few hours until dinner," she grumbles. "Ian, you'll have to borrow something of Charlie's to wear tonight."

"I can lend him a change of clothes," Miles offers. He seems ready to throw his body in front of Sonny's feet at the first opportunity.

"Ian, your shoulders." Louise shakes her head. I press my fingers along the burnt skin. My body is a combat zone of island injuries. If I keep going at this rate, I'll be on a helicopter to the hospital in Kos by the weekend.

"Come to think of it, I can't take a cab home," Miles says. "I left my wallet onboard."

Charlie stands on the bow of the black yacht, his cell phone stuck to his ear; in his other hand he holds a bottle of liquor. What's left of the sun finds the bottle and fills it with gold. His body is a black calligraphic *I* against the blue. We're all waving now, as if desperate for rescue. The distance between each of us on the shore is negligible, but between us and Charlie fraught and far. The beckoning is contagious, all of us trying to catch Charlie's attention, Miles hopping, Sonny and Louise making X's with their arms, me whistling with two fingers in my mouth, each in our own way needing him. We were all different people before we arrived on this island, which I suppose is why we're here.

"He doesn't see us," Louise says, dropping her arms.

"He'll see us." Sonny's certain voice breaks. "Well, maybe—"

But he does. And in the convoluted logic of boats and shorelines, when we get back onboard we relax into it like it's home.

THE NIGHT BEGINS as most nights never do: with a group hug. It was only meant as a demonstration, but we are huddled together in Charlie's sitting room, our arms around each other and our breath humid on each other's necks. Charlie, Sonny, Louise, and I, four fingers, and when Duck runs over and clamps onto her mother, the thumb. All evening I've felt like I've been floating, the sea still in my legs, and it is only this tight clutch that fixes me to Earth. I want to stay here, holding and held.

"It doesn't get any better than this," Charlie whispers. "It really doesn't."

Duck refused to hug Sonny good night, because the hug signaled bed. Christos's wife, Therese, a bony, gray-haired woman who speaks far better English than her husband, urged her toward her mother, but Duck stood firm. Withholding love meant staying up later. Sonny, in a red silk dress with a thin gold chain tight around her throat, kept her arms held out for her daughter to fill.

"I don't want to hug you," Duck whined.

"You're crazy not to," Charlie said, climbing the steps in a green polo and plaid shorts. "If you don't, I'm taking your place." He swooped his arms around Sonny, pawing her back. "Man, this feels good. Louise, get in here."

Louise had borrowed one of Sonny's linen dresses, and it hung stiffly on her body like a sheet draped over a piano. She walked over and entered the embrace.

I didn't wait to be invited. Charlie instantly gripped my shoulder, and Louise held my waist. Duck, stomping jealously, broke from Therese and added her weight.

It is just a demonstration, but we all stay here longer than we need to, a beating unit, temples pressing, complete. I agree with Charlie. It doesn't get any better, not younger or sweeter or surer. It is Duck who breaks away first, because for her this feeling isn't as rare.

"Say your prayers," Sonny orders.

Charlie looks like he's been ambushed. "Prayers?" He shakes his head diabolically. "You mean shopping lists?"

"What do you pray for?" Louise asks Duck as Therese reaches to confiscate her. Therese's teeth are worse than her husband's, grime-black and urine-yellow like February snow piles in New York.

Duck considers for a minute. "Peace on Earth?"

"Oh, my god, I love you," Sonny says, clapping her hands. "See, Lamb, you're always underestimating the Towsend women. A present for you tomorrow, Duckie. You pray hard for peace on Earth, and I will too, and eventually we'll convince him."

Sonny's response goes unheard. The girl is already hurtling down the stairs, chasing a frenzy of cartoon beeps that must be the ring on her cell phone. Duck has more important calls to take.

I've borrowed a pair of pants from Charlie as well as a white suit coat. I wear my T-shirt and swim trunks underneath, which prevents the need for a belt. Charlie's scent lingers in the silk coat lining, his familiar tang of lavender and metal. As we walk to dinner I find myself opening the coat to catch stray whiffs. Our voices echo down the stone corridor. The moonlight and the yellow shine from lit windows turn the walls soft.

Our dinner reservation is really a section at one of two never-ending tables that bisect the cobblestones like an equal sign. We're in the Plateia, not far from Charlie's house, but in a matter of steps, isolation is replaced by the loud pulse of late-night revelers. White Christmas lights flare out from the restaurant, the strands netting over our heads, and music blasts from the open windows. The tablecloths indicate previous consumption, stained with red wine and Brailled with salt. Miles is already seated. We're nestled in among other diners, some who know Charlie and Sonny, others who introduce themselves. Their names are hyphenated and foreign and loaded with consonants, like the rattling of silver dish sets. White pants, fresh makeup, ochre bodies fashionably starved, clove cigarettes that oversweeten the air, mouths in motion, left open between bouts of laughter. The drinks come swiftly, with a snap of the fingers, but the food order is forgotten. Sonny is in her element, her foot tapping to the pace of her conversation. Most often, we are beneficiaries of someone else's misfortune. "Lost all of his money. His money, his wife, his art. Haven't seen him since."

I'm three vodkas in and back at sea, adrift. I'm also comatose from my sunburn, and the salt on my skin feels as leaden as an X-ray vest in a dental office. Louise picks at a basket of bread and eyes me pleadingly as the bald man seated next to her prattles on about politics. It was interesting for the first ten minutes. He introduced himself as *the* French diplomat but speaks perfect American. Whether he's an

American diplomat to France or a French diplomat to somewhere else is never resolved. "What we're witnessing in the Middle East is the death of the nation state," he tells her. "It was an invention, and a clever one until it broke. The opposite is happening here in Greece with the European Union. The invention of an empire is failing right before our eyes."

His wife, an interior designer, explains that she only does houses she "feels."

Charlie sits across from Sonny, one minute smiling and listening, the next deep diving into the Mariana Trench of his thoughts. Charlie's attention span has always been short, and he's never learned to let his expression fly on autopilot. His eyes are candles snuffed.

"People think rococo was created for the French aristocracy, but it was actually a rejection of Versailles," Sonny lectures. "It was a more democratic aesthetic. Its tastelessness was its wit."

"A note scrawled on a torn take-out menu!" Miles erupts, nearly knocking over a bottle of wine. "That's my uncle's most prized possession. He lived upstairs from his flat in the seventies. 'Your music is too loud and is vibrating my ceiling.' Signed David Bowie."

A branzino finally arrives, but no one has silverware. The fish lies across the table, glimmering green and untouched, with the bulging eyes and drawn mouth of a bout of seasickness.

At a certain hour, the older diners disappear, and younger, drunker vacationers take their places. The corners are padded with ice buckets and leaning bodies. Portable credit-card machines zoom through the crowd like drones. My most successful eye contact is with the branzino. If the twentieth century had taken a different exit ramp, these eternal summer revelers would be the first in line to be shot. It's amazing that they haven't been, unreal that decadence won and the celebrations can still be heard far out at sea. At midnight, the restaurant turns on its outdoor lights to a roar of appreciation, the entire square overlit as tables are quickly dismantled. I brace my hands on the edge of our table, afraid it will be ripped from us. I suppose if I were less jet-lagged or hadn't already decided on

Louise, I might try my luck. I've always had better success in countries that don't speak my language, and more than a few socialites browse nervously, as if searching for someone worth the duration of their drinks. But in our tans, on vacation, under the glare of stadium wattage, individuality blurs like cantaloupe in a blender. A mutually agreed upon hysteria fills the emptiness, identities only reclaimed when it's time to pay the tab.

A squat, sweaty man with close-cropped hair approaches our table with staggered steps. He's introduced as Bence, a Hungarian with a title I don't catch, but he's only interested in Charlie. He pinches Charlie's shoulder roughly.

"You took my dock," he slurs. "That's where I wanted to park my boat, and you took it." He sounds furious, but he offers Charlie his hand to shake.

"There are plenty of spaces in Grikos," Charlie replies.

"Business," he huffs. "How much did you pay off the monastery for that business?" He grins at Sonny, as if he could kill her with his wrecked idea of charm.

"It was a fair deal."

"It didn't, no, I didn't say it wasn't, did I?" Bence stumbles in place. One hopes he'll have the decency to fall down. "But it stinks. I know a few captains. And to think those monks are getting a cut. Now here's what." He kneels, trying to catch his elbow on the table. Louise scoots toward the diplomat. "You need another backer? I can come in on it. I've got the money for that kind of operation. You'll never lose on yachts. What do you say about me coming in? A few million? One phone call. I own dogs worth that much."

"I'll consider it," Charlie says in a tone that works as a sobriety test: he won't.

"Good," Bence retorts. "I expect a call. You'd hate me as competition." He wrestles a business card out of his pocket and holds it between two manicured nails. The card hangs there for several seconds as vulnerable as a rose, before Louise plucks it to hurry him away.

Sonny and Miles stand to dance, Miles slipping his arm around her waist.

"Should we call a taxi?" Louise asks me. She begins to dial on her cell phone.

"But what about our bikes?"

"Helios can bring them to the cabins in the morning," Charlie says, offering a smile before standing. He lights a cigarette as he watches Sonny and Miles drift into the crowd. Sonny glances back at him, touching her chin to her shoulder, before she begins to sway in slow, narcotic movements. "Sorry, Ian," Charlie says, rolling his eyes at the evening. "It's August. What did I tell you?" He seems to understand the inherent problem with people: more of them only increases the loneliness.

"I can't hear the dispatcher," Louise reports, and she too gets up. "I'll be right back."

I sit at the half-deserted table while all around me are bones and noise. My chair looks upon the quiet, black alley that leads to Charlie's house, and I see a face stashed in the darkness, a face I recognize from the rooftop bar in Athens with a shaved head and a scar running from its mouth. Not all insects are attracted to the light. Some must wait to feed upon the ones that are. Several purses and wallets litter the remaining tables, waiting to be rounded up.

The interior designer finds herself alone and rubs her neck uncomfortably. She looks at me and, with a brave sigh of acceptance, leans forward to engage.

"Ian, isn't it? You haven't said a word all evening. Tell me about yourself. Who are you? How have you kept yourself busy all these years?"

CHAPTER 4

Google Ian Bledsoe. Insert my name into a search engine. Every potential employer since my time in Panama has. There for the record, in the collective historical cesspool, is the story of my offense. It follows me, haunts me, steps in front of me as I walk into a room, lingers long after I've fled offices and beds. It eats and eats and can't be killed—or if it can, it can only be eclipsed by something even more horrific. As with a cephalopodic alien monster in a sci-fi horror film, any attempt to destroy it simply makes it stronger. A response, a clarification, or an even-keeled defense written in a comments section will only piss it off. In some ways, in all ways but the one that really matters, it is me. It's the weather I live in now.

Type IAN BLEDSOE. Press SEARCH.

SON OF BABY-FOOD EXEC LINKED TO FOILED BOMB PLOT

SPOILED SCION TURNS RADICAL IN CENTRAL AMERICA, BETRAYS FAMILY BUSINESS

THE PRIVILEGES OF PRIVILEGE: BABY-FOOD HEIR AVOIDS CRIMINAL CHARGES IN CONNECTION TO DRUG CARTEL

These weren't headlines in national papers. They were small, fleeting, feel-bad items on page eight or ten of local rags, crammed alongside reports of George Washington Bridge jumpers or the dangers of owning a pit bull. As with the presumed motives of those jumpers or the savageness of those pets, the journalists realized what few facts they had in hand and misconstrued the details as sensationally as their editors allowed. The truth is simple and unworthy of note. There were no charges to avoid; I "turned radical" only in that I turned my back on the corporate offices of Kitterin Inc. and tried to help its working poor; the bomb plot consisted of a single rambling conversation at a party of which I took no part; *scion? heir?*

The story drifted from print as fast as a storm promising record snowfall and delivering a drizzle of rain. To their credit, Kitterin's PR flaks worked semi-assiduously to dismantle the coverage, releasing a single-sentence statement that read, "An internal review found that Edward Bledsoe's son had no participation in the alleged criminal events that unfolded in Panama City, and any reports to the contrary should be treated as libel." My father was given a one-month leave of absence to deal with "familial strife"—a blow he didn't take lightly and which finalized our estrangement. And that was it, except for me. Kitterin's official statement appears nowhere in the top Google searches of my name. There are only those blue radioactive headlines, clickable, linkable, a cloven-hoofed footprint visible from anywhere under the digital sun.

Infamy on the Internet is eternal. It has no sense of time. It eats backward—photos of me from college and my first years after graduation at charity benefits or food drives are tagged with anonymous comments. "Nice try handing out sandwiches to make amends for TRYING TO BOMB A FACTORY FULL OF INNOCENT WORKERS"; "look at that fucking, self-satisfied rich-brat smile. I hope the 'underprivileged youth' he's next to pulls a gun." And it eats forward, biting through every online outreach for donations I posted at the single job I managed to find, as operations manager at a Bronx-based drug and homeless nonprofit called We in Need. "Die, Ian, just go away. You made your bed and you're done." "This employee should be fired yesterday." "WTF? This guy is asking *us* for donations? Why doesn't he ring up his cartel friends? I hope he chokes on a spoonful of baby food."

Friends, I had some. Baby food, the Bledsoe specialty. Ironically it was in that processed, choke-free slurry where all my troubles began.

I FLEW ECONOMY on an MD-88 to Panama City in the rainy season. In this season, in the crooked intercontinental arm of Central America, the rain doesn't have an On and Off switch but only gradations of soft and brutal. Green is the dominion color here: the city is surrounded on all sides by stalled sea and jungle. And the real green, of course, is the reason for the nation's existence: the swamp-green money, collected and counted and flowing all hours through the world's most famous shortcut. The Canal passes through the city like a knife through a ghost. It seemed, after a few postcollegiate years struggling in the nonprofit sector, a good place to start a career in business.

My father arranged the assistant's job at the Panama headquarters of Kitterin Inc., but there was no special treatment for the vice president's son besides that solitary penny-loafer in the door. I was given a cubicle in a windowless office in one of the dust-green high-rises of the New City. My boss was an efficient, chinless executive who preferred to speak to me in English although I responded in Spanish to bolster my conversational skills. Her only individualizing traits were the two Harvard diplomas hanging in her office and the ritual reading of her horoscope in the mornings before the numbers came in from the factory. My job was specific and deadening: check the daily manufacture totals of 2.5 oz., 4 oz., and 6 oz. baby-food jars in its various flavors and varieties; oversee the weekly export shipping docket to North, Central, and South American suppliers; "liaise" via e-mail with jar, label, and package wholesalers (the jars were imported from Venezuela, and for that first month the parent company shifted almost daily from private to national ownership, wreaking havoc on the export price of glass). All of these responsibilities were actually conducted by corporate higher-ups; I was merely a second or third set of eyes, scanning for irregularities. When I missed aberrational spikes and dips, a computer program caught them and I was given a human-oversight warning. For the first month that I worked at Kitterin I never touched a single jar of baby food. However, the office was decorated with giant headshots of white, chubby babies, their lips twisted in digestive satisfaction and their eyes staring hungrily into your heart. Even the bathrooms with their automatic-flush urinals and automatic hand dryers weren't safe from these ravening eyes and ecstatic mouths. I had a joke—"baby brother is watching"—but I had no one to tell it to.

"Kitterin Baby Food®, made from the finest natural ingredients, organic and nutritious, tested on tiny taste buds, mom approved." It was a billion-dollar conglomerate. It fed the diapered future. The Spanish commercial showed a mom piloting a spoon of goop onto the pink landing strip of an infant's mouth.

I stayed in an eerily nondescript long-lease motel called the Royal Decameron Arms. It was located in the New City five blocks from the Kitterin offices and it shared a parking lot with a KFC. The room's walls were mint, its curtains sage, its heavy-breathing air conditioner the only new amenity. On my first day, the elderly American who ran the establishment gave me a map of the city with parts of the southern half x-ed out in red. "Red is for red zone," he informed me. "That means if you so much as walk those streets you're liable to be shot on sight." They were gang-owned, drug- and poverty-ridden, and rumor had it morgue vans cleared dead bodies off the streets with more regularity than garbage pickup.

"I thought the country was stable and prospering," I said to the landlord, who wore a hunter-green U.S. ARMY T-shirt.

"It *is* stable, and it *is* prospering, because it leaves the gangs alone. The last time the government interceded, Noriega became the leading drug trafficker in the Western Hemisphere. The day the government disperses the gangs is the day corruption starts. Don't worry. The rest of the city is as safe as a retirement home."

I kept to the un-x-ed areas of his map, wandering the rainy streets and admiring the sad Spanish haciendas with gated gardens pruned by teams of laborers. Catholic churches sang on Sunday with their wooden doors ajar. Occasionally I taxied out to the ruins of old forts and pirate prisons, the moss invading the stones as the jungle tried to reclaim its stolen ground. Every time I took a cab in Panama City, the first question the driver asked me was "when are you leaving?" The drivers would strike their palms together and let the top palm glide away like a plane. I knew they wanted the fare to the airport, but it became a constant chorus. *When are you leaving? What time is your flight? When will you go?*

At night I usually stayed in my room, masturbating to my computer. It's odd to travel so far to perform the same whipping ritual alone in a rented room—porn sites become as familiar as family photo albums. *There she is again, that girl, as memorable now as a distant cousin, with the black bob and shamrock tattoo; she's switched private schools again, her pleated jumper plaid instead of navy; same manicurist though, French tips.* Those were the most fulfilling ten seconds of my day, my body seizing, my mouth a volcano, my fist slowing in the aquatic glow of the monitor. Once a week I'd eat dinner with my father's only Panamanian friends at their mansion in the posh San Francisco district. They owned the national airline and told stories of the night in December 1989 when the United States invaded, how the American soldiers appeared at their gates in the fog of dawn, and how the couple brought food and drinks out for them. The soldiers only accepted cans of soda, as they were forbidden to consume anything unsealed. "In case we might be poisoning them," the wife told me. "I took down their names and phone numbers and called their families for them back in the States. We all cried that morning, me for my country and those parents for their sons."

I had the sense that real events were still taking place in Panama, just not in the parts that I knew. It was the same feeling that must befall those curious pockets of the United States that don't observe daylight savings—time moving peculiarly all around them, jumping forward and back, shifting and reacclimating, while their own clocks ticked on, dull and untouched. I had no plans to continue my career in food manufacturing, no intention of remaining at Kitterin longer than the minimum six months I'd pledged my father. I was lonelier in my cubicle than I was jacking off at night or drinking rum in an American ex-pat bar located next to the national airline's travel agency. My few sexual encounters—a shipping inspector from Gothenburg; a Texas grad student documenting the migration of surfers along the western isthmus—ended on my sage bedsheets with me repeating the taxi refrain. *When are you leaving? What time is your flight?*

Never underestimate the catalytic power of boredom. We put so much faith in the role of chance—the barely caught subway on which one's future wife sat reading last week's *New Yorker*; the yellow light, which resulted in a family of five crushed in the intersection. But boredom is the archangel of afternoon suicides and Craigslist affairs. Boredom places our heads in ovens, pushes us between stranger's legs, makes hobbies out of pharmacy aisles, and, if left untreated, turns solid floors into swamps of quicksand. Chance exonerates us, but boredom reveals us—the little flaws flower, urges itch.

Marisela Nuñez appeared one Monday morning in the cubicle bank of Kitterin like a Goth babysitter determined to stick to an undesirable job. She was an intern in our department and a fourth-year economics student at the university. Her hair was dyed fuchsia—an eccentricity that would have deterred me in New York—and her eyelids were so wide she looked permanently frightened. I explained spreadsheet procedures and invited her out to lunch. We sat under the rain-beaten umbrella of an outdoor KFC table, picking at deep-fried animal bones. "I thought you'd like food from your home country," she said. I decided our affair wouldn't extend beyond Panamanian borders. With twenty minutes remaining in our lunch break, we crossed the parking lot and had what I still consider one of the best sexual experiences of my life. Marisela single-handedly rendered my cherished porn sites irrelevant. Her breasts were wobbly teapots with long, impractical stems. My body was also a discovery for her. "I've never seen orange there before," she said, pointing to my pubic hair. We had sex standing, against two mint walls. After that first encounter, Marisela returned to the office first, me following five minutes behind, and the weekly shipping dockets took on a magical allure.

After three dates, I went with her to visit her family. Marisela said she was "middle class," but that term didn't carry the same over-broad designation that it does in the States nor the same promise of dependable comforts. She drove twenty minutes out of the city, into the muddy, humid outskirts where dogs and naked children ran across diarrhea-brown roads. Palm trees waved their fronds in stranded roadside emergency. Her tan Honda lacked the ordinary luxury of shock absorbers. "There are two classes of untouchables in Panama," she told me. "The poor and the rich. You never touch either if you live by honest means." There was a strangled sense in this visit of a lesson being taught. She pulled up in front of a single-story house painted the same color as her hair. It had fresh aluminum siding, indigo stained-glass windows, a covered above-ground pool, and a vegetable garden teeming with an exploded war chest of children's toys. Inside were many tidy linoleum-tiled rooms with plastic-wrapped sofas and plastic nosegays. If there was a lesson, it was one sweetened with kindness. I met her father—a moist, gentle hugger and the owner of a nearby mechanic shop—and her three younger brothers (her mother was away in the north visiting her sister). We ate goat stew and drank beer and I watched her brothers in the backyard perform endless choreographed dances. The rain abated for the afternoon, and neighbors drifted over, adding their radios and trays of ice to the picnic table. I was neither a curiosity nor an intruder, just another set of hands clapping to her eldest brother's impressive somersaults.

Marisela observed my enjoyment. "This must be different from what you're used to," she said.

"Yes," I said. "We don't have anything like this in New York."

"Like *this*," she repeated sarcastically and began to clear the dishes with vicious efficiency. I had passed her test by failing it, and while the Nuñez family seemed like the warm cultural entente I had been seeking in Panama, I decided right then to discontinue my daily post-KFC fuck-fests with their daughter on our lunch breaks.

"I'm sorry," she grumbled on the way back into the city, staring

irritably through the slashing windshield wipers. The rain had returned and so had Marisela's thoughtfulness. I later wished she
hadn't apologized. If only she hadn't muttered those two grudge-
erasing words. Worse circumstances would always be avoided if we
never lent those words any credence. But I did and kissed her knuckles as we jiggled and jolted back to the New City. It was that very
night, in a move as spontaneous as her brother's somersaults, that
Marisela asked if I had ever visited Kitterin's baby-food factory.

"No." We were lying naked in bed; the air-con provided the exotic
necessity of a blanket.

"Don't you want to see it? I'd like to. Surely the vice president's son
could arrange a tour."

The factory sat halfway between the Pacific and Atlantic oceans.
A mile before our approach, the roar of machines blurred the twin
acoustics of slapping rain and mating insects. The entire building
was barricaded in chain-link fencing, and yellow school buses and
white shipping trucks gridded the parking lot. In the visitors' hall,
lined with portraits of babies I could now identify from a book of
infant mug shots, Marisela and I were given plastic hairnets and
escorted through one of several connecting facilities. "You'll find
we observe the strictest sanitation codes," the tour guide, a short,
middle-aged man in a white lab coat announced in exclamatory English. "I trust you'll report what you see here back to your father."

A line of workers in hairnets, with paper mouth masks, latex
gloves, and white smocks stood at a conveyer belt covered with pears.
The workers split off the stemmed tops and threw the circumcised
fruit back on the belt. The pears continued up a ramp and into a
large vat, which whirred with loud, pulp-crushing intensity. Tubes
ran from the ceiling into its sides, pumping water and coagulates.
Another conveyor belt carried fresh glass jars—for a second I was
gratified to see that they had arrived from Venezuela—and the mixer's udders filled them with beige *peras* purée.

"This is the North American facility," the guide told us. "The
products made here go directly onto the shelves of the entire south-

eastern U.S. region." He had the pride of a middle manager in a far-flung outpost generating goods that would feed the empire. "Please note that we comply with all FDA regulations. As I'm sure you're aware, Mr. Bledsoe, the upside of a factory in Panama City allows not only for the import of the freshest ingredients but also for expedient shipping."

"Plus, the ridiculous tax breaks Kitterin receives from the government," Marisela said matter-of-factly. Our tour guide moved his eyes from me to Marisela for the first time, sensing an insurgent.

"Right this way, into the sorting room." He waved us through two sets of swinging doors and into a chilly warehouse where throngs of white-bibbed workers picked through crates of produce—apples, bananas, kiwi, carrots, peaches—separating the rotten or mushy or weevil-ridden from the fresh. Distinct wheelie bins were marked 1, for top quality, and 2, for castoffs. The sweet scent of decomposition filled the icy, fluorescent air.

"Many of these fruits are indigenous, which means we process far riper yields than our competitors. We take great care to ensure that our United States consumers receive the very finest ingredients."

"What about the rest of the Americas?" Marisela demanded. Her tone was sarcastically rhetorical, the kind of question that cannibalized its answer. "One-fourth of the baby food produced here goes to the Central and South American markets."

This time our tour guide did not deign to look at her.

"There are different regulatory requirements for each district," he exclaimed. "Kitterin follows them to the letter. As you must be aware, each consumer region exhibits unique tastes, thus the need for separate facilities."

"People outside the United States think they are getting the same quality, *American* quality," Marisela persisted. "But they're not, are they? What happens to the reject fruits that these employees are sorting?"

"We dispose of them," he replied cautiously. But even I knew from the neutral region of my computer terminal that the North

American facility was A and Central and South was B. It wasn't much of a stretch to speculate that the throwaway fruits were headed to sector B.

"Could we tour the B facility?" I asked. I figured that would put a stop to Marisela's outbursts.

"I'm only authorized to show you this one," the man said sheepishly. His pride had vanished along with his welcome. "I'm sorry. I thought you were only interested—"

"What about the pesticides, the synthetic sweeteners and additives, the trace amounts of lead?" Marisela interrupted. "In the past, studies have linked this product to mental impairments. The labels say organic, but even the USDA has found—"

"Miss," he stammered. "I was under the impression you were an employee."

I was about to apologize when Marisela crossed her arms. "One more question then."

"If it's about the composition of our product, I'm afraid I will have to consult my supervisor." He stared at me with beseeching eyes, as if his job hung in the balance.

"It's not about the food," she swore. "It's about the workers. How much are they paid by the hour?"

"We pay a *living* wage," he spat. "We offer dependable jobs in a country that needs them."

"What's your definition of living?" It was Marisela's tour now. We were merely an audience for her well-rehearsed indictment. "I know for a fact that they make thirteen dollars a day for eleven-hour shifts with only one break and no overtime. I know for a fact that you charge fifty cents to ship them each way on those school buses. I know there is no health care, even with the carcinogens and industrial hazards they've been exposed to at this plant." Marisela's speech had all of the sincere and unmerited rebellion of a college undergraduate, outrage meted with arrogance.

"These are questions to raise with *your* department supervisors, not mine." Our tour ended in the sorting room. The guide switched to demotic Spanish as he shepherded us back to the visitors' hall. The complimentary "experimental flavors" taste test promised at the start of the tour did not materialize (I was actually curious to sample "Beef Bourguignon Medley"). The guide took me aside, his fingers digging into my arm. "Whatever your animosities, you can only tell them I've done my job. I've done a good job, haven't I? You will tell them that?" A security guard escorted us to our car.

"You didn't have to attack him," I said on the drive back.

"Are you serious?" Marisela jammed the stick shift from first to third gear. "When are you going to open your eyes, Ian? That stuff we're making, sold with fat, smiling babies on the label, is poison for profit. Have you ever looked into the toxicity levels of a single six-ounce jar of Kitterin baby food? Did you see the workers peeling fruit on the assembly line, the ones missing fingers? Do that first and then tell me to keep my mouth shut."

"If you knew those facts already, why the hell did you take an internship at Kitterin?" In her minute of silence I knew the answer. It was the same as the answer to my unspoken follow-up question, Why would you sleep with the vice president's son?

"I'm not only studying economics," she finally said. "I'm also majoring in journalism."

I gazed out the window, at the squalls of tin-roofed dwellings and white-haired pigs suckling rain puddles and emerald jungle breaking in snatches through plowed fields that only grew telephone poles. The sky was steel gray, stressing the hinges of sanity. Three years before, I had left college as if high on a slapped-together commencement speech—"make a difference, snub money, change the world." The whole point of Panama had been to shake off that unviable hallucination. Sitting in the twitching Honda, I resorted to the standard response when faced with the kind of vengeful idealism I'd recently outgrown. I decided Marisela was naïve.

"I'd like to show you the workers as they board those buses in El Chorrillo," she said quietly. "Not as you saw them, masked and gloved, but their real faces."

"That neighborhood is too dangerous," I said, both embarrassed and rescued by my caution. "It's run by gangs." Neighborhoods like El Chorrillo were bloody news stories protected by a pay wall. You could glean the basic horrors around the edges, but accessing the full information came at a price—and that price was too high for a white American with red hair and an ATM card.

"I have a friend, Rafael, who could take us. He's in with the gangs. His brother is a member. No one would touch us if we went with him."

We took the viaduct over the brackish olive water, and the New City, a mini Miami of slender, liquid glass, rose against the Pacific storm clouds.

"The guide was right about one thing," Marisela said. "We should ask *our* supervisors those questions. You should ask them to your father."

"You can drop me off in the parking lot," I replied, gripping the door handle to prepare for a quick escape. "No need to come in."

My loyalty to Marisela meant that I wouldn't report her clandestine motives to Kitterin. I would close our relationship on that one last favor. That night, in lieu of porn, I Skyped with my mother.

"Did you feed me Kitterin baby food when I was little?" I asked her. It was already afternoon in India and she was drowsy with sun.

"Heavens no," she said. "I never liked the smell of it. Too sweet. And it wasn't organic like it is now. Your father brought home samples, but I dumped them out and made my own. I was ahead of my time in that way."

"Did Dad ever mention that the baby food was dangerous? That there were additives or chemicals?"

Helen yawned and took a sip of tea. "Your father," she said in her most indignant voice, "was only interested in one thing. And it wasn't nutrition. He might as well have been selling tires. I wouldn't be surprised by anything Kitterin did to bolster its bottom line. I think there were lawsuits about insecticides a decade ago, settled out of court, of course. Your father, as they say, was a one-man kingdom. He wasn't exactly a freedom fighter for the common good."

"That doesn't mean he's evil, Mom."

Even across ten thousand miles, my mother managed one of her victimized, you-know-better looks.

"You get your altruism gene from me. It's a shame you've decided to go against it. To be honest, I never really saw you in an office." After the divorce, my mother only spoke of my father in the past tense, and Helen Bledsoe was hardly a credible source. Still, in the heavy-lidded darkness, I kept picturing the tapioca-colored slurry leaking from the automatic mixers, marinating with mildly toxic chemicals on overstocked discount shelves, oozing across the mouths and chins of infants in various market-tested, "new-world" regions. "Tiny taste buds, mom approved." A possibility invaded my brain, rising high like a flame on a wick, gobbling oxygen, or more selfishly, a meaning inside all of the spreadsheets at my cubicle. I reached for my phone at two in the morning and texted Marisela. Okay.

Rafael was as lean as a palm tree (I'd discover his nickname as a kid was Flaco, which he despised) and he walked with a pronounced limp along the muddy grounds of the university. Marisela told me it was a birth defect, but his convulsive gait lent him a streetwise severity, the stature of a survivor of an unnamable assault. He wore his navy trousers with shortened cuffs, emphasizing white socks and black dress shoes that I'd later catch him spit polishing. Below his left eye were two tear-shaped cysts that could have been zapped off during a single dermatological visit in New York. He climbed into the passenger seat of Marisela's car. I sat in the back, invisibly.

"Do you have enough room?" Rafael asked.

"Oh, plenty," I assured him.

"I can scoot the seat forward."

"Don't worry about it. I'm totally cool." I wondered if I was playing up the nice American, positioning myself as the selfless exception to that reviled citizenry. Or was I trying to show how misjudged Americans in general were? We're really a wonderful, generous people who don't demand additional legroom. *We're totally cool.* In either case, there was no hiding the fact that I wanted Rafael to like me.

Barrio El Chorrillo was in the south of the city, a neighborhood studded intermittently with nineteenth-century Colonials built by Europeans in the decades before the creation of the Canal. Filigreed wrought-iron balconies and wide, French windows still decorated their melancholic facades. A New York visitor like myself would perceive them as exquisite bones, the kind of real estate to invest in and wait until the area slowly gentrified. But there was already a gentry in El Chorrillo, the Red Diamond Gang with its notorious ammunition supply and its ties to the cocaine cartels moving through the Central American corridor and into the Panamanian drug market. Rafael's older brother, Axel, was a low-level member who had vouched for Rafael, which was the reason I now sat scrunched in Marisela's backseat. Rain pounded on the car roof and on the empty weed lots and on the dense, knotted electrical wires that spun from window to window in shared circuitry. Sparrows burrowed in the deep bullet holes of brick and concrete. There were no white men roaming the streets, but there was every other color: black, brown, and golden yellow. After the Europeans abandoned the south side of the city, native Panamanians and Caribbean immigrants brought over to work the construction of the Canal claimed it as their home. I was surprised by how clean the sidewalks were. Not a single piece of trash littered the wet asphalt. Calypso music blared from fleeting storefronts, and old men dozed in lawn chairs under the shelter of dripping balconies, and young women in pastel shorts laughed as they jumped puddles and disappeared down alleys with their grocery bags. It was a cheerful scene, far more alive than the New City, like a dream bubbling from a nightmare, and my muscles eased as we passed tables of men tossing dice and slapping down dollars for the yellow tickets of the national lottery.

"Welcome to El Chorrillo," Rafael said as he rotated in his seat. "It's not what you expected, is it? The Kitterin buses leave in ten minutes."

Marisela swerved into an available parking spot and cut the engine. "We're getting out?" I asked.

"Don't worry," Rafael chanted. "You're safe with me."

I stuck by Rafael for four blocks, slowing my walking speed to match his limping rhythm. Passersby glared at me or smiled without eye contact, but none stopped us or swore under their breath or crossed the street. In the parking lot of a bombed-out church, seven yellow school buses idled with open doors. We watched as men and women, young and old, stood in line, holding Kitterin IDs and punch cards. The drivers punched holes, and one by one the workers climbed onto the buses, the beaten vehicles shaking with each heavy step. I didn't know exactly what Marisela expected me to witness, other than ordinary humans free of their work uniforms, happy or bored or sharing gossip. Several mothers hugged their kids good-bye. It was the inverse of American school buses, stay-at-home children seeing their parents off, trying to catch sight of them in the muddy windows. But I imagined their eleven-hour shifts ahead, peeling carrots, C-sectioning pea pods, digging through pineapples and loading them onto the belts. I felt, as I often did, not so much pity for these factory workers, but that I and so many like me had miraculously dodged hard labor like anemic children too fragile for gym class. *How do you feel sorry for a rich kid?* It was not Helen but Edward Bledsoe who understood.

"I thought you should see who Kitterin is cheating," Marisela whispered in English. She curled her finger around a lock of fuchsia. "Lives worth respecting, lives those like your father care nothing about."

I offered no defense. Thirteen dollars for eleven hours, one break, no overtime, children running through the streets at night to pick up their exhausted watchers. The buses pulled away in coughs of smog. It wasn't an extraordinary sight. An old woman leaned her arm against the blasted stone of the church, out of lethargy or nostalgia.

"The gangs take care of the people here. Keep watch over them.

Feed them if they need to. Take them to hospitals." Rafael shrugged. "The government does nothing. So who is worse?"

We walked toward the water. Rafael wanted to visit his brother, and for the first time I felt safe enough to stagger behind. Soon the Colonials dissolved, and slices of the fog-smeared Pacific appeared between the slabs of rebar and blackened concrete. I stared ahead, and even from this distance I could make out the container ships and yachts on the horizon waiting at sea for their turn in the locks.

In another country, the extraordinary sights go unnoticed by the locals. At first I confused him for a pile of clothes—the one heap of refuse in the rain-slick streets. It lay in a contorted clump on the sidewalk, and impulsively I steered toward it. But the muscles in my neck constricted, as if my neck understood before my brain did, and I realized it was a man, his blue shirt stained with brown fluid, blood leaking from the buttons, his thin legs bundled together and his hair matted over his eyes. It was a body, fresh, with the dust of bulleted brick sprinkled over the pooling red. The world went silent, as if even the street sounds were afraid of coming close.

"Keep walking," Rafael ordered. He and Marisela were hurrying on. "Don't stop, not for a second. Let's go." I caught up with them, terrified yet fighting the urge to glance back.

"He must have been a traitor," Rafael said. Marisela eyed me nervously and took my hand. I couldn't remember how far we walked before entering a building through an iron gate. A pinewood addition had been built onto the back of the red brick tenement, a labyrinth of jerry-rigged rooms and decks fitted with scrolls of leftover carpet. Posters of boxing champions and Hollywood Mafia characters covered the hallway walls. Rafael knocked twice on a steel door. A slat opened and then the door. Axel looked younger than Rafael, with a wispy pubescent mustache, and he wore a lime tank top that accentuated his biceps. He glowered at me menacingly, white man on Red Diamond green Astroturf, but Rafael opened his palms and claimed me as a friend. "Good to have someone on the inside."

"Cool, cool," Axel said, nodding. "Want a beer?" Where in another house vases and picture frames would have been set, a glass table by the door held a display of batons, hammers, and billy clubs. I noticed a machine gun tilted in the corner, and the blue light of a computer from a connecting room. The thin leg of a boy sitting just beyond the frame barricaded the door. Axel collected beers from a mini fridge. I passed by him and stepped out onto a slanted second-floor deck. The open courtyard below was decorated for a child's birthday party. The rain was pulping the paper hats and plates abandoned on the picnic table. A pink banner sagged in the downpour, FELIZ NOVENO CUMPLEAÑOS.

I practiced breathing. I took deep drags. Marisela touched my shoulder.

"I'm sorry you saw that," she said gently. "It's a violent place. There's no hiding it."

Some of my New York friends were wandering around the beaches of Southern Asia or posting photos of themselves holding dead leopards on safari hunts. Some were in grad school, or writing what passed for cultural criticism on snarky blogs, or starting careers in finance or art, and a few were trying their faces in modeling, putting their familiarity with expensive clothes and nonstop partying to practical use. Some, like Charlie, had simply disappeared. Standing on that slanted deck, I felt like I had been given an opportunity, admission into a world beyond anyone else's reach. Hadn't I been trying to do something bigger with my life, something meaningful and real? Selfish or selfless, I was twenty-five. I had been raised on Kitterin profits, cloistered and padded by green groves of money that were cultivated by invisible hands. Surely life could be made better for others or at least eased a bit. Good intentions. How many have ended in imaginary bomb plots?

"I want to help," I said. I still don't know how I could have.

THREE WEEKS LATER I flew to New York for my father's birthday. It was there in his town house, his face creased from an afternoon of smiling, that I recited the list of demands that Rafael, Marisela, and I had spent nights cooking up in my motel room. I presented the proposals under the guise of Kitterin ambassadorship. I exaggerated the growing antagonism for the company in its worker communities, perhaps even bragging of my chaperoned days in El Chorrillo where the gangs hosted cookouts and concerts and were in the process of building a medical-care unit for the elderly. "I've spoken directly to Kitterin workers," I said. "I've heard firsthand the conditions we're exposing them to. Some have actually lost limbs." Marisela's idealism was contagious, and only when I recited the mandates in my father's study, as he sat in his armchair clutching the tufted, pony-skin leather, did I grasp how deluded we actually were: a raise by two dollars a day for all of its factory workers; basic health-care coverage for full-time employees; weekly distributions of food to the poor; the assurance of quality control for all baby food, no matter the regional market—I didn't get to the day-care facility or sick days or free transportation on the school buses because I realized I had lost my audience. "These aren't unreasonable requests," I protested in a high-pitched wail that even I wanted to strangle. "It isn't threatening the company. It's assuring its future stability. You aren't there, Dad. You don't understand what's going on."

"Enough," he said. "Enough, enough. I don't own the company, Ian."

"But you could bring these matters to the board. You must know that Kitterin has a history of health-code violations and environmental lawsuits. These are new problems that can't be covered up anymore."

"I sent you to Panama to work for the company, not to investigate it," he hissed. "God dammit, one simple job."

We went on, and with each volley my father grew older and I younger until we each reached the age where we were unable to communicate. I returned to Panama, defeated, to find the rainy season over. The trade winds had cleared the storm clouds. The slashing white sun replaced the constant drizzle, and people ran for cover from the blinding light more quickly than they had from the rain.

"It's okay," Marisela said consolingly. "At least you spoke of the problems, made them known. It's a step. Most people don't dare stick their necks out. Maybe they're afraid to see how many want to cut their throats." She seemed friendlier to me after my failed, familial coup, although we gradually slowed on our daily fuck lunches. In the time-honored tradition of the martyr, I surrendered my sex drive. And often, when we were hanging out with Rafael, I noticed the secrets their eyes took on, and I wondered if they had always been a couple. I didn't call them out on it, because I needed Rafael to take me places I couldn't go alone.

"So your father didn't agree to the demands," Rafael acknowledged. "Now we print them up and distribute them in the church lot." No matter what we passed out in El Chorrillo, the residents happily accepted it—food, clothes, leaflets on unionizing labor. As much as I began to suspect the futility of our efforts, I enjoyed the warmth of neighborhood interaction, of families rushing from their doors in recognition, of afternoons spent on the slanted deck listening to music and watching young boys play video games. I often heard gunfire and later saw its aftermath, and I was the only one who flinched. The community appreciated our intentions, delighting in the fantasy of higher wages and longer breaks with such glee it seemed as if they were humoring us instead of the other way around. They often invited us into their homes for dinner where candle soot stained blue-marine walls and where black-and-white photographs of great-great-grandfathers digging through bomb-blasted jungle sat beside plaster icons of Mary and cartons of Marlboros smuggled out of the foreigners-only Free Zone in the even more dangerous city of Colón. I never met the leaders of Red Diamond, only their young, pistol-strapped foragers, some of whom helped us pass out our flyers, but Rafael assured me we had their absolute support. On the days I spent alone in the sanitized New City, I missed El Chorrillo's sticky residue of life. The sun also brought waves of tourists and snowbird retirees to Panama, and the daily newspaper reported muggings and murders—*Australian tourist stabbed in the stomach*—but they were described in a manner similar to climber deaths on Mount Everest, by brutal unseen forces that were beyond anyone's control.

When Rafael asked me one April morning to break into Kitterin computer records and print out the monthly profit sheets, I refused. He took the rejection lightly, slapping me on the arm. "You're right, forget it." The very next week Marisela was fired from her internship when my boss caught her at the copy machine with confidential sales-report binders. My boss stopped by my cubicle that afternoon, chewing on her lips as she studied my screen.

"How's it looking for Libra today?" I asked her. She slipped one of the leaflets we had circulated that compared the wages of Panamanian workers to their factory colleagues in Des Moines.

"Do you know anything about this?"

I waited until the next week to tender my resignation, hoping even the short delay would prevent any association. When I called my father to tell him the news, he seemed both aggravated and relieved that I would no longer be on the Kitterin dole. "Now you can commit yourself full-time to your suntan." I remained at the Royal Decameron Arms and dedicated myself to organizing a clothes drive for El Chorrillo. At my weekly dinner at the mansion, I didn't mention my resignation and instead invited them to contribute donations to my latest initiative alongside a local journalism student named Marisela Nuñez.

"I'm sure we can wrangle together something," the woman said. "I can even ask my friends. It's wonderful that you're getting so involved."

When I followed up later with phone calls, the housekeeper reported, so insistently I knew it was scripted, "Señora isn't here," "Señora is unavailable," "Señora would prefer if you didn't call back." She might have spoken with my father. Or maybe by then she had seen Marisela Nuñez's op-ed in the newspaper *El Siglo*.

Marisela channeled all of her accusations against Kitterin into a thousand-word missive, sharpening the facts into bayonets and in-dicting upper-management on charges of gross apathy and greed. The following day's paper printed a notice from Kitterin identifying the writer as a disgruntled intern who had been dismissed for poor performance. Marisela transferred her rage to an anonymous Twit-ter account, filled with gruesome pictures of on-site injuries, lists of reported baby-food poisonings stretching back to 1973, and one post that chilled me personally: "If Kitterin gets to feed our children, we should be allowed to feed theirs." The op-ed piece had raised the hackles of Kitterin, but it seemed to traffic little among the workers, who continued on, shift after shift. On the weekends we watched the cruise ships line up at sea and the crimes spike and in the night there were fireworks.

I stayed on, helping where I could, hanging out in El Chorrillo, picking up the tab for lunches with Marisela and Rafael, who chose to sit together across from me.

"Should we drive into the jungle for the weekend?" I asked. "Or we could organize a boat and visit the San Blas Islands."

"Everything we've done so far means nothing if there's no next step, no explosion." Rafael had grown increasingly fidgety and caffeinated, and I wondered if he was dipping into the supply his brother trafficked in the mornings along the promenade. Even his limp was more agitated, like a coffee stirrer whisking around an empty cup. "What we need next is a walkout. A protest outside of the factory."

I couldn't take it anymore. None of the workers had asked us to intercede on their behalf and now we were organizing them against their paychecks. In a moment of sanity, I realized the point at which our fantasy home was starting to undermine the value of the neigh-borhood.

"That's not practical," I said. "They'll all be fired. There is no union here. Kitterin can simply terminate them and hire fresh work-ers from someplace else."

"Not practical," Rafael wheezed. "Who are you to say? What have you really done to help? Do you think a trip to the San Blas Islands will help?"

"I don't think risking their jobs is helping them," I screamed in English. "What will they have once they're unemployed?" I was sick of speaking for people I hardly knew.

"You have a different idea of what a human being is," Rafael said as he picked his teeth. "You think only in terms of *I*. Our people will always look out for each other. That's what you'll never understand. Red Diamond is there because the community needs it. In this community, there is no individual." Our order arrived and we said no more.

That night in my room, Marisela tried to kiss me. I moved away.

"Rafael's insane," I said. "Whatever I thought I was doing, I don't want to be a part of it anymore."

"It's easy for you," she said stiffly. "You can just go back."

But I couldn't, not like before. "Did you ever stop to ask why the gangs have allowed me into El Chorrillo in the first place? Did you ever think that maybe Rafael and his brother wouldn't mind if everyone lost their jobs and had to rely solely on the charity of Red Diamond? You know what would really be a problem for them? If Kitterin started paying fair wages. Then they'd have no more need for the gangs. A boycotted factory would be a dream come true."

"You don't know what you're talking about." But as she grabbed her bag and left, I could tell my suspicions had taken root.

It all ended quickly. A few evenings later, Marisela, Rafael, and I arrived at the Red Diamond hangout for a party celebrating the high school graduation of a gang member's sister. There was cake in the boxing room, and kegs and chicken wings on the deck, and pot smoke as thick in the trapped air as the shake of musty curtains. The sight of bullet shells in spilled beer had long stopped surprising me. I knew now that no one here would ever give up their weapons freely, that every day would end in another dead body on the sidewalk, just as another kid's leg would barricade the door to the room where no one else was allowed to enter. Rafael sat by his brother, crouched gang-style. Marisela was fixing her hair in a cracked mirror. An inch of black had grown against the fuchsia. There was no air-conditioning, and the humidity was reaching a savage stillness, where just being around other warm bodies hurt. I could hear the punches on the leather bag down the hall, *thwak, thwak,* young muscles fatiguing on strokes of violence. They would hit harder tomorrow.

"A bomb," Rafael taunted. "That would get their attention."

"Sure," Axel agreed. "We got the dynamite. But the workers, Raf. You can't kill them. I don't care what you say."

I thought Rafael was joking. I spun around to gauge his expression. He wasn't joking. He was nodding, as if he had it all figured out.

"No, we do it at night. There's one hour between shifts. One A.M. No one's there but a few managers. We bomb it then. Won't kill any of our own."

Marisela stopped fastening her barrette.

"Good-bye factory."

"You're crazy, Flaco. Smart but crazy." Axel yanked his brother's ear. Rafael shoved his hand away.

"You don't believe I'd do it? I'll do it. And no one will see. You just lend me a little backup. A few guys and a truck is all I need."

Axel nodded, either in quiet agreement or because he knew that any response only encouraged his brother. I grabbed Marisela by the arm and dragged her out into the hall.

"I want to leave right now," I demanded.

"But it's dark, and the—"

"I want to go home!"

We held our breath until we reached the car. We drove back to the ew City in silence. Only after I opened my door in the KFC parking did Marisela lean over and speak.

'm sorry," she said, and once again I gave those words credence. ved she was sorry. "You were right about Rafael. He is insane."

next morning the police raided the Red Diamond hangout sted Axel and a few other minor, forfeitable members on to plant an explosive device. None of the leaders of Red

Diamond were touched. I wasn't sure if Marisela was questioned, because she stopped responding to my texts. I didn't place the call to the authorities, although I'm sure many suspected that I had. Maybe it was Marisela. But my guess is that the police had informants on the inside in case El Chorrillo violence ever threatened to spill beyond the neighborhood. I packed my bags and phoned the airline. As dusk was settling over the New City, I heard a tap at my window. I opened the curtains and found Rafael standing on the other side of the pane.

"I need to borrow some money," he pleaded. There were tears in his eyes. "Please. I need money. Just to get north for a while. Until it all settles down."

I didn't want to help him, just as I knew that he didn't want to ask for my help. But I was more afraid of him sought by the police than I was of him bragging in front of his brother. We walked together to KFC, and I went inside to use their ATM. Near the outdoor table, I handed him two hundred dollars. He stared at it, tapped his crippled foot on the ground, and asked for more. I went back inside and handed him two hundred more dollars. He folded the bills and tucked them into his shirt pocket.

"I'm leaving," he said. "You won't be seeing me." He seemed to expect me to give him a hug.

"I'm leaving too," I replied.

"Yeah." His tongue poked at his cheek as he scanned the avenue for cars. "Did you enjoy your vacation in Panama?"

As I began to walk away, he called after me.

"You know how I got my foot like this? Your father's plant."

I turned. "What? You worked there as an infant? Or are you blaming it on baby food. Jesus." I almost muttered *you people*, but I stopped myself.

He smiled angrily. "My mother worked there, the whole time she was pregnant with me. Eleven hours a day, no time off, like a slave with no rest, until she got sick, and she still worked up until the minute I came out. She's dead now." I didn't say anything. I wasn't sure he was even telling the truth, but the guilt flared nonetheless. "Thanks for the money," he said, patting his pocket. "You should go home. You're better off."

Rafael was caught the next day in Colón just as I was settling my bill at the Royal Decameron Arms. I'm not sure if he was the one who implicated me—once again, it could have been Marisela—but the city newspaper ran my name and photo as an accessory in a yearlong gang-related campaign to destabilize Kitterin among its workers that ended in a bomb plot. The police never questioned me, either because being within earshot of a man boasting of bombs didn't register as a crime for an American or because Kitterin called in a favor for one of its own. Until a blog in the States picked up the article two weeks later, I assumed it was another mistake I had left behind.

I put my luggage in the trunk of the taxi. The palm trees swayed like drunk, restless girls, and racks of sunscreen lined the sidewalk. The driver made the sign of a plane taking off with the palm of his hand. "That's right," I said. "Today's the day."

My father made baby food. I would have to live with that fact. I went back to New York.

CHAPTER 5

D reams.

I am one degree from nothing. The sea is placid, we have swallowed our valuables for safekeeping, but we are on high alert for pirates in the waves. A woman next to me is puking rubies and emeralds. Now I am a man in a suit pressed against a gate. Rough grasses blow in circles in the field, and there are goats grazing through it for the first time. Somewhere is the sound of a saw purring, maybe inside one of the goats' heads. Whales that are planes drop from the sky into the water, filled with people ooooohhh-ing. This needs to happen: the lessening. I don't have the number to call, to tell them it's over, they can stop now. The goats, but I need to speak to an ambassador. My feet are not guilty, but the path is guilty and I wander down it to the shore. Louise is pulling off her bathing suit, she's got the rubber suit halfway down, her arms digging like shovels at her waist, and she laughs so I know it is okay. "Come," she says, "closer, close."

I wake to the sound of a truck pulling up outside the cabin. Light moves aquatically across the ceiling, and dust motes Milky Way through it. The patio door is scythe-blade-streaked with glass cleaner. The sordid complications of dreams concede even to the bareness of a guest room, its white walls, its Lucite chairs, like a thumping, all-night party that goes magically still at dawn. I can't imagine a dream so tenacious, so portal-hopping, it could convince a man to desert his family and move to the opposite side of the Earth. But isn't that exactly what Sonny said happened with the psychologist pedophile from Chicago? Still, my dream was loud with color and there was a grip of captivity to it, as if I've just been released from a rockslide or a hot car on a hot day. I try to remember more but only catch the tail end, Louise in her bathing suit on the shore.

I was too tired last night to invite Louise into my room. On the taxi ride from Chora, her head on my shoulder, she gave an abridged version of her life in the past decade: she bounced around cities like Boston, Dallas, and San Francisco, taking temporary restaurant jobs, always returning to Lexington, always putting off the inevitable graduate school that ghosted her like a police cruiser on the highway, just waiting for her to break the speed limit to pull her over and return her to the sanity of a reliable order. Louise left me on the steps with a kiss on the cheek. She's now probably fifteen feet from me, her hip bones tipped against her mattress like a conch shell, her airplane reservation back to America tucked in the pocket of her suitcase. How can I compete with the entire continent of her life back home in the little time we have on this island?

I used to think I could read time the way Charlie reads the seas, that I was acutely sensitive to its passing, its thrusts and currents, its heavy iron roll. But fear isn't mastery, and, as a kid, time was simply the nightmare monster of the daylight shift. Yet, in moments like this one, lying on my back with the sun on my forehead and the blue outside finned with sails, it's hard for me not to recede into that boy so certain he can see the fragile seams that connect each second to the next. The conclusion after five minutes of out-of-focus staring: *I am alive, for this instant, on this bright August day.* It is almost enough.

I struggle out of bed. Louise was right: too much free time and you could end up devoting your life to entries in a dream journal. I'm almost relieved by my meeting with Charlie at his dock today. At least it's a worry I can do something about.

My tongue tastes toxic. Overnight, my mouth has transformed into a shriveled diving board slung over a septic pool. The grim condominium complex that surrounds it—i.e., the rest of my head—is experiencing a rash of small electrical fires. Less vodka at dinner from here on out. I run the shower, gulping down stray streams under the nozzle, and brush my teeth using an American-brand toothpaste that tastes more astringent than it does in America. "I am alive, for this instant, on this bright August day," I recite, but the magic is gone, the words failing at incantation, and as I spit toothpaste at the drain I see only my father buried below a fresh clump of dirt. The faucet turns and the towel is on my face, wiping the water away.

I slide open the patio door and plunge into the hottest day so far. When I look behind me, the sun is already sucking my footprints from the stone. Down below on the driveway, Helios wheels our two motorbikes from the truck bed. Their lean, yellow-and-black frames, with gleaming handlebars and spoke mirrors, have the look of lethal wasps.

Helios has on acid-wash jeans with machine-deconstructed rips at the knees; his black, long-sleeve T-shirt advertises an American rock band that has already crested in popularity back home and is now splashing up in the discount bins of dying music stores. He has a diamond stud in his ear, neon-rimmed sneakers, and a stringy goatee. Last night at dinner, someone mentioned that most of the young Greeks on Patmos spend the majority of the year in Athens, returning in the summers to work in their parents' tavernas and hotels. But I get the sense that Christos's son is a permanent islander, a left behind. He's like a bent antenna trying to pick up stray frequencies of youth transmitted from across the ocean. He walks in lazy circles, his sneakers kicking up dust clouds. He glances up at the cabins with his scabby lips pursed, and even after I wave, he doesn't seem to notice me. Maybe he's learned to erase tourists from his field of vision. Soon the last prehistoric Greeks will go extinct—with their unfitted housedresses and scratchy wool pants belted with rope—and the islands will be run by a legion of Helioses: manqué rock stars with mousse and tattoos and pot-smoke cologne, St. Marks Place on Santorini.

"Thanks for bringing the bikes back," I yell down. My voice startles him, and he lifts his arm in acknowledgment with vacant eyes. He gets into his truck, and in one graceful maneuver, backs up, rotates, and heads down the steep road. To be fair, he is diligent at doing what's asked of him. I wonder about the cold sores on his lips: Who does Helios kiss on Patmos? Is he one of the locals Charlie mentioned who cleans up on the rich vacationers full of alcohol and loneliness?

As I dress, I hear Louise climbing out of bed on the other side of the bolted door. Her feet pad across the wood, and her computer starts up with an organ groan. I reach into my bag and retrieve my phone.

From: <alexisbledsoe@motormail.com>
To: <ianb3@wirelive.com>
CC: <rosspbledsoe@triptime.com>
Subject: Where are you?

Ian, you weren't at the funeral. Ross, mom, and I assumed you'd be there. We're all shocked and angry—in the middle of grieving and making excuses for you to people paying their respects. Even the goddamn gardener found the time. We need to talk. You were the last one with dad and, at the very least, we'd like to hear what his final moments were like. Was he alert? Did he hear you? What did you say!? He's OUR father too. You can't just breeze in and out whenever you feel like it, not without answering any of our questions. Honestly, where the hell are you? I tried calling your phone, but it connects to a foreign ring and then a foreign computer-woman's voice comes on and there's not even an option to leave a message. I can't find Helen's e-mail (Ross, do you have it?) otherwise I'd bother your mother in India just to ask where her son is. WHY DOES NONE OF THIS SURPRISE ME!!!! Also, there's a suspicious withdrawal from the family account in the hours AFTER dad died. WTF? Mom's understandably too upset to pursue it, but I'm going to report it as a bank error unless I hear from you. I'm not leaving it alone. Call me. Immediately.
Lex

Ross responds in CC:

Ian, we really just want to talk and clear things up. You could swing by the house tomorrow, or if you're out of the country like Lex believes, we can all link up on three-way. Or are you back by the weekend? When? We're serious. Please let us know. We'd hate for anything to get ugly. R

Lex and Ross must each stand to inherit upward of two million dollars, with the majority of Edward Bledsoe's estate going to Lily. Two million for each of them, and yet Lex is chasing down nine thousand dollars like there's a tiny rip in her pocket and she's desperate to sew it shut before any more money falls out. But I'm more afraid of their questions—the final words I spoke to him, the begging and hatred and resentment as his hand grasped the sheet, and then let go. They think I'm to blame. They know my talent for speeding his suffering.

"Ian," Louise calls through the bolted door. "Are you awake? Are you making coffee?" She wiggles the knob. "I had a dream about the vultures."

I tiptoe toward the bike key on the nightstand, snatch it, and head for the door. I step outside and lock it behind me as quietly as I can. The e-mails from my half-siblings have made this morning's existential worries seem like vacations in themselves. I can't spend the morning trying to seduce Louise and contemplating the meaning of time when my entire future hangs in the balance. Would Lex really turn me in for raiding the family account? Is it even illegal to withdraw money in the hours after its primary account holder expired?

I walk my bike halfway down the hill before I start the motor. The sheep crowd the western-spilling shadow of a tree. In the distance, pink umbrellas bloom along the shoreline. This isn't vacation. It's a very warm exile.

ALONG THE ROAD leading to Charlie's port, jasmine buds droop in raw, gray grass, and seagulls pick at meat and rice in discarded

Styrofoam containers. The smell of algae blows inland. A red motorbike appears up ahead on the trail. It's Rasym flying over the bumpy terrain. I try to speed my bike elegantly over the divots to affect a more pronounced command. Rasym passes by without a word, casting an angry scowl in my direction before he zooms away. At the dock, a sleek, white yacht, freshly painted, with a satellite whirling on the roof, is preparing to embark. Greek crewmen in light-blue uniforms hurriedly lasso the lines. The orange splotch of a Cypriot flag hangs from a pole on the stern. The yacht glides into the harbor like a slowly exhaled breath, and a man wearing an olive shirt and thick glasses ambles down the dock while drumming a clipboard against his thigh. He walks into the hangar. I park my bike by the aluminum-sided trailer and peek through its dirty windows. It's an office with a chessboard already set up on a table, but Charlie isn't inside. I wander toward the hangar in search of him, practicing my speech.

"A nonprofit, multiformat, charitable wing of Konstantinou Engineering would be a fabulous PR move for your father's company. And while I wouldn't be nominally on the board, I could be the behind-the-scenes man, aligning vital causes with corporate and familial interests. For instance, I know your father is an art collector. What about sponsoring art schools among the underprivileged in the very Middle Eastern communities that are subject to Konstantinou contracts? Corporate altruism is tradecraft on which I've become something of an expert, and I'm uniquely qualified to oversee all handling and *liaising* from proposal to execution."

Admittedly, the pitch is a semi-incoherent word jumble, but Charlie is merely the gatekeeper to his father and I only hope to gild the idea enough to make it sound legitimate. The real work will come later, in research and presentation, when I finally secure a meeting with Mr. K or even Charlie's brother, Stefan. All I need is Charlie's blessing. For better or worse, this proposal is all I've managed to concoct for a secure position in the Konstantinou empire—the best view is that it's a contribution to humanity, the worst that I'm merely the smallest and most benevolent tick on the fat, hemophiliac body of a family fortune. Right now, either view looks pretty decent. At least it's a job I'm presenting in lieu of throwing myself at Charlie's feet or making bat swoops at his wallet.

As I enter the hangar's darkness, I'm hit by a wave of noxious fumes. The burning of butane issues from blowtorches that two young, shirtless workers inch along the hull of a harnessed yacht. They're welding a boxy, steel base to the refurbished luxury boat, patching its foundation with additional support. In the far corner, similar steel boxes are piled alongside cans of paint and timber. Oil leaks across the cement and across the workers' shoulders. Their eyes and skin gleam like wet horses in a stable, strong and easily spooked. The bespectacled man appears from around the yacht, shoving the clipboard under his arm. He sees me and begins to shout in a language I don't understand. The workers glare up at me, holding the blowtorches away from their eyes.

"I'm Charlie's friend," I say, raising my hands. "I'm supposed to meet him here at noon. I'm a little early."

"E-on? You are E-on?" The man's accent is so thick that for a second I don't recognize my name. He shuffles toward me. Both of his cheeks have a deep indent in their centers. He lifts his arm out, sword-straight, for me to shake.

"I am Ugur. I work for Charlie as manager." His grip is solid, and I'm so dizzy on the fumes that when I step backward for air, I pull him along with me. "Charlie tells me about you. Yes, I'm glad to meet. You joining team." He laughs, and I copy his laugh, relieved by the news that I'm being invited to join something. Thank god for Charlie. He hasn't forgotten me, and it's almost like this man's hand, unwilling to relax its grip, is saving me from drowning.

"I suppose I am. I haven't really worked out the details yet. Do you know—"

"We are securing the shells, you see? This is how we add the value. To make able to send into sea. Back and forth." Ugur raises his index finger and swings it from imaginary point A to B. Charlie must have told him that I know next to nothing about the business of boat rentals. I feign attention, as if his lesson has been instructive. I have no intention of learning the trade.

"Yes, very nice. But I should really speak with—"

"Old friends. Best friends." Ugur winks. "Charlie is in bad mood today." He circles his eye with his finger to communicate the source of Charlie's mood. Ugur must have overlooked something.

The sound of yelling reaches us, muffled inside the hangar. Ugur lets go of my hand, and we both step outside. Along the rocky shoreline, Charlie brandishes a stick, shouting angrily at the sea, his bad mood on full display. The back of his T-shirt is sweat-soaked in the shape of a stingray. At first it looks like that's all he is wearing, due to the skimpy yellow shorts that barely peek out under it.

"You're trespassing," he roars. "Get the fuck away from this area. There are limits, borders."

The intruder isn't the sea. I find his targets ten feet from him, a young man and woman of freckled, henna-blond persuasion in torn denim cutoffs. The man wears a red ANTI-BETHLEHEM T-shirt, and the woman's orange T-shirt traces the evolution of a stick figure from hunchback ape to hunchback desk worker. I fear we are reaching the end days of T-shirt irony; we are leaving very little material for future designers to work with. The couple has constructed crosses and daisy-chain necklaces from woven grass blades, and they stare at Charlie in pretty, stoned delirium.

"I thought all the beaches here were public," the woman says. She has a cloying New Jersey accent. "That's what we've been told."

"This isn't a beach," Charlie yells. "It's a port, and it's private. This is a business. Do you get that?" He slams his stick against the ground much like Duck did yesterday before our boat ride.

"We're having a barbecue," Anti-Bethlehem interjects. His thick blond beard is almost green in the morning light, and a gold loop hangs from his septum. His earlobes are stretched open like unlidded sewer holes from the raver plugs that once filled them. "At our camp. Vic would want us to invite you. All are welcome." Although his accent is Scandinavian, he seems to subscribe to the American belief that neighborly invitations will eradicate hostilities. Differences can be settled over hot food. And from there, religion might be found not far off in the tenderness of waves. I can't blame him for trying.

Charlie raises his face to the sky, as if seeking fortitude in the God he doesn't believe in. He slaps his forehead theatrically.

"Charlie does not like the hippies," Ugur whispers with an amused smile. "And he is right not to. They enter the hangar, steal supplies. Last week we find one asleep inside a boat."

"Turn around and go back to your camp," Charlie orders. "And tell Vic to shepherd her flock, otherwise the wolves will get to them. In case that wasn't clear, it's a threat. Come here again and I can't promise you'll make it out in one piece."

The man turns, but the woman is more obstinate—either more or less stoned than her companion. She steps forward and tilts her head. White foundation covers the moles and pimples along her jaw, giving the bottom of her face a blurry, lunar-like patina. Orange salamander tattoos creep up her ankles. "You're Charlie, right?" she asks. "Charles Konstantinou?"

"It's none of your business who I am!" Charlie stammers. "Go. I'm giving you ten seconds or I swear . . ." He shoos them with a fussy hand. They recede over the rocks, their hair lit like matchsticks in the sun. Charlie spins around, surprised at finding Ugur and me side by side, watching him. He nods and puts on an easy smile, briefly leaning down to pick up an empty chip bag caught in the weeds. But now I understand Ugur's bad-mood gesture. A purplish bruise hangs like a crescent moon under his right eye. I try to deduce who could have punched him in the last twelve hours: the drunk Hungarian in the square, scowling Rasym, a stoned Christian missionary? His smile doesn't defuse the black eye.

"They're getting braver," Charlie says to Ugur as he marches toward us scrunching the plastic bag, "so I had to put the fear in them. I take it you two have met."

"Oh, yes, we are friends now," Ugur says, but he backs away, as if to disclaim me. "Do you need anything?"

Charlie doesn't answer. He threads his arm around mine and steers me toward the trailer. Ugur melts into the darkness of the hangar.

"How did you sleep?" Charlie shoves his hand into his pocket and pulls out a key chain to unlock the glass-windowed office door.

"Okay. A few bad dreams."

"Tell Sonny," he says. "She's collecting them. She's probably at her psychic in Chora right now. I'm assuming they've run out of lines on Sonny's hands to study for three hundred euros an hour. You don't realize how ugly someone's hands are until each wrinkle is traced for a happy future."

"Sonny has a psychic?"

"Yeah," he replies wearily. "A psychic, a masseuse, a Pilates in-structor, an energy healer who also doubles as a facialist. I support an entire cottage industry of quacks. I keep expecting to find a little man in my bathroom, examining Sonny's bowel movements for fresh insights into who she is." Yesterday they had seemed so in love. I wonder if their relationship swings daily from one extreme to the other or if it ever levels out into wholesome boredom.

"Was it her psychic who punched you?" I ask.

Charlie touches the bruise. "Oh, this. No. That happened last night. Two tourists got in a fight, and my face was in their way. It looks worse than it is." I don't believe him. I've never encountered an eye that was punched by accident. But I'm not interested in getting on the wrong side of Charlie's mood.

He opens the door and directs me in with a wave. The tiny, rect-angular office has a plastic desk running under the bank of gritty windows. The desk is strewn with maps and paperwork, a telephone, and a microwave-size radio with three walkie-talkies Velcro-ed to its base. There's a computer monitor in the corner, its screen glowing an outline of the Aegean. Eleven blinking dots are scattered across it; one must indicate the boat that just left. Charlie tosses the chip bag on the desk and cracks open the window, glancing out to ensure that the hippies have left the vicinity. He crouches like a soldier staring from a trench.

"Maybe you should call the police if you're worried about trespassers," I say.

"The police?" Charlie taps his knuckles against the papers on the desk. "The ones on Patmos are useless. It's the old Greek system: three managers for every one worker, and they've all been trained that the best way to resolve a conflict is to wear the victim down with questions. *You say a man has entered your property, a human being, did I get that right, walking as a human does, onto land that is different from other land, that belongs to you, and you say you don't want that? Now this is a problem, indeed. Very troubling. Yes, yes, so tell us, this problem, what was it again?*" Charlie snorts and shakes his head. "God love them. It actually makes running a business easier in the long run, because they do their best to leave you alone. But I swear, Ian, don't let anyone steal your wallet. They'll find your mother in India before they find the thief."

"So they weren't much of a help when the bomb went off?"

Charlie whirls around, and in a millisecond his smile closes up shop, the plants and welcome sign taken in, the grate pulled over the glinting windows. The sag of his mouth matches the damage done to his eye. I wish I could choose a different day to discuss my future. But I can't wait any longer. I didn't stop at a restaurant while biking through Skala out of fear of spending extra money on breakfast. The sight of all those horny, hungry vacationers nestled around tables while posting pictures of themselves felt like watching the security-cam footage of a peaceful morning in the seconds before a catastrophe strikes.

"No," Charlie answers. "They weren't much help. You know, it wasn't just tourists who died. The owner of the taverna and his son were killed too. The locals started throwing chicken feed at the police because all they did was run around and squawk."

"There were fresh flowers in front of the bomb site today. I figured those weren't put there for the tourists."

"Doubtful," Charlie agrees. "You don't waste flowers on strangers whose whole purpose for being here is to turn their backs on the island to stare at the sea. One day it's blood, the next flowers, and then it's pavement again. That's the way it goes." He shrugs and points to the chair on the opposite side of the chessboard underneath a large framed photograph of his boat *Domitian*. Rounds of sunlight have aged it into nostalgia. "Quit stalling," he says. "You're black."

"I'm not sure I'm up for a game. Can't we just talk about the idea I had? It's important, I—"

"Come on." He swats my shoulder. I can tell he wants to anchor us in calmer water, and my role as his guest is to help provide that. "We can talk while we play. I always do my best thinking over chess. I'm guessing you haven't gotten any better."

Chess was always Charlie's sport. At the height of our marathon sessions, I won only a handful of times. I always suspected Charlie of allowing those wins because he understood the need for the occasional defeat in order to keep the competitor at the table. At Destroyers, I held the advantage, better when my back was against a wall than Charlie ever was with his blind faith that escape routes would magically materialize. At every other game, Charlie creamed me. And chess was indisputably his turf. I slide around the table and take a seat in the metal chair next to the radio. Charlie sits across from me, plucking his white rook from the board and dangling it between his fingers. The pieces are hand-carved wood.

"Do you still need a handicap?" he asks. Even with the Central Park regulars, Charlie often forfeited a rook in order to play a more equal game.

"It would be nice," I say with a smirk. This sacrifice gives me as much confidence in the game as it does in our friendship: we haven't lost it. And his beating me will instill a confidence in him: I haven't changed a bit. More often than not, my side of the board tends to approximate a feudal court that is trying to depose its own king and form a last-ditch democracy. Charlie places the rook sideways on the table, fallen castle, and launches with his knight. I mirror the move.

"How's it going with Louise?" he asks. "Are you getting anywhere?" The pawns ascend.

"Where am I supposed to have gotten with someone I haven't seen in years?"

Charlie expels a laugh, his hand fluttering over his pieces, as if my moves are merely mandatory rest stops. "You sound like you'd be a good candidate for the Patmian police force. *Now you say this human is someone for whom I have feelings and—*"

"I told you, I'm not here for the beach. Not for love either. I've got bigger problems. Charlie, it's bad." I want to make eye contact to emphasize just how serious I am, but we've hit the familiar stride of our game, and I'm like a jogger trying to keep up. He captures on a retreat.

For the past few days I've been trying to appear unfazed, the way you're told to affect normalcy when a ferocious animal enters your campground. Running off screaming will only make you its victim. Look bigger than it, show zero fear, stand your ground. But right now, alone with Charlie, I feel so close to screaming for help that I can barely keep seated. I latch my hands on the table, a tactic Charlie notices. His lips tighten.

"Okay, it's bad," he repeats. "No inheritance. You're broke." He stops to concentrate on my face. "So tell me, what did you have in mind?"

I feel my speech is moving nicely, lubricated for professional momentum, until I reach the word *fabulous*. "A fabulous PR move." *Fabulous. Fabula. Fable.* The word is a sinkhole, embedded in the English dictionary simply to swallow its user under the weight of its own flamboyance. Aren't all job interviews desperate acts of fabulism? *You need me, I possess a very special skill set, I can mountain your molehills and then molehill them again for a fee, Konstantinou Engineering can become the Apple of respectability under my constant watch.* I push on, doubly muddled, because Charlie's queen is eating horses, and a defensiveness creeps its way into my voice, as if Charlie is silently accusing me of being unable to organize a charitable wing of his father's company. I realize part of my anger stems from the fact that he's forcing me to play a board game while I'm begging for my life. "This is important, it could greatly impact your father's business if only you could see that, and corporate altruism is a field I've been focused on for the last few years." A small, fabulous lie. "I'm talking multiformat." Did I already use the word *liaise*? I use it again.

Charlie lets me finish. He pauses and doesn't check my king but instead makes an unnecessary opening in his battalion of pawns. I can't read this move as anything but charitable.

"You're my friend, Ian, my oldest friend." The information is hopeful, but the frank tone is crossing out hope in fat, black marker. He rubs his hand on the table, the skin on his fingers peeling from sun and tobacco exposure. "So trust me when I tell you that would never work."

"Why not?"

"Because my dad's not interested in that. He never has been. He already has a team of flaks to help him fly *under* the radar. Opening a few art schools in the Middle East is going to be more of a headache and a potential political shit storm than it is a, a"—he avoids the ugly word—"*good* PR move."

"Don't you think he should be the one to decide that? I'm only asking that you let me speak with him. If he's in New York I can fly back. I'm also pretty good at Skype."

"He's not well," Charlie rasps. "He has surgery for his lungs and heart every second week. His health is fading, and the doctors can't even manage a straight face on how long he's got. It could be months, a year, maybe two. Who knows?"

"I'm sorry. I knew he was sick, but I had no idea it was that bad." I didn't fully realize how much we have in common—both of us hitting that weird voodoo stretch of adulthood where parents evaporate one by one into hospitals and experimental procedures and family plots. But Charlie shakes his head, as if to ward off sympathy, his own and mine.

"The point is, my father's trying to tighten the strings, cutting the unnecessary fat so it's easier for Stefan to take over when it's time. Ian, I know this is meaningful, it's what you want, but it just isn't going to happen. Don't be mad because you've invented a job we can't offer you."

"The art school was only an example. It could be quieter, less risky endeavors. Maybe at this point in his life he'd appreciate the opportunity to give back. It could be an endowment, something in his name."

I worry I've overstepped—trying to tack my résumé on his father's bleak medical files—but Charlie's expression halts the apology on my tongue. His face is both knotted and serene, like a little Buddha statue folded up in painful contortions and yet expressing an uncomplicated peace. Then his mouth falls slack with the truth.

"Ian, you do realize that even my father knows how to Google."

The remark stings. I stare out the window, at the white, claustrophobic glare of light on water, as if the mutating code of the Internet has already infected those basic elements. I wouldn't be surprised if the Internet could be detected deep in the Earth's core, worming under the caskets and forgotten time capsules and decades of buried biohazard waste. There is nowhere I can go to escape Ian Bledsoe. A speck of island in the Aegean isn't far enough away.

"I'm just being honest," Charlie says through clenched teeth. "One search and your whole history is right there. It's probably not a fabulous PR move to hire you as the company goodwill ambassador." Charlie rises from his seat, abandoning the game he's on the verge of winning. He leans against the desk, pinching his chin.

"None of that stuff is true," I moan. "I had nothing to do with any fucking plot, because there was no plot. All I was trying to do was help. It's bullshit. I wish you'd believe me." I rest my elbows on the table. I have reached the age or state of decline where the head is a heavy appendage, in constant need of support. "Helping," I repeat helplessly. "That's all."

"Of course, I believe you. And quite honestly I find it courageous. You have what so few can even pretend to possess anymore. You don't care what others think about you." I stare up at him, my heart and eyelids beating arrhythmically. Charlie means it as a compliment, but the utter falsehood of that statement only shows how little he knows me. We *have* changed, and so has our sense of each other.

"I was stupid, not courageous. And now you see why I'm screwed. No one will hire me. I thought maybe your family might because at least they remember who I am. Jesus, you make one mistake and you're exiled to a life of unemployment and apologies. I suppose I could try China. They still have a ban on Google, don't they?" I'm only half kidding. Repressive dictatorships might be my only zone of freedom. "If I could just get away from that, move beyond it, but I can't! No one will let me! I wish they'd just throw rocks like they used to and be done with it."

"It's because of how we were raised," Charlie replies. I assume he means we were too coddled to bear hard falls, but he doesn't. "No one has pity for the rich. You were born in the wrong tax bracket if you expect even one drop of that. You knew the inside of mansions too young. Millionaire tears don't weigh much."

"I don't want pity," I whisper, although I realize that's all I have left to hope for.

Charlie draws his head to the side, studying me scientifically. "I always wondered why you've been so bent on this humanitarian crusade since college. All the volunteer work and passing out sandwiches and raising money for the next big cause." I'm not surprised by this reaction. It's always the good deed that needs to be defended, the selfless act that attracts suspicion and never the bad, self-seeking ones. "But now I think I know why," he says. "You feel guilty for how easy you've had it, like it's your own fault. Well, you aren't the only one trying to crawl out of that shadow. That's why I built this boat business. I needed to do something on my own, something that didn't already come prefurnished because of my family, something"—he searches for the word along the cracks in the floor—"not *haunted*, do you know what I mean?"

"I should never have taken that job at Kitterin. I shouldn't have gone to Panama."

Charlie nods, like we've resolved the problem, although I'm still sitting in front of a chessboard facing a checkmate that won't come. The sun hits the crumpled chip bag on the desk, a dense metallic sparkle, the ruthless sunlight of someone else's rush hour, and I think of all the jobs that brought this 1.5-oz. bag of potato chips to the beach grass of a Greek island: the decades of careful planning and market testing and boardroom strategizing, the factory time and package design, the negotiations with wholesalers and regional suppliers, the shipments and stocking and advertising that account for the bright glassine miracle of this bag's mere existence belying thousands of hours of people's lives. The lessons from Panama have been learned: a vision of the world, without the mess of work in it, is the most deluded luxury there is. All the labor that spins the planet, and yet I can barely find the strength to lift my head from my hands.

"You're right," I say. "We did have it too easy. And the sad part is I should have kept on like that."

Charlie glances despondently out the window, the ribbon of sea speckled with passing leisure boats. I think back to us as teens on the benches in Central Park with the miniature sailboats gliding through the tar-black pond water and the children standing like fidgety sentinels at the rim. The boats are bigger now and Charlie owns his own controls, but for the first time this morning I feel like we've found the quiet groove of our early friendship, two kids lightly damaged and stuck together in the spoiled orphanage of distracted families. We were junior champions of escape.

"Do you still need a little man to examine Sonny's entrails in the morning?" I ask him. You don't need to be good among old friends, only good enough. "Do I sound desperate? Because I am."

"I have an idea," Charlie says softly. "If you're willing to think outside the philanthropy racket. It's why I invited you here." His smile returns, his arms folded at his chest. "I was thinking you could work for me, be my number two. The pay is decent. And you wouldn't have to go back."

"Charlie," I wheeze. I'm stalling, sending his name slowly out of my mouth in a skid of air and spit, to gather all of the reasons why that wouldn't be a feasible arrangement. But all I can come up with is my lack of experience. That didn't prevent me from proposing art schools in the Middle East. "I don't know anything about yachts. Twenty feet out in the water and I wouldn't know how to steer one to shore. I appreciate it, really—"

"You can learn. And I'm not suggesting you become a captain. I was thinking more along the lines of support and development. Oh, and office upkeep." He picks up a few of the papers on the desk and lets gravity return them to their natural disorder. "If you can handle crack addicts, you can handle anything—even tourists who expect Folegandros to have the five-star amenities of Cap D'Antibes. The cleanup is probably similar."

"But you already have a staff. Ugur."

Charlie laughs. "Ugur is the brain of boat repair, and I'm lucky to have him. But you've heard his English. No, Ugur doesn't have the goods for upper management."

"What about Rasym? He's a sailor, isn't he?" I don't know why I'm trying to talk Charlie out of his proposal. Maybe I simply want to know whom I'm cutting in front of.

Charlie nods and reaches under the desk to retrieve a canvas tote bag. "Yeah, Rasym is competent on the water, no question. It's his first August on Patmos since I opened the company, and he did hope to come on board. He doesn't exactly do much besides errands for my uncle in Nicosia. But I want to keep the business out of the family. Rasym stopped by an hour ago. I told him I was going to offer you the job."

"No wonder he didn't look too pleased when I passed him on the road."

"He'll be fine. He doesn't warm instantly to outsiders. It's the Turkish side of his Cypriot. Invaders don't appreciate other invaders."

Support. Development. I'm only dimly aware that Charlie's company involves sending rich vacationers into the Aegean on refurbished vessels. The ports I can name are Athens, Patmos, Turkey, a few other Greek islands like Folegandros. I speak the global language of English, not the insider tongues that pull the tighter strings.

"It's kind of you, Charlie, really, but—"

"But what?" He stares at me as if he's tucked a check in my palm and I've dropped it at his feet. "I need you," he wails. "Do you know why? Because I can trust you. That's worth more to me than any nautical competence or five years handling invoices. I've had workers before, people I assumed I could trust, but they stole from me. Right out of the safe." He nods to the photograph of *Domitian* above my head. "It's nearly impossible to find someone you can trust, and we already have that. We're like brothers, aren't we? Better than brothers. We're not fighting over an inheritance like every scrap is a piece of our father's heart."

Charlie fishes his tobacco pouch and rolling papers from the tote bag and begins constructing one of his thin cigarettes. I pick up my queen and squeeze it. The game is over, but, like Charlie, I feel the need to busy my fingers.

"Look," he says, "there will be a lot to absorb and not all of it is pretty. Schedules and coordinates and dock reservations and even bribes." He nods at the last inclusion. "The ancient rule of baksheesh. You have to grease a few hands in this part of the world to keep a business going. It's just the way it is. And as much as I want this company to be my own, I had to call it Konstantinou Charters because the family name is worth something over here. My grandfather and father have been sailing the Aegean their whole lives. The locals value it. Every boat has a red *K* on the bow, a mark of safety and familiarity."

"Safety. Familiarity." I remember Charlie's own words about his family building the highways in the Middle East. "And intimidation."

He grins as he digs into the tote to locate a lighter. "Sure. The seas are still the Wild West sloshing up around the overpoliced borders. It's good to have the threat of a little financial muscle behind you. The job isn't saving poor kids, Ian. I can't give you that. But I can give you a place in what I've got."

Konstantinou Charters. Sometimes I think the Bronx nonprofit We in Need only hired me because of my last name. They were willing to forgive my infamy once they learned my father was a top executive of an international conglomerate. When I had trouble rounding up donations, colleagues asked why my father didn't fund a program. "I've seen your stepmom in the society photos of those fancy galas, why don't you ask her to get involved?" Perhaps they fired me once they understood they were only getting one Bledsoe, the least powerful and most unappealing, as a member of their team. *Haunted.* That's the right word for a last name, and saints are the only ones free of them. From here on out, I could just be Ian, two syllables, three letters, enough of an island on which to pitch a tent.

"I don't want you expecting a squeaky clean business," Charlie says flatly. "It's brutal and ugly and at times dishonest and it's wearing me thin because it's the fucking Old World out here. None of your idealism, okay?"

"Idealism hasn't gotten me very far."

He smiles. "Be honest. It won't kill you to be less idealistic?" I shake my head. "And who knows, you come back with me to Cyprus in the off-season and maybe we can talk about art schools. You'll be glad to know there's poverty everywhere. Every ten feet on this planet someone has a hand out."

Charlie shifts his leg on the desk, still scooping for his lighter in the bag. One of his testicles drops from the opening of his shorts, a prune-purple egg enveloped in a sweaty thatch of hair. It looks like the vulnerable head of a newborn. Growing up, I saw Charlie naked on an average of twice a week in the locker room after gym class. But for some reason I can't stop staring at this single oblong ball peeking from yellow fabric. It feels as intimate as entering the house of a stranger. I force my eyes back to Charlie's face, but that brief glimpse of nudity makes me love him more; he seems approachable now, his money and handsomeness and authority to offer me a job brought down to lopsided, pubic-blazing earth.

Charlie grows irritated by his lighter-finding mission and dumps the entire contents of the tote bag on the desk. An address book tumbles out, three pens, his car keys, and a turquoise earring as gaudy as a Venetian doorknocker. He grunts as he picks up the earring, clutching it in his hand.

"Sonny," he hisses. "She's still at it."

"I'm sure she's only trying to be funny. Are you two not doing well?"

He slides open a drawer and fingers a book of matches. He draws a match across the strike strip and lights his cigarette.

"You could say that," he replies as he exhales. The smoke clouds the trapped office air like clapped chalk erasers. "We've been arguing all morning." I now wonder if it was Sonny who gave him the black eye. Their fights might have reached a level of theatrics where physical violence felt like the only way to outdo their previous efforts. "Sonny wants to take Duck with us to Nicosia come November. One month is no longer enough. She says she's ready to be a full-time mom again."

"You don't seem so bad with Duck."

Charlie moves his cigarette an inch from his mouth and gives me a death stare. Stray stars would implode in the gravitational field of those eyes. But I sense loneliness in those eyes as well, like the most valuable accomplishment on my résumé might be "friend."

"Duck's great. But I'm not ready to be a dad. And Duck already happens to have a father in Los Angeles. Sonny thinks I can throw lawyers at him, dish out more money, get her a private tutor, a horse, a miniature replica of her ranch house in Topanga so she won't get homesick." He shakes his head and fastens the clasp of the earring onto his shirt. It jokingly hangs over his heart like a mock war medal. "I don't know. I sometimes wonder if we should take a break.

You give someone keys to your house, your checkbook becomes as communal as the medicine cabinet. I told you, every ten feet there's an open hand."

I smile queasily, conscious of the fact that I could be counted among the leeches. But Charlie doesn't seem to view me that way. He looks at me tenderly over a smoke-smeared mouth gritted in an uneven lock. There is an advantage in getting to someone young, the memory of the ten-year-old never quite expunged.

"Maybe it will just be you and me going back to Cyprus in November. If you're taking the job. Are you?" His stare transforms from black hole to sunshine. "I thought you'd be jumping at the offer. Come on, you want me to beg? Let me do this for you, all right? You've passed out enough free sandwiches. Why don't you take one for once? I know you're hungry. Take the sandwich, Ian."

I have no choice. And I'm not sure I even want one. "Of course I'm taking it. When do I start?"

He jumps from the desk, the smoke swirling from his fingers, and his grin is a streamer flapping in warm trade winds. "You just did," he exclaims, reaching both arms out. "Come here. No handshakes for us." My chair slams against the wall, and I knock over the pieces on the chessboard as I round the table to put my arms around him. The skin of his neck is still hot from the day, and I almost believe that we were destined to end up hugging in a metal trailer on the other side of the world. I feel the sneeze-like strain of tears about to break.

"Thank you," I whisper.

"Don't thank me. It's not going to be easy. But it will be ours."

Charlie drops back against the desk, and a minute of quiet intrudes. He twists his cigarette into an ashtray.

"So walk me through the procedure. Tourists call up and book a boat for a week and one of your captains takes them out to see the islands?"

He laughs faintly. "Something like that," he says. "Only a little more complicated. We'll get into it. *Deep* into it. But I have a meeting in five minutes so we'll have to wait. Why don't you go back to the cabins and unpack. I'm guessing your clothes are still in your suitcase."

"I didn't know how long I was staying."

He nods. "The cabin's your home now. Use the closets. I paid extra for cedar. We'll go over everything when I get back in a few days."

I look at him puzzled. "Where are you going?"

Charlie sighs and reaches for his tobacco pouch but reconsiders adding another link to his habit's chain.

"I need you to do something for me, a personal favor, and I promise the rest is on the level from here out."

"What?"

Charlie cocks his head. "I have some business in Turkey. There are people I need to meet in the port of Bodrum. It's urgent, a problem with the registration of some of the boats. It's a convenience-state loophole, nothing to worry about, but it's causing difficulties for our customers."

"Convenience state?"

Charlie nods. "Yeah, the reason the boats have Cypriot flags on their sterns. You'll learn. I'll teach you. But I need to skip out for a couple days—two, three at the most. The thing is, I don't want Sonny to know I'm gone."

"She must understand you have a company to run."

"Does she? I'm afraid Sonny thinks she's my full-time job." He wipes his hairline, the sweat slicking the curls straight. "Sonny will freak out if I leave her for a few days. She's paranoid. It'll become major warfare, and I just can't deal with it. So I want her to think I'm still on the island, just taking a little time out of the house."

"Why is Sonny paranoid?"

With a sharp tug, his hair turns tousled again, and his eyes sliver, as if simply mentioning a disease causes it to spread. Or maybe it's the frustration of someone unaccustomed to explaining himself. "It's that bomb that went off in Skala last month, okay? It scared her to the point she won't let me out of her sight for more than an afternoon. Two days away and she's likely to phone the police or hunt me down in Bodrum herself." Charlie stretches his neck and rotates his head like he's following a speeding clock. "Because of *where* that bomb went off."

"On this island."

"At that taverna, that particular taverna. I used to go there every morning at eleven on the dot. Nikos had been my ritual for years. Sonny was in Paris that day, and I got caught up in a phone call from my father. He never calls, but he did that morning because he'd just received bad news from his doctor, so for once I didn't go. The bomb exploded just a few minutes after eleven, right there at the tables where I always sit. I was fucking lucky, Ian, so lucky, because I should have been there. Any other day and I would have been."

I imagine the roar of that bomb in our past, a human-eating wound opening up in the world just a month behind us, and the small miracle of his being here, fighting the urge for another ciga-rette, dressed in too-tight, yellow shorts.

"Thank god for your father. Jesus, Charlie."

"Yeah." He wheezes. "His bad news saved my life. But Sonny has gotten it in her head that the bomb was meant for me. She won't listen. She's convinced of it, and I've had to do everything in my power to stop her from packing our bags and running back behind the gates of our house in Nicosia. Or worse, New York. I promised her if she stayed, I would too, so you see, my leaving will just bring all the fears back into her mind."

I picture Sonny at her psychic, an old Greek woman tracing her carcinogenic nail along Sonny's palm for a forecast of explosions and carnage. *Bomb? Do you see a bomb in my hand? What does it look like? Where will it explode?*

"What a minute," I say. "Why would Sonny think that bomb was for you? Charlie, what's going on?" For a second, I consider retract-ing my acceptance of employment. The rectangular metal office with its shut door has the ominous feeling of a trap.

"It wasn't for me!" he shouts, saliva cobwebbing his teeth. He says it so definitively I know he's spent nights weighing the possibility of another conclusion. "Not for me at all. Why would anyone try to kill me? If I could even conceive of a reason, do you think I'd be dumb enough to stay? My god, I wish I were that important. No, it's exactly what your taxi driver said, an antigovernment group trying to raise a bit of hysteria. And it worked. I've had Sonny asking Therese every morning if there are packages left in front of our door. She's finally gotten beyond it, and I don't want her starting up again. Greece is already as shaky as a roller coaster these days with its economy in the toilet and refugees washing up on all the islands. I go to Bodrum for three days and I know she won't be here when I get back."

"I thought you wouldn't mind a break."

Charlie looks down at his hands, where dry, yellow calluses line each joint. They're workman's hands, the kind scored from handling hard material, the kind that Buckland was meant to protect its students from earning. "I love her," he murmurs in the tone of an uneasy confession. "I do love her. I don't want her leaving me." This is honest Charlie. I remember the punctured-balloon sound from when we were kids, the pliant voice snagged on a sharp-metal emotion. Charlie could always handle being the leaver. He dropped out of college, split on his family and friends, waved good-bye to New York—his entire biography has hinged on him escaping first. When he died in our game of Destroyers, he'd actually get angry at me— "Come on, I can still get away, that's not fair, *not fair*, there's got to be a last way out"—on the verge of punching me for what he considered an act of betrayal. There are some people who have never been abandoned, and I get the sense that Sonny's departure would spiral him headfirst toward despair.

Charlie closes his hands and stares up at me. "Look, I know I haven't been a saint in relationships. And I'm not going to lie and tell you I've always been fair to Sonny either. We've had our low moments. But if any good came out of that bomb, it's that it taught me not to take her for granted. No more cheating. Never again. My new virtues are faithful and boring." I purse my lips, calling bullshit, and Charlie recoils with a laugh. "I swear. Almost getting caught in that explosion woke me up. You're looking at a changed man."

I want to ask why his newfound fidelity doesn't extend to lying about his whereabouts. But the bomb is back in my mind, and I hold on to my elbows as if my bones could shield the force of a blast.

"Be honest with me. Is this place safe? Could there be more bombs? Charlie, how are you sure it wasn't meant for you? I don't think I can—"

"Ian," he barks. "Bad shit happens. Real shit, even on vacation islands. Larger forces are at work than our own lives. You don't run every time there's a siren. New York happened, and everyone stayed, didn't they?" He's referring to a far bigger horror, but for a second I assume he means my father's death. I didn't stay. I did run. "I've made a life here, my company, my house. This is where I belong. Some lunatic group purposely planted a bomb at a smaller, local taverna. Enough fatalities to get the world's attention for five minutes, but they didn't pick the crowded cafés because killing twenty or thirty tourists would have meant an international incident. That's all it was." He brings two fingers to his mouth but finds they don't hold a cigarette. It's like he's kissing his fingertips. "You've got to learn not to take everything so personally. That's Sonny's problem. Don't let it be yours."

Charlie reaches out and latches onto my forearm.

"Don't let fear grow feet and walk all over you. You're with me, aren't you?"

"Yes, I'm with you." Five minutes into my job I don't want to be cast as a coward. I can't help thinking that this cooked-up chicanery with Sonny is a test of my loyalty. If I can't even smoke screen his girlfriend for two days, how can I be counted upon to handle the stickier operations of his boats? "So you need me to be your alibi."

"Alibi." He groans. "Why is everyone around me so dramatic?" He slips from the desk and sidesteps around the table. He unhooks the frame holding the picture of *Domitian*, and behind it is an iron safe with a combination lock protruding from its center. Charlie pinches it. When he turns the dial to the number 15, I know instantly the rest of the combination. It's the date of his last birthday backward—15–29–6. That was always his locker code at Buckland. Passwords, like habits, are hard to break. He pulls out a thin stack of aquamarine bills and shuts the door. "I don't need your help if one tiny lie is going to weigh like a fat man on your conscience. I just thought a bit of corroboration would put her at ease. Believe me, Sonny appreciates feeling at ease."

He offers me the money, and I take it, five one-hundred euro bills with an arch bridge stretching across each rubbery note.

"That should hold you until I get back."

"So what do I tell her?"

The sound of a car lumbers up the dirt road. An emergency brake is wrenched on the other side of the trailer.

"She'll think I'm staying on *Domitian*," Charlie says. "It'll be docked off the coast. Christos has me covered. All you need to do is pretend we hung out once or twice. Say you checked in on me and I'm still upset. I'm going to take one of the charter boats to Bodrum and be back before she realizes I'm gone."

Charlie bends down and rifles through a cardboard box. He resurfaces with a powder-blue baseball cap. A tilted ship's wheel is emblazoned on its crown under KONSTANTINOU CHARTERS in a breezy dark-blue font. He shoves the cap on my head, its band constricting against my temples.

"There's your uniform," he says. "If you lose it, the replacement fee is fifteen euros."

"I'll try to keep it clean," I joke. Charlie flicks the brim. "And I'll tell Sonny I visited you, but how are you going to get her to accept that you're spending a few days on your yacht in the first place?"

"Leave that to me. We're all meeting for drinks tonight in Skala. Ten P.M. Bring Louise." He slides in front of me, his eyes finding mine, darting from one eye to the other, as if to test their resemblance. "Thank you for the favor. You'll do it?"

"Yes."

He juts his head an inch from mine. "I can't tell you how much it means having you here. I'm serious, Ian. It's like we're both home."

"I hope I don't disappoint you."

"You could only if you tried."

He opens the door and clasps my shoulder as we step out into the thermonuclear heat. It is a day for avoiding the shine of metal, and the station wagon parked by the office isn't so much a color as a radiant star. But when the priest with the trimmed beard climbs out of the front seat, I identify the car as the white Mercedes that ran me off the road.

"Petros," Charlie chants and extends his hand. The priest steps forward in his long black robe, fitted tightly like the petticoats of a French bohemian. He cups Charlie's hand, a gold Rolex dangling from his wrist. His smile matches his automobile, and like the car, it has an element of speed to it, the purring grille hiding a mean motor.

"Petros is the priest of the St. Sofia church in Chora," Charlie tells me. "But he also manages some of the monastery's financial holdings. He's the landlord of my dock. Petros, this is Ian Bledsoe."

The priest's hands move from Charlie and offer themselves to me in their cupped arrangement. I have to slide my fingers between his palms, hot and soft, and he exerts a gentle pressure, like a nurse's on a child's forehead.

"Very nice to meet you," he says in a Greek soprano, like the un-spooling reel on a fishing pole when a line is cast. He first takes in my Charters cap and then my face. There's no visible sign that he recognizes me as the motorbiking tourist he nearly killed yesterday with his car. "Do you work here?"

"Yes, he does," Charlie intervenes. "Ian's just come from New York. He's my number two." I wish Charlie would stop calling me that. It now conjures the little man in the bathroom with a specialty in fecal analysis.

"Welcome," Petros says, dropping his hands away. "It is not a simple business, running boats. The water and transport are very difficult for the unacquainted. You're expected to know every island and port."

"Oh, Ian's a pro," Charlie says blithely. "He knows what he's doing. He's been working for me for a few months in the States, learning the operation on the business end." Charlie winks at me. Our new venture is joisted by little lies. "He's up to speed, very dependable. He's going to be an excellent fit. Customers will love him. He even speaks Spanish."

"What need? Everyone today speaks English if they can afford the sea."

Petros seems uncertain whether I will indeed be an excellent fit. He impatiently grinds his shoe in the dirt, as if I'm infringing upon his appointment.

"All right, Ian. Unpack your suitcase." Charlie eyes my bike. "I'm glad Helios felt well enough today to perform a few duties." He makes a screwdriver out of his finger and loosens the bolt of his temple. "Christos will be proud."

Charlie and Petros head into the office. I return to my bike. Before I swing my leg over the leather seat, I find I'm holding five-hundred euros in cash in one hand and, in the other by accident, the black hand-carved queen. It's substantially more than I had an hour ago.

I trade my work cap for my helmet and straddle the motor. I am all light, a man with a job, finally retired from the losing sport of philanthropy—a man who was so close to stop that it is almost unbearable now to be flying at high speeds along the kerosene blue, my whole heart pounding against the day. I am cutting fast through the dust and sun. To my new home on the island. And to Louise.

CHAPTER 6

I wait for her on the other side of the bolted door. Some decisions are akin to jumping from the top of a waterfall. No one will care if you don't do it, you can easily walk away. Who could blame you for not surrendering to the drop? But you'll know. And the fear is not to discover one day that the world has no meaning, but that, in fact, it does. Every decision counted. Against your better judgment, all of it mattered, the steps and choices, the pauses and delays. That's the real fear: an answerable life.

Or so it seems to me as the sun sets and I wait for her. The roosters grow agitated, staking one last claim to the land that is shrinking into invisibility in the dark. The sky bruises, and shadows pull at the bed and chairs. Even though while I was out a cleaning woman has come to scour the bathroom, change the sheets, and place two pink hibiscus flowers on the pillows, the money is still hidden in the nightstand.

The high beam of her bike sparkles up the drive. She climbs the steps and turns the latch on her cabin door. I hear the rush of feet, a bag dropped on the bed, and the hissing spray of the faucet in the bathroom. I place my ear against the door and catch her voice but can't make out the words through the running tap. Perhaps she's singing to herself. I wait until she stops. The alchemy of the purpling sky and the cool breeze flowing through the open patio door and the new-found confidence of a solid future has conspired to make every second significant, a now-or-never excitement of unbolting the door and finding Louise alone on the other side.

The toilet flushes twice—I ignore this detail, romance requires it. Her footsteps pound on the floorboards and an unidentifiable snapping of fabric traffics through the wood. "I've got to go," she says out loud. No more time. I clasp the bolt and dislodge it. I push, and the door swings wide.

Louise screams in terror, her head rotating like a police siren, and as in my dream, she has her bathing suit halfway down around her waist. Her forearm shoots to cover her chest, and her cell phone tumbles to the floor.

"God, Ian," she shouts. "What the fuck?" She glares at me.

"I, I, I—" No conclusion follows, except the most mundane. "I've just unpacked my suitcase."

"You scared me for that?" But a smile is softening the frightened edges of her lips. She picks up her phone and inspects the screen. "Well, it's not broken. I hope my brother hung up before he heard me scream."

"Sorry." I reach for the doorknob. "I wanted to share the good news."

"I can't tell you how thrilled I am to hear that you've emptied your suitcase," she says with a laugh. "And that you figured out how to unbolt the door."

"Not that." I laugh too. "I'm staying. Charlie's offered me a job at his boat company."

Louise flinches. Her eyebrows, bleached by sunscreen, dip, and her upper lip briefly contorts. She must realize the pessimism of this reaction because she instantly fixes her expression into a neutral lock.

"Really? I'm surprised."

"Why? I need a job. It's the reason I came here."

She tosses her phone on the bed. "No, I just . . . I don't know. I thought you were interested in doing more meaningful work, work that benefited others. That's what you always said you wanted, even back in school. It suits you." Dreams suit people. An astronaut suits most children.

"I *was* interested in that," I say. "But I need the money. And maybe it's time I grew up."

"And you think Charlie will make you an adult?" Her voice is thick with disappointment. I've forgotten Louise's skill at radiating judgment—or is that a demonstrable lack of skill, an inability to prune back the hostile flowers to encourage sweeter ones to grow in their place? Her lips are pierced to a dot just above the mole on her chin. I usually admire her unchecked responses—it must come from boundless fields of confidence, unbuyable real estate, immune to foreclosure—but not right now. I want to ask her what she's done to help the universe in the last eight years. I want to remind her that she's staying rent-free in this cabin out of Charlie's generosity. "It seems to me you're different than he is," she says, rubbing her toe across the fading light on the floor, as if trying to wipe out a wine stain. "There is still so much you could do besides indulging the rich, making money off of fun. I don't see you happy doing that."

"You might not know this about me, but it's not exactly easy for me to get a job these days." Of course she knows. Her cell phone is connected to the Internet and lies within reach on her bed. Even Duck could assess my occupational prospects given a few seconds alone with that device: my life has been rated on the Internet and I've received one star. "Charlie is doing me a favor by taking me on. I'm lucky. Things have been dark for a while. It's about time some good came my way."

"You really believe that's how it works?" she asks harshly. "Bad and good always balance each other out?"

"I'm broke," I snap. "I have no money. This isn't about what I'd like."

"I'm broke too," she replies, not resentfully but as if it were an ordinary observation, almost proud in its acceptance. "Always have been. Maybe I'm just used to it. I find it freeing in a way. Sometimes I think it's only the beggars who can be the choosers. You aren't always consulting the oracle of your lifestyle."

"All right," I say peevishly. I begin to close the door, but a flicker in Louise's eyes stops me.

"Wait," she says. "I'm sorry. Congratulations. Truly. What do I know? I care about you, that's all."

I so badly wish for the courage of three minutes ago. But it takes all of my strength to stand still and not shut the door. I don't need more courage, as it turns out. Louise has her own reserve. She drops her arm from her chest, her small breasts bobbing as she steps across the purple wood. Her white skin glows with what little light is left to the day. I let go of the doorknob, and she kisses me, pushing me backward. Kissing, arms yanking, we stumble together from her room to mine and fall against the bed. We hold each other tightly, as if to pull away for even a second might prompt reconsideration. But I don't see beyond this wanting. And like some dream of fighting the murderer of one's own blanket, even a swimsuit pulled halfway down proves difficult to remove with finesse.

THE SEX HAS left its marks. I'm used to this condition—my skin like a drop cloth recording each spill and grapple. It is the curse or boon of being so fair that the imprint of Louise's mouth lingers on my collarbone, her bony knees are embossed on my thighs, and her palm prints are etched on my rib cage as if I were a window she was frantically trying to open. Each follicle of chest hair is blushing.

"Sorry. Am I really that violent?" she asks with the sheet wrapped around her waist. At some point in our skirmish, Louise paused to turn on the bedside lamp—why, I didn't ask. Its paisley shade bathes our bodies in a yellow-green corona. Her breasts expand and contract with each breath. Her skin, varnished by a childhood under a brown Kentucky sun, holds no trace of the man who, until two minutes ago, was on top of her.

"You're very violent," I reply, although that wasn't quite the case. I lean in and kiss her, her top lip fatter than her bottom one, wet slivers of hair stuck against her cheeks.

Louise Wheeler and I had sex exactly six times when we dated in college. Was it as amazing then as it was just now? I can recall the dorm room, the foam-wafer mattress, the vintage Pink Floyd poster and the avuncular postcard of James Baldwin attached with blue putty to the cinder block wall beside her bed. But I can't summon whether or not it was satisfying—perhaps because at twenty simply being in the vicinity of a willing vagina was deep satisfaction in itself. Were we good then? Did I make an impact? Pure erasure, a personal history reduced to statistics—*six times!*—but failing to register the early tremors or the quiet aftermath. Maybe it's because at that age, sex is more like assisted orgasm.

Louise lowers her head and kisses my shoulder, purposefully without suction so as not to leave more evidence. We wrap our hands together and watch the night blow in from the patio under the slow radar of the ceiling fan. The impossible thread count of Charlie's guest sheets makes me feel like I've been sleeping on recycled climbing nets my entire life.

"We have to be down at Skala at ten," I say happily. I could say anything happily right now. Give me a page from the Book of Revelation and I'll make it sound like a thank-you note.

"Do we have to?" Louise whispers, pushing her palm against the hinge of my wrist. "I'd rather stay up here away from everyone."

I would too, but Charlie specifically asked that I come and I can't disappoint him. "I promised. We'll go for an hour."

"Every night is an obligation. You almost forget it's a vacation." She sighs. "I guess it isn't a vacation for you anymore."

"I have a few days until—" I stop myself from naming the reason; no one is supposed to know that Charlie is leaving the island. "He's letting me get settled."

"Very nice of him." Louise releases her grip and grabs the Henry Miller off the nightstand. She flips through it and stops on the underlined passages. "How is it?" she asks. "I saw you reading it on the beach."

"I found it in the room. Was anyone staying here before I showed up?"

She shakes her head. "No, it was empty. I asked Charlie if I could unbolt the door and have the whole place to myself, but he said he was saving it. I guess he thought you might be irritated if you found me camped out in your space. After all, we might not have hit it off again. Like car accidents, what's the chance you're going to hit the same person twice?" She runs her nail along the underlined sentences and gives up, tossing it away. "Do you remember my freshman roommate, Becky Holbrook? I took a class on Romantic poetry my second semester just so I could save money by borrowing her used textbooks. I'll never forget, Becky had underlined all of the verses on love and made little notes in the margins, 'yes, this is just what it feels like, love like a roaring river.'" Louise rolls over and shoves her face into the pillow, the muscles of her back cramping with silent laughter. She slaps the pillow to create an airhole for her mouth. "At that point Becky Holbrook had never had a boyfriend. Not a single date, not a kiss. A true virgin, if you can believe it. And it took every ounce of compassion not to shake her awake on her top bunk at night and say, 'Becky, I can't sleep. I have to tell you something. It's urgent and it's eating me up inside. Love is nothing like a roaring river. You need to know that. Good night.'" Louise whisks my hair back tenderly, curling stray strands around my ear.

I want to argue in defense of Becky Holbrook. The roaring river is much closer to what I feel right now than my usual default impression of love, which is something approximating a balloon drifting up in the night, battered by pockets of turbulence, with no hand far below in the city reaching up belatedly to retrieve it. Eventually deflated, it will return to Earth to suffocate an endangered ibis. Enough love in New York could wipe out an entire species.

Louise climbs off the mattress and gathers her swimsuit from the floor. Her thin hips jerk from side to side, as if she's slaloming a mountain. "My leg fell asleep," she says, reaching for the support of the door.

"So what do you think love is like, if rivers are out?"

I expect an answer along the lines of "short-range ballistic missiles" or "benignly swallowing razor blades." Or maybe it's "Argentina" or "soft rugs." I don't know what Louise is capable of, but I want some verification of the heat spreading in my chest and the cold knot twisting below it. She doesn't answer, or at least I don't take her next words as one.

"Do me a favor," she says as she turns. She covers her breasts with her swimsuit. The rest of her remains so delectably exposed. The skin along her arms and shoulders are different shades of tan like water stains in a bathtub. Her face and vagina are competing for my attention, so I glance down at the billiard rack of my penis and testicles. "Let's not tell Charlie and Sonny about us. Let's leave them out of it. You know how this kind of thing can become a telenovela for everyone else."

I nod. "At least tell me what happened to Becky Holbrook."

Louise stops in the doorway. "Married. Three kids. She owns her own import glass business and has a huge house in Marin County. Happy as a fly in a dirty kitchen by all accounts. It's a good thing I never woke her up."

THE POPULATION OF Skala spikes in the night like a murder rate. A whirlpool of motion that becomes more frenetic the closer we get to it. Metal-green faces shine above tooth-white shirts and peasant blouses. Cowboy boots are scuffed, studded, or inlaid with travertine and quartz. Tattoos pulse on waxed forearms or surface faintly through shawls of shoulder hair: an Italian flag; a happy face inside a pentagram; Gandhi leaning on a pot leaf. Tassels. Fringe. And the night is thick with gold chains, entire racetracks around necks and wrists. An oxidized cistern in the center of the village is a discard site for plastic cups. Children jump, one, two, three, invisible hopscotch. Outdoor flat screens in crowded bars play the same manic footage of fashion shows; agitated models march down planks draped in furs and capes. I can't decide if this obsessive runway broadcasting is meant to encourage or mock its audience. Paris fashion week. London. Tokyo. Milan. Seasons out of order.

The traffic is so extreme it's safe. Minicoupes clog the road, honking and blinking their headlights. Motorbikes fare a bit better, weaving through the pedestrians and rendering handholding a semilethal proposition. I extend my hand for Louise to take, but she ignores it as we cross the street. There are more bodies in Skala than beds on the island, but the arctic ice shelf of a ten-tiered cruise ship is docked in the harbor, and skiffs are running relay to cargo cabin-fevered vacationers. Everyone is hurrying, as if in search of some near-capacity trophy spot in the village and they haven't yet realized this is it. Jewelry shops and T-shirt stalls corral a small percentage of the foot market. Every so often a cheer ascends over the pop music, like a group rounding the top of a Ferris wheel, but it's merely a cluster of Germans or Italians toasting over metal ice buckets.

"Don't say it," Louise warns.

"Don't say what?"

"What you're thinking." She smiles at me. "It's not a nice word."

"What word is that?"

"You know what word," she says.

And I do know, or at least I can guess. *Eurotrash*. Except it doesn't look particularly *Euro* anymore. It could be Bogotá, Santa Cruz, Seoul, Moscow, Gaborone. The provincial sorting of trash seems like an outdated concept. It's just human flotsam washing up on August nights along the shores of another Greek island. I test out new words in my mind: *Humantrash. Caucasiangarbage. Globalcapitalistrefuse.* The language doesn't need more insults.

A shoulder slams into Louise, pitching her back, but is gone before we discover the assailant. "I told you we should have stayed home," she says.

Passing the closed police station, we come upon a young woman struggling to stand. Her knees below a tight floral skirt buckle and she falls back on the cobblestones with a visible bounce. Between her legs, as if she has given birth to it, is a pile of wheat-colored vomit. Her head is orbiting around, but she makes another noble attempt, the leather straps on her cork wedges straining against her toes, her feet bowed inward like a wobbly foal, her elbows slashing drunkenly for balance or to keep bystanders from interceding. I instantly become patriotic. I pray she isn't American, that we've boycotted this one-woman Olympic tournament against alcohol and gravity, an event we so often win. Each tectonic layer of her hair is a different ideation of blond.

"Don't fucking touch me," she cries, mercifully British, to no one in particular. She drops back to earth, narrowly missing the vomit. Finally a friend races over with a bottle of water. I grab Louise's arm, and we wind through the crowds. She looks back to make sure the woman is safe.

"When I waited tables at a bar in Lexington, I was the one who had to deal with the drunk women," Louise says. "Which always meant fending off men. I swear, everything about women's fashion is designed to hurt their chances—the high heels, the short skirts. I used to give them corkscrews to carry as a weapon before placing them in cabs. Civilization is a nice dream, isn't it?"

We finally locate Charlie and the rest of the group sitting at one of the quieter tavernas. Its outdoor chairs aren't metal but guava-green canvas and its drinks lack the tropical ornaments of cherries and orange slices. Ice is administered by elderly waiters via trembling silver tongs. Still the stainless steel table is a disk of whirling lights and a hidden speaker system plays propulsive techno tracks, just at a slightly less ear-splitting volume.

Charlie is wearing the same T-shirt and shorts from earlier; the gaudy earring is still clipped at his heart. He's slumped in his seat, downing the last of his drink and helping himself to the vodka bottle on the table. Sonny sits across from him next to Miles, who has his hair pulled back in a topknot. His pink oxford is buttoned prudishly to his neck.

"There you are," Sonny calls, waving her copper-painted fingernails. She has the preternatural ability to blend in even among the 10:00 P.M. chaos of a port town. The lurid greens and yellows of the night reflect against the sharp edges of her cheekbones, and her hair is braided in a ring around her head. She pushes one of the empty chairs closer to her, signaling that she wants Louise by her side. Adrian, whose happiness hasn't taken a single hit since I last saw him, grins as he pulls a bag off another chair. I won't be sitting next to Louise. Adrian wears a tank top with the sides cut open at the armpits. Every muscle of his rib cage is on display.

"Glad you could make it," Charlie drones stoically. "You're late." I can't tell if his somberness is part of his strategy to get himself evicted from his own house for a few days, but there's very little warmth in his voice. The aura of the table is one of nervous quiet, a morgue's hush between corpse deliveries.

"Yes," Miles chirps. He eyes us gratefully. "We had to guard these last two seats with our lives. Drinks, drinks, waiter, glasses please."

"Oh, I'm fine." Louise collapses into her chair. "That's quite a shiner," she says to Charlie, who doesn't bother to acknowledge her. Sonny places both hands on Louise's knee, as if she's claiming allies.

"You'll need a drink to be here," Sonny advises. "After two, Skala blurs just enough that it becomes fun. This isn't our usual spot. Charlie never likes it down here in the evening, but I guess he was feeling caged in by the Chora crowd." She tries for direct eye contact, but Charlie's staring out at the black water with his elbow on the armrest and his mouth resting in his palm. Smaller yachts are moored near the shore just beyond the yellow haze of the cruise ship. Jar-shaped lamps shine along the harbor, and bugs flutter around them like satellite debris. "I don't mind Skala," Sonny promises. "Good for people watching, right, Lamb?" She glances at me and scrunches her shoulders, as if to convey, *I can't get Charlie to engage, perhaps you can give it a try.*

Charlie responds but his hand is strapped against his mouth.

"What did you say?" I tap his shoulder. He flinches like I've poked a sunburn, and when he looks over at me I swear for a second I see the tussle of tears in his eyes. It could just be the way the village lights trouble any liquid surface. He turns his hand into a fist and coughs into it.

"I said, I picked Skala for Miles. I thought he might feel more comfortable down here."

Miles balks, not sure whether he's part of the joke or its punch line. The waiter places two clean glasses on the table and, with ceremonial attention, coaxes ice cube by cube from a bucket with his special tongs. Each ice cube is given emergency United Nations–summit level concentration. I resist the urge to grab the bucket and dump the ice in the glasses.

"Actually, the island has always been sequestered like this," Miles explains in a wise ethnographer's timbre. "All the way back to the Middle Ages. The monastery is the crown, and the rich built their homes around it for protection and prime views. The farther down the hillside, the poorer you were. And here—" Miles lifts his long hands from his lap to gesture around us; his shirt is buttoned at the wrists. "Here, Skala was for the workers and transients. And it's still that way. The more money you have, the closer you are to God. In fact, during the 1532 invasion of—"

Charlie crosses his legs impatiently and jerks his body forward.

"Can you please shut up with the history lessons? Honestly, how much will it cost for you to keep quiet?" He pulls his wallet from his pocket and slams it on the table. "Fifty euros? A hundred? Two hundred euros and you have to promise to sit there silent all night." I rescue my drink, disliking Charlie a bit. The target must be harder than Miles or it's really just cruelty out for a little exercise. I can't tell what's changed him in the hours since I left him at the dock.

Miles's face whitens like a pencil cleaned by a shaver. Sonny stretches her arm in front of his chest the way a mother does to a child in a fast-breaking car. I've finished my drink and pour another, caught among allegiances—to Charlie, to the new friends at the table, to what is becoming a menacing drinking habit. Damp, dark bodies pass through the night, and each one carries an electric current of desperation and restlessness. The heat of the day is rising off the ground, and the blaring music at competing tavernas is like its own form of torrential weather.

"What the hell's gotten into you?" Sonny wheezes. Her eyes freeze

on her turquoise earring pinned to Charlie's shirt, as if this accessory might be the root of the trouble. "Take that stupid thing off and
give it to me."

"No," he says, clutching it. "You put it in my bag. And, anyway,
your jewelry is safer with me." The allusion to her lost ring is an
ugly punch. Sonny's mouth shuts and her eyes widen; Louise leans
forward, as if to create a human barricade.

"I was thinking I'd visit the cave tomorrow," Louise announces,
trying to steer the conversation onto steadier shores. "The one John
wrote Revelation in. Ian, do you want to join me?"

"Yeah. Sonny, does the cave get crowded?"

"What?" She stares at me in clenched confusion. "Um, yes. No.
No, it's not crowded. Actually, I don't know." She barks an offended
laugh and returns her gaze to Charlie. A curl of tarnished hair falls
across her forehead.

"Are you sure you can come?" Louise asks me. "I don't want to
take up one of your last free days before you start your job."

"By the way, congratulations," Miles says sheepishly, holding up
his drink. "I knew you two were up to something." I tap his glass
with mine. He seems to want to say more, about the rigors of yacht
rentals or visitor statistics of the cave, but he worms his lips together,
fearful of censure.

"I've been to the cave," Adrian offers, his smile wide and innocent. "Go early. There's a monk inside who watches over the candles.
Sometimes on my morning swim, I see the monks bathing in the
sea. They go in naked, two at a time. I saw that one from the cave,
all hair up here"—he scoops an imaginary beard at his jawline—
"and totally hairless everywhere else. Almost like he's not Greek. I
heard they all have boys on the island that they meet on the beaches,
but I haven't seen any. They're actually excellent swimmers." Adrian
continues describing his morning swims, providing the buffer of
harmless conversation. Sonny begins to relax in the miles of his
story, enough to leave Charlie's nastiness behind her in the rearview
mirror. She pours a round of refills and surveys the couples that

shuffle like tired, unnumbered marathoners along the cobblestones. Older gay men, a few in beaded sarongs and others with the skin damage of too many summers, scan our group and settle hungrily on Adrian. Young, soccer-shirted straight guys do the same and land on Sonny. It's an odd feeling to be picked through and not chosen, left in the discard bin of sexual appetites. But on vacation, lust sticks to the standard archetypes.

"In the sea so early it's only monks and delivery ships," Adrian explains. "Couches, air conditioners, washing machines, supplies from Athens or Turkey for the houses in Chora. Sometimes even tiny boats of workers. Rasym thinks they're boat people, fleeing their home countries. Syrians or Afghanis sneaking onto shore at dawn. They're all over the islands this summer because of the wars."

Miles whimpers, indicating he has relevant information on the matter of migrants, if only someone would ask for his opinion.

"Why isn't the Greek coast guard stopping them?" Sonny asks.

"Because then they'd have to deal with them," Charlie grumbles.

An Italian teenager, too adolescent even to threaten Charlie in his current mood, points at Sonny from the sidewalk. He bunches his fingers together while his eyes roll back in simulated orgasm, and he unleashes a screeching mating call. Louise laughs, but the recipient of this hormonal call, to my surprise, is unappreciative. Sonny raises a middle finger, too late for him to catch. He skips on, pulling down his friend's shorts, nearly toppling into two girls carrying plastic cups of gelato, and glides into the darkness beyond the boarded storefront.

The former site of Nikos Taverna, thirty feet from our table, is the only square along the waterfront veiled in blackness. The rest of Skala is a fluorescent factory of consumption and noise. But this unlit void, drowned in its own absence, feels almost soothing by contrast. I try to imagine the chairs and tables set in the sun that morning, in the exact spot where stale clumps of flowers now lie, the food and the coffee cups and the ankles crossed, the milliseconds of normalcy before the event, with one table left empty where Charlie would usually sit. But every time I picture the blast, my brain pulls back and I watch it from a distance. I can't enter the white of the explosion, the deep thrash, the melt. By some failure of imagination, I'm ten feet away, twenty, now scanning the view from one of the yachts anchored in the water.

"I hope you won't be gone before August fifteenth," Sonny says to Louise. "They do a huge, all-night party on the beach by your cabins for the Assumption of Mary. It's really wonderful. I want to take Duck and dress her in little shells."

"What was Mary assuming?" Adrian asks. I can't tell if he's joking or just oblivious to Christianity.

"Hopefully the worst," Louise replies. "I always wondered if she even had a choice when God approached her. Like, could she have politely declined? *Sorry, I'd love to help, but virgin birth, public shaming, and exile is not exactly how I pictured my teens.* Better to be a distant observer. Keep the tragedies far away." She smiles weakly like she's confessed a shortcoming.

"Oh, I don't know." Sonny sighs as she chews on a stirrer, flattening it between her teeth. "What is that Chinese curse? May you live in interesting times. I mean, it must have been thrilling. She was probably one of those sad girls staring out windows, always listening to her iPod and waiting for the right car to come along."

"Rasym doesn't like Mary," Adrian says casually, as if she'd performed some personal slight against him.

Sonny laughs. "Why am I not surprised?"

I keep waiting for Louise to answer Sonny's question about staying. Lurching through the intoxication of my first two drinks, I'm dreading her departure.

"We could go to the party together," I suggest, as if my mere enthusiasm is reason enough for her to extend her vacation. "You won't leave before then, will you?" But my question is lost to the phone she has pointed at me.

"Ian, get closer to Charlie." I make an awkward incline toward Charlie's shoulder, but he keeps his face turned away. Louise presses the button and examines the shot. "Let's see, what should the caption be?"

A horn blows from the sea. A small commuter ferry enters the harbor, and the cruise ship blasts its horn, a playground bully with a louder, deafening baritone. Yachts begin to clear from its path, and several tourists scurry toward the dock with their luggage. Their hustling movement has the sense of rapid escape. My eye travels back to Nikos Taverna, and by reflex, I quickly examine the ground around our table for unattended bags or alarm clocks wired to suspicious packages. Only red straws and napkins litter the stones.

"You okay?" Louise asks.

"I'm fine," I reply. I pour more vodka into my glass. I need to slow down my intake. The back of my skull is threatening to blow open, as if by a slow-motion gunshot blast, and I'll be the one tomorrow picking brain matter off my pillow. I didn't drink like this back home.

Bodies move in the darkness of the boarded storefront. Flip-flops crunch the dead flowers. It's not entirely vacant. Teenagers have settled into its shadows as a temporary freedom zone, a parentless corner for the passing of a small metal pipe, oblivious of the carnage that has afforded their secret hideout. The commuter ferry releases a small congestion of arrivals. Old Greek women fly from door fronts like feeding starlings. They cross the street to proffer pictures of rooms for rent. A congregation of hippies with bloated backpacks and creased guidebooks ignores the signs and is greeted with hugs and fist bumps by friends. A few hippies are passing out yellow flyers by the taxi stand under the shiny green beards of eucalyptus trees.

"I've seen that girl before," Sonny says, gesturing to a young woman exiting the ferry with hair that runs to her waist. It shimmers gasoline pink in the lamplight and frames a delicate face with long eyes and a pronounced chin. "I swear I have. On this island."

"If it were the same one, she wouldn't be arriving on the ferry right now," Adrian notes.

"I guess they all start to look alike. Look how pretty she is," Sonny says magnanimously and then revises it. "Well, more cute than pretty. I kind of envy them. Just let everything grow and wash your clothes in the sea. When you're that young you don't need hygiene." Sonny slumps against Louise. "Should we try it?"

Louise rolls her eyes. "I once took a cross-country bus on three days of no showering. When we passed into Kentucky, the man behind me said, 'Kentucky is the lunatic capital of America!' I turned around and said, 'I'm from Kentucky,' which pretty much confirmed his impression."

The pretty, long-haired woman's T-shirt is screen-printed with NEW YORK in every conceivable font, running in every direction, a classic traffic jam of its own hysterical surplus.

"New York," Charlie whispers. Then he repeats it mockingly. "New York. That won't be the place."

"Won't be the place for what?" I ask. I keep hoping every time I look at him that his kindness has magically returned.

He eyes me darkly. "Can you believe we grew up there? Right in the lion's mouth." The water is still in his eyes, and red veins are invading the brown. "But he's a circus lion. The teeth are gone." Charlie's rambling like he's drunk, pulled by the riptides of the thinnest thoughts. Sonny watches him pained, as if on the shore, anxious to swim out to save him but knowing she'll likely be wrenched along. "Want to bet that girl's never even been to New York? It's better that she hasn't. Gives her something to dream about. Amnesia and insomnia. You can only go for so long under those conditions before it creates dead souls. You like New York, Miles?"

Miles's mouth jags tentatively. Like a timid cat tempted with a plate of food, he hangs back uncertain of the safety of the offering. He rubs his fingers around the side of his glass. Sonny signals with an encouraging nod for him to answer.

"Of course I do. It's not London, not home. But it's a damn fine city. Some of my best friends live there."

"So many best friends," Charlie sneers. Even if I ignored his angry smile, it's clear he doesn't mean it. "Damn fine."

"That's right." Miles sniggers skittishly.

"Jesus." Sonny moans, catching Charlie's intention.

"New York won't be the place for what?" Louise asks. She's not the sort of listener to be thwarted by rhetorical observations.

Charlie turns his attention on her as if he's only just realized she's here.

"It won't be the place to go if Greece finally folds under its own debt, gets evicted from its own currency, and this paper"—he taps his wallet on the table—"will be all the cash that's left to our names."

Adrian nods as he takes a swallow of his drink. "Greece got bailed out by Europe last time, but they might not be so lucky again. *Tick tock*, paradise on a timer. It's not their fault. What else do they produce besides getaways? I feel bad for them."

"The whole country is running on fumes, and the gears are stripped," Charlie shouts, his voice a raised hammer. "Don't you read the papers, Louise? There's no money left. They're completely bankrupt. Soon they'll be trading their children for food." He paints the destruction of Greece like it's a personal test of Louise's fortitude. "I hope you brought some extra U.S. dollars on your trip. Those will probably still be accepted."

I think of my plastic bag of cash tucked in the drawer of the nightstand. What had seemed the pit of desperation is possibly a prudent safety measure if Charlie's prediction of disaster proves true.

"None of the rich have their money in Greece anyway," Adrian says. "That's the problem. All the shipping magnates parked their fortunes in Zurich a long time ago. How there's even cash in those ATMs in Athens is a miracle." He leans back in his seat. "Want to bet the ink on those bills is still wet?"

"Stop, both of you," Sonny shrieks. "Nothing's going to happen. Charlie, just because you're in a bad mood doesn't mean the world is ending?" California sneaks into her voice, turning her attempt at assurance into a high-pitched question.

Miles throttles the arms of his chair, frantic to add his opinion, but he keeps his jaw locked, knowing that whatever he says will only win him Charlie's wrath.

"Countries, countries like this one," Sonny clarifies, "European countries, they don't devolve into bedlam. The world wouldn't allow it. America wouldn't." She reaches for her drink. Charlie must have realized he's overplayed his hand. He's making Sonny jumpy. He gently grabs her wrist across the table, as if he were handling a small nocturnal mammal.

"You're right. Nothing's going to happen," he says apologetically and nods at his own words. "Remember, I love you. I'll always make sure you're safe." Sonny retracts her arm. His spontaneous declaration of love seems so genuine I can tell she's questioning whether it's about to be turned against her. If it had sounded less sincere, she might have been able to trust it.

"Why?" she whispers. "Why are you acting like this tonight?"

A joint is tossed onto the table in front of Adrian. Rasym squats down next to his boyfriend's chair. He uncrumples a yellow flyer and flashes it at Charlie. It's an invitation to a barbecue at the hippie beach with the drawing of a cross rising from a bonfire. *All are welcome, some are called #RevelationParadise.* Adrian rolls the joint between his fingers and lights it. For a second, until he starts coughing with amateur convulsions, I feel as if I have discovered the source of his happiness.

"Man, this stuff is strong," he gasps. He extends the joint in my direction. I wave it off, and he continues the offer of impairment one by one. Sonny considers a drag but shakes her head. Adrian takes another puff and the coughing returns.

"I hope you didn't buy that off the hippies," Charlie warns Rasym.

"Would I?" he counters. "Helios gave it to me." I can feel Rasym's eyes on me and I turn away, to a bank of hotel balconies high above street level, where a man and a woman lean over a railing, both topless, neither touching. Far below them, near the hotel entrance, a guy has his back to the crowds, a stream of liquid running past his sneakers. I watch until he yanks up his fly, waiting for Rasym to stop staring at me. I don't want him asking about my job qualifications. *It's too late, I've already been hired instead of you*, I resist yelling.

"Whoa," Adrian whimpers, anchoring his hand on the table. His lips shrink with the threat of a vanquished smile and his white hair is slicked upward with sweat.

Louise tries again to reignite the conversation, asking Rasym about nearby islands. Charlie's cousin, more accommodating than I expect, ticks off two or three, before the Hungarian from dinner last night slides against our table. He's dressed in a white suit, a chubby dandy, the light of his cell phone giving the cast of embalmer's fluid to his face. A red wine stain decorates his lapel like a boutonnière.

"Charlie," he warbles. "You must check out this new app I invested in." Bence rotates the screen in front of Charlie's eyes. "It's the cool new thing. You take a picture of yourself and it turns you into whatever you want to be—a horse, a boat, a fur coat, a sexy rabbit. Anything! It's going to make me a fortune. The kids are eating it up! Too cool!" His excitement is embarrassing. *Too cool!* He pats Charlie's shoulder. "I got your message. I'm sorry I was out. What luck to find you down here."

Rasym darts his head to the side, watching Bence with wary concentration.

"I didn't call you," Charlie replies.

"But my housekeeper, she took a message about last night. She said—"

"I didn't call you," he repeats furiously.

"Okay." Bence releases his hand. "I got a call from someone. If you didn't, I expect you will. We have a lot to discuss. I won't wait forever."

"Bence," Miles interjects. "The Greek government." But Charlie shoots him a look and his resolve fades. "Never mind."

"Thieves," Bence gripes. "You don't take money from the hardworking people of Europe and then cry about not being able to pay it back. Does anyone actually think they'll pay it back? All this talk of Greek pride. If you are gifted ninety-five billion, you don't get to have your pride. Though if they do get booted from the Eurozone, even better for business, yes, Charlie? Makes it easier to run a company without all the European bureaucracy tangling you up. Call me, I mean it."

Charlie shakes his head as Bence lurches away. "I didn't call that asshole."

Adrian is chanting softly next to me, a man possessed with a message from another dimension. But I slowly realize he's singing along to the music playing from the speakers, a speedy techno poem about love and last chances. His face is serene, lost in the lyrics of the song like it's the only rope connecting his mind to earth. It's music crawling into him, building a home. I remember that feeling from as far back as my First Communion, dressed in a blue suit and waiting amid a sea of unfamiliar children in the Holy Redeemer vestibule to march up the aisle. The pews of the church rippled with parental anticipation, the whole incense-heavy edginess of a ritual about to descend. Somewhere in that melee, my mother and father were together, perhaps the last time they were ever together, because a young family friend named Lily was already pregnant. In the nervousness of the church, the only thing I had to hold on to was the organ calling from the altar and the familiar lyrics of love and salvation, and I sang those verses with all my heart before my foot stepped over the doorplate and onto the flame-polished stone: "And he will raise you up on eagle's wings." Intoxication chooses strange memories to freight with importance, but I am convinced all music for me has been about trying to get back to that moment where a song touched so fast and deep I felt admitted to a stateless place, an open arm of sound. "Last chance for love," Adrian croons, his watery eyes swollen with Skala's colored lights, "I'm falling through your heart." I wish we could all sing with him, wiring into each other, wiping the bad taste of the evening away.

"Adrian, drink some water," Sonny says, handing over a bottle. I reach for it to pass along and accidentally knock over the vodka bottle on the table.

"Ian," Charlie yells, saving the bottle, only to find it empty. He looks at me with fury, his lips snarled. I didn't expect his hostility to be aimed at me. "When did you start drinking so much? You didn't tell me you had a problem."

"I'm just nervous—" I choke.

"I can't take it anymore," Miles cries. He slaps his palms on his armrests. At first I assume he means Charlie's temper, but he's leering out at the sidewalk in the direction Bence went. What he can't take, apparently, is policed silence. "That man is an idiot. Why would being evicted from the European Union help a business? Doesn't he understand that vacationers aren't going to want to spend two weeks drifting around an unstable country? When did the facts stop mattering?"

"I thought you were going to be quiet," Charlie growls.

Miles exhales in irritation. "I'm allowed to speak my mind, Charles. I don't appreciate—"

"Then what about the facts on you?" Charlie says almost warmly. "Why don't you tell us about your time in London. I've asked a few friends."

Miles gawks at him, spooked, as if it never occurred to him that reputations could travel across borders, less worn than the men who run from them. I know that frightening math problem adding up on Miles's face; it's the look of the world catching up.

"How much do you owe back there? You can be honest with us."

"Stop," Sonny shouts so forcefully she attracts stares from neighboring tables. "Whatever you're doing, stop it right now." Miles places his hand on her leg to settle her. But that simple motion finally sends Charlie spiraling on the course he seems to have been hunting for all along.

"Sonny, if you don't tell him to stop fondling you, I will." Sonny and Miles both peer down at his hand as if it has inadvertently slipped inside her shorts.

"I haven't—"

"At least have the decency to admit what you are. A parasite. A little bug that feeds on the blood of others. It's okay. You've been that way since you were a kid. Just say it. I'm a little parasite. Say, I keep groping Sonny in hope that she'll feel sorry enough for me—"

"He doesn't grope me," Sonny says. "He's my friend. You're the one acting—"

"Charlie," I whisper, trying to pull him out of whatever kamikaze mission he's attempting merely to put two days' distance between him and his house. "Maybe we should take a walk along the water."

He ignores me, keeping his sights on Miles. "I guess we should all be thankful you haven't stolen from us yet." Charlie slaps me on the shoulder, his first gesture of friendship all night. "Ian, you can be objective. You're the most honest person I know. Would you trust Miles for a minute alone with your wallet? Think carefully. From what I hear, it's quite a risk."

Miles gets to his feet, whatever last ounce of pride pulsing into his fists. He steps menacingly around the table and stops in front of Charlie, glaring down. His teeth are pressed over the bitter, white onion of his lip, and a quiver runs through the muscles of his cheeks. There is an age one reaches where the possibility of a fistfight seems as improbable as fame or an advanced degree in medicine. Miles stands hesitantly, clearly astonished to find that the age limit has been extended.

Charlie smiles up at him. But I can see the tears unmistakably now, the sopped swollen pouches under his eyes, as if Charlie is the one who's hurt, as if he's sacrificing the best part of him to give Miles an opportunity to defend himself.

"Don't hit him!" Sonny yells. She nearly topples the table, and Louise springs up to steady her. "Miles, don't. He isn't worth it."

Rasym moves to catch Miles's arm but is blocked by the cordon of chairs. Just as Miles seems to have gotten a stranglehold on his anger, Charlie looks up at him. The condescending smile is waxed across his face. "You can't hurt anyone, can you?" he whispers. "Even when you try."

It takes a certain courage to punch a crying man. And in the second before the blow, a breeze runs through the port, carrying napkins from neighboring tables and sand from distant islands. The breeze is so soft I think it might even pacify Miles, but it doesn't. As the candles snuff, Charlie gets what he came for: a second black eye to match the first.

CHAPTER 7

This is the darkest place," Louise says stumbling. After hours of bleached morning sun, the cave is a blindfold, and we take tiny possum steps waiting for our eyes to adjust. The end of the world is nothing if not dark. Yellow, ropey flickers beat faintly on candles staked in dishes of sand. A tall, robed monk with a gray beard mutely stands watch amid the tight threads of smoke. His knuckles are as brassy as the sconces that hang around him in the fold beyond the entryway. His face pulses with the flames. The walls start to define themselves, billows of steel wool, and as we creep forward two wood benches bisect the widest region of the cave. A tourist sits with her head bent in prayer, and her companion, glowing with sweat, covertly eats grapes as brown as pennies out of a plastic bag. According to Louise's guidebook, the granite ceiling contains "a triple crack, which is said to be caused by the voice of God." But the low, brooding ceiling has a zillion cracks running and looping across it. We pause in front of an icon of a man lecturing his dwarfed assistant and an altarpiece of Jesus sitting amidst a gnat-like cloud of angels. A parallelogram of sharp white light punctures the darkness in the corner, a small window framing the Aegean like a hole drilled into a skull. The eastern half of the cave, the windowed half, is more spacious and chapel-like with its meticulous stonework, terrazzo floors, and spidery candelabras. I'm guessing John was exiled to the western lizard crevice. Saints must suffer, that seems to be the only rule. Louise moves toward a drape of red fabric smoothed along a shelf of rock. She holds her hand over it as if to pick up divine vibrations.

Most tourist attractions come stocked with pro forma associations: Venice, derelict romance; the Empire State Building, ruthless con-

quest. But in the Cave of the Apocalypse, I'm stuck for an appropriate response. It just feels heavy, sunken, an empty bomb shelter
left over from someone else's war. The two-euro entrance fee seems
entirely reasonable for the birthplace of mass annihilation.

Louise, however, is not stuck. "The darkest place," she repeats
solemnly. The lull of Kentucky rolls through her voice like moon-
shine vapors, but the cave doesn't echo it. It swallows voices. "On all
of Earth. Think what nightmares came from here, the plagues and
demons and reels of destruction, everything we still think of as the
end of the world. You can almost hear the beat of the horsemen's
gallop."

"I think that's water dripping from the spigot outside."

She pulls her nightstand Bible from her book bag, a tattered
white airport tag from CDG to ATH still taped around the strap.
She thumbs to the end. Her eyes are better at handling the gloom
than mine. *"And after that he must be loosed a little season."* She quotes
softly, the saliva of her lips shining in the shadows. "Frightening,
isn't it? *Must be. Must be loosed."* I never stopped to ask Louise if
she's religious. It seems to belong to the great antique trash heap of
get-to-know-you questions. For a moment, I picture Louise as a little
girl jumping on a trampoline in her backyard, trying to get airborne,
to break from gravity and into the chambers of a rain-clenched sky,
while inside her Kentucky house is a rickety kitchen table covered
with loaded revolvers.

Louise touches her palm to my chest. I flex my pectoral muscles.
For a reason I didn't quite understand, we slept last night in our separate beds. "I expected more visitors," she says.

"It's strange to visit a place dedicated to something that has yet to
happen. And I guess it isn't exactly uplifting as far as pilgrimages
go. Six-six-six. The beast with seven heads. The whore of Babylon.
Maybe John should have collected cats." I can sense rather than see
Louise's eyes straining to grasp my meaning.

"Huh?"

"Like Hemingway's house in Key West. It's just a writing room, isn't it? There's probably a gas leak in here, because honestly from what I remember, it's pretty much the recipe of a bad acid trip. It's like peering into a mirror smeared in feces. No matter what you look like, it can't be that bad."

Louise wanders off to a corner. I get the feeling I've disappointed her, not taken Armageddon seriously, and when I follow behind her I aim for gravity. We're again at the icon of John, a sword pointing from the sky toward the back of his head, as if he's reciting a list of hostage-negotiation requests.

"I read it over last night in bed," Louise says. "And, when it really gets nasty, I was surprised by how good it felt." She sounds like she's describing porn, and maybe that's what it is for the faithful, a faucet of release. "This part about Babylon on fire." She turns a page. "He gets so specific, like an auction catalog at Sotheby's. *The merchandise of gold, and silver, and precious stones, and of pearls, and fine linen, and purple, and silk, and scarlet, and all thyine wood, and all manner vessels of ivory, and all manner vessels of most precious wood, and of brass, and iron, and marble.* He mentions pearls like ten more times. He really hated pearls. But he overdoes it to the point that he sort of revels in each item he's destroying, like a shameful connoisseur."

"You know what I hate? Lapdogs on private jets. I wish he'd predicted that."

I finally succeed in making Louise laugh. She checks that the monk isn't monitoring us.

"Funny, I was making my own list last night. Diamond-encrusted cell phones. Monogrammed designer champagne holders. Orange Lamborghinis. A cafeteria table of stuck-up eighth-grade girls."

"Burn it. Burn it all. You're right, it feels good."

"Black-oak yachts with indentured servants on board."

It's a dig at Charlie, more transparent to me, perhaps, than it is to her, because Louise keeps grinning at our joke. I feign a closer examination of the altarpiece. After the scene last night in Skala, Charlie deserves some blowback. All morning I've been trying to rescue the kind, loving Charlie from the memory of him mowing down each of us with insults. Even if it had been his method of escaping to Bodrum for a few days undetected, he overperformed it, each attack too pointed and precise. Maybe Louise can afford to hate him, but I can't. I need Charlie, my employer, the generous friend. I hold on to his words at the dock: "more than brothers." I believe it because I've tested it, and it held.

The monk grabs a fistful of fresh candles from a hidden cache and beckons me over to take one. He nods to a brass box for coins by the dishes, and I slip a euro in the slot, a prayer jukebox. As I light the candle and wedge it in the sand, I ransack my head for a suitable prayer. Duck has peace on Earth covered, and asking for Louise to stay feels too petty and self-serving. *No end*, I think. *Or, no, a quick end for everyone, with no warning first. Maybe a minute of warning. Actually thirty seconds. Ten. Cancel that. I pray for the refugees, for everyone running, that they make it safely from their homes and never return.*

Louise pulls out her phone to snap a picture, but the monk lobs a warning to her in Greek while forming a stop sign with his hand in the universal *no photographs* gesture.

We take another lap around the cave, but all we find are more alcoves of leaden rock, cold and swept of dust. There isn't even a hole leading to a deeper cavern. Vital information seems to be missing, a reason or a clue. Finally, Louise and I step outside and blend into the sunlight. The dry air and sizzled hillside scrub feel like a homecoming. It's all still here, the gaudy, blue world.

"Do you know how it ends?" Louise asks, waving the Bible as we climb the stairs toward the exit.

"Yeah, it's Apocalyptic literature. It only ends one way."

"It ends with a wedding," she says, stuffing the book into her bag. "The bride waits for the groom at the altar. And he shows." She rubs her thumb across my upper lip. "You had a sweat mustache." I reach for her backpack and make my own adjustment, tearing the airport tag from the strap. I don't like the reminder of her being in transit. She balks, as if she might have been saving it, the way, as kids, we'd keep ski-lift passes on our coat zippers, letting the sticky paper fossils hang as emblems of heroic Christmas vacations careening down mountains in Aspen or Klosters-Serneus.

"Sorry. Did you want that?"

"No," she says, reddening. "Let's just go."

Passing through a gravel courtyard and the front gates with its warped white arch, we reach the blacktop. A sagging figure in scratchy brown burlap sits on a square of cardboard in the roadside weeds. Wedged in his fist is a waxy paper Coca-Cola cup, change filling enough to cover its base and make a plaintive rattle—likely, the coins are his own contribution to encourage the custom of giving. He looks like a rain-damaged watercolor of an old man, burns and rashes bubbling along his bloated arms and outstretched leg. It takes me a minute to realize his other leg is missing, just a pant strip balled against his upper thigh. There's no indication of how he managed to end up here in the half hour we were in the cave. He shakes his cup into a melody. I know that spare-change rhythm so well from New York I could sing along to it—*help, help the homeless, help, help the homeless.*

"Charity for one of the last devoted," he croaks, surprising us with his English. Louise digs into her pocket and withdraws two euros to drop in the cup.

"Pretty girl." He stares up admiringly, squinting even though his dirty face is covered in shade. "I'm disabled." He pats the empty area of his lost limb. "I got this in a long battle with s-, s-, s- . . ."

I try to imagine him as a soldier, thirty years younger, before he found religion, when he still had hope and bipedal aspirations. I want to help fill in his stutter: *S, S, S—. Cyprus? Syria? Sin?*

"Circulation," he finally utters. "They had to remove it. I had no choice. But do you think they cared how it left me?" He nods toward the gray monastery high above us. "Do you plan to visit the relics up there?"

"Not today," Louise says. "Is it worth visiting?"

He looks like he's tasted sour meat. "No," he spits. "I belonged to their order once. But they threw me out. Do you know why?" We don't have a clue. But in my years of working with homeless addicts, I've learned to park my expectations very close to the sidewalks of mistreatment and neglect. Right or wrong, the blame always lies in the hands of the door shutter, not in the face upon which the door is slammed. "Because I alone followed the rules of the Lord." He taps his remaining leg, and his black toes wiggle adroitly like spoiled pets. "I wouldn't put up with their sins. Each one rotten, pretending he is a servant of God. But do you know what god they serve in that castle? Money." The word reminds him of his cup and he jiggles it at me, Louise's contribution adding a tinny maraca. "You haven't given."

I open my wallet and tuck a five note into his instrument. His face beams.

"Don't look for the righteous in that monastery. Like wildflowers, you will find them in plainer sight. They tossed me out, a cripple, to fend for myself. All they are is wicked landowners, running every kind of atrocity, and they invent new sins each year. Can you believe they can still think of new ones? They do, and no one can stop them. New sins all the time!" His mouth is a sucking industrial toilet. I assume he's going to spit, as if on their memory, but he's merely clearing his throat. He reaches behind his back to collect a bottle of water, the seal breaking as he turns the cap. Someone cares for him, carpools him here for his afternoon playing the madman for tips, and ensures he has fresh drinking water. We say good-bye, and he screams after us, "It should end with Jude, not John! Do yourself a favor! Tear the last pages out! It's a wicked end!"

"I was beginning to think there weren't any beggars on Patmos," Louise says. "I passed a whole caravan of refugees on my way up here, just huddled together in the rocks by the port. It was the sad-dest thing. Women were holding on to their kids like life vests. But they weren't begging. I wonder where they'll go."

"I'm guessing not to the monastery."

"That's something you could do, if you're still looking for ways to help." She jabs her finger in my arm, the black cross tattoo faded under the lowest knuckle.

I smile tightly. "You, um, don't actually believe in Revelation, do you? You're not a real Christian. What I'm getting at is—"

"What?" Louise gasps, as if I've accused her of putting cigarette butts in the man's donation cup. "Oh my god, Ian, no." I enjoy getting a rise out of her. The harshness of her voice lifts, and a tiny season of unreliable weather breaks through the merciless pressure front of her control. "Although there are times I wish I could. It solves so much, doesn't it?" She stops on the road and looks at me. Her skin is the color of boat sails when the last of the sun hits them, a hazy desert pink. "My parents were big into religion. The extreme born-again variety. And I remember at fourteen, I sat them down and told them I didn't believe, that being born once was cool enough for me, and I wouldn't go to church anymore. I thought there would be a fight, I even had a bag packed. But they took it amazingly well. We hugged. It was fine. They loved me. I loved them. They went to church and I stayed home. They were really wonderful parents." Her brown eyes tighten and she turns her head to the traffic winding up the valley. A tinted tourist bus stops and reverses by the gates to the cave. The cup begins to rattle with insistence. "But the very night I told them and every night until I left for college, I locked my bedroom door before I went to sleep."

"Why?" I try to imagine a loving Kentucky family where its children ritually barricade their doors before bed. "What were you afraid of?"

"It was so long ago, I don't even know. Weird, isn't it? I was weird. Although they were the ones who believed in demons, so we were all a bit deranged. Most families are, aren't they? Weird?" She pulls my arm to keep us moving. I fight the urge to kiss her; she hasn't locked her bedroom door on me.

"You can't blame me for asking," I say. "You have a cross tattoo."

"Oh, it's a design I call a postcollege mistake," she says rubbing the knuckle. "I don't know what I was thinking. It could have been a diamond or the face of Jerry Garcia on a different day. Maybe I wanted to own my past, take it up as mine. But that's just putting an adult spin on a stupid decision. I've been a lot of people between the one you knew in college and now. Not all of them sensible. It's a souvenir of one of them, I suppose." She studies the error inked on her finger. "You see all these crosses and almost forget it's a sign of public execution. It might as well be an electric chair." She laughs. "We're going swimming, right? Let's hit Petra Beach. It's close, and there's a nice taverna there that Sonny took me to."

"Where did you park your bike?"

Louise and I met at the cave. I crept off this morning under the guise of visiting Charlie on *Domitian*. I can't convincingly report on his condition to Sonny if I didn't clear a few hours alone. What did he ask me to tell her? That he's still upset and not ready to come home? Instead of *Domitian*, I went to a restaurant in Kampos and ordered a breakfast of hummus and eggs. It felt human to be able to choose anything I wanted on the menu without worrying over the cost. I texted him while eating: MANAGE TO GET AWAY? No answer. YOU AND I ARE HANGING OUT RIGHT NOW. YOU'RE EXTREMELY SORRY FOR BEING A DICK. No answer. I texted him again as I paid the bill. WAITING FOR WORD. IN THE MEANTIME, I MIGHT GIVE MYSELF A RAISE. I grab my phone now to see if Charlie has responded. The screen is just a series of my sent messages, glowing green thought bubbles without a single reply.

"I'm over by the rock wall," Louise says. She casts her eye down at my phone, and when I cover it with my hand, she smirks. "Is it Charlie?"

"I saw him earlier," I say.

"I'm guessing he didn't apologize," she replies. I shrug vaguely. Lying to Louise feels a degree beyond my duties. "It's been a long time since I've seen someone behave like he did."

"He's never like that. I think he's just been overwhelmed with work. The stress was getting to him."

"Overwhelmed." She test-drives the word and finds it lacking horsepower. "When you're overwhelmed, do you lash out at those you presumably care about?"

"Well, he got punched for it, didn't he?"

Louise puffs her cheeks. "I didn't know Miles had it in him. I was actually impressed." She rubs her neck. "Not impressed. Startled is more like it. I was under the impression that Miles couldn't squash a mosquito, not unless Sonny was in danger of being bitten."

"You think he's obsessed with her?"

"No doubt about it," she says. "But who cares? Is it so awful to be infatuated with someone who doesn't love you back? He didn't deserve to be attacked like that. None of us did."

I so badly want to confide in her that it was all a ruse, that it was simply Charlie's tactic for creating a rift, with the additional benefit of dropping Miles from his constant periphery. But I keep my mouth shut as we approach her bike.

"I asked you the night you arrived if you thought Sonny was happy," she says. "Do you still think she is?"

"It was one fight. I'm sure they've had plenty. It seems to be their way." Louise nods, but the length of her stare, into worlds beyond the ground at our feet, indicates she doesn't agree. "You obviously don't think she's happy."

"I can't shake the feeling that she's always performing for him. Not as in former actress. Fine, she's dramatic. I mean in a deeper way. Maybe performing for herself too. Telling herself this is what she wants, this is the best she can hope for."

"And by this, you mean Charlie."

"It's like she's much realer without him. And when he enters the room a light hides behind a door and all you get is this faint incandescence. Charlie doesn't hide for her. Look how he behaves. He has the luxury of acting however he wants, and since he does, we can judge him by it. A hummingbird really does hum, you know."

"What does that mean? Is it a Kentucky expression?"

Louise stops at her bike, resting her hip against the black seat cushion.

"Most people turn out to be what they seem like. They usually aren't endless labyrinths of surprise."

I try to process how this depressing view of humanity applies to us. What do I seem like to Louise? Is she the only one allowed to be so many other people? For as smart as Louise is, she views the world too neatly. In her absolutism, there's no room for the in-between. Or maybe she feels that certain people need to earn their mistakes.

"I think you're reading too much into one bad night. And if we were all spectacularly ourselves all the time I'm pretty certain we'd be unbearable."

"We both know why she won't leave him," she says, patting my arm. "Just like you won't."

"Louise." Silence, a bird screaming in the bushes, and then an answer. "You've made your point. I could do something more fulfilling with my life. I get it. Can we please move on?" I'm almost ready to see her onto the ferry back to Athens if it provides a moratorium on these lectures on my moral inferiority. I could go on disappointing her from the distance of an ocean.

She races to explain herself. "All I'm saying is that he wasn't so nice to you last night either. And you've only been here a few days."

"I should stop drinking. I really don't have a problem." I sound exactly like a man with a problem. Admittedly, my hangovers are starting to ravage my mornings—not enough to leave me bed-wrecked, but to the degree that my brain cells are like passengers stranded at an airport, wasting hopeless hours until the weather lifts. "It's just the last of vacation for me. In a day or two I'll be working full-time for Charlie and I'll be going to bed at a reasonable hour."

"What are you doing for him? You never said." She pushes her bike off its stand and glides her leg over the seat.

"Support and development." Those duties seem so vague and vacuous, like code words for "hired friend," that I blush. Louise examines me, her crooked teeth trailing across her bottom lip. "And general office management. It's an expanding business. There's a lot to handle."

Louise inserts her key in the ignition. "Sounds hectic." She waits before turning the engine on, as if enjoying the warmth of the leather on her thighs. "What exactly about his business is expanding? What's his long-term plan anyway?"

"Aren't all businesses expanding? Boats. Tourists."

"I tried to find the Konstantinou Charters Web site on the Internet last night. His father's company, Konstantinou Engineering, has a zillion hits, not all of them very nice. Ugly really, with a rap sheet of violations a mile long. But I couldn't find Charlie's site."

"It's an elite clientele. They aren't promoting budget boat rentals on Yahoo. There are only ten or twelve yachts right now."

"Oh," she snaps in verdict. "Don't get too fancy, Ian. You're liable to forget the rest of us. We're not just people to sleep with."

"I didn't sign a lifetime contract," I say with a sigh. "All I'm doing is trying here. Can you please stop saving me from something I want?"

Louise nods, letting the subject drift. "I also did a search on Miles. I was curious about those accusations Charlie made about him. About owing money in London. Nothing came up. Just a zillion photos of him at boring social functions—all lawns and dinner parties and gravel driveways and ballrooms. Quite an extensive bow tie collection he has." *Lucky*, I think. Not everyone's worst transgressions end up in the septic tank of public consumption.

My phone vibrates with an incoming message. I hurry to read it, hoping to find a response from Charlie in Bodrum, news of him a-okay and heading back tomorrow, or maybe, benevolently, not to bother with the trumped-up alibi. But it's a message from my sister. My body goes cold.

DIDN'T HEAR FROM YOU. CALLING LAWYER. YOU REALLY NEED TO MAKE CONTACT. NOW. NONE OF US ARE OKAY WITH YOUR COMPLETE DISREGARD FOR OUR QUESTIONS AND CONCERNS AND WE MIGHT HAVE TO RESORT TO UNFORTUNATE ACTIONS. JUST WARNING YOU. FUCKING CALL, IAN! IS IT BEYOND YOU TO DIAL A PHONE NUMBER?

"What's wrong?" Louise asks.

"Nothing," I say, struggling to inject the ordinary levity of reading a message. "It's Charlie. He's very sorry about his behavior. Are you satisfied?"

"Beach then?" she says, securing her bag around her shoulders.

"Louise, you're a lawyer."

"Not yet. I've only done one year. I wouldn't represent myself. Why?"

"Is it illegal—" I try to frame the question so ambiguously it can't be traced to an actual situation implicating an actual person perspiring eight inches from her "—if say, someone were to die, and there was money that was for an entire party, a party like a family, and when that person died, one of the party took a little of the money, which they were regularly allowed to access, but they did so right after the death, although they never did before, because, well, anyway, my question is, would that or wouldn't it be illegal?" Running my own experience through the shredder of imprecise generalization in hopes of discovering a legal precedent is beyond me. The English language tightens into barbwire, each attempt to maneuver through it tangling me deeper in its teeth.

"Is that a question from Charlie? He must have access to better legal advice than I could provide. I haven't even taken Ethics of Finance yet. I guess technically it could be considered stealing, but only in the strictest sense. Only if the family pressed charges, and most families wouldn't. Maybe if you told me the exact situation."

"Forget it. Let me get my bike. I'll follow you."

Last night, while Louise was scouring the Internet in her cabin, I checked on the bag of money in my drawer, counting and recounting it. When Charlie returns from Bodrum, I'm going to ask him for a larger advance and send the nine thousand back to Lex and Ross in New York, no return address, just a note, *enjoy your inheritance, good luck in life.*

We roar up the hill into Chora. Although Louise is leading the way at full throttle, my skills at steering and angling the curves have become stronger with practice. Stability on a motorbike requires envisioning the road not as solid but as a yielding, permissive skin, the tires like a tongue licking the strip of an envelope. Focus too intently on the dangers, the cracks and potholes, and the fear takes over, a crash victim due to excess caution. I keep up with her on smooth blacktop, on mossy brick, on expectorating gravel, on un-mowed weed patches where stray kittens leap from the wheels like death is a ball of string. Before a steep descent from the star-white village, a little boy stands on the corner midtantrum. His mother is dressed in beach paraphernalia—a folding chair, a pair of flippers, and three towels conceal whatever swimsuit she might have on—and she tries to grab his arm, but he swings it away, feet-pounding, the fat tears rolling down his cheeks. He's not getting what he wants, a sufferer of island pleasure fatigue. I feel sorry for him. It's always the vacation tantrums that are remembered later by family members with mean fondness; vomit once at Disneyland, and you are forever age six vomiting on a wrought iron park bench whenever Disneyland is mentioned. The world is unforgiving to unhappy vacationers.

I have been trying to understand Charlie's tears all morning, why he was crying last night even as he launched his assault on Miles. There seemed to be a second, larger pain behind the first, a speeding train hiding a car crash on the other side of the tracks. It's those strange tears, even more than the dilemma of Sonny-versus-Bodrum, that leaves me aching for a single response from him.

The southlands flatten out by the sea, the weeds chirring with insects as we pass the timber skeletons of abandoned, half-built apartment complexes and the metal signs for GRIKOS. We're not far from Charlie's dock now, and Louise slows her speed, weaving through the low winds that smell of lavender and sting with salt. First it's one blue police car parked on the shoulder of the road; POLICE is written across the door in English. Then as we ascend a small hill and as the tin roof of Charlie's hangar gleams in the distance, another police car appears, this one with a siren on the roof revolving in the sun. Across the asphalt, in a field of yellow, waist-high weeds, three officers with leather bandoliers X-ed across their shirts stand in an awkward triangle, their eyes stuck on some disturbance in the grass. A young woman in tie-dye sits ten feet away on a slab of brick, sobbing into her hands; salamander tattoos writhe up her ankles. The oldest officer, his face ghosted like breath on a window, is snapping on a pair of light-blue latex gloves. It's the plastic gloves among all the loose details that puts the fear in me.

Louise and I brake simultaneously. Her mouth holds the first letter of a question—the angry kiss of a *W*. We stop our bikes beyond the police car, farther up the slant of road, and from that vantage point we both see the unmistakable line of a human arm stretching through the long, dry grass blades.

"Oh, shit." Louise clenches the handlebars, accidentally triggering the motor, which shoots her a few feet forward before she manages to stop again. The three Greek officers glance up in irritation. The youngest officer is prematurely trying to rope off the scene with yellow tape, but his clumsy attempt to yarn it through the weeds isn't working. The wind has the tape, tossing it playfully.

I'm sweating, my hands wet with perspiration, because we're so close to Charlie's dock and the fact that he hasn't responded to any of my texts hits me with terrible implication. I feel the heavy, clothy press of panic on my chest, and it takes enormous effort in those first few seconds to climb off my bike and sprint toward the body. I'm convinced it's Charlie in the grass. Every millisecond, as I'm kicking through the dust relearning how to run, I'm praying it isn't him, but I'm already bracing myself, already an hour in the future hearing Sonny's screams, a mouth like a window that will never shut, and the silence of my own mouth gone dry. The older officer whips around as I thread into the high grass, scything weeds. His plastic-covered hands lift out to catch me as he commands in gibberish, "*Rombaducke laf oxi.*" I pivot, push him aside by the shoulder, my jaw already hurting from its lock, and find the corpse splayed out in front of me.

A pair of hunter-green army shorts, a torn red T-shirt with an indecipherable insignia twisted across punctured ribs, a torn, meaty ear like an upturned bell toward the sky. The skin of the body is batiked in purples and greens, a bloated suitcase left out in the rain. Thick streams of blood cover the neck and jaw, not red but cellophane-clear in the sun glare. Dirt or flies are embedded in the shine. I take a careful step, straining to catch the face, just one rapid glance before reeling back, as if I can steal the identity and not the expression. A blond beard sprouts around a hollow of mouth. A gold hoop is clamped to the septum amid the rubble of smashed bone. My first relief is who it isn't: not Charlie. It's one of the Christian hippies, the ripped, red shirt once reading ANTI-BETHLEHEM. The side of his skull is dented into the earth, the one visible eye a flat, gray deposit. The expression, what's left of one, communicates shock: like a snapshot frozen at the moment of death saying *whoa, my turn already?* Not far from him lies the body of a woman, curled in the dirt. Long, blood-matted hair covers her face, and her bare leg is weighted down by the steel crumple of a motorbike. Shards of plastic and mirror are sprinkled across her orange T-shirt. Then the smell hits me, not harsh decomposing rot, but a faint *off* odor like cold cuts past their expiration date. I shut my breathing off to stop the smell from reaching me.

"You must get back," the older officer yells. "Off, back, away." The worry recedes, and the nausea of seeing two dead bodies fills its place. I no longer want to see, and with Charlie alive, breathing, still among us, I can't understand why I'm standing amid bodies and bike wreckage in an open field. Louise rises on tiptoes across the road, holding her stomach. "Do you know them?" the officer asks.

"No," I say, stepping back, the yellow tape caught around my shins. "I think they might be hippies from that camp not far from here." I relay this information so impassively, like a hypnotist's induction, I'm not certain he understands a word I'm speaking. "What happened?"

He shrugs. "That girl over there find them. Maybe driving bike they go off edge." He points upward, toward the sharp descent from a series of lower outlying hill cliffs. The placement of the bodies in this gulley seems a supernatural distance away from the drop. "Or maybe they hit by a car, run off the road when it is still dark. Vacationers very reckless on *motosikletes*. We get a few deaths from them every summer." He nods to our own bikes like they're complicit animals, local carnivores who prey on tourists. He's already pinning the blame on the dead.

The careening singsong of a European ambulance breaks the quiet, and, light-headed, I snap the tape from my legs and stagger across the road to Louise. She looks far more fragile in her shorts and tank top than she did two minutes ago. I want to put my arms around her and do what only the living can do: stand still and breathe and touch another person.

"What is it?" she demands, gripping my shoulder.

"Two hippies on a bike. They're dead." I lean against my seat, waiting for the face to dissolve from my mind and the spoiled smell to leave my nose. "Maybe an accident. They're bloody."

Louise grimaces as if she's fighting her own urge to vomit. "An accident. Why did you race over?" she asks. "I thought you'd lost your mind."

I can't tell her I feared it was Charlie. We were supposed to be texting only a few minutes ago. "I was worried it might be someone we knew," is all I manage.

Not far behind the sobbing girl, a woman lingers, late-fortyish, plump, wearing the floral-patterned shirt and shorts of a weekend gardener, gingerroot veins protruding from her thick calves, and her neck slung with hemp ropes. Three wristwatches are strapped to her right arm. Her round face looks too vulnerable for Mediterranean sunlight, the kind of pale skin accustomed to snowfall and calamitous winters behind storm windows. She watches the officers and us with surprising tranquility, as if she isn't experiencing but recalling this horrible incident from some easier future, calibrating and studying it. Her calmness unnerves me, and I'm briefly thankful when her lips contort in pain. But it's the beginning of a coughing fit. She balls her hand against her mouth. The ambulance roars over the bend and pulls to a stop, adding a belated sense of emergency, as if there has been hope of resuscitation all along, just lost on the winding Patmian roads.

"We should leave," I say to Louise. "I don't want to be here anymore. Those bodies—" But the images are still too clear in my mind to fit words onto them; they reach the boundary in the brain where language ends and all that's left is the orange whirl of broken syllables, a linguistic charnel house. Other bikers round the hill and pause to take in the activity. The young officer lifts a natty brown scarf from the grass and a sharp instrument that looks like a wooden spike. His two seniors in command step over to examine the discovery. I get the feeling that the island police force was trained by American crime shows on the virtues of appearing overly inquisitive to any random debris found near a body.

"Carrie, come along." The coughing woman takes the hand of the crying girl and tries to lead her away.

"But Dalia and Mikael," the tattooed girl murmurs. The New Jersey of her voice takes me back to the two trespassers on Charlie's dock. She was one of them, and the other with the gold nose ring now lies dead in the grass.

Louise looks over at me, her eyes shrunken. "I'm not up for the beach anymore."

"Me neither. I wish we had gone another way."

"I think I'll just go back and lie down. This must happen all the time." Louise swears, squeezing her neck.

"That's what the officer said."

"It's dangerous how they just rent these bikes to anyone."

"Promise me you'll wear your helmet from now on," I yell as I collect mine from the seat compartment.

"Are you coming back with me or not?" Louise asks.

"I told Charlie I'd visit Sonny. I'll see you at home."

We drive cautiously away from the scene, taking the hill in low gear, overly obedient to each stop sign. Gone is the thoughtless rhythm of speed. As I wave good-bye to Louise and make the turn toward Chora, my brain hones in on details I wish it could forget—

not the plastic gloves or the delicatessen odor or the nose piercing on the smashed, astonished face. I remember Charlie at his dock not twenty-four hours ago, screaming a threat to two hippies about not making it out in one piece.

At the top of the hill, I check my phone. Nothing. I try calling and after six aquatic rings a voice breaks through the electronic ocean.

This is Charlie. You know what to do. Leave a message.

CHAPTER 8

When my grandfather died in 2006, my father, half-sister, half-brother, and I flew to Michigan for the funeral. We watched a meteor shower rain sideways through the night over the parking lot of the airport Marriott, and the next day, we watched the casket lower into Muskegon Holy Catholic Cemetery beside my grandmother's grave. After that, to all of our surprise, there was very little of my grandfather to dispense with.

What did remain barely filled a few swept rooms of his white Sears Roebuck farmhouse. Most of his clothes had already been folded into grocery bags labeled for pickup by St. Vincent de Paul. The inventory of his kitchen cutlery consisted of one fork, two spoons, a butter knife, and a can opener. The refrigerator was bare, the shelves glowing antiseptic white like mopped hallways in a hospital, and his other appliances were stowed with their power cords cobra-ed around their bases. Post-it notes on his television, radio, and electrical panel ("turn on water heater ten minutes <u>after</u> pump") gave insightful instruction to anyone who cared to operate them. When we phoned the gas company to cancel service, we discovered that my grandfather had already terminated his contract—his propane tank had been filled in the spring and he told the technician to discontinue the annual visit. Every bill was paid, every signature witnessed, and belatedly (one day after the requiem mass) Lex found a list of funeral songs for which he'd always had a special fondness stuck in the front flap of his address book. When we opened the barn, I half expected the original boxes of the 1934 kit house to be stored inside, waiting for the dismantled parts to be returned to the manufacturer.

My father took palpable pride in the man's foresight to dwindle down the baggage of his estate. "So considerate, your grandpa, so like him, not to be a burden. He wanted to go as easily as he came. Did you ever once hear him complain about his years serving in Korea? He barely mentioned it, even when I was little. It just *was*, no whining. I hope you'll always think of him this way. Simple, clean." There was no denying that he had gone easily. *Clean*. Really, all that was needed was a realty sign in the front yard, and the entire Bledsoe foothold in Muskegon County would disappear like a few uncharacteristically mild days in a long and sweltering summer. Lex, Ross, and I, however, found the whole thing creepy. Clearly our rheumy-eyed, semimute grandfather had made a hobby out of his death preparations, and if he hadn't been felled by a heart attack in the meat aisle of IGA, we might have suspected suicide. It proved difficult to mourn a relative who had drawn such scrupulous plans for his own nonexistence, and deprived of grief in our weeklong visit, we devolved into greedy grandchildren. The three of us, or really me versus my half-siblings, fought like rival heirs over the smallest, cheapest, Post-it-less artifacts: a cracked softbound Bible; a collection of pewter tie clips; a pane of stained glass that might actually have just been a shoddy hardware-store patch job. We ran through the rooms in a frenzied game of hide-and-seek, except ours was find and keep.

Ross got the tie clips. Lex received two oak rush chairs that my grandmother had hand-braided. And I was directed toward the attic to claim the inheritance my father felt I deserved. "That's the real prize, anyway. You love history."

"Do I?"

"Well, more than your sister and brother."

The triangular attic doubled as a rodent hospice; amid piles of bright-blue poison pellets, the brown mice that hadn't yet succumbed were flinching and twisting in their final death throes. In the corner sat a cardboard Schlitz Beer box filled with newspapers and magazines. It rattled with mouse poop as I carried it down the ladder.

The box contained a century of headlines, and as I dealt them out one by one across the kitchen table, I realized my grandparents had spent their entire lives collecting souvenirs of the worst atrocities to beat a path to their front porch in the morning. Wars, famines, assassinations, blimp disasters, epidemics, celebrity suicides, mass graves, bombs dropped here, hostages taken there, sieges, explosions, congressional witch hunts, threats of nuclear annihilation, and shockingly for two devout Michigan Republicans, a seemingly endless obsession with *Newsweek*'s and the *Muskegon Star*'s coverage of Waco and AIDS. The box of horrors was pure and unmitigated. As I neared the bottom I hoped to unearth one solitary piece of good news—PEACE! or WAR OVER or Man on Moon or even "President Gerald Ford welcomes granddaughter." There lay only pink insulation balls that the mice had pilfered for winter nests.

Ross wore three tie clips along the placket of his button-down. Lex relaxed into the instability of her antique chair. I tossed the newspapers and magazines back in the box. "I don't want any of it," I groused.

"You might be able to eBay the Kennedy stuff," Lex said maliciously. "Ten, maybe fifteen dollars."

"Ha, ha, fuckface."

It wasn't about me being the slighted grandchild. Or, at least, not *only* that. The bizarre contents of the box ate away at my impression of my grandparents as preternaturally kind and oversweetened lemonade drinkers who sent mildewed, perfectly timed birthday cards and hugged at different ages on their doorstep in every snapshot we had of them. The fact that my grandfather didn't throw away this particular box when even the family photo albums were missing and presumed discarded only confirmed the sinister double life that began to superimpose itself onto my memory of them. I pictured my grandfather hurrying in with the morning newspaper, stomping his boots of snow on the mat. "Look, Jean! A famine in Ethiopia!" or "The *Challenger* exploded in midair!"; my grandmother advancing from the kitchen, steering around the walnut sideboard, her blue-veined hands clenched in mirth: "Quick, you fool! Add it to the box!"

Of course, it could have been that he simply didn't have the heart to go through those clippings one last time.

My father took enough notice of my disenchantment to inform me that I was never happy and wouldn't be and it was just like me to see the worst in every gift. I tried to explain that it was technically impossible not to see the worst—that's all that was in there, the absolute worst—but he was too busy working up a deal to sell the house and land to the farmer next door. The neighbor would absorb the forty acres, demo the residence, and keep the barn for storage. On the last day, driven mad by our own loud arguing in the quiet, polite weather of Michigan, we collected in the rental car as if it were a Manhattan life raft. If anyone wondered where the newspapers and magazines went, they didn't ask. I had returned them to the attic to await the mice and demolition crews.

As we were about to drive away, my father rolled down the window and sat silently for a few minutes, staring at the maples bickering with late-summer birds and the un-curtained hollows of the house.

"Good-bye, Dad. Thank you. Rest easy," he said before putting the car in reverse. Then he beamed over at me. "I sold it for two hundred K. That's an appreciate value of one hundred and eighty thousand in seventy years. Your grandpa would have been shocked out of his socks!"

AT FIRST I'M temporarily lost. Then, after twenty minutes of climbing sharp, lopsided steps and slewing down stone ramps and along passageways hemmed between endless retina-scorching, whitewashed walls, I'm officially lost. I can't locate Charlie's house. *Halfway down an alley. A red door with a brass doll-hand knocker.* The trouble is, doll-hand knockers and red doors and dark, leaky alleys multiply like clowns in a fun house, and every new, untried path spirals me through cat-puddled corners and grated windows and acute angles of stairs that lead through low claustrophobic archways. I'm hurrying at a jogger's pace, as if speed can extinguish the memory of the roadside accident with its blood and limbs and yellow tape. Aproned Greek women watering cacti watch me with feline disinterest and scurry into their homes before chancing a showdown with the incurably adrift. Six attempts and I'm once again at the entrance to Chora with its view of Skala and languid line of gift shops peddling painted rocks and maximalist confections of copper and amethyst.

Follow a wall through a maze and you will eventually reach the exit. But is there a rule for finding your way in? I should have asked Charlie to draw me a map. I should have asked Charlie a lot of things.

I enter the nearest gift shop and ask the elderly woman at the counter if she can point me in the direction of "Charlie Konstantinou's house."

She rubs the flecks of hair on her lips. "Char-lee Kon-stan-teen-o?"

"Yes. It's his father's house. His *grandfather's*. Konstantinou. Konstantinou."

She ponders the name, which I thought I had been pronouncing correctly my entire life but clearly my American accent is molesting it.

"His grandfather's house. Old house. Shipping house. Wealthy house."

"Oh," she roars hopefully. "You want take picture. Aga Khan house?"

"No, not Khan, not Iranian. Konstantinou. Cypriot."

She smiles and repeats, "Khan."

"Konstantinou."

She points out the iron-barred window at a jewelry store. "Across street, ask." I know it's simply her method of dispatching the idiot tourist onto the next shopkeeper. It hits me, the square that leads right into Charlie's alley.

"Can you tell me where the Plateia is?"

"Which?"

"Nighttime. Party. Big crowds." I flutter my fingers to indicate fun or champagne bubbles or fast, fleeting hordes.

"Too early," she says, tapping her watch. But she guides me to the doorway and signals up the road. Then her hand fins and swims in eight different directions like a demented water snake. I'm about to admit defeat when I catch a familiar figure walking by the jewelry store, a short, white-haired man with an untroubled smile, his thumb toying the ruby ring on his middle finger. I quickly thank the woman and step into the glassy sunlight.

"Prince Phillip," I call. The old man spins around, and his smile increases in intensity but not in size. "I'm Charlie's friend. I met you the morning I arrived."

"Of course, yes." He leans forward expectantly for the reception of a kiss on each cheek. "I'm afraid I've forgotten your name."

"You never had it. Ian. Charlie and I went to school together in New York."

"Oh, then you must be the custodian of all his juicy secrets. I'll bribe you with lunch sometime and you'll have to confess them to me. I do miss the wilds of New York. What a time my wife and I had there in the 1980s, the energy and commotion. Charlie will never discuss New York, but I know he has plenty of good stories up his sleeve. Why must I be acquainted with the only under-sharer of this young generation?"

"Well, Charlie's pretty private."

"There's nothing pretty about privacy amongst close friends," he rattles. "My motto is live, live as much as you can, and have the decency to tell others about it."

"Prince Phillip, could you—" But his attention is broken by a little boy with girlish features running by on clopping flip-flops.

"William," Phillip exclaims. "Aren't you supposed to be spending the day with my grandson?"

"I stopped by, but he wasn't there."

"They've all gone to the beach. You must have been late."

The boy shrugs. "Tell him I'll come by later. Before dinner."

"Very well," he says in dismissal and turns to me as the sound of the boy's galloping flip-flops fade. "That's evidently all I'm good for anymore. Arranging playdates. Relaying messages between children. William's a Von Blücher." When that fact doesn't prod recognition, he elaborates. "His great-great-great-grandfather defeated Napoleon. They live most of the year in Gstaad now for the obvious reasons. Well, it's still a fine place." Phillip winks at me and brandishes his open, ruby-streaked hand. His thin knuckles are pocked with red spots that fizzle like a firecracker to the blackened embers of his wrist. He seems to enjoy the classification of family and country, tracking rises and defeats by resort towns. But there's also a warm, mischievous flirtation in the old prince's manner that undercuts his devotion to the tired titles of Europe. Charlie called him a mystic, and he stops, Sphinx-still, his handsome, hawkish nose tilted up like a sundial, to read the lines on my face.

"Are you unwell, Ian? If you don't mind my saying, you don't look like a man on vacation."

"I'm sorry, Prince Phillip." I'm not sure why I'm apologizing any more than whether I'm allowed to drop the royal designation. He doesn't correct me on either account. "I just saw a horrible motorbike accident. Two dead bodies by Petra Beach."

"Oooh." He groans. "Those bikes are a fast form of suicide. You must be careful. We only have one doctor on this island, and notice I didn't say a decent doctor. Last summer, a lovely neighbor of mine was bitten by a viper. By the time the doctor determined it was serious enough that she needed to be flown to Leros, she was dead. I believe it was her death that prompted his diagnosis of the bite as serious." He waves his hand again, like a conductor who has the power to release the music but not the authority to change the program. "You must be very careful."

"I wear my helmet."

"I wish we could afford better facilities, but with the economy the way it is and the sad wildfire of immigrants pouring over the islands this summer, we simply have to make do. The Greek Crisis is a permanent condition. Like Swiss Punctuality or American—." He drawls off from completing the comparison, perhaps because he's speaking to an American.

"Don't you have some influence as a member of the royal family?"

"My dear," he gasps, "I don't have an ounce of Greek blood in my veins. I'm French by ancestry. And worse, Catholic. That doesn't get me very far in local politics among the holy robes of our monastery. They hate the Catholics. Better a turban than a tiara is an expression they like to use. And it bears. They take their orders directly from Constantinople. Don't believe the maps. Patmos is very much a territory of the Middle East. And if you weren't born on Patmos, you're a foreign invader no matter how much land you own." This too is concluded with a wave of his ruby ring, and he giggles sweetly, clasping my shoulder. "Give Charlie my love, will you? And tell that girlfriend of his to come for a visit."

"Actually, I was hoping you could show me where Charlie's house is. I'm—"

"Lost," he intuits, nodding at his skills of prediction. "I'm also good at directions. We do our part, we fossils." He locks his hands behind his back, and I follow him up the slanting road. Three ducking turns, and still the empty restaurants and taped posters for pottery exhibitions are unfamiliar guideposts.

"You've known the Konstantinous long?" I ask him.

"Why, yes, for half a century, perhaps more. I met Charlie's grandfather when he first bought on the island. And, of course, his father. All good men, tough men, as Cypriots tend to be. Stefan is my godson, an honor, don't misunderstand, but I've always felt more of a kinship with Charlie. He has that flint in the eye and gold kingdoms under his eyelids, that ease in the world that his poor brother never quite mastered. Maybe Stefan didn't have the option. He was recruited since he could wobble to take over the family business. And by all accounts he has. Dubai, I think it is. Or does he live in Doha now? He occasionally sends a Christmas card."

This time the ruby-streaked hand doesn't wave but reaches into his shirt pocket to extract a cigarette. The old prince is as jittery as a Brooklyn cement truck with its round mixer constantly rotating—he's always engaged in small, restless actions for fear of hardening. Phillip tears a few centimeters off the tip before he lights it. "I bought the wrong kind at duty-free, the long ones I can't stomach. But we must be frugal. We take what we are given." Phillip is the kind of smoker who doesn't inhale. He holds the cigarette like a stick of incense, swirling it in front of us as we pass a tiny taverna with its refrigerator motors purring through the lifeless noon. A young man stands in the doorway, his shirt open and his sweaty collarbone glistening through the soapy gray light. Phillip studies him, smirks, and passes on.

"For the record, I didn't approve of that nonsense of Charlie's father cutting him off." The news stalls me for a second and I take double steps to catch up. "What's the boy to do when he's never been raised to have a real profession. I told his father that. *You have the money. Let Charlie be. He can't survive on some arbitrary skinflint allowance. He's beautifully wild.* I think their time in America has had the deleterious effect of confusing moneymakers for strong characters. It's a lost art, the art of living, of taking small pleasures. I'll be honest and risk sounding like every other ancient crank drinking at the mahogany bar of nostalgia. They don't make people like they used to. Interesting people. People like destinations. People who are entertaining instead of entertained. One day there may be a wildlife sanctuary for the last remaining characters. I thought that might be New York. Sonny assured me on our first meeting that I was hopelessly out of touch."

Phillip shakes his head at a world of new humans forged without the vestigial appendages of personalities and puffs on the white filter like a senior citizen sipping soup.

"Charlie's father demanded he get a job." I avoid the tone of a question.

"What choice did he have anyway? I doubt Stefan would have welcomed him into the business with open arms. Once his mother was too sick to defend him, it was find a career or come home. Well, Charlie did, didn't he? He's done splendidly with his charter company. Perhaps I was wrong and his father was correct. *Bon.*"

"Have you been on one of Charlie's yachts?"

"Oh, dear, no. I'm too social to isolate myself on yachts for days on end. But I see Charlie's boats coming and going from that dock he rents. I can see it from my hilltop garden. It's a booming business, and I told his father so. When Charlie started it a few years back, I thought the idea was atrocious. No chance of making money on such a minor operation. On lugging tourists from island to island for a few hot months each year. On dressing up youths from nearby islands as captains. And you know Charlie's excitement over a new idea tends to be as lasting as his patience. But he proved himself and continues to, and slowly his father's clench on the family coffers loosens. I imagine he helps fund him now. Hoping for a child's success is constructive. Demanding it is altogether different." Phillip flashes his smile at me, then curtails it as if it has dawned on him that I haven't offered a single decent story to add to his collection plate. "You *are* close to Charlie, aren't you? I haven't been spilling secrets to a stranger?"

"Very close," I say reassuringly. "In fact, I'm joining the Konstantinou Charters team, so we may get to have that lunch soon."

"A lunch! What a lovely idea," he sings, as if the offer were mine. "You must promise to bring Sonny. I fear she'll be gone one day."

Phillip's fear echoes Charlie's, and yet nothing about Sonny seems to suggest she's on the verge of packing her bags. "Why would she? You don't think she likes Patmos?"

"It's not about liking," he rasps. "But do you see marriage in Charlie's future? I don't. And honestly why would there be? It's so much nicer to be free. Although I've often thought maybe it was all those bad marriages that created the pressure cooker of interesting souls." Phillips lifts his shoulders at the mystery of it all. "What do I know?

When you get to be my age you learn that youth is not a torch you pass on to the next generations. Youth is a state from which you are dethroned."

"You can still be young at heart, right?"

Phillip winks at me. "Let's have that lunch soon. I'll be gone in a week. A friend in Vienna has a ghost I must visit."

"To exorcize?"

"Oh, I wouldn't dare. I simply keep them company. It's horribly lonely on both sides." We cross through a tunnel and into the Plateia, the cracks between its rutted stone caulked with cigarette butts and wrappers. Phillip snuffs out his smoke on the wall and gently folds it in a tissue, which he places in his shirt pocket. "*Hoo hoo*. You're that way," he says, pointing toward the alley, then shuffles across a shaft of sunlight and is swallowed in the narrow passage on the opposite side of the square.

I push on down the alley, stopping at the red door and taking the flaccid doll hand in mine. I assume the hand is meant as a greeting, but it looks more like the appendage of a consumptive Victorian hanging from the side of a bed. I bang it three times against its brass ball. Inside, footsteps advance across the wood, a lock fumbles, and the door swings wide. Sonny stares out at me, her hair pulled back tightly, her plucked eyebrows arched, and her mouth an open oval. She leans out to search the alley for another presence, her bare feet curled over the threshold. Only when she realizes it's empty does she deflate against the door.

"Hi, Ian," she says without bothering to mask her disappointment. "I thought it might be Charlie."

On the subject of disappointment, we're evenly matched. A part of me hoped Charlie might answer the door, might have decided against Bodrum and already patched up the tear that he'd been so intent on ripping last night. After the dead hippies on the road, I'm not sure I have the strength to dangle a bunch of convincing lies Sonny's way. I've come to deliver a report of Charlie bruised but fine on *Domitian*. But it occurs to me that I'm actually here on the chance of gleaning news about him. *Come here again and I can't promise you'll make it out in one piece.* Even far from the ambulance siren, those words won't leave my head. Why hasn't he responded? I wrote him again after I parked my bike—ONE OF THE HIPPIES YOU THREAT-ENED IS DEAD—hoping the message would force an answer. There hasn't been one.

"Do you mind if I come in?"

Sonny shoots a worried glance into the darkness of the house before backing up. I slip into the chilly room lit with scented candles—jasmine and lavender—to cover its perpetual smell of old rain. In the sitting room, an ironing board is erected on the scarlet carpet, and tiny, candy-colored clothes are spread across its plank.

"Are Therese and Duck here?" I ask. I don't want to lie in front of a child. I can handle deception among adults, but any cross-examination from a seven-year-old might break my resolve.

"No, they're out," Sonny replies as she takes her place behind the ironing board. "I was just doing some chores." She grabs the iron and makes a few cursory swipes around a pink collar. There is something slightly staged about Sonny's middle-of-the-room domestic routine, as if she intended Charlie to catch her hard at work when he came crawling home, keeping up the slog of household activities to contrast his own irresponsibility. But I wonder if I'm being unfair to her; maybe everything Sonny does seems performed because she's so beautiful in motion, each movement planting a seed of previously uncultivated desire. For a second, as I watch her, I want to iron too, like it's some vital human ritual I'd never stopped to appreciate. The spell is broken when she jams the asthmatic appliance on its base and stares at me with agitation. "Why did you ask if Duck's here? Is everything all right?"

"Everything's fine."

"Because that's what people ask when they have bad news."

"I don't have bad news." I drop onto the couch. A glass bowl filled with melted ice cubes sits on the coffee table. "I suppose you haven't spoken to Charlie today?"

She laughs silently as she whips the pink dress off the stand and folds it in half. "No, not since last night. Not since I left him in Skala. I waited up half the night for him to come home. No dice. It takes Charlie longer than most for his conscious to kick in." I resist correcting *conscious* with *conscience*. "The evolution from how bad I am to how bad he is takes about as long as the life span of a mosquito." Her balled fists are putting new wrinkles in Duck's dress. "Still, I would have appreciated an apology. Not to Miles, but to me."

The promise of providing Charlie with an alibi was far easier in theory. An abstract angry Sonny was manageable; the combustible woman in front of me is an unfair fight. No throwaway excuse is going to pacify her.

"I know he's sorry. In fact—" A patter of gravel rises from the balcony, and I lean back on the couch to glance out the overbright window. A leg straddles the ledge as if the man it belongs to is considering a jump. It's three flights down into thorn branches, if the shrine doesn't break his fall along the way. Sonny looks at me almost humorously as she marches toward the balcony door.

"You can come in. It's not Charlie."

Miles appears in the doorway, his head bent timidly and his graying, wavy bangs covering one eye. Black and silver stubble rinses his chin. He tests a smile on me, unsure where my loyalties lie. I have no choice but to copy it.

"Hello," he says, holding his right hand in front of him like it's a toy he picked up and isn't sure where to stow. "Is the coast clear?"

"If it were any clearer, you could see Africa." Sonny studies me again. "Miles just dropped by."

"To apologize for last night," he quickly adds. "I don't know what came over me."

Sonny spins around. "What came over *you*?" Her feet keep rotating until she lands back on me. "Charlie's the one who needs to apologize. Tell him, Ian. Tell him he did nothing wrong."

"We all said things we didn't mean," Miles whispers. It's a generous assessment. I can't recall anyone else who said one nasty word all evening—not even Rasym. But it was Miles who brought the confrontation to a physical end. He slides around me and dips his right hand into the bowl of ice cubes. Bruises on two of his knuckles are yellowing to purple.

"I'm okay," he insists. "I swear I've never punched someone before. Not even in school. I've known Charles since we were both boys spending summers on this island, and we never once fought, let alone a punch." The memory of the blow seems to be contained in the bowl because he keeps his eyes fixed on it. "I'm really sorry. I feel, I feel—"

Sonny doesn't appear that interested in how Miles is feeling. She takes the opportunity of his bowl-centric distraction to roll her eyes and blow a clogged breath.

"You shouldn't have punched him," she snaps. "But that doesn't mean he didn't deserve it. Miles, it's fine. I forgive you. And I'm sure Charlie will too. We all had too much to drink. No one stays in their corner with that much alcohol." Miles must have been apologizing the entire time it took the ice cubes to melt. And what at first might have seemed a welcome consolation to Sonny is now clearly undermining her assessment of whom she regards as the real victim. I wonder if Miles mentioned Charlie's accusations last night, if he tried to explain them away or confessed. Miles lifts his hand from the bowl and wipes the excess water on his leg.

"I'll apologize to him myself. If you don't clear these misunderstandings up right away, they only grow bigger."

"I'd give it a day or two," Sonny advises. "And maybe it would be best if you aren't here when he gets back. After all—"

Miles nods and stands. "I'll make it up to you," he swears, reaching his unbruised hand for her shoulder with the hesitancy of someone who's been reprimanded for touching. "I'll fix it."

"There's nothing to fix." She presses her hand kindly over his. Miles's last smile is a sincere one. Having secured one friend, he seeks another.

"Ian, if you ever want to have a coffee. I know you're a permanent member of the group now, and since Patmos is a second home, I'd hate for you to think the worst of me."

"Sure."

He raises both hands in good-bye and sees himself out. When the door shuts, Sonny races to lock it.

"I never thought he'd leave," she wheezes. "My god. It's like everyone just assumes I have all the free time in the world."

"Do you think he really would have jumped if I had been Charlie?"

"If you had been Charlie." She smirks. "Depends on how angry you looked. Stupid of Miles to show up so soon. People say Americans are socially inept, but it's the Europeans who have zero sense of space. They crowd you with their anxiety. He would have stayed for dinner to tell me seventeen more times how bad he felt."

"He does seem sorry."

"Sorry." She sneers. "If I hear that word one more time today." But sorry is all I have to offer her. Sonny collapses into the medieval chair, toying her fingers along the armrest's pegs, her toes gripping the edge of the coffee table. Her tank top exposes the egg-white side of a breast.

"You must be used to men fighting over you." I mean it as a compliment, an appeal to her vanity, but Sonny regards me blankly. Splotches of pink line her eyes, from lack of sleep or freshly peeled skin. It's as if the varnish of ease has been scraped off her, like paper from a billboard.

"I'm used to everything," she says in a low, beaten voice. "But if you think I enjoy those kinds of incidents, you're out of your mind. I have enough to worry about without a demonstration of two adult men behaving like jealous children."

"What was Charlie saying about Miles owing money back in London?"

She lifts her hands up to catch an enormous, invisible ball.

"I don't know," she mutters. "And I didn't ask. How is it my business? Don't we all come to this kind of place so we don't have to think about the problems we left behind? If Miles got into trouble at home,

I'm sure he'll deal with it when he goes back. I mean, did you come to Patmos to be quizzed about every problem you had in New York?"

Nothing in her frank expression reveals an awareness of my situation, but the allusion is too well placed. She must know, at least, about Panama. And Charlie had to have told her how desperate I am for money, because she hasn't once asked why I'd be taking a job at his charter company. Sonny could be one of the last humans who doesn't find entertainment in the flailing lives that haunt her periphery. She seems compassionately uninterested in sore spots. But if I had any expectation of forging a bond with her, she shoots that prospect down with her next question.

"So why are you here?"

I'm still Charlie's friend, a perhaps not entirely welcome intruder. Charlie warned me that I'd be taken as competition. Worse, I'm an intruder without a return ticket. I'll be following them back to Cyprus in the fall like an injured dog discovered on a beach that's too pitiful and weak to be abandoned.

"I visited Charlie this morning," I broadcast loudly, to emphasize the purpose of my visit.

"What?" Sonny blinks and shifts forward in her seat. For the first time she seems genuinely interested in me, as if I have something that belongs to her. "You did? You visited him? Where is he?"

Probably lounging on the docks of Bodrum right now or eating sushi with his boat captains at the coastal outpost of an expensive Japanese restaurant. Chugging sake. Visually undressing Turkish girls.

"He spent the night on *Domitian*."

"He did?" Her head reels back. "I should have figured. The floating bachelor pad." Her hand grips the armrest. "You were on *Domitian*?"

"Yeah. Before I came here. He's still pretty upset. His eye isn't looking too good. Neither one is. He's like a raccoon. Who the hell punched him the night before?"

But Sonny isn't concerned with answering questions, only posing them. She stares at me intently.

"Where is *Domitian*? Where did you board?"

I can't remember if Charlie gave me an exact location of the yacht. Sonny knows his habitual mooring spots better than I do. I'm struggling for a safe reply, latching onto the first scenario that flares through my brain.

"He picked me up at the beach near Kampos. I swam out."

"That's weird. I saw Christos this morning and asked him if he saw Charlie. He said he hadn't. He said he'd spent the morning washing *Domitian*."

One foot in the quicksand of a lie is still too deep to escape. *Damn it, Charlie. You told me Christos was in on your cover.*

"He probably told Christos not to give him up," I say nonchalantly. "He's still a little hungover and hurt. Like you said, it will probably take him a day or two to come to his senses."

"A day or two?" Sonny screeches. "He's really that upset? You saw him, you swam out and saw him, and he said he's not coming home for a day or two?" Support. Development. Upkeep. I'm earning my salary on Sonny's ruthless fact check. I assume she's about to play another card that exposes my dishonesty—*were you wearing a swim- suit and, if so, what did you do with your cell phone and wallet? What does* Domitian *look like in the morning? Were the sails up or down?*— but she slumps back in the chair. "So like him. He wants me to call and beg him to come home. He wants me to wave the white flag so he doesn't have to feel guilty." She taps her nail on the armrest. "Well, that's not going to happen."

"He said he was sorry. Very sorry. He realizes he acted like an asshole."

"Oh, he wasn't acting. If I didn't have Duck here, I might consider taking a break from the island for a few days too. But he knows I'm stuck. Maybe I should text him and say I'm leaving. That will get him here within an hour."

A threatening text from Sonny will only signal that I've failed, that I've made the circumstances worse instead of better. Day one of em- ployment: torpedo Charlie's relationship. Still, Sonny doesn't reach for her phone, as if uncertain of the result. She must have learned that testing love often confirms its limits.

"He does love you," I say. I try to recall the weakness in Charlie's voice when he confessed that much to me in his office. "He's trying to be a better person and would be lost without you. He just needs time to cool off. But you're all he has and why he works so hard."

She gazes at me with amusement, one romantic pronouncement away from laughing in my face. I look away embarrassed, as if the confession were mine.

"Don't feel bad," Sonny says, rising from the chair and gathering the bowl from the coffee table. "It was a nice try. I'd love to meet whoever you're talking about."

"Those might not have been his exact words."

"Get back to me when you have them." The bowl sloshes as she carries it toward the kitchen. "Whatever he told you on the boat today, I'm sure it was a whole lot nastier. Otherwise, he'd be home right now."

"He also said you've been worried about him. Worried about being here on Patmos because of the bomb that went off."

Sonny picks up her pace and disappears through the doorway. After dumping the water in the sink, she calls from the kitchen. "Are you thirsty?"

"No. I'm good."

She returns with an emerald-green bottle of water and scans the bookshelf, gliding her finger across the leather bindings, the languid yellows and browns of autumn leaves before they break into rotting red. I see the green Bible where Charlie stowed his family snapshot. *If I die, shake my books.* I'm relieved, after the bike accident, that I won't need to. Sonny pulls out a large dusty volume, bouncing it off her leg and lugging it to the coffee table.

"I've been meaning to show Duck this atlas. The colors of the oceans and deserts are so gorgeous. When I first moved here I spent days flipping through it." She opens the book to a map of Saudi Arabia, washed in pellucid watercolors and calligraphied with the names of ancient towns. "They're almost like abstract paintings. Each country is done with such care. Charlie would have me close my eyes while he turned the pages and I'd randomly drop my finger down, and if the colors were beautiful enough we'd agree to go there in the winter. That's how we ended up in Lebanon last Thanksgiving." She smiles up at me, her blue eyes exerting a soft pressure. "Of course, it didn't take me long to catch onto the fact that Charlie was only pretending to turn the pages. There I was dropping my finger on the exact spot where he had already planned for us to go. I didn't call him out on his cheating. I felt it mattered to him somehow that I believed we were leaving it up to chance." I wonder if she ever called Charlie out on his cheating before he converted into a faithful man. Maybe, even then, she avoided sore spots.

Sonny flips a few pages, searching for a better country. "I'm going to show Duck Cyprus. The artist painted it red, so it looks like a deep-sea fish trying to swallow Western Asia. I want her to see it that way, so when she goes with us it's a sweet little creature swimming in her mind. Not the barbed wire and oil drums that split Nicosia in half."

"Even if it isn't by chance, at least you're seeing the world."

"Oh, I'm seeing it," she agrees. "Up close." A coldness creeps over her, its temperature measurable by the shrinking of her smile. "You asked about the bomb. I was in Paris that day. And when I heard the news, I was sure Charlie was dead. I had just left Louise at the Palais-Royal, actually. It took an hour to get him on the phone. And for every minute of that hour I was hysterical, like the world was skipping on its needle, and only when I finally got ahold of him and heard his voice did the music come back. I booked myself on the first plane, and when I got here, it was all the same, except that the taverna was blown apart and the army had descended. The Greek and German armies. Maybe some American forces. I paid a taxi double to hurry up the hill to Chora. And here Charlie was, lying across the couch you're sitting on, asking me what I was doing home from Paris so soon. Like the whole matter had been as minor as a headache."

Sonny takes a sip of water. In the silence of the room, I hear the thin moaning of a lamb in a field below Chora. It sounds like an animal lost, crying out at regular intervals for the rest of her flock.

"The bomb didn't worry me. It scared me half to death. It blew up at the exact time and place Charlie had his coffee every morning. What's the acceptable reaction for something like that? Charlie thinks I'm crazy, and some days I suppose I am. He says it's just a coincidence, the world being uglier than the people who live in it, that we're all soft targets wherever we go." Sonny leans forward and taps the atlas. "But, you see, he's been trying to convince me of the random nature of plans for a while now." She slumps on the carpet, her knees folded at impressive acute angles from her daily yoga sessions. Yoga, and palm reading, and Pilates, and a facialist—all the expensive hands that touch this body in front of me. "Maybe he's right. Nothing's happened. The world keeps spinning. The music plays."

"Why would someone try to kill Charlie?"

She gives me a look of absolute bewilderment. "I have no idea. None. But he's been stressed and nervous all summer, ever since we came here in April. He gets up in the middle of the night and paces on the balcony, smoking his lungs black. He says it's business or his father's health. But you know Charlie. You know him as well as I do. Or you did. The more you pummel him with questions, the more he shrinks from you. It's not that I don't ask, Ian. It's that I can't. And that's why I won't text him now. Bothering him when he isn't ready is the best way to keep him away."

Up until now, I haven't thought of Sonny as lonely. Lucky. Well matched. Smart. But loneliness is harder to detect when it's camouflaged in excess. I can understand how, surrounded by all the comforts of a house that doesn't belong to her and stuck with a boyfriend who sets the conditions of their confidences, Sonny might resort to psychics for a shred of predictability. What can psychics do but encourage you through a field of land mines you have to cross anyway. Yet it's precisely because Charlie hides so much from her that she imagines him someone who could be wanted dead.

"Thank god nothing else has happened," I say.

"Yeah. It proves I'm crazy. I can handle being crazy. Better crazy than Charlie gone."

I'm relieved that I didn't tell her about the dead hippies. The news might bring her running to *Domitian*, only to find it empty and washed.

"He didn't say anything to you, did he?" Sonny searches my face, as if scanning for a bird in thick birches. "About some reason he's been so on edge? I know he's your friend, and best friends stick together. But I hope you'd tell me. Since you'll be living with us, with Charlie, Duck, and me all year round now, I was hoping we could be friends too."

I shake my head and deliver the one word she's sick of hearing. "Sorry. I probably know less than you do. I haven't even started working for him yet."

She swallows hard, as if taking down a dry vitamin.

"Oh well. I thought I'd ask. If you do talk to Charlie again before I do, tell him his father's surgery was pushed up to tomorrow. Apparently his health took a turn in the night, and they decided it's best to operate immediately. I got a call on the house phone from his doctor about an hour ago."

"Is it serious?"

"It's always serious," she says lightly as she gets to her feet. "But he has surgery about once a month. We stopped lighting candles after the seventh scare. Even though Charlie's a devoted nonbeliever, he used to ask the monks to perform a special prayer, back when it felt like it might go badly. But Mr. K can afford the best doctors, and I guess if you have the money, they find a way to keep you alive. I swear, there must be claw marks in Manhattan as deep as the Grand Canyon from how desperately he's trying to hold on to the world." I think of how easily my father went in his bed, without much sound or struggle, his hands spread on the bed like two white, airless flags. Sonny pinches the tip of her tongue, pulling a piece of fuzz from it. "If it isn't his father's heart, it's his lungs or his kidneys. This time

it's his heart. I'm not allowed to send the flowers. That's one responsibility I'm free of."

"Why is that?"

She tilts her head to the side and eyes me belligerently.

"You know why. Don't act surprised. You grew up the same as he
did."

"Not exactly."

"Exact enough. They'll accept a total degenerate as a friend of the
family, sure, open arms, *mi casa, su casa*. But they're not so hospitable when it comes to a girlfriend. His family hates me. I think the
polite wording is, *doesn't approve*. They see me as a flyover person,
a pretty but low-rent stop on the route to somewhere better. You've
seen the way Rasym treats me, like I've managed to worm into their
lives on false papers. And Rasym's people in Nicosia, Charlie's relatives, are even worse. Maybe it's a class thing. Or a money thing. Or
that I started out in Hollywood and they've Googled all the wrong
photos of me because I had the audacity to pay my own bills when I
was young. Or maybe they just don't like me. Who the fuck knows?
But it's like the Konstantinous live at some high altitude, and the air
is so thin you can't even breathe."

"I doubt it matters to Charlie."

"No." She grins. "It doesn't." She wanders over to a marble end
table and clicks through her phone. "There's a song, a really old, rare
Chet Baker. I introduced Charlie to it. It's our song. Once I heard
him playing it for someone else. He said, *check out this song I found*,
and I thought, *you shit, I gave you that*. But that's love, right? You let
go of who brought what to it. It's ours, so it's his. And if the Konstantinous took away everything else, the house and boats and all the
trips and even this island, we'd still have that song. You can't strip
everything away."

I'm familiar with that feeling of jealous proprietorship over
one's own tastes. Even in my early twenties I became a one-man
paramilitary every time an esoteric band I loved gained a mass
following. But that resentment exposes its own internal weakness:

there is so little that sets you apart, you can't afford to lose a single distinction.

Sonny's about to press PLAY on her rare Chet Baker when four knocks boom from the door.

"Charlie!" I yell. But Sonny doesn't share my hope. She stumbles sluggishly across the rug, her feet leaving scarlet wave crests in her wake.

She opens the door to a diminutive Malaysian woman with gray pigtails and a navy canvas robe. The woman steps inside wielding a flat metal suitcase.

"Good afternoon," she announces with phonetic buoyancy, each vowel a rickety chain on a wooden roller coaster. She dips her head at me as Sonny points toward the ironing board.

"Right there is fine, Andrea."

Andrea makes a peace sign with her hand and I'm about to return the universe-affirming gesture, when she asks, "Is it for two today?"

"No. Ian's just leaving."

Andrea begins transforming her suitcase into a foldout massage table.

"Do you mind if I use your bathroom?" I ask. Sonny nods as she shakes her hair free from the band. As I pass by she latches onto my arm.

"Thank you for coming. For bringing news of him. I bet you Charlie is home by dusk. He gets bored of his stances after a few hours."

I descend the dark staircase for one last task as Charlie's emissary. It's a chance to counterbalance the deceitful message with a deceitful act that might convince Sonny she still takes up the whole of his heart. Learn the game, and anyone can play it. I pull the black, hand-carved queen from my pocket, the one I accidentally pinched from Charlie's board. On the staircase, the lamb's moaning becomes louder and more insistent. I pass Stefan's empty room with the blanket smoothed across the cot. As I pass the second half-open door, I catch sight of Adrian and Rasym, both naked, hunched together in a Heimlich lock over the corner of their bed. Rasym is on top, his thin, velvet-haired ass dimpling with each thrust, his cheeks yellow with sweat, his small brassy hands flat on ivory shoulders. Adrian is below him, his muscular arms splayed across the mattress, his mouth and eyes open, making small plaintive cries. For a second, I don't even realize that I've stopped in the hallway mesmerized, struck not only by the fact that it's Rasym who fucks Adrian and not the reverse, but by the vision of Adrian's angelic face, creased in pain and yet transported, held in that impossible harmony of hurt and ecstasy, with every muscle operating to unfasten the brain and dissolve the world. His whole face is fluttering, drowsy, a wire carrying too much current. He's like an ancient Roman statue being smashed, finally, decisively, by a baseball bat.

I move into the master bedroom, hunting for Sonny's purse. Her straw beach satchel sits on the dresser, loaded with a bikini top and three different bottles of French sunscreen. I drop the queen below the bottles, hoping she'll find it, one more volley in their ongoing smuggling competition of who can trick whom and almost get away with it. Sonny didn't trust my generic avowals of love because that's not the way she and Charlie communicate. They speak the language of gentle deceptions.

Upstairs in the sitting room, Sonny is already sprawled on her stomach, her bare, oiled back flickering in the candlelight. Andrea is applying her thumbs, digging deeply into the lumbar region, telling her how and when to breathe. Sonny's blond hair spills over the edge, her face hidden, inhaling and exhaling, her lubricated ribs moving against the puncturing fingers, her polished nails digging into the vinyl.

"Easy," Andrea warns. "Too tight here. Bad tight. Hold. Now breathe."

I step into the alley and decide to attempt an untried path back to my bike. At the end of the long corridor, a young Greek guy exits from a crevice door, his greasy hand balled around a red wad of euros. I recognize him from Charlie's hangar as one of the teenagers running a blowtorch along the hull. He disappears through an alley before I can call to him to ask if he's seen Charlie. But in the small, screened window next to the door, I find the gauzy gray face of the Chicago pedophile peeking out. He draws a red curtain like a priest cutting off a confession.

It must be a holy day. A throng of monks chants a hymn as they carry a golden box on inlaid silver poles through Chora, either from or to or simply around the monastery, taking God for a stroll. I press against the white concrete as they march by in their black robes and hornet-like hats, mere indents of mouths singing through their beards. A gift shop ahead with a sprinkling of souvenir goat bells suggests I'm near the main road with its northern view of Skala. But as I ascend a sharp stone passage, vine-veined with the occasional burst capillaries of hibiscus buds, I realize I'm turned around. The view drops into the hazy green southlands, with its mammoth tan-hide haunches sloping into the sea.

A tiny cemetery is nestled in the hillcrest ten feet from me, not a relic but a functioning burial ground—all burial grounds are functioning, but this one accepts new customers. A few Patmians stand as still as storks amid clean granite headstones lined with pots of carnations and geraniums. On the mounds, photographs of smiling faces lean amid gaudy plastic flowers, stuffed teddy bears, and spinning homemade ornaments—all crayon-bright the way a child might color over death. I try not to wonder where the bodies of the two dead hippies are right now, in the island hospital, preparing to be shipped back in containers to their home countries. Perhaps somewhere in the air around me are the voices of their parents, crying into their receivers, bouncing from satellites down onto the warm Aegean that can't supply a comforting answer. I stare out at the coppery shine of the sea. Far along the coast, I make out one of Charlie's chartered yachts casting off from his dock toward the east.

CHAPTER 9

For a few minutes after sunset, the sky goes eerily white. Darkness waits in the mountains, camps in the trees, and covers the horseshoe of sand at the beach in Kampos where Louise and I are eating. The first stars are visible, solid silver against the white, like dense metal globes that the Air Aegean jets dodge as they descend toward the larger islands of the Dodecanese. It is Louise's opinion that Patmos has been spared the leviathan of mass tourism due to the lack of an airport. Louise, whose syrupy Coca-Cola–colored hair matches the darkness, dips bread in olive oil and chews with an open mouth. She tells me that every so often a billionaire prospector arrives on Patmos with plans to buy a huge chunk of land and convert it into a five-star resort—infinity pools and minimalist beach bars, five hundred rooms with sliding-door sea views, light jazz twinkling from speakers buried in shorn Bermuda green. Full service, sterling service, service like a pistol, military-issued fun. The billionaire is usually an American, a scion of a hotel chain, and the plans inevitably include the gratis construction of an inland airport.

"Only the monks in the monastery won't approve an airport," she says, prodding a zucchini blossom onto her fork. "Because as soon as there's a transportation hub, they'd lose all of their influence. They couldn't control what gets built. So God says no direct flights from Athens. Just as well. It would be a shame if all the raw beauty were destroyed." She bites into the blossom, and oil drips onto the paper tablecloth that's sutured to the edges by rusty clips. Below the table I'm rubbing Louise's leg. "They distrust Americans over here, don't you think? My great-grandfather served in World War II. He finally took a European vacation in the 1980s, a sort of budget Grand Tour with those matching vinyl shoulder bags. It was his first time out of the country since the war. And everywhere he went he said, 'you're welcome.' You know, for saving them. That might have been the last time an American could travel through Europe and say 'you're welcome.' Now it's like we just want to eat the place."

"You've done a lot of thinking about the tourism industry," I say, pinching her knee.

"Well, before you came, I was here for two weeks. I had a lot of free time. There are only so many days you can go to the beach alone. That Hungarian, Bence, had this awful idea to turn all of the Syrian refugees into construction workers. Put them to use by building cheap vacation condos in cash-strapped Greece, and then that solves two problems. You know what sucks about greedy capitalists? Sometimes their ideas actually make a degree of sense."

A group of guitarists in flossy linen shirts have been sitting at a table across the road, shooting dice until their time to play. Suddenly, they begin to strum. And when I look up, the white is gone. The sky is black, and along the water, two sets of fluorescent-green bikinis float like ghosts on holiday.

"Anyway, I thought you'd be interested," Louise says with a wink. "Since you're working in the tourism sector now. By the way, I texted Sonny your cell number. Charlie hasn't come home yet."

"Oh, I imagine he'll be back tomorrow." I feel I've done my part in mortaring their relationship. Charlie can take over when he returns from Bodrum. I'm appreciating a night alone with Louise, off-time from our jobs as houseguests.

"Sonny's anxious," Louise says.

"When I left her she was getting a massage." I try to reach my hand farther up Louise's thigh. My attempts at tenderizing her for romance don't appear to be effective. She's all one appetite, dumping another helping of tomatoes and feta on her plate.

"Did she tell you about wanting to bring Duck back to Cyprus?"

"Charlie told me."

"That's why she's anxious. Duck's father is broke."

"The director in L.A.?"

"Yeah." She hums. "It's horrible. He's using that child as a poker chip. If Sonny wants full custody, she's going to have to pay. So she needs Charlie to write him a check. Otherwise, no daughter. I really think that's all Sonny wants, now that she's gotten back on her feet and found a place she feels settled. And it's pretty horrible of Charlie too, not to give her an answer. It's not like he can't afford it."

"Maybe Charlie doesn't want to be a father," I say in defense. This afternoon, Sonny put on a convincing performance about her indifference to wealth—*all of it could be stripped away*—but the facts snag against the memory.

Louise scoffs. "People come with attachments. We aren't sold separately."

"Let's not talk about them tonight," I whisper. "I'd rather just be with you."

Our pompadoured waiter hides for most of his shift in the restaurant. When he does stroll out onto the sand, so many customers are waving for his attention that he briefly becomes a celebrity. I want to ask him for another Mythos beer, but I've already promised Louise I'd slow my drinking. Yet the self-imposed denial only makes me thirstier. Nervousness was my excuse when Charlie raised it, but it seems as if I'm chronically nervous the moment the sun goes down. Maybe I'm anxious about Charlie's failure to respond to my texts, or maybe it's due to being alone with the person I want. Around us, at beachfront tables, couples sit across from each other, staring out at the sea or deep diving into the wine list or holding limp, sunburned hands. Their long spells of silence, as if they've traveled all this way to run out of conversation, accentuates our stilted stabs at talking. We're amateurs at sharing a meal.

I try to engage her with a tale of my first Grand Tour of Europe, as a kid with my father and stepmom—"you better enjoy every second of this vacation, Ian"—and how my only vivid memory of that trip amid all the churches and leaning towers and iridescent mirrored hallways of Versailles was the tits on public television, the copious topless women jiggling in the greens and yellows of the hotel sets. "That to me was Europe," I say. "A continent of free boobs. But when I finally went to the hotel swimming pool with my father, I was so terrified by actually seeing—"

"Are you okay about your father?" she asks, like she's missed the point of my story. Louise is an emotional storm chaser; she drives right toward the eye. "You haven't talked much about his death."

"I'm fine," I say abruptly.

"Have you spoken to your family?"

"No." But since we're on the subject of losses, I decide to ask her about her return to the States. "When exactly are you planning on leaving?" I drop my hand from her leg. I want to keep exploring, but the table leg is in the way. And the mention of my father has killed my hard-on.

Louise smiles. She wears a black Hard Rock Café Paris T-shirt; I can't decide whether it's an ironostalgic flourish, a tourist souvenir, or simple indifference to whatever advertisement ends up emblazoned across her chest.

"My ticket back to D.C. is booked for next Wednesday." That's five days, and the sorrow of the timetable hits me like a slap. "I could always push it back a bit if I swallow the fee."

"Why don't you? I could pay the difference." My hand scrunches the blue map of Patmos printed on the tablecloth.

"Ian." She breathes. "I've already been on vacation for so long. I'm forgetting what home looks like."

"Keep forgetting," I say. "Forget it entirely. Come on."

"Some of us aren't allowed to forget."

"Aren't you having a good time here?" And un-artfully I add, "With me?"

"One swallow doesn't make a summer. Or one swallow is enough for a summer. Either way . . ."

"Louise," I stammer. I'm about to confess my feelings. But she squeezes my hand, and I don't have to speak.

We wear our helmets on the ride home, astronautic lovers tapping fiberglass to fiberglass. On the stone porch, in the hot, mountain air, we grapple with our clothing, which, in the darkness, becomes as complicated as mountaineering gear. Her black shirt around her neck, mine unbuttoned, our shorts and underwear slid to our ankles, we seem to be moving at avalanche speed and also, unfortunately, with avalanche precision. I feel the tight clench and beyond it the soft release, and with every thrust, as my forearm pillows her skull from the stone, I want to cry a small bleat of "stay." *Stay with me, Louise, right here, in the confusion of this summer, in this lost perfect dot on the globe that no planes can reach, just stay, and I will be whatever you want from me, the volunteer, the provider, the man behind the unlocked door.* I inspect her eyes, searching for that shudder in the lids, the whorl like a fingerprint so specific to each person, to know I'm making an impact, moving the furniture around in her head, leaving even a temporary trace. But Louise's eyes don't flinch. They stay on me, not coldly but methodically, no Adrian-like convulsion racking her face. The meat of her eyes is light blue from the moonlight, the irises as forebodingly black as inner-city parks at night. I come, and my lips scoop for her collarbone, caught in the folds of her Hard Rock Café shirt. I roll off of her, and for several minutes we remain that way, lying on our backs, unspeaking. Every so often, after sex, you realize that you might not be any good at it and all it amounted to was a childish tantrum on top of another body.

I'm grateful when Louise takes my hand. "I want to say I'm sorry for giving you such a hard time about working for Charlie. Sorry for the soapbox treatment. It's just that part of me is envious of all those years after college when you tried to help people. I wish I had done that."

"Don't be. It's not a talent. Anyone could have."

"But so few do. I have a theory that most humans don't actually like each other. It must have been rewarding. Didn't it, even for a little while, feel good?"

"Maybe. But no matter how much I did, I never felt like it was enough. The suffering, it doesn't have a limit. It just goes on and on."

"I wasted the last decade trying to figure myself out. And that doesn't have a limit, either. It also goes on and on. At least you fed people and gave them a bed."

"I was let go from that job. Fired."

"Still, you tried. Most people just keeping walking." She tightens her hand. "Thank god I don't believe in reincarnation. I can't imagine what I've doomed myself to come back as."

"For two nonbelievers, we talk about religion a lot."

"It's this island. I *am* going to miss it. What are you hoping for now that you're here?"

Everything.

When I don't answer, Louise pulls my hand to her lips and kisses it.

"I'm curious to hear how it goes at Charlie's company," she says. "Maybe I will push my ticket back."

That promise seems to be all I need to take with me into sleep, because I wake an hour later, alone on the porch. I expect to find Louise in my bed, but the sheets are still made and the door to her room is shut.

NIGHTMARES—A KILLER ON a boat; asking for directions while burning up in the sun. The phantasmal merry-go-round is only halted in the late morning by the sound of a key turning in the cabin door.

"Forgive me," Therese says as she steps inside wearing a flowery plastic apron, black socks, and slippers. She stalls in the doorway as I climb out of bed. "I come early today because I have to watch Duck."

"No problem," I reply, grabbing a pair of pants and hurrying toward the bathroom. "What time is it?"

"After eleven."

I stop briefly at the presence of a much younger woman behind Therese, with a matching apron tied around her waist.

"My daughter, Vesna," Therese says. "She helps clean."

Vesna issues a brief, curt smile. She looks as grungy as her brother, but unlike Helios, there's a sharp owl-like intelligence to her face, with large wayward eyes that settle like flowers on a murky pond. Streams of bright dyed blue snake through her hair, and a collection of charms and beads engulf her fingers and wrists. Maybe it's the hair dye or the troubled teenager lurking in her expression, but she reminds me of Marisela. For that reason alone, I decide it's best to avoid her and scurry faster into the bathroom. When I re-emerge, Therese is on the porch, scouring the stove, and Vesna is disdainfully pushing a rag across the window ledge. She turns when she spots me, bundling the rag in her ringed fingers.

"You're a friend of Charlie's from America?"

"Yes." I grab a clean shirt and quickly pull it on.

She nods coolly. "I don't . . . I mean, I'm not only a cleaning lady." Her English is fluid but leveed with distrust. "I study at the university in Athens. I come back only in the summer to help my parents."

"What do you study?"

Her eyes narrow. "Communications." And as if it almost pains her to elaborate, as if it's required of her major and nothing more, she says unwillingly, "My parents expect me here for summers. I wouldn't come otherwise."

"Your brother lives here year-round, right? Helios isn't in school?"

"Helios," she rasps dismissively.

"You two don't get along?" She glares at me, although I'm not sure if that isn't just her resting expression. "I don't get along with my siblings, either," I say to defuse the accusation.

"I'm not like my brother. I want to make my own life, a future. My home is Athens now. Helios is a lost cause." She measures our distance from her mother. "It's our parents' fault. They want Helios to take over for them. But take over what? They have nothing, and they don't even realize it. So Helios is stuck here, doing nothing, and now he's dead in the head. But my parents are blind islanders, as if the rest of the world doesn't exist, like problems beyond the sea don't

touch them. Only their precious son learning to be the errand boy
for the Konstantinous. That isn't a future. It's the past. Have you met
my father?"

"Yeah."

"He's very hard on Helios. Always disappointed. He's hard on me
too, but I don't put up with it. Maybe they let me leave because I'm
only a daughter. But I'm the one who's going to do something with
my life."

I should have expected a motive behind Vesna's unsolicited information dump. But I'm still taken off guard when she steps toward
me, barking a gruff, conspiratorial "hey."

I stand still. "Hey, what?"

She attempts a smile. "Could I ask a favor? A little one?"

"What?"

Her lips tremble toward their mission, like a horse gathering
speed to jump a fence. "Could I borrow some money?" By reflex
I'm about to claim poverty, simulating a search of the pockets and
coming up with waving hands in the manner of a magician who has
failed to conjure a rabbit. But it occurs to me that Vesna has been
regularly cleaning my room and might have noticed the plastic bag
of cash in the nightstand drawer. "I usually ask Charlie," she says.
"He always gives me a little extra without my parents knowing. But
he isn't around."

"You've looked for him?"

She nods. "Everywhere. He's not at home, not at his dock. I
thought he might be on *Domitian*. But when I went to clean, there
was only an awful mess. No Charlie."

"I thought your father cleaned *Domitian*."

"I do the insides, the galley. He does the rest. Charlie leaves me
extra in one of his trophies, my secret tip, but he must have forgot. I
tried calling him. No answer."

Charlie said he'd likely be back today. I was hoping he'd already
returned, saving me from continuing the lie.

"Helios is looking for him too," Vesna says. "He gives us both extra. Maybe you should try calling him if you don't believe me. He's very generous."

"It's not that I don't believe you."

"Just eighty euros," she says, unclenching the rag. "You see, I need to take the ferry to Athens tonight." She checks again to make sure her mother is out of earshot. There is a goat-like quality to Vesna's face in profile, with its large, crested eye spaced far from her nose. "Tomorrow there is a rally in Syntagma Square to protest our government's alliance with the European Union. It's very important! We will never be a free country, our own people, with the West bleeding us dry with their impossible restrictions. It's our country! Not the capitalists who are determined to put us in our place!" Perhaps she's merely prepping for the rally, or her politics are still in their early formation when every statement is expressed as a vehement argument, but I no longer remember if I'm the target of her antagonism or the person she's asking for help. "You must know how awful it is here. Half the Greeks my age can't find a job. We have to be independent if we ever want to escape this nightmare of poverty and dependence. They have decided what Greek people are and they are making us be those people whether we like it or not. So you see, I have to be there!"

"Wasn't the bomb in Skala last month set by a leftist group that was trying to send the same message? I hope you don't agree with their tactics."

"That bomb." She snorts. "Who says it was set by us? You think liberal minds are the only ones who use explosives? It was two sticks of dynamite. All the islands are loaded with dynamite. How do you think Greek fishermen used to fish before it became illegal. String a fuse on a timer, drop the sticks in the water"—Vesna mimes a hunk of explosives in her hand and proceeds to detonate a switch—"and all the fish come to the surface. Haven't you seen old men with missing fingers in the villages? They were fishermen of the old Greek style. *Boom.*" Vesna brags of her knowledge of explosives the way American college students show off their music tastes. I'm not sure whether to be impressed or frightened, and when pulled between those two reactions I tend to become aroused. *Remember Marisela*, I tell myself. "If you walk down this hill I bet you'd run across a hoard of dynamite piled under tarps. Anyone could have gotten their hands on it. It's just easier to blame the group that is trying to execute real change." As an afterthought, Vesna adds, "I didn't mean to say *execute*. I believe in nonviolence. So will you help me? Charlie will pay you back. He understands."

I reach for yesterday's clothes on the floor and milk my wallet from my shorts pocket.

"And you can't ask your parents for the money?"

"No. They don't want me going. They think it's dangerous. But I told you, they live in another century. Please don't tell them about Charlie giving me money. They wouldn't approve because of their pride." As if to apologize for asking, she touches my arm with her chilly rings. "It's our pride that gets in our way."

I open my wallet and pull out the last aquamarine hundred from my advance. After last night's dinner, I'm down to less than two hundred euros when counting up all the bills. Vesna snatches the hundred before I have time to hand it over and doesn't offer me the twenty euros in change.

"Thank you," she says and leans close, her grimace twitching at the corners. "Another thing, because you have been kind. I would hide that money you have in the nightstand somewhere safer. Thieves know that vacationers have brought extra cash with them this summer in case the bank machines run out. I've heard of break-ins and robberies on the islands. They come in and out on the ferries, so they're never caught. You should be careful."

"Where should I hide it?" I ask, tossing my arm around the room.

Vesna shrugs and tucks the hundred-euro bill in her apron pocket.

"How about under the mattress? It is safer these days than the banks."

"Vesna?" Therese cries from the sliding door. The mop handle is tight at her chest. She notices us close together with an open wallet between us. "Why aren't you cleaning? Why are you bothering Charlie's best friend?" Therese's ashen face, with sunspots circling like lace around her eyes, seems to hope for the least upsetting conclusion. She sucks air through her yellowed teeth.

"We were just talking about how generous Charlie is," Vesna answers. I catch a trace of sarcasm in her voice, as if Charlie might not regularly supply her with covert funds. Have I just been duped by the housekeeper's daughter? Should I be grateful she didn't stage a robbery to dip into the nine thousand in cash?

"Oh, Charlie is very generous," Therese proclaims while she touches her forehead in the opening volley of the sign of the cross. "We owe our lives to the Konstantinous. They're family. Charlie is our second son. Where would we be without him?" I'm accustomed to domestic workers of richer friends swearing their allegiance in the chance that I might pass along their praises, but Therese's devotion strikes me as genuine. It must strike Vesna that way too, because she pauses from stripping the pillowcases to glance at her mother like she's in need of senior care. "And not only us," Therese continues. "Charlie funded the playground of the children's school last year when the government couldn't afford to keep it up. He brought in his own engineers and builders so the kids could have their games. And he pays for Vesna's studies too, doesn't he?" She prods her daughter with her eyes to confirm it. The nape of Vesna's neck glows red. "So many people today who buy houses on Patmos don't care about our island. They see it only as summer fun. Not the Konstantinous. Christos and I are very proud to be working for them all these years. I worry about Mr. Konstantinou's health. He is too sick, now, to make the trip to see us. Sonny told me he has one of his operations today."

"Why does he even bother to leave the hospital?" her daughter mutters.

I ask Vesna where *Domitian* is docked. She lifts from the bed with a tired breath. Her mother races over to finish fitting the sheets.

"In Grikos," she mumbles. She's staring over my shoulder, and when I turn I find a sweaty, dark-suited man with a black mustache standing in the rectangle of sunlight. His belly swells over a tightly buckled belt. Two blue-shirted officers fill the void around him. He's putting a crumpled pack of cigarettes into his blazer.

"Excuse me," he says, tapping belatedly on the door. "Are you Ian Bledsoe? I am Inspector Martis." For a second, my stomach plummets, and the air is knocked from my lungs. "I was hoping we might have a word down at the station. It is about your friend, Charlie." He gauges my expression and smiles. "Nothing has happened. It is merely an informal inquiry, involving an accident yesterday with two young foreigners on a motorbike. I promise it will only take a few minutes of your time."

Therese, hugging one of the pillows, barks at him in Greek, and he gesticulates wildly as he replies.

"It's okay," Therese reassures me. "He says you are not in trouble. He says you can follow him on your bike."

"I could have told him that," he balks. "I do speak English, Mrs.—"

"Stamatis. Therese Stamatis. We work for the family. And this is my daughter—" But Vesna, clearly averse to cops, has disappeared into the bathroom.

I collect my wallet and keys and step outside. The two officers have returned to the police car, no doubt to prevent the sense that I am being taken into custody.

"I really don't know anything," I swear to the inspector, as if my ignorance could absolve me from having to make the trip to the port.

"All the same, a few questions, very minor," Martis replies warmly and stares down the hill at the sea. "I forget how beautiful Patmos is. A rare island. They say it vibrates."

"You aren't from here?"

"Oh, no," he says laughing as he claps my shoulder. "I'm from district headquarters in Kos. I only come to Patmos when there's a mess that the local police can't handle."

"I thought you said it was very minor."

Martis's response is to smile at the view.

THE POLICE STATION in Skala shares a building with the Tourist In-formation Office. The squat Venetian structure with domed archways and a gingerbread tower sits across from the ferry dock boasting a tattered Greek flag. In Venice, the building would be declared a public eyesore; here, due to its bell-tower height, it possesses an imposing majesty. Yet nothing about the building suggests that either the tourist office or the police station is open to visitors. The windows are closed and curtained. Only a small rusted plaque announces its municipal purpose. Palm trees and parked rental cars barricade its entrances. Drifting all around the reclusive white cube of bureaucracy are the restless tans and fluorescents of August vacationers: bag-weighted couples in board shorts; children Breathalyzer-testing inflatable rafts; cherry ice cream lickers; collectors of day-cruise leaflets. A family of seven from Sweden, fleeing the confines of their yacht, jogs along the waterfront wearing shorts that bear the name of their boat, *Princess Octopus*—the name means something different sewn across the ass of each family member. They run so happily, so unencumbered, a family portrait in blond, bouncing motion, their terry cloth shorts free of the bulk of wallets or IDs, that it strikes me that only the obscenely rich are permitted the comfort of carrying nothing. I park my bike while Martis and his officers wait across the road.

"You will have your beach today, do not worry," Martis promises. We head toward the station, the inspector leading the way as the two officers flank me. I force a smile to downplay the impression I'm under arrest and scan the port for anyone I might know. Standing at the to-bacco stall, not twenty feet away, is the thief from the Athens hotel. He steps from the shade. And as on the Grande Palace rooftop, our sights cross uneasily like two unfamiliar hunters through riflescopes.

Martis motions to a set of steps running up the side of the build-ing. A white arrow points skyward with the words TO THE POLICE STA-TION written modestly across it.

"Is this necessary?" I ask, not exactly sure what I even mean be-sides some need to register noncompliance, in case this is an arrest, in case I'm about to be told a Mediterranean rendition of my Miranda rights. A phone call? A lawyer? An arraignment in front of a judge? Is there a standard arrest procedure in Greece? Is there even a judge on this island? All of these questions barrel through my head before I realize I've done nothing wrong.

"I said not to worry," Martis replies. "We are very civilized. We have no death penalty."

At the top of the staircase, a different visitor chaos spills across the yellow terrace, hidden from the tourists below. Nearly twenty dark bodies, some slumped in corners, others squatting over swaddled infants, some upright with eyes fixed on their toes. Men of all ages, in dirty T-shirts, hoodies, and jeans, barefoot with raw, ulcerous skin, jaws etched with days of facial hair; women in their early twenties, roped in hijabs and dense fabrics of maroons and browns, most wearing sandals, a few clutching plastic bags. The smell of the sea is on them, and the silence of the sea too, the hopelessness of lost places, of valuables irretrievably dropped. Tiredness weighs in their eyes but also elation, a nervous, festive mood of relief. Only a pear-skinned kid of ten or eleven acknowledges me. "Hello," he shouts, blinking his uneven eyes—one big and brown, the other slivered almost shut. He sits under a cabinet shrine to a saint. The boy is dressed in a too-large sweatshirt, his black hair parted by the plastic comb in his hand. He smiles as he glides the comb across his scalp, wanting to meet the new continent with the polish of a first day at school. I give him a thumbs-up, as my heart ripens—ripens, falls, and is scorched by the acid in my stomach until the pain of it waters my eyes. Martis doesn't have to tell me that these are refugees from the east. Life vests are piled next to pallets of bottled water. A rug has been left unrolled for prayer. An orange bucket by a drain offers what I can only imagine is a receptacle for seasickness.

I want to believe that this terrace is like a fire escape in Manhattan, a safe spot for sitting, a converted outdoor room, and not a last-ditch measure for people fleeing a blaze but still a dangerous distance from solid ground. An officer appears from a doorway by the shrine and grabs the closest man by the upper arm. He wears the same light-blue latex gloves that were snapped on at the motorbike crash, as if each migrant body is the scene of a crime.

Martis taps me on the back to urge me toward the main door of the station. As I stumble forward, I feel as if my shadow is being ripped from me, the remnant of who I was that needs to stay and help. *Do something, do something.* I reach for my wallet, at least to give the boy a few euros, but Martis practically pushes me into the station. We sweep through a tapioca-colored waiting room, and Martis motions me into a glass-enclosed office. I take a seat in a walnut chair directly below a blinking light fixture with wires poking from its sconce. The inspector lingers in the doorway, speaking to the officer who tried to stop me from getting near the bodies yesterday. The other uniformed men greet Martis obsequiously. As with any unchallenged authority, Martis remains relaxed and convivial. The desk in the office he's borrowing is a Sahara of disheveled paperwork, beige dunes of files and perforated documents. Framed, waterlogged photographs of men fishing, drinking, and posing with saturnine monks crowd the tops of the metal cabinets. I recall Charlie's warning about the uselessness of the Patmian police force; it does appear from the look of the desk as if their primary occupation consists of filling out and misplacing forms.

Martis lumbers in and squeezes himself into the chair behind the desk. His bottom teeth are engaged in the effort of trying to bite the tips of his mustache. The dusty sunlight reveals the craters and hairline scars running across his cheeks. The skin around his eyes is bunched like the creased corners of a folded map.

"Those refugees outside," I say. "Are you arresting them?"

"Syrians," he replies, spinning a ballpoint pen on the blotter. "No, not arrest. Process. Once they set foot on European soil, they claim the right to stay. Most of them don't have papers. And, of course, they can never remember the names of their smugglers. They've spent days in a boat with these traffickers, but ask them to describe these men, they all go hazy in the head. We do what we can, which is not much. No one knows what to do with the refugees this summer."

"What will happen to them now?"

Martis smiles as he scrunches his shoulders. "They are seeking asylum. Not in Greece. Even Syrians are aware of how bad our circumstances are right now. Would you risk your life at sea to join the long lines of the poor and starving in Athens? No, they want to get to Germany or Denmark. And perhaps that is why we don't stop them. Germany gives us so much trouble in the E.U., we shall give them something back." He winks and takes a deep breath. "Most of the boats don't get as far as Patmos. They land on the islands closer to Turkey, like my island. You should see our shores on Kos, littered with life vests and rubber boats and growing camps of despair. The beaches are like war zones now. But they can't control the currents, they are prisoners to the mind of the water, and some do wash up as far as here. They will be sent to the detention center in Lesbos, and from there?" He tosses his hands. "It is a very bad summer for refugees. And where is the money to patrol our borders? There isn't any. It is open season on the seas. What is that line on your statue? *We take your poor, your tired, your huddled breathers?* We should move that statue to the Aegean. It makes more sense for us now." Even this dark forecast is treated with Martis's personable mirth. He chomps at his mustache. "Where are you from in America?"

"New York."

He slaps the desk. "One day I hope to visit. I have cousins in Astoria, Queens. Do you know where that is?"

"Sure."

Martis points a peremptory finger and struggles with his blazer pocket. He fishes out his cell phone and taps. "I follow my cousins on Facebook. They are very happy in New York. Every weekend is baseball games. You and I could be friends on Facebook too. And when I visit, you could come to Astoria to greet my family."

"I'm not on the Internet."

Martis glances at me perplexed, as if I've just admitted that I don't intend to go to heaven. "You must be. All young people are on the Internet. Let me type in your name. Ian Bledsoe." I can't decide if he's staged this conversation to lead us to the disclosure of my past or he's simply unwilling to accept a refusal of friendship. No day is safe from friendship. Gone is a world of passing acquaintances; one is either nonexistent or a certified friend. He switches his phone's keyboard from Greek to English. *I-A-N.*

"I'm not on there," I yelp, digging my foot against the chair leg. "Ian Bledsoe is a very common name in America. You won't find me. But I promise I'll join Facebook and I'll send you a friend request." I don't want him dredging through my history of bombs and cartels and a tourist with a record for turning against his family. "I'm sorry, I actually have somewhere to be. I'm not on vacation. I work on this island, at Charlie's charter company. So if we could just get to the questions you have for me?"

"Yes, yes," Martis agrees apologetically. He swats his phone aside. "I am sorry. It is addictive, this device, making friends, looking into the lives of others." He smiles without a hint of duplicity. "My questions involve your friend, Charlie. That is why we are here. I haven't been able to track him down."

"No?"

"I have learned from my colleague that you were witness to the two young foreigners who died yesterday near Grikos."

"I witnessed the police finding them. I didn't see them die."

"No, no. That is what I meant," he corrects jovially. "My English. Yes, a man and a woman, backpackers who were part of the Christian camp on the beach. According to their parents, they had been traveling around the Mediterranean for several months. Not together. They didn't seem to know each other before Patmos. The man, Mikael, was Norwegian, and the girl, Dalia, was Dutch. I have pictures of their passports. Now let me find them." He makes a show of searching the desk but locates the folder instantly and slides two printouts in front of me. Both Dalia and Mikael are of the age when passport photos are still flattering—Dalia grinning prettily through stage curtains of long, straight hair; Mikael, pre-nose ring and earlobe plugs, serious and strong-jawed and blank. They could be any twenty-somethings patiently submitting themselves to the red tape of documentation for the freedom that waits on the other side. It hits me how archaic passports are, tiny, mobile stamp collections recording the pit stops of the wandering soul. And they're like yawns—the sight of one induces me to clutch my pockets for my own. I left mine in the cabin.

"Have you ever seen them before?" Martis asks.

I check my answer. I saw Dalia exiting the ferry in her New York T-shirt the night we met for drinks in Skala. And I saw Mikael trespassing on Charlie's dock.

"I'm not sure," I say. "Those hippies all tend to look alike."

Martis chuckles. "Yes, they do. What a scene down at their camp. No clothes and food on the bonfire and so much blasting music. Who can blame them for wanting to join in? Not a bad way to spend the summer."

I stare at their pictures again, but the memory of Mikael's smashed face in the grass intervenes and I drop my hand over his image.

"May I ask why you're showing me their pictures? I thought they died in a motorbike accident."

The inspector leans back, running his teeth over his mustache.

"An accident is the likely cause. Hit by a car or more probable they drove off one of the hilltop cliffs in the dark. They are nearly fifteen meters high at some of the turns. The village should erect guardrails. It is very unsafe. We are checking all of the cars on the island for evidence of a, how do you call it, a hit and go? In any case, my colleagues here concluded it was an accident. Unfortunately, there are three or four such deaths on Patmos each summer. Motorbikes are irresistible to vacationers."

Martis's chubby fingers amble across the desk toward his phone, like a piano player following the rhythm of a song. But he catches himself and tightens his fist.

"But you don't think it's an accident?"

"Ah, but that's just it," he says beaming. "I do. The doctor at the hospital examined their injuries. His report was inconclusive."

"I've heard that doctor isn't very reliable."

Martis juts his jaw out. "He is decent enough, a good man. Their bodies sustained a great deal of damage, consistent with a very serious accident. Obviously this island doesn't have the resources that you are accustomed to in America. We are not in the business of autopsies. We've already sent their bodies home."

I snort at the ineptitude of Greek protocol. Martis responds with a wry smile, as if to assert, *you want definite answers, you should have stayed at home.*

"When I pressed the doctor," he continues, "he could not rule out homicide, the kind of injuries that could be caused, say, by the blunt force of a bat." I think of Martis's cousins and their newfound love of baseball, attending Yankees games and posting photos of themselves in the nosebleed seats holding hot dogs laced with ketchup. "However, he feels it is most likely that they drove over a cliff's edge. And the simplest answer is usually the correct one."

"So what's the problem? If everyone agrees it's an accident, why are you investigating? I hope they don't bring you to Patmos every time a foreigner runs off the road."

Martis finally manages to trap his mustache in his teeth. The victory is short-lived.

"No, they do not. I am a very busy man, I assure you. The problem is that someone has come forward. A young woman has made a report. An American like yourself. She claims that the deaths of Dalia and Mikael might be more serious than a random accident." Even before Martis identifies her, I picture the crying girl with the salamander tattoos writhing up her ankles, Mikael's companion that morning at the dock. "She told the police she was with the young man when your friend, Charlie, made a direct threat on their lives. That was only a day before the accident." He watches me for a response, like a man searching a fetid aquarium for signs of life. "She was very upset, very shaken. Understandably. She had just lost her friend. Maybe Mikael was her boyfriend? Now, we do not put stock in the hysterical suspicions of a grieving girl. But the difficulty is, when a report such as this is made, one of possible murder, we are required by law to investigate it. So that is why I am here." He jabs the pen in the blotter. "It is highly sensitive. As you know, Charlie is from a very respectable family, a family with much esteem on our islands. The Konstantinous have been with us for generations, very good people, and we do not want to offend them with the allegations of a disturbed young woman. So please do not take my questions as an interrogation. All of this can easily be resolved. We do not wish to alarm anyone."

I nod.

"I looked for Charlie at the dock of his yacht business, and I found only his worker, a Turk named Ugur. The girl mentioned there was a man fitting his description there when the threat was made. I asked this Ugur, but he said his English is so poor, he couldn't understand what was spoken between them." I'm jealous of Ugur's excuse; the best alibi is total ignorance of a foreign language. "What a strange little man he is, yes? Rather unsavory, if I may be honest. I think I frightened him with my questions. And I do my best to frighten no one." Martis laughs, as if his charm is as involuntary as his heart-beat. "But the girl said a young man with red hair was also present. As you say, you work for Charlie." He drops the pen. "So may I ask, did you hear any threat made?"

Charlie must be on his way home right now, his boat on the sea, the motor at full blast, at any second the black ripple of the island breaking across his horizon. He will be home soon, and he will speak with Inspector Martis, and the incident will disappear as quietly as the bodies of the backpackers to their home countries. I'm so lost in the vision of Charlie's return, I almost forget I'm sitting in a police station fielding possible grounds for murder.

Martis's face rumples with concern.

"Do you need some water, Ian?" He raises his hand as if to call a waiter.

"No, I'm okay. Now that you mention it, I was at the dock that morning and I did see two hippies from the camp. I think they were stoned. They were trespassing, and Charlie told them to leave. He might have yelled at them a bit excessively, but I wouldn't go as far as calling it a threat. Nothing that would be a reason to kill them." I copy the inspector's ingratiating laugh. "I get the sense there's some hostility between the locals and the members of that camp. Apparently they treat the whole island like their own backyard. But, really, that's all it was. You have my word. Charlie wouldn't kill anyone over trespassing. Why would he?" I'm surprised by the sincerity in my voice, as if I can convince both of us of Charlie's innocence. It was a minor threat in the heat of the moment, just a coincidence that it arrived right before one of them was killed.

"You see," Martis cries, banging the desk. "The fantasy of a troubled girl. That is all. No reason for me to bother with my trip."

"Have you spoken to the woman who runs the camp? If by some chance there was foul play, it might have nothing to do with Charlie. Aren't they down there praying for the end of the world?"

Martis opens his mouth, exposing a silver mine shaft of dental work.

"Christians and their Apocalypse!" he retorts. "Why are you Westerners more fond of that book than the rest of us? The luckiest on Earth are the ones who want it to end the fastest." He shakes his head. "Yes, I did speak with that woman, Vic. She was very nice, very welcoming. She was the one who provided me with their passports."

"What did she say?"

"Oh, she thinks the same as we do. That this young woman, Carrie Dorr, is mistaken, gone a bit confused in the head. Vic told me some of the youths who join her group can be unstable. She said she tried to reason with her and talk her out of coming to us with the claim. So, you see, everyone is in agreement. A tragic accident. Maybe one day they will erect guardrails!" Martis pushes back in his chair, his swollen stomach curled on his lap like a sleeping dog. "So it is only this young woman who is scared for no reason. Just as I thought."

"She's scared?"

His nostrils flare. "Quite scared. Paranoid, I would say. She believes she's in some danger. I always warn my children not to smoke the *marichouana* that is so popular now on the islands. It is much stronger than it used to be. Bad for sensitive heads." He laughs with his hand on his stomach, each wave of it growing fainter like the sea leveling in a boat's wake. He sighs deeply when he's finished, and I begin to lift from my seat. But Martis isn't done. He leans forward, braiding his fingers.

"So now there is only the last necessity of speaking with Charlie myself. When he tells me there was no ill will with these young foreigners, the matter will be settled." Martis stares at me greedily, as if counting the seconds before I produce Charlie between the blinks of the overhead light. I cling to my smile like a life raft.

"Well?" he grunts. "Could you tell me where he is? According to Ugur, you are his number two."

"I'm not sure, I—"

"I visited the Konstantinou house in Chora this morning. I spoke with Charlie's wife."

"Girlfriend. Sonny is his girlfriend."

"Ahh," he sings. "He should marry that one." Martis pretends to fuss with his shirt collar. "I plan to come back as a playboy and have a wife like that." He waits patiently, his grin frozen. He is the controller of time in this office. "She tells me she has not seen Charlie in two days, but that you have seen him, been with him, just yesterday. So if you could tell me where I could find him?"

One lie. That was all that was asked of me. One lie concocted between old friends to keep a house in order. And now the lie is growing to the size of an island and must be watered and pruned and fed. I consider coming clean, confessing the ruse to provide Charlie with an alibi while he's busy handling business in Bodrum. But mentioning one deceit suggests the presence of others, and what have I offered the inspector but my word? To admit that Charlie needs an alibi might suggest some credence in the young woman's claim. Charlie will be back from Turkey at any minute, and he can speak with Martis and clear up the confusion. In the meantime, he won't appreciate it if I've helped to finger him as a possible suspect to the police.

"Charlie and his girlfriend had a fight," I say, "so he was sleeping on one of his boats. I think he might be out on one now. His job is mostly at sea. He told me he had a little business off the island to take care of."

"Ugur did not tell me he had taken out one of the company boats."

"He has others, family boats. *Domitian* is a big, black sailing yacht." In case Martis checks on *Domitian*, I add vaguely, "and I think there are others too."

"So many boats the Konstantinous have!" Martis roars. "What fortunate people. To be a billionaire in paradise." He fans himself with his hand. "Will he be back onshore today?"

"I couldn't say," I answer meekly. "Most likely. He's working, and phone reception is so spotty off the island."

"But you saw Charlie yesterday. Was it after you witnessed the finding of the bodies?"

Now the alibi is working backward, pinning Charlie to the island when the fact of his absence would absolve him of blame. I have no idea what time he left for Bodrum. It must have been in the early morning. I move back the clock hands of the lie, for his protection and for mine.

"No, much earlier. Almost dawn. He might have been at sea all of yesterday for all I know. So he probably wasn't even here when those hippies were killed."

"The doctor couldn't determine an exact hour of death. They had been in the grass for some time. It was probably still darkness, still some night left. Did Charlie seem normal to you when you last saw him?"

The last time I saw him he was anything but normal, lobbing insults in the hope of being punched. "Yes, absolutely," I assure him. "Maybe a little hungover. We only spoke for a few minutes."

"On one of his boats?"

"Listen, Inspector, I'm late for work. I'm sure Charlie will be back today, and if I see him, I will tell him to talk to you right away. He'll want this cleared up as quickly as you do. I feel terrible about this misunderstanding. The poor families of those accident victims."

"Yes," he says, wiping a fist over his mustache. "The officer who telephoned them has the hardest job there is. I wish you visitors would be careful on your holidays. If my children died far from home, I would hope the police would be thorough. To see the injuries done to those young people, it was not a painless end."

For the first time, I catch a tremor of doubt in the inspector's voice, as if the case isn't nearly as settled in his gut as it is in his head. I can't shake the sense there is information he isn't sharing, a fact that's stopping him from surrendering the case folder to the desert of lost documents on the desk. Martis glances at his phone and then, less trustingly, at me. He knows about my past. He's read up on me.

"Just so you know, Charlie's a good person," I say. "He'd never kill anyone. We've been friends since we were little. I've known him my whole life. So even if you do think those two were murdered, Charlie wouldn't have done it. The whole idea is preposterous. I mean, honestly, they were just trespassing."

He nods and slides another piece of paper from the file. It lands on top of the passport printouts, a photo of a sharp wood nail lying on a steel tabletop.

"That was found next to the bodies," Martis says. "That and a scarf, the sort that Middle Eastern women wear around their heads. Do you know what that instrument is?"

"No. Were the backpackers stabbed with it?"

"Not stabbed. But it was there at the scene right beside them. It's a hand-carved spike, the kind that refugees carry when crossing on their rubber rafts. In case the coast guard finds them floating at sea, they puncture their raft with it. By law, the coast guard must rescue a sinking vessel. It assures they will be taken in instead of ordered back."

"So you're saying they could have been killed by refugees sneaking onto the island? Is that why they're at the station? You're questioning them?"

Martis again scrunches his shoulders. "They are here to be processed. But it could be that migrants entered Patmos in the early morning when it is still dark and were discovered by the two foreigners. They might have resorted to killing so they could not be reported. They can get to the north much faster if they are not detained. It is only a theory." He gathers the papers and returns them to the file. "The refugees have been very peaceful. There has been no violence against tourists yet. But it is always possible a few wolves sneak in with the lambs. And it is my job to consider all possibilities. Again, I do not mean to alarm you. I agree, trespassing would be an unlikely motive. Very foolish. After all, Charlie is a Konstantinou." He glances at me with an expression that verges on pity. "With the terrorist bomb last month, this island has been through enough. We would like this to be an accident. My superiors would like that very much."

Martis stands and reaches his hand out for me to shake. "Thank you, Ian. Please tell Charlie to stop by, and I will relay what a dependable employee he has. And I will wait for that friend request you've promised. I hope we can always be friends."

When I return to the outside terrace, the detainees have vanished. Only empty plastic bottles litter the freshly hosed brick. I follow the sound of scraping feet and whispered voices over the inner wall, where the building forms a square courtyard cut off from the rest of Skala. In the courtyard below, the refugees are huddled in corners on silver blankets. The boy with the comb sits alone on a bench.

I can still do something right, score a small, symbolic point against the tromping of the undefeated team whose mascot is anybody hunched and suffering. I pull a twenty-euro bill from my wallet and whistle to catch the boy's attention. His eyes search the blue of the sky and meet mine. "Hello," he calls again. I wave the bill, and he hurries to the wall, dropping his comb to open his hands. But his action has not gone unnoticed. Three men run over, their palms also clapping the air, nearly knocking the boy to the ground, and their shouts reverberate against the stone. "Here!" "Thank you!" "Sir, for me!" A lottery of hands below me, mouths wild with teeth, and I'm dangling money over them like food over starving inmates. I can't manage to drop the bill so it will find the boy's hands. When two officers race into the courtyard, alerted by the noise, I quickly step back with the twenty still in my grip. When I peek over again the officers are wielding batons.

My shirt soaked, my face burning, I take the steps down to the street. I race to my bike and fumble with my helmet, the shame holding me like a fever. Will the boy remember me, years into the future, a white Westerner high in the sky taunting him with money and then disappearing without dropping a single note?

Two dogs tied to a lamppost are barking. The red is on the water, breaking across its silver crests. I am sick of the uselessness I call helping. I'm more disgusted by this failure than by the twenty minutes I spent lying to the police.

I hope the boy will forgive me. I can barely forgive Charlie for leaving me here to deal with his mess. I told Martis I've known Charlie my whole life, but I haven't truly known him the past eight years. When I picture the refugees clamoring in the courtyard, it's not me but Charlie at the top. He waves his cash, his handsome face burnished like promise. He smiles. He disappears.

BY THE TIME I park my bike at the Charters dock, my phone has been beeping and vibrating in my pocket like a smoke detector that will be silenced only by smashing it to the ground. The country code is +30. At least it isn't my half-sister. But it isn't Charlie either. As soon as I pick up, Sonny's voice is a crowbar in my ear.

"There you are!" she shouts, her vocal chords corroded. As I expected, the detective's visit this morning hasn't been a balm to her nerves. "Police were at my door today. Police! Looking for Charlie!

Ian, what's this about?" There is a brusque command to Sonny's tone, not an appeal to a friend but a direct order from the boss's wife. I wonder how long would it have taken otherwise for our relationship to settle into this natural imbalance. By the time we land in Cyprus, will I be carrying her suitcases off the plane? Still, I can't blame her for being frightened. "What does this inspector want with Charlie?"

"Good afternoon, Sonny." In the second's ensuing silence, I can feel the willful stemming of her temper. "Didn't the inspector tell you?" I ask.

"No, he didn't. He said it was a minor matter. But in all of my time here, there's never been a cop at my door. You can't get a cop to come to your door when there's a *major* matter let alone a minor one."

I'm impressed that Martis had the foresight not to mention the deaths of the backpackers to her. Perhaps he realized how quickly panic spreads in the closed confines of a house.

"But it *is* minor," I assure her. "At least for us. I spoke with the inspector. There was a motorbike accident near Charlie's dock yesterday. No one you know. Some hippies died in a crash. He was just asking if anyone saw anything."

"If Charlie saw anything?" she drawls. "Why would he have?" And as if the news has finally caught up with her, she whispers, "That's awful. You say they're dead? But Charlie . . . I've been trying to call him and he isn't picking up. He hasn't come home yet. Where the hell is he, Ian? What's going on?"

A figure shifts in the shadows of the hangar, a tall, wire-thin body ducking around the corner. I'm suddenly aware of how quiet the dock is, without a single sound of activity or repair. There is only the mournful swaying of the crane's hooks overhead and the surf slapping along the rocks. Seagulls nestle on the vacant pier.

"Ian, are you there?"

"I've got to go, Sonny. Try not to worry. I'll call you later." Her protests dissolve with the press of a button.

I drop my helmet in the seat and head toward the hangar. One of the garage doors is pulled down, the other open to reveal the swampy darkness of the interior. Now that I'm alone, in the silence of the island, the inspector's suggestion of murder is hard to shake. Could the hippies really have been killed deliberately on this barren coastal stretch, the boats too far out at sea to protect them, the empty fields of thistle and scrub offering no shelter or hiding spot, only the goat bells clanging in the night? Even in the brittle sunlight, the landscape holds a mad desert stillness. Charlie called the camp a death cult. I wonder if it's the custom to return the clothes of the dead to the families and what Mikael's parents might make of the ripped Anti-Bethlehem slogan covered in their son's dried blood.

Before I reach the hangar, a peal of metal echoes from around the corner. "Hello?" I call. The metal object continues to swivel, rotating like a spun coin. There's no answer. "Hello?" I try again. I step into the shadow and steady my hand against the concrete as I turn.

Helios sits halfway down the building's side, just beyond the lid of an oil drum settling on the pavement. His knees are bunched at his chest, his sneakers projecting out like turtle heads, the cuffs of his long-sleeve T-shirt bunched in his palms. He rises when he sees me, sliding his back up the concrete wall like an execution in reverse.

"What are you doing?" I ask sharply. My anxiety has instantly converted into unjustifiable anger.

Helios wipes his mouth with his T-shirt sleeve.

"What does it look like?" he grumbles in his stiff English. "Taking a break. Hiding out from my father. He wants me working all the time." Helios prefers to stare out at the gated field beyond the hangar that encloses nothing but dry dirt. But an idea must have flared through his dim mind because he quickly rotates his head to me, his blistered lips easing into a smile. One of the blisters is dotted with pus. "How do you like the cabin? The hot water okay?"

"The hot water's fine."

He nods, *good, good.* "My job," he says, jabbing his chest. "I did plumbing. The locks too. I do it nice for Charlie."

"I met your sister, Vesna, this morning."

He scowls, rolls his head back, and takes in more of the view.

Either the original idea is reinstated or an entirely new one drops its bags in his head. "Soon, next year, the year after, if you stay, you will be able to drink at my bar." He runs his hand across invisible signage. "Helios's Lounge. You bring your friends, okay? Leather stools. First-rate sound system. Stage and dance floor. I will put it here by the sea or maybe in Skala. Charlie is helping me. He promises. Maybe I put it where Nikos's was. Something will have to open there. Bad to see it empty and black, and the family will not reopen."

"That's a good dream," I tell him. I can't imagine Helios's Lounge will ever see the electric light of day. Charlie must have factored lazy ambition in the lounge's launch schedule.

"One year, maybe two or three. Soon." Helios twists a few goatee hairs with his bruised fingertips. His back is still pressed against the hangar, as if it's his job to keep it from toppling over. I wonder if he's considered on the winning side of the country's youth employment statistics. "Charlie is a good friend. Have you seen him today?"

"No. Have you?"

He chews on his pus-dotted lip. "I have to find him, have to ask him for a small favor. Very little." He glances at me, gauging my cash potential, his eyes fleeing to my pockets for the imprint of a wallet. I finally get to perform my universal poverty gesture with empty waving hands. "That's okay," he replies contritely, shivering a bit in the building's shadow. Helios is far less aggressive than Vesna about borrowing funds, maybe because he has nowhere urgent to be. "Charlie helps me out. He is my pal. It can wait until I see him."

"Has your father seen him?"

He glides a hand through his gelled hair. The back of his neck is sunburned, but his pocked forehead is as pale as moth wings.

"No, I do not think so. Charlie gave him day off. He might still be out on his rowboat fishing. *Fffff.* I hate fishing. My father won't let me play music. He says it scares the fish. He is an old man, out of touch. Doesn't want me to open my bar, either. Doesn't understand what money it brings. Money, girls, real nice first-class place." Christos must view Helios's Lounge the way my father did charity work:

solar-powered fantasies on which no practical machines can run. "Charlie never gives my father days off in August," he says. "That means Charlie is off the island. I was hoping he would be back by now. He always comes right back."

I'm relieved by even this vague, hash-muddled confirmation of Charlie's plans. Without realizing it, Helios has restored my faith in the timetable. To express my thanks, I pull the twenty-euro bill from my pocket and hold it out to him.

Helios gazes at it waywardly, one eye closing, as if steadying on a mark.

"What is that?" he says, as if he has already forgotten asking for money.

"For you. Take it. It's not a problem just this once."

"Are you sure?" He snatches it and wads it in his palm. "Thank you." For the first time there's a healthy color to his cheeks. "I appreciate. A free drink for you at my lounge." He slaps my shoulder, holding his hand there to momentarily balance himself. "Tell Charlie I find him tomorrow, okay? Thank you for the tip, dude."

Dude. With that last triumphant Americanism, Helios wanders with a sideways stagger into the field, dropping out of sight into a gulley. Unlike with the hippies, Patmos actually *is* his backyard. He grew up here and must know every beach and cove in which to hide from his father, who also grew up here and probably knows exactly where to look for him.

I return to the front of the hangar, inspecting the horizon for a white yacht with a red *K* on the bow drifting in from Bodrum. Out in the deeper channels is a mini-UN of luxury vessels, flags from Turkey, Malta, Nicaragua, Spain, Australia, Italy. The faint glittery beige of human bodies collects at the tips of the decks like expensive hood ornaments. A few black orbs dot the water, swimmers treading around their crafts. The shimmer of the sea reminds me of the fiber-optic whirl of technology, as if those swimmers are floating in the electrodes of boundless information, bobbing through screen-like waves of transference. They are tiny glitches that spark and fade.

I step into the hangar, its silence reeking of butane and paint thinner. The brass frame of the refurbished boat gleams in the blackness, the *K* already painted across its peak. Two small squares sparkle a few feet behind it. Ugur shuffles forward, pushing his glasses higher on his nose. He has the reluctant, mole-like expression of a man caught hiding.

"E-on," he wheezes, nervously scanning the area behind me. "The police were here today. I do not like the police."

I concur that most people don't.

"I did not answer his questions," he says. "We have understanding with the local police, but not this one. Do you think he will come back?"

"Not if Charlie talks to him."

That response prompts no perceptible consolation. "I do not want him asking for my papers, to have my name down." He inches forward, still distrusting the light.

"Ugur, where are the workers?" I gesture around the empty hangar.

"I tell them not to come. I did not think it was good idea with that inspector from Kos turning up. They too have names, families, papers. I wait for Charlie to tell me it is safe."

"He's not from the Better Business Bureau." I laugh. Ugur heaves a flummoxed sigh that underscores what little humor there is in undocumented labor. I try to inject the command of a number two in my voice, to exert a firm authority over my future workplace. I channel Edward Bledsoe. "We can't shut down just because an officer has a few questions about a traffic accident. What about the customers? Aren't there bookings? Someone besides Charlie has to be handling the reservations and dock schedules."

"Customers?" Ugur repeats.

"The tourists. The vacationers. The charterers."

"I, I do not handle," he stutters. If only Ugur would step into the sun we could have a reasonable conversation, but I'm staring at the twin reflections of his glasses and the charcoal color of his lips. "I think booking this week with family from Moldova. To Agathonisi?"

"One booking this week? What about the yachts out now? It's high season!"

"I do not handle," he cries again. "That is your job. Like man who came before you. I handle boats. I do not *liaise* with customers." It's as if Ugur and I are only proficient in the universal language of corporate catchwords. "Customers! The customers are not my problem! Why you not ask Charlie? Where is he?"

I'm startled, tossed back, someone who had mistaken this planet the last few hours for Earth. Of anyone on this island, it is Ugur who should know where Charlie is.

"What do you mean? You don't know? He's in Bodrum. He should be back any second. He went to deal with some problem about"— what did he call the problem?—"*ports*. Didn't he take one of the charter boats out yesterday morning?"

One step back, and Ugur fades into the shadows. Maybe he doesn't want me to see him shaking, but I can feel it, the air running cold between us.

"He was supposed to, yes. On a boat scheduled to leave at seven A.M. But he did not show up. He never show up yesterday. The boat leave without him."

"So he's not in Bodrum?" Silence, only silence. "Could he have taken another boat?"

"No. Not one of ours. I radio captains at sea. They never hear from him. And I call his phone all yesterday and today. He does not answer."

"Where the hell is he then?"

Ugur scoots closer to the boat, and his mouth issues a panicked sound midway between a growl and a bleat. "I thought you would tell me. You are his best friend. Now your job. E-on, where is he? Charlie needs to be in Bodrum yesterday. That meeting was very important. He would not miss it. Tell me what to do now!"

There are prayers for the faithful. And there are prayers even for the faithless, quieter maybe, but no more certain of their futility. I try one. *Answer, appear, just show up right now in your skimpy yellow shorts with your bob-and-weave smile, end this by being here, for fuck's sake, appear.* A dirty brown mutt lopes into the hangar and sniffs the door grate, his curled tongue lolling. He notices the two pathetic inhabitants and scampers off. I suppose the faithful might take it as a sign.

"So he's still on the island?" I yell toward Ugur's glowing lenses.

"Yes. I think. Where else would he be? But he would be here now. Very bad. Very, very bad. Eon, you do not know how bad this is."

It's odd that the moment I realize my friend is missing I feel in some way that he's found. Against all logic, Charlie is still on Patmos, out of sight, not answering his phone. But if he is on the island why isn't he at home with Sonny or down at the dock running his boats? All I can picture are the strange tears in his eyes the last time I saw him that night in Skala, as if a star he loved had finally stopped transmitting light. Or were the tears over a less poetic blow that resulted in the last-minute change of plan?

"Charlie!" I scream into the darkness of the hangar. Ugur's lenses are no longer visible. He must have backed into a corner where even indirect light can't reach him, behind the steel shells and paint buckets and boxes of folded towels.

I spin into the sun and march toward my bike, the need to find Charlie pressing on me, tightening each nerve like a string. The problem is, I can't think of anywhere in particular to look. I would go to the police if they weren't already searching for him. I would notify Sonny if she weren't already agonizing over his whereabouts. Even Helios is stalking the island trying to hunt him down. Without my lifting a finger, the search parties have all been dispatched. And yet it is little solace that every lie I told about Charlie being here has stumbled backward into the truth.

I rev the motor—*where are you? where are you?*—and take the thin trail away from the beach. On the main road, where the dirt meets the blacktop, a white Mercedes station wagon idles. I see Petros through the windshield with his thin, Rolex-ed arm dangling from the window. As I turn, he flashes his headlights in recognition. Petros must be looking for Charlie too. It occurs to me that if anyone ran two foreigners off the road in the night, Petros is the likely suspect. I would offer his name up to Martis for questioning, but even I know the futility of that accusation. The clergy owns the island, more immune even than the Konstantinous to suspicion.

I speed along the pavement, worried the station wagon might appear at any moment in my rearview mirrors, its grille hungry for more casualties. When it hits me that *Domitian* is the only place I haven't checked, I swerve the bike into the dusty village of Grikos. Whitewashed homes are built into the hillside like rice terraces on an Asian steppe. Their walls stream with meaty bougainvillea and the circuitry of rust-brown grapevines. At the port, just beyond tables of yellow wine and heat-exhausted families, Charlie's black yacht is moored with a beige canvas strapped over its hatch. But I'm too late. Martis, using an officer as a support beam, is jumping onto its polished deck.

After dialing and redialing Charlie's number, I have nowhere left to go but home. I pull a bottle of vodka from the minifridge. I turn out the lights. I slide the lock on the connecting door. A passing rainsquall beats across the roof like the feet of running children. When Louise knocks gently from her room, I swallow a shot and whisper that I'm sick. I sit in the minutes and hours trying to conceive of what might have happened to Charlie that night after Miles punched him and we all drifted back to our beds. Where did he go? Where is he now? He must know that everyone is worried, that I couldn't hold them off indefinitely with a phony alibi. I don't need to check whether Charlie's resurfaced. As evening sets, my phone vibrates with Sonny's incoming number—one missed call, twelve, twenty-two.

Not every lie I told has proved true. I claimed to be the last to see him, and blame rests on the last known visitor, the one who sat in the rocking chair, the one who still had the power to breathe when he exited the room. There's too little left in the bottle not to finish it.

Ian, what did you do?

CHAPTER 10

S onny's calls stopped at 3:14 A.M. When I wake late, my head throbbing and my stomach in the midst of a fulminous congressional debate about whether I should run immediately to the toilet to vomit or wait agonizingly for a unanimous decision, the bleary sunlight a mean double operative, I'm relieved that her calls haven't resumed this morning. That gives me hope that Charlie is back. Instead I've slept through three Skype requests from my mother. Unable to reach me, she resorted to text message.

Mom: IAN? YOU THERE? CAN WE TALK?

Mom: WHERE EXACTLY ARE YOU?

Mom: I'M ASKING BECAUSE I GOT A DISTURBING CALL FROM ALEXIS. HONEY, SHE SAYS SHE'S BEEN TRYING TO TRACK YOU DOWN ABOUT MISSING MONEY FROM YOUR FATHER'S ACCOUNT??? THAT GIRL IS A PIECE OF WORK, SHE REALLY DOES TAKE AFTER YOUR FATHER. BUT SHE SEEMS TO BELIEVE YOU RAN OFF WITH 9K—WHICH I TOLD HER MUST BE A MISTAKE. YOU ARE MY HONEST IAN, EVEN IF YOU DID SEND ME THAT ODD AND, I MUST ADMIT, UNNERVING SYMBOL OF A POLICE SIREN. AND WHILE I'M SURE YOUR FATHER

Mom: WAS NO DOUBT MISERLY IN HIS WILL—BELIEVE ME I KNOW EXACTLY WHAT IT'S LIKE TO TRY TO EXTRACT DESERVED MONEY FROM THAT MAN—HE MUST HAVE LOOKED AFTER YOU SOMEHOW? YES/NO? AT ANY RATE, SHE WOULDN'T GET OFF THE PHONE UNTIL I PROMISED TO REACH OUT TO YOU. I GOT THE FEELING SHE HAD MORE PRESSING REASONS THAN 9K. QUESTIONS, QUESTIONS ABOUT YOUR

Mom: FATHER, LAST WORDS? WAS HE EVEN ABLE TO SPEAK AT THE END? JUST OUT OF CURIOSITY, DID HE MENTION ME AT ALL? I HIGHLY DOUBT LILY WOULD HAVE ALLOWED THAT, BUT I DO WONDER. I'VE BEEN

THINKING A LOT ABOUT OUR MARRIAGE THESE LAST FEW DAYS. BEFORE YOU, IT WAS AS IF ALL THAT YOUR FATHER NEEDED WAS THE SOUND OF SOMEONE IN THE NEXT ROOM. THAT WAS HIS IDEA OF MARRIAGE: A NOISE IN THE BACKGROUND. BUT THEN YOU WERE

Mom: BORN AND IT MADE THOSE YEARS WORTH IT. YOU WERE A BIG, BEAUTIFUL NOISE. I DON'T KNOW WHY I'M TELLING YOU THIS. MAYBE SOME WISH TO TALK ABOUT YOUR FATHER AND HERE IN INDIA THERE IS NO ONE WITH ANY CONNECTION TO MY PAST. I USUALLY FIND THAT A GIFT. AT ANY RATE, PLEASE CALL ALEXIS. SHE SOUNDED VERY ANGRY. ANSWERING HER QUESTIONS MIGHT PUT THE MATTER TO REST. RE-MEMBER, I LOVE YOU. I LOVE YOU SO MUCH. AND IF I DO MANAGE TO OPEN THIS

Mom: ORPHANAGE—THE POLITICS OF SUCH AN ENDEAVOR IS NOT EASY IN BACKWARD DELHI WHERE, AS I'VE TOLD YOU, THEY BE-LIEVE NOT THAT YOU MAKE YOUR DESTINY BUT THAT YOUR DESTINY MAKES YOU SO GOD WANTS YOU TO DIE OF HUNGER IN THE STREET—PERHAPS YOU COULD GIVE A SMALL CONTRIBUTION FROM YOUR INHERITANCE. YOU ARE MY GOOD HEART. I LOVE

Mom: YOU. PLEASE SEND A SIGN YOU ARE FINE. I WORRY. LOVE, HELEN

The vote is unanimous. I cover my hand over my mouth as I fly toward the bathroom, the heaving so perfectly choreographed that I reach the porcelain mouth at the exact moment a flood of yellow syrup shoots from my throat. I don't even kneel, just bend my head like a professional as five retching doses fill the bowl, the pain mi-grating from my stomach to my temples.

I wipe my chin with a towel, avoiding the quicksand of the mirror, and attempt to insert the prodding finger of the toothbrush in my mouth. Stumbling back into the bedroom, I check that the money is still in the nightstand as I tap a text to my mother: I'M IN GREECE. I'LL HANDLE IT. JUST A MISUNDERSTANDING. AND NO, THERE IS NO IN-HERITANCE FOR ME. I DIDN'T MAKE THE CUT. As I'm trying to figure out a better hiding spot for the money, another text beeps.

GOOD MORNING, IAN. IT'S MILES. DO YOU WANT TO GET THAT COFFEE? I'D REALLY LIKE TO EXPLAIN.

I respond: HAS CHARLIE COME HOME?

No.

I wish my stomach had something left to oust. A different, far heavier queasiness descends, irremediable by sips of water or whiling hours from the final intake: the fact that Miles was one of the last to see Charlie, and he ended it with a punch. If Charlie's disappearance is in any way involuntary, could it be that Miles's conscience is inducing a need to explain? But I don't want to think what "in any way involuntary" might begin to mean. My hangover won't let me. A hangover is not so much an unwanted by-product of last night's drinking as a destination in itself. It's a safe room from overthinking, the outside world so full of excruciating, bomb-blasting sights and sounds, the worst thoughts merely blend into the scenery.

I'LL COME TO YOU, I write him. WHERE'S YOUR HOUSE?

I'M WATCHING DUCK. LET'S MEET AT A TAVERNA IN CHORA?

I HAVE TO DO SOMETHING FIRST. BEST IF I JUST COME TO YOUR PLACE. I DON'T KNOW HOW LONG I'LL BE. OKAY, MILES?

I open the empty cedar closets, searching for a hiding spot for the money as I await his answer. After five minutes, he finally responds: UH, OKAY, HOUSE RIGHT BY ROAD IN CHORA, OVERLOOKING TAXI STAND. GREEN DOOR WITH WHITE AWNING.

There is no better hiding spot than the nightstand. My clothes are still piled in my suitcase. Against Charlie's advice, I haven't unpacked, haven't hung my shirts on the hangers or arranged my toiletries like a toy train along the medicine-cabinet shelves. At some point in adulthood, I've learned that the sanest way of existing is never to feel at home. Today should be the first day of my new job at Konstantinou Charters. Instead, I'm going to visit *Domitian*, searching for the man who was supposed to rescue me.

GRIKOS IS A vanishing village, the white gulls scattering off the stucco rooftops like exploding stone. Even in the August high season, Grikos's condos stare vacantly at the sea, its balconies rarely flash a swimsuit drying across a railing, and its gunmetal shop grates are pulled shut to serve as peeling announcement boards for summer concerts a month out of date. The tourists who drift along the port have the disappointed expressions of failed explorers, and the liveliest spot along the water is a restaurant offering pizza, and in newer signage sushi, and, in a final gastronomic gamble, a cartoon drawing of a taco, as if to tempt vacationers island-ed out on feta and squid. Still the village manages to appear overcrowded simply because of the compact houses packed tightly against the meager sliver of sand. I stop in a pharmacy, its neon-green plus sign blinking like an American dollar. Two hippies congregate in an aisle gathering rolls of cloth bandages, the kind to wrap around sore ankles and knees. I study the two young men with horsey German faces, one with a silver piercing in his cheek. The smell of pot and cloves drifts from their tourist shirts. They must belong to Vic's camp.

"Do you have more bandages like these?" the taller, cheek-pierced guy asks the woman at the counter.

I buy a bottle of aspirin, cherry-flavored for children. A slice of lemon sits on the cash register, which the clerk dabs with her fingertips before counting out my change. I only have about seventy euros left from the advance Charlie gave me. Back outside, in the breezy blur of the bay, I curse myself for not saving more of it. When Charlie returns . . . But that thought echoes without resolution, *when Charlie returns, when Charlie returns . . .*

I'm chewing on two aspirin tablets as I approach *Domitian*. Christos stands on the pier, hosing down a pile of life vests and corralling one with the side of his flip-flop. His shirt is off, and from the back his body appears younger, a caramel hide over lean, taut muscles. He shuts off the spray, and turning, he becomes his age. There's an apprehension to his darting, missing-teeth smile. Vesna said that he's hard on his children, demanding too much. For some reason, strictness in a Greek father who makes his money tending boats seems more forgivable to me than in a wealthy New York businessman who managed to limit all contact with his son. And yet I wouldn't want to be the recipient of Christos's abbreviated gestures and barking commands. Charlie brought out the occasional warmth in the captain, but, of course, Charlie was paying him.

"Christos," I say. He wipes the water on his shorts before extending his hand. "Have you spoken to Charlie? Have you seen him in the past day?"

He blinks at me in confusion. "No," he bellows. "I hear nothing. I not know if he want *Domitian* today. No word." He motions to the boat, as if it's someone's pet he's forced to care for, which is exactly what it is. He grooms it, he cleans up after it, he knows its tricks and shortcomings better than its owners do. But there's no sense of usufruct with *Domitian*; yesterday Helios told me that his father took a rowboat out to fish, as if borrowing the Konstantinou trophy for his own enjoyment would be a breach of conduct or of personal pride. "I leave here. I wait for him call." Christos grabs his phone from his pocket and waves it. "He no call. Not for days. Want boat today or no want? I must move *Domitian* to Skala. He not tell me."

I pray that Christos is better at understanding English than at speaking it.

"I have to ask you an important question. Three nights ago, did Charlie say anything to you about staying on *Domitian* for the night? Or about anchoring it out at sea for a few days until he got back from where he was going?"

Christos watches my lips carefully, his own lips cracked, lined with silver stubble, miming syllables.

"Charlie tell me leave *Domitian* here in Grikos. Leave galley unlocked. He say he sleep here and we speak early in morning about putting boat at sea. But I come next day, very early, he not here. He leave me no word. No call. No instruction. I keep boat here, but not hear anything from him." He looks uneasy without a check-in from his employer, no doubt in his decades as the captain for the Konstantinous a trustworthy operative in whatever bizarre requests a billionaire family has asked of him. I imagine there have been many over the decades. He must be the caretaker of a zillion secrets that have flourished and faded in their summers on the island. A boat is a house with no neighbors, a mobile playground.

"You did the right thing," I say. He seems indifferent to my attempt at assurance.

"You work at company now for Charlie?" he asks gruffly, tightening his eyes on me. In those eyes, we are now both employees.

"I haven't started yet. What do you know about that business?"

"Not my business," he hammers, poking his chest. "I no part. I do family boat only, for Mr. Konstantinou. I no interest in tourists." A gold medallion hangs in the tinseled fauna of his chest hair. On the medallion is the engraving of an older, straining man, his back bent, with a child mounted on his shoulders like a beleaguered father carrying his son. I recognize the figure from taxi dashboards and from the necks of superstitious vacationers and from my childhood memorizing saints in church. It's St. Christopher, Christos's namesake, the patron saint of travelers. I remember the story: Christopher, by occupation, presumably before the invention of boats, carried voyagers across a river. One day a little boy stood waiting to cross. Christopher took him on his back, and as the water deepened and turned treacherous, the boy grew heavier and heavier until he was the weight of lead. But the soon-to-be saint prevailed to save the boy, and once onshore he realized the child was Christ. It seems less a case study in voyage miracles than it does in a fervent work ethic. But I can't help wishing that Helios was worth the burden of his muling father, or that Edward Bledsoe had taken me as something more valuable than stubborn weight: to keep my mouth above the water even as his slipped under. The real lesson, when stripped of its Christian pieties, seems to be that serving the future means putting a weaker body before your own, a future of defenseless boys riding their drowning fathers in the waves.

Christos frowns as he lassos the hose. "Mr. Konstantinou, he has operation yesterday. Is he better? Awake soon? Out of hospital?"

I had forgotten about Mr. K's surgery. "I don't know," I tell him. "I'll ask Sonny when I see her." He nods and tucks his chin against his neck, as if praying for a quick recovery. Tears glaze his brown eyes.

"Are you okay?" I ask.

"My daughter, Vesna. I not find today. Gone. And Helios I not find also." I consider informing him of Vesna's protest rally in Athens, the one I surreptitiously financed, but I'm not interested in implicating myself in a Stamatis family crisis. I have Charlie to worry about.

I ask Christos if I can check out *Domitian*. After we both hop aboard, the captain unsnaps the canvas cover from the galley hatch.

"My daughter clean," he tells me as he slides open the rosewood door. "I coffee." He points to the shoreline restaurant as I steady my feet on the ladder rungs.

The galley is dark, the chrome glowing green, and the carpet soft on the barely rocking floor. My hand slides along the recessed wood until it finds the dimmer switch. The silent, sunken room, under the constellation of track lighting, is a headachy gleam. While I've always appreciated Charlie's taste, there's something garish about *Domitian*'s interior, like a lavish midtown condo that an oligarch bought predecorated but never visited. Fashion and boating magazines are stacked on the table. Two glass tumblers have been washed and left to dry upside down in the kitchen's dish rack. Vesna has straightened and cleaned, at least in her mildly incompetent manner; on a low shelf next to the opal-inlaid chessboard sits a dirty ashtray she's missed. I walk over and peer into it. Six hand-rolled butts fill the dish. The chessboard is frozen midgame, white winning, cornering the black king, although both sides have suffered heavy casualties. But now I know for certain that Charlie is the one who's been sitting here. A castle lies on the side of the board, his signature forfeit to ensure an even match.

Two glass tumblers in the dish rack, a chessboard halted one move from victory—Charlie's been here and he wasn't alone. I try to recall if he mentioned visiting *Domitian* between the afternoon we sailed around the island and the night we met for drinks in Skala. Or is this evidence that he did come back to the yacht that night to sleep, just as Christos confirmed was his plan? If so, he had company. Someone must have visited, someone he knew well enough to offer a drink. And maybe that someone had a serious matter to discuss, prompting the second offer of chess. Chess is how Charlie swore he did his best thinking—how he wanted me, jammed in the corner of his office, strung over a board, to prove he could beat me as I was begging for his help. Even in charity, the game was still to win. The memory infuriates me now as much as his disappearance. Did he want me to understand which one of us was the loser? He could have at least chosen a game in which I had a fighting chance. *Three gunmen in black balaclavas burst into the room. What do you do?* Was it ever one gunman? One would be enough.

I move into the bedroom. The king-size bed hasn't been slept in since Vesna made it up. Only a slight pond's ripple is frozen across the purple wool. I scan the shelves of trophies, old Roman coins encased in plastic, a few bottles of cologne, and paperback novels warped by their home on the sea. At the end of a shelf is a small, yellowed book with a Polaroid sticking out. I pull the book out, and it falls open to a blue-lined page.

The crude handwriting is unsteady, the *e*'s backward, the *g*'s fattened into hourglasses, the *P*'s hovering like streetlamps. It's a childhood diary dated 1993, when Charlie was seven:

the winters are cold. The sun sets arond 5:30 but rises before I wake up. When it isn't cloudy, the sun is warm and it feels good to stand under but your not alowed to look up at it or else it hurts your eyes. The churches are old. The shops are loud and angry. The food is just okay, but you should not order the same thing all the time because its boring. Most people are nice. A few are not. But people like you if you tell a funny joke. Old people walk to slow under umbrelas. I like night the best because its dark but you can see farther in the sky. Mom says we wont stay long.

Maybe it was a trip with his family that Charlie was recording, or maybe it was a winter in New York. But it reads like practical advice for living, a Yelp review of planet Earth.

I pluck the Polaroid from its pages. It's a photo of Charlie, undated, but he's at least ten years younger than he is now. He's midsway on a rope swing, night the only background, a yellow flannel shirt open to reveal his hairless chest. His legs are splayed, with the white blob of a sneaker kicking out toward the camera and catching most of the flash. But it's his face that fascinates me, pitched back but staring directly at the lens, somewhere between startled and self-possessed. It's like some phantom point on a horizon, beautiful and untouchable, for once free of all context, even of its arrogant smile. Whether it's the past I'm thinking of or the present, I find myself missing him and worried for him and wanting him back, as if I could reach out and still the ropes and hold him by the neck. *Where are you, Charlie? What happened? It doesn't have to turn out this way. We can still be whatever we want.* But I realize I'm talking to a boy ten years gone in a photograph. The white blob did meet the ground. The swing stopped. We are both too old to be whatever we want.

I slip the Polaroid between the pages. Time is too often gauged by what could have been prevented. History is a palace of mistakes.

First it's just a sound, distant but subterranean. I stop to listen. The sound rises again, rustling, scraping. There's something down in the boat with me. I pass back into the main room where the pale sunlight catches the frame of Charlie and his father. *Skk, skk.* The sound is beckoning from behind the closed bathroom door by the kitchen. I imagine Charlie on the other side, his legs and mouth and wrists taped, rubbing a torn fingernail across the wood. As crazy as it might be, I consider this scenario the most optimistic one—or at least the easiest scenario to explain why he never made it to his meeting in Bodrum.

The scratching is low to the floor, as patient as a branch against the side of a house. I grab the knob and wrench it open. Terry, the gray boat cat, sits on the marble bathroom tiles.

"You scared the shit out of me," I yell, picking him up and bring-ing him to my chest. I feel his thin bones under the unkempt fur. My feet crunch the spilled litter around the tray under the sink, the marble tiles streaked with Vesna's mopping. I stand for a minute in the bright quadrilateral, where a large portal window frames the seamless confluence of sky and sea. It's so perfect, that fine, hazy blue, I almost want to punch a hole through it, press some button to make the unbearable beauty stop.

"Are you hungry?" I ask the green eyes and white whiskers, lifting the cat in front of the mirror. In the reflection, a tiny blotch of brown covers the fur of his front paw. It's the color of dried blood. I grab at Terry's paw, but the cat turns feral, clawing at me, digging into my wrist, drawing more blood. As I let go, he races into the kitchen. Dried blood on his paw, and now on the bathroom floor I notice two brown splotches missed by Vesna's mop. Fear switches the heart's motor to its emergency-fuel reserve—Charlie's blood, Charlie bleed-ing in this bathroom, Charlie never finishing the last move on the chessboard. Vesna's own words yesterday ring in my ears, a pass-ing observation that I stupidly didn't stop to question. *But when I went to clean, there was only an awful mess. No Charlie.* What kind of awful mess? The mess of a scuffle, a fight? Or the mess of someone who never learned to pick up after himself? If only I could ask her, but right now Vesna is thrusting an anti-Eurozone sign toward the sky in Syntagma Square, chanting along with her compatriots for the rights of a free and independent nation. Fucking good that does when she might have mopped up a crime scene. Where does Vesna dispose of the garbage she collects from *Domitian?* Is there a trash bag on a barge floating out at sea with all of the evidence of some-thing I can't force myself to imagine?

I'm about to sound an alarm—in my mind, I'm already hur-tling down the dock screaming for the police—when I remember my injured toe on the day we sailed around the island. Relief floods through me as fast as fear. The blood is probably mine. I hobbled down here after Sonny bandaged it.

The fresh scratch marks on my wrist are leaking red, and a drip falls onto the floor, further contaminating a contaminated scene. I run the cut under the faucet and apply pressure. *You're paranoid*, I say to myself in the mirror. Paranoid, definitely. But Charlie has still been missing for more than two days.

I return to the chessboard and pull out the chair that Charlie sat in with the ashtray by my right hand. I inspect the wood and opal inlay, pinching my fingers along the surface and checking them for specks of red. The table is clean. My fingertips trace the groove of a small drawer on the side of the table. I slide it open. Resting on the padded velvet is the gaudy turquoise earring that Charlie had pinned to his shirt that night in Skala. I lift the earring by its hook. He was here, has been here, on *Domitian*. He did come back. But then what? I can't be absolutely sure the blood is mine.

Clutching the earring, I climb the ladder. Christos sits at the restaurant on the shore, his bony legs crossed. He spots me and gets to his feet, stumbling around the tables and a cluster of tourist bags. We meet halfway along the dock, by a row of plastic buckets where dead sardines float on their stewing surfaces.

I flash the earring. "I found this. Charlie had it on in Skala."

Christos studies it skeptically. "Sonny earring," he replies, plucking his earlobes. "Charlie no."

"That's not what I mean. He had it with him. It proves he came back to the boat that night. And you said he wasn't here early the next morning?"

He must sense hostility in my voice because his skeptical expression passes from the earring onto me. He begins to cluck, like a lawn mower cord being pulled to jump-start an engine.

"He not there," he hollers as he flails his hands. "*Domitian* empty."

"Was there a mess? Or any sign of a struggle when you checked that morning? Did your daughter clean up anything toppled over? Christos, did she clean up blood and not tell anyone?"

I shouldn't have included Vesna in my accusations, but the rush of anxiety has turned my questions into swinging fists. Christos's face reddens. Then it pales. As I'm reaching out in apology, he grits his teeth. I find I don't have the courage to touch his shoulder. My hand hovers in front of him, as if to prevent an attack.

"My Vesna, she do nothing but clean. What you say not tell of blood? No blood there. Nothing. Empty. We do our job only."

"I didn't mean it that way. It's just that I found small traces—"

"We not work for you. We work for Charlie. Charlie and Mr. Konstantinou. Who are you, eh?" He flicks his fingers against my bicep.

"I'm sorry," I say. "But I can't find Charlie. No one can. I'm trying to figure out where he is."

"He gone. Not on boat. I come, he not there. But Charlie—" He can't summon the words in English, tapping his palm roughly against his chest. I know the words. Charlie is strong, Charlie is an adult, Charlie is a free man, Charlie can take care of himself. I nod, wishing I could believe that. But Christos is right about one thing: he does work for the Konstantinous and not for me. If, by chance, Charlie is hiding out on the island, purposely out of sight, he might have asked Christos to keep that secret safe. In any case, I've already lost the captain as an accomplice in concern. He eyes me distrustfully, like I'm a cyclone he could get sucked up in.

"This not okay," he grumbles. His eyes are already off me, glaring at the rocking, black-oak sixty footer, clearly regretful of letting a stranger on board. "I want speak Mr. Konstantinou."

"Fine. I understand that. But will you let me know if you see Charlie? Or let Sonny know? Or anyone? Or will you just tell him to come home? I didn't mean anything about Vesna. I'm sure you'll see her soon. And Helios too."

Christos shakes his head, digs his feet deeper into his flip-flops, and strides down the dock. "I only speak Mr. Konstantinou!" he shouts.

I've managed to offend the one man who could have been a crucial ally. When is the moment that doing nothing serves a crisis better than throwing yourself blindly into its midst? I almost convince myself to stop the search. But as I climb onto my bike, I stare down at the earring. It's the only proof I have of Charlie's existence after I last saw him. At some point after midnight in Skala and before Christos arrived early in the morning, he was on his yacht. And he wasn't alone. For the first time, I let myself imagine a scenario that would explain his failure to meet the charter boat to Bodrum and the long days of silence since: Charlie taken by surprise in the galley, injured or incapacitated, weighted down and thrown overboard, erased underneath the waves. The imagination is a wild dog. It runs happily toward the meanest end.

In the distance, *Domitian* glides from the port, its sails wrapped around its mast, the motor churning a sapphire wake. Christos is moving the boat to Skala. Here on a holiday island, nothing, not even a room, stays in place.

MILES IS THE one person I can think of who had a reason to visit Charlie that night on his boat. Thankfully, his mansion sits directly opposite the taxi stand at the entrance to Chora. I doubt I'd be able to find it otherwise. The egg-white awning, ripped on one side, shades a door scabbed with pistachio-green paint. The slender, white-washed mansion rises three stories. The tall windows of the first two floors give way to the small square windows of a garret, from which top-forty hits blare, mingling with chanting prayers from a nearby shrine. Unlike most houses, no antique knocker decorates the door. There's only a rusted screw that once held one.

I'm about to knock when the door swings open and three attractive Asian vacationers bolt into the daylight. They litter the air with smiles and loud voices singing along to the upstairs pop music. Two men and a woman, barely out of their teenage years, step back to close the door and study me. Their sunglasses are diamond-encrusted. The woman's hair is bone-marrow white and plaited in neon barrettes. Their swimsuits are adorned in the garish tartans and mismatched stripes of popular European fashion brands.

"I think I have the wrong house," I say.

They find my mistake hilarious, jostling each other by the shoulders. Or maybe they're just wildly happy to be on Patmos. They speak to each other in clipped Mandarin, which induces further laughter, and one guy attempts to twist the other's nipple.

"No, Ian, you have the right house," a voice booms from behind them. Miles ducks his head from the darkness, gaunt-cheeked and puffy-eyed. He smiles in embarrassment and turns to the three beachgoers. "You have your key? I leave it locked."

"Okay, captain," one of the young men says, saluting sarcastically.

Miles beckons me into the hallway. A crooked staircase leads to a sun-drenched landing, but we remain on the ground floor, passing along the peeling, brick-tiled hall.

"Who were those three?" I ask.

"Guests," he replies nonchalantly. "I've been renting out the top two floors this summer on one of those destination websites." He takes my silence as an accusation. "Not all of us can pray to the patron saint of richer friends when we're having trouble."

"I'm not judging."

His face eases a bit. "I'm sorry. I don't know why I said that. We're a tiny anthill up here, everyone crawling on top of each other. Even if Charlie hadn't mentioned my recent difficulties the other night, I'm sure you would have heard about it sooner or later." The memory causes him to massage his punching hand, as if still trying to relax it out of a fist. "The new renters are Chinese kids. *Fuerdai*. You know, the children of the Beijing elite. You wouldn't believe what they're willing to pay." Miles seems to want me to be impressed with his boarders, as if their money reflects onto him. "This house was built in 1429, owned by the farming and sheep-rearing gentry, thus the northern view of the valley. It's my father's house, but I'm the one who comes every summer. And, honestly, what do I need all the extra rooms for? Really, I see it as an ethnological experiment," he adds. "What's left of ethnology anyway. Some advice. Don't rent to Brazilians. They aren't housebroken. They shattered a seventeenth-century whale-oil lamp and didn't even bother to sweep up the glass." He glances at me, shame weighing on his face, as if he had never imagined himself part-innkeeper, part-domestic policeman. "It's only for this one summer!"

"There's nothing wrong with taking in guests," I assure him.

He stops at the door to his quarters. "We'll talk more about it in a minute."

We enter a large, sparse living room, the light a dusty gray through the grime-mottled windows. White sheets are draped over two long couches, as if Miles hasn't found the energy to release them from their winter hibernation. The décor is sea themed—ceramic starfish, abstract prints of blue blotches that approximate the shapes of fish, a coffee table mosaicked with mirror and seashells, large knots of fishermen's rope. It's the same design scheme that infects the mansions of the Hamptons and Cape Cod, weekend homes where the senile wealthy surround themselves in reminders of where they are. The only unexpected feature is a giant canvas sac hanging from the ceiling by a chain; it vibrates from the upstairs music. The chandelier has been bagged, protecting the heart of the house, like the pouch of internal organs stuffed inside a store-bought turkey. Clearly, Miles didn't expect to entertain this summer, but the swaying gray canvas over our heads exposes his desperation even more than his boarders did. The elegance of a gold and crystal chandelier would dangle like a reminder of better days.

Duck is sprawled on the floor, half hidden behind the coffee table in a tangerine jumper. She's coloring on a sketch pad, duplicating two figures from a glossy magazine, pushing hard on a peach marker while her head rests dreamily on her arm. Miles's pause on any discussion of his finances is purely for the benefit of a seven-year-old. Maybe he worried the news would get back to her mother.

"Hello, Duck," I say. "How's it going?"

She glances up at me, her eyes phosphorescent blue over sunburned cheeks. "Hi, Ian." Now I'm the one submitting to the clout of a seven-year-old. I feel strangely honored that she remembers my name.

"What are you coloring?"

"People."

I make a show of studying her work, leaning my head sagaciously to the side. Duck is not yet of the age where every artistic attempt is torturously private, concealed by a guarding arm or a shielding shoulder. As with her toplessness on the beach, she hasn't yet learned the American virtue of deep shame in exposure.

Peach splotches cover the sketch paper, approximations of two celebrities caught paparazzi-style in Mediterranean water. They must be European celebrities because I don't recognize them, and without any clues to their importance, they condense into lopsided specimens, not particularly attractive, hardly worth the photographer's mesmerized focus. They're human flesh blobs on vacation, and Duck's bloated, fish-slop rendering is deft.

"You want a drink?" Miles asks. "I have a bottle of vodka open, and grapefruit juice in the fridge."

"No, thanks. I've been drinking too much." I take a seat on one of the couches.

"I had a friend who visited last summer," Miles says as he wanders to a small bar in the corner with its bottles and decanters organized like a home chemistry set. Alcohol is one luxury Miles isn't skimping on. "She neglected to warn me that she was in AA. Or I neglected to warn her that there was no such thing as an AA meeting in the Dodecanese. She lasted thirty hours before booking herself on the next boat. Abstinence is not exactly the culture here." He pours himself a vodka and falls onto the opposite couch.

"We haven't gotten to talk much since you arrived," he says, smiling tartly as he takes a sip. "How are you liking Patmos? It's the holy island. You can feel it vibrate." I'm beginning to wonder how much of the island's renowned vibrations are due to alcoholic shakes.

"To be honest, I'm worried about Charlie, about why he hasn't come home in the past few days. Between you and me—"

Miles widens his eyes and motions toward Duck to caution me about saying anything upsetting. I have nothing to say to Miles that isn't upsetting.

"Charles will be fine," he swears. "Didn't you see him two mornings ago?"

I clear my throat, unsure whether Miles is calling my bluff. "But I haven't since. Not a word since. And really that was only a few hours after we were all in Skala together so it hardly counts. He's"—I avoid the word *missing*—"out of touch."

"Well, you know how he can be. Or perhaps you don't anymore. From what I understand, you two haven't seen each other in several years." He swills the vodka in his glass. "I've watched him closely the past few summers. He's just blowing off steam. For a man who works in tourism, he tires quickly of all of the socializing and commitments. He's getting some distance, no doubt to antagonize Sonny. I wouldn't be surprised if he's holed up in a hotel room on the other side of the island, laughing at all of us. It's only been a couple of days. You know how his kind can be." He wipes his hand down his chest. "Irresponsible."

I stare at the lonely drinker in front of me. I want to tell him about Charlie missing the boat to Bodrum, about his empty yacht with the chessboard midgame, about the fact that Charlie's own charter staff hasn't heard from him. But these are all upsetting topics to mention in front of Duck. So is the single glaring incident that might render Miles the prime suspect should Charlie actually be declared missing: the last time anyone saw Charlie, Miles punched him in the face. In the fire of that thought, his swollen eyes and haggard cheeks take on the appearance of festering guilt. But I don't directly accuse Miles of visiting *Domitian* that night, in case the conversation might upset a child.

"Where's Sonny?" I ask instead. "She called me a zillion times last night, but I haven't heard from her today."

Miles takes a hard sip and checks on Duck. There's a fatherly devotion in the way he watches out for her, one ear and eye radar–ing for signals of the slightest distress.

"Sonny's gone sailing for the day," he says simply. "She brought Louise with her. On Bence's boat. He invited her this morning. At first she said no. But then she figured, why not? Bence has one of those wretched mega-yachts, where everything transforms by remote control. What's its name? *Velociraptor?* Something savage and meat-eating."

"I was too tired," Duck declares from the floor. "I'm tired of the sun."

Miles's news stuns me. Nothing in Sonny's afternoon of yachting jibes with the frantic girlfriend who phoned me nearly thirty times yesterday. Charlie goes missing two days, she's hysterical; on day three, she's diving off a remote-controlled dinosaur. What is the attention span on this island for the disappeared?

"You look surprised," Miles proclaims. "I was too. Who would want to be stuck on a boat with that Hungarian? Maybe Sonny went because she knew it would piss off Charles. They sailed to Marathi, a tiny island to the east. Great family-run restaurant there, Italians but they pretend to be Greek. I'm sure Bence will be trying to charm Louise out of her—" He fingers his jacquard shirt. "She doesn't strike me as the type to be charmed."

"I thought Sonny was worried about Charlie."

"Oh." Miles tosses his hand. "She came to her senses. She thinks the same as I do. That Charles is purposefully staying away to punish her. You remember how he treated her in Skala. Not very nice. Apparently, they had one of their arguments right before we all met up. She didn't tell me what it was about. But this morning she found something in her bag, an item that proves Charles has been to the house while she was out. They play these childish games with each other." The hand-carved queen. I could shoot myself for putting it in her bag. I meant it as a sign of affection, but now it's another lie I've buoyed to give the impression that Charlie is alive and well. It is far too simple to fool the willing. "You know," Miles says, "when you play too many games as a couple, nothing's sacred. Everything, even avoiding each other, can be written off as a joke. It's possible to treat love too lightly." A fleeting storm crosses Miles's eyes, cutting through the calm in his voice. One second he's relaxed and jovial, the next sullen and jumpy. I'm not sure which to blame on the vodka.

"Charlie could have put that item in her bag before he vanished. That hardly confirms anything."

"No, Sonny said she used that bag right after Skala and it hadn't been in there. But that wasn't the real confirmation."

"What was?"

"I saw Charlie this morning," Duck announces as she switches markers.

"What? You did?" I rise from the couch. "You saw Charlie?"

"Yeah. Miles and I were down in Skala buying supplies."

"Groceries," Miles clarifies. "And magazines. Duck, remember not to show those magazines to your mother. You know how depressed they make her."

"Charlie was on the other side of the square. At the entrance to where the real people live. Behind the stores."

"Patmians," Miles schools her. "We're all real people. Even Charles."

"Patmians. Whatever," she gripes. "He was standing, like, fifty feet away. Or what's the length of a pool? I yelled to him. I yelled, and he turned around and looked at me and ran off." She slaps her sketchbook. "He ran away when I called his name."

"Are you sure it was him?" I ask.

"Yes," she whines. "It was Charlie. He saw me, and he ran away. Why would he do that?"

"You can be very frightening," Miles teases. "He was probably scared you were going to ask him to buy you something." Duck rolls her eyes. Miles turns to me. "I was in the shop, so I didn't see him."

"Are you absolutely sure, Duck?" I plead, almost standing to get a full look at her. "You're telling the truth, right? It couldn't have been someone else?"

She is not too young to suffer doubters. "Why doesn't anyone believe me? Mom asked the same thing. I swear I saw him. He was dressed funny, like in black. And he had on a baseball cap. But it was him! A stranger wouldn't run away when you called their name."

"Nor would most familiars," Miles adds. "But that sounds like Charles all right. That's Charles all over."

"It was him! I swear. I saw him!"

"Can I hug you?" I ask, extending both arms. Duck shakes her head, not even giving the offer a second's thought. My whole body is warm with relief. Charlie is safe. He's on the island. Of course, he's on the island; he didn't take his charter boat out. Even the resentment I feel for him is warm now.

"Sonny wasn't too pleased when we phoned her with the news," Miles says. "But she was, at least, reassured. I think she was beginning to wonder if you might have been hiding something from her. Last night I did everything I could to keep her from calling the police."

They're already looking for him, I stop myself from replying. The memory of the dead hippies returns, along with the inspector's suspicions. Now that the worst scenario has been ruled out, I worry that Charlie's unwillingness to be located might have something to do with the threat he made. Could he be hiding out because he's somehow responsible? But I won't let paranoia puncture my happiness. It's Charlie's mess to clean up now. I'm no longer the last person to have seen him. And he can't hide on Patmos forever. Maybe Christos's irritation with me was simply annoyance at having to lie for him. The idea so strong in my mind two minutes ago—that Charlie could have been murdered, that the blood on the boat was his—now seems so ludicrous I can barely recognize the Ian Bledsoe who stood quaking at the front door. How can I expect to understand what's going on in Charlie's head? Miles is right, I haven't really known him in eight years. It took less time for Duck to join planet Earth and grow into a chubby Californian girl lounging in a ramshackle mansion in the Aegean.

"I think I'll have that drink," I say. "No grapefruit."

Miles gets to his feet, snapping his fingers. "Duck, you're late for your nap. Ian and I have some adult talking to do. You can sleep in my bedroom."

"Do I have to?"

"Mother's orders. She won't want you crabby when she's back from her swim."

Duck grudgingly picks up her sketchbook, extending it in front of us. She's drawn gastric brown scribbles for stomachs and tiny yellow crosses on their foreheads. She wants what every artist wants: a second of recognition.

"Excellent," I say. "The next El Greco. Or who was that woman artist who painted the French royalty?"

"I'd give it to you, but Mom will want to keep it. Or maybe she won't now?" She gazes at Miles for guidance in the unpredictable jungle of adulthood. "Will she still want my drawings now that I'm going to be living with her in Cyprus? Or will I have to send them to Dad?"

"Of course she'll want them," he says. "And if she doesn't, I'll keep it. Now naptime."

As Duck teeters into the adjoining room, Miles pours me a drink and refreshes his own. His hands quiver as he passes me the glass. Released from his role as doting uncle, Miles devolves into a more nervous creature, gulping even when he isn't sipping vodka. He pushes his unwashed hair back with chalky nails.

"I appreciate your stopping in," he whispers. "I'm glad we have this chance to talk. I feel like my reputation has taken a hit. Charles's attack was enough of an insult. But there's the further insult of having to explain myself to everyone who heard him."

"I'm just relieved that Charlie's been spotted. I don't want to tell you what was going through my head. The worst. The very worst." The first gulp of vodka travels straight to the drought.

Miles watches me curiously, as if he'd like to ask the specifics of what the worst might be. The bruises on his knuckles have faded to the color of sunlight on snow. I'm glad he doesn't ask because I might tell him that the only person I could imagine wishing Charlie harm is Miles.

"Unless I shouldn't believe Duck? You don't think she's lying, do you?"

Miles shakes his head. "Duck doesn't tell lies. Charles, on the other hand . . ." He sighs bitterly, again slashing at invisible crumbs on his chest. "Well, as I said, he can be irresponsible when it comes to others. I suppose if you have enough money you can afford to be irresponsible. I wouldn't take his silence personally. There are two kinds of rich—those who solve their own problems, and those who throw money at them until they go away. Which camp do you figure Charles is a member of?"

Miles sets his glass on the mirrored coffee table and pushes it toward the center to make reaching for it only slightly less easy. If I still believed that Charlie was a victim of foul play, would Miles's honesty make him more or less likely a suspect? Few talk badly about those they've already taken care of. And it also stands to reason that, had Miles done something to Charlie, his jealousy would have vanished. Jealousy dies along with its target—it mutates into respect. No one is jealous of the dead.

"Sorry. He's your oldest friend," Miles says. "Perhaps you see more in him than I do."

"I'm not defending him."

"The truth is I actually like Charles half the time. Don't forget he and I have known each other since we were kids spending summers on this island. Not that we were particularly close then, but we did often get thrown together to play. I'm looking forward to clearing the air once he's home. I know we can patch this up. That fistfight in Skala, I'm ashamed of it." I don't comment on the fact that technically it wasn't a fistfight; it was one man clocking another. A fistfight requires two punchers. "He already had one black eye before I gave him another. It's as if he were collecting them. Well, I've been under a lot of stress lately, and something broke in me that night, and unfortunately I resorted to violence. I'm human. What can I say?"

"Miles, you don't have to explain anything to me."

"But I *want* to explain," he drones. "Because you live here now and we'll see each other and I hope that you and I can be friends. Just as Charles and I will be again. I don't like this resentment hanging over us."

Miles doesn't seem to realize that the purpose of Charlie's attack that night was not a lapse in friendship but a refutation of it. There is no Charlie and Miles. But I get the sense that Miles might be the sort who procures friends by wearing them down into white-flagged submission. Some are terrorists in their friendship.

"Why does it matter what Charlie thinks about you anyway?" I ask.

A blush floods his face, more blue than red in the dimness. "He's Sonny's boyfriend. And I care about her. She's a very close friend. She means a lot to me." He stares at me defensively, teeth jammed together, as if daring me to state the obvious. But what good would it do to pressure him into admitting his obsession with her? Charlie's absence has probably been a boon to his prospects. "And there's no getting around Charles on this island. The fact is, I may be staying on in Patmos indefinitely. I was thinking I'd try out the winter here. People say it's beautiful in December if you don't mind monasticism and cooking at home. It's just you and about eight other souls giving the fireplaces a workout." He inspects the tall room, as if evaluating its ability to keep out the cold.

"You wouldn't go back to London?" Sonny trusts Miles with her daughter, and yet Charlie warned me about leaving my wallet out around him. I take a chance on a touchy subject, almost touching the soft spot to test it for a reaction. "Does it have anything to do with money you owe back there?"

Miles shuts his eyes as he sinks into the cushions. He reaches blindly and unsuccessfully for his drink. His eyes open mechanically one at a time. Miles is the kind of talker who actually stares at the person he's addressing, the surreal way actors stare at each other in movies, eyes never flicking away, never caught distractedly among word formation, other private worries, and mindless fascination with nearby objects.

"I was stupid to expect Charles to have enough tact not to bring that up in front of everyone. But, yes, I did get saddled with some trouble in London. From what I've heard, you and I aren't in such different circumstances." He smiles tactfully, tapping his fingers along his hairless arm. "I'll just say it, so you don't imagine the worst. I've fallen into a bit of debt. Gambling. Poker, mostly. It was small change at first. A friend, the son of a very prominent art dealer, set up a little ring on Wednesday nights in the backroom of his mother's gallery. That gallery was always loaded with millions upon millions in contemporary art. Awful work. How they made their fortune in it, I'll never understand. The biggest detriment to the cultural value of contemporary art is actually looking at the stuff." Miles shakes his head to jettison his tirade on art. "Anyway, I really did take it as all light fun. My mistake wasn't losing; it was to whom I was losing. I didn't realize a few of the other players at the table were professionals, some well-dressed Russians with bags of cash. I figured they were just friends I hadn't met yet, like the actors and footballers who sometimes appeared on Wednesdays, dropping or winning a few thousand and waving off my losses. It was more of a social night. Or so I thought."

"You should always be careful when people show up with bags of cash."

He nods. "Thanks, but you're ten months too late with helpful advice. At some point the Wednesday nights took a dark turn, and my former friend didn't have the decency to warn me that the game had gotten real. I think I was marked as easy prey, although how was I to know? I trusted this friend. Before I knew it, I was in the red. Red up to my neck. And these new players were no longer happily waving off my debts." Miles crosses his legs and jerks his shoulders forward. "The problem with gambling is you're convinced the next hand will save you from the last one. But, I swear, cards sense desperation. I owe some money. I've drained a few accounts, and that still hasn't been enough. How can you be held responsible when you don't know who you're playing against?"

"You can't ask your family for help?"

Miles's face holds the manic expression of someone who traced his descendants back to royalty only to be told that they were actually murderers and barmaids. It's a purely English face.

"We're a prominent family," he says, "but we're not particularly flush these days. My father wasn't exactly sympathetic, even when I told him that these gangsters were threatening to borrow parts of my body and send them back to me a few days later. To be honest, old Albrecht's gone a bit lost in the head. He's the cousin to the seventeenth Earl of Winchelsea, a real seat, not like these Mediterranean princes. *Ne pas mélanger les torchons et les serviettes.* Not that it matters to my father anymore. In his retirement he's devoted himself to his rock band. He plays the bass. They specialize in Queen covers. You can rent him out for weddings. So much for dignity even if you do have a passion." Miles reaches out to capture his drink and takes two gulps to make up for lost time. "It's my fault, entirely my fault, and I'll fix the mess I've gotten in. I'm not looking for sympathy. I'd have preferred not to bore you with any of this, and I hope you'll keep it to yourself. But it did get scary for me, Ian. I gave what I could to keep them at bay."

"Will you ever be able to go back?"

Miles laughs, as if I've misunderstood the gravity of his confession.

"Oh, god, yes. I'm not in hiding. It's not *that* serious. That's why I'm explaining, in case you took Charles's insinuations to mean that I was some kind of petty crook. I have a small property I inherited in Covent Garden that's on the market. If that goes through, I should be more than all right. But in the meantime, I decided it was best to disappear for a while. I was sick of London anyway. I've always felt so much more at home here. *La graziosa isola. Die hubsche Insel.*" He swings his leg, free in his last zone of safety as his exhausted aristocracy dissolves into meaninglessness behind him. What did Charlie say about the weight of millionaire tears? Tears of nobility are even lighter. "So, there you have it. Thank you, Charles, for broadcasting that embarrassment to all of Skala. Really, it will all work out. The whole world is driving off the rails. It's getting scarier out there each day. Don't you feel it? Like there's a hole blown through the netting? Like the fear is starting to win? But I'm going to hang on."

Miles laughs blithely, although I suspect he's dug himself even deeper than he's letting on. Maybe Charlie knew the extent of it. I wonder if Miles tried asking him for a loan.

"You don't play chess, do you?" I ask.

He eyes me cautiously, as if he senses a motive behind the question.

"No. I never much cared for chess. I don't like games where your opponent has unlimited time to strategize. It's a fascinating game though. If you're black, you start with an immediate disadvantage. White is always one step ahead, so all black can do is disrupt the order. Lay traps in the system. As I told you, I'm no good at traps. I think losers tend to be the better humans, don't you? Who wants a face so cold it never shows its pain?" As if to test out his theory, he offers me two wounded eyes over oblong, woodcut cheekbones. It's a vision of Miles twenty years older, tapped out, still referencing some earl he's indirectly related to like it might make sense of him being a tall white man with impeccable posture riding on a London bus through neighborhoods of fear and Georgian architecture. "Wait a minute. Why did you ask about chess?"

"When I visited Charlie's yacht today, I noticed his chess board set up. I thought maybe you visited him after your fight. To try to patch things up."

Miles downs the remainder of his drink. He glances at his wrist and is visibly disappointed to find no watch on it. "No, I didn't visit him. Maybe I should have. But I was certainly in no mood for a game that night. And I've learned my lesson on who not to play with. Charles would cheat before he lost. He cheats, doesn't he, your best friend? He probably always did, am I right?" Miles smiles at me as if it's now my turn to make a confession.

"I don't know, does he?"

"I didn't have to punch him. I could have inflicted far worse damage if I'd just opened my mouth. But I'm not the type to spill secrets vindictively. And it would have hurt someone I care about."

"Something that would have hurt Sonny? What, that Charlie cheats on her?" Even though Charlie declared himself a new man, there is no statute of limitations on past failings. I imagine Miles has witnessed plenty over the years.

He waves his hands, his face sour, as if his tact has finally failed him.

"Forget I mentioned it," he snaps. "For her sake, forget it. Honestly, maybe one day she'll realize she deserves more. But I'm not going to plant that splinter. All I can do is be there for her. I think she's lonely. She likes ideas more than the reality behind them. You can get stuck on a good idea. It's the good ideas that have their way with you." He stares at his empty glass, as if to blame the alcohol for the direction his mind has taken. It was another good idea. "If Sonny decides to open her eyes, she'll see what he's like. Maybe she's seeing now, with him gone like this."

Miles would love nothing more than if Charlie never returned. He'd be free to spend his days with her, adopting Duck as a seasonal daughter, waiting onshore with their towels as they swim in the sea. But, of course, Charlie is what keeps Sonny on Patmos. His enemy is his provider. I've finished my drink and set it on the table.

"I should be going."

"One final shot," Miles exclaims. "A toast." He gathers our glasses and jumps up, his feet less steady, tripping over an invisible rug.

"I really shouldn't." I'm already feeling the vaporizing lift that the first drink provides, the brain buzzing like an alien spaceship over prudent farm fields.

"Oh, come on," he says, pouring. No one likes to drink alone; alcohol is an informant you should never meet without backup. That was my mistake last night. "You can't start working for Charles if he isn't here. One for the road. Let's have a toast, one last shot at redemption."

He hands me my glass.

"Redemption for what?"

Miles considers his tightly laced boat shoes. "How about for all things I could have done? I always thought I'd get my act together, that one of my interests would bear some fruit or purpose. All the knowledge I trapped in my mind. And now that I'm nearly middle age, I'm still waiting. The person who messes up your life most is you, isn't it? You get out of bed like it's the same every day, the same two arms and then . . ." He doesn't finish the thought, maybe because it would lose its poetry if released from his head. It's a risk he can't afford to take.

"You're still young, Miles. How old are you? Thirty-seven?"

"I'm thirty-five."

"That's young."

"So says a guy in his twenties. Well." He clinks my glass, and we drink. "I'm still young enough to see the good in people. That goes away too, doesn't it?"

As I step into the daylight, I'm struck, childlike, by a profound appreciation for the beauty of simple objects. I shut the door to Miles's house and leave his sadness trapped in there with him. Forget the wheel. The door is the most brilliant human invention: portal-stoppering, the suture on a bleeding cut. At the top of the hillside, the island is warm with explosions of sun beating down in scattered patches through the shaggy firs. I make a list of all the things I'll do tomorrow: wake early and go to the beach, maybe not even bother with a swimsuit; brew coffee with Louise, guide her to my bed; if Charlie's back, I'll ask him for a loan and return the money by FedEx to Lex and Ross; I'll be easier on myself; I'll live.

Descending the cobblestones, I feel a jab on my thigh and pull the turquoise earring from my pocket. A garbage can sits by the taxi stand, and I consider tossing it. But it's got to match a second earring, and Sonny might want it back. I sing along to a pop song I heard blaring from the top floor of Miles's house, a song whose lyrics I didn't even realize I had memorized. It must have been playing undetected around me all summer, the contagious auto-tuned pollen blowing from the industrial culture farms of America. Tomorrow I'll download the song and play it over and over until its joy has beaten me into submission. There must be a few islands left in the world that have yet to be touched by the noise of invaders. Dense islands, tiny as freckles, with lackluster beaches and of no mineral import. I wonder if their inhabitants are told that the world outside is the stuff of dreams, or if upon waking, they stop a moment to imagine the rest of us and the sounds we make. Or am I the last one dreaming, and everyone, everywhere, has already heard us?

CHAPTER 11

The note on my bed is written in black ballpoint.

Ian—
Meet me tonight 11 p.m. down at the charter dock.

It's unsigned, although the stationery is embossed at the top with a tilted ship's wheel and below it, in powder-blue ink, KONSTANTINOU CHARTERS. I'm not a specialist of Charlie's handwriting. In fact, I have nothing to go on except for the childhood diary entry I read on his boat. But those fat, puckish letters must have evolved through teenage years of frantic note taking followed by a decade of scarcely ever needing to wield a pen into the spiked, wiry scrawl across the stationery. The door to my cabin was locked when I returned, although Therese has been in to clean; the bed is made, the floors reek of Lysol, and a candle is lit on the nightstand, its orange flame reflecting on the glass sliding door. I open the drawer and rummage under the sweater. The plastic bag of cash is still safe. I walk over to the connecting door and check that it's bolted. Charlie clearly has keys to the cabin and must have stopped by while I was out. I don't understand why he didn't text me, unless he lost his phone. That would explain why he hasn't answered my calls.

The only thing I am certain of is Charlie's decision to remain out of sight. Otherwise he wouldn't ask to meet late at night in such an isolated spot. Perhaps he's waiting until Inspector Martis gets tired of sniffing around and returns to Kos with no other option but to mark the case an accident.

I stash the note in my pocket, toss the earring in the drawer, and strip out of my clothes to take a shower. As I stand under the nozzle, it strikes me that Charlie might have arranged this meeting to ask for one more favor, one more lie to keep him hidden, one more errand that lands me in the center of everyone's worry. Tonight could be the right moment to tender my resignation. I imagine him pulling more money from his office safe and waving it at me until I agree. *What's your price, Ian?*

My body hair is pale orange in the lather, and, for a man who barely exercises, my hip bones still jut without a pinch of fat on my waist. Even if my brain is close to collapse, at least my metabolism refuses to give up on me. It is so hard to pull out of zero. Maybe if Greece closes its doors, I could go back to D.C. with Louise and live with her in her tiny, grad-school apartment. I could take just enough cash from the Ziploc bag to buy an economy ticket and find a job busing tables in Georgetown, selling shirts in Foggy Bottom, standing outside of banks begging for signatures on renewable energy sources. I could do all of that until Louise grows tired of her degenerate boyfriend or a hacker collective finally strikes the Internet and wipes all memory of Panama clean. I'm worn thin on too many futures, a clotted hairball of possible escape routes.

I dry off and put on a fresh pair of pants. The last clean shirt in my bag is a silk button-down the color of rubber cement. It was a Christmas present from my father and Lily, mailed to me in the new year with the receipt folded in the pocket. As I slip it on, I hear a knock on the connecting door.

"Ian," Louise yells. "Are you feeling better?"

She must have returned when I was in the shower. I slide the bolt free.

"Much," I say. "It must have been something I ate."

"I don't know why you keep that locked." She steps into my room, bringing the coconut smell of suntan lotion with her.

"Habit. I'll break it."

The afternoon on Bence's yacht has turned her skin hickory, with her arms ghosted by tiny white hairs. She wears a yellow bikini top that radiates through a sheer gray shirt. Her brown eyes have the dazed expression of entering a dark room after a long time in open sun. I have the urge to pull her onto the bed, and she stands in front of me smiling, as if surprised I don't.

"I have good news," she says. "I changed my ticket. One more week in Patmos. I'm really pushing it. I'll have, like, thirty hours before classes start. But you've got me for the next seven days."

It is good news. Louise is the only good news on the entire island, and I'd suggest we spend the week floating around other parts of the Aegean if either of us had the money. We're stuck here on Charlie's generosity. We're already scratching the tin of our bank accounts, and I'm not sure we could scrape together the price of a hostel in any other port.

"I thought you'd be happier." She chews on a white gob of gum.

"I am happier," I say. I reach my arms around her waist, her skin the temperature of a teakettle. "At least I want to be. I'm going to force myself."

"What's bothering you? The general state of the world or the safety of those closest to you?"

It's an odd question. Before I realize she's joking, I answer honestly. "The general state of my world is the safety of those closest to me."

She exhales and presses her forehead on my shoulder. *Poor Ian,* the rubbing forehead implies. *How did I fall for such a loser twice?* I get the sense she might have had a few glasses of champagne on the yacht. A little jab of jealousy passes through me that she spent the day with Bence.

"All I meant was, you don't have to worry," she says. "Charlie's been spotted. Now we can all be grateful for his continued existence. I'm expecting fireworks along the harbor when he finally returns home."

"Yeah, that's good news too. It's all good news. Still, it doesn't answer why he's been avoiding everyone."

"Sonny told me they had a fight." It's exactly what Miles said, and yet Sonny didn't mention a fight when I visited her.

"What about?"

"Duck, I'm guessing." Louise shrugs. "To be or not to be a father. That explains his mood the night we met for drinks. Maybe he's trying to prove just how unreliable he is by disappearing for a few days. Sonny's taking it rather well, considering."

I briefly wonder if Sonny might have visited *Domitian* that night after Skala to reignite their argument. But I let the thought go. It doesn't matter anymore.

"How was Bence's boat?"

"Oh, god." She steadies her hand on her stomach. "I think it has its own zip code. The ugliest monster I've ever seen. There's a pool on the back. A freshwater pool in the middle of the sea! Every surface is that sparkly shade of beige, which always reminds me of cheap makeup, but is supposed to connote money and taste. He has a crew of fifteen, all blond, none of them Greek, very young and staring at the monitors trying to figure out where the hell we were. I'm amazed we found his slip when we docked." Her tongue works at kneading the gum. "I really shouldn't be so awful about Bence. It was nice of him to take us out. He's not from royalty, FYI. He's proudly self-made. Kind of a pig about it really, blatant about swooping in and investing in countries in the midst of extreme economic crises. Guess what he said to me." Louise raises her arm, as if swearing to tell the whole truth. "I'm not joking. I'll always remember it. He said that for all the analysts he pays to discover opportunities in 'emerging markets,' the best indicator is prostitutes."

"Prostitutes? Like their clients spill insider secrets?"

"No. Like where the prostitutes are from. Determine the origin of the latest crop of sex workers flowing into Western capitals— Slovenia, Romania, Sri Lanka, or wherever they're coming from now—and that's where to target your speculation. He said, 'I don't need my investment portfolio to reflect my morals.' What morals?

It was pretty fascinating, a real behind-the-curtain peek at finance. Now he's got an itch up his ass for phone apps. And for Charlie's yacht business. He gave a long, sincere lecture about wanting a cut of it. He swears Charlie called him about investing."

"I doubt he'd find Charlie's business lurid enough. Or even in coherent shape. To be honest, I'm not sure it's still running. Not with Charlie gone."

Louise cocks her head and swivels her jaw. She waits a second before continuing.

"Anyway, that might have been why Bence invited us out. To butter Sonny up, get her on his side. You know, she's not too happy with you right now."

"Why not?"

"She knows you didn't meet Charlie on *Domitian* that morning. She asked Christos. He said not unless you met him before he checked on the boat. Sonny figures you're aiding and abetting, stringing her along on boss's orders." Louise makes a *tsk*-ing sound. "Are you?"

I consider coming clean, but in a few hours, when I meet him at his dock, the whole mess will be resolved—or at least explained. Charlie can do the work of patching up his lies for a change.

"I'm officially no longer getting in the middle of their relationship," I say. "I'm out."

"You can't be out if you're working for him. Isn't he expecting a good solider?" Before I can defend myself, Louise spins around in a room suddenly tinted sepia. She grabs my hand. "We're missing the sunset!"

We step out onto the terrace, Louise tugging me toward the edge. The sun is a Vaseline smear along the gray striated knife of land, the whole sky bloodshot in reds and oranges.

Louise takes her phone from her pocket. "It's so beautiful," she says. "It's like I forget how beautiful the last one was, and I'm seeing a sunset for the first time." She snaps a few shots, the colors on the screen muddy, in no way replicating the miracle of a fireball descending below the horizon. The chirring of insects rises around us, like an impatient roar in an arena, cheering on the night.

"How are the posts?" I ask her.

"Posts?"

"Your vacation photos. Are they getting an appropriate number of likes?"

"Oh, yeah. The one I took of you and Charlie the day you arrived, a bonanza of likes. Someone commented that you looked like two out-laws who escaped into paradise." She jams her fingers into my side. "Don't make fun of me. Don't act superior just because you're not on social media. I hate that new form of snobbery. As if you appreciate life more if you never share it."

"I'm not making fun of you."

"This trip is special. Europe isn't a place I get to visit like the rest of you do."

I stand behind her, arms around her, feeling the smallness of her bones and the dampness of her hair on my chin. Another day. And there are seven more of them, and eventually all of the anxiety of the moment will be forgotten, and I'll have Louise's permanent record of muddy sunsets, and maybe I'll wonder why I didn't ask her for more than the time of a ticket pushed back.

In the distance, the monastery darkens on the hill, and I imagine the candles lit and the prayers in the dungeons, men moving silently in their robes through chilly corridors that hold no exit.

"Do you want to hear something funny?" I ask. "Something Char-lie and I did as kids?"

I don't know why I tell Louise about Destroyers. Maybe it was the escaping comment or the need to share an embarrassing fact that would make her laugh at my expense. Or maybe it's because all thoughts on Patmos eventually lead to Charlie. I explain the rules and our favorite locations. I describe the killers in black balaclavas, number variable, who enter with rounds of gunfire. I list a few of our wilier strategies: the smoke of burst fire extinguishers for cover; hiding inside coat bags so our feet don't touch the ground;

turning appliance cords into trip wires; the dead janitor's heavy body, flipping it over to locate a master key. Louise listens silently, not even grinding her gum, and she continues to stare out at the sea after I finish.

"Were we demented kids?" I ask. "Describing it out loud, it is kind of sick."

"Not sick. Not any sicker than most games kids play. You don't want to know the tortures my brother and I inflicted on my dolls. I admit to slicing off their fingers and giving them buzz cuts. But it was my brother who ended every scenario with a Dream House hanging."

"I guess it's light fun when you're little. Playing at how awful life can be."

She's quiet for a minute. The faint breaking waves echo up the valley.

"It's not light," she finally says. "Haven't you ever watched children play? They're insanely serious." She takes a receipt from her pocket and spits her gum into it. "I often think I should have noticed those early warning signs. Not with me, but my brother." She shakes her head, clenching my knuckle like a rosary bead. "I told you I didn't go to grad school right away. But it wasn't exactly by choice."

"That never did make sense to me."

"My brother had problems in Lexington, and I went home to take care of him. Each time I moved away, off to another city, he'd eventually relapse, and my parents, god bless them, couldn't handle it. So I'd go back again, and that would be another six months off my life. It got to the point that every time I packed up somewhere, I assumed it'd be temporary. Thus the 'finding myself' trip. All you can do is find a few spare parts when you know you aren't staying long."

It occurs to me that as close as we've gotten in the past week and as much as Louise espouses sharing and the needlessness of the bolt on the door, she's kept our relationship on her terms. She hasn't slept a single night in my bed, as if to wake up next to me would certify a contract she enjoyed drawing up but never intended to sign. She's learned to be cautious. Why bother with the aching fingers of practicing a new instrument, if it's only going to be ripped away?

"What kind of relapse?" I ask hesitantly, afraid of spooking her into silence.

"He was an addict. *Is* an addict," she clarifies. "The worst stuff, the stuff that's burning cigarette holes right through every family photo album in America. It's like headlights to deer. It stops people. It doesn't knock them over. I wish it did that. It just leaves them standing, vacant and twitching." She lets go of my knuckle. "That's what it did to Luke. It deleted him from our lives, even if he was still just sitting on the couch. Well, he's clean now. He has been for a year. But you're constantly waiting for the news that he isn't, and the worst part is, he knows you're waiting, and the whole thing becomes a flinch test. Will today push you over edge? How about tomorrow? Meanwhile, congratulations on washing the dishes and driving to and from the grocery store. It's like talking about the weather to a ticking bomb."

She turns to me. I expect tears in her eyes, but there aren't any. It's an old wound. I hug her anyway, worming my hand along her shoulder bone.

"I'm not sad, Ian," comes her muffled, midhug retort. "I'm not asking for pity. I just wanted to explain. I felt like I was making no sense to you without that information. I guess that's why I've been so noncommittal about everything. Law school for one."

"I get it."

She pulls away, apparently for the urgent need to run her fingers along the stone ledge, feeling for sharp edges.

"I keep asking myself what the limit is? How many times you can rescue someone from the same river? If he does it again, I'm honestly not sure I'll . . ." She trails off. "What about you? Why did you mention that game you and Charlie played as kids? You think that's what he's doing now?"

I don't follow. "I haven't been aware of any gunmen."

"No, but maybe he's running away from something worse than a seven-year-old."

"Maybe," I say. "But I don't know what that would be. There's a detective from Kos who's hoping to ask him a few questions."

"A detective? The police?"

"Because of that motorbike accident. But it can't be that. All the guy wants is to ask if Charlie saw anything." There's no reason to alarm her with details. "I really don't know Charlie as well as I thought. I'm not even sure if I'm going to keep working for him. It's not the secure employment I signed up for, with him vanishing like this."

"So you'll quit?" she asks almost hopefully.

"It's not that simple. I'm screwed if I do. I need the money. I just want Charlie to come back and tell me what's going on. But quitting might be more practical. He might do this all the time for all I know. Maybe he is playing Destroyers. He wasn't very good at it. He had a knack for making bad choices."

Louise opens her mouth, her lips warped on a word.

"What?"

"Nothing," she says.

"If I did quit, if I did go back to the States"—I'm squeezing the tail of my shirt, on the verge of backing down, every defender in my brain advising me to abort the next sentence, *don't say it, retreat, retreat*—"maybe I could try D.C. That could be a good place to start over. After all, you're there. We could see each other, or—"

"Ian." She breathes, stepping forward. It is only a few feet between us but it feels like miles.

"It's just an idea."

She grabs my arm. But just as quickly, she loosens her grip. "I don't know if that make sense."

"No, you're right. It doesn't."

"We've only seen each other again for a few days."

"It was a stupid suggestion."

"It's not stupid. It's just fast. I care about you, very much—"

"Don't worry about it." I lift my arm to touch her face, but my jerking movement knocks her hands away, which ultimately feels like the more appropriate reaction. "Sorry. Forget I brought it up. I wasn't thinking."

"Don't."

"Don't what?" But the logic of *don't what* baffles both of us.

"I'm, I'm . . ." She licks her lips and starts again. "I'm on my own in D.C. For the first time I'm trying—"

"You don't need to explain. It's been great having these days with you here. It's been wonderful." I'm already writing her a postcard. There's a picture of Patmos on the front. I'm even about to list a few vacuum-packed memories: sharing a motorbike, lying in the sun. It's not a postcard. It's a eulogy, and no one reads those more than once.

"Let's talk about it when I leave in a week, okay?"

When the tears finally arrive, they're mine, and I walk to the kitchen counter. I pretend to explore the innards of the refrigerator, but the frosted yellow bulb spotlights what I'm hiding and I shut the door.

"Are you hungry?" I ask.

"I'm here for seven days," she says, gathering her hair at her neck. "Maybe if you're serious and you do decide to go back, we can discuss it then. We can see how it goes."

"Okay."

She's white eyes and white teeth in the darkness.

"And, yes, I'm hungry. *Starving*," she moans with exaggeration. "Let's have dinner down in Kampos by the water. My treat. You paid the last time. Maybe that band is playing. We could dance on the—"

I don't want Louise to save me. I don't want her to feel that she should. "Louise?"

"Yeah?" The word is breathless, practically begging for pardon from any more talk of the future.

"It will have to be a short dinner. I have to meet someone at eleven. It's a work matter for Charlie's business."

"So you aren't getting out? You're staying on with him?"

I belong where I am welcome. I go inside and gather my wallet. Outside, from deep down the hillside, I hear the rumble of clapping as the band starts up.

AFTER A BRISK, dispiriting dinner with Louise, I head south on the island past Skala and the village of Grikos. My bike judders down the dirt trail, the headlight eking out desert scrub a mere three feet beyond the handlebars. The sea ahead is wet with moonlight, and ridges of the island to the north are pocked with gatherings of yellow. The area leading to Charlie's dock, however, is a total blackout, and, stripped of scenery, it feels like a longer drive from the main road than I remember. It's the kind of place that refutes the notion of screaming as a warning call; here a scream would be purely ornamental, a fleeting human trace. I'm reminded of that strange idiom still used in semirural enclaves, "we live within screaming distance of our neighbors," measuring distance on the wise metric of emergency.

When the beam finds the concrete hangar, I slow the motor and park next to the crane. Moths swarm the headlight before I switch it off—creatures throwing their bodies against the brightness. The night we dressed for dinner at the Plateia, Duck had asked, "If moths love light so much, why don't they come out in the day? They'd be so happy then." None of us could wager a decent answer.

Close to the water, there's enough shine to discern the hangar with its grates pulled down. It must be a few minutes after eleven, but there's no sign of Charlie. The dock is empty of charter boats, and far into the horizon, the murky rectangles of freighter ships sit motionless like islands unto themselves. The odor of algae and low tide blows inward, and goat bells from a nearby field clang and fade.

"Charlie?" I call. I march toward the trailer. No lights are on in the office and the door is locked, but moonlight pours through the windows. The long plastic desk, once cluttered with documents, is bare. Not a single paper rests on it, every messy layer that Charlie burrowed through to demonstrate his need for my organization skills gone. The hard drive under the computer has been removed. The walkie-talkies on the radio are also missing. The framed picture of *Domitian* hangs crookedly on the wall. The whole office signals a rapid and thorough purge, and I wonder if I opened the grates to the hangar whether the refurbished yacht would still be on its blocks. There's such little indication of a thriving boat business that a needle passes through me, that this meeting isn't a reunion but a good-bye.

He must have been standing by the corner of the hangar all along, but drowned in the night, I didn't see him. I remain by the trailer as the faint, indistinguishable shape of a human crosses the lot.

"Charlie?" I shout, but the figure doesn't respond. It simply walks straight toward me. I quickly ransack my body for items I know that it doesn't possess: a flashlight, or as the figure keeps coming with no word or hesitation, a knife. "Charlie or whoever you are, answer!"

But now I glimpse solid features under the moon: a shaved head with patchy skin, a set of starved, lidless eyes, a mouth with a scar running from its corner. It's the thief from Athens, and I flatten myself against the trailer's siding, pulling my bike key from my pocket.

The thief stops a few feet from me. "You got my note," he says with a frank American accent.

"*Your* note?"

He notices the key poking between my fingers and smiles. "What? You're going to stab me with that? And to think I was about to thank you for coming."

"You wrote that note? How do you even know my name?"

"Ian," he shouts to prove his familiarity with it. "You don't recognize me? I guess it has been a long time. I didn't used to look this beat-up. You should take it as a warning of what a few summers with Charlie can do."

"I don't know you. We've never met."

He laughs, or at least his mouth mimes laughter.

"Met? We graduated together. Buckland Academy, go Blue Knights! You don't remember me? I guess I *was* closer with Charlie.

You and I never really hit it off. It's Gideon, Gideon Frost. We had bio together, and weren't we conversation partners junior year in French?" The name is an excavator, a backhoe digging up bones of memory down to a scrawny, disturbingly prepubescent boy save for about eight black hairs of an anticipatory mustache, too many in number not to be deliberate and too few to attract the wrath of the school's strict no-facial-hair code. Gideon lived in Queens, which, at Buckland, served as shorthand to indicate that the Frosts weren't rich. But now I recall that Gideon was friendly with Charlie; they'd been in chess club together. I can picture the name FROST embla- zoned on the back of Charlie's maroon alumni shirt, a thief hiding all along in plain sight.

"What the hell are you doing here, Gideon? All the way here?" I mean on Patmos; I mean a decade later in time. "Why did you leave me a note in my cabin?"

"Your cabin?" This too induces a silent laugh. "It was my cabin before it was yours. It was mine for almost three years until about a month and a half ago. I still have my key. That's how I got in." I feel a sting at the memory of the initials *G.F.* in the front of the Henry Miller novel. "Who do you think had the job of being Charlie's whip- ping boy before you were shipped in and taken out of your box? I started up this business with Charlie." He waves his arm, as if pre- senting his estate. "I suppose he didn't bother to tell you. Does he still call our job his number two? Man, I hated that. I never wore that stupid cap, either. At first, he didn't mind. At first, he still treated me like a friend. Those are the honeymoon days. I hope you're enjoying them."

There's no hint of the child I remember in Gideon's face. That kid has long died in him and the scar of that murder is a face sunken at the cheeks and shrouded in sweat. This face would prevent me from spending an hour at a bar reminiscing about school days if I'd accidentally run into Gideon on a Manhattan street. Alone, on an Aegean island, on this purposefully vacant stretch of coastline, it causes me to bunch my hand protectively over my wallet.

at the sky, his throat a white, crooked pillar with bruises at the base. "Is that what you think this business is about? Oh my god. Don't tell me you're that naïve?"

My throat closes on me, and even if I did have an answer, I couldn't get it out.

"Ian, pal, wake up! Have you ever seen a single tourist at this dock? The few that come only serve as cover. To be fair, we did try that route at first, the up-and-up chartered vacation route. It just wasn't profitable. And Charlie needed to show some sort of profit or Papa would have cut him off." Prince Phillip said as much: *find a career or come home* . . . but Charlie proved himself, and his father's stranglehold on his money loosened. I want to refute Gideon's claims, but the few boats I've watched cast off from Konstantinou Charters have lacked the tanning, demanding renters that would justify the entire apparatus. It's been all luxury and no one paying to appreciate it.

"I guess Charlie hasn't filled you in on the whole picture yet." Gideon shakes his head in mock disappointment. "Let me help you out. What do you think those shells Ugur welds to the bottom of the hulls are for? I had a hand in that invention," he says proudly. "There's a little button wired on the console, and if by chance the Greek coast guard stopped a yacht, which, of course they never do because they know what that red *K* painted on the bow stands for, but if they ever did. . . ." Gideon leaves the cigarette dangling from his mouth and forms a trapdoor with his hands. "One press of the button and it all dumps into the sea." His hands flip open. "*Sure. Come aboard, officer. You're welcome to search the boat.* Pretty clever, huh?"

"What are you saying?" But it's already said. Charlie warned me that his business wasn't squeaky clean, although he neglected to mention the variety of dirt he's been smuggling underneath the polished oak.

"With all of the shit going on out in the Aegean these days, who's going to get suspicious about expensive white yachts helmed by a crew in blue uniforms?" Gideon asks. "Especially when they're owned and operated by one of the wealthiest families. The best way to hide bad money is in a bundle of cash."

"What is Charlie smuggling?"

Gideon takes one last drag and flicks his cigarette. A tiny firework blazes against the trailer.

"You need to have a chat with Charlie. He can answer the rest of your questions. I'm not your fucking oracle, Ian. Sad to say, I didn't invite you down here because I'm concerned about your well-being." He rubs his palms together, keeping his thumb bundled over the nub of his pointer. "In fact, when I realized you were taking my job, I decided I might as well head back here and make a proposal. What do they call it? A golden parachute? I tried to talk to Charlie that night in Chora, but he refused to listen. So I need you, his number two, to deliver a message. Can you do that?" He nods encouragingly, as if I'm just intelligent enough to understand simple English. "I want money to go away."

"I'm sure he'll be surprised to hear that."

He laughs resentfully. "You're hilarious, Ian. Don't ever lose your sense of humor."

"It went a long time ago."

"Yeah. Panama knock it out of you? You always were a prick at Buckland."

"Thanks."

"I want two hundred grand. Don't worry, Charlie can afford it. I'm sure he tosses out that amount monthly for the upkeep on his cunt of a girlfriend. You two getting along? She was never nice to me, steered ten feet around me to prevent so much as a hello."

"But you're so charming."

"Just deliver the message. He might be surprised I upped it from one sixty, but he shouldn't have waited. He should have talked to me last month. I was more reasonable then." Gideon folds his arms over his stomach. His vexed smile extends the scar's trajectory. "I want it in cash, American dollars. And you tell him, if he waits any longer, someone else has shown interest in what I have to say, someone Charlie wouldn't want me talking to. I might have to if he doesn't pay."

"The inspector from Kos? Is that who you mean?" But my bullet doesn't seem to hit its mark. Gideon's smile remains intact.

"I saw you go into the police station down in Skala. Haven't you learned yet that the police are useless on the islands? It won't matter what you tell them. All they're interested in is keeping their jobs—that's their idea of keeping the peace. You rat out anyone with means, they'll just cut in front of you in the bribe line. And they won't touch the Konstantinous. So you be a good boy and deliver my message. And good luck, Ian. Good luck keeping your head down here."

Gideon turns to go.

"I can't find him," I say. "No one can. He's on Patmos, but he's not answering his phone. He missed a meeting in Bodrum. Even Ugur doesn't know where he is." There's a joy in relaying the truth to Gideon. Even the slightest sabotage to his plans feels like a victory.

"What?" His voice rises. "Don't lie to me. He didn't go to Bodrum? He must have."

"He didn't."

"But then how—"

White light pours over us, and we're exposed. Two headlights shine from the road, our flinching bodies bleached, as if caught in an extended camera flash. We squint, hands against our eyebrows.

"Did someone follow you here?" Gideon hisses.

My eyes adjust to make out the hood of the white Mercedes station wagon, moths flittering around the shine. Petros, priest of vehicular homicides, steps forward, blocking one of the headlights with his thin silhouette. But there's movement behind him, the shapes of two men climbing out of the backseat, bulky, dressed in midnight colors. Their faces are covered in black scarves except for the meager human trace of eye slits. The light catches the muzzle of a rifle.

"Oh, shit," Gideon squeals. "Oh, shit!" He takes off toward the beach, sprinting as his feet kick the dust into clouds. Petros gestures in a sideways dice-throwing motion, and one of his goons races after him. I hear their competing, scattered footsteps along the pebbled shore. I stand against the trailer, fear overriding my brain, unable to transmit basic signals to my legs. The goon by the car jiggles the rifle on his shoulder, the muzzle pointed toward the sky, and Petros, in his long, tailored robe, walks toward me. His grin is framed by a manicured beard, and he extends his hand, as if to give assistance to an injured man.

"Won't you come with us?" he asks me softly. "We need you in the car."

"What for?" I hear my voice answer.

His grin stiffens but doesn't fade. I would prefer no grin.

"It will be easy," is all he says.

I keep standing in place, incapable of complying with Petros's simple request. There's a long pause of silence before Gideon stumbles into the light, the dust clouds reclaiming him. The goon holds his arms behind his back, and a wet trail runs from his crotch down the side of his pant leg. He glowers at me as he's pushed forward, whatever ounce of toughness he possessed giving way to the panic of a little boy.

"You didn't even run," he howls. "You should have, you idiot. What's wrong with you? You didn't even try to run!"

When he gets to the station wagon, his wrists are tied and a burlap sack is placed over his head. He's tossed, like collapsible cardboard, into the backseat. Petros grabs my arm to steer me across the lot. It's like we're dancing, I don't even feel the ground on my feet.

"That's a nice shirt," Petros says, touching the silk cuff. "Is it from America?"

The men in the makeshift balaclavas wait by the open car doors, one of them lifting a sack to cover my head.

"Please don't," I beg as I stare into the brown eyes surrounded by the frayed purple stitches of the scarf's seam. "I'm afraid—" But the bag slips over me, fit snugly like a cover over a birdcage. My wrists are bound behind my back.

The coarse fabric fills my mouth when I breathe. I exhale hard and try to spit the itchy twill from my tongue. A hand clamps on my head to prevent my hitting it as I'm placed in the back of the car. The goon slides in next to me, and I'm wedged against Gideon, his body warm and reeking of piss.

"It will be a short drive," Petros promises from the front seat as he slams his door. In another second we're potholing down the dirt road, each divot throwing me onto my hip. My fingers latch onto a seat belt buckle jammed in the leather cushions, my left leg tapping against the rifle that leans from the seat well.

Gideon tries to knock me away from his shoulder and screams in Greek. The man next to me laughs faintly. Petros utters two syllables in his dog-whistle pitch, which must be a form of "shut up" because Gideon does.

I feel the smoothness of concrete as we turn on the main road, rising and sinking along the hills. A car Dopplers by us, a liquid *whoosh* that I follow with my ears until every atom of it evaporates. There are only the sounds of men breathing, a key ring jingling, and the electronic patter of buttons—whizzing, jackpot beeps as if the man next to me is playing a game on a cell phone. Then we are shaken, tires over cobblestone, and for an instant voices crowd around the windows—an Italian man shouting, a young American woman screaming for "Katie!" I wonder if I cried out whether they'd turn in the direction of the backseat and what they could even do if they saw us. "Katieeeee, bring me my bag!" Music erupts suddenly from the car speakers, quickly lowered, tinny percussions slapping against a wailing flute. We speed on.

However short of a ride was promised, it's too long to be staring at death. Did Charlie know the danger he put me in? Did he use me to buy time and plan his own escape? Is this what he's afraid of happening to him if he returns to his house? He's right to be afraid. I imagine all the freedom of twenty-nine years up until five minutes ago, the wasted freedom, the days of doing nothing, the resentful slog of morning and noon, Louise right now lying in her cabin, New York right now in its flea-like haze nearing sunset, the traffic flowing into oblivion, nasty Panama where an end like this one could have been expected, and again I'm in the backseat of a Mercedes with burlap scratching my cheeks and a rifle butt banging against my ankle. Numbers go berserk on a clock, with every second out of order. And yet the lines between the past and present seem so straight this ride feels like nothing so much as a punishment. The world has been very lenient; now it isn't.

We dip down into coolness, into chambered darkness. We brake abruptly, tires squealing on cement. The Mercedes I never wanted to sit in is now the car I don't want to leave. The doors open, and Gideon flails around, his elbow knocking into my ribs, but they must have pulled him from the seat because he's no longer next to me.

I'm treated more delicately. A hand again protects my head as I'm brought to my feet. I don't know if it's the tenderness of this hand or what it is bringing me toward, but I begin to weep. A poke to my back informs me to walk.

"This is a mistake," I yell.

"*Shhh*," the man behind me hisses.

I speak more quietly. "This is a mistake. You've got the wrong person. I haven't done anything."

"Step."

I sample the floor with my foot and locate the step's edge. There are two more steps before another poke steers me into a rancid-smelling tunnel. I'm gliding through shapeless darkness. When I stop, I'm shoved forward. The floor is slippery, and beating orange light bleeds through the burlap. Fingers grapple at my neck, and my head swims free of the sack.

I half-expected a chop shop, the kind found in Panama basements with grimy tiles, a table of saws, and a floor drain clotted in blood. Instead, I'm standing inside a cramped, golden shrine lit by electric chandeliers. Frescos cover the walls, steroidal saints and lumps of naked men. Carved wood crosses are gathered in a corner, next to a column of stacked metal chairs. Two linoleum-sided box speakers hang from chains, one swinging from where the gun muzzle struck it, and a microphone is curled up on a marble table. On more uplifting days, this church must be a site of community worship.

Inside a wooden cubicle in the far corner, half-hidden behind a velvet curtain, sits a Greek boy of eleven or twelve. He is wearing headphones; his foot taps silently as he folds papers. I wait for him to turn his head to us but he never does. He keeps folding the papers with devotion, once, twice, into panels, and adds the finished missalette to a growing stack. But his presence is comforting: they wouldn't do anything violent in front of a child.

Gideon leans, de-hooded, against the marble table, his teeth bared, part maniac smile, part I-will-not-show-fear. His hands, like mine, are still tied behind his back. One of the goons reaches up to steady the speaker.

"I wish we didn't have to do this," Petros says wearily, spinning his Rolex on his wrist. "It's a waste of time for all of us. If only you would respect deadlines."

"Nice god you have," Gideon retorts, glancing around the church. "For fuck's sake, wasn't my finger enough for you?" He stares at the goon without the gun. "Hi, Argus. How are you?" The goon bunches his scarf higher up the bridge of his nose. "All of you look like a joke." I'm relieved by Gideon's show of insolence, although there's still the urine stain running down his leg.

"You seem to have trouble learning lessons," Petros responds. "I have my orders and so do you." He turns to me, the silent, compliant one, as if my hands aren't tied behind my back but tucked there dutifully. "Ian, we haven't worked together much, but I'm a stickler for conditions. They must be met."

"We haven't worked together at all," I correct him.

His cheeks dimple. "Oh, but we have, all along. As you know, it's our dock that Konstantinou Charters uses and it's our protection and permission that you enjoy. Do you not work for Charlie as his number two?"

So it's the underlings who take the fall. They wouldn't treat

Charlie this way, wouldn't dare drive him here at gunpoint or slice off one of his fingers. Or would they? Perhaps the only enterprise impervious to a powerful family is the church. Puke spears up my throat. Do they always take a finger off a new recruit? I'm thankful my hands are tied behind my back; they might look tempting out in the open.

"We've been looking for your boss," Petros says. "Waiting and looking. Only we haven't been able to locate him." Gideon darts his eyes at me. I shrug, *I told you.* "It's unlike him to be absent for so long. Unlike him to forget the terms of our arrangement. It reminds me of our first summer, when we had to clarify the importance of meeting the conditions."

Gideon lets out a dry laugh.

Petros turns to him. "Why do you laugh?"

"You're funny," he says. "*Clarify.*"

"That's funny to you?" Petros pierces his lips in a pose of contemplation. "Well, we may have to *clarify* again. We want our money, fifty thousand euros for August, and Charlie is three days late. That's three days we have to put off our own commitments. It's simple accounting: if you keep money past the due date, we're loaning *you* funds, and you're earning on what we're losing. We require timely payment. Charlie knows there are penalties." Petros has descended into the logic of the unpaid New York freelancer, which happens to be the logic of national debts. I suppose his oversimplification of imbursement structures is for my benefit. He steps in front of Gideon, who jerks up straight as if to be measured for a suit. "Gideon, where is Charlie? When will we receive our money?" The boy in the cubicle taps his foot in a slower rhythm, his fingers sliding a crease down the paper.

Gideon gives a flaunting smile.

"Sorry. I don't work for Charlie anymore." He shoots his smile in my direction. "That's Ian's job now. He's the one you have to deal with. He's my replacement. Aren't you, Ian?"

I didn't expect loyalty from Gideon, but as Petros eyes me with new appreciation, his deflection feels like a betrayal. Is there such thing as a betrayal when the threat of violence is at stake? For a second, Petros's handsome eyes hold a glimmer of compassion for me, as if it might pain him to hurt me. It's so much easier to hurt the one you've hurt before.

"Is that so?" Petros says with a sigh. He turns back to Gideon. "Then what good are you if you can't help us? There's no need to keep you."

"That's right," Gideon agrees. But then his smile drops like a flag without wind. "Wait. What?"

The priest nods to the goon who may or may not be Argus. Up until this moment, I held out hope that they were merely playing at being thugs. But when the man thrusts the sack over Gideon's head and reaches around Gideon's waist to unsnap his pants, I realize the seriousness of the performance.

"What are you doing?" Gideon shrieks. "Stop touching me!" A punch to his back knocks the wind out of him. His pants are pulled to his ankles, uncovering fragile white briefs, the cotton in the front soaked to gray. These too are tugged to his knees. The tiny walnut of testicles is covered in brown moss, a skeletal ass blooming as he squats to hide his nakedness. The goon shoves Gideon against the table, where the two worming inches of his penis flap onto the marble. The goon presses against him to keep the shriveled, circumcised head fixed there.

Petros looks away in disgust and finds my eyes. "Ian, where is Charlie?"

"I don't know," I wheeze. "He's on the island, but I haven't seen him for days."

"Don't give me more excuses," he yells. "Charlie isn't that irresponsible. Are you saying he's having trouble making the payment?"

When I don't answer, the goon unfastens a sheath on his belt buckle and extracts a steel hunting knife. Gideon's burlap head rotates at the sound of its release from the leather. The goon steadies the blade directly over Gideon's penis.

"What is he doing?" I scream. The question is contagious.

"What is he doing?" Gideon cries. "What's happening?" The burlap oscillates between deep intakes and exhalations.

"Don't do this," I plead. I wrench forward as if my own penis is on the table.

"Then tell me when we will get our money."

"I don't know! I only just arrived! I don't know where Charlie is!"

Petros nods to the goon. I turn my gaze to the boy who is tapping his foot and folding papers, his face buried behind the curtain. Then I shut my eyes, tight as fists.

"Open your eyes," Petros orders.

But I can't. I can't watch the mutilation. I listen for the sickening sound of the knife striking the marble. My breath is failing to clear my throat, and light-headed, I feel my knees begin to buckle.

"I said, open your eyes."

When I don't, footsteps race toward me and the cold coin of the gun tip is pressed against my temple. I force my eyes open, as if in salt water. The whole room is swirling, pieces of Petros and saints and electric bulbs and a marble table. The puke climbs to my tongue. Some of it leaks on my lips.

"Ian, please help me!" Gideon begs. Yesterday's criminal is today's victim, but I'm the one who has to watch.

"See!" Petros holds my chin, so I can't look away. "See what we are forced to do when our conditions aren't met!"

"I will get you the money. I will find Charlie. I promise." The goon raises the knife in a hacking motion, and the world crashes down so softly it's like I'm floating. I slowly sink into my heartbeat. The trap snaps. The connection is lost. The goats are grazing in a distant country.

CHAPTER 12

The pleated shade over the window bleeds apricot. It rattles against the frame when a breeze hits it. A wooden door is built crookedly into the wall, and from its handle, a goat bell hangs by a rope knot. I must have fallen back asleep because the apricot has deepened to peach, and the goat bell clangs as the door swings open. Before I have time to do much more than register that I'm lying on a cot, a woman enters carrying a tray. Her mustard slippers whisk across the brick floor, which sends two birds perched on the window ledge flying—one hitting its wing against the shade. The woman is older, with white tissue-paper hair around her ears. The rest is stapled back in a metal barrette. Her shy, hesitant smile, affection set low on a dimmer, fights the panic gathering its forces in my head. I quickly frisk my body, patting for injuries or gross violations incurred while I was out. Except for the film of sweat on my skin, I'm all right.

"Do you still have fever?" the woman asks, her voice soft and hoarse. "You were very sick last night." She settles the tray on the mattress.

My pants are on, but my silk shirt is folded next to my shoes on the dresser. One of my shoes cups my phone and wallet.

"Where am I? What's going on?"

The woman reaches in slow motion for a wet rag on the tray and swabs my forehead. "You pass out, you faint, in our church, and we bring you into our son's room to rest. I am Petros's wife." I'm not sure which revelation surprises me more: that Greek Orthodox priests can take wives, or that a man like Petros could find one. What's more, he's a father. The only indication of a boy inhabiting this whitewashed room is a badly glued model of a ship on the dresser. Was it the same boy who folded the papers in the confessional box last night? She eases the warm rag around my eyes. "We were so worried. Petros checked on you often in the night. He will be happy you are better. We like when vacationers take the time to visit our church."

"That's what he told you? That I was visiting?"

She steers the rag down my nose and wipes my mouth, like a mother cleaning baby food off a toddler. A needlepoint of cysts and freckles line her neck.

"You don't remember? He open Saint Sofia for you to see. It is small church. There are many on island. Three hundred, three hundred—" She can't find the right numbers in English. "One for each day. I hope you like ours. I take much care to make it nice. Inside the—"

But *inside the* reminds me of Gideon and where and how I left him.

"What about the guy I was with?" I ask urgently, pulling back from the rag. She balls it on the tray. "My friend with the shaved head? Did you see him?"

"Gideon." Troughs form around her lips. "I think he is not such a friend. He leave you last night. Run off."

"Was he hurt?" By reflex, I clutch my groin.

She's either confused by the question or by the grab at my crotch. "No. He only leave. Not even help to carry you." She wipes her wet hands in the folds of her skirt. "I think he not so good for Patmos. Petros say he is trouble. *Apateonas*," she exhales in insult. So it was only a fear tactic after all, a demo of terror, a lesson that body parts are only slightly more permanent than luggage if you aren't careful to keep watch over them.

"Is Petros here?" I demand, swinging my legs off the bed. How could I have slept for hours in his house?

She lifts the tray, mistaking my question for the desire to see her husband again. "I am sorry, no. He very busy. He do much work for the monastery. He is good man. We do not have it easy here. We lose our son last year. He drown." Their boy wasn't the one folding papers. It explains why this bedroom is so empty. Maybe it also explains Petros's cruelty, but I'm not looking for reasons to forgive him.

I place my shoes on the floor and wrestle my feet into them.

"I'm sorry to hear that."

"It is hard, losing son. All we have now is church. Our Saint Sofia. Please tell your friends to visit."

"I will," I lie. I whisk my arms through my shirt. She watches me as if she enjoyed even a poor substitute filling her son's bed for a night. "Thank you," I say. "For taking care of me."

"Petros tells me to. I promise to be sure you are okay. He was very worried. Are you hungry? I make—" She's disappointed when I shake my head. I get the feeling she'd appreciate the company. "Your *motosiklete*, it is outside," she says. "Argus brings it." As I follow her out of the room, she scurries down a ceramic-tiled hall. "Wait," she calls. "I have for you." The hallway is decorated with family portraits, many of a small child I make an effort not to study. I want to leave him, forgotten, in this hallway.

She returns waving a white, sealed envelope.

"From Petros," she says. She seems curious for me to open it, but I slip it in my back pocket. I thank her again and step out into the sunlight. The fringed, yellow sun is already high over the domed white church of St. Sofia, its tin roof glowing pharmaceutical orange in the light. Attached to the house is a pen of chickens sticking their warty beaks through the mesh. Two roosters crow, as if promising new sunrises, better ones, so late in the morning. *When is the next ferry to Athens? Patmos to Athens. Athens to anywhere. All my fingers and organs scanned through the metal detector and carried on board.*

The real question, though, is why Petros has let me escape so easily—with just my word that I'd get him his money.

Sitting on my bike, I rip open the envelope and unfold the paper. Greek letters are littered across the white like matchsticks dropped randomly in the snow.

A CHALKBOARD OUTSIDE of the Blue Star office in Skala lists the weekly ferry departure times to every port: SYROS, LIPSOS, LEROS,

KALYMNOS, KOS, SYMI, RHODES, AGATHONISI, SAMOS, PIRAEUS. Surprisingly, ferries to Piraeus only run twice a week—and in high season, they're probably booked. The smaller islands offer daily departures, and quick escapes to the capital require a cat's cradle of connections, winding east to slip toward the west. I wish a developer had succeeded in building an airport. Right now, a smog-eaten ferry is trembling into the harbor. Ticketed travelers begin to make their pilgrimage toward the metal gates. I pass into the Blue Star office, which seems to have shared the interior decorator who did the police station: a man whose death is recorded in the microfiche of the last century, content that his wood veneers, atomic-green filing cabinets, and plastic crenulated ashtrays would persevere for several bankrupt generations. The office radiates an unremitting atmosphere of frustration. Time is eternal on Greek islands, but in here it is a finger pressing at the rate of one computer key every thirty seconds. I feel the sweat climbing on my skin, last night's imaginary fever yielding to a real one.

I can't stay on Patmos after last night's threat. Picturing another encounter with Petros or Gideon puts a spur in my throat. Nor can I wait around for Charlie to appear and fix the chaos his absence has unleashed—or the chaos he unleashed and left to run wild in his absence. *Fucking Charlie. Fuck you, Charlie, my rescuer, my friend.*

I'm stuck waiting behind a wrinkled British woman in a straw hat who is committed to arriving in Santorini on Thursday—any Thursday—like she has all the Thursdays in the universe at her disposal. She seems to have cashed out her life savings on the Byzantine gold in the jewelry shops. Outside, the ferry glides against the dock, and crewmen bind the ropes to the moorings. Tourists and locals collect across the sidewalk in nervous states of welcome and farewell.

Every day the world blows up, quietly, one life at a time, and each life already holds among its clutter the bomb and the switch, the germ that could detonate, the dark secret not yet revealed. When was Charlie going to tell me the true nature of his business? After a week? After I got settled? Next year? I feel the loss of a future that never actually existed. I fold my arm on the counter and press my head into it. Even the loss of unreal futures hurt. And there are other losses too, like telling Louise of my departure after she extended her own ticket. It's strange comfort that she practically spelled out to me last night that we didn't owe each other much beyond this trip. Seven more days wouldn't be enough time to change her mind.

When I glance up, the British woman is watching me irritably while she fans herself.

"I waited forever," she grumbles. "Now it's your turn."

A worker slides into a chair at the next desk, sips on a Diet Coke, and finally beckons to me. I race to her station, clamping my hands on the counter.

"When's the next ferry to Piraeus?" I ask.

She points out the window.

"That one, now." Which means the next one isn't for four more days.

"Is there a seat?"

She types and studies the screen.

"One seat, yes."

It isn't Louise that stops me from booking the ticket. It's the nine thousand dollars in the nightstand—that and my passport in my suitcase. I'd never get to the cabin and back in time. Everything else I could shed—the clothes, my toiletries, Charlie, even Louise. What is the definition of a tourist but a person who disappears so cleanly and completely they leave no trace? No wonder Louise is so insistent on taking photos—*I was here*—because no one here would miss you if you weren't. Does anyone miss the two dead hippies, now that their bodies have been shipped back home? A phrase occurs to me, one from a time or country I can't pinpoint: *to keep you is no benefit, to destroy you is no loss.* I don't remember where that's from, but it's the perfect advertising slogan for vacations. All it needs is a palm tree.

"And the next ferry after that to Piraeus?" I ask.

She confirms what was written on the chalkboard. "Saturday, but no seats. You could see if there's a cancellation in a day or two. Or go to Kos and then Kos to Mykonos and hope from there? Kos ferry leaves tonight at six."

A young couple is sighing theatrically behind me as I consider my options.

"Okay. That sounds good. I'll get my bags and come back." But before I go, I pull Petros's letter from my pocket and hold it out in front of her. "Can you tell me what this says?"

She grabs the paper as she raises the Diet Coke to her lips. But her eyes narrow and she doesn't sip.

"It says, well . . . it says you promised." She pauses. I can hear the carbonation of the soda at her lips.

"That's it?"

"It says to remember your promise. And if you leave without saying good-bye it would hurt the one you care about." She struggles to make sense of it. "A love letter?"

"Sort of." It is Louise, in the end, who keeps me from booking a ticket. And maybe I'm no longer a tourist here, because there is something I can't afford to risk.

In the bright air of the port, ripe with jet streams of cheap tobacco smoke, I watch the sun-brown passengers board and the pale passengers disembark. Two hippie backpackers are descending the ferry ramp, the taller one with a horselike face spinning a silver piercing in his cheek. He's familiar to me, I've seen him before, but I can't place where. Maybe all the hippies do look alike, because he's clearly a new arrival, ambling down the dock in red-laced hiking boots and a fresh I ♥ ATHENS T-shirt with JESUS WAS A HUSTLER scrawled in rainbow colors across the Greek flag.

From the flapping shade of a taverna, an olive-shirted man with thick glasses hurries toward the ferry, dragging a steel suitcase behind him. It's Charlie's boat manager, Ugur, fishing his ticket from his shirt pocket. I race to catch up to him, weaving around bodies, nearly caught in a fishnet of children with their arms interlocked.

"Ugur," I call.

He flinches and speeds faster toward the boat.

I shoot across the cobblestones, slipping between bumpers of stalled traffic. I reach his side as he's passing through the gates. He takes no notice of me, as if I'm begging for change with a cup in my hand. *Help. Help the homeless.*

"Ugur," I repeat. "It's me."

"Hello, E-on," he says dismissively, neither slowing down nor bothering to look up.

"Where are you going?"

He scrunches his ticket tightly in his grip.

"Back."

"Back where?"

Ugur adds himself to the line of passengers waiting for the guard to check their tickets. He rises on his tiptoes and impatiently leans one way and another like a cobra in a basket. His glasses slide down his nose from the sweat that glistens his skin.

"Ugur, why are you leaving?"

He glances behind him, and I notice Inspector Martis standing by the bronze-green bust of a military figure in the square. We both step forward in the shrinking line.

"Charlie should have made that meeting in Bodrum," Ugur murmurs. "He should have been there, and he should be here now."

I tip into him, so close I smell his bitter cologne and the perspiration it's trying to neutralize.

"I know about the shells."

For the first time, he gazes at me, his eyes giant and lashless behind their lenses.

"I thought you already knew. Then you know Charlie should have made that meeting. Something went bad."

"Is that why you cleaned out the office?" He doesn't respond.

We step forward.

Between my clenched teeth, as if to filter out clarity in case of eavesdroppers, I whisper, "What was he smuggling?" Ugur flaps his hand between us, as if fighting off a mosquito.

"Do not bring up. It is over. I can't be here. I already wait too many days. I go back on flight to Izmir. Not safe here for me anymore."

"Ugur," I plead. "Petros needs to be paid. He's threatening my life and others. Where do I get the money? Please, just stay until the next boat and help me."

We're standing in front of a heavyset guard armed with a red laser gun. Ugur extends his ticket. The guard swipes the laser over the bar code. I reach out to grab onto Ugur, but he snakes past the guard before I can make contact. The guard stares dully at my hands waiting for me to produce my ticket.

"Ugur," I yell. "Please!"

Ugur turns as he collapses the handle of his suitcase.

"The money is in Bodrum. Why do you think it was so important he be there? And now too many come with their questions." He lifts his suitcase, climbs the steps, and disappears into the metal innards of the boat.

I smile at the guard. "Sir, could I go aboard until the ferry leaves? I have to talk to my friend."

"Need ticket."

"I'll just be a minute."

He thrusts me aside with his arm and accepts the next passenger.

"Could I buy the ticket on board?" I ask him. If I could have a few minutes trapped with Ugur, he might confess the entire operation and where and why Charlie needs to remain in hiding. He might know the location of additional money, presuming it isn't already stuffed in his suitcase. He's the only person I can think of who can answer how deeply Charlie's in trouble—or I am—and what to do if he doesn't reappear.

"We depart now," the guard says. "Piraeus sold out."

"The woman at the office said there was one seat left."

He checks his watch. "You buy ticket at desk on level two of ship. Must hurry."

I glance back at Skala, at the white cubes shining through car exhaust and golden dust. Fresh flowers have been placed once again in front of the bomb site. I try to gauge the seriousness of Petros's threat. He's a man who takes fingertips and maybe even the lives of hippies on motorbikes. I could call Louise from the rooftop bar of the Grande Palace and ask her to send my suitcase and passport to the hotel, along with the Ziploc of cash. I'd trust her with the money. I could even explain the danger she might be in and tell her to bring my things herself. I could pay for us to stay in Athens with the nine thousand dollars. Wasn't that its intended purpose: *in case of emergency*, from Edward Bledsoe to his disaster-prone children? There was only one child who would ever have needed to use it.

At first he's a mirage, a little dream bubbling from the stalls of overpriced swimsuits and souvenir beach towels. I blink and refocus. He's wearing a black baseball cap and a black T-shirt, the visor shielding his eyes. He's standing in the center of Skala in the direction of the harbor, like a lion sauntering through the pea-green grasses of the savanna utterly unaware that hunters have been camping out for weeks and shitting in jars just to get a glimpse of him through their rifle scopes. He appears so simply it's almost a disappointment, no strategic cornering, no shattering trumpet blast. But for a millisecond he lifts his head, and the sun dumps its light, and Charlie squints. He's staring right at me, the wide, round penny of his face flashing through waves of traffic and strolling sightseers. I feel as if the mere sight of him has touched the most private place in me, that combustive part where love and hate take turns breathing through the same apparatus.

I break into a run, abandoning the ferry and hurtling straight toward him. I don't even give myself time to call his name. He already sees me and begins to step back. I barrel through the jaws of the gray port gates. A flatbed truck loaded with watermelons glides into my path, its tires slow over the rutted stone, briefly cutting him from my view. When it passes, I make out the black shirt fleeing deep into the jumble of pre-lunchtime Skala. I dodge a bicycle and sprint across the street. Inspector Martis is holding up a finger, smiling warmly in greeting, his bulky legs marching toward me.

"Mister Ian," he calls. "Could we please talk—"

"Later," I scream, full propulsion toward the darting fish of black shirt. I won't lose him. Destroyers wasn't the only game we played as children in which I had a fighting chance. I beat Charlie seven out of ten at Buckland sprints. His years of smoking can't have given him the adult advantage.

I thread beyond the police station with its bright yellow mailbox, through the crowded outdoor tavernas and the aproned waiters leaning against their menu stations, down a paved artery half blocked with motorbikes and fat parked quads for rent. The black shirt gallops thirty feet ahead of me.

"Charlie!" I shout. "Charlie stop!" But even those few syllables seem to push against my velocity. We're bolting through a long straight alley of dress shops and jewelry stores and piteously empty lounges blasting techno music to entice or scare off customers with apotropaic drumbeats. The length of the alley gives me hope—if this were Chora I'd lose him instantly in its labyrinth. Up ahead is a wrought iron gate, which Charlie shoves open. It swings back, clicking its pin into the lock. Reaching to unhook it, I watch the black shirt veer wide and glide left beyond a cypress. As I fumble with the lock, my body has time to register its exertion and lack of oxygen. It's with every last, food- and air-starved cell that I continue the pursuit. I push the gate open, lurching into a run, and tack left.

A concrete path stretches between two rust-brown apartment buildings. Lines of laundry bow overhead. Corroded toys are embedded in a central strip of grass. The three floors of balconies are barricaded by domestic junk piles, and children peek their heads between the bars like archaic surveillance devices. Radios and televisions bicker from competing corners. Rusted rebar spaghettis from the buildings' sides. The whole place is like a Soviet housing complex hidden behind the Potemkin facade of an amiable island fishing village. I remember Duck's words—*where the real people live.*

I catch the echo of feet driving up interior steps and chase after it. Entering a dim cavern of cement, I hear Charlie's feet pass onto the second-floor landing. As quietly as I can, I double jump the stairs. So this is where he's stashed himself, buried in the unscenic slog of the working locals. No one would think to look here—it's about as accommodating to outsiders as a caliphate on Christmas. When I finally reach the landing, I just have time to see the last door along the exterior corridor shut. I use the distance to catch my breath and wipe the sweat from my cheeks, my pulse thrumming like it's picking up stray radio signals.

The door is sun-faded to mauve. There's no eyehole. A bank of windows next to it is covered in plastic-lined curtains.

I knock.

"Charlie, open the door. I saw you go in." I wait. "Come on, dammit. We need to talk."

A muscular man in a wifebeater staggers out of the neighboring apartment. He stares at me, summing me up as he balls his hands in his track pants. I smile benignly.

"My friend's in here," I explain. He continues leering from his doorway, fists rolling around in his pockets, his eyes pitted like pistachio shells. In a lighter moment, if I had less to lose, I might suggest he bring out a chair and watch my through-the-door tantrum in comfort. Right now, in this silent showdown, all we can do is estimate each other's potential for violence.

I raise my palms, and even though I'm not sure he'll understand, I say, "I mean no harm."

After another minute, he eases himself from the frame and retreats into his cell.

I knock again. When I hear no advancing footsteps, I try the knob. "Please, Charlie. Open the door. Talk to me."

Nothing.

I push my lips against the crevice.

"I'm not mad at you," I lie. "I just want to know what's going on. I can help. Whatever's wrong, we can fix it *together*. I'm on your side."

Nothing. I pound on the door, my knuckles scalloping the paint.

"I'm not leaving until you open up. I'll stay out here all night if

I have to. Please, Charlie. *I need you.*" The honesty of those words brings tears to my eyes, or the mere fact of my being within an inch of compacted vertical sawdust from the person I'm desperate to recover. I press my forehead against the door. I know he's listening on the other side. And maybe I'm a better Catholic than I thought, because this thin screen between two chambers of silence seems like nothing so much as a confessional box.

"You were there for me when I needed help," I whisper into the crevice. "And now I'm here for you. Whatever you've done, whatever trouble you're in, we can work it out. I've done terrible things too. Nothing you've done is worse than I have. Please, Charlie. I know about your company. I know the truth about Ugur and what you've been—"

The knob jingles. The mauve door swings wide. In the rectangle of darkness, a squat shape hovers indistinguishably. The loss of the barrier between us erases my promises of trust. It takes all my restraint not to perform a Gideon or a Miles by punching him right in the eye.

He grabs a switch threaded on a glassy cord, and the lamp on the dresser brightens. Charlie's face gleams momentarily in the shine before it distorts, widening, aging. Stefan. Just the sight of Charlie's brother is like provoking coldness by remembering previous winters. Our disenchantment with each other couldn't be more apparent, both of our faces set on identical registers of disgust.

"For fuck's sake, why did you run from me?" I blurt out. "Why did you let me think you were Charlie?" I stumble backward and consider making a sprint for the stairs.

"Wait," Stefan says. He takes an irritable breath and folds his arms. The years have given his face a lizard-like severity, eyes and lips pinched, and the opaline smoothness of his skin suggests a regime of creams that has the inverse effect of spotlighting an older man's obsession with wrinkles. There is just enough Charlie in his face that he must be accustomed to unfavorable comparisons, of eyes brightening up for him at a distance before they go dark.

"What are you even doing here?" I ask.

"I'm sorry to disappoint you," Stefan replies insolently. That familiar tone in his voice returns me to the kids we were, the ones I thought had been left behind long ago. "I suppose I've been doing the same thing you are. Only you seem to have gotten a bit farther along on the question of what my brother's been up to. Will you please come in and shut the door? Unlike you, I have an aversion to scenes in front of strangers."

I submissively step inside and pull the door shut. I don't have any fight left to make things harder on myself.

The ugly, daisy-wallpapered room smells of previous occupants' late-night nicotine orgies. It has a shadowy budget-vacation interior that practically assaults its inhabitants into enjoying the outside. An ascetic's resolve would be required in order to stay here, and in Stefan it's found its ideal boarder. A brown leather suitcase sits open on a chair with clothes folded in its cashmere casing. Files are stacked neatly on the nightstand on top of a silver laptop. The one item that offers a whiff of personality is a tennis racket by the door, zippered in a purple cover.

Stefan leans against the wallpaper, his foot toying with the spring of the doorstop. A constant ticking invades the room, which I first assume is a clock but must be the dripping of a leaky shower nozzle.

"Take a seat," he says, pointing to the bed covered in a synthetic duvet. I follow his order and let myself sag into it. Stefan's presence on the island feels like the delivery of bad news, but like all bad news it at least offers a sense of finality. It's good news that blows the future open. If anyone has the means to locate Charlie, it's Stefan.

"How long have you been on Patmos?" I ask. "You do realize there's an empty room up in Charlie's house with your name on it?"

"Charlie's house," he repeats caustically. He places his cap on the dresser, next to a small cache of orange medication vials. They match the one I saw on his bathroom counter up at the house. I wonder if the pills are for nerves or for pain. As Stefan stares down at the *boing-*ing doorstop, a halo of light shines on his nascent bald spot. All I can think of is how much Charlie must hate that bald spot on his older brother—a signpost of the destruction ahead.

"The point of my being here is to go about *undetected*. Why do you think I was running from you? Jesus, Ian, if I want to get to the bottom of how royally my brother's been fucking up in the family name, I'm not dumb enough to announce myself. You think Charlie's going to walk me down to that port he's rented and show me the paperwork?"

"So you've been here a few days," I reply sarcastically. Stefan nods, crosses the room to a minifridge, pulls out a bottle of water, and drinks it down. The fridge is stocked with several more bottles, but he doesn't offer me one. He reaches for a vial on the dresser and swallows down two pills.

"Long enough to determine that you've been recruited as an accomplice in Charlie's charter disaster." Stefan shakes his head at the lunacy of it—or at the onset of a cold headache from guzzling water too quickly. He hunches over and touches his left eyeball, moving his fingertip in circles over the iris. "The fucking pollen on this island!" He blinks rapidly to reset his contact lens. "I know we've never been fond of each other, but I have to say I feel you've let my brother down."

"I have? I've let *him* down?"

"You were always the sensible one, Ian. And my family was so good to you when you were young and having all of those problems with your parents." He makes it sound like I was an orphan that the Konstantinous were forced to take in out of moral obligation. It stuns me that Stefan interpreted my entire childhood friendship with Charlie as some sort of charity project. "When I arrived a few days ago and found you among Charlie's drinking party, I thought, well, at the very least, a friend has come who can talk sense into him. Then I learned you were simply taking advantage."

"I think you've got the wrong idea."

He smiles at me with the smugness of a meticulous researcher. How could I have ever considered meeting with Charlie's brother to secure a job in the family business? Last week's plans are moving past me as if they exist in a separate dimension, traveling god knows where at the blissful speed of ignorance.

"Did you or did you not come to Patmos to sponge off *our* money?" Of course it doesn't matter how Stefan frames the past. It's the embarrassing accuracy of the present that counts.

"I was in trouble. Charlie wanted to help me."

A juvenile laugh erupts from his lips.

"Help you to help yourself? After what you did to your poor father in Panama—"

"Please don't mention my father," I say curtly. He's not such an accomplished researcher that he's studied recent obituaries. Or has he?

"My brother has particular weaknesses, and you know that. Among them, depravity, recklessness, and one too many soft spots for old friends."

"Those aren't all bad qualities."

"They are when they're on someone else's dime! It's not Charlie's money!" I'm about to respond *is it yours?*, but Stefan lifts his hand in the sign of détente. "Look, I'm not here to argue with you. There's no gain in that. I'm glad you've showed up, because I need your help. Living like an animal is one thing—the fucking and fighting and smoking and drinking and coasting and sailing. I'm not Charlie's keeper, even if I do find it pathetic. But I'm sure as hell not going to let him destroy the family name."

"So you've come to spy on him."

He looks at me sadly, and for once the ruthless executive in him is replaced by the burden of the responsible sibling, the one who didn't get to do any of the fucking and fighting and smoking and drinking and coasting and sailing because someone had to keep their head. If there had been no Stefan, there would be no Charlie.

"My parents let Charlie behave like a child for too long. Eventually everyone has to grow up and stop existing like an overindulged pet. A few years ago, I convinced our father to stop the incessant cash flow. It was only my naïve mother who was permitting it to go on for as long as it did. Charlie needed to build a career. It was for *his* benefit as well as ours. So, typical Charlie, his imagination extends only as far as his eyesight. He concocted his ridiculous boat business. Fine. Let him have his little break-even odyssey in Greece. Better that than him interfering in the family firm. As long as he showed some profit we wouldn't intervene."

"So what's the problem?" I ask as if I don't already see the problem, as if it isn't sticking up like a tetanus-laced thumbtack on Stefan's immaculate brass-plated desk.

"The *problem* is it's not Charalambos Charters. It's *Konstantinou* Charters!" He jabs at his chest, his anger redoubling. "It's our name on those boats, those bright red *K*'s! Which means it's tied to us. And my gullible father has been funding it as a subsidiary behind my back! Which means, *Ian*, if there is anything untoward about Charlie's business, it jeopardizes Konstantinou Engineering! Do you get what I'm saying now?"

He clomps across the marsupial-brown rug, which is surprisingly sound absorbent, and grabs the files on his nightstand. "I don't know if you are aware, I don't know if Charlie's *bothered* to tell you, but my father is extremely unwell. He doesn't have much longer, and it's fallen on me to take over as chief of the construction business. I have enough on my plate dealing with certain trumped-up violations that the ITUC and its proxy labor activism groups can't wait to crack over my head as soon as my father dies. That way they can break the hold we have over our contracted clients. When a figurehead passes, that's when they go right for a company's knees." He tosses the folders on the bed, three of which, due to the mattress's inherent sag, immediately spill onto the floor. Stefan bends down stiffly, his mouth registering the pain in his legs, and begins collecting the papers. The type on them is so microscopic and consists of so many numerals and competing languages it appears like Babel run through a Manhattan taxi's receipt printer. "I'm cleaning KE up, every part of it, so spotless it squeaks, so sanitary you can eat your breakfast on it. When those inspectors and journalists put on their sanctimonious white gloves and run their fingers along the edges"—he stands again and drops the fallen papers on the bed—"not one speck of dirt."

Charlie isn't a speck; he's a spreading oil spill. "Charlie told me about your father," I say gently. "I'm very sorry. How did his surgery go the other day?"

This small act of compassion seems to bewilder Stefan. His eyes immediately scan the room as if searching for his cell phone.

"That's nice of you," he replies mildly. "It went okay. He's a tough one. He hasn't regained consciousness, but they moved him out of the ICU. The doctors are encouraging. They need to go back into his chest, when he's stronger, to replace a valve."

"Did you tell your father that you were coming here before he went under?"

"Of course not," he whines. "He might have told Charlie, and that would have blown the whole purpose of my being on Patmos. To figure out what's really going on with that charter outfit, which is the reason I've stayed out of sight. To make sure it isn't a pile of dirt floating out in the middle of the Aegean that could be flung across the headlines to prove just how unethical the Konstantinous are!"

Charlie's voice, a whimpering child: *We built the highways in the Middle East.* Haven't the Konstantinous always been unethical? Isn't that the secret of their success? I wonder how clean Stefan can make an empire constructed on the backs of slave migrant labor to build up the infrastructure of precarious midnight regimes. How many unscrupulous deals must the Konstantinous have forged with decades of conflicting powers to secure their own survival in the Middle East, and still soldiers bleed out daily along those roads to claim that ground, and refugees are spilling across them to escape it. I can't even begin to understand the politics of that region, but I suspect that Stefan, for all of his years inside Dubai's KE corporate headquarters, doesn't understand it either. Prince Phillip might. You can't scrub old ghosts away so easily; all you can do is try to make peace with them. Stefan strikes me as dangerous, not because his intentions are nefarious but because they aren't. He believes he can perform quick conversions. I don't suppose Konstantinou Engineering will last long under his watch. It's more likely he won't last long as he is under its terms.

I lift my head and try for direct eye contact. His allergy-damp eyes meet mine in the form of a challenge.

"So what have you found?" I ask.

"Not enough. Charlie's created a tight little barrier around himself, people unwilling, and, I assume, *paid* not to talk. But I know his charter company is a front for something."

"How?"

"You think I'm here on a whim?" He snorts. "Do I seem like I have unlimited quantities of free time? I've got better things to do than spend my vacation days checking up on my brother. I should be on Mallorca right now at the tennis clinic!" His right hand clenches an invisible racket. "I received an e-mail on August first from one of Charlie's former employees informing me that I might be interested in what's really going on with those refurbished boats. This employee asked for compensation in exchange for his information, which, naturally, I refused. But I can't let that sort of accusation slide." Gideon. He must have made contact with Stefan after he saw me in Athens and knew he wouldn't be getting his job back. And now he's hoping to squeeze two hundred K out of Charlie so as not to rat him out to his brother. "I canceled Mallorca and flew directly to Patmos."

"You flew? There's no airport."

"Helicopter," he clucks. "The point is, Ian, I haven't gotten very far on those I've approached. And I can't approach too many without Charlie catching wind. I've always been close to Therese, she's a blessing, but she'd likely tell Christos, and that old man is Charlie's captain. He might as well be sitting in my brother's pocket. Thankfully, there has been someone, a trustworthy source, who's shed a little bit of light. But he could only tell me what Konstantinou Charters *isn't*—a venture taking vacationers around the islands." I want to ask Stefan the identity of his source but I already know he won't provide it. "I got so fed up I cornered that bizarre little man, Ugur, down at the port yesterday. He was useless. Charlie's thumb might as well have been pressing on his tongue."

Stefan does something unexpected: he grins. He rests one of his legs on the dresser, leaning his weight into it in the way a salesman tries for a casual demeanor right before he presents his best offer.

"So that's where you come in," he says. "What you said through the door about knowing the truth of his company." He waits expectantly for a response.

If the hairy, twill curtains weren't closed, I might search for a distraction out the window. All I can do is stare at the slick purple cover of the tennis racket. Stefan is still frozen in an awkward half-stand on the dresser, not so much like a salesman now as a county prosecutor waiting for the first jolt of the electric chair to pronounce his problem officially contained.

"Tell me what you know, Ian," he orders. "I realize you're working for Charlie and you might think it's in your best interest to protect him, but that business of his isn't going to make it to the end of the year. I'm going to see to that."

It doesn't occur to Stefan that I might want to protect Charlie out of loyalty to whatever friendship we have left, that it isn't only my interest I'm looking out for. I could tell him about Bodrum, about some vague smuggling operation and the shells welded to the hulls. But how will Stefan's knowing help Charlie? And won't he be more likely to hunt Charlie down if he remains in the dark?

Stefan lifts his foot from the dresser and marches to the nightstand. He pulls out a checkbook, smacking it twice against his palm. He reaches for a pen, jots a number in the box, and signs his autograph.

"I know you need money. My source told me that. He said you've dug yourself into a hole and that your father cut you out of your inheritance. I'm willing to provide remuneration for your help." He rips the check along its perforated seam.

"Why don't you just pay the former employee? Wouldn't that be simpler?"

It's clear by his smile that I'm a novice across the net. "Blackmail-ers never stop blackmailing. Pay once, you'll pay for life. And how can I trust his information? With you, I know it's legit. We go back. You'd be doing the family that was kind to you a favor. And I feel it matters to help a friend." He holds out the green paper between his fingers as if tipping a maître d'. $50,000 is written in the box. "This is what you came for, isn't it? Don't be proud. Proud people don't sleep well."

I should take the money. I should deposit it and send the 9K to Lex and leave the island as soon as possible with Louise. What's one more rotten transaction between adults in the history of rented rooms? Charlie thought he could buy me too, but in his case I was asking to be sold.

"I get it," Stefan says when I don't reach for the check. "You think Charlie might give you more. Well, he can't. When my father does regain consciousness, I'm going to report what I've learned and Charlie won't have the resources to buy you a drink. It's going to be hard times ahead for him. My father doesn't like to be duped. As soon as he's conscious and strong enough to talk, Charlie will be lucky if he can scrounge together the price of an airline ticket back to New York." Stefan waves the check between his yellow fingers. "I'm going to find out the truth. If you don't talk, someone else will for much less. Do the smart thing here. I hope I spelled Bledsoe correctly. *Oh ee*, right?"

It's as if a meteorite has fallen from the sky and landed a few inches from my feet. You can get stuck on the impossible statistics of being crushed to death by astral debris or you can obsess over all the exchanges in time—the pause for the elevator, the speed of boiling water—that allowed you to stand mere inches away from that particular square meter of landing space. In either case, you walk away lighter, a survivor of the near miss. A swell of warmth spreads through me as I commit to my decision. It's like tasting myself again, the *Ian*-ness, a bland, earthy flavor of Michigan cornmeal. Without meaning to, Stefan has given me the rare opportunity to become the person I've wanted to be—someone who doesn't always cave to the highest bidder.

"No. I'm not taking it. You're right. I am broke. But I'm not betraying him."

Stefan's only weapon is money. When it fails, so does he. His mouth approximates an aerial photograph I once saw of an L.A. mansion caught in a mudslide. Half the mansion remained pristine, but the lower half sagged down the hillside, the swimming pool buckling free of its perfect ellipsoid. Stefan folds the check and shoves it in his pocket.

"But if you're interested at all in Charlie's well-being," I continue, "you can do something to help him."

The juvenile laugh returns as Stefan moves to the door to pull it open for me.

"He's in trouble. He's missing. And the worst part is, everyone only thinks he's safe because Sonny's daughter saw you in Skala and made the same mistake I did."

"That loud little girl?" Stefan asks. "I figured that was her kid. I've heard a lot about Sonny Towsend, about the kind of woman she is, but I haven't had the pleasure. Has Charlie dressed her up to match the house?"

I ignore the insult. "He's been missing for four days. No one has seen him. I'm not even sure he's on the island. But he wouldn't have just left everything the way it is. He wouldn't have just left—" I stop short of adding *me*.

Stefan stands watching me, clenching and unclenching his jaw in a series of physiognomic calisthenics.

"Did you hear me?" I yell. "Your brother is missing. The business you're so worried about is basically obsolete."

"Exactly!" he hisses. "Exactly the kind of thing Charlie would do to avoid a confrontation." Stefan notices the doubt creeping over my face. "Don't you think it's a bit of a coincidence that my brother goes missing at the exact moment I'm on the island? He's probably learned I'm here. Much easier for him to disappear rather than face the consequences. And what better way to hide the truth of that charter operation than to fold up shop. I bet you if I left today he'd be hosting a cocktail party up in Chora by sunset."

There is no doubt that Charlie would have panicked if he had discovered that his brother was snooping around the island. His tears and violent mood that night in Skala jibe with someone whose luck was in danger of running out. I remember his words about New York not being the place he'd go if Greece collapsed, and maybe his Greece was collapsing right then, his little kingdom expiring as we sat drinking vodka and expected him to pick up the tab. Was he hunting for places to run? Louise asked if Charlie was still playing Destroyers: use every tool available to buy time and search for an escape.

"The only way to be sure is to find him," I say. "Don't you have people?"

"People? What kind?"

What's the term for those who look after the rich and do their bidding and perform the various dirty work that keep them out of trouble? I recall the team of black-clothed servants in the Konstantinou's Fifth Avenue duplex, nameless, interchangeable, efficient—the ones who never seemed to have headaches or hangovers or birthdays or children. "Staff. People who could track him down and make sure he's okay."

Stefan winces at my childish understanding of wealth. He actually seems to feel sorry for me.

"You mean nannies? I'm afraid even Charlie aged out of them. No, Ian, I'm not going to hire *people* to track him down and then sob when I discover he's still breathing and tell him all is forgiven." He pauses before shouting, "I'm not, I'm not!" as if for a split second the wadded-up possibility hovered on the rim of the garbage can.

"Then you need to go up to the house and tell Sonny he's missing and the family isn't going to get involved."

"Now why would I do that? You aren't willing to help me, fine, but I'd appreciate it if you didn't give me ultimatums."

"Well, there is one thing you have to do." Stefan's curiosity is only moderately disguised by his anger. He opens the cap on a vial and swallows down another pill. "Charlie owes fifty thousand euros to the monastery. It's for his port, and he's late on the payment. Stefan, it's urgent. You have to pay them."

He laughs. "Why on Earth would I pay Charlie's bills?"

"Because they're threatening those around him." I can't mention myself. Stefan would exploit that fact to his advantage. I bend the truth to help the cause. "Like Therese and her family. You know that the monastery runs this island and they're capable of hurting the people who live on it. Do it for her, at least."

Stefan cocks his head and sucks on the lozenge of his tongue. He doesn't speak, but his unwillingness to pull the trigger on a deeply satisfying *NO* means I've finally managed to reach him.

"You have to give the money to a guy named Petros. He's the priest at Saint Sofia in Chora. It's a white-domed church with a tin—"

"I know where Saint Sofia is," he snaps. "Don't forget, I have been coming to this island since I was a child too."

"So you'll do it."

"I'll think about it."

"You should be careful. Petros means business."

Stefan refolds his arms and smirks at me, as if to broadcast, *I run a billion-dollar construction firm with military dictators and emirs as my main customer base. I can handle a solitary priest of a moribund parish on a minor island in the Aegean.* Part of me enjoys the idea of Stefan strolling into Petros's church and trying to argue with him over his brother's expenses. How soon before Argus and the other goon collect their favorite convincing instruments to demonstrate how little an expensive last name intimidates them?

Stefan opens the door and brings the sunlight into the room, recasting it as even smaller and more crooked. The ticking of the shower stops, like the room's heartbeat has finally surrendered.

"I'm sure we'll talk again soon," he says.

I pause in front of him.

"I care about your brother."

No wince, no smirk, no condescending reply.

"So do I. Very much. And that's why, ultimately, this will be good for him. Charlie's adept at treading up to his neck, but he's never learned how to pull himself out. If Charlie could, he might not have ended up like you."

"Like me?"

"Disinherited. Some people need to be in order to take responsibility for their lives."

As I pass down the walkway, I stop at the neighboring window. The man in the wifebeater is standing in the center of the room, a barbell frozen in his hand, his body glazed by the light of the television set. On the screen, refugees in tattered, bloodstained clothes are scrambling off a boat, tripping over the waves and over each other, pulling the dead bodies of two children onto the shore. It's news footage that would have been banned in America for graphic content, but here it keeps playing, the drowned, swollen faces with water-swollen legs and water-swollen shoes. It rips your heart out, and the man keeps watching, never lifting the weight into the curl of his bicep. There are more boats behind the first and more scrambling, and the body of an old man who is not dragged free of the water as if the sea might take him back.

L ouise's text wakes me. It's almost two-thirty in the afternoon, the white daylight flavorless compared to a dream I was having of being in a castle without exits. Louise and Sonny are at Petra Beach not far from the village of Grikos. WHY DON'T YOU COME? As I struggle into my black swim trunks, I try to decide if my conversation with Stefan has neutralized the threat of Petros. Is Louise still at risk? Should I be taking a taxi instead of the motorbike? I check my wallet. The last of the euros from Charlie's advance total up to seven and change. I still have a few hundred dollars in my bank account, and that's my net worth aside from the Ziploc bag. I feel a brief pang at refusing Stefan's $50,000, but I wait for it to pass as I scroll through the messages on my phone.

Lex sent an e-mail last night entitled, A LETTER FROM THE LAWYER, PLEASE READ. I don't read it. I double click on her e-mail address and write:

> Yes, I took the money. Jesus Christ, Lex, does it really matter that much to you? If you're so bent on leaving me with nothing just to prove how little I mean to the family, I will send it back. Happy now?

But I press DELETE, and the words fly from the screen as if they have been written on water. Even I know an e-mail like that would be an admission of guilt forwarded on to her lawyer. I start again:

> Hi Lex, I'm out of the country and for some reason all of your messages keep coming up blank. I hope nothing's the matter. I'm sorry I wasn't at the funeral.

Maybe one day you, Ross, and Lily will forgive me. Question, assuming your next message will come through: what's your mailing address? I want to send you something. Love, I.

I have searched my brain for the moment when my half-siblings and I declared war on each other. What point was it when these two doe-eyed, raven-haired children formed their axis of evil in the West Village compound, resisting my every-other-weekend settlement in their lavish dominion? Did my mere presence disrupt their otherwise undisputed claims to kitchen seat arrangements, the hierarchy of drinking cups, and bathroom schedules? Or was it simply that I had beaten them to Earth, and that slight, considering the limited territory of my father's heart, induced their joint crusade against me? Lex and Ross are both younger, but when their combined ages overtook mine, they became an indomitable anti-firstborn front. Maybe their loathing of me is the glue that's kept them close. Or maybe they saw me for what I am, the redheaded monster that would ruin the family if allotted the opportunity and space.

On the drive across the island, I'm on high alert for the white Mercedes slithering into my rearview mirror. By the time I cruise the dirt trail by Petra Beach, the afternoon shadows are collecting like tide pools along the pebbled shore. The overgrown fields, not far from the roadside accident, are peppered with red anemones. A giant rock formation swells from the sea, which snorklers attempt and fail to climb. Behind the boulder and a swirl of cormorants, *Domitian* is anchored, a black dart with Christos on deck dropping its sails. The pebbles on Petra are fatter than they are on the northern beaches, the size of charcoal briquettes licked white by fire. Here and there, the pebbles give way to chalky strips of sand.

I find Louise, Sonny, and Miles sitting on a pale green sheet with blue diamonds batiked across it. Black *Domitian* towels are stretched along its sides like caravan buffet tables, and white china dishes are arranged on them, filled with the residue of figs, tomatoes, and anchovies. A bottle of champagne smokestacks from a silver ice bucket, and plastic cups are secured in the pebbles at their feet. The wind flips the pages of a rococo art book. Miles shuffles a deck of cards while Louise leans into Sonny, laughing. Louise wears a yellow bikini, and Sonny a red one, their skin oiled and catching the sun. It's an ordinary day at the beach, as if nothing has happened, as if one of us isn't missing. Duck paddles in the shallows, pretending to drown.

"Ian, you made it," Louise yells with an exaggerated wave. I see the tender dents of her expanding rib cage. "I was beginning to think you hated the beach."

Miles grins, his whole clumsy face squinting at me as I drop onto the sheet. He seems less anxious and despondent than he did yesterday locked up in his house, as if the hours with Sonny have reminded him that there's still life to be hopeful about, that the nervous system isn't the body's only governing force. Sonny looks over at me coolly. After a few seconds, she manually overrides her initial reaction and offers a frail smile.

"Hi, Ian." Like the whetting of a blade. She tops up her champagne. Louise grabs the bottle, pours the topaz liquid into a fresh cup, and hands it to me.

"We were on the boat all day or I would have invited you earlier," Louise says. "Miles almost went into the water."

"Not by choice!" he howls. "Christos wasn't so smooth today. He lacked his usual finesse. To be honest, I think he was trying to knock me overboard."

"Honey, it's the only way you're going to learn," Sonny chides him. She looks at Miles and Louise—and not at me—and laughs. The thick tube of Miles's spinal cord stretches as he reaches to slap her lightly on the knee. "Prince Phillip agrees," she swears. "He told me to push you in. He told me you're being deprived of one of the last pleasures that humanity hasn't figured out how to ruin. And he's right." She brushes a piece of towel lint off Louise's shoulder. "It's too bad you couldn't come to dinner last night. And now he's left, and you'll never get to meet him."

"He's gone to comfort ghosts," I add in a lame attempt to join the conversation.

"What?" Sonny's expression wilts as she looks in my direction.

"Prince Phillip. He went to Vienna to sort out a haunting. He's a mystic."

Sonny turns her head away, examining the winding helix of the beach where a group of lithe, Italian teenagers are rolling on top of each other, their waists as narrow as saplings and their skin as dark as redwood bark.

"How did your meeting go last night?" Louise asks me.

Sonny whips her head around. "What meeting?"

"For the charter company," Louise explains. "Ian's been working."

"*You've* been working. Who were you meeting?" Sonny's voice is prosecutorial, but her trembling lips are those of the victim on the stand.

I decide to be honest. "Gideon Frost. You know him, don't you? He and Charlie were old friends from school."

Sonny gets to her feet, her slender body advancing toward the blue shelf of water.

"Duckie, come in. Enough drowning," she calls.

"I don't wanna," the girl whines, slapping up sea spray. "I'm not done yet."

"I don't care if you don't *wanna*." Something catches Sonny's eye in the surf. She bends down and collects a piece of ringed plastic. She brandishes it at us as Duck crawls from the water on all fours.

"Look at this!" she says angrily. "Tourist litter washing up. I swear, there's no respect for the environment." Her expression is so distressed it's alarming. "I really think this is it. The world is dying. The seas are warming, the glaciers are melting, there are new droughts and extinctions every day. And we just keep polluting. We just keep attacking the mother ship. I really think it's over." So much for the woman who swore the world wasn't ending over drinks in Skala. Sonny seizes her daughter around the waist and hugs her tightly, pulling the girl's chubby shoulders against her breasts, as if trying to melt her back into her body. She kisses her on the many water-warped cowlicks of her head. "I'm sorry, Duck. I'm sorry about the world you're inheriting. I'm sorry we didn't do better and you'll be the one to pay for our mistakes."

Duck's face blanches in confusion. "Huh?"

"Soon you won't even be able to swim here. We failed you. We didn't leave you anything to hope for."

"It's okay, Mommy. I don't mind."

Sonny releases her daughter and covers her face with her hands, her glistening back quivering like the sun on the sea. Miles eyes me knowingly, *I told you this would happen sooner or later*, before he drops his pack of cards and hurries over to comfort her.

"She was doing so well today," Louise whispers as she squeezes my ankle. "All she said was how much Charlie would love to be here and what an idiot he was for missing out on such a gorgeous afternoon."

"Until I showed up," I conclude. I should have seen this coming. And yet a part of me is jealous of Charlie. He disappears for four days, and everyone's life falls apart. When I disappear indefinitely, my relatives want their money back.

Sonny battles free of Miles's arms. "He didn't *go* missing!" she shrieks. The Italian teens stop dry humping down the beach. I notice Adrian farther out in the water, submerged up to his shoulders, sparkling like an albino seal. I search for Rasym in the waves but don't find him. "What does *go missing* even mean? That's how the inspector phrased it to me this morning. You don't *go missing*. You're either missing or you're not. You leave or someone's taken you." Stomping across the pebbles, she steams toward us. She leans down an inch from my face, and I see that her blue eyes are blurry with tears, like rain on airplane windows. "Where is he?" she shouts. "You talked to him last! Why isn't he home? For Christ's sake, tell me what you know!"

I scoot backward, dragging the plates along with the sheet and knocking over the champagne bottle.

"Sonny," Louise says. "Don't. Calm down."

Sonny jerks up and uses the heel of her palm to wipe her eyes. Miles stands behind her with his arms open, as if waiting for her to return to them.

"Miles, let's go into the water," Louise proposes. She jumps to her feet and readjusts the yellow fabric over her ass. "Come on. I'm teaching you to swim, no arguing. Duck will help me, won't you?"

"No."

"Well, you can swim next to us and show him how it's done."

Duck bolts into the waves.

"Oh, good luck with that," Sonny says, laughing through her slowing breath. She no longer looks at me, cordoning off her line of vision to the slosh of champagne foam on the rocks.

"I can only go in to my waist," Miles gripes playfully.

"Then we'll see how you do an inch above your waist and take it from there."

"The trick," Sonny says tiredly. "The trick—" But she gives up explaining what the trick is.

Louise holds Miles's elbow and steers him like a ward nurse toward the sea. I nervously pinch the sheet with my toes as Sonny continues to watch the champagne bubbles dissolve and two flies land on the sweetened pebbles. She slumps onto the towels as if someone has kicked her legs out, but she doesn't take her eyes off the flies. Their hairy, gilded bodies are phosphorescent green, rivaling the opal ring she wears. Sonny positions her middle finger against her thumb, but keeps her hand frozen in that position without flicking them away. Her cuticles are pushed so impeccably against the nail bed they are perfect white seams. She takes more care with each cuticle than I do with my hair. And yet the scaffolding of her face is hollow.

"We had a fight that night, before we all met up," she mumbles. "Before Miles punched him. It was about Duck. He wanted to wait a year before bringing her back to Cyprus. He said everything had suddenly gotten too crazy, and it was no time to be making rash decisions. I'd never seen him so angry. I did send flowers by the way."

She realizes that I'm not following. "To his father in the hospital. Yesterday, I sent a huge bouquet and signed both of our names on the card. So when he wakes up . . ."

"That was good of you." She either doesn't hear me or isn't interested in my approval.

"I thought maybe Charlie was getting some space because of our argument. Now I know that can't be the reason." The flies spin from the rocks. Sonny moves her hand to the sheet, not far from my toes, and her finger finally flicks away nothing. "Do you remember that weird thing he said to me in Skala? That he loved me and would always make sure I'm safe. Safe from what? Why would he bother to say that and then vanish? He wouldn't just leave like this, Ian. He's a lot of things, but absent isn't one of them. I wish you'd tell me the truth."

So I do. I recount my conversation with Charlie in his office that morning, about his needing to go to Bodrum for work and my promise to provide an alibi to keep her from freaking out. Sonny blushes at the mention of her paranoia, and her blush deepens at the orchestration of lies to put her at ease. People want to be lied to; it's the failure of a lie to smother the truth entirely that angers us. Her tongue travels around her mouth, lingering at each tooth like they're stations of the cross.

"I would have understood," she says in an offended tone that suggests she wouldn't have. "I'm not a child. I understand he has his business to look after. And, all things considered, a bomb is a pretty decent reason to be paranoid. Is that how he makes sure I'm safe? By feeding me a bunch of garbage?" She burrows her hand in the pebbles. "So you lied for him. How do I know you're not lying to me now?"

"You don't have to believe me. If that doesn't sound like something Charlie would cook up, you have every right to doubt me. You know him better than I do."

Sonny doesn't respond. She taps her chin against her shoulder and stares out at the water where Louise and Miles are up to their waists in the ribbon of light blue, just before the seabed drops off into darkness.

"Charlie's the child," she murmurs. "Does it ever occur to him that it's his safety and not mine I'm worried about? Of course not."

I could stop here and let Sonny go on believing that Charlie is merely avoiding her while he's dealing with business. But I've done enough damage under the banner of helping a friend.

"Listen," I say. "You should be worried. I am. The man Duck saw in Skala, it wasn't Charlie."

"What?" I pray she doesn't mention the hand-carved queen. I can't admit to another deception. "If that wasn't Charlie, and you didn't talk to him the next day—"

"No one's seen him since that night in Skala. And he never went to Bodrum."

"So he *is* missing," she cries. "And all this time, you let me think he was fine!" She bunches her knees to her chest. Tears begin to clot where they had been wiped. "He could be dead or injured somewhere for days and you let me think he was safe! You mother-fucker! Why did you come here, Ian? Why did we ever let you into our house?" Saliva strings from her teeth. She lunges for her shoes or her phone or maybe a weapon to use against me in her straw satchel. "I even went down to the station this morning and asked that inspector if he had talked to Charlie, when I should have been filing a missing person's report!" Her shoes and her phone aren't in the bag. They're on *Domitian*. She possesses no useful tool to get her off the beach.

I grab her arm, and she struggles to free herself.

"I think Charlie might be purposely hiding."

"I don't want to listen to you anymore! All you've done since you've gotten here is lie to me!"

"That man in Skala who Duck saw. It was his brother, Stefan." The revelation stops her from fighting my grip. She does know Charlie better than anyone. I can see the pieces fitting together behind her eyes, the jigsaw starting to assemble the border of a picture. "He's here to check on Charlie's company. He thinks there's something bad about it."

"Bad?"

"Illegal. And I'm afraid he might be correct."

She shakes her head, a coldness settling over her face. I loosen my grip, and she yanks her arm free.

"I don't know anything about that," she says automatically, as if that's how she'd been instructed to respond if the subject ever arose. Or maybe, if she had her own suspicions, that pledge of total ignorance is how she dispelled those thoughts. "I told you, I've never been allowed to know. But if Stefan's here, why isn't he using his room at the house?"

"He was staying out of sight. He thought he'd discover more that way. He's rented a hole in the wall in that housing complex behind Skala. I'm sure he'll probably pay you a visit now that his cover is blown. But I think Charlie might be keeping his distance to avoid a confrontation with him."

She expels air and rocks back and forth, caught without a strategy in her allegiance to Charlie. If she reports him as a missing person to the police, whatever's *bad* about the charter company is likely to come under investigation.

"Are you lying now, Ian? So help me god—"

"Charlie was the one who lied. I was just the messenger. And I only found out about Stefan a few hours ago."

"If Stefan's here trying to catch Charlie, I wouldn't put it past him to disappear until he's gone. I've never understood the animosity between them. But if Stefan learns anything—"

"Then he's going to report it to their father." I don't need to elucidate. Her eyes widen and close. For a few minutes neither of us speaks. Louise and Duck are scooping up seawater and dumping it baptismally over Miles's head.

"The money," Sonny finally utters. *The money* is the short answer to every question. I could have run onto the beach screaming *money* and everyone would have instantly understood. She laughs in exasperation, at the one entity that Charlie might cherish more than his commitment to her. Or, I'm guessing, she realizes that money is the one provision that will keep her safe. "He's not going to lose his inheritance," she snaps. "No way. I don't care what his brother told you. His father adores him and would never abandon him like that. A parent doesn't do that to a child." She's not so lost in her own head that she doesn't recognize the inadvertent slight. "I didn't mean—"

"It's okay."

"Why weren't you honest with me right away?" Her eyes are on Duck, who's now swimming around Miles with her hand finned at her head like a lurking shark. "Maybe I could have done something. Do you think Charlie knew that night we had drinks? No wonder he was so pissed off. Is that why everything had suddenly gotten *too crazy*?"

Nothing about Charlie in the trailer on the morning we hatched the alibi suggests that he was aware of his brother's presence on Patmos. And yet everything about his behavior that night in Skala seems to confirm that he had learned of it. I wonder if the change of plan happened then—to redirect the alibi for a different and darker advantage. I don't have the heart to mention that Charlie might not be waiting Stefan out, that he could have disappeared altogether, leaving us to deal with the disaster in his wake. Could Charlie already be in Cyprus collecting whatever money he has stashed away, while Sonny is left waiting for him and I'm left holding the reins of a smuggling ring? He couldn't be that callous.

"When you say *illegal*—"

"I don't know," I answer, crouched halfway between a lie and the truth. "Honestly, I don't want to know. I'm not working for him any longer. You can trust me on that."

"I'm almost glad Miles decked him. Only that was Charlie's intention, wasn't it? He started that fight to give me a reason not to want him home." She scrapes off a line of brown polish from her toenail. "Is Stefan as awful as Charlie always said? Do you think he'd listen if I spoke to him? I could smooth things over. I could appeal to him, out of respect for his brother or for my daughter and me."

She's patriotic in her vanity. I get the sense that patriotism has won her a number of early wars and has led her to believe in its supreme capabilities.

"Stefan can be like talking to a corporation with a really strong backhand."

Sonny stares dazed, moving her eyes from *Domitian* to the hilltop monastery in Chora and then rolling her vision back down the cliffs to her daughter in the sea. It's as if she's calibrating what she's at risk of losing, itemizing it before it's snatched from her hands.

"I didn't mean those words I said that night. That Charlie wasn't worth it. He is worth it. To me. It's like I told you. I don't care about the rest of it. All I need from it is Charlie and Duck. That's the thing, Ian, the only value in that money is for Duck, to be a family again. And now with Rasym here and Stefan turning up, it's *their* house, isn't it? Just like Cyprus is their country, and there won't be room for us. How is anything safe?" You can prepare for the worst, you can stab your heart a million times to harden it for the blow, but when the blow comes it still destroys you. Because it does so in ways you can't anticipate.

"When I was a kid," she whispers desolately, scratching at the rest of the polish, "my father worked for a rich family who had a cabin in the San Gabriel Mountains outside of L.A. We'd go up there, my mother and I, for the summers to watch over the place. We were up there every June through September, we loved it, not a day without dancing under the pines and drawing birds and my mother reciting her feminist earth poems." I want to ask Sonny how she went from the daughter of a feminist poet to a Hollywood actress and on to the girlfriend of a billionaire's son, but I know it's only in fantasy that the search for a better life is always progressive. We are not so much evolving as swimming for our lives. "It was our heaven, our haven. The family only used it for one week in July. Before they came we'd have to move all of our stuff from the main house into the tiny guest cottage. And for seven days, we'd watch that family use the house and break the things we cared for and trample the flowers we planted and sleep in *our* beds. I knew they owned the place, but I also knew it belonged to us. Those states were entirely separate in my head. And they still are. But it doesn't matter. When my dad was fired, we lost our summers there." She presses her forehead against her knee. "I guess I have no choice but to wait and see. Become a guest now. Tell Duck she might not be coming back with us. How do I tell Duck that? Charlie promised me!"

She exhales sharply and climbs to her feet, watching Miles back away now that the water has advanced above his navel. Louise pushes against his resistant back, as if she's trying to force him through the emergency doors of a crashing plane.

"Thanks for telling me the truth," she says. "For warning me. I'm sorry I screamed at you. I didn't know that Charlie was jerking both of us around." It's as if some visible shift comes over her as she stands in front of me, an alteration in her shoulder and hips. "But, no, I'm not going to give up hope. I mean, Stefan might not learn anything. And really how illegal can that business be? It's not like Charlie's devouring children. And he's only been gone a couple of days. Charlie wouldn't leave me. I know he hasn't. He's out there figuring it out. And as long as he's alive and okay, we're still here."

"It's important to stay positive."

She squints down at me with a barely suppressed smile, the tips of her curly hair frizzled in a soft halo against the gauzy sun.

"You don't know everything," she says. "I know Charlie's fine. He sent me a message that he is."

"You spoke to him?" For a second, I wonder if our entire exchange has been a performance. Was she aware of my deception even on that first afternoon I visited her? Has she been privy to Charlie's movements all along? "Sonny, if you've talked to him—"

She shakes her head. "He left me something, a sign only I would be able to interpret. No one else would understand it. You see, we play a little game." She kicks her satchel. "He left me something to let me know he's with me."

Her voice is so certain, her sun-blasted American face so sure of its own optimism, I can't find it in me to admit her mistake. I can't strip her of the last thing she believes in, a two-inch piece of wood that prevents her world from breaking apart.

MILES NEVER SWIMS. He gets close. Sonny and I watch from the beach, but when it comes time to dunk his head below the surface he reaches a line he can't cross. He treads back to shore, slipping on the loose pebbles in the charging current, lunging for the safety of dry land.

"I tried," he tells Sonny with a wounded voice. "I knew you were watching. I tried. I really did, for you." Maybe he wants to crush censure by couching his failure in devotion. But I get the feeling by the way he stares at Sonny with probing, golden-retriever eyes that he's being sincere.

"You should do it for yourself," she replies but clearly enjoys the idea that her mere presence could annihilate lifelong phobias.

"It's just that going under is like wrapping my head in plastic. I'm scared about breathing, even though I know you aren't supposed to. It's like being trapped in an elevator with fish."

"It really isn't," Sonny promises. "You're going to have to learn sooner or later. You're surrounded by the stuff."

He rubs his hair with a towel. "I've made it this long."

Louise rises from the waves, lifting her thin, brown arms to indicate that she did her best. Behind her, the tender is cutting a direct path toward the beach, Christos's silver hair blazing against low clouds. Miles begins to pack up the china, and Duck worms onto her mother's lap. Sonny rubs cream across her shoulders.

"My little empress," she coos. "Not a princess. Who wants to be princess when they could be an empress?"

"Emperor," Duck amends but agrees.

Louise winks at me before putting on her aviators. "Do you want to go back on *Domitian* with us?"

"I have my bike," I say. "I'll see you at the cabins later?"

"Wait a minute. What's going on between you two?" Sonny asks, sharing her smile first with Louise and then with me as if they are separate ceremonies. She's doing a noble job of hiding her anxiety. "I'm sensing something. The emperor and her handmaiden demand to know."

"Nothing," Louise stammers.

"Uh-huh." She turns to me. "At least you'll come by for a late lunch tomorrow. I've asked Therese to make her special Patmian fish stew."

"*Bleeeh*," sounds Duck.

"I wonder if Stefan will be joining us. Do you think he'll have moved up from his pied-à-terre behind Skala by then? Or should we send him an invitation?" When I don't answer she smiles mechanically. "Well, it will be a nice afternoon, no matter."

"So it wasn't Charles that Duck saw that morning in Skala?" Miles surmises. "I'm sorry. But that doesn't mean Charles isn't—"

"It's okay," Sonny replies. "It's the Konstantinou's island, not mine. That much is clear. We'll just have to put on our best fake smiles, Duckie. You can do that for me, can't you? We'll make a game of it."

"Can't Therese cook something else?" Duck begs.

Miles palms her wet head. "I'll smuggle in a hamburger for you."

And like that, the day returns to normal. I wonder how long it could continue, afternoons on the beach, plans for lunch, rides on the yacht, all without Charlie and yet cocooned in his money and name. Christos motors up to the shore and reaches for the supplies to place in the dinghy. He accidentally drops two plates in the water and curses as he climbs out to gather them. He purposely avoids looking at me. I want to ask if he's found his son and daughter, but he's clearly in no mood for outside interference, especially from the man he's already cast as a loudmouth infiltrator. He claps his hands impatiently for everyone to hop aboard. Even with Charlie gone, he's forced into service, meeting the relaxation needs of tangentials of the man who writes his paycheck. Better that than no man writing his paycheck, which is one imminent danger he shares with Sonny. Of everyone on this beach, I think it's Christos who understands the gravity of the situation. What would the Stamatis family do without the last Konstantinou who relies on them?

I pull Louise aside as she's scooping her arms through her shirt.

"Be careful on your way home. On your bike."

She knits her brow. "Why, Dad?"

"Just wear your helmet. There's a lunatic priest driving a white Mercedes. If you see that car, pull off the road. He nearly took me out. I'm serious."

"Okay. First you don't come home last night. Now you're lecturing me on driver's safety. Mind telling me what's up?"

"We can talk tonight. I—" *think I really might be close to loving you* "want to convince you to take a trip to—" But my mind goes blank at naming a nearby island. "We'll talk tonight."

I wave as they blur into molecules of color and a motor's hum. I pick up two playing cards that Miles overlooked. A tiny tear mars the top of a red ace, either by accident or a sharp's mark.

A gang of hippies roars far down the beach. There are five of them, perhaps the youngest of their delegation. Their skin is the brown mingling of dirt and sun, accented with cowrie-shell belts, flip-flops caked in mud, bikini bottoms decorated with skulls and smiley faces, dreadlocks arrayed like the armature of brass chandeliers, pierced mouths open like flame-swallowers, two with leather headbands strapped across their foreheads. The shirtless guy with a handlebar mustache does a backflip on the pebbles, a trick he must have performed a zillion times because his friends take no notice when he sticks the landing. A giant green crucifix is tattooed on his back. Their giggling and wrestling is so pure, so joyous, it feels threatening, youths high in the altitudes of their own promised land. They look like the mutant spawn of whatever remained at Spahn

Ranch, hovering life-thirsty on a scanned and pixilated horizon. A few mutts circle them, barking, but it's a purebred, collared Dalmatian that they're trying to coax into the water.

I should feel a measure of relief in admitting the alibi to Sonny. But it's as if I proved to myself as well as to her the sham I'd been holding on to. The lie was a willingness to hope, because a part of me still believed that Charlie could reappear that easily. Wandering along the beach, I'm struck all over again by the shock of his absence, the total and traceless vanishing. Or almost traceless. He was on *Domitian* that night after Skala, and there's still the chance the blood on the floor was his. I try to think of anyone who'd have a motive to do Charlie in. Not Gideon or Petros or anyone who expects to be paid. Miles comes to mind, but the very reason I suspect him seems to clear him from blame: who punches someone in public and then murders him hours later in private? Unless it wasn't premeditated, *unless, unless, unless* . . . I'm grabbing at invisible bodies to blame for an invisible death. The only other source of friction I recall in the days leading up to Charlie's disappearance is the hippies, his most despised form of island invaders. I watch them frolicking along the waterline, happy, ragtag, self-drafted soldiers of the world's end.

If Mr. K were even semiconscious, I'd call him now and convince him to send help. Stefan isn't an option. I search the beach for his only other relative within reach. Rasym is all I have.

Adrian stands in the sea, tossing his head back to let the water slick his hair. He climbs from the surf, the swells of his back tapering toward the small, swiveling disc of his hips. I'm surprised by his boldness, catching sight of me and lifting his arm just as he rises enough from the waves to reveal no swim trunks—only the white trace of its occasional necessity around a triangle of dark, curly blond. A thick, uncircumcised penis beats against the plum of his scrotum. His nudity is more pronounced by the two black water shoes on his feet. Seawater beads across the arch of his ass. Even the hippies stop to watch him, like he's a new and potentially disruptive species evolving in sped-up time lapse from the deep, skipping all of the messy undextrous development of primates. I was hoping for the justice of a very small penis.

He hops toward me, smiling, almost clueless of his own beauty, *almost* because his abdominal muscles are too sculpted to be unintentional.

"You missed the boat," I tell him. He clasps my arm for balance as he unfastens the shoes.

"I wasn't on it." He nods toward two towels weighted in their corners by rocks. Two towels are encouraging.

"Is Rasym with you? I need to talk to him."

"Not yet. He should be here soon. What time is it?" He bends over to pick up his iPad, the feather of his ass crack blazing a chapped red. I'm amazed he wasn't worried about someone stealing the device during his swim, but I remember what Louise said about the billionaire Kromers of Kraków. Adrian can afford losses. "He'll be here any second. Why don't you lie down with me? Take his towel. It's too cold for him to go in now." Adrian flips onto his back, burrows against the towel to make a comfortable crater, and hooks his arm behind his head. Blue veins cable from his fuzzy armpit. His smile isn't flirtatious, it's loving and careless and calm.

As I lean sideways on the adjoining towel, I experience the gratifying sense of being in the company of a person who has nothing to do with Charlie—no motive, no loss, no grief, no gain. Adrian is a holiday from the last few days of trouble, a purely uninvolved party floating in his own escape hatch. I'm jealous of him, the sun soaking into him, the water cresting at his feet, the unfailing agreement of smooth body and mind. He doesn't even care who's watching him. A naked man has the advantage of honesty: there are no pockets to empty. The police would ask a naked man to dress so they could search his pockets for secrets.

"How do you do it?" I ask, 2 percent sarcastic, 98 percent serious.

"Do what?"

"Be so happy all the time."

"It's beautiful here, so hospitable and warm." I honestly think he means Earth. "How can you not be happy?"

"It just seems like you have it all figured out."

"I try not to figure it out. All I do is try to put myself in its path. I'm alive."

I'm alive, I mouth silently. A jet ski whisks around the giant boulder, a fun machine shaped like the head of a killer whale. After a few minutes of listening to the tides play across the rocks, I ask him where Rasym is.

"A group of refugees washed ashore last night," he tells me. Even an escalating humanitarian crisis is spoken of with an unflagging smile. Nothing will destroy Adrian's happiness. "Rasym is handing out head scarves for the women and copies of the Quran for the men. He had a shipment sent here, and he's befriended a few of the commissioners dealing with the migrants for the UN. I offered to help, but he says my presence might confuse them. He wants to make them feel at home."

Yes, a gay blond Adonis would disrupt the dispersal of piety. Adrian passing out Qurans might be a disquieting introduction to the West—promising and threatening far more than they'll find.

"Are you religious?" I ask him.

"Perfectly faithless," he says, examining a mosquito bite on his elbow. His buttonhole of a navel shrinks to a slit. "On my long morning swims I get close to something. The goats on that tiny, vacant island. I believe in them." His smile amplifies. "I should say faithful. Faithful to what's here."

"Is it strange for you that Rasym is so religious? I saw him praying that day we went out on the boat."

"You mean in terms of us being together and Rasym being Muslim." Adrian rolls onto his side and uses his bicep as a pillow. "You're intent on us having a serious conversation, aren't you?"

"I'm just curious," I say, blushing.

"Yes, it has its challenges. Not so much for me but for him. When I first met Rasym a few years ago in London, he was much more devout. Or, rather, devout in the traditional way. I shouldn't tell you this," he says, laughing in preparation. "Rasym would kill me. He's sworn me never to bring it up. But he was in a writing program in London. He wanted to be a fiction writer, and his teachers kept encouraging the students to get under the reader's skin. Go for the throat. So Rasym did as he was instructed. I read the story later. An American businessman boards a plane and is seated next to a Muslim guy wearing a tunic and turban. The businessman is very nervous and afraid. He's filled with prejudices. But eventually the two get to talking and they realize how much they have in common. Rasym wrote the scene very tenderly. They share photos of their wives and children, they laugh about politicians and argue about sports. They bond. They see each other for once as fellow humans, and the businessman is so moved by his change of heart that he invites his seatmate to dinner at his home. It is very touching."

"Does he accept?"

"The Muslim man says he couldn't possibly. *It's no trouble. I want you to meet my family and we can all break bread and they can see you as I do, another member of the world.* That kind of thing. *No, no, that will never happen, but thank you.* Finally the Muslim man says, *it's been great talking to you.* He gets up from his seat, slits the throat of the flight attendant, and hijacks the plane. Right before it crashes, the businessman yells through the cockpit door, *I thought we were friends.* The voice replies, *we are friends and I'll think of you as one for as long as I live. But please return to your seat. I must finish my duty.* The end."

My smile isn't so much an expression of satisfaction as a face that doesn't know what to do with itself. "What did his teachers think?"

"He was basically expelled from the program," Adrian replies. "I think they suspected him of being a budding terrorist. Yes, it's a horrible story. But they were asking for the brutal truth, and he gave it to them. I guess what they really wanted was brutal compassion, a truly fictional version of the world." For the first time, Adrian's mouth contracts. The sun moves the shadow of a tree across his forehead. "I shouldn't have told you that story. It makes Rasym sound like something he's not. But it answers your question. I met Rasym the week he was kicked out. He was struggling with his faith. You pray, you follow the dictates and the rituals, but there are only so many times you can watch innocent gay boys hanged or thrown off rooftops in the name of Islam and not begin to question the version of god you're serving—especially if you happen to be gay yourself. Aren't they too young to be damned?"

"How old does one have to be?"

"The point is, Rasym had to learn to be Rasym, which is Muslim but also his own self. He finally found a more accepting route, his own route, not the kind his mother subscribes to. She's become quite fundamentalist on her side of Nicosia, the Turkish side."

"And his father is Charlie's uncle, the Greek side."

Adrian nods, his smile reappearing, first a testing fire and then a full explosion of teeth. "They married young. Apparently, it was a scandal for such a prominent family. It's still very much the Berlin Wall in Nicosia, east versus west. Or north versus south for them. They call it the Green Line. I think he held on to that fundamentalist approach as a way of holding on to his mother after she moved back to the statelet in the north. Now she won't talk to him. It's sad. She feels he's aligned himself with the infidels of the West. Like she didn't once choose who she loved."

"At least Rasym has you."

"Between you and me, I think homosexuality has saved many a man. It turns them good if they let it." Adrian flips onto his back and peers over at me. The shadow falls into the space between us. "Do you like boys, Ian?"

I shake my head. "I mean, I experimented in college like everyone does." Adrian doesn't seem disappointed by the news, as if a gay version of myself wouldn't have been a temptation.

"I wondered," Adrian says, "if maybe you and Charlie, when you were younger, because he was so excited for you to arrive—"

"It wasn't like that." The idea of Charlie being excited for my arrival hits me in the gut.

"Rasym is very fond of Charlie. Admires him. Out of all the Konstantinous, it's Charlie he loves most."

"Rasym's father is also in the family business, isn't he?"

"Not so much anymore. Charlie's father sidelined him years ago. He still gets a cut of the profits. I'm sure they're all worried what will happen when Stefan takes control. *Be nice to Stefan if you ever meet him*, Rasym always tells me. And I guess I will soon, since he's on the island." How does Adrian know that Stefan is here? But, of course, Rasym is probably Stefan's trustworthy source—the one who informed him about what the charter company *isn't*. I'm about to ask Adrian about it when he begins to laugh. "But you and I, we have gotten too serious. We're on a beach, man!"

"Sorry."

"It happens as soon as money comes up. It sucks the life out."

I drop onto my back and pinch the edge of the towel.

"Do you like living in Nicosia?"

I assumed this question registered on the less serious side of the scale, but Adrian pushes himself onto his elbows. "Oh, I don't live with Rasym. I'm mostly between Kraków and London. He comes to visit me for a week each month, but otherwise we're on our own. You steal a person from their old life when you find them. We just steal each other a little less. I like to be stolen more than Rasym does."

"Did you ever meet Miles in London?"

"Never," he mutters, turning his eyes to the sea, watching its crests through the sun-bleached valley of his thighs and pubic hair. "That fancy circle he's so obsessed with was never my thing. I guess it's no longer his thing either, now that he can't afford it. Or rather, their thing is no longer a broke Miles. Poor guy. I heard he's had to sell his apartment to pay his debts. No, I'm the opposite. I went to London when I was twenty to escape. I wanted more by wanting less. Does that make any sense?"

Amid the echoing laughter of the hippies and the blackening

waves in the late afternoon heat, Adrian recounts his first years in London, traveling there by train from Poland, refusing his parents' money, not out of any grudge against it, but in the self-interest of surviving on his own. He slept in parks, then in apartment shares, taking small, lurid side jobs—nude house cleaning, go-go dancing in bars—never reaching the point of full-fledged hustling but passing over all of its contingent steps. He tells me about trips to Amsterdam and Stockholm, hitchhiking and getting by on a diet of vending machines or the refrigerators of one-night stands. Many of his friends were actual prostitutes, and he never divulged the vaults of money open to him back in Kraków. Adrian paints that period a bit too much like a fairy tale, prince to pauper without any of its scars. I get the impression that his time hunkered on park benches and gyrating for tips, the prodigal son of the man who privatized Poland, was a far shorter stint than he's letting on. It's hardly his fault: early experiences grow larger than the days that hold them, while entire stable years drift away in a blink.

"I had to stop when *Fakt*, a Polish newspaper, found out about me. For my family, I had to pretend to be the spoiled son. Everyone was more comfortable with that."

He tells me that he still lives humbly in London, not *as* humbly, but his friends are mostly the ones he met on the streets and in the bars. He grabs his iPad and shows me a few photos: gay men, coarser in eye and skin than Adrian, faces haunted but stronger for having survived the ricochets of their youth. Adrian smiles at them in the tender way people used to look at photographs, not as vectors of competition but as reminders of distant ports. After scouring several albums my interest begins to wane. Adrian seems to sense my boredom.

"Do you want to see your friend, Louise?" he asks. "I found her Instagram account. It was locked, but she accepted me as a friend." He clicks on an icon and pulls up louisealtheawheeler (Althea is Louise's middle name? Her parents must have been Dead Heads before they were Born Agains).

I flick through her shots of Patmos—sunsets, beaches, a plate of fried octopus, a view of the monastery from the handlebars of her bike. None of the photos she took of Charlie and me are uploaded. No sign of all the likes that first picture of us on the balcony accrued. *Two outlaws who escaped into paradise.* I continue flicking, tracking her movements back to Paris (a shot of her and Sonny in front of the glass pyramid at the Louvre), London, Copenhagen, Berlin. Eight weeks back, she's in Lexington, Kentucky, her arms wrapped around a tall, bearded guy in a cowboy shirt, the caption below an emoji of a swollen heart. Before I can search the inventory of her life any further, Adrian yanks the tablet away and aims it at the hippies. They're lighting a small fire on the beach with sword grass and the ripped-out pages of a book. He clicks a few shots.

I am still eight weeks back in Lexington, mentally unplucking Louise's arms from the bearded guy's neck. Jealousy is the presiding emotion of the Internet—it feeds on the banquet of soft filters and precision-fit moments that never expire. *Who is he?* I imagine asking Louise in the cabins tonight, the question a torpedo locking on its target. And I imagine an answer that dispels the entire scene: *You idiot, it's my drug-addicted brother, Luke. How dare you accuse me? Seven days. That's all I promised.* And she'd be right.

"Look at them," Adrian says jubilantly, his eyes on the hippies bent around the fire, their faces like stone lions watching it grow. "I like them. Who cares if they read the Book of Revelation? Maybe it's their way of enjoying every minute." He uses the screen as a tray and begins to roll a joint from a small stash in his bag. "Rasym is convinced the hippies planted that bomb last month. He thinks they celebrate destruction. To me, it looks more like they celebrate life."

An empty chair at 11:00 A.M. at Nikos Taverna. Charlie's chair, the one he sat in every morning. A bomb on a timer in a crowded port. What if Sonny is right that the bomb was meant for him? If something terrible did happen to Charlie that night on *Domitian*, if he isn't simply hiding out until his brother leaves, could it have been a second attempt to succeed where the first one failed? All this time Charlie might have been a man with a mark on his back—a motive that goes far deeper than a fistfight in a square. I stare at the hippies perched around their afternoon campfire. Maybe they're celebrating the vanquishing of the godless. They unbuckle the collar from the Dalmatian's neck and toss it, laughing, in the flames.

"Go slow on that," a voice booms above us. I look up to find Rasym peering down, black sunglasses insecting his eyes.

"I only want a few drags," Adrian protests, lighting his badly rolled joint. Half of the paper catches fire, a miniature *Hindenburg* hanging from his lips. Loose white ash blows through the air.

I get to my feet. Rasym is dressed in a tan T-shirt and chinos, dirt slicked across the front. He drops a heavy zippered bag next to Adrian's towel, the weight of it still imprinted on his crooked shoulders.

"I was hoping we could talk," I say to him. "How about a walk down the beach?"

Rasym chews on his lips as he kicks off his shoes. After a second's hesitation, he begins to march in the opposite direction of the hippies. I jog to catch up.

"Adrian told me what you were doing for the refugees." This comment is met with silence. "That's really good of you."

"People are suffering," he replies matter-of-factly. "It's not like Greek islands have an endless supply of Qurans and hijabs lying around." I think of the natty, brown head scarf found next to the hippies' bodies in the roadside accident. All around me, stray details seem to be adding together, but, like a dream set in math class, I can't understand the equation. "It's going to get worse."

"What is?"

His forehead wrinkles. "This crisis. The camps are already at their maximum capacity. Even the winter won't stop them. This is a beginning without an end."

We continue along the shore, Rasym swerving toward the water's edge to sink his feet into the wet pebbles. His ankles, exposed under

his pant cuffs, are reedy and swathed in long, black hairs like fluttering eyelashes.

"Charlie," I say aloud to set the course of the conversation. This
too is met with silence. He's the polar opposite of his boyfriend. Perhaps that's what first drew them to each other, the so easily likeable
challenged by aloof resistance, the hard-to-like floored by the per-
sistence to connect. "Rasym, I'm concerned. *Very* concerned. Charlie's missing."

"I know that," he snaps and walks more quickly. As I pick up my
pace to catch him, he stops altogether, forcing me to spin around. His
lips sandpaper together as he glances out at the water in the direction
of Charlie's port. In profile, the bruise on his forehead bulges.

"Do you know where he is?"

He doesn't speak. I need Adrian to interpret his silences for me.
An interpreter or some muscle to shake a straight answer out of him.
Finally, hands slipping tiredly into pant pockets, he replies. "I was
going to ask you the same question."

"So we're both in the dark. Don't you think we should do something?"

"Like what?"

"Can't you call your father? Charlie's a Konstantinou, for god's
sake. Don't they have a private army of helpers or something?"

"It's not that simple."

"Why isn't it that simple?" I cry.

He watches me, as if determining whether I'm worth more words.

"Charlie's made a point of being on his own here. *Mind your own
business* has pretty much been his ethos when it comes to my side of
the family. And my father has been cut off from any real power for
a long time. There isn't much he could do." I catch bitterness in his
voice, the weak branch of the Konstantinou oak rattling its inferior,
sun-deprived leaves. "He would suggest we contact Stefan or his own
father if he were in any condition to help. No, you know what he'd do?
He'd ask me if Charlie going off like this was out of character, and
what am I supposed to tell him?"

The fact that Rasym isn't sounding alarms over his favorite cousin's disappearance convinces me he knows more than he's letting on. I take a gamble.

"You spoke to Stefan, didn't you? You told him that Charlie's charter company might not be so clean."

He sways, as if the truth is upsetting his balance. He shoots a scowl at me before jamming his feet in the rocks.

"Who told you that?"

"Rasym, I'm not stupid. Not completely anyway."

"If only you hadn't come," he snipes. "Then I'd have your job. Then at least I'd have been able to learn the truth and could have done something to help him. I asked Charlie if I could be his manager that morning before he offered you the job. I had every right to it. I'm family. But he refused. He said you were a better match. You, who have zero experience with sailing, who sat there sick and bleeding on your first trip out on a boat. Why you over me? Honestly, why?"

The answer is clear to me. Charlie figured my desperation would ensure a more agreeable party to his smuggling venture. After all, my résumé involves wrangling with Panamanian gangs. Or maybe the explanation is even simpler: he could afford to put me at risk more than he could a member of his family. Rasym's fingers are more precious than mine.

"Yeah, I was angry," he admits. "And after I left Charlie's office I did talk to Stefan. You don't understand. It's not your family. You have nothing at stake. We are relying on Stefan. We need his support when he takes over. I had to be honest with him! And it's clear tourists aren't lining up at that dock to be taken on vacations." His skinny arms knife through the air as he begins to walk away. When he doesn't hear me following behind him, he turns around. "I don't regret it. If Charlie's doing something illegal, Stefan should put a stop to it. There is already too much wrong in these waters to take advantage of the chaos." Where is the fiction writer who had no qualms about downing a passenger plane? Rasym gathers the neck

of his shirt at his throat. "What I regret is feeling guilty about it afterward. I went back to the port that afternoon and told Charlie that
Stefan was nosing around. I guess I wanted confirmation that his
boat business wasn't all that he claimed it was. He went ballistic, full
panic mode. I didn't tell him I said anything, but it's my last name
on those boats too! What choice did I have? Why do I have to choose
between Charlie and the rest of my family?"

His anger is his only comfort, and he stands shaking in the golden
heat, his eyes searching the infinite recesses of the stony shore. I
have never wanted to hug Rasym before and I don't dare to now.
Instead I offer him my hand, palm-side up. From a distance it must
look like I'm asking him for something. When he turns and kicks
the advancing tide, it feels as if I am.

"I'm the reason he's gone," he murmurs. "I shouldn't have warned
him. I should have just let Stefan confront him. It's my fault he's disappeared."

"It's not your fault. It's Charlie's. I didn't know about his business
either. I still don't." Just as I'm about to drop my hand, he rushes
forward and grabs it. His teeth are gritted like he's intent on bearing
the electric shock of physical contact.

"Do you think he might have left the island?"

Rasym shrugs.

"But he'll come back, right?"

"You know what I think?" he asks. "Remember when that crass
Hungarian Bence came to the table that night and swore that Charlie had called him? I think that was Charlie trying to sell his stake
as fast as he could. Dump the business. Transfer the title. Paint a K
into a B. Get out and move on. He could be anywhere now. Athens.
Cyprus. Polynesia."

"I hope not. For Sonny's sake."

At the mention of her name, he lets go of my hand. "That woman,"
he hisses. "Did she wear her burka for you yet? She finds it very
funny. If she's so wonderful, why didn't he take her with him?"

Rasym stumbles forward, and we head back down the beach. For a moment he leans against me for stability. I'm strangely moved by the warmth of his body and the earth-metal scent of his skin, the whole bony being that is Rasym, where religion does battle with desire.

"Can I ask why you think the hippies planted the bomb last month?"

"Uh, have you read the last chapter of the Bible? Are you familiar with the Apocalypse?" He clops his feet to indicate horses.

"But you don't think they have anything to do with Charlie's disappearance. What I'm saying is, he couldn't have been a victim of foul play?"

"Foul play? Why would the hippies want Charlie dead? Sure they hate each other, but I don't see how offing Charlie would advance their cause. It's good to have enemies. An enemy is more honest than a friend. You know exactly where you stand." I wonder if that explains his open hatred of Sonny. In Rasym's moral universe, tolerating her would give her a false sense of trust. He's erected his own Green Line, and there will be no crossing, no confusion as to who belongs where. He shakes his head. "Hippies murdering him. Now you sound like Charlie."

"How so?"

"He's been paranoid. Maybe it's because of whatever he got up to with his boats. Maybe it's due to that guy he fired. What's his name?" He snaps his finger. "You saw that cat on *Domitian*."

It hasn't occurred to Rasym that Charlie might be dead. He's never even considered the possibility that his disappearance is in any way involuntary.

"So what? He has a cat."

Rasym snorts. "You don't know anything about boats, do you? God, you would have made a terrible manager. The gas lines on yachts are notoriously easy to cut. A silent killer. There's only one reason you leave an animal on a boat. To make sure it's still breathing when you climb on board."

He observes the shock on my face, and it seems to me he takes a certain pleasure in delivering it.

"Charlie won't be gone forever," he assures me. "You're forgetting something he left behind. In the meantime, we're just going to have to wait until Stefan gives up and goes back to Dubai."

He pats me on the back, and we approach Adrian sprawled on his towel. He's staring up at the dome of blue, his eyes glassy.

"You detach yourself from it, and then you submit to it," he warbles, his voice distorted, as if it's issuing from an old apartment intercom. "Can't you feel it? Time pressing its thumb on us. We're deep in its ridges. What does it want?"

He's as high as a human lying on his back can go.

Rasym sits cross-legged at Adrian's feet and flings a shirt over them to prevent their burning. It might be more prudent to cover Adrian's genitals. The beginning of an erection is rearranging the hard geometry of his body. Rasym looks up at me.

"His inheritance," he says. "That's what you're forgetting. You don't stand to gain a few hundred million in a year or two and run off with nothing but the clothes on your back."

LOUISE AND I sit at the patio table. The candles between us burn low on their wicks. Earlier, Louise opened a bottle of vodka and poured out three fingers for both of us. I'm now on my fourth three fingers. It's almost midnight but the heat of the day is beating around us like a bass drummer who lost his marching band. Sheep are moving in the fields, scurrying and swarming with anxious bleating. Why are they so restless tonight? I'm alert to every set of headlights skirting up the valley, fearful of a priest at the wheel. I follow their incline through the darkness, spinning and twisting like children holding flashlights, along the winding road, before they overshoot our turn-off and disappear.

There's a rattle in a bush close to the driveway.

"Did you hear that?"

"Hear what?" Louise asks.

I lift from my chair; it could be my imagination but I see a figure dissolving into the black shrubbery. I wait for a minute, but the darkness remains total and unyielding.

"I thought I just saw someone on the driveway."

"It could be a neighbor. Or I noticed one of those girls from the hippie camp walking through the fields earlier."

"But not a priest or any beefy Greek men?"

Louise shakes her head, and I sit down.

"You're acting funny," she says with concern.

"I'm sorry. I've been a bit stressed."

"Will you tell me what's going on?" It's more a demand than a question; the harshness has returned to her voice.

"Everything's falling apart without Charlie," I answer vaguely. I wrap my hand around the vodka bottle, not to pour more but to collect its coldness. "He owes money to the monastery, and since he's not here, they're bothering me about it. What would you say about a few days on another island? We could leave tomorrow and try Folegandros? I hear they have spectacular cliffs. Okay, that might be too far. But what about—"

Louise's face creases. "We can't. I can't, anyway. I don't have the funds. Europe's wiped me out. And Sonny asked us to lunch tomorrow. I can't abandon her." She holds her drink to her mouth but doesn't take a sip. It's just as well. If Stefan paid the debt, Louise is safe.

"What's going on with Konstantinou Charters?" she asks.

"Your guess is as good as mine."

She reaches her hand across the table and touches my elbow.

"I feel like you're not telling me everything."

Who is the bearded guy in the cowboy shirt? Why didn't you post the pictures of me and Charlie? Did you remove them before the bearded guy could see them and ask you about other men? I don't ask these questions because I don't want to know their answers, because Louise is here for only five more days.

"But you're still working for him?"

"I suppose," I answer with a nod.

"And there's nothing strange going on with its operations?"

I gaze at her over my nearly empty glass.

"Strange how?"

She picks up one of the candles and waves it in front of her like a beacon.

"Earth to Ian, Earth to Ian," she says laughing. "It's high season for boat rentals. Charlie's missing. You're not exactly keeping office hours. I wondered if anything is wrong." She pulls the bottle from my grip and fills my glass. My fifth three fingers. I put my hand over the rim to discourage myself from drinking it. "Talk to me. You can tell me. Maybe I can help."

"You can't help."

"Try me."

The e-mail tonight from my sister:

YOU MOTHERFUCKER, CALL ME! I COULD GO TO THE POLICE AND THEY WOULD ARREST YOU FOR LARCENY. THAT'S A FELONY, IN CASE YOU DON'T HAVE THE BRAINCELLS TO FIGURE IT OUT. SO HERE'S MY FINAL OFFER. IF YOU RETURN THE MONEY AND ANSWER ALL MY QUESTIONS ABOUT DAD, THEN ROSS AND I WILL RECONSIDER FILING CHARGES.

On the bright side, Lex did supply her mailing address.

"Are you looking forward to going home?" I ask.

Louise rests her forehead in her hands.

"You're changing the subject."

"I wish we had run into each other again a year ago. Six months ago. Hell, next year. Just not now. I'm at my lowest." I remove my hand from the rim and take a drink.

To have always had money: the burn for things that can't be named; a crowded room with no lights on; the dependability of automatic doors, the *whooshing* sound when they open and the cold air on shivering skin.

To have never had money: the work and the work and the work and barely a time for prayer; a jacket not made for seasons; grass growing around a shrinking house.

To have once had money and lost it: a hole in the shoe and to never get accustomed to it, to feel the hole with each advancing step until the hole is bigger than your body.

"Please, Ian. Just tell me what's going on!" Louise reaches over again, but I move my elbow away.

There's no reason to burden her with the truth. Let her have her five days of vacation. Let me not be a lesson in her traveling story. Let her think of me later, somewhere in D.C. or Lexington, as a man not broken, as someone clean.

"Even if it's something bad, I'd like to hear it. You can tell me the worst."

"Will you visit your brother before classes start?" I ask. "What did you say he looks like?"

Louise gets up from the table and perches on the wall. Then she's up again, walking around the table, and she puts her arms around my shoulders.

"I'm really happy I'm here with you," she whispers. "Whatever happens. For as long as it lasts. You know that, right?"

"Do me a favor," I say, pushing the drink away. I look up at her, gravity forming a kiss on her lips, this person embedded with the mystery of wanting to be with me for reasons I can't explain. Dig it up later, excavate it from the dirt, hold the bones up to the sun and try to figure out what kind of creature it was. It had some life, it moved, it breathed. It mattered for as long as it lasted.

She cocks her head to the side. "What?"

"Sleep in my room tonight. Don't go back to your bed."

We have reached the stage where we are asking each other for easy, impossible things.

CHAPTER 14

Her name is Vic and she has a nagging cough. This much I know of their leader.

I walk north from the beach at Grikos on the first day of dark skies. Low storm clouds streak like the dirty fur of huskies. The lack of sun turns the town's whitewashed walls a drab cream, exposing plaster gouges and chalky patch jobs. Fresh spray paint mars a few of them: "Smash Troika," "Tote Me Tanks, Tope Me Banks," "Eat the Rich." Tattered taverna awnings droop from their frames. Paradise is a trick of light.

I veer along the rocky shoreline. The harbor is mostly clear of yachts, and only a few dilapidated fishing boats trawl the deeper channels. As the cliffs rise and the beach narrows, I hear and smell the camp, a microclimate of sweetened smoke and gusts of blasting music, a hip-hop song dissolving into the amphetamine heartbeat of trance. Their dogs must hear and smell me first too, because three mutts, two with severe underbites, scamper toward me and sniff at my shoes. The tiniest one lifts its brawny leg, and I have to sidestep into the water to prevent it from marking me. But I'm accepted into their pack; they scuttle around me like fawning ambassadors as I approach the cluster of tents.

Gold. Red. Hunter green. Each tent is emblazoned with a cross on its side. A bonfire flares midbeach; a man in a felt hat is dancing around the flames, touching the heads of those who are feeding the fire with twigs, oregano leaves, and squeezes of lighter fluid. Two young women with long matted hair, not so unlike their dead friend Dalia, clip T-shirts to a line tied between olive trees; one of the shirts flapping in the wind is the rainbow I ♥ ATHENS shirt that I saw on their latest arrival. A short, gaunt kid, each bone cripplingly visible in his back, his hair a knot of fuchsia dreads, raps in Portuguese as he spins a baton stick in the air. He's so focused on his rhythm, he nearly steps into the bonfire, and the girls feeding it yell at him with croupy fits of laughter.

"Gibby, you have chores," one of the T-shirt clippers screams. She wears a cheap plastic tiara.

"No, not on Wed nees dee," he answers, fracturing the word until it loses its reference to a weekday. His lip is so distended a word tattooed across its pink underside hangs exposed. *Count? Cunt? Comet?*

A group of men, nude and hairy, dive-bombs into the water, their legs and asses an accumulation of bruises and welts. Empty sardine tins, cigarette packs, bent spoons, and dented cans lie scattered close to the advancing tide. A topless girl in cherry velour track pants, one nipple punctured with a brass rod, scrubs the gristle off a grill; her tits jostle from the effort, and when she stands erect to wipe her forehead, I see she's several months pregnant. Two Spanish-speaking guys, strangely collegiate in their close-cropped hair and soiled button-downs, wrestle violently along the rocks; their giggling fails to disguise the intensity of their fight. A forearm pins the smaller one by the throat. Tattooed bluebirds on the arm fatten and vein.

It's not accurate to call them hippies. They're more like cultural scavengers, picking promiscuously at the scrap heap of history and novelty shops and romantic teenage tokens rotted for years in suburban closets before taken up again as badges of burned innocence. Their armor is in their expressions, the sharp eyes and crooked mouths of a starved vitality, a pent-up momentum, hysteria on a tightened leash. And yet they are beautiful, most of them, because they are young, a state they haven't figured out how to demolish, and their attempts to do so—tattoos, greasepaint, ear plugs the size of silver dollars, cocaine lines of white razor blade scars on their arms— only prove how young they are. I imagine when it's sunny and hot, a light madness greases the bare bodies of the camp and turns the sea hallucinogenic, and God does feel very close to a zombie super returning to pick the recyclables from the trash. Amid the soundtrack of barking dogs, manic laughter, and unctuous speed-music, I'm struck most but what is lacking: not a single cell phone in sight. They are humans stripped of the gleaming remora of upload and transmit.

I track my eyes farther down the beach, where a circle forms around the morose Dalmatian. Girls hum as they braid grass wreaths around its neck. The muscular guy with the handlebar mustache squats on an upturned bucket. He's eating sardines out of a peeled-back tin. Two silver loops pierce his lower lip, and a knife is strapped to his army shorts. But it's the person next to him who captures my attention. Helios sits with a beach towel shrouding half of his head, like a child's idea of a veil. His face looks both happier and more lost than it did the last time I saw him; an expired joint is lodged between his fingers. He grope-rubs the Dalmatian distractedly, his eyes tuned to the humming contest of the girls, one of whom is dancing topless, arms swaying like branches, waving her ANTI-BETHLEHEM shirt like a banner.

A Latin boy with long, surfer-permed hair and orange fingernails, wearing a nylon sports bra, passes by, speaking into a walkie-talkie. "You arrive at three-ten," he barks into the device. He struts up the beach and enters a large caravan tent constructed out of blue tarpaulin and green-brown camo netting. Its front metal pole quivers as a white flag snaps at the tip; on the flag two gold horns crisscross. Next to the tent is a plastic outdoor bin, where a girl is sorting through heaps of backpacks.

"Does anyone know where Regina's gear is?" she yells in a Nordic timbre.

The guy with the handlebar mustache glances at her. But before he replies, his eyes drift over to me.

"Hey," he shouts. "Who the fuck are you? What are you doing?"

My eyes go immediately to Helios, who is also staring at me, almost as if he's frightened to find me here where even his father probably wouldn't dare to look for him. Helios doesn't say a word as the guy rushes toward me, his soles scattering the rocks with each thrust.

A flap in the caravan tent opens, and Vic steps outside, her hand shielding her eyes from the nonexistent sun. She has on a different floral ensemble, pale cornflower shorts and a shirt patterned with daisies. She immediately lifts her arm in a gesture that stops the guy from hurtling forward. Vic tilts her head and walks calmly toward me.

"It's fine, Noah. All are welcome." Noah doesn't like that I'm fine. He clasps his hips to accentuate the broadness of his chest, and his teeth nibble at his piercings.

"We have too many," he grumbles. "It's not safe."

She examines me curiously, her soft blue eyes filled with compassion, not as if she's the one stepping closer but as if I'm leaning out of a train window and she's watching me depart, a friend she's going to miss. She reaches her chubby arms out and her hands cup an invisible bowl.

"Welcome," she says. "Welcome to Camp Revelation. Are you tired yet?"

I stand still. "Tired of what?"

"Tired of searching," she says with a rehearsed smile. "Tired of looking for fulfillment in all the noise and glitter. Tired of fighting the battle you know you've already lost. Because that's what we offer. A way out." Her voice modulates into the hushed, lulling tone of a librarian reading a picture book to a child. "We could make you better. We could take all of that hurt inside of you and throw it in the sea. There's no fear here. All you have to do is want it. Want for the hurt and worry to stop." It's like she's staring inside of me; I do want that. But suddenly her chest convulses and a volcanic cough erupts. The cough takes full possession, leaving her gasping between its thrashes, like one of those fake pro wrestlers stunned by an amateur blow of actual pain.

Noah races to a cooler and retrieves a bottle of water. She sips tentatively, keeping her eyes shut, evaluating her body for further activity. She gulps down the rest of the water.

"Excuse me," she says, when at last she opens her eyes. "My name is Vic. I'm glad you've come."

"I know your name."

The noisy, glittery world is not so far away that she doesn't appreciate a reputation. She smiles.

"And I know you," she replies. "I saw you the morning our sister and brother had their bike accident." She taps out a sign of the cross on her daisy shirt. "We miss them. I found it very moving the way you sprinted toward their bodies in the field. It stayed with me, that image of you running with all of your heart toward their deaths."

"I thought it might be someone I knew," I retort. I can feel my defensiveness taking control. I don't want Vic returning to her conversion mode. I don't want her seeing inside of me.

"Ahh." Her smile tightens. "Well, we're not much for tourists at our camp. This is a place for the lost and the found."

"What about for the missing?" I hope this question might hint at Charlie, but Vic doesn't take the bait.

"You've never been missing. Not for a single day. She's always been with you. You just need to reach out your hand."

"Is that girl here with you? I think her name is Carrie Dorr, the one who found the bodies."

Vic's smile vanishes. She nods toward her tent. "Why don't we talk inside?"

I follow her up the beach. Noah studies me carefully. I search behind him for Helios, who is now sitting with his back to me, the towel fully obscuring his face. Vic lifts the flap, and I duck inside. Yellow scrolls of carpet cover the floor. Cheap sequined pillows and rolled sleeping bags in the center create an improvised lounging area; one of the pillows is needlepointed with the numbers 5:47:31, which I assume is a biblical verse. The interior smells stale and damp, like summer locked in an unused cabin. On one side of the tent, wooden shelves house a stockpile of canned goods and stacks of tourist T-shirts still wrapped in their factory cellophane. On the bottom shelf is a row of plastic bins, one of which appears to hold a cache of cell phones and laptops; in another, piles of passports. One open bin teems with Greek guidebooks and cracked leather Bibles. On the other side of the tent, a laminated map of the Greek islands is taped to a piece of particleboard. Pushpins of various colors cover the map in an amoebic constellation. A small chalkboard, not dissimilar to one in Skala, lists the weekly ferry schedule to and from Patmos along with port connections to adjoining island chains. But it's a black metal container secured with a padlock that takes up most of the space. A lace tablecloth and a pile of candlesticks cover it. But I can't help wondering if it's filled with fishermen's dynamite and detonators, in case the Apocalypse needs a little encouragement to get under way.

The boy in the sports bra is standing at the map, shifting a pin.

"Thank you, Leif," Vic says in dismissal. He nods obsequiously, sweeps his hair back in a ponytail, which accentuates his beautiful eyebrows, and departs.

"Have a seat." She folds her stocky legs under her and adjusts the pillows around her hips and calves. There is something of a den mother in Vic, because of her age or because of her unassuming, vaguely midwestern features, or because she's the only one at the camp wearing a watch. She has three strapped to her right wrist. She notices me staring at them.

"Two tell Greek time," she explains. "But even I am not entirely free of the past. It's my last indulgence. Rapid City, Mountain Standard, paused eternally at 5:47:31, the very second I found the Lord."

"How long ago was that?"

"Six years and so many months. I don't remember how many, nor do I care to. It's no longer important." I recall Charlie telling me that Patmos gets its share of insanity cases lured by the dream to live on the island of Revelation, as it did for the Chicago pedophile. Although his reasons are sharply different from Vic's. "I've been on these islands ever since, devoting my life to Her, preparing for Her coming, for the battle and the feast."

"You mean the end of the world."

She smiles. "If you think only in losses, the end of this world, yes. But it's just the beginning of a better one. Is this old world really so good? Read a paper. I dare you to read two of them without feeling sick. It's far too late to save it. I'm not saying anything your scientists haven't already determined. Two strokes to midnight. The second hand is circling fast. Are you ready?" She chews at her cheek. "What's your name?"

"Ian."

"Ian." She studies me as if watching a sparrow at her window, fascinated by the survival skills of the bland and ordinary. "I can feel it in you. Has anyone told you that? Has anyone ever bothered to really look inside of you before? You have so much pain and confusion and doubt scored deep, and I sense you are struggling to find a lasting place. I'm sorry. There won't be one. Not where you're looking." She leans over and pats my knee. "I don't ask anyone to believe. Every member of the camp chooses freely to be here, chooses to wish for something greater than what they've been programmed to accept. How would you feel if you let go of all that hurt? Would you still be Ian? Do you need him?"

"What's the map for?" I ask, redirecting her away from Ian.

She glances behind her, as if admiring the number of pins.

"The word is getting out. Young people are coming, more and more. We help them find their way. We plan their routes and lead them home. Every single one of those young people outside have been tortured and abused, warped by their parents, bankrupted by their education, let down by their governments and communities, ridiculed for who they are. Most of our contingent started out as backpackers, traveling in search of a little meaning, and those who don't find us end up back at home knowing less than they did when they began. Pictures on a phone. That's not meaning, Ian, is it? A few sunsets? Trivial public intimacies? We are the antidote, the backpackers who didn't return, the empty chairs at the table, the last army." Vic exhales what sounds like petrified lung tissue, and her coughing resumes. She lunges for a tissue behind the needlepoint pillow and crushes it against her mouth.

"Are you okay?"

"Fine," she insists. I wonder if the 5:47:31 on the pillow also marks the exact time of her diagnosis. Nothing makes for a quicker believer than a terminal disease. Befriend the beast and ride it into the grave. Take the world with you. Because we all know what we are told not to believe: the world does end, some essential golden part of it, when you die.

"Why all the tourist T-shirts?" I ask.

"Oh, those." She sighs. "Bulk surplus. It's a cheap way to clothe the kids. We're a free community, but we still need supplies. We don't mind dressing like the enemy. It's easier to circulate that way, to make inroads, to deliver God's verdict, righteous millennialists disguised as self-righteous millennials." She laughs. "I thought that up myself. Some of the members donate what savings they have, although, of course, that isn't a requirement. We take in all sorts. Yesterday, we had a girl, a Swede, who joined us. She left her family's yacht to embrace her freedom with our group. I don't take that sacrifice lightly. She insisted on bringing her Dalmatian. Our dogs don't like him. I had to keep them from attacking him in the night." She clears her throat. "We live humbly on these rocks. And the island allows us to be close to the cave as long as we stay on public ground. We weren't always on Patmos. This is our first full summer here. Last year we tried Leros, but the locals weren't sympathetic. The monks here understand the emergency of the hour. The Omega is where we are."

She stares at me, one half of her mouth retaining its smile, the other half deflated. "I don't think you're ready, Ian. I don't feel I'm reaching you at all. You aren't humble enough. You prefer to be scared. And that's okay. We don't recruit the timid."

"Do you know Charlie Konstantinou? He isn't very humble, is he?"

She doesn't feign bewilderment at the mention of his name. Vic must already be apprised of the fact that I'm his friend, and perhaps that's why she's taken a special interest in me: a pet project to poach from the enemy side.

"Not humble a bit by the look of him. Gluttonous, selfish, insatiable. Pretty girlfriend. He's a type of person, which is the saddest person, don't you think? He's a childhood wrapped in an adult's body. He's a kind."

"You don't like him."

She laughs sweetly. "Do I like him? He embodies every malady that's corrupted and destroyed the planet. All that shimmering excess, the *me, me, me* that feeds the engine and continues to steamroll. Hasn't his family done their part in the atrocities of the Middle East? They build a war and they float away on yachts. But make no mistake, you can't be a prince twice. You must choose your dominion. And on the day of battle, the birds will feed on your friend's body. They will pick him clean outside the gates. That's God's prophecy, not mine. It was put down on paper on this very island." It would be difficult for even the most fanatical to make avian torture sound upbeat, but Vic achieves a buoyant sanguinity, as if she's scored front-row tickets to the final annihilation show. "I prefer to picture him like a shark in a sea soon lacking any prey. There will be nothing left for him to devour. Think of an ocean with just one shark in it, alone."

"So you wouldn't be too upset if something happened to him?"

"To Charlie?" Vic clasps her legs. "You misunderstand. I don't wish Charlie harm. In fact, he's a secret collaborator. So secret he isn't even aware of the good he's doing our cause."

"How is he your collaborator?"

"We need more like him. His greed, his arrogance, his apathy, his religion of money. What do you think are the signs of the coming end? He's speeding the second hand along. I told you, there's no going backward. The canker is already on the stem. This is how God wins, not by fighting the Devil but by letting him do his work. Charlie's evil, I won't deny that. But he's a necessary one. I hope no one touches a hair on his head. Please, make more of them who roll in their fortunes while so many starve. Only God knows the hour, but we can certainly oil the clock."

Vic smiles at me, fully aware of how she's coming across, like a true believer, like Marx off his meds.

"I was once like you," she says solemnly. "You think gravity doesn't apply and the market just keeps going up and the poor will eventually find some way to get rich. Well, that won't happen. We've tried the century of the merciful Jesus. It didn't take. Now it's time for the vindicator, the furious judge, the thief. How can you watch the horrors on this planet and still hope humanity will right itself? That's belief to the point of delusion. We're realists by comparison. God has given us the answer. You don't understand a book unless you read its last chapter. Revelation. It's ugly, but it's also sweet."

Noah sticks his head through the flap—or has been sticking his head there for some time.

"Everything all right?" he asks.

"Perfect." Vic beams. "I think I'm being interviewed. It's too bad he hasn't brought a photographer." She jokingly pats her hair. "We're almost finished. Get the wine and juice ready for prayer. Check the expiration dates on the cartons." She turns to me. "You won't be staying for that."

I get to the point when Noah departs.

"That bomb that went off last month in Skala. Your congregation wouldn't have happened to have set it to hurry the destruction along?"

Vic coughs into her ball of tissue, and a few blood spots bloom on the white. She tries to conceal them by tightening the tissue in her hand.

"Is that what the tourists are saying?" she replies nonchalantly. "We wouldn't need to. There's so much destruction already. Didn't they conclude it was some anti-Eurozone faction? Or maybe it was Al-Qaeda or ISIS or the Jabhat al-Nusra or any of the black-flag wavers running around the Levant." She ticks off terrorist groups as if listing other secret accomplices. "Or maybe it was a summer vacationer who spent a week being massaged and fucked by strangers and having her room cleaned by maids and her mouth stuffed with grape leaves and her snorkel gear adjusted by staff and she just couldn't take it anymore. The emptiness in the postcard was too severe. The pleasure only increased her pain, so she blew herself up. Ian, we believe in the end, but we're a mostly peaceful people. We don't have to lift a finger to bring it about. The world is doing it for us. Whether they know it or not, everyone on Earth is doing what they can. We're only a few more collapses away now. Haven't you seen the refugees washing ashore? Poor souls. There's a passage in chapter—"

"If you're really a Christian, shouldn't you do something to help them? Why don't you stop praying for the Apocalypse and lift a finger for good? Wouldn't your god like that too? Isn't there room for mercy?"

Vic hangs her head in disappointment. Outside, a bell is clanging and the sound of feet and laughter gathering close to the entrance of the tent.

"Do you know what sin is?" she asks in a whisper. "The essence of sin is doing what's right in your own eyes. Sin is conforming God to your own moral code. It doesn't work that way if you really believe. All suffering upsets me. But once you embrace the horror, you're no longer scared of it."

We have reached the moment where lines grow fuzzy, where the lunatic has the facts of the world on her side and my attempt at rational humanity is equivalent to hugging trees during a forest fire. Vic begins to climb from the floor, but she pauses on one knee.

"Why did you ask about Carrie?"

"She went to the police after Dalia and Mikael were found. She told them Charlie might have had something to do with their deaths. I wanted to talk to her about that."

Vic swats her hands dismissively and rises to her feet. "That girl is confused. She came to me confused two weeks ago. I shouldn't have let her in. All she did from day one was doubt me. I love misfits. I love the kids who have been hurt so much all they need is love around them. That's what we offer, unconditional acceptance. But Carrie wasn't interested in that. She's a tourist, and unfortunately a romantic when she set her eyes on Mikael. He was one of my most dependable members. I cared for him dearly. Dalia too. They had both been with us since June."

"I thought I saw Dalia the night before she died exiting a ferry. Didn't she just arrive?"

Vic lifts the tent flap. She staunches a rumble in her chest.

"You're mistaken," she says, staring out at the young men and women assembling around the campfire. "And so was Carrie. If Charlie had anything to do with their deaths, I would have been delighted to point that inspector his way. But the truth is, Mikael was always careless on a motorbike. He enjoyed taking turns too fast." She sighs with motherly obligation. "I have to slow some of these kids down. Their lives are precious, but they're too young to realize it."

"Can I talk to Carrie?" I ask.

She gawks at me as if I've invited her to a rally to protest Arctic drilling.

"She's gone," Vic says, looping her fingers around her necklace. The hemp digs into the fat of her neck. "She took her phone and passport and left. I tell you, the girl was completely off her rocker. All you would have gotten from her is nonsense. But she went back to America. I'm sure she's home in New Jersey by now taking selfies of her tears."

Noah glides up to the tent entrance. He taps his dirty fingers along his knife handle.

"Leif needs to pick up two who are arriving from Kos in an hour."

Vic studies her watches, comparing one face with the other.

"He still has time for prayer. In honor of our guest's visit today, we'll sing chapter seventeen." As she turns to me, the compassion is absent from her eyes, but her smile remains. "Okay, Ian. I hope you'll consider what we discussed." She waves me over and hugs my shoulder while pointing to her flock around the fire. They are passing around a crate of instruments and filling plastic cups with green juice from cartons and red wine from a fiasco bottle. I can't find Helios among them.

"I ask, before you judge us, look at the joy, the camaraderie, the lack of pain. There is no night here. I might not make it to see the end, but some of them will." They are dancing, they are laughing and kissing, they are beating tambourines. They are high on the waves of an atomic blast and they look unprepared for winter. A cough is worming up Vic's throat, but she stalls it, a red blush ballooning on her face. "John prophesied the Apocalypse from Patmos, but he didn't set the final battle here. That takes place in Armageddon, a town, to no one's surprise, in Israel. How's that for the accuracy of prediction?"

Convenient of him. As convenient and distant as a drone strike.

As if she's read my mind, Vic releases my shoulder.

"We aren't trying to win your thoughts," she says. "What we want are your feelings."

WHEN MY MOTHER and I moved postdivorce into the garden apartment on Riverside Drive, Helen took to decorating with the gusto of a person forced against her will into the mania of a midlife crisis. The new apartment offered, among other prospects, the opportunity for ornamental retaliation against Edward Bledsoe's bland Michigan tastes.

Charlie called our place the Jungle House. Gaudily embroidered Mexican curtains hung across the windows; the sofa was a tropical motif of palm fronds and soaring parrots, where even food spills took on a second life as Amazonian flora; bamboo was the go-to material for tables and cabinetry. And for many Saturdays of that first year as our decidedly *not-abandoned-but-released!* mother-son unit, we'd plunder the last shrinking Chelsea flea markets set up in purgatorial parking lots (soon to be the ground floors of glass condo towers) for gilded birdcages, carved picture frames, beaded pillow shams that hinted of a South American origin, and artisan glass the colors of cough drops. Exotic plants came and went, delivered blooming, dying as melodramatically as stage actresses, one leaf at a time. My mother installed two yellow canaries, named Lovely and Lovelier, in a hanging brass cage by the window that sang their hearts out in the morning.

The one space that resisted the tropics was my bedroom. To my mother's irritation, I left the walls white and blank. I preferred hardwood to the handwoven rugs that began to pile up in the living room like daises (our Peruvian cleaning lady had played intermediary to a textile importer in Queens). I changed my laptop's screen saver on a weekly basis, but even as I aged into the double digits I didn't so much as tack a postcard above my desk. It was a room where shadows collected, mine mixing with those from a century of previous occupants.

Eventually, in her ongoing fit of *horror vacui*, Helen took my indifference to décor as a silent revolt, a refusal to be devoured into our not-so-new life.

"Don't you want anything up?" she'd ask pleadingly.

"I like it the way it is."

"How about we buy a poster of the galaxy. A huge one. It could go—"

"No thanks."

"Or we can dash over to the Met and get a nice framed poster of—"

"Not interested."

She'd release a troubled breath.

"Do you need to talk to someone?"

"We are talking."

"A professional. A psychologist. You're clearly depressed."

"I'm not, Mom. I swear."

"It's been years now, and you're still having difficulty adjusting. You're refusing to commit. You don't see this as your home." The tears would come then, worse for being so tentative. "Just one poster. A hockey player. You liked hockey last winter. A woman, is that what you're holding out for? Go ahead. Bikini it up! A sports car, maybe? A band? That singer you and Charlie love whose lyrics I didn't approve of? A fashion model? Is that what this is about? I'm okay with it. I like fashion! A man in a swimsuit! That's absolutely fine!" She wanted me to have full freedom over my room, and it was my freedom to do nothing that proved to her the extent of my unhappiness.

"It's just that the rest of the apartment has so much stuff," I'd say. "And New York is right outside the front door. It's nice to have a quiet place."

"Please hang something."

"I have my computer. I'm not even in my room that much."

"Anything. Please. We'll paint the walls!"

"I like them the way they are."

"Ian, I don't want you existing like this."

She started dating. It took a while, and I was far too young to realize what a bear market New York is for smart, older women who have already suffered the disappointment of a marriage. She'd pin a flower to her chest and fold her coat over her arm so as not to squash the petals. She'd return a few hours later, the flower still pristine but her face wilted underneath her makeup.

I encouraged her volunteering. First it was dogs; she'd walk hapless mutts with orange ADOPT-ME vests up and down Riverside Park and spend her free time cleaning cages at the no-kill shelter in Morningside Heights. Our refrigerator door became a photographic record of successful adoptions. Helen gained weight, which filled the hollows of her face and suited her, and she laughed more, or rather her laughing stopped feeling like a symptom of nervousness and resentment. Her expensive clothes no longer fit and she began buying more comfortable smocks and silk pajama pants that were probably just as expensive but didn't read as trying so hard. Dogs gave way to a solid year of volunteer horticultural services at the Riverside Park Conservancy—a passion that killed her interest in houseplants—and I'd quiz her delicately about some of the male retirees I'd find her with on hands and knees in the dirt, dumping out jars of worms to enhance the soil.

"Oh, it's not like that," she'd say, blushing. "Just friends. But if it ever were, would you, I mean, might it—"

"Of course it would be okay!" I'd exclaim.

Those men never materialized at our door. By the time I entered high school, the home décor began to shift, as if slowly ravaged by global warming. Indian tapestries and a gurgling miniature water fountain found their way among the bamboo—items sold at the yoga studio where Helen took classes on meditation and Ayurvedic massage. Lovely and Lovelier, perhaps realizing the fading interest in their roots, developed umpteen minor illnesses, which required constant veterinary appointments. The vet diagnosed them as "stressed."

"Why do we have all of these dumb little baubles?" Helen would ask me, grabbing a glass jaguar.

"It was yours from an earlier phase," I'd answer.

"I really don't remember buying this. Would you want these in your room?" My room had remained adamantly untouched.

"Just throw them away."

"We'll donate them. I'll bring them to the Center."

The Center was a senior-care home, where, for nearly two years, my mother spent afternoons washing the elderly and keeping them company while they watched TV. At Christmas our hearth was lined in cards from her favorite patients with notes of thanks that she'd actually written for them to herself.

"Sometimes I wish—" And I could hear the needle in her brain sweep onto the groove of a sad, relentless song. I knew by then not to bring up dating, so I'd sit on the sofa and hug her.

"You're going to be fine," I'd promise her. "Keep looking ahead."

She exchanged the old for the young in my last years of high school. First, infants with incurable diseases and with so many wires strapped to them they looked like jumped car batteries in their hospital incubators. Then fund-raisers for runaways and at-risk youth at the Broadway New Heart Shelter. Soon it was vulnerable children from all over the world tacked to our refrigerator, and while her spirituality was drifting toward new age transcendentalism, she exploited her ties to Catholicism to join a Christian missionary program that ventured to orphanages in New World countries.

"There's a trip coming up," she mentioned to me. "To China."

"Are you going?"

"Well, you see, I'd have to leave the afternoon of your graduation."

"You should go."

"I wouldn't miss the actual ceremony, but I'd have to leave right after." She frowned. "I can't do that."

"Mom, go. I can celebrate with Charlie. He rented out the Rainbow Room. I was planning on doing that anyway."

"It's your special day. I can't *not* be there for you."

"Mom, please go. You need this." I was rebelling like a lunatic outside of the house (mostly under Charlie's influence), but my gift to Helen was the illusion of a calm-and-steady son. Appearing morally upright for a parent is life's longest con. But I wanted her happy. I wanted her to think I was already taken care of.

"Are you sure?" she asked. "Really sure? It could be good for me."

"It *will* be good for you. Try it."

"I don't know. Maybe. I just feel so lost."

We both moved out at the end of the summer. I went to college in the Berkshires, and Helen sold the Riverside apartment and bought the static-electric midtown studio, which she decorated in costly Zen minimalism (the tropics had finally been bulldozed off the Bledsoe map). There was no second bedroom—no place for me to leave bare—but she did purchase a sofa bed. Lovely died by Thanksgiving, but Lovelier persisted. After three subsequent missionary trips with the Christians, my mother fell out with the program's leaders when she decided they were milking her for funds. "They think I'm rich," she told me squarely. And she was rich, sort of, thanks to her divorce settlement, but Helen continued in her delusion that she lived just above the white-Manhattan-divorcée poverty line. She began to travel, not for humanitarian purposes, but simply to see the world on her own. Indonesia. Tibet. Morocco. She'd plan her trips to coincide with my breaks from college so someone could be there to feed Lovelier.

It was in India that she found herself. Mumbai. Udaipur. Jaipur. Jaisalmer. Agra. She came back thinner from a stomach virus, but her eyes had turned a brighter hazel, like two distant planets that had finally locked into orbit. "The things I saw!" she kept repeating in an ecstatic form of post-traumatic shock. "I saw things I'd never thought I'd see! The colors alone! The peach silk of a Sikh's turban moving against the orange sky!" That image, in particular, seemed to haunt her—far more than even the dead body she saw floating in the Yamuna River. Her phone calls to my dorm room followed the methodology of Freudian analysis, the playing and replaying of her Indian adventure as if one day, with enough clarity, she'd be able to process it and move on.

She did not move on. She called me in the spring of my last semester, after a late-season blizzard dumped a foot of snow on New York.

"I miss India," she said.

"I know you do. But the great thing about it is it's not going anywhere."

"Neither is Manhattan. Not for me. I don't think I like it here. I tell you, it's this snow. I loved it in Michigan, but not in this city. Not anymore." She paused for a very long time. "If it weren't for you, I'd up and move to Delhi. I'd leave next month if I could sell the studio."

"Why would I stop you?"

"Honey, if I left, you'd have no one in New York."

"I'd have Dad."

"I repeat, you'd have no one in New York."

I knew what she was asking from me. My permission.

"Mom, if that's where you want to live, you should go. Don't worry about me. I'll be fine. I'm an adult if you haven't noticed. I'd rather you happy in India than miserable while I slept on your couch."

"But what about Lovelier?" she cried, as if I were the one being impulsive. "I can't take him with me."

"You're really going to stay for a bird?"

"He's been with us for twelve years! That's very old for a canary. He's a member of our family."

"Snap his neck."

"Murderer." She laughed. "No. I'm only daydreaming. It's not feasible."

"Listen to me. If you really want this, I order you to go. It's your life, Mom. Your *life*."

"And I'm telling you, it's simply not feasible. End of conversation!"

Helen sold the studio for a sizeable profit, donated her furniture, made her good-bye rounds at the Center to the few residents still alive and coherent enough to remember her, reallocated her stock portfolio for minimal risk, and began her course of malaria pills. I purposely didn't ask about the fate of Lovelier. On her ride to the airport she phoned, her voice stiff and fragmented, shuffling around in the highest register.

"I'm scared, Ian. This was a mistake."

"No it isn't. It's exciting."

"I don't know why I let you talk me into this. I don't know anybody in Delhi. All I have is a one-month rental. I could be murdered my first night, and no one would find me for weeks."

"No one's going to murder you. You can do this."

"I just don't think I can. I just don't . . . oh, look, the skyline. There it goes. My god. Driver, slow down. All the yellow and gray."

"Call me when you land."

"Okay," she said in a whisper, trying to muffle her sobs. "I'll call you. And when you're back in New York, keep your eyes out. Maybe you'll see him."

"Who? Lovelier? Mom, you didn't."

"I'm not saying what I did. But keep your eyes on the trees. Oh, Ian, I feel like I'm going to throw up."

"I love you so much."

I had done all I could for her. I waved good-bye from a mountain in Massachusetts as she blasted off on a Delta 747 toward the unknown. Helen was finally on her way.

AUGUST CROWDS HAVE overtaken Chora. A cruise ship must have docked in Skala this morning. Lots of golf hats and ergonomic walking shoes. Tour guides barely visible in the throngs hold up metal antenna wire with bright orange pennants at the tips. The ticket line leaks from the monastery and down its stone steps, a drool of single-file sightseers that ends under the UNESCO WORLD HERITAGE plaque. I have to fight my way through the mêlée of broken conversations—*I hear the Greek islands are so bankrupt they can't even get shipments of bottled water. That's why I brought mine from the boat. What, they don't allow photography inside? Cheap way to get you to buy a postcard. No monks in the chapel? What's the blasted point of a monastery if you don't get to see no monks? Colin, your wallet is showing in your back pocket. Cheryl, this is where . . . Cheryl, this is where they wrote the Bo . . . Cheryl?*

In the narrows of the Choran maze, a three-minute walk from the monastery, the sounds of the multitudes fade into the clatter and hum of occupied houses. Large jugs of tea sit on a roof ledge, waiting for the sun to appear. I'm two hours early for Sonny's lunch, but it was either drift around Chora or search out Stefan or Inspector Martis, and I chose the easier option. On a hilltop peak in the distance, three stone windmills beat, and I can taste the bitter pollen in the air, more in my throat than on my tongue. I make a few stabs toward Charlie's house, climbing the skull of a cobblestone hill and winding along a passage that ends in a tiny courtyard. A flock of nuns draped in heavy black wool hurries through a carved wooden doorway. One of the nuns pulls a rope that activates a bell above the entrance. She continues ringing it until each nun has stepped over the threshold. They disappear like coats collected in a cabinet.

"Ian," a child's voice shouts behind me. I turn to find Duck skipping down the passage in her white linen caftan. Therese and Vesna follow, their arms loaded with netted bags of groceries. "Are you going to see the three eyes?"

"Three eyes?" I ask.

"In the convent," Duck says, pointing to the door that has just slammed shut. "There's a painting in there that Mommy loves. Mary has three eyes. It's a miracle. The third eye just appeared one day."

Therese smiles at me. "They do not let men inside today." She shifts her arms and two oranges fall from the netting, which Vesna quickly gathers. When she lifts up, I make a point to catch her eye.

"Hi, Vesna, how was—" But I remember the secret of her Athens protest rally and cut the question off. Her lips stiffen but eventually relax when it's clear I am not going to rat her out. Her black and blue hair is tied in a braid, and her gray shirt glitters with plastic rhinestones. "I saw your brother an hour ago."

Now the lips of both Stamatis women stiffen, and they exchange glances.

"Where did you see Helios?" Vesna asks. "My father has been looking for him."

"Down at the beach by Grikos. He was at—" I stop myself again. I'm guessing Helios doesn't want to be found.

"He hasn't shown up for work the past few days," Vesna says. Her mother nudges her to stop her from airing family problems. Vesna doesn't take the nudge lightly, turning to Therese and unleashing a thunderstorm of Greek.

"Today Miles started following me," Duck brags. The declaration sounds mildly alarming until Duck inches her pink cell phone from her caftan pocket and pulls up her Instagram account. "He liked my picture of the three eyes."

"Duck, you are not to take photos of the icons," Therese scolds.

"Why not? We paid. Mommy always gives the nuns money. She says it's not fair that tourists only give to the monks."

Therese manages to disguise her frustration with a put-upon smile. Her bony arms adjust the groceries. When I reach for the bag of oranges, she deflects my attempts to help.

"I hope you are hungry. We make big lunch," she announces. "My stew. Sonny tells me Stefan is on island. So I make extra in case he comes."

"Did Sonny invite him?"

Therese shrugs. "Just in case. I know my Stefan will want to see us. I always keep his room ready so he can come whenever he wants. And Charlie, he love my stew also. Maybe he come home too, all the boys."

Vesna stares at me, her tongue moving over her teeth as if hungry to ask me a question about Charlie or her brother. Or maybe she wants another loan. I have a question for her too, about the nature of the mess she cleaned up on *Domitian*. Before either of us can speak, Duck bundles her hands over her stomach and moans.

"My tummy hurts," she whines.

"We still have more food to buy," Therese says softly.

"Can't I go back with Ian?" She rocks in half-circles.

"I'll take her. And I can carry some of your groceries." I grab a few of Therese's bags before she has time to resist. "Do I need your key?"

"We left it unlocked this morning," Vesna says. "For Stefan. If he does show up."

Duck is already galloping down the passage, and I lift the bags to signal good-bye. I chase after my child guide. Her sandals bang like pans on the cobblestones, her hands grabbing fists of air. A few rays of afternoon sun have conquered the clouds, and yellow light slides across the white walls. Duck races ahead, veering through a tunnel, and we arrive on a familiar path.

"Duck," I call. "Wait up. What happened to your stomachache?"

She scrunches her nose at me as she leans against the dirty brick. "I was acting. I didn't want to go to the markets anymore."

"Acting runs in your family," I tell her.

"Have you seen Mom's movies? I'm not old enough yet. She says I'll be too young for some of them even when I'm thirteen."

"Where is your mom?"

Duck waves her hand to indicate a manicurist or a palm reader. She keeps beside me as we hike the incline. Up ahead a woman stands in a corner archway knocking on a door. It takes me a second to realize it's Louise. She has on the same black silk blouse and navy trousers she wore my first day on Patmos. But just as I'm about to call her name, the door opens and she steps inside. When we reach the door, I stop. The window beside it is covered in a red curtain.

Duck snatches for my hand, but I'm holding too many bags.

"We have to walk quickly and hold our breath," she says. "This is the house of the bad man." The Chicago pedophile. But why would Louise be visiting him? Has she taken over the chore of defending Sonny's daughter? Louise would be a more intimidating ambassador than Miles. We're all doing our part to shoulder Charlie's absence. Duck runs full throttle into the darkness of the alley. When I make my way through it, the door to Charlie's house is already open.

I set the bags in the kitchen. A giant copper pot is simmering on the stove and releasing a cloud of mussels and squid. I put a jug of goat milk in the refrigerator. The shelves are packed with green cheeses and bagged oysters and warty truffles and black porcelain jars of caviar and a plate of white butter, each square pressed with the seal of a Parisian dairy. A bulk carton of emerald water bottles is open on the floor. When I cross into the sitting room, a pale yellow tablecloth covers a large round table. The china is set around it, silver-white discs with a simple brown line drawn around the rims. Lime napkins are folded on each chair in the shape of sailboats. A bouquet of white irises sits in the center, their petals still studded with slivers of ice. They must be imported. It strikes me that Sonny is spending an unwarranted amount of money on her late-afternoon lunch, reveling in luxuries the way someone does when they're uncertain how long they will last. I count ten settings. Duck has scrawled names in crayon on paper cards. Sonny, Ian, Miles, Rasym, Adrian, Duck, Louise, Chiara, Lorenzo, and a question mark.

"Mom and I did the table this morning before we all went out," Duck says proudly as she fidgets at the top of the stairs.

"Who are Chiara and Lorenzo?" I ask.

"Mom's friends from Rome. They're supposed to be sailing in on their yacht this afternoon. Lorenzo is *figo*."

"And the question mark?"

"In case there's a tenth guest. I hope it's Charlie. I miss him."

There's no sound in the house to indicate that Stefan has returned. I swap my card with Chiara's so that I'm sitting next to Louise.

"A game!" Duck demands. Now that my hands are free, she's quick to intercept one, leading me down the flight of stairs. The bedroom doors are closed along the hallway, and she drags me down another flight, where storage crates mix with surplus furniture, bins filled with beach and garden gear, and minor marble statues, presumably less consequential for being anatomically complete. A pipe must be leaking because a drip of water has formed on the plaster ceiling and there's a tiny puddle on the terra-cotta tiles. Duck opens a stained-glass door to pull me into the back garden. Spiderwebs hang in the thornbushes, and white stars of jasmine shield the entrance to the tiny shrine. Duck watches as I battle the overgrown branches to peer through its window. I can't control the hunch that Charlie might have been hiding in this backyard bunker all along. Could it be that simple, that obvious? But whatever I expect to find in the shrine isn't there—only rusted candelabras and blasted mosaics, household saints varnished with grime. *I'm sorry, Charlie. I haven't helped you at all. I haven't even filed a missing person's report.*

"Marco Polo," Duck declares. "You hide in the house. And when I say Marco, you say Polo."

"Isn't that played in a swimming pool?"

"We don't have one," she replies sadly. "Houses up here aren't allowed to have them. Except for Iranian pools, you know, covered with a roof." Duck is already a specialist on island code. "I keep my eyes closed. I only get seven Marcos. After seven, if I don't find you, you win."

"You don't want to hide first?"

"I like finding. Go! I'm counting down from sixty."

I dutifully return to the house. Some childhood tingle envelops me, the fear and thrill of being hunted, the search dependent on the searcher's patience. I climb the steps to the second floor and open the door to the master bedroom. I hear Duck in the garden, *forty-seven, forty-six, forty-five* . . . One half of the bed has been slept in, the dented next to the undented pillow. I slide open the mirrored closet door. The whiff of lavender and metal hits me, Charlie's smell. His shirts and coats are spaced evenly on the hangers, and his shoes cup the darkness on the floor. How long does the scent of a person last in a weave of fabric? What's the life span of their trace? I can't bring myself to sit in Charlie's closet, wrapped in his belongings while I wait to be discovered. I reach for the sleeve of a seersucker jacket, but stop myself from bringing it to my nose. Sonny's jewelry is spread out on the dresser, the gaudy turquoise earring matching the one in my cabin, the black hand-carved queen standing sentinel-like among streams of silver and gold. A jar of face scrub announces that its ingredients are made of the finest ground-up mountains.

I move into the hallway and linger in front of Duck's room. She might deem that hiding place an invasion of privacy. *Sixteen, fifteen, fourteen* . . . I knock on Rasym and Adrian's door before entering. I briefly try to squeeze under their bed, but suitcases block any successful concealment. Plus there are condom wrappers scattered on the brick. *Three, two, one, zero. Ready or not.* Now I risk utter failure, standing dumbly in the middle of a room. It's a game for children, but I'm panicking, savoring the panic of nearly being found and the ridiculous need to win. To prove to a seven-year-old that I'm capable of vanishing too.

"Mar-*co*," she calls from the garden.

"Polo."

I hear her tug on the handle of the stained-glass door. I race into the hallway. I consider hiding under the upstairs lunch table. But Duck is already on the stairs, and my footsteps would be detectable. I hurry toward Stefan's room.

"Mar-*co*."

"Polo," I murmur faintly, trying to sound far away.

I turn the knob onto the darkness. The curtain is drawn over the window. Papers litter the floor, contracts and documents in English and Arabic. A laptop sits open on the bed, its screen dark. Around it are empty vials and empty emerald water bottles. As I walk up to it, I notice a photograph lying on the keyboard of two boys side by side in their suits. It's the photo of Charlie and Stefan I found on the morning I arrived.

"Mar-*co*."

"Polo."

I tap my finger on the computer's space bar, and the screen brightens. A short text is written in a Word document, the cursor blinking after the last word.

I'M SORRY, DAD. I CAN'T HANDLE IT. I CAN'T MAKE YOUR SINS MINE. WE HAVE DONE TOO MUCH DAMAGE AND THERE'S NO WAY TO ERASE OUR NAME. SYRIA WAS ONE DEAL TOO MANY. I HOPE I'LL BE FORGIVEN.

I hear the tick of a faucet. A pair of shorts, underwear, and a T-shirt are carefully folded by the bathroom door. When I step onto the red marble, liquid laps around my shoes. Stefan's eyes are open, staring up in the flooded tub. He's naked, motionless. His body is as white as a bar of soap with stray hairs stuck to it. One hand is folded at his chest, and the other has fallen against his thigh. He's submerged in thirty inches of water, but he feels as far away as a strange country inaccessible by hands or helicopter.

"Mar-*co*."

"Duck, stop! Don't come in!" I sprint from the bathroom in time to find her dancing in victory from the hall.

CHAPTER 15

S uicide leaves too much to imagine and very little to do. But even a burned-out life gives off heat, and, for the two hours I sat in the upstairs living room slumped in the medieval chair, I felt the cooling star of Stefan's body radiate through the floorboards. Inspector Martis sealed himself off in the bedroom, and I watched as one by one the lunch guests arrived to be greeted with the news. Like watching sightseers eaten by a lion.

Rasym returned to the house just as I was dragging Duck by the arm up the stairs. I didn't know where the phone was, and Duck didn't know the number for the police. Rasym grabbed the cordless house phone and disappeared down the steps, his whimpering breaths receding as I led Duck onto the balcony.

The parade of grief that followed was interrupted only by the phalanx of officers and the island's doctor. He wore a short-sleeve linen shirt with O's of sweat bleeding from his armpits, and he swung his black leather case loosely at his side, as if relieved that he was too late to be called upon to use it. First Therese appeared, then Sonny, both turning white and shaking, moans of *no*'s and *what*'s and *not possible*'s, as if each decided separately not to believe. Therese broke down in the kitchen, until Christos arrived to take her back to their house. Christos's voice was a frantic baritone. He gazed at me before he left, his eyes wet, his chest weighted by his wife, and on his face was a look of innocence I had never seen on him before.

"I can't . . . I can't understand," he shouted. "Why no one tell me Stefan here? Why no one tell me? How he dead?"

Louise. Miles. The dark-blond Italian couple armed with champagne and flowers. Sonny sat with Duck on the balcony, calling hotels to find a room for the night, all of which were booked. Rasym, between check-ins with the officers, was also on the phone—to his father in Nicosia, to Mr. Konstantinou's assistants in New York, to Stefan's staff in Dubai, and around and around in a carousel of sympathy and arbitration. He must have texted his boyfriend and told him to stay away because Adrian never showed. Louise cleared the table of the plates, the seating cards, and the silverware. All that was left were the irises hovering above their puddle of ice.

I wanted to mention Charlie. I wanted to say his name out loud, some simple declaration like, "Charlie is Stefan's brother," but I didn't. And no one else mentioned Charlie either, out of respect or fear, but I was sure we were all thinking of him and maybe waiting for him to appear too. Miles drifted onto the balcony, sat down in one of the metal chairs, and offered Sonny his arms.

"I'm going back to the cabins," I told Louise as she continued cleaning, picking up stray glasses, stacking two magazines, the green Bible, and the oversize atlas on the coffee table, beating the sofa pillows back to life. I was jealous of her busyness.

"I'll stay a little longer, just in case Sonny needs anything." She looked at me, *crazy*, and glanced at Rasym, who was on his phone in the corner conducting a hushed argument with a New York attorney. "Stefan's father is still unconscious. Can you imagine him waking up in the hospital to hear that his son is gone?"

Which one? I thought.

Hours later, greased in moonlight on the cabin patio, I am still asking myself that question. *Which one? Or is it both?*

I try Charlie's cell phone. It goes directly to voice mail. The battery must have died long ago. *This is Charlie. You know what to do.* But I don't. I stare at the open bottle of vodka and my empty glass. Far below along the beach, against the gleaming waves, teenagers are screaming in each other's arms.

I want to believe in suicide. I want to believe Stefan had that strangling vine growing inside of him on my visit to his rented room. But nothing about his promises to clean up Konstantinou

Engineering suggested a man waylaid with guilt. There's another answer, the best friend I can't find. Charlie could have waited for the opportunity to do away with Stefan before he discovered the truth and spoke. The problem with the missing is that you can dream any crime on them.

Two high beams cut up the hill and disappear around the bend. I hear the motor lumber up the final ascent. A tiny silver car glides onto the driveway. I walk through my room and down the front steps. Rasym slams the driver's side door, and I wait for the passenger's side door to open, searching the windshield for the blur of Louise.

"She's staying with Sonny and Duck tonight on *Domitian*," he says. "Sonny asked her to." Rasym's had a grueling afternoon, but the hours of phone calls and strategizing seem to have invested him with a new vitality. He stares at me with his jawline hardened, as if ready to weather a few trivial commiserations before he gets to the reason for his visit.

"I'm sorry about Stefan," I say anyway. His thin lips eke out a pained smile. "When you spoke to him the other day, did you get the feeling he was depressed?"

"Not everyone puts their troubles on a billboard." Rasym's eyes flicker over the cabins. Perhaps he's looking for a sign of Charlie. "He wasn't in his right mind, that much is clear. Stefan and I weren't that close." He crosses his arms, irritated by the need to explain. "What I mean is, we didn't speak much about personal matters. Still, I wouldn't have guessed he'd end up doing something like that."

"Me neither. If anything, when I spoke to him, he seemed thirsty for the future, ready to make his mark on the company."

"Exactly," Rasym agrees, leaning rigidly against the car hood. I can tell he wants to leave but is determined not to. He takes a few dry breaths and studies me. "Obviously this isn't an easy time for the family. My father wanted to fly in, but I told him I could handle things here. A lawyer is on his way from Athens, a representative in case the situation gets ugly."

How much uglier could it get? One son dead, the other missing, and a father who is still comatose in a hospital bed eight thousand miles away.

"Did the police confirm it was a suicide?" I ask.

Rasym stares at his shoes as he pinches his nose. He's unpracticed in asking strangers for favors. The Rasym cut from family power yesterday did not anticipate the Rasym today charged with it. It occurs to me that he no longer has to exist under the mantra *be nice to Stefan,* in order to keep the money flowing. Maybe that's why he told Adrian not to come back to the house this afternoon. His boyfriend might have witnessed a disturbing transformation, the erratic butterfly back into the prudent, green-eating caterpillar.

"Inspector Martis is asking that you stop by the station tomorrow morning," he says. "You were the one who discovered the body. I suppose he just wants to check with you before the death certificate is processed and we can send Stefan back to Nicosia for burial."

"Okay."

Rasym drops his hand and stares up at me, stares or glares, his eyes squinted as if snow blind.

"There's something you need to do for me. *For us.*" He starts over, lightening his tone. "There's something I need to ask you to do for my family. For Charlie if not for the rest of us. Did you see Stefan's computer on the bed?"

"Yeah. I read the note."

Rasym winces. "Ian, listen to me. There is no note."

"But there—"

"I erased it. I erased it before the police arrived." He grips the car behind him, as if for the reassurance of a warm machine. "I had to. If it got out that Stefan killed himself because of his involvement with Konstantinou Engineering that would be the end of the company. It would basically be seen as a confession of guilt, and the media would take those words and run. Not just the end, but also a public investigation. That thing he wrote about Syria, as if the crisis there has anything to do with us! Can you imagine how that would read in the world? I spoke to my father, and we agreed it should be deleted. We were doing what's best for the family. I told you, Stefan wasn't in his right mind."

Rasym reaches into his pocket and pulls out a pouch of tobacco and rolling papers. I've never seen him smoke before, and it strikes me as a habit he purposely picked up to model himself after his favorite cousin. His fingers shake as he threads the tobacco across the seam of white.

"But doesn't that note verify it was a suicide? The police might—"

"The police might what?" he repeats as a dare. "The island police? I told them Stefan had been depressed. It's an open secret in the family that he took those pain pills for years. They're running a toxicology test. Even that incompetent island doctor is capable of drawing blood. It will prove he was high on painkillers. There's little question that his death was self-inflicted. But it doesn't have to be ruled a suicide. Suicide is another declaration of guilt."

"What are they listing as the cause of death?"

"Accidental drowning." Rasym pats his body for a match and grows impatient when he can't locate one. He tucks the rolled cigarette behind his ear. "That *is* technically what killed him. And that's what we'd prefer his father thinks. When he comes to. If he does."

"What do you mean, *if?*"

Rasym turns to the view down the valley. The wind tosses a neon beach umbrella along the shore. There's no wind up here, hot and static with the smell of dry shrubbery and only a vague sense of the sea.

"Between you and me, and only you and me, he's not doing so well. They're not certain he's going to regain consciousness. Apparently there have been complications. They're taking him back into the operating room tomorrow. We'll have a better idea after that surgery." He rotates back to me. "So will you do it? All you have to do is not mention the note. Please, I'm begging you. Please just do our family this one favor."'

Even the billionaire son isn't allowed his last words. Especially the billionaire son, presuming those were his words. If Stefan mattered less, his death could be his own. I wonder, had the note remained on the screen, whether Martis would have checked the fingerprints on the keyboard.

"Rasym, you don't think Charlie could have been involved?"

Rasym opens the car door and ducks inside to scrounge the glove compartment for a lighter. He returns with the cigarette burning at his lips.

"That's the other thing you have to do."

"What's that?"

"You told Sonny that Charlie was off on business in Bodrum. We feel he should be."

"I don't follow."

"You need to tell the inspector that Charlie is away for work. It's best if no one thinks he's anywhere near the island."

"I already told the inspector that."

"Good," he says with an unconvincing grin. "Then repeat it." A bank of smoke gathers along his teeth. "As far as any of us knows, he is. He's only been gone a few days. I spoke with Sonny. She understands why it's important to maintain that belief. He was nowhere near the house when Stefan died."

"But Rasym, what if Charlie's in trouble? What if he really is missing? He could be out there hurt and we haven't even looked for him. Or what if he did have something to do with Stefan's death? Don't you want to know the truth?"

Where is the Rasym from yesterday who was so sunk in regret over his lost cousin? One dose of power and all of that concern is shed. He's bent on protecting the family more than its members. Who are the Konstantinous? Not people anymore.

"I'm tired of lying," I say. "I can't keep doing it."

"Why is it a lie? Isn't that the last thing Charlie told you he was doing? That he was going away on business? Don't you see, we're doing this *for* him. And once we handle this disaster of Stefan, we're sending our own private team to track Charlie down. Quietly. And we'll get him whatever help he needs. I promise you that." Finally, the bullet of loss punctures Rasym. His head reels back, and he blinks his eyelids, as if holding back tears. He lets his cigarette drop from his fingers. "I don't like this either, all right. I cared for Stefan. But I have to look out for the ones I love. This is what has to happen. We have the company to consider."

"Your finances, you mean."

His principles have already taken enough of a thrashing for my remark to draw much blood.

"Transnationally we employ what amounts to the size of a small country. It isn't only *us* on the line here."

I don't imagine Rasym will be passing out Qurans and head scarves any longer. You can't hold dual citizenship on two different religions.

"You didn't answer my question. Do you think Charlie is behind this?"

Rasym clutches his keys in his pocket. His eyes close and for a while he goes still, as if trying to find sleep while standing on a long ride home in a subway car.

"I really hope not," he utters without opening his eyes. "I honestly don't think Charlie's cold enough to put his own brother in a tub and watch him sink. Maybe abstractly he could have wanted Stefan dead. But to do it himself." He shakes his head. "Did Sonny do it? That crossed my mind. She has as much to lose as anyone. Maybe you shouldn't have told her that Stefan was on the island yesterday. Did you mention to her where he was staying?"

"You should try to be nicer to Sonny. She's already lost enough."

His left eye opens. "I'm not obligated to like her. I'm obligated not to kick her and her daughter from the house."

"Maybe if more people had liked Stefan, his death wouldn't be so easy to sweep under the rug."

I realize I can only speak to him like this because he needs a favor from me. Rasym stomps out his cigarette and gets in the car.

"Maybe you're right. We should make sure there are people who love us. They're our protection. Stefan didn't have many. Charlie will be glad he has you."

"You could still look out for Stefan. He's your cousin."

"I'm not enough." He starts the engine. "Ian, I won't insult you by offering you money. But if you do help us, we'll make sure you're taken care of. I promise you that. I know you've been hit hard lately. Thank you for your cooperation." He attempts a tender expression.

I begin to walk toward the steps but quickly spin around. Rasym is making small, inept reversals in order to maneuver the car down the drive.

"If Charlie never reappears and Mr. K doesn't pull through, what happens to it all? Who takes over?"

The final yank of the wheel clears the way. Rasym raises his hand in good-bye, and the red taillights smolder down the hill.

Charlie is permanently away on business. His brother drowns by accident in a tub. It is not enough to be loved. All you're left with is the mess of your own version of the story, and others will happily scrub it clean for you. That counts as love too, I suppose. Suicide or accidental drowning. Either is better than murder, and better is how the Konstantinous choose to live. In the distance, across the harbor, the brown monastery is lit with floodlights, like the scorched launch pad of a rocket at takeoff.

I return to the cabin and drag my suitcase onto the bed. The connecting door to Louise's room is open and the darkness holds a curious emptiness, which I wish her presence would break. I want to see her one last time to say good-bye. I fold my clothes and place them in the case. Another time and other places, strangers and accidents and a little lust conducted in a corner. I've never been to Madrid, never seen the Goyas that Sonny said reduces a visitor to tears, but I speak the language. If the planet owes you anything, it's anonymity. After my meeting with Martis tomorrow morning, I'll buy the cheapest ticket on any boat. It is sometimes good to be such a tiny creature in the world.

I open the drawer of the nightstand. On a day of surprises, this one shouldn't register as the worst. But what I find bores a hole in my heart.

I toss the empty sweater from the drawer. The bag of cash is gone. Stolen. I cry as if I've earned it.

"WILL YOU TAKE our picture?"

An American couple, around my age, is standing by the waterfront in Skala, at the choice spot where the gray gates end and the sea comes uninterrupted to the pier. They have first-day sunburns on their forearms and the bloom of expectation on their faces. The woman in a crop top and azure shorts holds her phone out toward me, as if I'm required by some ethic of tourism to obey her command. The man in an orange Adidas T-shirt already has his smile glued on and his arm wrapped around her waist. The 10:00 A.M. sun is blaring down, and at their feet are a number of white plastic bags. They've already been to the shops. Flip-flops, a bath mat, two bottles of olive oil, one bottle of ouzo.

"Just a few," she orders when I lift the phone in front of them. "Make sure you get the boats and the sea." A squat Greek woman stands beside them with a loose bouquet of red roses in her hands. Each rose is one euro. The flower sellers usually work the cafés and tavernas at night, when romance is less frugal, but the tough economy has brought peddling out at all hours. The American couple is her best bet this morning for love. I snap some shots of the three of them, the young man and woman and their inadvertently adopted aunt. When the woman briefly scans the photos she asks me to "hold on a sec" and turns to the rose seller.

"Can you move?" she snaps. "Mark, can you get her to move?"

Mark drops his smile.

"We don't want any roses," he tells the woman. She plucks two from her bouquet and offers them. "*Nooo rooosess.*" She will not be dispatched so easily. She steps closer and shakes her flowers, grinning innocently.

"Mark, do something!" The American woman looks at me with harried kindness followed by a roll of the eyes. "I'm sorry. Just a sec!"

"We don't want." Mark drawls out the words while waving his hands. She gathers another and now it's three stems practically shoved against his chest. "She's not going," he reports.

"God, they're vicious. This is exactly what Tara said they were like. Remember?"

"Don't yell at me about it! How is it my fault?"

The Greek woman is clever. She's not selling roses. What she's selling is her absence in their memories. It ends up costing Mark five euros to convince her to leave the frame, so their photo is perfect, just the woman and Mark against the sun and sea, smiling wildly, the caption already written: *day two in Greece! #peaceful #sea #patmoslover #romantic #whywearealive*

I'm down to my last euros and searching the port for an ATM to withdraw the remains of my bank account. I'm poorer now than I was when I arrived. The escape boat out will have to wait.

I pass the bomb site of Nikos Taverna where, once again, some last invisible mourner has left fresh roses on the ground. I could pick them up and sell them for one euro apiece. At a café on the corner, facing the statue of the military figure, Petros sits at a silver table. He's in his black robe, and his aviator sunglasses reflect the furry print of the newspaper in his hands. It already occurred to me that I led Stefan straight to the priest, and if Stefan refused to pay, I'm not sure it would have been beyond the island's holy landlord to retaliate.

I slip into the empty chair across from him. His head lifts from the paper, his lips drawn in distress.

"Hi, Petros," I say dully. "How about buying me a cup of coffee?"

He slaps his paper down and turns to the street. His fingers toy with the hair on his throat. I signal to the waiter and order.

"Put it on his tab." The waiter checks with his regular, and Petros hesitantly nods his consent.

"What do you want?" he asks when the coffee arrives. He's fidgeting, fixing the Rolex on his wrist and straightening the packets of sugar along his saucer rim. He refuses the intimacy of taking off his sunglasses. Intimidation cannot have brown eyes.

"Did Stefan Konstantinou visit you at your church?"

He exhales petulantly. "It is over. Do not bring up such matters again."

"What's over? Did he pay you or not?"

"It is no longer your concern."

"I'm guessing you heard what happened."

"Of course I heard," he concedes. "Terrible. That is why it is over."

"And you wouldn't have anything to do with it."

His breath comes as a whistle now, his sharp teeth exposed.

"Me? I only wanted what was owed. I am not a murderer. From what the doctor tells me, it is suicide. It is not my fault what trouble that family gets into. I lease them a property. I ask for the rent on time. I mind my own business otherwise." But he is not quite ready to mind his own business. He leans across the table. "I have watched people like them. It is always the kids of the wealthy who end up so badly. It is unhappy to be that unburdened. There are two types of people. Those with troubles and those who look for them." He stiffens back in his seat, so rigidly it's as if I'm talking to a spinal cord.

"What about next month's rent? What will you do if Charlie doesn't pay then? More fingers? Maybe a bullet to the skull?"

Petros collects his paper, distracted for a moment as he waves to a man in a fisherman's cap parking his bicycle against a streetlamp. He fakes a leisurely smile.

"There will be no next time," he whispers. "We will not renew the lease of the dock. Too many are asking questions now. I should never have allowed it." He reaches into his robe and tosses a few coins on the table. "You mention fingers. Your friend, Gideon, he was here that morning the bomb went off. He was sitting at the tables outside Nikos. It's a surprise that he lives when some of our own are killed, no? Does Charlie think that he and his friends will always come away without a scrape? It was a mistake to rent the dock to Charlie. He forgets who the island belongs to."

"And it's your job to show them who owns it. Did the two hippies on the motorbike need a reminder?"

Petros doesn't answer. He rises from his chair, and as he passes me, he taps the corner of his newspaper on my shoulder. I can smell the expensive cologne on his robe, sweet and acrid like spring in New York when all the trees are in heat. "Enjoy your coffee." He walks from the table, slaps the back of the man in the fisherman's cap, and the two stroll slowly along the cobblestones.

I finish my coffee and take the steps up to the police station. The terrace at the top is empty, the cabinet shrine open, and a column of fresh water bottles is wrapped in plastic, awaiting the next influx of remanded visitors.

"Inspector Martis," I say to the officer behind the desk. He points to the glass office as if I've been expected. Martis is on the phone, the cord wrapped around his elbow. He indicates with a nod for me to take a seat as he reclines in the chair shouting jovial Greek into the receiver. He's gotten a haircut. A militant side part lends his chubby face a boyish rebellion, and the whiskers of his mustache have been cut in a straight line high above his upper lip. He will no longer be able to bite at it. He yanks the phone from the unwilling crook of his neck and places the phone on its cradle, the warmth of the call lingering in his expression.

"Mister Bledsoe," he says, "thank you for coming. The last time I saw you in Skala, you were running away from me."

"I thought I saw someone I knew."

"Did you catch him?"

"Not really."

"Well, it is a small island. There will be a next time." He braids his fingers over his belly and studies me. I think he might be on the verge of asking why I haven't sent him a friendship request on Facebook. But the cheer drains from his face. "The Konstantinous," he says with a long sigh. "Not so fortunate as we thought, are they? This

Stefan, he travels from very far away to kill himself in his family vacation home. Perhaps he wanted one last time where he spent summers as a child."

"Perhaps."

He looks at me shrewdly. "Although the doctor and I have been hounded this morning by a solicitor from Athens who demands his death be declared an accident. Even a Konstantinou's end is a matter of legality. We are accustomed to their many requests in life, but now it extends to their preference of death."

"Maybe they want to bury him in a Christian cemetery."

His fingers scratch the back of his head.

"You were the one who found him, yes?" I nod. "I ask because you've been helpful to me. A little window into a family that resists. I'm not expecting you to betray your confidences. But out of curiosity, was there anything that suggested to you that his death was deliberate?" Deliberate to whom, Martis doesn't say.

I pretend to recall the scene, my eyes drifting over the photos on the tops of the filing cabinets. "No. Just papers spread around the room. And then I walked into the bathroom, and there he was in the tub. That's really all I know."

Martis waits, as if more will be remembered if he gives me time. Time seems to be the great decider in Greece. He finishes rooting his tongue around his gums for missing specks of his breakfast and speaks.

"His suitcase and personal items were found in the closet. It appears he had just come to the house to put his things away, be sloppy about his papers, take too much pain medication, and run a bath. His medication was for his knees. From years of tennis, his cousin told me, although he also suffered from depression."

I think of the old medication vial that was on his bathroom sink the first day I arrived. I try to recall if it was still there when I found his body. But all images of that moment gravitate to the contents of the tub, and I squeeze my eyes shut to erase the drowned man from my mind.

"No one saw him arrive," Martis says.

"If he did deliberately take his life, he probably knew he wouldn't have the house to himself for long. But you can't blame the family for preferring to believe it was an accident."

"No, no," he assures me. "I do not blame them. I blame no one. I am sympathetic to the family's suffering. Barring any unforeseen results, the doctor has agreed to list it as an accident. I hope that will provide some comfort."

This is the second time Martis has invited me to the station to chat about a death that has been officially deemed an accident. And as with the hippies on the motorbike, he seems hazily unwilling to accept the official report. The two hippies must be buried by now, and Martis is still hanging around Patmos getting his hair cut and waiting for his suspicions to magically resolve.

"It only surprises me how quickly the Konstantinous have released their solicitors. Most families want answers. Most families are not so ready to supply them."

"The Konstantinous aren't most families."

"That is true," he says somberly. "But a little doubt is to be expected. I checked the flight manifest at the heliport on the island's military base. Out of curiosity. Stefan comes by private helicopter a week ago. Does that not seem odd to you? Stefan is on the island for a week before he goes to his family house and decides to take his life. Why did he not go to his house right away? What was he doing all those days by himself?"

"Maybe he wanted to be alone," I offer. "I only knew Stefan as a kid. I'm afraid I can't enlighten you on his mind-set. Rasym is the one to talk to for that."

"My police brain," he says and knocks his palm against his temple. "It is just so many questions about the Konstantinous all of a sudden. They are quiet for so long, and now one brother after another." He looks at me curiously. "You have not spoken to Charlie, have you? You did relay my request to speak with him?"

"I haven't seen him since the last time I was here."

"Odd too that he is not around even after his own brother dies. Rasym tells me Charlie is away on business. You said yourself he was off on a boat. But his girlfriend, Sonny, visited me the other morning to ask if I had tracked him down. She was very upset. Now when I speak to her this morning, she tells me she was confused. She too says he is away on business. It must be important business for him not to come back for his own brother. And yet when I go down to his charter dock, it looks as if the whole place is shuttered for good."

We have reached the purpose of my visit, my betrayal of Rasym, and I'm hesitating, holding the words on my tongue like they're insects that could sting if I move too fast.

"Can I speak off the record? Can you promise what I say doesn't get back to Charlie's family?"

Martis smiles, appreciating collusion. I get the sense he's nailed me for the weakest member of the Konstantinou entourage. Perhaps he's already tallied my betrayals on the Internet, the quisling wanderer who turns on his own family if left to his devices for too long. It is hard enough not to believe what you read about yourself. And there might be some merit to the public account: *makes terrible decisions based on his own warped idea of good.*

"Certainly, Ian. You have my discretion. There is no case against the Konstantinous. You have no one to protect."

"Charlie's missing. I think something's happened to him. He hasn't been reachable since that last time I saw him, before the hippies were killed."

"You mean he is in some sort of trouble?"

"Yes. But I don't know what. He's just vanished. The family is planning to conduct their own investigation. They want to do it quietly. But something's not right. You said it. Charlie would be back here if he knew that Stefan had died. First it's one brother, and then the other. The two sons, both gone."

I expected Martis to jump at this disclosure, but he leans back in his seat, his eyes tiredly trailing along the same set of photographs that I was pretending to study. He presses his fingertips together as if trying to align their whorls.

"Did you hear me?" I yell. "My friend, the guy you're looking for, is missing. No one's heard from him. You should authorize a formal search."

"I had thought of that," he admits quietly. "Two boys of a wealthy family. But the father is alive, yes? So the money is not in their name."

"He's barely alive. He's in New York having another surgery today. I'm pretty certain this qualifies as a police matter." I'm one second away from reaching over the desk to shake Martis into action. He was the last card up my sleeve.

"Charlie did not tell you he was going away on business?"

"He did. But that was days ago."

"And yet that is what he said he was doing."

"Inspector Martis, no disrespect, but I'm—"

He raises his hands in capitulation.

"Please, Ian. Do not be angry. I understand the concern. I am the nosy investigator who has been ordered by my superiors to return to Kos. The Konstantinous' solicitors have put their pressure on the heads of the Hellenic force as well. You and I are in agreement, something is not right, and I would like nothing more than to act on this news. The problem is that it is not illegal for a man to leave the island. And, sadly, it is also not illegal for a man not to return even when his brother dies. My hands are tied unless a member of the family reports Charlie as missing. Unless I have an official report from his family, I am not authorized to conduct a search."

"And I can't report it."

Martis stares solemnly at the blotter pad. "That is the reason I asked you here," he says queasily. "I was hoping you could convince the family to cooperate. If not to investigate Stefan's death, then to find your friend. Perhaps you could speak to them, reason with them, to come down and file a report, which would allow me to stay on. Otherwise—" He opens his palms in defeat. "Otherwise Charlie's been gone less than a week."

I have no faith in my ability to reason with Rasym. But an idea springs from the déjà vu of sitting in this obsolete office. A crime might rescue Charlie. His culpability could be his salvation. To be wanted for murder is still to be wanted.

"What about the hippies? You have doubts about their deaths. Charlie's your suspect. He could have murdered them. He threatened them just before they died. If he's your prime suspect, you'd be required to hunt him down."

Martis clucks and rolls back in his chair. "You are very clever, Ian, but what proof? I have no proof that he is responsible. You told me yourself, it was only an idle threat. I have more evidence to suspect fleeing refugees than I do your friend. I'm afraid, without any solid proof, that case is closed. My superiors have demanded it closed. We are not a detective agency. I was only dispatched here to confirm it was an accident and comfort a hysterical American girl. Without proof . . ." Again the open hands.

I don't have proof—not even of the smuggling operation. The police station might as well be an annex of the tourist office one flight down. It satisfies the illusion of protection. If I had any confidence in its abilities, I might file a report on the theft of nine thousand dollars in a Ziploc bag. I rise from my seat with nothing else to say.

"I encourage you to speak to his family," Martis says. "Surely, they will want him found as soon as possible. I could help, but they need to allow it. I can't search for someone who is away on business."

"I almost wonder if they'd prefer it this way. If Charlie's gone, he could still be alive and innocent. It might risk too much to have him home."

"I have learned over the years that some crimes don't want to be solved. Picking at them only draws more blood. I have never been good at learning my lessons. Pick, pick." He laughs wearily.

I stop at the door. "You know, Charlie was supposed to be at Nikos Taverna the day the bomb went off. That was his spot, every morning at eleven. Maybe his disappearance is linked to that."

"Is he the murderer or the victim? The suspect or the target? You keep changing your mind." I want to tell him that it's possible to be both. "You sound like that girl, Carrie Dorr," he says with a snort. "She also mentioned the bomb in connection to your friend. She even had something in her possession that she took as proof that she was right. I'm afraid I might have indulged her suspicions. But I came to my senses. It was nothing. That girl is quite unstable. And the bomb is a scab not worth picking. We have picked it too much already. It is best to let it heal."

"I visited the hippie camp. Vic told me that Carrie went back to the States."

Martis raises his eyebrows in surprise. "I don't believe she's left yet. When she came by two days ago she was renting a room above the supermarket. You didn't speak to her?"

"Why would I have?"

"She asked where you were staying. I thought she would have paid you a visit. Ah, just as well. Perhaps she has gone home." Martis withdraws a business card from his pocket and, in an impressive maneuver, hurls it across the room right into my chest. "I leave in two hours. If you talk to the family before then, I could stay. Otherwise, my contact information is on my card. And remember, I'm reachable on Facebook."

I think I would enjoy being haunted by posts of Martis—fishing trips, old men at wicker tables toasting with ouzo, photos of his growing children turning him into ancient history. One day they might link a camera to users' graves so you could continue to visit them and leave electronic flowers.

"What will you do now, Ian?" He taps the arms of his chair and swings his legs out from under the desk. His suitcase sits on the plastic scruff mat. It's clear Martis doesn't expect me to succeed in changing the Konstantinous' minds. "Are you planning on going home?"

It is a question people ask when they don't think they will see you again. I suppose, for most, home is the sweetest term for good-bye.

I TAKE THE zigzagging asphalt past the Cave of the Apocalypse and up through the scratchy pine and eucalyptus groves. Chora is no longer a puzzle that's impossible to solve. I locate Charlie's house in a record five minutes. The red door is open a crack and voices bleed through it. I let myself in. After the temporary blackout of the interior, I find Duck in a turquoise swimsuit and plastic jelly shoes chasing the gray cat around the sitting room.

"Terry, Terry." She stops when she sees me. "We brought Terry home. He was lonely on the boat."

"Leave him alone, honey," erupts a low, prickled voice from the couch. Sonny lies across the cushions. Her body is covered in a white, wool throw, which she keeps bundled around her as she lifts into a seated position. The skin around her eyes is pinched and red, and the eyes themselves have a blue-gray fixity, like iron fire doors at the end of school hallways. It's a face no longer accepting disappointments— it's reached its fill of them. I scan the room, hoping to find Louise, but I don't see her. Faint music emanates from somewhere beyond the house. Rasym and Adrian are on the balcony. Rasym stands, wearing khakis and a starched, white button-down. Adrian is reclining in a teetering chair, his muscular legs crossed on the ledge and his bare shoulders gathering sun. He drinks from an emerald bottle. Rasym is speaking to him with hands gesticulating in circles, and Adrian watches him between impatient stretches of his neck. Even through the glass, I detect a rabid energy in Rasym of a man between appointments.

"Terry was an orphan," Duck blurts out. "Mom and Charlie found him by a Dumpster on the side of the road. Someone ran over his leg, and the other cats abandoned him. He was dying, and so they rescued—"

"Duck, let's not talk about that. I don't want to hear that story again, okay?" Sonny turns to me, trying to decide between a smile and a grimace. Neither surfaces. "Rasym has workers in the basement fixing the water damage to the ceiling. And Vesna's downstairs cleaning the room. Therese is still too shaken, so I gave her the day off. She stayed at home with Christos." She pats the couch for her phone. "Christos keeps texting me about Charlie's father. He's asking to speak to him. I think they're worried if Charlie doesn't—" But she can't say it, can't state the obvious possibility that Charlie might not come back. Instead she gathers Duck in her arms and concentrates on the doorway to the kitchen. "Miles," she shouts. "I said I'd make it myself." Her eyes divert back to me. "He was making tea, like, twenty minutes ago."

"I'll help him." I pass into the kitchen where Miles is lodged against the freezer door, returning a bottle of vodka to the shelf. He's dressed in a black silk shirt, untucked over madras shorts, and his cheeks are splotched and sweaty from alcohol. The bulk box of water bottles is still on the floor by the stove, which Stefan must have plundered before his last walk down the steps. I can't resist thinking how easy it would be to mix Stefan's old medication in a bottle of water and wait until he passed out. Then it would just be the labor of dragging him into the tub.

"Charles is going to come back," Miles says in lieu of a hello as he picks up his drink. "I keep telling Sonny that because she needs to believe it. And I believe it. Don't you?" Miles stares at me and then at the floor, humiliated by the sound of his own optimism. "He's just been kept away." He takes a sip of vodka and speaks in a quieter tone. "He'll be back and he'll need Sonny to break the news about his brother. So we have to keep her spirits up. Will you help me do that?" He touches his wrist. "What time do you have?" He asks like it's a matter of minutes until Charlie returns.

I check my phone. "Almost twelve-thirty."

"Then there's a whole day ahead for hoping." He pulls a tea bag from a steaming cup and steadies his fingers around the handle. "Rasym says that Stefan was depressed. He says he was under too much pressure and he cracked. I hadn't seen Stefan since we were kids on this island, so I hope this doesn't sound rotten. But I wish he had done it back in Dubai. Why did he have to come here to kill himself? Now it's always going to be the house where his brother died for them. I had a cousin who—"

"Miles," I bark as if snapping him sober. "You don't really think Charlie's going to come back, do you? Like he's just going to walk through the door any second?"

Miles's expression is a wonder of determination. He seems to genuinely believe that fortunes change for the better on a dime. It's got to be the alcohol that's keeping him afloat. He reminds me of someone who snorted their first line of cocaine at four in the morning and thinks as long as he continues to talk and smile and tweeze the conversation toward the crazily positive the hard postmortem dawn will never arrive with its chaser of pain and lonely beds.

"It's possible that Charles found out about his brother dying, and he's in a state of shock," he says. "I wouldn't be surprised if he's on a plane to New York to be with his father. Or maybe he's still out at sea on a boat that's lost all signal. He could be somewhere and have no clue what's happened. Ian, you've got to have some faith. What's the point of presuming the worst? It's not going to help Sonny, and that's what I'm here to do. It's not a miracle for someone to return from the blue."

Tea in one hand, vodka in the other, he hurries into the sitting room. He seems to have found his calling as nurse and comforter, the man I once thought had the only conceivable motive to wish Charlie harm. Now he's the only one of us who expects to see him again. Sonny takes her tea and leans against him. Miles attempts what must be an inside joke about a waiter dropping a tray at the beach. Sonny isn't listening, or rather she's listening to a sound at a higher register. She spins her head toward the window.

"Who the fuck is blasting music? Are they playing music outside? Someone dies, and the island just goes on with the party." She shakes her head. "This place is unreal. Why can't he just be here! Where is he!" Miles holds her, and Duck collapses on the floor, as if pretending to be dead.

"Someone pour ketchup on me," she murmurs.

I open the glass door, which ratchets up the volume of the music, and step out on the balcony. The decaying reverb of a dance track drifts from a neighboring rooftop. Young men and women barely in their college years are clamoring with raised drinks along to the lyrics, *get the honeys, take the moneys, feel the paper, kill it with me, I ain't your hostage but a brand-new Bugatti, zero to ninety, fat girl, fat girl, you're the free world leader* . . . Everyone on the rooftop knows the words and not their meaning. The red canvas shades behind them make them appear as if pulsing in a wine stain. The blue sky with its sporadic paint chips of gulls seems very dreary by comparison. I recall Prince Phillip's comment about being dethroned from youth, and I can't shake the sense that the army is at the gate and these sloppy, gyrating kids have already won. We had our chance and did too little with it. It's been a long time since I've had that feeling of restless possibility, walking through Greenwich Village with the belief that every door was open to me and all the architecture I needed was spring weather, the princeliness that money can't buy and is only owned by the young. Whatever I was hunting for back then, I never found it. To find it would have ruined the search.

Adrian snaps his fingers to the music, rocking on the back legs of the chair. His swimsuit is fluorescent pink with white palm fronds patterned across it.

"How did the talk go with the inspector?" Rasym asks me. He hasn't shaved today.

Since I failed in stirring Martis into action, there's no reason to cover my tracks. Worse, now that the cash is gone from the nightstand, I might need to rely on the money he offered. *Be nice to Rasym.*

"Okay. I didn't mention anything he didn't already know."

"Did you tell him Charlie was away on business?"

I nod and lean against the ledge, trying to fight the feeling of a dutiful dog.

"When are you organizing the search party?" I ask.

Adrian gazes up at Rasym, as if the answer is a test of his honesty.

"My father is arranging a team from Nicosia. If all goes as planned, they should arrive tomorrow or the next day at the latest. We have to be careful. Stefan will be buried on Monday." I have no idea what day it is and how many more days come between now and then. I have an overstaying vacationer's concept of the calendar—time without nouns, just infinite cube-like blocks of light broken by sleep.

"Don't you think it might help to get the island police involved?" I ask. "Two more days is a long time to wait."

Rasym stares out at the water with his hands on his hips.

"You have to trust that we know what we're doing."

"Rasym," Adrian snaps. It's the first harsh word I've ever heard out of his mouth, and Rasym spins around coldly to receive it.

"They'll also be handling any of the material that was left in the Charters office and hangar." The team sounds less like a search party than a cleanup crew.

"But finding Charlie is the priority," I clarify.

"I don't know what your plans are," Rasym says curtly, "but you aren't obligated to stay. If you want to go back to New York, you should. It could be a good idea, considering that you were covering for him. There might be questions about your involvement."

"Jesus." Adrian moans. "Have some subtlety. Charlie is his best friend. He wants to help."

Rasym flinches, but the defensiveness is already building. He turns to me. "Last night you said you thought Charlie might have been behind Stefan's death." I'm fairly certain this reminder is for Adrian's benefit, so he understands the kind of best friend currently sharing their balcony. "That's been going through my head ever since. If that's the case, Charlie doesn't need to be found."

"Only if that's the case."

He smirks.

"Charlie wouldn't do that," Adrian swears. "What would you say about me if I went missing? Excuses like I deserved it?"

Rasym ignores him. "Look, I promise you, we're going to find him. I'm sorry if I don't seem sympathetic. My cousin just died. I'm doing everything I can here."

To be fair, someone had to step in and be the pillar to the crumbling house. Someone had to arrange the transport of the body and keep the worry from ransacking the valuables and the floor from caving in. I feel I've been too harsh on Rasym. Underneath the fledgling beard, the bruised, obedient forehead, and the calculating eyes is a tired and frightened pallbearer unsure of the weight he's expected to carry. Is it one body or two?

I move toward the door. "How's Charlie's father?"

"We'll find out soon," Rasym grumbles. "Please keep his surgery today between us. All we need is more hysteria." He gestures toward the bundled occupant of the sitting room.

Adrian lets his feet drop from the railing. He reaches down for the hose and pulls the trigger on the sprayer, rinsing his chest and legs. Someone screams at the rooftop party. An important guest has arrived.

"How can a whole side of a family go at once?" Adrian asks. "That quickly? A week ago they had everything, and it all blows to—"

I step inside. Duck and Miles are no longer keeping Sonny company. I close the door, thankful that the blasting music will drown our voices out. Sonny is staring at the tea in her cup like it's a phone screen.

"They're having a party next door," I tell her. "Where did everyone go?"

"Miles took Duck to the store." She exhales with resolve. "He's been a good friend, even if I do blame him for punching Charlie. Because if there hadn't been that fight, if Miles had just walked away. . . ." She kicks the coffee table with her bare foot. "I told them they should go to the beach. I'd go too, but I'm afraid to leave. Afraid if I come back, my bags will be by the door. Rasym's holding up very nicely, don't you think? A real rock, huh?"

I kneel down in front of her. "Where's Louise?"

"She left about an hour ago. Sorry I stole her from you." She again attempts a smile, but it only drags the corners of her eyes down. "Sleeping alone on Charlie's boat would have been too much for me.

I actually spent most of the night up on deck. I didn't want to go down into that hole with all of his things."

"Sonny, I think you should consider going to the police station and talking to the inspector. I know Rasym's promised a private team, but if you filed a missing-person's report he could start the search right away."

"Rasym promised me they're hiring the best people."

"I'm sure they are, but they won't get here for another couple of days. If Charlie's injured"—*still alive*—"or in trouble, he needs to be found right now. We've already wasted too much time."

Sonny could mention that I was complicit in the days that passed without alarm, and it's decent of her not to bring it up. But I can tell that my pleading on my knees isn't getting through to her.

"You haven't been here long enough to realize that the island police are useless. Utterly useless. It will be twenty questions for twenty days, and they'd still only find him if he walked through Skala on fire."

"Inspector Martis is different. I trust him. All you have to do is explain that he's not away on business. We know he isn't. You know that, right?"

"Rasym promised me they'd find him," she repeats. What she won't say induces the hopeless refrain. If there's any chance that Charlie had something to do with Stefan's death, the police are the last party she wants involved. She catches her breath after a minute of holding it. Terry slinks across the arm of the sofa and stops to lick its paw. I reach over to pet its head, and it bats its claws at me. It's more demoralizing to be snubbed by an animal than by a human. It implies the fault lies in you—a rot at the core that predators with more heightened instincts detect. Terry jumps onto Sonny's lap, but she doesn't take any notice. Her eyes are on the atlas on the coffee table, pinned under the green Bible.

"Anyway, it's not so simple as that," she says quietly. "I have to do it their way now. They have me in a corner."

"Who has you?"

She lets the blanket slide from her shoulders, as if unwillingly giving herself up to the room. She's dressed in muted, anorexic gray.

"Rasym says, no matter what happens, I can still keep our house in Nicosia. And more than that, he's agreed to front the money I need for Duck. Money for her father, really. Money so I can bring her back to Cyprus with me. So, you see, they have me. I don't have a choice." It's one thing to be had on your terms, and quite another to be had on theirs. But I can't blame Sonny for putting her daughter first. We both seem to be mourning the woman a few days ago who prided herself on being willing to lose it all.

"But what about Charlie?" I need her to believe in his return in order for me to go on doubting it. Otherwise, the loss is too complete.

"Rasym promised me they're hiring the best people!" She tosses Terry onto the floor and sweeps her palms over her eyes. "You trust he's going to do that, don't you?" I set my face to twelve o'clock. Midnight. Noon.

"Can you keep a secret?" she asks, reaching to clasp my hands. "Can you?"

"Yes."

"There is something they don't know. No one does. Remember the ring I was looking for, that diamond I left on *Domitian?* Charlie and I had a secret ceremony in Cairo last December. I'm honestly not even sure it would hold up legally. It probably wouldn't. We did it on the spur of the moment, wore these white djellabas we bought at the market, and Charlie dredged up some Egyptian judge who recited an Arabic blessing. Charlie didn't want his family to know. He was sure there'd be a big blowup. I never wore the ring in Cyprus. In fact, I never wore it off this island, which is why I didn't take it with me to Paris. It wasn't even supposed to count, except between us. Mostly, I was the one who said it didn't count. But I swear, if it comes to it, if Rasym demands one more sacrifice or doesn't follow through on his promises—" She clears her throat. "They're going to find him. They're sending professionals. He's got to be somewhere. No one disappears forever. You can't be deleted off the planet."

I can't imagine even Charlie would be reckless enough to marry without a prenup, although back in December he probably didn't have that much in his name. Still, if the ceremony is legal, Sonny stands to inherit far more than she did a day ago, and certainly more than what was in store if Stefan had his chance to speak. It flashes through me that Sonny might have tried to talk to Stefan, that she might have gone to see him to smooth things over or invited him up to the house. Stefan would have come willingly to anyone with information on his brother.

"Sonny, you didn't—"

Her mouth widens, and her eyebrows arch. She lets go of my hand. She must have guessed what I'm thinking by the gravel in my voice.

"Oh, not you too. Not the worst from you, along with all the others."

I reach for her, but she knocks my arm away, and marches to the staircase.

"I'm on your side," I tell her. "It might be smart for you to contact a lawyer."

She stares at me, with her mouth frozen in a circle of disdain. She's seen herself as others see her. She's watched people watch her—on screens, in photographs, in life. She's an expert in gauging the reaction she makes. She puts her foot on the first step and pauses.

"I haven't known you long," she says, "but it's funny. You were on Charlie's side until a few days ago. This morning Rasym said you were on his. Now you're on mine. You always seem to end up on the side with the nicest view."

THE CHARTERS PORT is barren, except for a wandering donkey that stands by one of the iron-cradled boats, chewing the grasses that spike around the unfinished hull. The grates are still pulled down and padlocked on the hangar, but a white yacht painted with a red *K* is moored against the dock. Pink vinyl buoys bob around it. There isn't a soul on board. It must have been returned by one of the young captains, who promptly abandoned it along with the island. I have no doubt Ugur warned the crew that the game was up. I step onto its flybridge, examining the inert navigational equipment underneath a dry, water-stained windshield. One of the console buttons must release the trapdoor shell. The cabin contains no beach towels or guidebooks or any other indication of seafaring vacationers. It is one of Charlie's Trojan horses.

As I leap back onto the dock, I catch sight of a man and woman weaving along the shoreline. Their long, wet clothes are licorice black from the water. The man holds a toddler at his hip, and the woman has an orange life vest dangling from her arm. Their raft must be farther down the beach, or maybe they swam in from a boat at sea. They stop when they spot me, but their eyes are still running, scanning me and the hills and the long road inland. I wave with my arms raised high, making broad U's and X's. The man gathers the back of his child's head, as if to indicate that whatever I want, I will not be taking their boy.

I run toward them. I have nothing to offer, nothing but welcome, on an island that isn't even mine.

"Hello," I say. "Welcome to Patmos."

The woman is heaving, her breasts expanding in her heavy cotton tunic. But she pulls a phone from a plastic bag, lifts it out in front of her, and takes a picture of herself. She turns around to document her husband and son.

"I can take one of the three of you," I say. The husband shakes his head, but the woman with deep eye sockets smiles and hands me her phone. She steps back to join her family, but the boy isn't looking at the camera.

"What's your son's name?"

"Ibrahim," the woman shouts.

"Ibrahim, over here, over here. Look!"

His plump face is examining the new geography with a detached expression, like a brain too busy recording to be recorded, carbon paper for eyes.

I take five shots of them, trying to get more land behind them than sea.

"Thank you," the woman says as she grabs her phone. "We will send to our family so they know we made it." Belatedly, the tears come, from the shock of survival or the family they've left behind. "They would rather us drown than save us. Five boats went by while we were in the water. They wouldn't have cared if we died."

Her husband begins taking small, hesitant side steps, as if now that they're onshore, time is even more of a necessity.

"Sir," he says. "Which way to the central port?" They both speak faultless English.

I point up the road and fin my hand right.

"It's a few miles to Skala. A few kilometers."

"And police?" he asks. "Do you know if they are taking us in?" I'm not sure if he means asylum or arrest and perhaps neither does he. The woman reels out a few sentences in Arabic and yanks her son onto her shoulder. The man checks a plastic pouch hidden underneath his shirt.

"There's a station," I tell him. "They've been processing refugees. I believe they're being sent to a camp in Lesbos. I could drive your wife and child on my bike. I don't know if I can hold all three of you."

"No, we prefer to walk," he answers. "We stay together."

I wish I had euros to give them. Automatically, I make my pocket-patting poverty gesture.

"We have money," the woman replies breathlessly. "We need crossing to the north. But Europe. This is Europe." And with a last smile and the toss of her life vest, they begin to hurry along the dirt road. When you say welcome, you cannot say good-bye. I watch their retreat, the boy's face bouncing against his mother's shoulder, until the dust and distance claim them. I picture Charlie bobbing out in the water, miles from land in every direction, boats passing another dark head caught in the waves, and if he went under how many of the newly dead would he join? I squat down and press my fingers in the dry, royal earth.

The office door is locked, and its bank of windows is latched from the inside. The purpose for my visit lies inside the trailer. I'm prodded by the loss of nine thousand in cash and Rasym's promise of the private team stripping the place of any lingering material. Checking that no one's around, I grab a heavy, sharp-sided rock and strike it against the door's window until the glass shatters. Reaching my hand over the shards, I turn the knob.

Ugur has indeed swept the office clean. Even the garbage bin under the desk is empty. All that's left is the chess set and the box of caps and tote bags. I unhook the photograph of *Domitian* from the wall. A series of dents runs along the safe's edges. Ugur or Gideon or someone else must have tried to pry it open. But I watched Charlie work the combination. I spin the dial through the numbers of his last birthday backward, 15, 29, 6, and feel the shackle's release. The iron door is heavier than I expected, and a black leather-bound book drops to the floor. It's a log listing dock times and shipments, from last week all the way to the first of May. There's no indication of the contraband being transported, but the cell phone number of G. Frost is penciled at the top of the first page. From the look of the registry, the fleet of yachts must have been moving nonstop between Turkey and Greece all summer, from Bodrum to Athens and a town called Thessaloniki. I place the book on the desk and reach my hands inside the safe.

Nine thousand is all I had to save me from oblivion. Now that it's stolen, I don't have enough to buy a plane ticket home. I'm hoping for a few thousand, a few hundred, whatever petty cash of a doomed boat business might remain. Part of me also hopes that the safe is empty. If Charlie did make a last-minute escape, he might have collected whatever available money he had on hand. A bare safe could signal his survival. But my fingers hit upon the paper stacks, ten of them piled together like unmortared bricks.

I pull out one of the thick, rubber-banded stacks and flip my thumb along the pink, five-hundred-euro bills. My heart skips. The mere physical weight of so much money in my hand induces fear, like coming across lions mating or a bag of knives on a playground. There must be two hundred bills tied in the rubber band. Ten times five hundred times two hundred—I'm incapable of arithmetic just as I'm incapable of speech. But there's got to be upward of one million euros in cash. No wonder Charlie fired Gideon for getting anywhere near it. People have been hacked to pieces for so much less.

I transfer the stacks onto the desk, a flock of ten flamingo-colored squares, fluid and redeemable anywhere on the planet. This is my future lying on the table, the rescue I wanted, the reason I came to Patmos in the first place. From here on out, each step is like putting my foot on the gas. Why, then, does it feel like I've already been thrown through the windshield?

The office is too quiet, except for the chatter of dry teeth. I grab a tote bag from the box and load the stacks into it. I add the shipping log to the top of the cache. Am I saving this money or stealing it, preserving it in case of Charlie's return or giving myself an accidental motive for wishing him gone? I'm too poor to leave it. I reach back into the safe and root around for any last bills. In the corner are two more bricks, not paper, but gummy rock wrapped in plastic. The bricks are feces brown, the plastic sliced open, and an Arabic word is written across them in black marker. They smell of spoiled vinegar.

I would have preferred not to know what Charlie was smuggling in his underwater shells, taking the mystery of it to bed with me along with the visions of places I never traveled and people I never got to love. The not knowing would have kept some hope alive of good. It could have been ammunition or medical supplies. But the sad, obvious truth is two brown bricks of heroin, discards on the dope route from East to West. Would Charlie have been forgiven if Stefan had learned the truth? If he's alive now, does he even want forgiveness? I stare out the window where the sun whitens the sea like pavement.

His father built the highways in the Middle East.

CHAPTER 16

One motorbike parked among thirty along the port-side road of Skala attracts no particular interest. Its black-and-yellow frame is dented and streaked in mud. Its metal license plate hangs by a piece of wire at the tail. Its front fender is slightly askew. A helmet dangles by its strap from the handgrip. In high season, the island is a blur and buzz of identical machines swarming through the towns and beaches like summer locusts. It would be impossible to guess that stuffed inside the seat compartment of this bike is a substantial fortune. Anyone with a screwdriver could bust the seat open and run off with its contents in five seconds.

I have nowhere else to hide the money. Even the cabin is no longer safe from thieves. I wonder if Vesna or her brother, sensing their family's dire situation in light of the vanishing Konstantinous, decided it might be wise to pilfer a spare bag of cash that practically begged to be stolen in the first place. Or maybe Gideon used his key. I hesitate a few feet from my bike, my senses heightened, now less free for having so much to lose. But I pick up my pace and head toward the center of town. God giveth, god taketh . . . in other words, God doesn't care.

Martis said that Carrie Dorr had rented a room above the grocery store. There's still a chance she hasn't left the island. The supermarket's narrow aisles are crowded with loud voices and quiet, sunburned children and Greek boys mopping during peak hours. Green plastic baskets are overflowing American-style with food. I slide up to the woman at the register.

"Excuse me," I say, ignoring the line of customers. "I'm looking for my friend. She rented a room upstairs. An American. Carrie Dorr."

The clerk stops scanning a jug of milk to the irritation of the man she's helping. His yellow hair and blue complexion under the fluorescent lights precisely match the Swedish flag.

"We rent many rooms upstairs."

"Salamander tattoos on her ankles. Orange lizards."

"Oh, that girl. No, she left. She moved to a room above the oil merchant on the other side of Skala. Maybe two or three days ago."

I make my way across town. The oil merchant guides me to a jeweler who directs me on to a souvenir shop. Carrie must have changed accommodations nightly, too frightened to overstay but underestimating the watchfulness of a tiny Greek village. I remember that Martis described her as paranoid—as if she were in some danger. But it is what she has in her possession connecting Charlie to the bomb that drives my interest in tracking her down. I assume she'll agree to speak to me. She did ask for my whereabouts.

The clerk at the souvenir shop points me up a flight of stairs. "She take room this morning." I knock on a door painted cerulean blue and press my ear against it. I try the handle.

"She isn't in," I tell the shopkeeper back downstairs. "I'm her brother from America. I'm supposed to be staying with her."

Previously hard of hearing, he's now alert to the economics of a second guest. "You are staying too? She did not mention. It will be double, even if it is one bed."

"That's fine. Could I use a spare key?"

"Seventy euros," he shouts, demanding to be paid in advance in case the Dorr siblings are tempted to skip out on their bill.

I pull a crisp, pink note from my pocket. "Can you make change for five hundred?" Flamingo paper. And yet this money might well have cost innumerable lives.

He fumbles through his lockbox and hands me a key attached to a yellow tassel. I climb the stairs and knock again, quietly this time. When there's still no answer, I slip the key in the lock. As I open the door, stale air escapes with its reek of air freshener and synthetic bedding. No lights or windows make sense of the darkness. I reach my hand along the stucco wall in search of the switch. Just as I flick it on, a sparkling object shoots toward me. I duck, and right above my head is a loud explosion. Glass splinters rain on my shoulders and feet.

I rise to find Carrie Dorr with her hand around a plastic handle that was once attached to a coffeepot. Her face is flushed through a layer of thick, white concealer. She's silent just long enough to study my identity. "No, not you!" she shrieks. "Stay away from me!"

She hurtles backward, but the room is so tiny, she immediately falls onto the bed. Her hair-stubbled, salamander legs kick as she drops the pot handle and lunges for the bedside lamp.

"Stop," I whisper. "I'm not here to hurt you." I shut the door to prevent the clerk downstairs from overhearing.

Carrie is simultaneously wielding the brass lamp and desperately trying to unplug its cord from the wall. I race over and pull the lamp from her grip.

"Please, don't!" she screams, raising her arms, her wrists crossed above her face.

I drop the lamp on the bed and lift my hands.

"Carrie, I just want to talk. Didn't you want to talk to me? You asked Martis where I lived."

"Not to talk!" she wails. "To look for evidence! That's all! I didn't take anything!"

So Carrie is the one who stole the nine thousand in cash from my nightstand. She must have been waiting until the cabins were unoccupied. Louise said she saw a girl from the camp wandering in the nearby fields. My door was locked, but Louise leaves hers open, and I stopped latching the bolt between our rooms. I can't accuse Carrie of stealing it right now, because it would only protract her fit of screaming.

"Listen. We could help each other. I could be your friend."

"You're *his* friend," she moans. Tears fill her eyes, runny with black mascara like motor oil for a crying machine. Her picnic tablecloth-patterned shirt is twisted above her freckled ribs.

"You mean, Charlie's friend?" I ask.

"Uh-huh. Did he send you to finish the job?"

On a wooden drying rack that blocks the path to the bathroom hangs a patchwork of clothes, which Carrie must have washed in the sink. It's the T-shirt with New York written in a traffic jam of fonts that catches my attention. The room is otherwise empty, aside from a half-eaten box of biscuits on a table and a duffel bag at the foot of the bed. But at the bottom of a small, open closet I notice a cheap hotel safe. I have no doubt it holds my money.

"I *am* Charlie's friend, but he didn't send me. He's missing."

"Missing?" She lowers her arms and wipes her eyes. "What do you mean?"

"He's disappeared. He's been unreachable for a week."

Her sympathy is short-lived. "Good. He's a fucking asshole."

"Do you know him?"

"No," she wheezes.

"Then what evidence were you looking for in my room?"

"I said I didn't take—" The souvenir clerk is knocking and shouting in Greek from the hallway. Carrie stumbles to the door.

"It's okay, Mr. Pachis. I just broke something. Sorry to bother you."

"You pay for damage!" he demands. "Two is too many for room!" His footsteps disintegrate down the steps.

"Thanks a lot," she says sarcastically, eyeing me with snotty hatred. At least she had the courtesy not to turn me in. She can't be more than twenty underneath the mortuary makeup. The pimples on her chin and the childlike slouch of her shoulders radiate a girl who has not altogether lifted herself out of the snug New Jersey suburbs. She looks like an ideal candidate for Vic's brainwashing end-of-the-world camp, but she's hardly an impressive witness for Martis's case against the Konstantinous. I can see why he weighed his suspicions against Charlie and chose to let the investigation drift. Carrie Dorr versus any one of Rasym's lawyers would have been like tossing a mouse in a python cage—very cute right up to the moment it's swallowed whole.

Still, she's doing her best to look tough, with her hands on her hips and her mouth wrenched in a snarl. The tears are dripping onto her teeth.

"So, what do you want? Or do you enjoy breaking into women's rooms and scaring the shit out of them?" I don't mention that she broke into mine. "Because I'm already scared enough. This island is the worst place I've ever been. And you've done a great job of convincing me it's time to go home."

"I spoke with Martis. He told me you thought Charlie was behind the death of your friends, Dalia and Mikael."

"Because he threatened our lives," she squeals. "You were there. I saw you. Maybe he was worried I was on to him."

"On to him about what?"

"I mean, it's not a coincidence. I was supposed to be on that bike with Mikael. He was my . . ." Her lips begin to twitch. "That night the three of us were on the beach together, me, Dalia, and Mikael. We built a fire away from the camp. Dalia and I swapped shirts." She nods to the New York shirt on the drying rack. "That's my shirt from home, but Dalia borrowed it. She was obsessed with New York and hated wearing the stupid tourist crap that Vic was always pushing on everyone. Anyway, we traded back that night after she got off the ferry from Athens. She had on the orange shirt I was wearing at the dock! Your friend must have thought it was *me* on the bike. He probably ran them off the road and clubbed them to death while they were lying in the grass. And it would have been me if I hadn't fallen asleep. Why not kill both sisters? What is he, part of the Cypriot mafia?"

I have no idea what Carrie is rambling on about. *Both sisters?* How much can I attribute her belief that she's worth murdering to the narcissism of a twenty-year-old? Maybe if she and Mikael had trespassed and discovered the truth, there might be some merit to her story. But they had simply walked away.

"Did you find out about Charlie's boat company?" I ask her.

She stares at me puzzled. "No. What about it?"

"Carrie, why would Charlie want to kill you? I don't understand."

She picks up her duffel and tosses it on the bed. Unzipping the bag, she burrows through her scant belongings and hands me a crumpled postcard that was tucked in her passport.

On the front, a curved beach hugs smooth, turquoise waters. Only a white church in the distance and PATMOS emblazoned in maraschino red distinguishes it from any other airbrushed paradise.

"Read the back, idiot." Her eyes are wetter than they were before.

I flip the postcard over.

"My sister wrote that. She sent it to me before she died. Her name was Elise. She was here with her friend on vacation last month when the explosion went off. I got it a day after her funeral. Not that we had anything to bury."

I recall the two American tourists who were killed at Nikos while waiting to board a ferry. Every day there have been fresh flowers at the bombsite, which Carrie must be leaving for her sister.

I read the short note written in bubbly cursive.

"Did you get to the part about the extremely sketchy Cypriot dude with the expensive yacht?" she asks.

I did. I also got to the part about her friend f***ing him. Sonny was off in Paris, giving Charlie a window to pick up a pretty visitor, the safest prospect for an unmessy conquest; vacationers arrive with termination dates stamped on their foreheads. No wonder the bomb converted Charlie into a faithful man. The last girl he cheated with died in the blast, sitting right where he was supposed to be. I'm glad Sonny isn't here to read the postcard.

"She was my only sister," Carrie cries. "Those are her last words. The American embassy, the Greek government, that joke of a special task force of the Hellenic police, they all told us the bomb was a random act of terrorism set by some left-wing radicals. That's it, no deeper explanation, no justice, like we're just supposed to accept that and move on." She sits down on the corner of the bed, her hands braced on her knees. She blows out two sharp breaths. "Never mind the fact that no one claimed responsibility. Don't you find that weird? Who goes to the trouble of setting off a bomb and murdering people and doesn't take responsibility for it?"

Most murderers, I think. Most kill with the expectation that they won't be caught, let alone take bragging rights. It hits me as news so often does: What kind of new world is this, where the perpetrator is expected to claim their crime?

"My sister died as an empty symbol!" she shouts. "I'm sorry, but that makes no sense. I can't accept that. So I decided to come to Patmos and see for myself what was going on. I spent all my savings to get here. My parents didn't want me to come, but I had to. Elise deserves that. I wanted to be where she died. Even if it was just a stupid pilgrimage."

I stare down at her, trying for tenderness. "Just because Charlie is mentioned in the postcard doesn't mean he had anything to do with the bomb."

"He's all I had to go on," she says sniveling. "I asked around. He always went to that taverna, every morning at eleven. Why wasn't he there that day? Turns out he has a girlfriend who might not have been too happy to discover he was cheating on her."

"You really think he'd blow up a café full of people to keep your sister's friend from talking?"

"Don't make fun of me," she howls. "That's why I went to your cabin. I wanted to find proof. I knew you worked for him."

"I'm sorry," I say. "But bad things happen. Sometimes there's no explanation."

"Yeah, dickhead, I live on Earth too," she yells. "I'm aware of how life works. So it's just another coincidence that Elise is killed and then someone tries to do away with me after I'd been asking around the island about Charlie Konstantinou?" She shakes her head. "I told Martis about my sister. I told him that Dalia was wearing the shirt I had on. I showed him the postcard. It all leads back to your friend. I thought Martis believed me, but in the end he's just as bad as all the other police. All he gave me was a Kleenex and a hug." She glances piteously around the rented room the size of a penalty box. The only movement is the flutter of sheets from the air-conditioning unit in the wall. "I haven't been sleeping. I know I should just go home. I don't feel safe here. But what about Elise?"

She climbs to her feet and walks to the clothes rack. She folds the New York shirt and bunches it in her bag. "I tried," she mumbles to herself. "You're right. Bad things happen. People blow up. No answers. Maybe the refugees did kill Mikael and Dalia. What the fuck do I know?" She grabs an extra-large T-shirt off the rack, the novelty emblem on the front translating Greek alcoholic drinks into English. "This was Mikael's," she says. "He told me bad shit was going down. He promised he'd tell me what it was. He never got to. He was going to leave the camp. He was sick of it. I was hoping he'd come back to the States with me." She lifts the shirt to her nose.

"Why were you even part of Vic's group?"

She drops the shirt in her bag. "They're not bad people. Well, maybe they are, but they're nice enough when you get past all that garbage about Revelation and the kingdom awaiting them when this world dies. I think only half of them seriously believe that crap. The others just have nowhere else to go." She stares over at me as if I'm judging her. "They know the island. I figured they'd be able to shed some light. It wasn't like I was getting anywhere on my own. Plus, sleeping in their camp was free. I don't exactly have any money."

I give her a knowing look, but she ignores it.

"All I had to do was clap along at their prayer meetings and smoke a bunch of joints. Oh, and tell Vic I was lost and alone. Which I am. She gets into you, like, inside of you. Honestly, it felt good for a while, like the past and future could disappear, and you could just exist in this perfect, dirty now. If I didn't have my family waiting for me, I might have stayed. Underneath all of that worship of destruction, it did get near to love. Like a vibration that filled some hole." She carefully tucks the postcard in her passport. "And Vic hates Charlie. She considers him the Nero of greed. You'd think she would at least have humored me that he was behind the bomb."

"Did you tell Vic the real reason you're here?"

"Yeah," she hisses. "I finally did. That night with Mikael. I told her that Charlie threatened us at his port. She was so pissed, like I had betrayed the camp by not being a true believer. She said I was out of my mind. This woman who prays for the Apocalypse was telling *me* I was out of *my* mind." She jabs her finger against her chest. "She and Mikael screamed at each other. Vic's whole trip had gotten too much for him. That's when we left and met up with Dalia down the beach. I mean, I liked Vic, but, Christ, I wasn't going to devote my life to her. And Mikael was tired of being her drug mule."

The words catch in my ear, two little wasps with lethal stingers. I spin around, to where Carrie is trying to maneuver the clothes rack so that she can slip into the bathroom.

"Wait. What did you say? Drug mule?"

Now I'm the naïve one. Carrie purses her lips and rolls her eyes. "I don't want to get anyone in trouble. Never mind. It doesn't matter."

"It does matter. It's important."

"That's how Vic makes the money to keep the camp going. Look, I know it's awful, but I wasn't involved. She only lets the ones she really trusts go."

"Go where? What do you mean?"

"Heroin," she exclaims. "She has some supplier on Patmos. Maybe they bring it in at night on boats. I don't know. I tried not to know. All the party islands have drugs crawling all over them and plenty who will pay a fortune for it during the summer. If the camp didn't do it, someone else would. But don't you get the point of the tourist shirts? Vic would send her favorites out on the ferries dressed like typical backpackers, young, fresh-faced Americans and Europeans, because the police aren't going to think twice about naïve vacationers waving guidebooks with those embarrassing T-shirts on. Only their backpacks are crammed with packets. They even wrap them around their stomachs with cloth bandages. They deliver them to other islands and come right back on the ferry. Mikael told me they're always coming and going. They even reach the Ionian Islands on the other side of Greece through Athens. That's what Dalia was doing when she returned that night. Vic and her henchman, Noah, have it all worked out. She has a big, locked container in her tent filled with the stuff."

There's only one supplier on Patmos who matches that M.O. The police wouldn't think to search a bunch of green, young island-hoppers, any more than the coast guard would stop a yacht owned by a billionaire family. Charlie *is* Vic's secret collaborator. And the best way to hide an accomplice is to disguise her as an enemy.

"And Mikael was getting out?"

"Yeah," she whispers dejectedly. "That's what he told Vic that night. I wish he'd stayed at the camp. He was safer there." Her eyes are too red and worn from crying. She pinches a centimeter of space between her fingers. "I was this close to loving him. I thought maybe Elise had brought us together. Now I know how dumb that sounds because the opposite happened. Maybe, because he got mixed up with me, someone killed him. I don't want be the reason he died."

"Did you tell Inspector Martis about the drugs?"

She clenches her teeth. "No. Why would I? It doesn't have anything to do with my sister. Elise never touched drugs. I get it, they're bad. They're narcotics traffickers. You can spare me the guilt trip. They took me in. They were kind to me. Some of them are my friends. I might not have agreed with their mission, but I'm not going to rat them out and ruin the only community some of the weaker ones have found. I honestly think Vic sees what she's doing as the Lord's work, keep the evil flowing through the world, inject it right into the blood system of greedy, white Westerners, feed the addiction and watch the despair win. Yeah, it's super fucked-up. I'm not nominating her for a peace prize. But she does feed and shelter a bunch of kids whose families have given up on them." Carrie stamps her foot, as if to kick-start a broken conscience. "There *is* something good about that camp. You wouldn't understand from the outside. But it helped me. I stopped fighting. I'm not personally handcuffed to every misery that befalls the planet. Maybe misery is how the world runs."

She plunks back onto the bed, staring down at the triangle of space between her legs, as if it's the only real estate she owns.

"I know I need to let it go," she says. "Let Elise go. Accept her as gone. I spoke with Mikael's parents in Oslo. It was so spooky, the flatness of their voices, like they just accepted it, almost like they had been waiting for that kind of news and now they could live the rest of their lives no longer worrying about receiving that call. It's like Vic said, the worst news sets you free." She rubs her eye with her wrist. "I'm taking the ferry to Athens tomorrow. Ironically, it's the same ferry that Vic is using to send a huge shipment to the other side of Greece. At least I'll get to see some of my friends one last time."

A few minutes ago, Carrie tried to bash my head in with a coffeepot. Now I sit down next to her and put my arms around her to comfort her. Even if she did steal money from me, the world has stolen far more from her. Slowly she does the same to me. I know I won't remember this feeling later, time will warp and distort it or dump a landfill of other memories on top of it, but in the moment, hugging a near stranger, I'm swept up in its delicate warmth.

"I'm sorry about your sister."

"They say she wouldn't have felt it. I hope so. If those are her last words, at least she was happy. At least she died looking out at the sea."

When I walk to the door, I notice a plastic Ziploc bag on the table next to the box of biscuits. Although it doesn't hold any cash, I know it's my bag because the yellow bank bands are stuffed inside like snapped hospital bracelets. I'm going to let Carrie keep the nine thousand. But I can't resist pulling out my wallet.

"Do you want me to pay for the coffeepot?"

"No," she says, wiping her nose. "I will. It's my fault. I have enough to get home." She's like an awkward teenager trying to coax an expression that matches the weather in her head. It takes a minute, but finally her lips release the short, crooked line. "Thanks for listening. I hope you find your friend."

I PARK MY bike on the side of the road as the late afternoon sun tilts the island's shadows toward the east. I'm a few feet from a cliff's edge.

Musk thistle and flowering weeds are harassed by black mosquitoes. Far below, bodies are stretched out on towels, the day's last sun worshippers with their tans blurring into the pebbles. Two yachts drift in the cove of blue. On the back of the larger one with a green flag, a Saudi family dances. The teenage daughters are testing their seduction moves, rubbing their long hair in their own faces to arouse each other or some imaginary future admirer, while their chubby mother snaps her fingers in an energy-efficient version of a polka. At home, they can't dance like this out in the open, but here on the water they are free. On the other side of the road, stone walls crisscross through fawn-brown fields, and sheep huddle in the shadow of a tree. A man turns his head, sitting among his sheep. I unlock the seat compartment and remove the black-leather log. I turn to the first page and tap the number into my phone.

Four rings. Then five. But before the sixth, the texture of the static changes, and I hear a voice on the line.

"Ela? Hello?"

"Hi, Gideon. It's Ian."

There's a short, reluctant pause followed by an irritated sigh.

"What do you want?"

"Where are you?"

"Not where you are, mate." I get the sense he's purposely modifying his accent, sampling a range of possible new identities. He sounds less weasely as an Australian. "Halfway to Crete, if you need to know. How about not looking for me?"

"You heard about Stefan, then?"

Another pause. I imagine his stub finger prone over the disconnect button.

"Don't even try to pin that on me. I had nothing to do with it. But I know when my run is over. I hitched a ride on the boat of a new friend, an older Scottish lady. She's the widow of a Greek shipping magnate. Full staff and everything. Warhol did her portrait. I'm looking at the painting right now. The Warhol's on the boat!"

"Congratulations." Some people should come with a warning label.

"That Stefan situation is seriously messed up. He committed suicide, right?" A jolt of fear quickens his words. "So even if they look through his e-mails and find something I wrote him, it doesn't matter, right? He took his own life. I'm not responsible! Look, tell Charlie or his family or whoever that I don't want anything to do with them. All is forgiven. *Ma'a salama.* Send them my sympathies. Actually, you'd better not. Don't say you talked to me. How the hell did you get my number?"

"I found it."

"Un-find it. If you call me again I'm going to chuck this phone in the Med." I had hoped Gideon would be more hospitable due to the fact that I'm partially responsible for the continued multitasking of his penis.

"Just one question and then I won't bother you anymore."

"All right. Be quick."

"You were at Nikos the morning the bomb went off."

"Is that a question?" he snaps. "Yeah. I was fucking there. You know what saved me? Smoking. Don't let anyone tell you it's a killer. If I hadn't run out of cigarettes and walked over to the tobacco stand, I would have been one of the casualties. Disgusting how they targeted the nicest taverna on the richest island. Of course they did. And what did it matter in the end? Did you read the papers? Greece made a deal. They're staying in the Eurozone. All those dead tourists for nothing. As usual, politicians make a joke of our lives."

"Why were you there?" I ask. "To meet Charlie? That was his spot."

"Well, he had just fired me. As you know, I wanted my job back, and he wouldn't talk to me. I'd made a bunch of dumb threats I didn't mean. I told you the corner I was in. So I had someone arrange a meeting. I didn't speak with Charlie myself. Anyway, what difference does it make now?"

"Gideon, who arranged the meeting?"

He goes silent, and I hear a lilting Scottish voice in the background demanding a game of backgammon. The voice fades—*play me, play me.* Gideon must be moving to a more private area on deck.

"Was it Vic?" I ask. "You can stop the charade. I know she and Charlie have been working together."

He laughs. "God damn, how did you figure that one out? Impressive. I underestimated you, Ian. Even Ugur didn't know. Best to keep the network as buried as possible. That way one hand can't slap the other. Two enemies, no connections. It was civil in its hostility. Yeah, I asked Vic to talk to Charlie for me. She and I always had an understanding. She told me to meet him at Nikos that morning. Of course, I was suspicious about the timing of the bomb, but when I confronted Vic afterward, she admitted that the meeting wasn't nearly as arranged as she let on. Charlie refused to see me—that's why he wasn't there that morning. He said I had to go home. Vic offered to let me stay at her camp, but that whole hippie death-wish thing isn't my scene, even if they do have a steady supply. It's a good thing Charlie didn't show up. I swear, he's a wizard at dodging bullets. It's all win win for him, isn't it? Look at him now."

"How do you mean?"

"With Stefan out of the picture, he stands to inherit, *what*, a billion dollars. There's no need to bother with the Charters outfit anymore. Sucks for you to come all this way for nothing." I hear the tick of a spark wheel, the hard suck, and the long exhale. "Honestly, I'm better off. In a way, he did me a favor by firing me. That stuff was plowing me under. You thought he canned me for stealing money, but it wasn't that. I'm clean now."

"Eventually, you have to choose a better way of living."

He laughs again, like I've told a good joke. "Nice talking to you. Maybe I'll see you at a Buckland reunion. Maybe when we're seventy. We can sit on the gym bleachers and cry. I often wonder what happened to—" The call drops. It's just as well. I didn't want to go back to the place he was visiting.

I toss the leather book in the compartment, climb back on the bike, and head north toward the cabins. Maybe Charlie didn't know what Vic was planning. Maybe one hand can cock the gun while the other is typing a text message, wiping sleep from the eyes, or opening imperial doors and reaching for a pouch of tobacco. If Vic understands anything, it's the horror of the hour. Take out one potential threat to her camp's survival by detonating a terrorist bomb; remove two others in the manner of a bike accident, but leave a few stray items at the scene to implicate fleeing refugees. I have no proof of her involvement, but I'm certain her henchman, Noah, or a few of her most devoted executed her holy orders. The messier the better. Her world needs more nightmares. Otherwise, who would bother to believe?

Yet, like all seemingly random acts of violence, what it offers in atrocity, it lacks in aim.

BY THE TIME I return home, the skies are different colors. The eastern sky has already darkened to blue, the western sky is sprawling with translucent-yellow spirals. I carry the tote bag of money up the cabin steps. Inside, through the open connecting door, I hear the shower running and Louise sing-humming a country song. A half-full bottle of vodka sits on the outdoor counter. I want a drink, the mind's teat-seeking fingers already wrapped around the bottle. But I decide, for the foreseeable future, I'm going to let the anxiety and self-doubt have their way with me. Who knows, if Charlie hadn't gone missing and I'd become his number two, I might have ended up like Gideon, sampling the merchandise.

Across the front of a large manila envelope I bought at the stationery store in Skala, I write Alexis Bledsoe's name and address on Central Park West. I count out nine thousand euros from the bag and stuff it inside the envelope (the remainder in conversion to dollars should more than cover two weeks of interest). I print my name in the upper corner. Tomorrow morning I'll send it by certified mail. Maybe it will reach New York on the same day that Louise touches down in Washington. Back to her life of law school and quiet, cough-averse libraries congested with graduate students memorizing legal precedents to restrict freedom in order to secure it. And back to her brother Luke not smoking meth and to the tall, bearded guy in the cowboy shirt worthy of a digital heart.

How can the future be foreseeable when the present is as fuzzy as the sun seen through shut eyelids?

Quietly, I step through the doorway of our connecting cabins. In all of my days on Patmos, I haven't once ventured into Louise's room. She always came into mine and retreated here every night to sleep. Her bed is smaller. A circle of light glows on her nightstand from a nickel-plated lamp that wasn't smuggled in from Israel inside Sonny's suitcase. There's a rattan chair under the window and a flat-screen television on which a pair of damp jeans hang. The air smells of lilac perfume and sugary chewing gum. Country music is for people who can't sing, and Louise can't sing really well. Her scrubbing shadow bleeds across the bathroom wall.

Two suitcases rest on the floor by the bed, and her phone snakes between them on its charging cord. The phone is a half-full bottle of vodka; it wants me to drink its contents. The man who merited the heart emoji could be Luke. I could go on believing that, and we could have dinner tonight on the beach and sex afterward before we sleep in separate beds, and I could see her down to the ferry on her last day of vacation, and we could say things to each other about staying in touch, and I could remember her for months after she's gone, strolling the edges of the Ganges one day, still wondering how our lives might intersect.

I press the power button on her phone. I hate myself for invading her privacy, but my hatred does not extend to my fingers.

The most recent text is to Sonny, the one before that to an unidentified number in Greece, and the third to a man named Grant. I click on Grant's name and read in reverse order.

DON'T WORRY. BE HOME IN NO TIME. MORE TOMORROW.

BE CAREFUL. PLEASE!

I HAVEN'T REALLY HAD THE TIME TO GIVE ANYTHING A THOUGHT. ESPECIALLY COHABITATION. YOU WOULDN'T BELIEVE THE SHIT HERE.

BUT IT'S ALMOST COME TO NOTHING. I WANT TO NAIL THE FUCKER BEFORE HE GETS AWAY WITH IT. SEEMS LIKE HE WILL.

HA. HA. JUST GET BACK HERE. I HOPE YOU'VE GIVEN SOME THOUGHT TO MOVING IN. GREAT 1BR IN ADAMS MORGAN, SEPT 1.

I BET I KNOW WHERE IT HURTS.

SURE THING, BABE. I'LL BRING BALLOONS TO THE GATE. MISSING YOU SO MUCH IT HURTS.

I CAN'T WAIT TO SEE YOU. WILL YOU PICK ME UP FROM THE AIRPORT?

My fingers are trembling. I click on the unidentified Greek number. There are no responses from the recipient, only Louise's green message bubbles forming a list of names and photo attachments. There's the photo of Charlie and me on the night he went missing, his face turned away at the table in Skala and mine staring warmly at the lens. Farther up, backward in time, I find a still life of a business card, BENCE ARPAD, INVESTOR with a note "call him, mentioned buying into KC at dinner in Chora tonight." I thumb through the series of pictures Louise took of the charter port on the afternoon we went sailing—the Greek boys scouring the hull, multiple angles of the open hangar, *Domitian* floating at the dock with Christos on deck. I scroll up the screen and land on the shot from the day I arrived. Charlie and I stand side by side on the balcony in the crystal-bright sun, our heads tilted together to form a steeple, our grins broad and contagious, two outlaws who escaped into paradise. "Ian Bledsoe on left, Google Panama."

"Did you find what you're looking for?"

Louise stands at the door to the bathroom. She's wearing her Hard Rock Café T-shirt and a pair of white underwear. Her hair falls in wet tangles across her cheeks. Every person with a phone is a spy, but Louise is a double operative. I never should have left my door unbolted. Not for a night or a minute.

"Yeah, unfortunately I did."

She walks over, squats down, and pulls the phone by its cord from my hands. My first instinct is to hit her, and I bundle my fist on the mattress.

"How much did you read?" she asks matter-of-factly. A drip of water runs down her forehead, and she wipes it away before it nears her eye.

"I don't know. How much information on Charlie have you been supplying *to nail the fucker*? I read enough. Ian Bledsoe on left, Google Panama."

"Ian." She reaches for my hand, but I keep it balled in a fist. "It doesn't make any difference now."

The feeling is like an ice shelf breaking off into the ocean, the weird serenity of a fast and irreversible end. Louise was never anything more than the girl in the computer room of Stearns Hall, draining water from her ear. I'm mourning a person who never existed, and my hope for that person's spontaneous return only makes the mourning more humiliating.

"You are an awful human being." I want my voice to sound cold and remote, but it doesn't.

"No. Charlie is the awful human being. He's the one smuggling drugs while taking advantage of a humanitarian crisis. I can forgive the petty dealer who doesn't have a choice. But I can't forgive Charlie. I'm sorry. I can't."

"Is Sonny aware that you're narc-ing on her husband?"

Her expression doesn't crack, not even a flinch. It might hurt one degree less if Louise were crying. Her face is a steady, deliberate blank, as if she's being compared to her passport photo.

"I care about Sonny. I care about you too, very much. But—"

"But what?"

She accepts the dare, raising her chin. "But some principles are more important than friendship."

"Would my arrest for drug trafficking have been worth your principles? Fuck you, Louise." She reaches for my hand again but decides against it, coiling her fingers at her chest. All the days and nights we were alone, Louise kept asking about the nature of Charlie's business, prodding me with alcohol and sex for any information that could be used against him. It was Charlie, all along, who interested her. "Is cheating on Grant worth your principles? Jesus, what exactly are your principles? You could have at least told me you have a boyfriend back in D.C."

"Grant's a friend," she corrects.

"And we've learned how much you value your friends."

She squeezes her lips together and then releases them. "He's someone I'm seeing, that's all. I didn't make him any promises. I didn't make you any, either. Grant has nothing to do with you and me." Louise is more like Charlie than she realizes. They don't seem to view the people they ensnare as inhabitants of the same planet. Each collision is a separate incident.

"So this is why you came to Europe. How hard did you have to work to become Sonny's friend in Paris?"

"It wasn't like that," she says, shaking her head. "Will you let me explain? I didn't ask to be put in this position. A few days after I got to Patmos, a man approached me. He saw me with Charlie, and he did his research. He found out I was in law school at Georgetown. He's an agent with the DEA who caught wind of Charlie's operation. Just so you know, I didn't rat anyone out. Charlie was already being investigated."

"That's one weight off your conscience."

"Please, listen. I was only trying—"

"What's a DEA agent even doing on this side of the world? Greece isn't Mexico."

Louise nods, as if thankful for the change in subject. It's much easier for us to discuss politics than what we've done to each other.

"It's because of the whole mess with the Eurozone and the fact that Greece is too broke to patrol its own coast. The U.S. government stepped in to interdict criminal contraband. That war in Syria isn't an isolated massacre. It also disrupted the usual narcotics flow from the Middle East to Europe by land. Borders tightened. Just like with the refugees, new routes had to be improvised across the water. That's where your best friend stepped in with his fleet of flailing vacation yachts. He took advantage, Ian. And he was smart. The agent was having trouble gathering information on exactly how Charlie was managing it. He's restricted on how much he can do on foreign soil."

Louise speaks like she's defending her dissertation. I want to shake the cold integrity right out of her, but touching is no longer an option for us. She already has someone in Washington to touch. It's that betrayal over all the others that revives my hatred for her. I remember her yesterday, ahead of me on a footpath in Chora, knocking on the door of a strange house, back when I still thought we belonged together.

"The Chicago pedophile," I say. "He's your agent."

"Yeah, the pedophile," she confirms. It's a brilliant cover. Who would get close enough to him to learn the truth?

"I thought you said you didn't want to do anything criminal with your degree. What happened to staying far away from tragedies? Have you said anything sincere since day one? I hope you're getting paid a lot to inform on your friends."

For the first time, her face is pierced by something human, the rancid aftertaste of genuine hurt. It's not the accusation of cheating that breaks her composure but the suggestion that she has a price.

"I'm getting paid nothing," she snaps. "Once the agent explained to me what Charlie's been doing, it wasn't hard to convince me to help. I told you about my brother and what drugs did to him. *That* was sincere. What about all the lives destroyed by the junk Charlie's smuggling from Turkey? You think I'd just sit by and say, *sorry, I'm on vacation, ask someone else.* It was my duty to do what I could. Yes, I felt guilty. But that's worth more to me than Sonny or—" She pauses and I don't think she'll say it. "Or you."

"I'm glad you're finally being honest."

She exhales a pained breath and sinks against the wall. "What was I supposed to think? My god, your history is all over the Internet. You were practically in league with drug cartels. You show up as his new manager, and it all makes perfect sense." An hour ago, I would have rushed to convince her that I'm better than the searches of my name. But I no longer owe Louise an explanation. I don't have to sanitize my mistakes.

"All I said I'd do is keep my eyes open. That's all. If I came across anything that implicated Charlie, I promised to pass it along. I wasn't investigating. And I warned you not to take that job. I did everything I could to convince you not to join Charlie's company. I hope you remember that."

Her brown eyes lock on mine, two trowels digging into loose dirt.

"And you came across me."

She tosses her head back, knocking it against the wall. "I was hoping you would tell me what you knew so I could put an end to it before you got in any deeper. That's all!" *That's all,* she keeps repeating, just one more step, one more ugly little action and nothing further. But both sides are infinitely greedy. Virtue will take as much from you as it can. "I don't blame you for hating me. I'd probably hate me too."

"Probably?"

"Yeah, I'd hate me, all right? But I care about you no matter what you think." Her forehead creases, and her lips begin to fray at their seams. "Our time together meant a lot to me—"

"Stop!"

"—and there's good in you, I know that. There's still that guy from college who dreamed of doing good. Do you really want Charlie to win no matter what the price is? Beyond all the money and summers he can throw at you?" She shakes her head so certainly, as if goodness is a blood type. "I don't care if you were best friends as kids. That's not you, Ian. It just isn't. You tell me if a man came to you to help stop so much misery that you'd turn your back and enjoy the beach and nights up in Chora, eating out of Charlie's hand? You wouldn't. I know you wouldn't. You're not like that. I've seen you up close. You're one of the good."

Louise has my address. She's found the right street and the right house. But I've already moved. It's a stranger who opens the door.

"I'm not that good anymore," I say simply. "I'm really not. You haven't seen me at all."

"Bullshit. Even if you did accept a bag of cash from Charlie when you got here, I can't believe you knew the full extent of it."

Louise must have gone through my room. If I hadn't kept my phone on me, she probably would have read my e-mails.

"Charlie didn't give me that money. It was mine."

She shakes her head furiously, as if her thoughts have gotten stuck. "What? Who travels with a bag of money like that? What did you do, knock over a cash machine on your way to Patmos?"

"I took it from my father. It was all I could get."

"All you could get?" There's doubt in her voice, sweet vicious doubt. Maybe her memory is homing in on the vague question I asked the day we visited the cave, about the legality of stealing money after a relative dies. I decide to be clearer. Right now I hate Louise most for her childish universe of absolute right and wrong. I want to destroy that universe inside of her where Ian Bledsoe lives under the permanent status of "good." I'm going to annihilate him for her and I want her to suffer every second of his loss. I want us both to walk out of this room violated.

"I stole it after he died."

She flattens her hand on the floor. "I'm sure you had your reasons."

"Right after he died, I went straight to the bank. I didn't withdraw more because I was worried I'd be caught. I didn't go to his funeral, either. I just skipped town."

"Before you arrived, Charlie told us your father was too hard on you. He said he never supported you, that he was always putting you down."

"I watched him die." I don't even recognize the voice coming out of me as my own. I'm smiling, though, the way a gazelle seems to be smiling when its neck is being drained in a predator's mouth— and maybe the gazelle is smiling, *this is finally over, I'm out of this constant hell of fear and running.* It's hard work to destroy Ian Bledsoe, but I'm committed. "I sat there alone with him in his room. He'd already had two strokes and could barely move. I was right by his bed."

"Okay, enough." Louise climbs to her knees.

"He made this sound, like an extended gasp, and his hand fluttered up. More like swatted up, really, like he was trying to keep something away. But I'm pretty sure he was signaling for me to get the nurse."

Louise's mouth cringes. She doesn't know what to do with her hands except to hold them out for balance as she stands.

"Fifteen seconds of that sound and that swatting, maybe twenty."

"I get it. You can stop."

"I hated him so much for how he treated me and what a useless, piece-of-shit son I was to him. It hit me that it would be easier if he died. The money I thought would come to me, yes, but it was so much more than that, not what I was getting but what I was losing. Pain. He went so fast, and I sat right through it."

"All right! I don't want to hear it!"

"I couldn't move, or I didn't. In the end, there wouldn't have been time to get the nurse. But his eyes were open, and he was alert. He must have realized in those last seconds that his son wasn't moving a muscle, wasn't running for help or even trying to say good-bye. He hated every single move I made in my life. So for once, I just sat there and let it happen."

I'm not even aware that I'm crying until I taste the runoff. Louise doesn't try to comfort me. She stands at a safe distance from the bed, her face turned away.

"You said there wasn't time to get the nurse. You couldn't have done anything. Twenty seconds isn't very long." Her universe is more durable than I expected. It won't exterminate its good creatures easily. "You were in shock!"

"No. I wasn't. I knew exactly what I was doing. And twenty seconds is a long time to watch someone die. His eyes were pleading. He looked right at me. He was scared."

"I don't believe you. You're remembering wrong. You're grieving and you're—"

I'm no longer listening. Whatever is coming out of me needs to spread before I can pull it back. I wrestle my phone from my pocket and find Lex's e-mail.

I took the money. I'm sending it back to you. Do what you want about filing charges.

"What are you doing?" Louise shouts.

But I'll answer your question. Yes, I saw him take his last breath. Yes, it's my fault. I didn't say a word to him even though there was time, no last mention of you or Ross or Lily or me. I just sat there instead of calling the nurse and let him go.

"Ian, don't write anything when you're this upset," Louise orders. "Seriously, do not press SEND. You're not in your right mind."

I will be exactly what you want me to be, your evil, poisonous, destructive, selfish brother. That's my parting gift to you. Someone to blame. Good-bye Lex.

My thumb jerks to the SEND button, where it will slip from guilty hands into the electronic bloodstream, and the virus will be permanent and terminal. Technology offers new ways to kill yourself.

Before my thumb touches the button, I feel a blinding punch against my cheek. As I reel back, Louise wrenches the phone from my grip. She glances down at the screen and then at me.

"Give me back my phone!"

She's a flash of black shirt and white underwear disappearing through the connecting door. I'm close behind her, but she gets to the sliding door and shoves it open. Out in the hot night, chalky with stars, she sprints to the edge of the patio and lifts the phone high. As

I swing for it, she uses all of her strength to slam it down. The screen shatters, and pieces streak across the stone.

"There," she yells, as if she's fixed it. I'm gawking at her, fear and hate so out-of-breath I've passed over into astonishment. "I had to," she says harshly. "You needed someone to look out for you."

Is there any worse feeling than the world not ending right when you accepted that it would? I threw parts of myself into that hope for a quick conclusion that I'm certain I will never regain. I feel dizzy and sit down on the wall. Louise uses her foot to sweep some of the glass into a pile and she sits too, a few feet away. The night is too humid for touching, although the urge is still there. I wish we could go back to that first afternoon on Charlie's balcony, four nearly young bodies that had not yet deceived or disappeared or had to keep their eyes open. But I'd have to go back even further to undo all the errors to make that moment complete. The glitches were already in place.

"Thank you," I whisper.

"It's okay."

"No, it isn't."

Goat bells ring in the darkness.

"Do you want me to stay with you tonight?" she asks. I can't tell if she means under the same roof or in the same bed. "Just to be sure you're okay?"

I shake my head.

She wipes her eyes. "I'll get my bags and find a hotel. My ferry is the day after tomorrow. I won't—" She pauses. "I'm not going to say good-bye. Not to Sonny or anyone. I'll e-mail her when I'm back in the States and try to explain." Her hands are shaking.

"You're quitting your mission?"

I can feel her watching me, but I continue to stare down at my shoes, pretending to find some fascination in them.

"Charlie's gone," she says. "I thought maybe he was just avoiding everyone, but the fact that he hasn't come back even when his brother died makes it pretty clear he's fled. Who knows, maybe he found out that there was an agent onto him. Maybe he realized what I was up to. The dock is closed. The boats aren't running. The agent still hopes he'll turn up, but if he doesn't, there's nothing left to catch. If it's my fault, I'm sorry. He's gone." Perhaps Louise is hoping I'll provide some last-minute information that will verify the good in me. Or perhaps she's right and all along it was Louise that caused him to run. It doesn't matter now. I'm going to hold her to her promise of no good-bye.

She gets to her feet and walks to the sliding door. I sense her standing at it, but when I finally look up it's just the reflection of white moonlight on the glass. It could have been five minutes. Or ten. Or a few seconds acting like hours. But eventually a car weaves up the hillside, and one of the island's silver taxis lurches onto the driveway.

Louise carries her suitcases down the stairs, and the driver pops the trunk. However long she waited for her taxi in the darkness of the cabins, it gave me time to inventory all the reasons why I hate her and the one thing she did to save my life. I dart through my bedroom and down the steps. I'm almost too late. Louise is climbing into the backseat, half her hair beaten around by the car's blasting air-con.

"Louise," I call.

She turns to look at me, a different woman from each angle, all of them somber, none of them less sure of themselves.

"Before you go, I do know something. It isn't Charlie. But you and the pedophile can stop a shipment from going out."

Every morning in August the boat guides line the port of Skala. Older white-haired islanders with charbroiled skin linger along the quay, the chalkboards next to them promoting FULL-DAY TOUR WITH SUNBATH, SNORKEL, PATMOS COAST AND SWIM COVES, FRESH FISH LUNCH €50. The captains' shirt collars are flipped up to protect their necks from the sun, which lends them a hustler's coolness, and for all their claps and whistles of encouragement, they never muster direct eye contact. They remind me of the tuxedo-ed maître d's on the last, dying blocks of Little Italy, grabbing tourists by the shoulder and pulling them toward their doomed establishments. "Everything you are looking for! All you want!" As with the restaurants in Little Italy, each vessel is nearly identical: a steel guardrail surrounds a floating clothes iron draped in antique lifesavers and fleshy buoys. Gangplanks connect the boats to the port like a row of World War II field stretchers. Cash only. Time of your life.

It is 9:45 A.M. and the ferry to Athens doesn't arrive until eleven. I have no desire to witness the outcome of the tip I gave Louise last night. Maybe the agents are already in place, crouched behind the blooming bougainvillea and desiccated palms, awaiting the hippies with their tourist T-shirts and bloated backpacks and round-trip tickets tucked into their guidebooks. Carrie won't be whiling away the eight-hour ferry ride with her friends, after all. She'll also probably never learn that Vic was responsible for her sister's death.

I scan the excursion boats. One is already packed with crouton-colored Americans stuffed in red life vests. Another holds a clutch of screaming toddlers and their indifferent, zinc-nosed parents. Farther down, I notice a smaller craft with three young tourists slumped under the deck's nylon shade. A pair of thin Eastern European grandparents smokes in synchronicity at the bow.

"What time are you leaving?" I ask the captain, whose sunglasses are affixed around his enormous ears by a purple cord.

"Ten," he shouts.

"And when do you return?"

"Four."

I hand him the money. I won't be back on solid ground until the raid is over. But at least some justice will be served today. The good Ian Bledsoe—he's hard to kill. This morning I mailed the manila envelope International First Class to Lex in New York.

I walk the rickety plank and sit on one of the wooden storage compartments that doubles as a bench. The boat's name is *Tadita*, and it has none of the comforts and amenities of *Domitian*. When the captain removes a trapdoor to punch the engine switch and pour oil over the gears like salad dressing, a black heifer of smoke heaves around the guardrails. The motor sets the entire deck jittering, and I use my towel as a seat cushion to soak up some of the vibration. A heavyset Italian family makes a last-minute assault on *Tadita*, extinguishing my prayers for legroom. They squeeze sun lotion over themselves with ejaculatory fervor. The captain unwinds the ropes, offers the grim smile of a prison guard, and passes out plastic bags.

"What's this for?" I ask him.

"Protect your phone."

I wad up the bag. It's another favor Louise did me. Break all contact with the whistling beast. Smash the antenna you've voluntarily stuck in your pocket. I should have destroyed it a long time ago.

When it's clear there aren't any other latecomers joining us, we cast off into the harbor.

Perfect blue. Miles of it in every direction, the sea and sky traveling in adjacent lanes. We motor north along the island, and our Patmian captain refuses to cede to the oligarchs and plutocrats of sleek yachts as sharp and shiny as carving knives. Their crewmen yell at him with maraca-ing arms, but he shrugs them off and keeps *Tadita* swerving along in its phantom path. A white wake trails behind us like feet kicking under a sheet. The captain points out the basalt formations rising along the cliffs, the lunar shrines, and the huddled village of Kampos. We pass Goat Island and the pebble beach where Charlie's boat once moored. I spot the peach taverna halfway up the hillside. We sail on.

The three youths laze under *Tadita*'s deck shade, a guy and two girls in their early twenties, dark-haired and dark-eyed with their swimsuits loose around their skinny waists. One of the girls is holding a strand of her brown hair up against the sun, mesmerized by it. The other girl might be her twin sister with the same slender nose and overly spaced teeth. The guy keeps staring at me in that curious way that could either be sexual attraction or an urge to inflict violence. He pulls his flip-flops off his feet and ventures a question.

"Where do you come from?"

I smile. "America."

"Told you," he says with a nudge to his companions. "New York?"

"Michigan."

He's momentarily disappointed.

"What about you?" I ask.

"Spain," the girl who isn't absorbed in her hair answers. "I'm Branca. That's Andres. And here"—she pats her twin gently—"is Julia."

"Are you two sisters?"

Branca slaps her stomach and laughs, indicating that they aren't.

They tell me they've been traveling the islands for the past two weeks, crashing in hostels and sleeping on ferry decks. *Me too*, I say. Yesterday they splurged on a hotel in Skala. I tell them I just arrived and haven't yet found a place.

"All alone?" Andres asks.

"Yep." Not the entire truth, a few scattered lies, but enough of the truth that I believe what I am saying. Right now, off the island and the grid, I feel released, a free-floating human who could spend nights in cramped hostels and wash up in unexpected beds. Their faces hold the griminess of infrequent showers. My face, I decide, is too clean. Maybe it's the American in me, but I'm struck with the sense that I'm never too damaged to start over: life with unlimited free refills.

Julia lurches to the side of the boat, her head dangling over the guardrail.

"Is she seasick?" I ask.

Branca shoots her foot onto my leg, wiggling her dirty toes on my thigh.

"No, she took a half-tab of acid this morning. We told her not to. But she wanted to experience the Apocalypse."

"We got it in Mykonos," Andres brags. "Very weak."

Branca laughs. "Weak, yeah? Do you miss the donkey you asked to marry you?"

Andres blushes and casts his eyes on the view.

We reach Patmos's northern point and dip south, flying down the seahorse spine of the island. The western beaches are more barren, the pebbles larger and the waves more vicious. Rambling shacks built along the sea have none of the elegance of Choran mansions. Our captain steers us into an empty turquoise cove, where the cliffs fall straight into dappled water. The sound of our motor echoes against the rocks. He drops anchor. The Italian family uses their beach towels as private dressing rooms, shimmying off their shorts and underwear and yanking on their swimsuits.

I lose my new Spanish friends in the melee of swimming preparations. I ask the captain what time it is. Eleven-thirty. Vic's backpackers have already been escorted off the ferry, their bags stripped from their shoulders, the elastic gutted from their stomachs. They're probably hunkered in the station's inner courtyard, praying to god or to Vic or to the leniency of Greek trafficking laws or to the empty square of blue above them. I try to go as deep into the sea as I can, down past the moment where my ears ache with pressure and all my eyes process is cold, velvet blackness. Above me, the Eastern European grandparents bob in the nude.

I surface and paddle to the front of the boat. On the other side, Branca, Andres, and Julia tread in a fluid circle. They are speaking in Spanish.

"I find him cute," Branca says.

"Yes, I do too," Andres admits. "But an American."

"We should love everyone, even Americans," Julia offers.

Andres splashes water at her. "You said they were only good for buying drinks."

"I like his red hair," she replies.

Branca spots me and lifts her hand.

"Having fun?" she asks in English.

"Such nice water," I answer in my most earnest midwestern accent.

On board, the captain slices precooked sea bream wrapped in aluminum foil. We spray lemon on their silver bodies and pick through their bones with plastic forks. I want to ask the captain if he knows the Konstantinous or the Stamatis family, who looks after them, but those questions would blow my cover. I'm enjoying the company of the Spaniards too much, eating together under the awning, listening to them bicker about which island they'll hit next. They're not as beautiful as Charlie's group, no Sonnys or Adrians among them. Julia's back is flecked with faint purple acne splotches. Branca's shoulders and hips are rounded. Andres's tiny rib cage doesn't flex with playground speed bumps. Maybe that's why I feel so at ease among them. We roar past the backside of Skala and continue south, sleepy on gas fumes and the rocking current. When Andres fetches sodas from the cooler, Branca nudges me with her hip.

"I think Andres likes you," she says. I can tell she's trying to assess my proclivities.

"He seems like a really sweet guy," I reply evasively. I can't help it. It feels limiting and unadventurous for the new Ian Bledsoe to winnow his options. Julia informs us she's coming down, that her brain almost exploded ten minutes ago and none of us noticed.

A black oil spill looms ahead in the sea. *Tadita* motors toward it, and we all gather along the guardrail for a glimpse. It's not an oil slick but a deflated rubber raft, warped and grooved like a giant record. The captain wields a long wooden pole, latching onto it and pulling it against the hull. Andres and I do our best to help him lift it from the water, but the raft is heavy and slippery, and ultimately it drifts beyond our reach.

"They could have made it!" Julia hopes aloud. Everyone turns to the coastline, searching the rocks for happy endings.

I fall asleep, secluded in the haze of Branca's patchouli smell. When I awake, we're near the southland tip. A ribbon of sand flattens at the edge of a harbor, real sand, Caribbean smooth, with Frisbees and volleyballs sailing across it.

"Psili Ammos Beach," the captain proclaims. "Soon we will have one last swim before the end." We head north, passing more populated shores. I stand watch, my fingers gripping the guardrail.

"What are you looking for?" Andres asks. He's loitering shyly next to me with his shirt on and his arms bundled under it for warmth.

"I'm just taking it all in."

The Charters port rockets by, the hangar and trailer vacant. Not long after is the white blast of Grikos village. I see *Domitian* moored in the marina. We follow the thread of pebble beach and then it comes into view: black entrails of a doused bonfire collected among the rocks. Red, green, gold—the hippie tents are punctured and flattened like jellyfish. Bibles, shoes, broken instruments, and sleeping bags are strewn along the beach. Vic's caravan tent is just a skeleton of metal poles, the flag of crossed trumpets still snapping at its mast. The plastic bins are upturned and the pillows shredded. The large black container from her tent has been pried open and left on its side. A pregnant woman is crying on her knees by the water. The mutts are barking around her. She's weeping into her hands, the last remaining member of Camp Revelation, left behind in the clutter of no one's salvation.

"What was that?" Branca bellows. "Crazy party or something?"

I shrug and sit down in the shade.

On our last swim, we stick together, letting the tide ripple through us. The Italian family is too tired to go in. The grandparents are filming underwater. Branca and Julia hold hands, and when the waves bump me against Julia's leg, she reaches out and guides me next to her. Andres grabs onto my arm, and for a few minutes we hover in a four-pointed star, our undersides syrupy cold and our backs baking like asphalt. It took so little for me to be invited. And I don't care now if Charlie is ever found—let him stay running, let him be that figure ahead of me in a crowd, someone I think I know, who escaped before he was caught, who made terrible decisions and realized the light wasn't going to shine forever. Louise is right. He is gone.

After the boat returns to Skala, Branca and Andres trade glances as we disembark.

"Hey, Ian, do you want to come to our hotel room?" Andres says coolly, but the sunburn on his face is intensifying from the inside out. "We have beer. We could make a party and play some music."

"I'd love to," I respond.

"And if you don't have a room for the night," Branca mumbles, "we have two beds we could push together. It's hard to find a place here in high summer."

"That sounds great. Thank you." I'm so high on what's to come and the love I feel for them at this moment, I barely recognize Therese tearing down the cobblestones on a motorbike. Her cheeks are slicked with tears, and her hair is a tangled steel sponge. I've only been off Patmos for six hours, but the sight of her is like a memory returning at full force from the crypts of childhood. Instinctively, I step out in the road and raise my arms. She's like the first fallen leaf streaming through the air to signal summer's collapse. Therese brakes and topples off the bike.

"Ian," she wails as she falls against my chest. "Did you hear? Or have you been in your cabin all day? Or were you out on the yacht with Sonny?"

The Spaniards are idling within listening distance. Andres's eyes have the hostile squint that economy passengers contract at the baggage carousel after a long flight, when the first-class suitcases tumble out ahead of all the others. But I can't worry about them now.

"What's the matter?" I hold Therese by the wrists. "What happened?"

"Rasym just told me," she sobs. "I go now to break the news to Christos. I'm worried how he will take it. We've been with him so long. He was like a son to us. What will we do now without him?"

I don't realize how brutally I'm squeezing her wrists until she peers down at my hands.

"Is it Charlie? Have they found him?"

She gazes up at me with lava-black eyes. "Charlie, no. It's his father. He passed away in New York this afternoon. He died in the hospital."

When I turn around, my new friends have gone.

THE RED DOOR is locked. I use the flaccid doll hand, banging a pulse into it. I hear Miles advancing from the sitting room, his voice a squealing fire alarm. "It's Charles! I know it is!" The thirty seconds it takes for him to negotiate the locks gives me time to prepare for my role as the undesirable door prize—a pin popping Miles's helium dreams of reunions. When his red face peers out of the darkness and settles upon me, he barely manages to hide his disappointment.

"Ian!" He stumbles backward. "Have you heard from Charles today?" I admire Miles's palliative faith. He seems determined to maintain Sonny's optimism no matter how excessive the life support. At what point will the machines be turned off, the curtain pulled, and the facts chill the body? Will Miles still stare out of his mansion window long after the summer people have fled and the first frost creeps up the Choran hillside? *Maybe today, for Sonny's sake, Charles will pass along the monastery, heading toward his home, and the world will go on like it always has, and every summer will be like the last.*

Sonny is sitting in the medieval chair, her hair tied back. In a tan blouse and matching pants, her skin registers as an extension of her outfit. Adrian lies across the couch in a pair of shorts, distractedly magazine-flipping the pages of the green Bible. He sets it down on the coffee table, where the childhood photo of Charlie and Stefan lies. Rasym must have taken it from Stefan's laptop and put it there after he deleted the note. The atlas has been returned to the shelf. Aside from Miles's hysterical hopefulness, there is no indication of sudden distress. The bad news about Mr. K must not have reached them yet. For another few minutes, the marble statues and creaking chandelier and dusty icon paintings—all the way down to the turquoise Venini lamp and the cheap teacup ashtray dish—still safely belong to them. Next summer, if Charlie never shows, the house and all of its contents could be in unfamiliar hands. Obituary writers across the world are currently darkening their computer screens with lists of Konstantinou accomplishments. But this room is still dumb to the facts that will destroy it.

"Where's Louise?" Sonny asks quietly as Miles hurries to retrieve his drink on the table. "She was supposed to meet me this morning on the boat. She's not answering my texts."

I don't have the heart to tell her the truth. Or the strength. Or even the right words to inflict it. Sonny never had many friends here. And if she doesn't have them here, where does she?

"We had a fight," I reply. "A bad one. She packed her bags and left."

Sonny puffs her cheeks and offers a tight, compassionate frown. "I'm sorry," she whispers. "I was hoping for you two. I know she had some guy back home who she wasn't all that crazy about. I thought you might change her mind."

"Me too." *And still if you asked me to meet you, and set a time and place, I might walk halfway there before turning around. And if you e-mailed me, I might write a short reply and save it in the draft folder.*

"Did you see all the police activity this morning?" Adrian asks me.

"What police?" Miles interrupts. He uses the moisture of his glass to slick his bangs back. "On Patmos?"

"Some sort of raid on the hippies," Adrian says with his immaculate smile. "Drugs, I heard. Selling or smuggling." Sonny darts her eyes at me, the connection to Charlie's boat company hovering. But whatever she almost grasps falls away and she sets her sights on the light in the window. "I feel bad for them. When you're young you should be allowed to make mistakes. There should be laws *protecting* mistakes."

"The dragon stood on the shore of the sea," Miles quotes. He unleashes a squawking laugh. "Who would have imagined the Hellenic police force was actually capable of arresting anyone?"

"I guess that's what the camp was praying for in a way," Sonny murmurs. "An end. Some things do come to an end. Even if it's not how they envisioned it."

Miles catches the pain in her voice. He kneels down next to her, staring up with drunken love. "I would take it back if I could. If I could go back to that night and not have punched Charles, I would. You know that, don't you?"

"Miles," she warns through gritted teeth. "I told you it's not your fault."

He grabs the photo on the coffee table, gazing at the two Konstantinou boys he knew as a kid during summers on the island. "He's alive," Miles says. "Don't give up hope. If he's not back by tomorrow, Rasym's search party will find him." He's relied on alcohol to keep his hope alive, but alcohol only fools the drinker.

Sonny balls her fingers and rises from the chair. She walks to the window. Miles remains draped across the floor like a man who has lost function of his legs. His glass of vodka could be a cup of spare change.

"Are you going to Cyprus with Rasym this weekend?" Sonny asks Adrian.

Adrian's smile briefly stalls. "No," he replies. "I'm not sure where I'll go. It's still too hot for Kraków, and there's so much August left. I was thinking Stromboli, or Biarritz, or maybe Sharm el-Sheikh. A friend has a house in Tenerife." Adrian lists places like flowers he's cultivated in his garden, as if they bloom in summer simply for him. I may temporarily be a millionaire, but Adrian has the whole world in his pocket. He has all of the days that his looks endure not to settle down.

"I'd kill to go with you," Sonny says. "I'd do anything to get off this island for a week. I'd take a boat tomorrow."

"You can't leave," Miles pleads from the floor. "You and Duck will stay, won't you? Sonny, I swear to you, he's going to come back, he's—" Sonny tightens her fists, and Miles finally realizes he's overplayed his optimism. He tucks the snapshot into the Bible, as if to hide any trace of Charlie from her. "Once Rasym's gone, you'll have the house to yourself. And I can watch Duck if you need time alone. It can be however you want."

But it can't. Because what isn't here is yelling right into her eyes. She steps toward the balcony to escape the claustrophobia of the room. But as she reaches for the handle, Rasym's voice erupts from the doorway. None of us heard him enter, and Sonny and Miles both briefly convulse in fright. Rasym's beard is surprisingly thick for two days of growth.

"Charlie's father died this afternoon," he announces flatly. For a second, the room goes silent, and the faint bleeps of a video game ping from downstairs.

"What?" Miles yells, climbing to his feet. "His father? You can't be serious?"

Adrian rises from the couch and heads toward Rasym. Once he nears his boyfriend, he seems uncertain how to navigate a consoling gesture. I wonder if they've had an argument, but eventually Adrian finds his way in and pulls him close. Sonny squints at Rasym, her mouth moving underneath closed lips. She has no one to comfort but herself.

"Are you sure? Are you absolutely sure?" Miles groans with such anguish you'd have thought it was his own father. He latches his arm around his stomach.

"Of course I'm sure," Rasym responds. "There had been positive signs this morning of a recovery. He was even awake for a few minutes. But it didn't last."

"He was awake?" Sonny asks delicately. She must realize what little grief is allotted to her in front of Charlie's cousin. "Did he say anything? Anything about what's happened to Charlie or Stefan?"

Rasym shakes his head. "He was told they were on their way to see him."

Miles is careening around the room, wiping his mouth, gripping the edges of the sofa and chairs. Sonny extends her hand to stop the constant circling, but he pushes by her, quickening his speed.

"It can't end like that," he rattles. "Without a word from his sons? What's the point then, if they weren't even there? Alone in a hospital! All by himself!" Of everyone in the room, Miles has the least reason to mourn Mr. K. But his intoxication seems to have invested this death with particular tragedy. He isn't wrong. There will be two funerals now for the Konstantinous in Nicosia. How much longer until it's three? "All for nothing!" he cries. "Without ever hearing the truth!" The rest of us stand in the eye of Miles's hurricane.

"They decided it was best not to tell him about Stefan." Rasym's voice takes on a defensive edge. "They thought he might fight harder to live if he knew his sons were on their way. He even managed to write Charlie a note. All it said was that he loved him and hoped he'd see him again. Exactly that: *I hope I see you again, son.*" Rasym chokes on the last words.

"But the search party is still coming tomorrow, isn't it?" Sonny asks. "That hasn't changed, has it? They will still look for Charlie?"

For the first time a flicker of sympathy for Sonny passes over Rasym's face.

"Yes. And you and Duck are still welcome in Nicosia. Have you told her she's not going back to California? There's an English school a few blocks from the house. My father has already spoken to them. It will be a good place for her. I promise."

The room is eerily peaceful. Miles is no longer circling. A puncture of daylight brightens the foyer as he steps out the front door without saying good-bye.

Sonny drifts onto the balcony and takes a seat at the metal table.

Adrian's blue eyes glisten like windshield cleaner. "I'll go with you to Nicosia," he tells Rasym. "I'll help."

"My family is there," he demurs, trying to harness Stefan's aloof, professional tone. After all, Rasym is primed to inherit a thriving business. He didn't get my job with Charlie, but he might have gotten Stefan's at the firm. Now isn't the time for him to show the weakness of a human being. "It will be too hectic. It's better if you stay behind."

Adrian steadies his hands on his boyfriend's shoulders. "We're going to Nicosia as men, and let them be children if they don't want to meet me. What does it matter if they accept you abstractly, if they aren't willing to see my face? You have to decide."

I give them their privacy and step onto the balcony. A motorcycle gang of ants is crossing the stucco, and maroon bees suck the centers of wilted flowers. Birds whistle below in the garden. Sonny isn't staring out at the view. Her focus is on her thumbs, pressed against the table, as if committing their prints to ink.

"How are you holding up?" I say.

"Am I losing my mind or finally regaining it?" she asks. "Why do I feel so lucid? Why?" She motions for me to take the chair across from her. "I suppose it was inevitable. He was so sick."

"No matter how inevitable, it's always a surprise."

She nods, adjusting her elbows on the table and sliding her hand through her hair.

"I want to thank you for your advice yesterday. My former manager hooked me up with a lawyer. You were right. It was smart to talk to her."

"What did the lawyer say?"

Sonny lets out a feeble laugh. "She was so excited when I explained my situation you'd have thought God cold-called her. As soon as I mentioned the name Konstantinou, she nearly crashed the car she was driving. She says even if the marriage isn't official, it's enough of a threat that they'll throw money at me to shut me up. Imagine the payday now that Mr. K is dead." It's as if Sonny is purposely beefing up her role as gold digger. I sense she's using me as a dry run for all of the invectives she'll be bombarded with if she proceeds with her claim. But the muscles of her jaw stiffen, and she looks up at me with the burden of someone who wins at a heavy price. I'm not sure whether to offer her my congratulations or condolences.

"I know what you're thinking," she says. "If I had more dignity I'd just walk away. If I had an ounce of self-respect, I'd take Duck and go back to California and never ask for a dime from them. It would prove I loved him if I didn't take a cent."

"I'm not judging you. It isn't an easy world." But that response sounds too pat, so I apply a dose of naïve hope. "There's still a chance Charlie could be found. Maybe he did take a boat out and is lost at sea. It happens."

Sonny drops her shoulders. She searches the blue above us.

"Please don't be Miles," she says. "I don't need the comfort of insanity. No, there are only two possibilities. Either Charlie is dead, or he purposely disappeared because he didn't want to get caught. In either case, he's not coming back." She's handling reality rather well. The late afternoon shadows are encroaching on our small islet of sun. We'll sit here until the shadows cover us. "If he's alive and did run, I forgive him. I've been thinking all day about what kind of person I am. Not was, even up to a week ago, but am now. I can take what I need and still love him. I can be greedy for Duck and sincere when it comes to him. You're right. The world isn't easy and it will call me whatever it wants to, and even the good names won't be right." She breathes heavily. "Unless you're a woman, you can't understand the number of names you get called in one lifetime. But I'm done believing in any of them. I'm too old to be tricked into dignity."

She leans her head against her shoulder, as if needing physical contact with her own body. Tears blur her eyes. "I'm not doing this only for me."

"I know you're not."

Somewhere in Chora, a steeple bell begins to ring. I count the clangs to determine the time, but it rolls past twelve and other bells join it.

"You'll keep in touch, won't you?" she asks. "When you go. Even if Charlie vanishes forever, it'd be nice to hear from you once in a while. Check in, will you? Tell me you're doing well. You can still lie to me."

"I hope I won't have to lie," I say with a smile. "And I bet Charlie would be glad that you got some of his family's money. Maybe that's what he meant that night in Skala about always making sure you're safe."

"You've always been good at covering for him," she says, patting the table. "Like that chess piece. Charlie didn't put the queen in my bag. You did."

I don't confirm or deny it. I dig my fingers in my pocket and fish out the gaudy earring I've been carrying around to return to its owner. I push it across the table. Sonny smirks when she realizes what it is.

"I found it on *Domitian*. It's the earring from—"

"I remember." She picks it up.

"Charlie got back to his yacht, that much is clear. So he really could be anywhere now." She doesn't bite. She's not interested in false faith.

"So ugly," she moans. "Charlie always had great taste, except when it came to jewelry." I suppose talking about him in the past tense is a sign of acceptance. "I figured it got lost when Miles punched him." She clips the earring onto her shirt like Charlie did and lets it dangle over her heart. On her tan uniform, it does look like a war medal. "Can you imagine if Charlie did return looking like a shipwreck victim and discovered that the only person who kept hope alive for him was Miles. He'd be so pissed. Charlie hated him even when they were kids playing together. I guess you never know who your real friends are."

That sentence sends a chill through my skull. I clasp the table and let go.

"Are you still taking Duck to Nicosia in the fall?" I ask her.

She shrugs. "Who knows? For once, I'm not thinking that far ahead. This weekend is the festival for the Assumption of Mary. They float an icon of her in the sea by Kampos and set these little paper boats on fire. It's beautiful. I want Duck to see it." She laces her hands behind her head and gazes out at the southern tip of the island. The monster star is turning the dirt fields red and the sea a glass-blown yellow. "You know, I don't think I ever experienced real happiness until Greece," she says. "Back home it was never direct happiness. I always needed someone else's confirmation that I was in a good place. But here it just is. Pure. Like it doesn't even care if it's remembered." She stares at the sky with wonder. "I'm twenty-seven, Ian. And I have the weirdest feeling I'm going to live to be a hundred."

I turn to the horizon, where the future always looks less crowded.

THE SCALY, PISTACHIO door across from the taxi stand creaks open when I tap my knuckles on it. Pop music blasts from far upstairs, and the rooms on the main floor are sheeted and empty. I climb the crooked staircase, following the synthesizer bass line and the screaming-girl lyrics. I pass through a tiny oval door that's cut into a larger one. Inside, the garret apartment lies in shambles. A ceramic vase is shattered on a table. An entire bottle's worth of red wine stains an embroidered sofa. A modest impressionistic painting of a port on fire has been revived by a slash through its canvas. The Beijing *fuerdai* weren't such respectable renters after all. The knob on the stereo is missing, so I pull the plug to kill the music. I take a narrow spiral staircase up to the roof, turning in six circles to reach the sky.

Miles stands barefoot on the tarry, whitewashed rooftop with his arms outstretched. The dense brown slab of the monastery looms above him, and bells from every church and shrine are pealing from all directions. The fuzzy laughter of tourists reverberates from far below. He must have heard me climbing the steps, but he keeps his back to me. He's swaying and his arms are soaring, as if drifting on some invisible current.

I should have figured it out as soon as I realized Charlie and Vic were only pretending to be enemies. If a method proves effective, it tends to be exploited repeatedly. And Charlie never had much of an imagination; even at Destroyers, he always resorted to the same nearest-window strategy. I knew that Charlie staged the fight with Miles that night in Skala, but I didn't know that Miles was in on the act. Who would suspect him of cleaning up his enemy's mess?

"He was supposed to be back by now," Miles whimpers, wrapping his arms around his sides. "He has to come back." An empty bottle lies by his foot.

"Yes," I reply. "Otherwise you won't get your money. You must owe a lot in London to have taken care of Stefan for him. Did Charlie promise you a cut of his inheritance?" Miles spins around, but it isn't fear that grips his face. He's somewhere far beyond that. I almost feel sorry for him. He murdered for no reason. Mr. K died before there would have been time for Stefan to tell him the truth.

"We played games as kids," Miles slurs. "On summers here as children. Charles always wanted to play the same game he made up. It's too hard to explain the rules. It was about running away from murderers." I'm not surprised that Charlie took Destroyers as his own invention, any more than Sonny was when he took their song as his own discovery. *It's ours, so it's his.* Even if Charlie hated Miles, Destroyers must have forged a lasting bond between them. "He wasn't very good at it. He always found the worst corner, and I'd have to invent a last-minute escape. Keys or windows where they shouldn't be. A hole in the wall."

"Miles, did you lure Stefan up to the house by promising him information on the charter company, or did Stefan reach out to you on his own?"

"Charles said he'd only be in Bodrum for a few days," he cries. "People don't just disappear. Where is he? The refugees, more each hour, so many of them, endless gobs of flesh, but no Charles." He loses his balance and lifts his arms to steady himself.

"You shouldn't have included the photo of Charlie and Stefan with the suicide note."

"This is an island of refugees. Are you aware of that? Have you bothered to learn the history of this place? No history for an American, right? Only beaches. In 1453, after the fall of Constantinople, a horde of refugees took shelter here."

"I saw Charlie stash that photo in the Bible on his bookshelf. There's no way Stefan would have known where it was."

"More refugees with the conquest of Rhodes by the Turks in 1522." Miles wipes his mouth with his sleeve. "And again, in 1669, when Crete fell. I won't even bore you with the Venetians. Greece is a very young country."

"Charlie must have told you where to find the photo. You put it back in the Bible today when you were talking to Sonny. You're too thorough of a cleaner."

"And now London is falling. *London falling*," he sings. "My vespers, yeah? When I was little, we used to come to this house every Easter as well. It's the prettiest time of year. The youngest monk always plays Judas. If you can play Judas, you can play anyone." He stumbles forward as if to hug me, but the momentum of his first few steps peters out. He looks down at his feet. "We had horses in the country back home. I knew each one so well I could recognize them by their smell. We'd have to put them down too. It was out of principle. If you ride them and feed them, you have to be able to end their suffering. You see, that's how he and I are different. The first time I held the rifle, I was nervous. And I asked my father, *where do I shoot her?*" He laughs and brings his finger to his temple. "The head, of course. These are my stories, Ian, and they can't be taken or touched. I have so many I want to tell you. We had horses and a rare-book room and a greenhouse for herbs and two Alfa Romeos that never did run and bright, long meadows and the devil wasn't there."

"Miles," I whisper, trying to pull him out of his spell. "Why don't I take you down to your bed?"

His shaggy eyes fix on me, and I see red dents in his bottom lip from where he's bitten into it. Where he is, there is no backward.

"It was all for what? For time? To keep in a name? My god, what difference did it make? All I did and no point to it." I'm not sure if he means the murder or his life. Too many memories are sloshing through his brain. I grab for his wrist, but he dodges my arm and marches with quick, deliberate steps toward the ledge.

"Miles," I yell. "Come here. Closer. Come close."

"Remember our toast?" he asks. "You're Catholic, aren't you? Can you ask for forgiveness in advance? I was given everything but a purpose. When you have everything I guess you don't need one. All you can do is watch the loss. Come back in the spring. Blue anemones bloom up the hill. I lost my virginity there to a Greek girl. It was like paradise." He steps over the edge, a millisecond of swirling white shirt and tan skin, and then nothing, and then the screams in front of the monastery.

Miles never learned to swim. It wouldn't have saved him. He couldn't fly.

CHAPTER 18

H e sits cross-legged by the wheel of my bike. His jeans are caked in dirt. His lips are dotted with sores. The diamond stud is missing from his ear. A fresh, short-sleeve Anti-Bethlehem shirt reveals long, sinewy arms with bite-like scabs running down their pale undersides. He's staring out at the view of Skala at dusk, and even the yowling ambulance that pulls to a halt by the taxi stand doesn't distract him. At first, I don't recognize him as anyone other than a nationless stray of Vic's camp, a postraid orphan reduced to sleeping far away from the policed beaches. But as I fit my key into the seat compartment to collect my helmet, he lifts his head. It's Helios's sickly eyes that catch mine. He winces out a smile, as if the air is a wall he keeps hitting his head against.

"Ian," he says limply, as if it sapped all of his strength to remember my name and there isn't much left over to utter it. "Hey."

I squat down, and he flinches. He reeks of smoke and armpits.

"Your parents are looking for you," I say softly. "They could do with seeing you now. Charlie's dad died. Do you want me to give you a ride to their house?"

He shakes his head. "No. No way. Charlie back?"

"I'm afraid not."

He raises his arm and lets it drop hopelessly onto his lap. "I've been waiting for you. I knew this was your bike."

"Where can I take you?"

His tongue greases his lips. "Take me someplace better."

"Where's that?"

"Camp gone," he mutters. "I need to borrow from you, dude. Just a little. Please. Anything. I'll do anything." His skittish eyes move to the space between my legs, either to my crotch or my pockets.

I stand up to fish out a bill.

"Helios, you've got to take care of yourself." I try to make the advice sound *dude*-like, free of parental lecturing. "I really wish you'd consider going home. Your parents are worried. They haven't seen you in days. What about talking to Vesna?"

"Stop!" He moans and flings his hand flipper-like against his cheek. "No! Just give me. Please, Ian, just give!"

I fold the fifty-euro bill twice and extend it toward him. He gawks up at it as if it's a meaningless piece of scrap paper.

"What's that?" he asks.

I'm growing aggravated by the zombie-ed out son of Charlie's boat captain. The men in the ambulance have already raced toward the scene of a fall, and the dark atmosphere is thick with emergency. I don't want to be in Chora any longer.

"It's money," I reply, shaking it. "Take it. It's what you want. You don't have to do anything for it. And you don't have to pay me back."

Helios lets out a gutting cry and tips onto his hip. "I don't need money," he yells. "There's nowhere on the island now to use it. I can't buy it anymore with the camp closed. Give me what you have! You've got to have some left! Give!"

"Helios, I'm sorry, but—"

He rolls into a crouch, and his entire face curdles with the effort of standing. He breaks into a staggered run, hopping over a wall, and is lost in the maze of painted stone.

The lamps of Chora blink on, paling the lights of the ambulance. It's cocktail hour at the Apocalypse.

NIGHT HAS FALLEN by the time I approach Grikos. Mid-August traffic has intensified along the winding roads. Rental cars thrash around corners like dying fish. Even sleepy Grikos glitters with the romance of candles and glassware. I park my bike and walk along the port. Families gather on the back decks of their yachts, eating and drinking and cheering each other on at games, like tailgaters in the world's most expensive parking lot. I turn onto the concrete dock where *Domitian* is tied, its sails down, its black-oak hull swaying against the buoys. Hazy yellow light bleeds from the portal windows. Someone's home.

A breeze lifts off the water, and I wait for it to die before jumping on deck. The wood floor has been freshly mopped and waxed after Sonny's morning excursion. I climb down the rungs of the ladder. The galley is empty, but the track lighting is turned high and speakers play a late Beethoven string quartet at low volume. I take a seat at the opal chessboard and set the pieces in place. Charlie was always white. Now I am. The ashtray lies upside down on the kitchen drying rack.

Christos steps from the bathroom with a caddy of cleaning supplies. Grease is smeared on the front of his shirt, and his gold St. Christopher medallion is tangled around his collar. He pauses when he spots me and grunts in acknowledgment before stowing the caddy under the sink. His eyes are bloodshot. Why do people read palms when they should read faces? I can read his. He's had a brutal day with the news of Mr. K's death. He's spent his life as a faithful servant for the Konstantinous. I wonder if Rasym's side of the family will bother to keep him on.

"I close boat now," he tells me as he stacks glasses in the cupboard.

"I'm just waiting to see someone."

"No more boat. No more . . ." For a second, he glances at me with fleeting hope but doesn't find what he's looking for. Instead he grips the counter, as if *Domitian* is riding treacherous waves.

"How about a game?" I ask. He shakes his head. "Charlie and I played a lot as kids. I'm sure you two did too. Come on. Just one game."

Tentatively he approaches the board and slumps down in the chair across from me. He points his finger at my white rook.

"No," I say. "No handicap. I'm not as good as Charlie. We start even."

I open with a pawn to e4. He counters with a pawn to c5. Classic Sicilian Defense, and my only strategy is a quick attack. We play in silence, annihilating little men.

"I saw Helios tonight."

Christos's outstretched hand trembles, and he shoots it onto his lap. He stares down at the board, refusing eye contact.

"He's still in bad shape. I worked at a place in New York for guys like him. Withdrawal is vicious. How long has he been hooked?"

Christos escorts his bishop to a square in the direct path of my queen. It's either a novice mistake or an offering. A bead of sweat drops from his nose. I don't take the easy meal.

"Christos?"

He won't look up.

"Christos, I understand. He's your only son."

His throat chokes, and there must be more waves now because he's clenching the table.

"You did what you had to do to protect him. He wasn't going to stop on his own. And Charlie wasn't going to stop either."

Christos lifts his face. Tears stream from brown eyes as haunted as churches, the deep, quiet alcoves of desperate prayers. He presses his fist to his chest.

"What did you do to Charlie?" I ask.

"Helios my son," he wails with iron syllables. "*My son.* And all light go out of him. Dead boy that Charlie hurt." His shoulders quake, and his knee bangs against the table, irrevocably shifting the pieces. "Charlie plan go to Bodrum that night. Plan to bring more drug to Patmos. My island, Helios home. He destroy my family. I have no choice. Only stop to save my boy."

I nod. My eyes are watering too because I'm not sure I'm brave enough to hear how Christos stopped him. Charlie must have been sitting in this very seat, facing the same opponent over the same game, closing in on his captain's king. That's when Christos inflicted his surprise attack. *Christos is trustworthy*, Charlie assured me on the morning I arrived. He must never have seen it coming.

"What did you do to him?"

"Charlie like son to me," he pleads. "Boy I help raise since small. But he change, he forget, and he become." He jolts back in his chair as if shot. "For Helios, my future, you see! Helios change this summer too. I only stop Charlie. Not kill him, not tell police for arrest. Stop him only from Bodrum. My wife, she not even know." His gnarled fingers sprout at odd angles over the board; tourists might take pictures of those ancient instruments. "I know you make alibi for Charlie. He tell me so. He tell me he will be gone few days and you lie for him. That give me time. I try call Charlie's father. I try every hour to speak to him in New York. To tell what his son does and to come get him. Only he can fix. But Mr. Konstantinou in hospital. I wait for him wake up. I wait and pray every day. He does not wake. He only get worse and now—" His hands aren't useless. One slaps against the varnished wall.

And now. And now there is no Mr. K, no last resort on the other end of the line to clean up his son's mess. A red blaze funnels through the windows, and an air horn raids the galley. Christos's eyes rifle into me as if I've betrayed him. But it's only a party yacht sailing through the harbor. Singing men and laughing women pass by as they prepare to disembark.

"Where is he?" I ask, extending my arms. "Is he still alive? I want to see him."

Christos clambers from his seat and walks with a bent back to a wooden bin. He opens its lid and rummages through the contents.

"Konstantinous," he curses. "My life, yes, but not my son. They will not steal it. I will bring you where you want to go. I will take you, and you will be with him. It will be over then, and you will see." Christos's English, so garbled in past and present, becomes magically fluent in the future tense. And it's the future that scares me. I picture the specks of Charlie's blood on the floor and consider making a break for the ladder rungs. How far up would I get before he drags me under, while all around us restless boats party into the night?

"I am sorry." Christos is almost weeping as he reaches into the bin. "He all I have."

"Christos!"

He pulls out an orange life vest. "To get there, you will need to swim."

GOAT ISLAND IS pitch-black, its contours only distinguishable as land from where it blocks out the glimmering sea and sky. The captain steers *Domitian* thirty feet from the island's lowest slant and shines a flashlight on a cluster of boulders that billow like fossilized clouds from black-velvet ripples of water. Any place seen through a flashlight's beam looks nefarious. I try to recall the island as I first glimpsed it, its ram's horn peaks and mossy slopes and thin, steely trees poking out like wires, peaceful and unpopulated. Behind us, the distant monastery glows over its dominion of tiny orbs. A ferry is revolving in the harbor, a sugar cube crawling with ants. Christos can't sail the boat any closer for fear of running aground. I secure the clips of my lifejacket over my chest.

As kids, long after midnight, Charlie and I would press our foreheads to the floor-to-ceiling windows of his parents' Fifth Avenue apartment. We'd watch the traffic below stream south, and we'd pick out cars to ambush with stories. Destroyers didn't work in vehicles: too many doors, no room to run, the black-balaclava gunmen sitting docilely next to us in the backseat like ride-sharing companions. *The woman in that taxi just left her sleeping husband; she's hurrying down to SoHo to meet her girlfriend at the Mercer who is also her gallerist; her art career is failing. There's a hip-hop producer in that white stretch limo with a male escort, but the producer's mother from Indianapolis is also with them; she surprised him with a visit and now the escort is pretending to be a tour guide showing her the sights. That yellow Oldsmobile is packed with Buddhist monks and religious icons that they're going to pawn for casino money.*

Charlie's favorite destination was the airport; every other taxi was headed there. Even at that age, he was dreaming of someplace else. As I got older, I understood why. For us, where you happened to be born or raised—that meaningless factoid beloved of biographical synopses—didn't matter as much as where you went. We were already from Dream City. Later, when fresh arrivals from sleepier parts of the country moved in, we'd shrug or roll our eyes. All they brought with them were their ecstatic delusions of New York, but the natives were defeated by the fantasies of the immigrants. They squatted in our normal lives, and maybe we hated them because they seemed to own the city out of sheer determination to possess it. Someplace else, far away, unknown air, two children's foreheads slicked against tinted glass high above Manhattan, refusing to dissolve into the wavering mercury of the skyline. Did Charlie and I hold hands as we made up those stories? Why do I picture us holding hands?

I strip my pockets of my keys and wallet. Christos signals for me to remove my shoes, but I leave them on. I slip off the stern and paddle through the freezing current. The vest prevents swift strokes, but as my legs scrape against hidden reefs, I realize its necessity at night. If I go under, Christos won't be able to find me. He follows, treading without a vest, the flashlight lodged in his mouth, the blue light illuminating his skull. I reach the boulders, out of breath, and locate a slender divot in the bedrock. It takes all of my strength to drag myself out of the water. The smell of dill weed and fresh earth pours from above. I climb the boulders and reach the beginning of a dirt path. Christos has already caught up to me. He aims the flashlight up the trail.

Faint rustling stirs the darkness, soft bleating, hooves on stone. For two minutes we hike the incline, and Christos's beam attracts a whirl of flying insects. A small fluorescent-white shrine glimmers up ahead. The glass in its oval windows is blown out, the cross at its crown tilted and the nails loose in its rotted wood. Greek text is written in red milk paint above the doorframe. I catch sight of my very first goat, a matted gray male with boomerang horns lapping at a spigot. It glances up at us, its silver eyes contracting in the shine, and kicks off for higher ground.

Christos switches off the flashlight. "Wait," he orders and enters the shrine. I hear the wrench of metal and the moan of a generator starting up. Electric orange fills the church from a strand of bulbs in the rafters. I step into the damp ruin, its walls peeling and tapestried with mold. Scabs of stonework cling to the edges of a deep crater in the center where the floor has fallen through. Mosaicked saints dissolve into mud at the drop. I notice Charlie's phone and wallet on top of a stack of bottles and sardine tins. A coiled rope hangs from a hook by the door. Christos nods toward the hole, refusing to look at me, and walks outside.

I test my weight with each foot forward and stare over the edge of the pit. Water bottles, a bucket with a board over its top, empty tins, and sheaves of Konstantinou Charters stationery cover the bottom like a raven's nest. For a second I mistake him for a pile of blankets. But there he is, my oldest friend, lying on his side, his face and legs covered in dirt, a filthy bandage wrapped around his forehead. No door, no window, no clever improvised ladder for him to use as an escape. It cuts my heart to see him trapped.

Charlie squints, disbelieving, his eyes trying to blink me away. "Ian?" he murmurs. And now his voice rising like hands that have discovered crevices in the dirt, "Ian, oh my god, Ian. I never thought I'd see you again!" He struggles unsteadily to his feet.

"Christos brought me. Are you all right?"

"Do I look all right!" he shouts in a pitch nearing laughter. "I've been down here for so many days. I've almost lost count. The sun comes through the roof. All I've done is watch it. Oh, my god, Ian. You're too late. I already gave up hope." He's sobbing as he stamps the blood back in his legs. Even now, he is a beautiful man.

I kneel down and worm my chest against the floor. I dangle my arms, and Charlie reaches on tiptoe. Our fingers touch, cupping, and whatever it is I thought we had lost passes between us, a feeling so mortal and raw it seems to tell my years to me.

"You know, don't you?" he says. "You wouldn't be here if you didn't."

I nod.

"All of it?"

"Pretty much."

"I'm sorry. I'm sorry I got you involved in my mess. I never meant for that to happen." He drops his hands to wipe the wet grit on his cheeks. "I didn't plant that bomb. All I got was a text from Vic telling me not to go near the taverna that morning. I had no idea what she was going to do."

"That counts for something."

"Does it?" He stares up, his expression caught halfway between sentenced and pardoned, as if he's trying to determine whose side I'm on.

"How—" I begin. *How did we get here, Charlie?*

"Don't ask a man in a hole for a confession. He'll tell you whatever you want to hear."

"It's not me you owe answers to." I extend my arm again and wiggle my fingers. He doesn't reach for them. He merely gazes around at his prison walls of rock and mud. It occurs to me that he hasn't yet asked for the one thing I can give him: a way out.

"How's Sonny?"

"Desperate to see you again. As worried as you can imagine. We've all been worried. No one has any clue where you are."

"Does she know what I've done?"

"No."

"Miles didn't crack and tell her about Stefan?"

"Miles is dead."

He absorbs that information with a stagger of his feet.

"What about the dock? Have they found—"

"It's closed. Ugur shut it down and left."

His eyes flicker, some last brown spark of a fire that's gone cold.

"So it's only you who knows? You and Christos. Is he up there with you?"

I turn to search the doorway, but Christos is nowhere in sight.

"He's outside."

Charlie's open mouth issues a series of sharp, dry breaths.

"Do you understand what this means?" He pants. "We can take care of him. We can bribe him to keep his mouth shut. Or if he won't accept that, when we get to the water, we can—" He's pleading deliriously, trapped in a corner and expecting me to supply one final method of escape. He must have waylaid Miles with a similar speech. The panicked plotting is so familiar, like a song I loved in youth, that for a moment I fall victim to it, confusing its rhythm for sense. "We can do this, and it can be just like it was supposed to go. You and I. Oh my god, listen, Ian, it's not too late."

"It is too late," I say. "I won't do that to Christos. There have already been too many."

"Why?" he begs, dropping onto the dirt. His eyes welt in the overhead lights. "Why is it too late?" But the whine of that last question holds a comprehension of its futility.

"There's an agent on the island waiting for you to return. It's going to come out eventually. Maybe not all of it, but enough. Let's get you out of here and talk about it once you're home. We can make a plan then. A real one."

Charlie doesn't move, except to kick weakly at a water bottle. When he does look up at me, he's no longer a boy playing Destroyers but the defeated player of a different game.

"I'm not going back," he says quietly.

"What do you mean?"

"Do you know the prison term for drug trafficking in Greece? It's life. Can you imagine how much the world will celebrate a Konstantinou convicted of a felony like that? And one crime exposes others. If the truth ever comes out about Stefan, I wouldn't be able to take it. I told you, I'm not going to confess. What I've done can't be forgiven. I know that now, and I won't ask for it."

"You don't have to confess. Rasym brought over a family lawyer. You can—"

"I was going to do it this morning. But the light was so beautiful through the roof."

He crawls toward the loose papers, snatching at one and brushing off the dirt. He checks his notes for the date, writes it across the top, and folds the paper twice. He hands it up to me.

"I've asked you for too many favors. But do one more for me, will you? Take that. Say you found it on *Domitian*."

I unfold the letter.

"Don't read it!" he yells. "Just say you found it and leave it alone!"

To whom it may concern, I married Sonny Towsend on December 13, 2014, in Cairo at the Oberoi by a judge named Abdel Barakat. The certificate is in my desk in Nicosia. I leave her all of my money and assets. While this might be a suicide note, I am of sound mind and body. Also, please allocate $2.1 million to the Patmos Children's Day School to be bequeathed under the name of Stefan Konstantinou.

Sincerely, Charalambos Konstantinou

It is an insane piece of paper written by a sane man.

"Charlie, come on!" I stretch my arms to him, my hands snapping like jaws. I'm certain if he sees my face he'll change his mind. If that doesn't work, I'll crawl into the hole with him. "You aren't thinking straight. When you're back on the island we can figure it out."

"Don't!" he shouts. "There's no other way free, okay? You can't make someone live if they don't want to. Even you can't do that for me. Time down here"—he swallows hard—"it's made me live with myself. I'm not sure I ever have before."

His eyes are unfocused as he stares at the moths orbiting the bulbs.

"Listen," I beg. "I was wrong. We can try to bribe Christos. Let's do that."

"And the agent?"

"Maybe he can be paid off too. There's still a chance it can be like you planned. Please, Charlie. I won't say a word, I promise. You have your inheritance. Are you listening? You *are* free." For a second, I wonder if I'm being tricked by a brain more cunning than my own: I'll void his guilt to save his life. I'll invent a last, make-believe window for him to jump through. I'll tailor the universe to suit him. But in this moment I mean every word I'm speaking. "Please," I cry. "We'll pay the whole world off if we have to."

"No," he says simply. He juts his tongue to the side and brings his fingers to his teeth, tweezing out a tiny metal arrowhead from the back of his gums. He must have spent his days honing that weapon on the tins.

"Come on, Charlie," I stammer. "Don't do this. There are other ways to make amends. And Sonny is up at the house waiting for you, and I'm here, and your father needs you in New York. He's in the hospital. He sent a message that his only wish is to see you one last time. At least do that for him, dammit."

"This isn't a rash decision. I've already decided. Don't make it harder for me."

"I love you too much to make it easy."

"I love you too," he says. "I'm glad I got the chance to tell you that. But now I need you to go. For once, I'm okay with this. Did you hear me? I'm okay." As he looks up at me, I know that nothing I can say will change his mind. I couldn't stop Charlie any more than I could ever hold him in place.

He reaches out his hand and I take it, all of us in the tips of our fingers. It's as close as we will ever get.

"Tell Christos to come back tomorrow. Break the generator, will you? Make it so he can't get me until the morning."

When I don't answer, he screams, "Say you'll do that. Please."

"Fine," I reply, wiping my eyes. "But you have to do one final thing for me."

"What? Money? I have some in the safe. The code is—"

I hurry to the rope. Knotting it tightly on the hook, I thread the coil across the floor and toss the remainder down the hole. The last curls land at his feet.

"You can climb out if you want to. It's another option. It's not too far to swim. And there will be ferries tomorrow to anywhere you want to go. I think you'll change your mind if you see the sunrise. And there are plenty more after that one, I swear. Just consider it. You don't have to be Charlie Konstantinou anymore. You could be anyone in the world."

He fights the furious smile that's threatening to destroy his resolve.

"You're a fucking asshole," he says. "You're a piece of shit for doing that. Don't leave it dangling down here. Ian, pull it up! It's not fair!"

"I know."

I walk to the generator and pry open the side hatch. As I yank the plastic gas tank from the machine, the orange lights sputter into darkness. The entire shrine is swallowed in the hole.

Out in the hot night, I find Christos sitting at a distance on a rock.

"The generator broke," I tell him. "Charlie asked that you get him tomorrow."

Christos lifts his head and glances behind me.

"He wants one more night there. Penance. Tomorrow you take him to the police."

We return down the trail. Crawling into the water, I aim for the white, rocking glow of *Domitian*, holding the letter above the waves. I dip my face into the sea to wipe the tears and sweat away. Far beyond the swaying mast is the Monastery of St. John the Divine. What are the monks praying for in their isolated cells as the entire island erupts in celebration around them? Are they praying for peace or for the end or for another day exactly like this one, filled with its ferocious stake of beauty and rage? On the very day that Charlie was made a billionaire, he became free.

EPILOGUE

The Athens airport is a frenzy of arrivals and departures, a luminous buffer zone between land and sky. Heretics scream at check-in counters clutching canceled tickets. A Nigerian family in yellow dashikis lines up for frozen lattes. Lonely single men slink into magazine stalls and into interfaith prayer rooms. Trapped birds perch on surveillance equipment. Two teenagers kiss passionately by the security scanners. But mostly it's commuters crisscrossing the terminal like sleepwalkers plagued with nightmares of impending deadlines. I grab my suitcase and stroll over to the blinking monitor to check the departure times.

I, Ian Bledsoe, am in search of salvation. The good news is I have one million euros to find it. That's $1,138,050 U.S., according to today's exchange rate. Don't ask me how that's determined. Tomorrow or yesterday the amount would be different. A little more, a little less.

17:01 Athens ➋ Madrid

Wheels down just after sunset. I'll find a room at one of the old hotels across from the Prado, and in the first light of tomorrow I'll recoup my losses. New dress shirts, made to measure, new pants, a camel sport coat, black crocodile loafers, underwear—everything but a phone. I'll rent an apartment with herringbone floors and leave it unfurnished except for a mattress and an upright piano by the window. There will be time for lessons: piano, painting, botany, Castilian. I'll take the days slow, a rambler of boulevards, a lurker in the parks, steering clear of bars until I get too solitary, and even then, club soda only. I will choose my acquaintances carefully, a nonrestless set prone to outdoor concerts and weekend drives in the country. The sex will be good, and the food better, and the nights won't hurt, and I'll grow. I will build a new Ian out of this rubble, a shining man.

17:23 Athens ➲ New Delhi

I will land in a sunrise of pea-green smog, hot sulfur, burning tin, and oxygen laced with the finest particulate matter on the planet. I will taxi past homes that look and sound like car collisions, past bored cows and naked children with naked eyes. The smells alone will be otherworldly. Delhi will be like walking through a haunted house with all the lights on, and the tourist museums won't be bastions of culture but brief respites from it. I will surprise Helen Bledsoe on her doorstep. After our reunion, we will have hard work ahead. Even in India, one million dollars won't be much seed money to start an orphanage. But a family, by nature, is an infinitely expandable enterprise, and the Bledsoes will be committed to doing our share. To love, to help, to make the world one degree less wicked. Maybe one day, standing beside my mother, I will come to feel I've earned my life.

17:58 Athens ➲ Cape Town
18:12 Athens ➲ Prague
18:46 Athens ➲ Singapore
19:18 Athens ➲ Buenos Aires

The whole world is reachable from here.

For a second, I catch sight of them, the men in black balaclavas crouching behind the benches, running with bent backs along-side luggage trolleys, collecting their rifles in the restroom alcoves. They're gathering for their assault, and they mean to steal every-thing from us. But in another blink they vanish, a glitch in the eye or the shadow of a plane taking off.

The good news is that the time is still not near. We have hours, we have years to go.

ACKNOWLEDGMENTS

As much as I hope to have gotten down the island of Patmos accurately in physical description, I hope no reader takes any of the characters in this book as reflections of actual persons. The citizens of *The Destroyers*, their histories, and their actions are entirely fictional, dreamed up in the cave of my writing room and as true to life as the creatures that haunt the Book of Revelation (special thanks to St. John the Divine for the constant inspiration). That said, I'm eternally grateful to all the Patmian regulars and locals who offered me their time, stories, houses, boats, advice, and a seat at their tables on my many trips to the island for research. Chief among them are Owen Madden, Marios Photiades, Prince Michael of Greece, Marina Karella, Tobias Meyer, Maddalena and Raffaele Mincione (for the test-run boat ride to Turkey), Stavros the captain, Scott Morse, Vassilis, Yannis Strata, John Stefanidis (for the tour of his exquisite grounds), Karla Otto, and Angela Ismailos. Thank you to Dennis Freedman and Dakis Joannou for essential introductions. Thank you to Athens attorneys Theodore N. Rakintzis and Leonidas C. Georgopoulos for the education in Greek law. Thank you to Michael Barasch for pointing me in the right direction and to Howard G. McPherson (Mac) for the vital mentoring in maritime law.

This book would never have been written without the help and encouragement of its dedicatee, my friend and agent, Bill Clegg. It also would never have come together without the deft touch and sagacious eyes of my editor, Jennifer Barth. Thank you to the whole Harper team, particularly Jonathan Burnham for his support and understanding of the territory. Across the water, deepest appreciation goes to Simon & Schuster UK, including Suzanne Baboneau,

Jo Dickinson, Rowan Cope, and the mighty sentence-sharpener Sophie Orme.

I wouldn't be anywhere without the friends and family who get me through, a few of whom are mentioned here: George Miscamble, James Oakley, Wade Guyton, Thomas Alexander, Joseph Logan, the folks at *Interview Magazine*, Adam Kimmel (for the chess lessons), Alexei Hay, Claudia Aranow, Patrik Ervell, T. Cole Rachel, Will Chancellor, Ana and Danko Steiner, and Edmund White. And, of course, my Ohio family of mom, grandmother, Heather, and Sam. We had to draw pictures inspired by the Book of Revelation in Catholic school; I'm sure that helped feed the beast.

ABOUT THE AUTHOR

Christopher Bollen is the author of *Orient*, an NPR Best Book of the Year, and the critically acclaimed *Lightning People*. He is the editor at large at *Interview Magazine*. His work has appeared in the *New York Times*, *New York Magazine*, *GQ*, and *Artforum*, among others. He lives in New York.